The intruder slid back into unconsciousness, which meant he wasn't going to be causing any more trouble for at least the next few moments. Nick turned away, shutting all thought of the man out of his mind—the most effective way to keep his rage from coming back and spiraling out of control.

He sat down on the bed next to Melody. "That should hold the bastard for a couple of minutes while I say a proper hello."

"Hello." Her smile wobbled, but she held on to it. Her voice was still husky with stress. "You're supposed to be in New York."

"Cancún seemed a lot more appealing. Sun versus sleet, Melody versus Mac. It was no contest."

She gave a tight laugh. "You have to admit I arranged a spectacular welcome for you."

"You sure did. Although for future planning, the sexy outfit is more than enough excitement for me. The fistfight was overkill."

JASMINE
CRESSWELL

FINAL JUSTICE

MIRA®

ISBN 0-7783-2140-1

FINAL JUSTICE

Copyright © 2005 by Jasmine Cresswell.

All rights reserved. Except for use in any review, the reproduction or
utilization of this work in whole or in part in any form by any electronic,
mechanical or other means, now known or hereafter invented, including
xerography, photocopying and recording, or in any information storage or
retrieval system, is forbidden without the written permission of the publisher,
MIRA Books, 225 Duncan Mill Road, Don Mills, Ontario, Canada M3B 3K9.

All characters in this book have no existence outside the imagination of the
author and have no relation whatsoever to anyone bearing the same name
or names. They are not even distantly inspired by any individual known or
unknown to the author, and all incidents are pure invention.

MIRA and the Star Colophon are trademarks used under license and registered
in Australia, New Zealand, Philippines, United States Patent and Trademark
Office and in other countries.

www.MIRABooks.com

Printed in U.S.A.

For Malcolm, with love.

Here's to our new house—
and our new new house!

One

The motel room smelled of cigarette smoke and old carpet, overlaid by a thin veneer of cheap cleaning products. The heating unit was churning full blast, intensifying the stuffiness with intermittent blasts of hot, dead air. The sagging curtains had been drawn shut, not to close out the dreary view of rain falling onto the icy parking lot, but to conceal the activities of the occupants from any chance passersby.

Melody Beecham sat at the rickety table, her laptop open, her SIG Pro pistol within easy reach. Her blank expression concealed the intensity of her focus on her partner, Nikolai Anwar, and the other two men in the room. So far, her role in Unit One's latest operation had merely been to look decorative, but in a few moments she would have to fake the transfer of two million dollars into Bryce Merton's bank account in Western Samoa, a newly popular hot spot for illegal banking activities, and it was vitally important for the transaction to proceed with apparent smoothness.

Bryce was a lab tech employed by the Seneschal Corporation, where he worked under the direction of the renowned physicist Dr. Simon Feng. Dr. Feng was one of the world's leading authorities on the application of nanotechnology to the problem of energy generation. In return for two million bucks, Bryce had promised to provide Nick with a CD-ROM he had stolen from his employers. The disk reportedly contained complete details of Dr. Feng's groundbreaking research into photovoltaic materials that could generate electricity directly from sunlight. Nick had heard rumors that the disk was for sale during the course of another Unit One operation, and had approached Bryce with an offer to buy. After two weeks of hard bargaining, this afternoon's meeting had been arranged.

Bryce Merton's appearance was as greasy and unappetizing as his ethics, but provided he didn't get spooked and start shooting, he didn't pose much of a physical threat. Although only a few pounds overweight, he was seriously out of shape, his body flabby and shapeless beneath his too-tight pants and sweater. Melody didn't anticipate any trouble when they arrested him, even though he was flashing a pearl-handled Beretta that he seemed to have no clue how to use. Amateurs and guns often made for a dangerous cocktail, but Bryce was both arrogant and incompetent, thus providing a soft target. Having observed him closely for the past fifteen minutes, she was confident she would be able to disarm him without much difficulty.

Bryce's hired bodyguard wouldn't be so easy to handle. Jesse Appolito was at least six foot two, and he appeared bulky with steroid-grown muscle. Jesse was carrying a businesslike Glock and, in contrast to his client, he gave every impression of knowing how to use it. He wasn't easy to distract, either. Melody's short leather skirt and long legs encased in tight zippered boots had won nothing from him beyond a single, assessing glance. Any longing looks Jesse cast toward her corner of the room had been aimed at her SIG rather than her body.

Unit One was a covert organization, not officially acknowledged by the government and not bound by the strict procedural rules of agencies such as the FBI, or the looser regulations of the CIA. Unit One operations were always secret, aimed at targets within the United States, and usually kept confidential even after they were completed. Consequently, many of Unit One's most successful missions didn't end in legal prosecutions. Even when they did, Unit One handed off most of the actual arrests to local law enforcement or the FBI. But today Nick and Melody would be acting as the arresting officers, which meant they were required to offer Jesse and Bryce all the protections guaranteed by the Constitution. However, since both suspects were armed and likely to shoot their way out of the motel room the moment they felt threatened, Nick and Melody could legitimately disarm them before announcing the arrest. But first, they had to have evidence against the pair that would hold up in court. That meant Bryce had to accept the two-million-dollar payment for the stolen research.

Bryce handed the promised disk to Nick with an elaborate flourish. "Here you are, then. Everything you need to start a revolution in the world's energy markets."

"I look forward to doing just that," Nick said. He spoke with a slight Russian accent, since he had conducted his negotiations with Bryce in the role of Nikolai Anwar, a businessman with connections to the Russian oil cartels and their associated criminal underworld.

Bryce gave a hoarse laugh. "Hell, when you get down to it, I'm a regular patriot. By selling you this research, I'm fucking over all those Arab dictators who want to hold America to ransom by charging a fortune for their oil."

"I am impressed by the intensity of your desire to serve your country," Nick said.

Bryce scowled. "Yeah, well, we can't all be goddamn heroes." He scratched at a pimple on his chin. "Anyway, I've given you the disk and now it's your turn. I want my money."

Nick tapped the slim plastic case containing the CD-ROM. "Before I hand over any money, I need to be sure that you are not selling me garbage."

Bryce appeared insulted. "You have my word that the disk contains all of Feng's current research materials."

"Your word?" Nick allowed a moment of withering silence and then smiled coldly. "My thanks, but I prefer to review the disk for myself."

Bryce Merton flushed, stung by Nick's contempt although he tried not to show it. He shrugged, almost visibly consoling himself with a reminder of how much sun and fun he would be able to buy with two million bucks.

"Be my guest," Bryce said. "Here, use my laptop." He sat on the edge of one of the beds and slipped the disk into his computer. He keyed in a command and the computer hummed quietly. After thirty seconds or so he swiveled the screen around so that it faced Nick.

"There you go, hotshot. I've pulled up the table of contents. Take your pick of any file. They're all loaded with good stuff. Feng has no clue about how to keep his files secure. You know what his password is in the lab? His wife's name." Bryce shook his head, genuinely appalled. "What a loser."

"In fact, he almost deserves to be robbed," Nick said.

"You got that right," Bryce said, sublimely unaware of Nick's irony. He gave his pimple another quick scratch. "Feng may be a genius at physics, but he's sure short on common sense. The guy needs a keeper to remind him to tuck his dick inside his pants."

Nick sat down on the bed. He actually understood no more about nanotechnology than Melody, which meant he understood next to nothing. However, he'd been extensively briefed by Dr. Feng, and he knew which files contained the most confidential and innovative elements of Seneschal's research project. He swiveled Bryce's laptop around on the bed, opened an appropriate file and started reading, searching for the crucial equations that Feng had helped him memorize in order to identify the contents of the CD-ROM as stolen property.

In fact, Nick's insistence on examining the contents of the disk was mostly for appearances' sake, since Bryce Merton would be toast once he took the two million bucks even if the disk contained nothing but gobbledygook. If he couldn't be arrested for the sale of stolen research, he could be arrested for extortion.

Melody watched Nick as he read, ruefully aware that she must have fallen dangerously deep into the minefields of love when even his frown of concentration struck her as sexy. Neither Bryce nor Jesse spoke, and the roar of the heating unit fan sounded loud in the stuffy room, the only other sound being the creak of Jesse's boots as he rocked backward and forward in monotonous rhythm.

After less than five minutes, Nick ejected the disk, slipped it into its case and tucked it into his shirt pocket. The fact that he put the disk into his pocket using his right hand was a prearranged signal to Melody indicating that, as far as he could tell, the disk contained exactly what Bryce had promised. Honor among thieves, if you could call it that, had apparently prevailed.

Nick pushed the laptop back across the bed to Bryce. "I am satisfied you have delivered Dr. Feng's research materials."

"Impressive stuff, right?" Bryce sounded as proud as if the research were his own.

"Very impressive," Nick acknowledged. "Dr. Feng is clearly a genius."

"Yeah. Also a major pain in the ass." Bryce grimaced, then glanced toward Melody. "Okay, enough already with the socializing. Let's move on to the good stuff. Where's my money?"

Melody looked at Nick, as if for approval. "Shall I start the transfer of the payment?" she asked.

He nodded. "Yes, that is acceptable to me."

"The motel only has a dial-up connection," Melody said as she entered the codes that connected her laptop to the computer system at Unit One headquarters. She keyed in the numerical combination and the password that indicated she was ready to begin the fake transfer of two million dollars to Bryce's account. "It's going to take several minutes to complete the transaction."

"That's okay." Bryce smiled. "My plane doesn't leave for another four hours."

"Where are you going?" Nick asked, propping himself casually against the wall of the motel.

Bryce laughed, increasingly excited now that the money was almost in his grasp. "That would be telling, wouldn't it? Somewhere warm, that's for sure. I'm sick to death of freezing my ass off through five months of goddamn Midwestern winter. That bastard Feng insists on starting work at seven in the morning." He sounded outraged. "You know what it's like getting up before dawn at this time of year? Fucking miserable, in case you couldn't guess."

"Well, now you are about to enjoy several years free of Feng's demands." Nick delivered a bland smile.

"Yeah, and I'm lovin' it."

Dr. Feng and starting work at 7:00 a.m. were going to seem like fond memories when Bryce was in prison, Melody reflected, waiting for her laptop to connect with Unit One. The link was finally established. Thanks to the outstanding computer skills of Bob Spinard, the director of intelligence, Melody's laptop whirred through several screens and then displayed what appeared to be a Nigerian bank account in the name of Nikolai Anwar. Bob Spinard had enjoyed himself, Melody saw, and given Nick a supposed bank balance of over seventeen million dollars, although only two million were shown as immediately available.

Melody gestured to Bryce, indicating the screen and showing him that Nick had sufficient funds to pay for the disk. "You notified us that you want your two million dollars transferred to the Presidential Bank of Western Samoa," she said. "I'm accessing the Web site of that bank now."

The monitor went blank for a full minute and then displayed a screen that supposedly welcomed her to the Presidential Bank. So far, so good. "For the next step I need to enter your account number, Mr. Merton." She moved her mouse to highlight the box asking for account details.

"I'll type in the account number myself," Bryce said hoarsely. Now that the two million dollars were only moments away from his possession, his excitement had escalated to the point that his breathing had become quick and shallow. "I'm not stupid enough to give my passwords to you. You could take the two million back out of my account as soon as I leave here."

"We never expected you to give us your account passwords," Melody said, turning her laptop toward him. "Go ahead. Enter them yourself."

Bryce merely grunted. Hunching one arm over the keyboard so that nobody could see what he typed, he pecked out a series of numbers using only his left hand.

The screen blinked and then returned with a request for him to enter his password. Bryce repeated his one-handed entry system, which effectively prevented any-one in the room from learning his passcodes even if they managed to sneak a clear view of the screen. Unfortu-nately for him, every stroke was being recorded back at Unit One headquarters, giving Bob Spinard imme-diate access to Bryce's account.

From Bryce's perspective, however, all was well, and he gave a satisfied grunt when a window popped up on the screen asking him what transaction he wanted to complete. He clicked the box "Make a Deposit."

"Okay, it's all ready for you to transfer the two mil-lions bucks into my account," he informed Melody, stepping aside so that she could access the keyboard. He moved behind her, hanging over her shoulder, and she pointedly asked him to move away while she typed in the symbols that supposedly gave her access to the funds in Nick's Nigerian account.

"I'm transferring the money now," she said, entering the final command that created the illusion of two mil-lion dollars winging their way into Bryce's account.

Bob Spinard was such a computer whiz that Melody had never anticipated any serious problems. Still, it was a relief that there had been no glitches in this crucial part of the operation. She let out a breath she hadn't real-ized she'd been holding when a window finally ap-peared announcing that the transfer was complete.

Bryce used the sleeve of his sweater to wipe his fore-head. "Show me my new balance," he demanded.

Melody swiveled the laptop in his direction. "You

need to enter your password again for that screen to come up."

"Okay, I'll type it in." For a second time, Bryce hunched over the keyboard and pecked away. A few seconds later, a banner flashed onto the screen containing the information that his account now held two million, two thousand, three hundred and eleven dollars and sixty-three cents.

Thank you, Bob Spinard.

"Hey, how's that for a healthy bank balance?" Bryce beamed. "Two million and change!" He gulped in air and then laughed as he shut down his laptop and zipped it into its carrying case. "Come on, Jesse, let's get out of here. We've got a plane to catch."

"Not so fast." Jesse spoke almost for the first time since the meeting had begun. He stepped in front of Bryce, extending his arm to stop his buddy's rush toward the door. "You need to check that transfer of funds again. This time run the check on your own computer, not hers."

Bryce's gaze narrowed. He clearly wasn't a man who reacted well to having his decisions questioned. "Why?" He jerked his head toward Melody. "I watched what she did. I keyed in my account number myself. There's no way for her to have screwed us over."

"Are you sure?"

"Of course I'm sure." Bryce's voice was riddled with doubt, despite his confident words.

"Humor me," Jesse said. "Double-check the balance on your own computer. Did she really put the funds into your bank, or did she just make pretty pictures on her computer?"

Melody rose to her feet, tucking her SIG into her waistband, the movement fluid and deceptively casual. She and Nick had considered the possibility that Bryce would insist on checking the transfer of funds on his own computer, and Bob Spinard had promised to arrange a diversion from the Web site of the Presidential Bank. Anyone attempting to access Bryce's account for the next twenty-four hours would actually be reading information generated by Unit One. She hoped to God the link and the diversion were in place and would function as advertised. It would be much easier to disarm Bryce and Jesse if they were relaxed and happy, not anticipating problems. She didn't want this afternoon's operation to end in a shootout, or serious injury to Bryce and Jesse, even if the two men had all the appeal of rancid lard.

"Check all you want," she said to Bryce. "The money's in your account, as you'll discover."

"It'd better be." Scowling, Bryce shoved his revolver into the holster hidden under his sweater. Then he slid his computer case onto the table Melody had just vacated. He extracted his laptop and plugged in the modem, his fingers tapping impatiently as he waited to get online. Standing behind him, Melody hid a rush of relief when his Presidential account came up, once again displaying the promised balance.

"Nasty suspicious minds you and your buddy have," she said mildly.

"Better safe than sorry." Bryce delivered the cliché with as much aplomb as if he'd just invented it.

Melody shrugged, using the gesture to conceal that she was looking to Nick for instructions. This operation had gone on long enough. Bryce had incriminated himself a dozen times over, and Jesse was apparently never going to put away his gun, so they might as well get on with the business of arresting them.

Nick clearly shared her opinion that it was time to move. His hand hanging loosely at his side, he pointed his index finger almost imperceptibly toward Bryce, their agreed signal to indicate that she should disarm him while Nick, who was a master of unarmed combat, concentrated on taking down Jesse, the stronger and more dangerous target.

She gave Nick the briefest of nods and positioned herself directly in front of Bryce, her attention focused on getting his gun away from him without injury to anyone. She acted immediately, without warning, throwing a hard punch to the region of Bryce's solar plexus. Her hand sank into at least an inch of flabby flesh, and Bryce reacted as if she'd sliced his liver with a stiletto. He shrieked and doubled over, probably as much from shock as from pain. Melody quickly moved in close, screening out the thuds and bumps of Nick's fight with Jesse so as not to become distracted.

She grabbed Bryce's right arm. Almost simultaneously, she brought her right leg forward and hooked it around Bryce's leg, forcing it toward her. He fell backward, crashing into the table. She pulled his fancy Beretta out of his holster as he careened off the table and collapsed to the floor. He lay there moaning, although his total injuries didn't amount to much more than a few bruises and maybe a couple of pulled muscles.

"You're under arrest," she said, keeping the Beretta aimed squarely at his heart. "Don't move until I say you can. You have the right to remain silent. If you choose to speak—"

"You're a fucking *cop?*" Bryce spat the words out.

"Something like that," Melody said.

Behind her, she heard the crash of a chair tumbling to the floor and the thud of hard blows landing on flesh. Jesse was apparently proving as tough a target as he looked, and he had enough skill in unarmed combat that Nick hadn't been able to disarm him within the first couple of seconds. Nick yelled out her name as she heard the explosive sound of a gun firing.

A sudden searing heat burned through her side. Pain blossomed, spreading out to envelop her body so completely that she could no longer think. She tried to focus on keeping the Beretta aimed at Bryce, but it was impossible. Her eyes were open—weren't they?—but she couldn't see. The room had gone dark.

More noise. More shots. More crashes. More thuds. It required too much effort to work out what was happening. Then Nick was suddenly leaning over her and she realized she was on the floor. She felt him take her hand. She sighed in relief and closed her eyes.

"Stay with me, Melody!" he pleaded. "Melody, for God's sake, you can't die on me, dammit!"

I'll try not to.

"I'm calling the paramedics now. Just hang in there, Melody. Promise me you'll hang in there."

She would have answered him if she could. Promised him that she would fight to stay alive, since he seemed so frantic, but the link between her thoughts and her voice had been severed. Sound and light vanished, and she slid into the comfort of darkness, where there was no more pain.

Two

Martin McShane, director general of Unit One, bounced out of his chair as soon as he saw Nick. "What's the latest on Melody?" he asked, tugging at his ratty Bears sweatshirt, signed by the great Walter Payton himself. Mac had lived his entire life on the East Coast, but for some obscure reason, he was a rabid Bears fan. "Is she back in New York? Did the flight go smoothly?"

Nick nodded. "She's home. The flight was fine. Jasper's with her right now."

Mac grunted. "Jasper driving her crazy?"

Jasper Fowles was the owner of the famous Van der Meer Gallery in Manhattan. Melody nominally still worked there as his executive assistant, a job that provided cover for her role as a Unit One operative. Jasper was also the commander-in-chief of Unit One and a friend of Melody's since her childhood. Most of the world considered Jasper flamboyant and shallow, albeit witty and entertaining. The very few people who knew of his role as leader of the most effective covert organization within the United States considered him brilliant, ruthless, and exceptionally good at navigating the treacherous waters of Washington politics.

Since Jasper was also deeply attached to Melody, whom he regarded as the daughter he would never have, her recent brush with death had been a devastating experience for him. All the more so because, when Melody first learned the truth about his double life, their relationship had dived into the sticky tar pits of misunderstanding and had never quite climbed out. Her sense of having been betrayed by a much-loved mentor had been exacerbated six months ago when she discovered that Jasper knew the true identity of her biological father and had chosen to withhold that information from her.

Clandestine work was hell on relationships, Nick reflected wryly.

"Jasper's definitely hovering," he told Mac. "But Melody will warn him to back off if he becomes too impossible. Lately, I've noticed that she and Jasper are getting along better—well enough for her to stop being so polite to him all the time."

"Noticed the same thing." Mac was never a man to waste words, and when he was worried, he rarely produced a full sentence. "What did our doctor say about her condition?"

"That she survived the journey just fine, but that she's lucky to be alive," Nick said. "That if the bullet Jesse Appolito fired had been a quarter-centimeter farther right, it would have destroyed the functionality of her pancreas. Also that the surgeon from Chicago did a great job sewing her up, although she's going to have some impressive scars from the surgery."

"Better to have scars than be dead." Mac's bushy eyebrows wriggled as he shot a shrewd glance toward his director of operations. Nick wasn't looking too happy, despite all the positive news about Melody. Although he would have undergone torture before admitting it, Nick held a special place in Mac's heart. Mac had worked at the CIA with Nick's father and had been selected as point person by the agency when Nick's father, mother and teenaged sister were blown up by a car bomb planted by order of the KGB. Nick had been a freshman in college at the time of the triple murder and, for at least a year after the tragedy, Mac had been fairly sure that only a burning desire for vengeance kept Nick alive.

Mac spoke with deliberate casualness, knowing how cautious he needed to be about intruding on Nick's well-guarded emotions. "For a man whose main squeeze just survived a bullet, you don't look too cheerful."

Nick was silent for so long that Mac assumed he was searching for ways to dodge the implicit question. In the end, though, Nick decided not to prevaricate. "I can't work with Melody anymore," he said. "No more partnering her in the field. No more planning her mission profiles. I need to back right off."

"Why?" Mac asked, although he could make a pretty good guess.

"You know why."

"Might guess, but I don't *know*."

"I'm in love with her," Nick responded tersely.

"And real happy about the situation, I can see." From the point of view of smooth operations over the next couple of months, the fact that the director of Unit One operations had fallen in love with one of his field agents was a damn nuisance. From a personal point of view, Mac was delighted to hear that Nick was capable of succumbing to an emotion powerful enough to take precedence over his work. Six months earlier, at the start of Unit One's mission to disband the Soldiers of Jordan, Mac had ordered Nick to break up with Melody. To his dismay, Nick had obeyed the order. Mac was deeply relieved that Nick was now exhibiting signs of regular human emotion and had begun to draw some boundaries around his dedication to Unit One. Without that sense of limitation, Nick could never have been promoted to the position of director general. The person who ran Unit One had a lot of power—far too much to trust to a potential fanatic.

Mac expressed none of his thoughts, not wanting to affect Nick's answers. "Care to explain why you can't work with the woman you love?" he asked.

"That should be obvious." Nick rolled his eyes. "We're not talking about the two of us sharing duties in a flower shop. We're in a business that exposes us to life-threatening danger on a regular basis, and I'm not able to function rationally when she's around. My feelings for her have already caused one negative outcome. I don't want any more."

"What negative outcome?"

Nick's expression became even grimmer. "I shot and killed Jesse Appolito before he could be questioned."

"With adequate cause," Mac said crisply. "According to your report last week, Jesse had already fired at Melody when you shot him."

"That's true."

"So what's your problem? It's not as if Jesse Appolito is the first person you've ever killed."

Nick ran his hand through his hair, pacing. "The moment Jesse grabbed the gun off the floor and fired at Melody, I wasn't in control anymore. Usually a crisis brings the situation into more intense focus. But all I remember after Melody went down is white-hot rage, alternating with overwhelming fear. I squeezed off shots at Jesse without any calculation—"

"You're overdramatizing," Mac said. "If any other Unit One agent had been lying on the floor wounded, your reaction would have been the same—"

"No." Nick shook his head, then qualified. "My actions might have been the same. My emotions would have been entirely different."

"True but irrelevant. Quit beating yourself up over what happened. Your emotions in no way affected your judgment. Jesse had already fired once with murderous intent and he'd have fired again if you hadn't taken him down. You did the right thing. There's no suggestion otherwise from anyone."

"Maybe. But that reinforces my point about the difficulty of working with Melody. It's been fourteen days since she was wounded, and I'm still second-guessing every action I took that afternoon. My judgment's literally shot to hell where she's concerned. That means I shouldn't be working with her."

Mac glanced longingly at his espresso machine, which hadn't provided its comforting hisses and aromas in over a week. Damn drama-queen doctors and their dire warnings about blood pressure, stress and caffeine. And why was he listening to the doctors, anyway? He never had before. He sighed, turning his back on the machine. "I'll consider your request regarding Melody," he said.

"Thank you."

"Humph. Take a couple of days off, Nick, and that's an order. The FBI is handling Bryce Merton's prosecution, so our involvement in the Seneschal case is over. Go sit at Melody's bedside. Hold her hand and tell her she'll feel better soon."

"I've already taken fourteen days off. I can't take any more. The Vergoni operation had reached a critical point when Melody and I took time out to go to Indiana and nail Merton. I have to follow up on Vergoni in the next twenty-four hours—"

Mac had no intention of taking Nick up on his offer. If Nick was going to take over Mac's role as director general, they needed to start grooming some of the newer Unit One operatives to find out if any of them were capable of working in the field with the sort of flair that Nick had been demonstrating for the past decade.

"I've assigned the Vergoni mission to Tony," Mac said.

"Tony will need a partner to go with him to San Francisco. This is a two-man op."

"He can take Josh Straiker." Mac raised Josh's name on purpose. Josh was the only operative Mac had encountered in a thirty-five-year career who came close to being as good as Nick. Predictably, the two men had been circling each other like cougars staking out territory ever since Josh had been recruited from the CIA.

"Josh is brand-new and the Vergoni operation is complicated." Nick's words were clipped.

"Yep, it is complicated. I guess we're about to find out if Josh is as good in the field as the bigwigs in Langley promised us when they sent him over."

"Dammit, Mac! Vergoni's ex-wife is attempting to sabotage the vineyards. Two of his brothers have died in suspicious accidents, and that's only the start of it—"

"All our operations are complicated," Mac said dryly. "Hand this one off, Nick. Take a couple of days away from headquarters. Go play at being a normal human being."

"At a minimum I have to brief Tony and check out Josh's readi—"

"No," Mac said. "*I'll* brief Tony. *I'll* check out Josh's readiness. You're good, Nick. Damn good. But you're not indispensable. None of us is. Now get the hell out of here."

Mac remained standing until Nick had left the room, then returned to his desk and sat down heavily. Nick was the best field agent he'd encountered in the course of a long career. Even distracted by love, Nick was more effective than ninety-nine percent of operatives working at the top of their game. Trouble was, at this precise moment, Mac really needed Nick to be functioning at one-hundred-and-ten-percent capacity, and that wasn't going to happen until Melody was fully recuperated.

Mac scowled at his espresso machine. Got up, walked toward it, and then sat down again. Damn doctors. Whichever way you looked at it, getting old really sucked.

Nick let himself into his apartment and made his way to the master bedroom, where Melody was recovering from the stresses of the flight from Indiana. The medical team dispatched by Unit One had left, but Jasper still sat in the corner armchair, a pile of newspapers from around the world stacked neatly beside him. The two men exchanged silent nods of greeting, but Melody woke up anyway.

She appeared less of an invalid without all the hospital monitors hooked up to various portions of her anatomy, Nick saw with relief. She was pale, though, and her face was thin after two weeks of barely eating while she recovered from surgery to remove the bullet, followed by an infection that had been considered life-threatening for a terrible twenty-four hours.

Her eyes lit up when she saw him, and Nick's heart turned over. For the past six months, he had been telling himself that he would probably fall out of love with Melody as inexplicably as he'd fallen in. That hadn't happened, and he was about ready to acknowledge that he'd been deluding himself. Ever since he'd helped the paramedics load her blood-soaked body onto the stretcher in that miserable motel room, he'd realized that his feelings for her weren't going away. On the contrary, they were getting worse. Or deeper, or more important, or however the hell you wanted to describe them.

When his parents and teenage sister died, Nick had learned the bitter lesson that love came with a high price tag, and that the loss of love caused a pain almost too intense to bear. Unwilling to pay such a price ever again, Nick had disciplined himself to avoid falling in love. But somehow Melody had slipped under his guard, perhaps because they worked together and their relationship had leaped over most of the introductory stages, over his defenses. One morning he'd woken up and discovered he'd surrendered his heart before he'd even noticed that it was under siege.

He liked that explanation marginally better than the idea that falling in love with Melody was an inescapable fact of his destiny, and would have happened however and whenever he met her.

"Perfect timing," Jasper said to him, putting down the newspaper. "Melody has been sleeping almost since you left. She woke up just a minute ago."

"Did you enjoy your nap?" Nick asked, sitting on the edge of the bed and taking Melody's hand into his. He leaned over and kissed her softly, taking care not to scrape the stubble of his beard against her cheek.

"The best." She leaned back against the stack of pillows. "I didn't realize how uncomfortable that hospital bed was until I got home."

Technically speaking, Melody wasn't home, since she was in Nick's condo and she had never officially moved in. She still rented a one-bedroom apartment near Bellevue Hospital, but over the past six months it had gradually been transformed from the place where she lived to a place that served mostly as storage space for their excess belongings. However, since Melody wasn't much better than Nick at verbalizing her feelings, they'd both managed to rub along for the past several months without ever actually discussing the fact that they were now, for all intents and purposes, living together. That they were a couple.

The amazing thought didn't set off alarm bells. On the contrary, Nick rather liked the idea, strange as it felt for someone who'd been alone since the age of nineteen. He stroked the back of Melody's hand, his thumb brushing over the fading bruise where an IV needle had been inserted into her vein.

"Mac is so relieved to have you safely back in New York that he spoke at least a couple of complete sentences."

Melody laughed. "Probably to inquire when I would be back at my desk."

Nick shook his head. "You're maligning him. He's anxious for you to take all the time you need to heal. In fact, he's insisting I should take the next couple of days off and stay with you."

"I'm touched," Melody said. "I know how busy everyone is at work and how much Mac relies on you."

"Speaking of work…" Jasper rose to his feet and came to stand on the other side of the bed. "I have a cocktail party I need to attend this evening, so I'll leave you two to enjoy a night of reckless adventure together."

"What adventure is that?" Melody asked wryly. "Discovering if I can sleep without painkillers?"

"Whatever turns you on, sweetie." Jasper leaned over and kissed Melody's forehead, then took a step back and looked at her, allowing both his worry and his affection to show in his aquiline features. "Are you still in a lot of pain?"

"No, not much," Melody said, a little too quickly.

"That bad, huh?" Jasper touched her lightly on the shoulder.

Melody managed a shrug. "The surgeon explained that he was forced to cut through quite a bit of muscle to get to the bullet. And the post-op infection didn't help."

Jasper feigned a shudder. "Just hearing about all you've been through sets my nerve endings tingling." He gave her hand another gentle squeeze. "Would it ease the pain somewhat if I told you I heard this morning that Zachary Wharton reached a plea deal with the Feds, and he'll be serving eighteen years on charges of conspiracy to murder Bashir al-Hassan and former vice president Johnston Yates?"

"Federal prison is too good for Zachary Wharton," Nick said. "If I'd been in charge of his prosecution, I'd have turned the hypocritical bastard over to the Syrians—and they'd have executed him."

"Better yet, he should have been kept alive and leg-shackled to Dave Ramsdell for a few years," Melody said. "Now there's a couple that deserves each other."

Jasper chuckled, then sobered. "The evidence that Zachary knew exactly what Dave Ramsdell was planning is slim," he said. "Eighteen years is probably the most severe sentence we could hope for."

Nick sighed, but nodded. "Realistically, Zachary might have walked if the trial had ever gone in front of a jury. The man was brilliant as a preacher, and he would have been even more compelling as a witness in his own defense."

"He's so persuasive, he'd probably have had the judge and jury volunteering to join the Soldiers of Jordan," Melody agreed ruefully. "He held his community in White Falls together by sheer force of personality, and in lots of ways the place worked, thanks to him."

"Did you see the memo from the local sheriff saying that, at last count, there were only twenty-two Soldiers of Jordan left on the White Falls campus?" Jasper asked.

Nick nodded. "Yeah, I saw it. Along with the note informing us that the former members of the community are all suing each other, trying to recover some of their vanished life savings. If they hadn't held such unpleasant views, I could almost feel sorry for them."

"Well, let's not go overboard," Jasper said. "If you recall, most of the recruits to Zachary Wharton's nasty little sect were quite willing to go out and kill anybody Zachary targeted as an enemy, even if the enemy happened to be a former vice president of their own country, or a moderate Muslim cleric working his ass off to bring peace and stability to the Middle East. By the way, Melody, speaking of former vice presidents, Johnston called me yesterday to find out how you're doing."

"Did he?" Melody gave a small smile. "He already sent some extravagantly beautiful flowers to the hospital in Gary."

"He's very worried about you, naturally. I told him you were getting better, but still in need of lots of TLC." Jasper paused. "He and Cynthia are planning to take their yacht on a Caribbean cruise starting a week from Saturday. It's the first time Johnston will have sailed in the Caribbean since your mother died."

"He mentioned that trip to me," Melody admitted. "Actually, he invited me to join him."

"And last week he asked me to encourage you to accept the invitation," Jasper said.

"Well, of course I can't accept. I'm way behind at work. I'm planning to go into headquarters next week to catch up on paperwork, then start fitness training again the week after that—"

"Absolutely not," Nick said, worry making his tone of voice harsher than he had intended. "Are you insane? The doctor said a minimum of six weeks before you would be fit to return to active duty."

"The boy is taking the words right out of my mouth," Jasper said. "My dear Melody, kindly display some grain of the intelligence with which you were fortunate enough to have been born. You will be nothing but a liability at work until you've regained your strength. Meanwhile Johnston Yates is longing to have the chance to help you recuperate, and at the same time enable you to visit the place where your mother's life ended with such tragic unexpectedness. I can't order you to accept Johnston's invitation, but I can tell you that you will be barred from Unit One headquarters for the next three weeks at least. And that's a threat I *can* implement."

"I can see that I might as well say yes to my father." Melody scowled at Jasper, who merely raised a supercilious eyebrow. She sighed, then finally laughed. "Did I ever mention, Jasper, that you have a tendency to be a bully?"

"My dear girl, you are quite wrong. I don't have a tendency to be a bully—I *am* a bully, and take considerable pride in the fact, since I only bully people for their own good."

"And you always know what's good for people better than they do themselves, of course."

"Of course. I'm an old soul, who arrived in this world full of wisdom from my many previous lives."

Melody sent him a surprised glance. "Since when did you decide to believe in reincarnation?"

"Since I realized I was a wise old soul." Jasper patted her hand. "So I expect to hear shortly that you are leaving for a cruise in the warm waters of the Caribbean."

"Yes, Jasper. But only because I'm much too tired to argue with you. I'll call Johnston tomorrow."

"I'm delighted you've decided not to waste your substandard levels of energy in a vain attempt to defy me. Good night, my dear. Sleep well. Nick, I'll see you at work the day after tomorrow. No, don't bother to show me out. It's evident that you're dying to get into bed with Melody and far be it from me to keep you from your heart's desire."

Nick barely waited for Jasper to leave the room before he kicked off his shoes and lay down next to Melody, stretching out his arm so that she could rest her head on his shoulder.

"Jasper's right as always," he murmured, burying his face in her hair. "I've wanted to hold you like this every moment of the past two weeks, but each time I got close to you an alarm would go off and bring the nurses running."

She rubbed her cheek against his shirt. "I never understood before how dehumanizing a hospital can be, even when you're out of Intensive Care. It feels so good to be lying on your shoulder instead of on sheets of plastic protectors, with all those damn tubes trailing every time I turned over. I finally feel reconnected to the world."

Nick gestured to the puffy comforter that covered the lower half of her body. "A few moments ago, you told Jasper that you were glad to be home. Do you think of this apartment as your home?"

A faint trace of color appeared in Melody's cheeks. "It was a figure of speech—"

"Was that all?" Nick asked quietly. "I hoped you might mean it."

Melody looked at him, her extraordinary blue eyes still clouded with the remnants of pain and medications, but her gaze straightforward. "Taking a bullet to the belly seems to have blown away some of my inhibitions. What are you asking me, Nick? Are you suggesting we should make it official that we're living together?"

"I guess that's exactly what I'm asking. How would

you feel about that?" Nick realized he was holding his breath as he waited for her answer.

She kept him in suspense for what felt like half of eternity. Then she smiled and nestled more closely against him. "I'd like that. I'd like it a lot."

Her answer made Nick happy enough that he almost forgot to be scared by how much he cared.

Three

The waters of the Caribbean stretched out in a shining azure sheet, with only the jump of frightened fish, chased by hungry predators, to ripple the calm surface. Nursing a mug of hot chocolate—the air was cool despite the brilliant sunshine—Melody adjusted the brim of her cotton deck cap and watched Cynthia Yates attempt to reel in her catch: an extremely angry grouper at least three feet long. Squinting against the sun, Melody sipped her cocoa and yawned. Utter laziness was turning out to be one of the major attractions of convalescence.

"You're rooting for the fish," Johnston Yates said, drawing up a deck chair and coming to sit beside her. "I can tell by your expression."

Melody laughed. "And I thought I was doing such a good job of hiding my feelings."

"I'm learning to interpret the subtleties of your expressions. The more polite control outwardly, the more you're seething inwardly."

Johnston still managed to surprise her quite often with how well he had her character nailed. Melody smiled at him. "My grandfather accuses me of being a complete hypocrite, and he's right. I'm one of those frauds who loves to eat meat and fish, but works hard to avoid thinking about the gruesome details of how my meal got to the table."

"Oh pish darn!" A resounding splash marked the victory of the grouper over Cynthia Yates. She stood, hands on chubby hips, muttering quaintly old-fashioned insults at the lost fish.

Johnston glanced toward his wife, smothering an affectionate chuckle. "I'd say you just got lucky. It seems fresh grouper isn't going to be on tonight's dinner menu after all." After a moment, his smile faded and he turned around, sitting sideways on the cushioned lounger. He leaned hesitantly toward Melody, then pulled back, still wary of physical demonstrations of affection despite six months of guarded but increasing intimacy between the two of them.

If Melody had ever wondered where her own emotional inhibitions sprang from, her speculation had been answered six months ago when she discovered that Johnston Yates was her father. It was amazing how similar many of their personality traits were, given that they had barely spoken to each other for the first thirty years of her life. Johnston had been vice president of the United States when Melody was conceived during the course of his extramarital affair with the notorious Lady Rosalind Carruthers Beecham. Johnston demonstrated all the easy charm and charisma of a successful politician when he was in a group setting. However, when he had to deal one-on-one with an emotionally fraught situation, he either bumbled around hopelessly lost for words, or froze into seeming hauteur. When she met Johnston Yates, she'd not only met her biological father, she'd met her personality doppelgänger, Melody reflected wryly.

Guessing that her father wanted to talk about Roz's death, she took pity on him and brought up the subject herself. "Did you come to tell me we're getting close to the spot where my mother was swept overboard?" she asked. "I studied the reports from the Mexican Coast Guard. We must be getting near the place where the accident happened."

Johnston sighed with relief that the painful subject of the death of Melody's mother, and his one-time mistress, had been broached. "Yes, we're getting very close to the spot…. I thought you would want me to tell you." He cleared his throat. "Nobody can be sure precisely where your mother fell overboard, of course. Obviously, nobody was around at the time, or she would have been saved. However, I spoke with the captain this morning—he was with us then, too—and he confirmed that we must have lost her somewhere in this general area."

Melody stood up and walked to the side of the yacht, resting against the rail. She realized only after she leaned forward that her wound had finally healed to the point that she no longer instinctively protected that area of her midriff.

Johnston followed her to the rail. Melody zipped up

her jacket, feeling a sudden chill. The sunshine was dazzling, but tomorrow would be the first of December and the sea breeze carried a nip of winter even this far south. Or perhaps her mother's death still carried enough of a sting to provoke a physical reaction.

Johnston laid his hand on her arm. "We don't have to talk about this if you would prefer not to."

"No, I want to talk. I very much want to talk." Melody had resigned herself months ago to the fact that her mother's body would have been eaten by predatory sea creatures within a few days of her death, so it was absurd to stare into the hypnotic depths of the ocean as if she somehow expected to identify the precise spot where the body lay.

Not for the first time since Roz died, Melody realized that logic carried her only so far when it came to dealing with the grief. Regrets seemed to catch her unawares for the most trivial of reasons. How could she have known, for example, that the absence of a grave—a symbol she would have believed entirely unimportant to her—would become a tiny but constant ache in her heart?

Johnston kept his gaze fixed on the slight swell of the waves. "The sea is so calm today, it may be difficult for you to imagine how threatening this stretch of ocean looked the night your mother died."

Melody shook her head. "It's not hard at all. After my mother divorced Wallis and we went back to England, the house we lived in was only five miles from the ocean. I grew up seeing firsthand the effects that strong currents and high winds can produce out at sea.

The report prepared by the Mexican authorities indicated that the winds were blowing at more than fifty kilometers an hour, with gusts reaching much higher. That's not a hurricane, but there's no way my mother should have been on deck without her life jacket."

"She shouldn't have been on deck, period," Johnston said. "The captain specifically warned us not to come on deck without taking adequate safety precautions, such as hitching on to a lifeline. Most of our guests didn't want to come on deck, of course. They became quite seasick, especially after dinner, and retired to their cabins early."

"But not my mother," Melody said.

"No," Johnston agreed. "Not Roz. She didn't feel sick at all, whereas two or three of our guests were almost prostrate. She was one of those fortunate women who never seemed to suffer from minor aches and pains like the rest of us. I remember the days when she could climb a mountain in the morning, ski down in the afternoon, and drink the rest of us under the table at night. I used to tease her that she would live to be a hundred." He was silent for a moment, and his voice was husky when he spoke again. "I wish to God I'd been correct."

From the corner of her eye, Melody noticed that Cynthia Yates had abandoned her attempt to catch another fish. Having neatly stowed her tackle, she went below deck. Given the current location of the yacht, Cynthia probably guessed what her husband and Melody were talking about and had chosen to slip away without intruding. Melody was grateful for Cynthia's tact. Left alone with her father, she felt free to probe the relationship that had existed between him and Roz, a luxury that had presented itself only rarely in the six months since she discovered that Johnston was her father.

"I didn't realize you and my mother had ever gone skiing together," she said. "How in the world did you manage that? I know the media were more discreet in those days, but still…"

"Well, we couldn't go skiing as a twosome, of course. Quite apart from the press corps, I always had a Secret Service escort, so we could never have slipped away together without letting them in on our plans, which I wasn't willing to do. But Roz and I moved in much the same circles, so it was easy for us to arrange to be in the same place at the same time. Roz was masterful at pretending to find me rather pompous and annoying, which prevented people ever imagining that we were…attracted to each other. I think she actually found the deception fun." Johnston shook his head, looking bemused. "God help me, when I was with her, I found myself agreeing with her."

"My mother *was* fun to be with," Melody agreed. "Even when she was at her most exasperating, it was hard to be angry with her."

"That was even more true when she was younger. When we first met, Roz was in some ways still quite naive. Combined with her stunning looks, that hint of naiveté made her totally enchanting. She was one of the most sought-after guests in Washington because she enlivened any gathering, and not simply because of her beauty."

Melody had heard the same thing from many people but she could never quite picture her mother as naive. She wondered if her father might be confusing indifference to convention with innocence. Right up until her death, Roz had possessed a rare talent for creating an environment in which people were so captivated by her charisma that they found themselves playing her game, and following her rules. She had rarely allowed conventional moral standards to interfere with how she chose to lead her life and had probably never worried that her affair with Johnston Yates might be ethically wrong, or hurtful to others. From Roz's perspective, the inconvenient detail that Johnston was married to Cynthia, and she herself was married to Wallis Beecham, would merely have added spice to the excitement of their liaison. The fact that Johnston risked his position as vice president of the United States, and that Wallis Beecham was a pathologically jealous man, wouldn't have deterred her. Roz would probably have considered an extramarital affair barely worth pursuing unless it was high risk.

Johnston Yates was still married to Cynthia, the same woman he'd betrayed thirty-two years earlier, which added another layer of complexity to Melody's desire for an honest discussion of his relationship with her mother. Unlike Roz, Johnston had plenty of moral inhibitions, and she could see he regretted the deceptions and betrayals that were implicit in the skiing anecdote he'd just recounted. Still, she had been born because of his liaison with Roz, and she was hungry for details of the time her parents had spent together.

"You told me once that you fell passionately in love with my mother," she said. "Was that true, or were you just saying what you thought I wanted to hear?"

Johnston avoided the uncomfortable intimacy of holding her gaze by watching a school of fish leap into the air and arc back into the water. "It was the truth. I loved Roz, although I was never blind to the fact that she wasn't always an easy woman to like. She was self-centered and spoiled, but I was self-centered, too, with a damn good opinion of myself, and I admired her ability to go after what she wanted with ruthless single-mindedness."

"She was nothing like her parents, or her brothers," Melody said. "They're all salt-of-the-earth type people, very modest and unassuming, despite the fact that my grandfather is an earl. Most of my relatives love English country life. Farming is their favorite topic of conversation, and their definition of wild entertainment is a trip to London for a symphony concert—opera being a bit too melodramatic for their tastes. I think my mother must have felt hopelessly out of place within her own family."

"I'm sure she did. She glittered, and she craved a stage where she could shine to maximum effect." The fish had stopped jumping, but Johnston still didn't look at Melody. Instead, he stared off at the horizon, where the sun was just beginning to dip toward the sea. "Roz was unfortunate enough to be both smart and beautiful at a time when society, at best, allowed women to be one or the other. She coped by emphasizing her physical beauty and working very hard to appear dumb."

"It was such a waste of her potential," Melody said.

"Don't be too harsh on her. A lot of beautiful women did the same thing. Think of Marilyn Monroe, who also happened to be one of the great actors of the twentieth century. She struggled her whole career to hide just how extraordinarily talented she was, and how smart. Roz was from the same era, and utilized many of the same tricks to get by."

"It's sad to think that if my mother had been born a generation later, she'd probably have been president of a giant commercial enterprise by the time she was forty."

Johnston smiled. "Yes, she probably would have, unless she decided to become prime minister instead."

"My God, Roz as prime minister!" Melody gave a wry laugh. "The world doesn't know what a narrow escape it had."

"I think she'd have been brilliant." Johnston sounded as if he meant it. "As it was, Roz had to be content with exploiting her looks and learning to manipulate people, especially men. She cast a sexual spell over the majority of the men she came into contact with, and I was no exception. I fell hard and fast, but in my case, it wasn't only a physical attraction. Roz was a much softer, sweeter person when I first met her than the woman she later became, and I took advantage of that sweetness." He paused for a moment, his eyes dark with regrets. "Looking back, I can see that our affair left her a lot more cynical than she'd been before, which adds another black mark to my lifetime account. And yet I can't say I regret the affair, because without it you wouldn't exist."

"You may be glad to have a daughter now, but you played no role in my life. I can understand that marrying my mother might have been difficult, but that didn't mean you had to ignore me." Melody tried to keep her voice neutral, but didn't succeed. She heard the sharp edge to her comments and didn't really care. Johnston had never provided an adequate explanation for his years of neglect, and she was still struggling to come to terms with his failure. In the past six months, it often seemed that he sought out her company whenever he could. But she still wondered if he would ever have acknowledged their relationship if she hadn't forced the confrontation.

"You're right that I refused to acknowledge that the child Roz was carrying was mine," Johnston said. He finally brought his gaze back to meet hers. "I wanted to be president of the United States and that's a powerful dream. Powerful enough to hold your mother's enchantment at bay. Powerful enough to make me neglect you."

He'd hinted before that presidential ambitions had kept him silent about their relationship, and his answer should have been entirely credible. At the time of her birth, Johnston had been vice president of the United States. For four years, he'd lived with the knowledge that he was a heartbeat away from becoming the most powerful man in the world. It wasn't surprising to hear that he'd craved the ultimate accolade of the presidency. The only problem was, Johnston had never held public office after his single term as vice president. Instead, he'd retired into lucrative commercial ventures, seemingly content to remain a behind-the-scenes authority figure in the Republican Party.

"I've never understood what happened to your political career," Melody said. "You say you rejected Roz and me because of your political ambitions, but you never even campaigned for your party's nomination, although you were one of the most admired and successful vice presidents ever. Instead of capitalizing on your popularity, you simply retired from public life."

Johnston hesitated, then shrugged. "Cynthia became seriously ill and the rigors of a campaign would have been too much for her. I owed my wife more than you can imagine, Melody. I still do. The fact that I'd been unfaithful was only part of my debt to her, so you can imagine how great the sum total was."

Melody had read everything she could find about Johnston's decision not to campaign for the presidency, and his wife's health had been the reason cited for his decision to retire from public life. Johnston had certainly owed Cynthia big-time. But he owed his daughter a debt, too, Melody reflected. After all, she was the one person in the nasty triangle of Cynthia, Roz and Johnston who had played no role whatsoever in the original mess. She didn't give voice to her thought, but Johnston seemed to be as good at reading her mind as he claimed. His cheeks flushed a dark, guilty red as he looked at her.

"The truth is, I put myself in an impossible position when I started the affair with Roz. Your mother was married to a brute who later turned out to be capable of murder, but I was married to a good and loving woman, who had been a loyal wife. Whatever my feelings for your mother, I had already made promises to Cynthia that should never have been broken. When Roz became pregnant, I had two conflicting sets of obligations, and there was no way to make everything turn out right. The circle couldn't be squared."

He paused and when he spoke again, his voice was strained. "I like to think I would behave better if I had to cope with the situation all over again. The frightening truth is, though, that I'm not sure what *better* might have meant once Roz and I made the initial mistake of starting the affair."

"I'm sorry," Melody said. "I've stirred the pot of difficult memories to no real purpose. Whether or not you chose to marry Roz was something between the two of you—"

"And Cynthia," he corrected quietly.

"Yes, of course. But it's not something between you and me. Especially not now, three decades later."

"You're letting me off the hook too easily." Johnston grimaced. "My decision not to marry your mother affected you enormously and, at the very least, you have the right to know if you were born as the result of a casual liaison or something more important." He cleared his throat, patently ill at ease discussing such intimate and emotional subjects. "As I've grown older, I've realized that it's invariably the innocent bystanders who get hurt when people decide to break the rules. Your mother and I enjoyed six magical months together, and other people paid the price for our enjoyment. I promise you, though, my relationship with your mother may have been illicit and short-lived, but it was neither casual nor trivial. And if it's any consolation, in the end I think both Roz and I paid dearly for our six months of pleasure."

"You and Roz seemed to remain friends after the affair ended," Melody said. "Did you?"

"Not really." Johnston gave a bleak smile. "Passion and betrayal don't translate very well into friendship. But Roz and I continued to move in the same circles, and we couldn't suddenly appear hostile to one another, any more than we could previously show how attracted we were. Those forced meetings were painful for me and I assume they were equally painful for your mother. Gradually, though, enough time passed that the facade of friendship became the reality."

Melody was surprised that their friendship had warmed back up to the point that Johnston had been willing to invite Roz to join him cruising in the Caribbean, and she said as much. "When my mother called to say that she was going to spend her fiftieth birthday with you, it didn't strike me as strange, but given everything I've learned since, it seems…unlikely, to say the least."

"Lawrence Springer asked me to invite Roz," Johnston said. "Otherwise, I have to admit, I would never have issued the invitation. Springer was briefly between wives at the time and it seemed a less bad idea than you might imagine. I checked with Cynthia, and she agreed that Roz's presence might actually make the voyage a little less tense for everyone."

Melody winced. "That was optimistic, considering almost everyone on board was connected in some way to the Bonita Partnership. With my mother scrambling to collect material so that she could continue to black-mail Wallis, I imagine the tension levels during that cruise must have been off the charts."

"You underestimate your mother's ability to charm and entertain," Johnston said quietly. "I'd invited those particular guests because I'd had a disturbing conversation with Lawrence Springer regarding the Bonita Partnership and I wanted to pursue my questions in a relaxed and informal setting. I was beginning to worry that I'd invested my money and my reputation in something a lot more dubious than offshore stem cell research. I wanted to find out if Senator Cranford had developed any doubts similar to my own. Cranford, however, was exceptionally difficult to pin down, which is no surprise in view of what we've discovered about him since then."

Johnston's smile was bitterly self-mocking. "It seems I was the only partner in the Bonita Project who wasn't aware that Wallis Beecham was planning to clone human babies as a commercial enterprise. Since I've always prided myself on being astute, the realization of how I was duped still shocks me. It's humiliating to realize I was being used as window dressing to create a veneer of legitimacy for a project I would have rejected if I'd guessed its true nature."

"Unless you'd grown up with Wallis, as I did, those good ole country-boy manners of his were quite convincing. It's no surprise he fooled you. He fools everyone."

"It was more a case of stubbornly refusing to see what was shoved right under my nose," Johnston said.

"Wallis Beecham played me. He knew I considered the limitations imposed by the Bush administration on stem cell research to be too rigid and likely to send many of our cutting-edge research scientists fleeing abroad. He exploited those fears to get me on board. I'd harbored doubts about Wallis Beecham's ethics from the time I first met him, and I'd had thirty-plus years to confirm my original negative impression. And yet he convinced me the Bonita Partnership was a breakthrough combination of cutting-edge science and commercial interests." He grimaced. "I'd be dishonest if I didn't admit that I was attracted to the chance of doubling my investment within two years."

"Wallis Beecham has a talent for deceiving smart people," Melody said. "In addition to that, he's power hungry to a point that's literally pathological. He has—had—a real need to be in control of all the people in his orbit, and the more power he grabbed, the wider the universe that he wanted to dominate."

"I wouldn't disagree with your assessment. In fact, Roz was one of the few people who didn't seem intimidated by him."

"She wasn't in the least intimidated, and I think Wallis hated that. Actually, I'm convinced he'd grown to hate everything about Roz." She hesitated for a moment, then told her father the truth. "To be honest, it's been a long time since I accepted that my mother's death was accidental."

Johnston blinked. "What do you mean?" There was a nervousness to his question that suggested he understood exactly what she meant.

"It occurred to me at least a year ago that Wallis Beecham probably arranged to have my mother murdered," Melody said.

Johnston looked appalled. "Oh no, my dear! Don't torment yourself with ideas like that! Have you forgotten that Wallis wasn't even on board when she died?"

Melody shrugged. "I didn't forget. But that's not proof of his innocence. Wallis rarely did his own dirty work, and he had two of his favorite surrogates on board—Lawrence Springer and Lewis Cranford. You just told me that Springer wrangled the invitation for Roz, and that makes me even more suspicious that Wallis is implicated in her death."

"You can't be suggesting that Lawrence Springer pushed Roz overboard? No, absolutely not. It couldn't have happened." Johnston shook his head, emphasizing his denial. "It's not possible."

"Physically impossible? Or is murdering my mother something you believe Lawrence Springer wouldn't have done?"

"Either. Both." Johnston's fingers drummed nervously on the deck rail.

"Lawrence Springer is known to have contracted at least two murders on Wallis Beecham's behalf, and probably more. And Senator Cranford tried to have you killed. In fact, just six months ago, Cranford constructed an elaborate plot in which your death was an essential element. Cranford's only motive for killing you was anger that you were insisting he should resign his Senate seat. Why on earth wouldn't the pair of them have been willing to murder Roz? They're strong enough to be physically capable, and obviously neither one of them quailed at the idea of murder."

"Given what we've learned in the past year about Springer and Cranford, it would be foolish to pretend they were incapable of plotting to kill your mother," Johnston conceded. "I just don't believe they did. Apart from anything else, it would have been terribly difficult from a practical point of view. This is a relatively small yacht, not a giant cruise ship. Roz would have screamed and struggled if anyone attacked her. The crew, or one of the other guests, would surely have heard—"

"Not if Cranford and Springer were working together. They could have overpowered Roz before she could produce a single squeak of protest."

"But what was their motive?" Johnston sounded plaintive. "To be capable of killing isn't enough. They needed a *reason* for murder."

"Wallis wanted her dead. Plain and simple. Plus my mother had almost certainly tried to blackmail Lawrence Springer, and she was causing trouble in Cranford's marriage. There were plenty of reasons for both those men to want her dead, and no very good reasons for them to want her alive. Given everything that's been uncovered about Springer and Cranford in the past year, don't you agree that it would be a huge coincidence if my mother's death turned out to be accidental?"

"No, I don't agree." Johnston spoke slowly. "Planning to kill Roz by pushing her overboard would have meant taking huge risks. For example, nobody could have predicted that convenient storm—"

"The storm may have been convenient, but it wasn't

essential. If there'd been no storm, would the outcome of the investigation have been much different?" Melody answered her own question. "I don't believe so. I think Roz's death would still have been declared accidental. You're an important man. Your guests were all important people. There's a strong temptation on the part of the investigating authorities not to cause unpleasantness if it can be avoided."

"True, but there was absolutely no evidence of anything happening on board this yacht except a tragic accident. There had been no arguments, no confrontations...."

"But why would there be? If Springer and/or Cranford planned to murder Roz, presumably they would avoid having a blazing row with the intended victim."

Johnston gripped the rail, his body language stiff with rejection. "It's true that when your mother died I had no reason to be suspicious of either Lawrence Springer or Lewis Cranford, so we automatically assumed her loss was accidental. However, all the signs pointed to an accident. Nothing pointed to murder. Your mother's bed hadn't been slept in that night, which presumably means that if somebody came into the room with the intention of killing her, she would have been awake. Since Roz was awake, she couldn't have been surprised by an intruder. She would have had time to scream before she was overpowered."

"Why would she scream at the sight of Cranford and Springer? Two men who'd both been her lovers. They could have knocked my mother unconscious before she realized there was any need to cry for help. There's no body for an autopsy, no way to prove what condition she was in before she went into the water. Her head could have been blown off for all we know to the contrary."

"If she was injured, there would have been bloodstains. We would have heard the sound of a shot."

"Not if they used a silencer on the gun. And with all the rough weather, any footprints her attackers made would have been washed away by rain and waves within minutes."

"But Eleanor Cranford is an honorable woman. She would never have covered for her husband and she would surely have noticed if Lewis had gone wandering around the ship in the middle of the night."

Melody was surprised at how strongly Johnston was resisting the idea that Roz had been murdered. She supposed he felt guilty for having invited Springer and Cranford to join the cruise, although nobody could blame him for not suspecting the chairman of a major corporation and a senior U.S. senator of being potential murderers.

Johnston started to press his point, and then broke off when he saw his wife approaching them. Not surprisingly, he appeared relieved at the interruption. "Cynthia, my dear, come join us. I hope you aren't too unhappy at losing the fish?"

Cynthia laughed. "I'm devastated, but resigned to the inevitable. After forty years, you know as well as I do that I'm the world's worst fisherwoman."

"Melody will be relieved to hear you admit that. She confessed to me that she was secretly championing the cause of the grouper."

Cynthia directed a smile toward Melody. "I can almost guarantee that if you bet on the fish, you're always going to come up a winner when I'm the one holding the rod. My attempts at deep-sea fishing are an ongoing triumph of hope over experience." She sobered, keeping her gaze fixed on Melody. "But I didn't come up on deck to talk about fishing, and I'm sure you and Johnston weren't talking about that, either. I know we're close to the area in which your mother lost her life, and I want to tell you again how deeply sorry we are that such a tragedy happened when Lady Rosalind was a guest on board our yacht."

Cynthia was the daughter of a former U.S. senator, and she'd probably grown up being gracious to people she didn't especially care for. Melody had always assumed she would be among those people, since it didn't take a giant leap of the imagination to assume that Cynthia would have no reason to like the child born as a result of her husband's extramarital affair. Even the fact that Melody had been instrumental in saving Johnston's life six months ago wouldn't provide cause for gratitude, since Unit One's role in that incident remained completely secret. However, there was no doubting the sincerity of Cynthia's condolences, and Melody thanked her for her sympathy.

"I heard a little bit of what you were discussing just now with Johnston," Cynthia said. "I don't know if it will set your mind to rest to hear that Johnston and I were up quite a lot the night your mother died. My fault, I'm afraid. I was wretchedly seasick, despite the fact that I'd taken a hefty dose of anti-nausea medication. Seasickness pills make me sleepy and I went to bed right after dinner. I woke up around two, disturbing Johnston in the process. I fought and lost another battle against nausea, spent twenty minutes in the head up-chucking, and then couldn't for the life of me get back to sleep. The wind was certainly making a lot of noise, but I'm fairly sure we would have heard any sounds of an argument or a struggle. After all, we were awake, and Roz was in the cabin right next door to ours."

Johnston nodded. "As it was, Cynthia was the person who eventually raised the alarm."

"Yes, I did. Around three, the wind finally died down. I heard Roz's cabin door banging and went to find out what the problem was. That's when I realized she wasn't in her bed." Cynthia gave a little cough. "To be honest, at first I still didn't imagine there was anything wrong. I…um…I…" Cynthia's cheeks flushed bright red with embarrassment and she avoided both her husband's and Melody's eyes.

"You thought my mother might be sleeping in somebody else's cabin," Melody supplied.

"Yes." Cynthia didn't disguise her relief that Melody understood. "So I shut the cabin door and started to walk back to my own room. At that moment, Lawrence Springer came out of his cabin. He looked dreadful, and thoroughly relieved to see me. He'd been ill, too, and had come out in search of more seasickness pills. Well, once I realized Roz and Lawrence weren't…um… weren't sleeping together, I began to get worried. The Cranfords were sharing a cabin, so Roz couldn't be there. Her life jacket was on the shelf in her cabin, and her bed hadn't been slept in. So where was she? That's when I went to find a crew member and we started to search for her." Cynthia pulled herself back from memories that were visibly painful. "Well, there's no point in going over all those grim details again. It's not helpful to keep raking over the events of that tragic night."

"But I've never heard what happened," Melody said. "I've only read the report from the Mexican authorities, and that's very short on details. I really would like to hear a firsthand account."

Cynthia exchanged glances with her husband, and he gave an almost imperceptible nod, as if reassuring her that she could tell the truth without sending Melody into hysterics. When she spoke again, Cynthia's voice was shaky.

"It was terrible to search and to become more and more certain that Roz was nowhere on board. We began to look in the most unlikely places, desperate to find a trace of her. We all went from rather mild worry at not being able to find her to a sort of mingled horror and disbelief when we began to realize that we might never find her. We had to wake the Cranford girls in case for some reason Roz had gone into their cabin. They were both in floods of tears, poor things, and their mother was trying to comfort them when she hardly knew how to comfort herself."

"Cynthia was a rock that morning." Johnston looked at his wife with quiet pride. "I was in a state of complete shock, and wasn't as much help as I should have been."

"I'd always been so jealous of Roz, you see." Cynthia swallowed hard. "Now, when it was too late, I realized what a terrible and destructive waste of emotion that had been. All that beauty and liveliness just…gone. Too late, I realized I wished passionately that she could come back." She shook her head, her expression sad. "Why is it that we always need the finality of a death, or a tragedy of some sort, before we realize how trivial most of our hurt and anger is?"

Melody had read the report prepared by the Mexican authorities more than once, but it was quite different to read a bare-bones account and to hear Cynthia's story. Grief welled up, renewed by the immediacy of Cynthia's words. She fought the grief with questions. Had she allowed her loathing of Wallis Beecham to overcome her judgment? It had seemed such a coincidence that Roz should die when she was on board a yacht with two men who were criminal partners to Wallis, and who themselves had reason to want Roz silenced. But life tended to be full of coincidences, and perhaps she ought to accept that her mother's death had been caused by nothing more criminal than a cruel spin of the wheel of Fate.

She made one last attempt to resuscitate her belief that Roz had been murdered. "You mentioned that you saw Lawrence Springer come out of his cabin," she said. "Are you sure that's where he came from? Or is it possible that he had been somewhere else and then, when he saw you, invented the need for seasickness pills as an excuse to justify being out and about?"

Cynthia shook her head. "I'm absolutely sure Lawrence came from inside his cabin. I was standing in the corridor, walking somewhat cautiously back to our room since the boat was heaving quite a bit. I saw him open the door to his room, and he stepped into the corridor from inside the cabin." She exchanged another questioning glance with her husband, but this time Johnston responded with a tiny shake of denial.

"What is it?" Melody demanded. "What is it that you're not telling me?"

"Nothing," Cynthia said, but she was a bad liar and her cheeks turned pink.

"Tell me what you're hiding," Melody repeated. "Please."

Cynthia and Johnston exchanged another glance. After forty years, they had the art of silent communication down pat. Johnston finally spread his hands in a gesture of defeat.

"At my urging, Cynthia is avoiding telling you that the Mexican authorities were convinced your mother committed suicide," he said, his words clipped. "The mayor of Cancún informed me privately that since there was no proof one way or another, they decided to spare everyone's feelings by delivering a verdict of accidental death."

Melody drew in a breath that was less than steady. "Do *you* believe my mother killed herself?" she asked Johnston. If he did, it would explain why he'd been so forceful in arguing against the idea that Roz had been murdered.

He hesitated, choosing his words with visible care. "It's true that Roz was a little melancholy beneath her veneer of birthday cheer, but that doesn't mean the idea

of suicide ever crossed her mind. All in all, I'm very relieved the Mexican authorities didn't mention suicide in
their report. I'm sure it was the correct decision on their
part."

As far as Melody was concerned, her father might
as well have come right out and admitted that he believed Roz killed herself. She was silenced by the pain
of what was being suggested and felt unexpectedly
grateful when Cynthia patted her arm, the gesture
clumsy but well-meaning.

"My mother died twenty years ago next month and
I still miss her dreadfully. But with each year that
passes, I remember more of the happy times we shared,
and the pain of her loss is less acute. I know you must
have been offered similar attempts at comfort often
enough for it to become annoying, but it's true nonethe-
less. Try to bear in mind, Melody, that time is the ultimate healer for even the most jagged wounds."

Melody made a polite reply, although she suspected
her grief would heal more easily if there were fewer un-
answered questions about exactly how and why her
mother died. Still, almost three years had now passed and
it was time to let go, since answers weren't likely to be
uncovered at this late date. Springer was dead; Cranford
and Beecham were behind bars. If they had killed Roz,
her death was certainly avenged. If she had committed
suicide, heartache and regrets wouldn't bring her back.

The yacht was scheduled to dock in Cancún the next
day. Johnston and Cynthia both went out of their way
to make the final dinner at sea a pleasant meal, with the

conversation focused on safe subjects such as art and foreign travel. It was only when Johnston claimed that he needed an early night if they were going to brave the shopping markets next morning that Melody had the chance to speak privately with Cynthia.

There seemed no point in trying to ease into the subject of Roz's death, so Melody posed her question bluntly. "I can see that Johnston really hates the idea that my mother's death was anything other than accidental. I also noticed that you deliberately avoided endorsing his opinion. Do you agree with the Mexican authorities, Cynthia? Do you believe my mother committed suicide?"

"Oh, no. I'm sure she didn't." Cynthia gave a bright, flustered smile.

"I wish you'd stop worrying about hurting my feelings and tell me the truth. Nothing is more painful than the suspicion that people are lying to me."

Cynthia opened her mouth to speak but stopped, seeming to change her mind. "You know, I'm not quite sure why we're all trying so hard to hide the truth. It obviously isn't protecting you, because you don't believe our attempts to be reassuring. Here's my honest opinion. The truth is, to anyone who knew her well and could read beneath the surface charm and her vivacious manner, your mother seemed miserable for the entire trip. She seemed especially miserable on her birthday. She hated being fifty, although she must have been the most gorgeous fifty-year-old I've ever laid eyes on. She definitely drank rather more than she should have at dinner, and we discovered another bottle of wine in her cabin that was half empty."

"So you believe my mother committed suicide?"

"Not exactly." Cynthia looked apologetic. "I'm not avoiding the question, Melody, I'm trying to tell you what I really think. I don't believe your mother was the sort of woman who would deliberately set out to kill herself, but I'm afraid she drank enough that her judgment and her physical abilities were impaired. There's no other rational explanation of her decision to go up on deck, in the height of a storm, without a life jacket, and wearing, as far as we can tell, nothing except a strapless evening gown."

"In other words, you believe it was a sort of self-induced accident. My mother died as a result of too much alcohol and an attack of low-grade melancholy that made her careless."

Cynthia hesitated, then spoke firmly. "To be honest, yes. I do think that's exactly what happened."

Her mother drunk and careless was an all-too-credible scenario. She'd pressed Johnston and Cynthia until she got answers about her mother's death that finally sounded honest. It was a pity, Melody reflected, that the truth had turned out to be so depressing.

Four

Nick paid off the cab that had brought him from Cancún airport to the Caribe Azul Hotel, adding a tip big enough to make the driver smile. He had to be back at Unit One headquarters in just over twenty-four hours, and the flight from Cancún to Newark, with a change in Miami, would take him the best part of eight hours, even assuming security checks at the airports went smoothly. Right now, however, Nick wasn't focused on the journey home. He was focusing on the fact that he had sixteen whole hours to spend with Melody here. Best of all, the six weeks of recuperation from her surgery were over, which meant that her injuries and incisions were healed and the doctors had given her permission to resume normal activities. Nick had entertained himself during the long flight south by visualizing all the interesting ways in which the two of them could improvise on the theme of "normal activities."

Skirting a man polishing the granite-tiled floor of the

lobby, he made his way to the reception desk. Melody had called in to headquarters to confirm the hotel where she was spending the night now that the yacht was docked and the Yateses had left for Mexico City. However, the Caribe Azul sprawled over almost four acres, and he needed directions to her room.

"Room 2404?" the receptionist repeated. She looked tired, and her makeup was caked as if it had been a long time since she'd last had the chance to freshen up. "*Sí, señor*. That is on the second floor of our Chantico Building. The room is located on the corner, overlooking the ocean."

"And how do I find the Chantico Building?"

The receptionist gave a smile that clearly owed more to rote than to feeling. "You can reach it through our gardens. There are signposts for you to follow, and you will be able to identify the building by the wall mosaic over the entrance. Chantico is the Aztec goddess of volcanoes."

Nick thanked her and strolled into the balmy night. It was almost one o'clock in the morning, and it seemed to him that the receptionist ought to have inquired if he was a registered guest, or at least requested identification, before handing out directions to a room. He shook off mild disapproval of the hotel's lax security and reminded himself that for the next twenty-four hours he was on vacation; in other words, he was free to focus on sex, sun and frozen margaritas as opposed to crime, criminals and hotel security systems. Melody didn't know he was in Cancún and he wanted to surprise her, so he should actually be thanking the receptionist for her casual attitude.

The scent of frangipani and night-blooming jasmine filled the air, a pleasant reminder that he was in the tropics. As he passed a little twenty-four-hour café, the smell of roasting chili peppers wafted toward him. Nick grinned, his spirits lightening at the prospect of some authentic chimichangas for lunch tomorrow. Damn, but it was good to be here. He breathed deeply, admiring the profusion of flowers, the clever lighting of the tropical foliage and the attractive wrought-iron balconies that adorned many of the rooms.

He followed the signposts for the building dedicated to the goddess Chantico. It seemed to be the one closest to the ocean and farthest from the main hotel reception area. The signs led him over a footbridge that crossed an ornamental stream, which meandered around clumps of dark green elephant ears and bird-of-paradise plants before ending in a lily pond where frogs had taken up residence. The croaking of dozens of bullfrogs attempting to attract mates formed a pulsing backdrop to the thud of his footsteps on the little bridge.

Nick slowed down to watch one bullfrog that was puffing himself up until he looked like a cartoon creature on the point of explosion. Despite his monumental efforts, no female was sufficiently impressed to emerge from her hiding place. The bullfrog deflated to half size, his rosy chest collapsing into a collar of limp skin. After resting for a couple of seconds, he started the inflation all over again. It seemed an even more harrowing way of finding a mate than braving a New York singles bar. Nick walked on, wishing the poor guy luck in finding a lady toad with lots of cute warts sometime very soon.

Grinning, he tipped his head back, stretching his arms and flexing his shoulder muscles to rid himself of the kinks produced by too many hours on a cramped plane. The multiple stresses of New York, miserable weather, and a work schedule that seemed to get more crowded by the minute fell away. He and the bullfrog were working toward the same goal, he thought in silent amusement. Right now, he had nothing to worry about beyond finding his mate and impressing her with his masculine prowess. And he intended to be major-league impressive. Replete with goodwill toward humanity, he smiled at a couple who walked past him in the moonlight, hands clasped.

In contrast to his cheerful mood, the Goddess Chantico seemed less than happy with the human race. She glared down from her dominant position over the entrance to the building named in her honor, obsidian eyes flashing, nostrils breathing fire. She looked more than ready to blow flames and foul smoke at anyone who annoyed her. Nick played it safe by tipping his hand to her in a respectful salute.

He identified Melody's corner room on the second floor. Despite his efforts to cultivate a more laid-back attitude, he couldn't entirely cut off his analytical skills and he noticed that the balconies presented a major security weakness. Several of the guests had their windows open, presumably taking advantage of the mild temperatures to sleep in fresh air instead of air-conditioning. Melody's window was one of those that had been opened. Nick frowned. Any reasonably agile burglar—or rapist—would be able to climb from balcony to balcony, using the open windows to gain entrance to the rooms. Hell, the climb was simple enough that even Melody, with her phobia about heights, would be able to make it.

On the point of entering the lobby of the Chantico Building, an idea struck Nick, and his frown vanished. Climbing up onto Melody's balcony would be the perfect way to surprise her. About the only weakness Melody had as a field operative was her fear of heights, and the fact that they so often needed to make quick getaways by rappelling down the side of various buildings had become something of a running joke between the two of them. Her phobia was powerful enough that he doubted if she'd even stepped to the edge of the balcony to admire the view. The balcony doors would definitely be the best way for him to make a grand surprise entrance, he decided.

He had been carrying his small flight bag slung over his shoulder. He would need two hands free to make the climb, so he adjusted the strap and moved the bag onto his back. The sliding balcony doors to the room directly beneath Melody's were closed, and the drapes drawn. Good. He didn't want to disturb any sleeping hotel guests.

Checking to make sure nobody was around to watch him, he quietly vaulted onto the first-floor balcony. He'd traveled from New York in jeans and sneakers, so he was fairly well dressed for his plan. Based on his experiences of the hotel thus far, it didn't seem likely that he needed to worry about zealous security guards springing out of the shadows and demanding to know what he was doing.

As if to prove him wrong, he'd no sooner landed on the balcony than he heard the hum of a motorized cart approaching. Nick leaned casually against the railing, pretending to admire the gardens before turning in for the night. Forty feet away, a hotel employee drove past in an electric maintenance cart, the rear cargo area stuffed with withered palm fronds. The employee paid no attention to Nick.

With the cart safely out of sight, Nick climbed onto the balcony ledge. It wasn't more than four inches wide and the top was slightly curved, but his sense of balance was good and it posed no problem for him to stand upright. As soon as he straightened, it was a cinch for him to reach up and grab the balustrades of Melody's balcony on the floor above. With the confidence of many similar climbs—most of them in situations rife with danger—Nick quickly pulled himself up onto the second floor, rolled over the ledge and then jumped down silently onto Melody's balcony. At least, he hoped it was Melody's balcony. If the receptionist had made a mistake identifying the room, he was soon likely to find himself confronting some extremely annoyed and frightened guests.

Nick took no more than a single step toward Melody's room before he heard the ominous sounds of people fighting on the other side of the closed curtains. He'd been involved in too many fights to harbor any doubts about what he was hearing. He didn't stop to debate how or why, or even whether this really was Melody's room. He simply dropped his flight bag and burst through the open doors at a run.

Enough light filtered through the curtains for him to see that Melody was pinned against the bed, struggling to defend herself against a stocky, dark-haired man. The flash of metal in the moonlight revealed a double-edged knife blade arcing toward her throat.

Jesus! Nick aimed his first kick at the attacker's wrist, followed by a swift downward chop with the edge of his hand. The knife fell onto the carpet with a soft clunk, almost drowned out by the attacker's cry of pain.

Momentum carried Nick around in a full circle. He changed feet in mid-spin, swinging his other leg to connect with the side of the attacker's head. The man staggered and then lurched sideways, allowing Melody to escape, although her attacker managed to land one more vicious punch to her midriff. She gasped and doubled over, but she didn't dare give up and leave Nick to win the fight on her behalf. Catching her breath, she clenched her fists together and thrust upward, connecting squarely with her attacker's chin. Nick finished him off by grabbing his hair and banging his head against the wall. The man toppled to the ground, unconscious.

Melody collapsed onto the bed, panting, arms wrapped around her belly. "Thank you." Her voice was hoarse with pain. "I'm seriously out of shape, or he would never have cornered me like that."

"You look in pretty fine shape to me." Nick sat beside her, spreading his hands comfortingly over hers. "Did he do any real damage? Open any wounds?"

"No, the bullet wounds are all healed. He just gave me a cluster of new bruises." She leaned down, reached

under the bed and used her index finger to pull a revolver out from behind the dust ruffle. "At least I managed to disarm him before he could use this. There's a
silencer attached…well, I guess you noticed that. Anyway, the police should be able to lift some fingerprints
if he tries to pretend he wasn't armed."

She sounded coherent enough, but Nick could hear
the strain behind the calm. She was shaking, and her
eyes were glazed with shock. This attack had come too
soon after the shooting in Gary for her to brush it off.
He wrapped a cotton blanket around her shoulders, feeling a burst of rage against her attacker that was so blinding he was forced to walk away to prevent himself from
kicking the man's unconscious body. He could tell that
Melody wasn't ready yet for sympathy, much less for
rational analysis of what had just happened.

"I'll get you a washcloth," he said, deliberately casual. "You have a scratch on your cheek."

Once in the bathroom, he ran the water until it was
scalding, wringing out the washcloth with meticulous
care as he strove for calm. In a moment, he would have
to call hotel security and arrange for Melody's attacker
to be turned over to the police, but first he wanted to find
out exactly what had occurred. This might be nothing
more than a robbery gone wrong, but he needed to rule
out the possibility of any link to a Unit One operation.
If Melody's attacker was simply a thief who got caught,
why had he seemed so interested in taking Melody
down rather than making good his escape?

Nick returned to the bedroom with the hot washcloth.
Sensing that Melody still wanted another few seconds

to get herself together, he turned his attention to her attacker, who was beginning to stir. With his urge to kick the shit out of the guy more or less under lock and key, he pulled the belt off a toweling robe hanging in the bathroom and used it to tie the man's left hand to the leg of the armoire. The man's right hand was puffy from the blows Nick had delivered. The wrist was probably broken, he thought without emotion. He patted the man down, found another knife tucked into an ankle sheath, and pulled it out, slipping it into his own pocket. Then he took off his belt and used it to strap the man's ankles together.

The intruder slid back into unconsciousness, which meant he wasn't going to be causing any more trouble for at least the next few minutes. Nick turned away, shutting all thoughts of the man out of his mind—the most effective way to keep his rage from coming back and spiraling out of control.

He sat down on the bed next to Melody. "That should hold the bastard for a couple of minutes while I say a proper hello."

"Hello." Her smile wobbled, but she held on to it. Her voice was still husky with stress. "You're supposed to be in New York."

"Cancún seemed a lot more appealing. Sun versus sleet. Melody versus Mac. It was no contest."

She gave a tight laugh. "You have to admit I arranged a spectacular welcome for you."

"You sure did. Although for future planning, the sexy outfit is more than enough excitement for me. The fistfight was overkill."

"Sexy outfit?" She glanced at her gray cotton knit boxers and skimpy athletic shirt and gave a rueful grimace.

"It's incredibly sexy," he said, with perfect truth. She had a model's ability to don virtually any scrap of clothing and make it appear a high-fashion statement. He carried her hand to his lips and pressed a kiss into her palm. "You look beyond beautiful."

She laughed, denying the possibility, but let her hand curve softly against his cheek. "And you saved my life again. Thank you."

He shrugged. "You're welcome, but you'd have taken him down if I hadn't happened to arrive when I did."

"I'm not sure. It's frightening how uncoordinated I was. How...weak."

"We'll soon fix that. Ten days of strength training and you'll be in decent shape. A month and you'll be in top form again."

"I hope so."

"I know so." He traced the scooped neckline of her shirt with his index finger. "Okay, enough with the trivia. Now let's talk about the really important stuff."

Her breathing had finally steadied. "I'm ready. What would the important stuff be?"

"That I've missed you like hell." Nick had reached the point where he could sometimes express the truth about his own emotions. He wasn't quite brave enough to ask if she'd also missed him. Instead, he tilted her face upward and slowly lowered his mouth to hers. He was more than willing to be gentle, at least until he was sure she'd recovered her equilibrium, but her response to his kiss was immediate and powerful, the two weeks of separation and the adrenaline rush of combating her attacker combining with explosive force. The kiss accelerated from friendly to full-throttle passion in seconds.

A year had passed since he and Melody had first become lovers, a fact that was incredible in itself. More incredible still, the urgency of the desire he felt for her hadn't diminished. But even that urgency was less bewildering to Nick than the tenderness that always seemed to accompany it. It was a mystery to him that he could feel tender toward Melody while wanting to rip her clothes off, find the nearest horizontal surface and climb on top of her. He'd felt sexual attraction for other women on plenty of occasions, but until he and Melody became lovers, he'd never experienced the accompanying tenderness.

He desperately wanted to make love to her right now. After six weeks of abstinence, his desire for her was even more intense than usual. However, the urge to have sex wasn't quite compelling enough to make him forget that the man who had tried to kill Melody was tied to the armoire and would certainly not remain unconscious for much longer.

A moan from the corner of the room punctuated his thought, and Nick reluctantly pulled away from Melody. She followed his gaze toward her attacker, who was tugging angrily at his tether.

"Did he come in via the balcony?" Nick asked.

"No, he came in through the regular door. Fortunately, I wasn't deeply asleep and I woke up when he jimmied the lock, but there wasn't time to do more than hide behind the door before he burst in."

For the first time, Nick noticed that the door to the corridor had been forced open, which said something amazing about where his attention had been focused for the past several minutes. It was almost beyond belief that it had taken him this long to notice that the main door stood slightly ajar. The safety chain wasn't broken, but the latch it was attached to had ripped out of the doorjamb. The protection provided by a chain was dependent on the strength of the screws holding it in the wood, and in this case that had meant almost no protection at all.

"Hotel burglars don't usually break in to occupied rooms," he said. "As soon as he realized the chain was latched, he should have run like hell. They don't work at night, either. They prefer the middle of the day when guests are likely to be out and about."

"I don't think he's a regular hotel burglar," Melody said. "Or maybe not even a burglar at all. He came in with a gun in one hand and the crowbar he'd used to jimmy the lock in the other. He immediately started walking toward the bed, as opposed to looking around for something to steal. I managed to kick the gun out of his hand, and then the crowbar, but that was only because I surprised him. He's very strong and he's a vicious fighter. Once he pulled that knife from the sheath on his arm, I was on the defensive. To dodge the knife, I started giving ground, and pretty soon he had me backed up against the bed." She swallowed hard. "If you hadn't arrived when you did, I would be dead by now."

Nick couldn't allow himself to acknowledge that she was correct. He put his arm around her waist. "You did

a great job of defending yourself. The man had a gun,
a crowbar and two knives. You had no weapon, and
you're alive to tell the tale. I'd say you did pretty damn
good."

"I'm alive because you arrived. Do you think—?"
She took a quick breath. "Do you think he planned to
rape me?"

"We'll find out," Nick said grimly. "Let's start asking him some questions, shall we?"

She nodded. The man's eyes were closed again, his
chin slumped onto his chest, so Nick filled a glass from
the bathroom with tepid water and threw it onto the attacker's face. The man groaned once more and opened
his eyes.

He looked up, saw Nick standing next to Melody and
pretended to pass out again. Nick grabbed a handful of
hair and pulled the man's head up, putting an end to that
game.

"What's your name?" he asked.

"No hablo inglés," the man muttered.

"Fine," Nick said in Spanish. "We'll talk in Spanish.
What's your name?"

The man sent Nick a look of utter loathing. "Go fuck
yourself," he said in English.

"Weird name," Melody said. "What could his mother
have been thinking of?"

The man scowled at her, then let rip with a string of
expletives that Nick cut off in midstream by jerking the
man's head back and banging it against the armoire.
"I'm really angry about what you did to my friend tonight, so if you're smart, you'll act very polite toward

her. I want information, lots of it, and I'm warning you that I don't plan to keep asking the same questions and getting insulted by way of reply." He tugged the man's hair again to emphasize his point.

"Next time it'll be your broken wrist getting banged," he said. "The time after that, I'm going to kick your balls, and keep kicking until you decide to talk. Now, let's start over, shall we? What's your name?"

If the man had a grain of sense, of course, he'd give a fake name. Nick had a suspicion, however, that Melody's attacker wasn't over-gifted with brains and that he was in sufficient pain that dissembling wouldn't come easy.

"Jorge," the man said, his voice hoarse. "My name's Jorge."

"You got a second name, Jorge?"

He hesitated. "Morrero."

The hesitation might be a symptom of reluctance to give up the truth. Or it might be a belated realization that he needed to lie. While Jorge was almost certainly his first name, Morrero might or might not be his surname. Nick let the uncertainty slide. At this moment, it was a lot more important to find out why Jorge had been in Melody's room than to uncover his identity. Fingerprints would most likely provide an unequivocal answer to that.

"Well, Jorge, now that we've been officially introduced, let's move on," Nick said. "Why did you break into my friend's room tonight?"

"I was looking for something to steal. It was jus' chance I picked her room. I don't know nothing about who she is. No special reason I picked her room. None."

His lies were transparent. Melody and Nick exchanged glances. Jorge, it seemed, was willing to admit he was a thief in order to convince them that he hadn't specifically targeted Melody.

Melody dismissed his lies with a sweep of her hand. "You weren't trying to steal anything. You were trying to kill me. Why?" she asked, cutting to the chase.

"No! No, I wasn't trying to kill—"

From the corner of his eye, Nick saw Melody wince as he banged Jorge's broken wrist against the armoire. The man either passed out, or was smart enough to fake it.

"You don't have to watch," Nick said to her, his gaze still on Jorge.

She drew in a shaky breath. "If I'm willing to have you beat him up for the sake of information, I need to be willing to watch."

Nick didn't dispute her logic. "I'll get some more water."

Jorge came around, his mouth twisted with pain. Nick squatted on his haunches, so that the two of them were more or less at eye level. "Let me tell you what your choices are, Jorge. You've got two of them. We can call the police and tell them that you tried to rape and kill my friend here—"

"I wasn't gonna rape her. I ain't no rapist." Even Jorge realized his answer suggested that, while he might not have planned to rape Melody, he had intended to kill her. He rested his injured wrist on the back of his other hand and scowled at them both. "Anyway, you can't prove nothing."

"Sure we can," Nick said. "There's the broken door-jamb, which is evidence of violent entry. There's the crowbar, the gun and the knife, all with your fingerprints plastered over them. On top of that, there's our word about what happened here tonight. When you stack our word against yours, somehow I think the cops are going to believe us. We're respectable American tourists. What about you, Jorge? Are you a respectable Mexican citizen? I don't think so. I bet you have a list of priors longer than my arm. In the States as well as in Mexico, most likely."

"I didn't do nothing," Jorge repeated, but he looked increasingly unhappy. "I got a wife and kids to feed. I jus' needed some quick money."

"Have you ever considered getting a job?" Melody asked. "I know, it's a wild and crazy suggestion, but some people find that working hard is a really great way to make money."

"There's no goddamn jobs in Mexico," Jorge said. "That's why I spent the last five years working my ass off in a goddamn meat-packing plant in Nebraska. Until it got shut down for health violations."

"Let's get back to the subject of what happened here tonight," Nick said. "If you don't want us to hand you over to the police, along with your gun and all the other weapons, you can tell us why you're really here, what you were planning to do and who paid you to do it, and then—"

"And then you'll turn me over to the police anyway." Jorge looked at Nick with hatred. "You must think I'm some real stupid dickhead."

Nick resisted the urge to agree that he did, indeed. "Here's the deal, Jorge. If you answer my questions, my friend and I will lose the gun and we won't dispute your story that you were only planning to rob us. That cuts your prison time down from life to a couple of years. Even if you have as many priors as I suspect you do, an arrest for attempted robbery will be better for you than an arrest for armed robbery and attempted murder."

Jorge's expression indicated that some hard thinking was going on. "How do I know that you'll keep your side of the deal?"

"You don't," Nick said promptly. "But your alternative is to refuse to answer, at which point, I'll beat the crap out of you until you give up the truth. After which, I'll still turn you over to the police. Or you can hope I'm going to uphold my side of the bargain and answer my questions the first time I ask them. Either way, you'll end up telling me the truth. And if I were you, Jorge, I really wouldn't go the beat-the-crap-out-of-me route."

Nick held his breath. In Jorge's position, he would no more believe the interrogator would stick to his deal than he believed fairies built pearl palaces out of discarded baby teeth. Jorge, thank God, apparently believed the beat-the-crap part, even if not the part about Nick sticking to his word.

"What do you wanna know?" he asked, his voice surly, but defeated.

Nick pointed to Melody. "What's this woman's name?"

Jorge sighed. "Melody Beecham."

"Were you sent to kill her?"

"Yeah."

"Why?"

He shrugged. "I got no clue. She musta made some-body mad. She's a rich bitch. They sent me colored pictures torn from a magazine so as I could recognize her. Showed her sailing on some old dude's yacht."

"Those pictures were everywhere," Melody said to Nick. "Anybody could have seen them, here or in the States. The media took a ghoulish interest in the fact that I was sailing in the Caribbean with the Yateses. 'Will She Meet the Same Fate as Lady Roz?' That seemed to be a favorite headline."

Tonight she'd come way too close to meeting the same fate as Lady Roz, Nick reflected, turning back to Jorge. "Just so we're crystal clear about what you were planning to do tonight—you have no personal grudge against Melody Beecham. You'd been hired to kill her, is that right?"

Jorge hesitated, then shrugged. "Yeah."

"How much did you get paid?"

"Seven thousand dollars American up front. I was gonna get a bonus of eight thousand more when she was dead."

"Only fifteen K," Melody said, her mouth turning down. "Getting rid of me came pretty cheap. Who ordered the hit, Jorge?"

Jorge looked at her, showing not the slightest trace of remorse or guilt for having attempted to kill her. His whole attitude reeked of resentment that he'd been caught, as if Nick and Melody hadn't played fair by defending themselves. "I dunno nothing about who ordered the hit."

Nick grabbed Jorge's hair. "Try again. Who hired you?"

"I told you, I dunno nothing."

It seemed likely that he was telling the truth. "Then how did you get your seven thousand bucks if you don't know who was paying you?"

"The job came through my cousin, Alejandro Garcia. I didn't ask no questions. I was jus' glad for the money. One of his business partners paid me the money, and I don't know his name, neither."

"Okay. Where can we find your cousin Alejandro?"

Jorge gave a crack of laughter. "In Memphis, Tennessee."

"Address?" Nick demanded.

"John A. Denie Road." Jorge's moment of mirth faded. "He's in jail. Federal prison. Serving fifteen years on drug charges. Done six, got five more to go if he don't fuck up."

Nick and Melody persisted with their questions, but they got nothing out of Jorge, probably because he knew as little as he claimed. His up-front money had been delivered to him in cash, and his instructions had come by phone calls, either from Alejandro, or from one of Alejandro's associates. Cousin Alejandro, it seemed, was connected to a powerful drug cartel and could pull strings from inside prison without much difficulty. Jorge had first heard about the job two weeks ago, but had been told only yesterday that Melody was staying at the Caribe Azul. He'd received a phone call late in the afternoon notifying him of her room number and instructing him to get the job finished tonight.

Unfortunately, Jorge's revelations didn't point toward any particular culprit as the purchaser of the hit. Between the media coverage of Melody's trip with the Yateses and the slipshod security at the hotel itself, whoever hired Jorge would have experienced no difficulty finding out where she was spending the night. After an hour of intensive questioning, Nick gave up. The unpalatable truth was that they had little better idea of who had hired Jorge than they had before they started.

"Let's hope Cousin Alejandro knows who's behind the hit," Melody said as she and Nick waited for hotel security to respond to their call.

"Not only knows more, but is willing to give up what he knows." Nick made a frustrated sound. "Why were *you* targeted, Melody? Okay, it seems pretty clear this was a revenge killing, but every major mission you've worked on for the past year, I've been involved. Why would somebody target you and not me?"

"Maybe you *have* been targeted," Melody said. "Maybe the hit against you is scheduled for later. Or maybe you already had a lucky escape and don't even know it. Did you get jostled on the subway station and almost fall off the platform? Get chased by mysterious cars? Dodge a tile falling from a roof?"

"None of the above," Nick said. "I'm positive there have been no attempts on my life. Which means there's somebody out there who is more pissed off at you than me."

She smiled, albeit wanly. "How could that be possible? And me so sweet and gentle, too."

"I just remembered one person who probably dislikes you more than he dislikes me," Nick said. "Plus he's already proven he's capable of planning a long-distance murder."

"Who's that?" Melody asked.

"Zachary Wharton."

Melody thought for a moment before shaking her head. "Zachary is a snob and a racist. He established the Soldiers of Jordan in Idaho because it's the state with the fewest ethnic minorities. I can't believe he'd ever get friendly enough with a Mexican drug dealer to hire him as a hit man."

Nick gave a short laugh. "Zachary's in prison. His circle of acquaintances doesn't leave much room for snobbery."

"Maybe not, but I think Zachary would cling to his racism even when he was forced to give up everything else. Besides, prison is an extremely racist environment with plenty of white supremacist groups available for him to join. The Aryan Brotherhood would be his natural allies, not Mexican drug dealers."

Nick acknowledged her point. "But does Zachary need to be 'friendly' with somebody he's hiring as a killer?"

Melody gave a quick nod. "Absolutely he does. Zachary is behind bars, allowed very limited contact with the outside world. How can he be sure the person he hires will do the job unless he trusts him?"

"In Zachary's situation he might be forced to trust a

man he doesn't like." Nick shrugged. "Still, you're probably right. The timing's wrong for Zachary to have hired Jorge. Zachary only worked out his deal with the Feds three weeks ago. Until now, he's been held in the D.C. area, so he wouldn't have had time to get acquainted with Alejandro in Tennessee."

"And there's no reason for Jorge to lie about where his cousin is incarcerated," Melody added.

Which seemed to rule out Zachary as the would-be killer. Nevertheless, tomorrow morning it would be worth calling in to headquarters and asking Bob Spinard to run a check looking for any intersection of the movements of Zachary Wharton and Alejandro Garcia, Nick decided. Since Alejandro was imprisoned for drug dealing, it was possible that he and Zachary had crossed paths in the days when Zachary ran drug rehab programs as a cover for raising money to fund his dream of a separatist colony in Idaho.

The hotel security team arrived and arranged for Jorge to be removed to a holding room to wait for the local police. The chief security officer agreed that Melody and Nick could make statements and sign off on the official paperwork the next day, before they left for the airport. Jorge complained bitterly about his broken wrist, accusing Nick of wanton brutality. He demonstrated no gratitude whatsoever when Nick kept his promise and didn't mention that Jorge had been planning a murder rather than a robbery, or that Jorge had broken into Melody's room armed with a gun fitted with a silencer.

By the time the hotel carpenter had provided a temporary fix for the smashed lock on the door, it was almost four o'clock in the morning. Bolting the door behind the handyman, Nick returned to the room to find Melody standing in the bathroom, her hands braced against the counter. She was staring into the mirror, but Nick would have bet large sums of money that she wasn't seeing her own reflection.

His suspicion was born out when he walked up behind her and folded his arms around her waist, holding her close. She jumped, her startled gaze meeting his in the mirror as she returned from whatever place she'd been mentally hiding.

"Are you sure you don't need to see a doctor?" he asked, his cheek nuzzling hers. "And don't bother to tell me you're not hurting."

"No doctors. I've had enough of them over the past few weeks to last me for a while." Melody let out a breath, and some of the tension left her as she leaned back, relaxing her weight against him. "Jorge didn't do any serious physical damage. I'm just more shaken up than I would have expected."

Still standing behind her, Nick separated her shirt from her boxers, exposing her midriff with its virulent red scar. The imprints of Jorge's fists were clearly visible, already darkening into a string of dark-hued bruises. Not speaking—he was afraid his voice might crack—Nick traced the scar with his fingers. Thank God, it didn't feel hot or inflamed, suggesting there was no internal damage.

Melody watched him in the mirror. "It's ugly, isn't it? And it's not going to go away, although it should fade somewhat."

"It's not ugly. It's just part of you."

She grimaced. "A yucky part."

Nick smiled at her reflection. "It's like a Japanese garden where you must always leave at least one leaf or twig not swept up so that the sheer perfection doesn't seem lifeless."

She laughed. "Well, that's the first time my stomach has ever been compared to a Japanese garden."

"It's the perfection part you were supposed to concentrate on, not the garden." He turned her around within the circle of his arms and bent his head to kiss the bruised area.

Her breath caught, and he quickly drew away. "I'm sorry. Did I hurt you?"

"No. It felt good." She cradled his head between her hands and lifted him up until his mouth was level with hers. "But kissing me here would work even better."

Passion flared the moment their lips touched. The turbulent emotions of the past six weeks burst out from behind the wall where Nick had stashed them, rioting in triumphant liberation.

"Come to bed," Melody said. She wrapped her arms around him, her mouth almost touching his. "God, Nick, I've missed this. I've missed you."

They made love with the ferocity of six weeks' abstinence, softened by the tenderness that had been growing between them for the past year. Afterward, they lay sweating and exhausted in the tangle of damp sheets, watching the pale fingers of dawn streak light across the sky. Melody lay with her head nestled in the crook of his arm, her fingers splayed across his chest, her legs twined with his. It felt goddamn wonderful, Nick thought.

His heartbeat slowly returned to normal, and he realized that he was poised somewhere between bliss and terror, a state of being that had become all too frequent over the past couple of months. The shooting in Gary had been bad enough, but he'd retained his sanity by dismissing the incident as a one-off. Tonight's episode reminded him of the simple truth that as long as Melody worked for Unit One, she was going to face this sort of danger on a daily basis. He wished he could simply order her to stop taking field assignments for Unit One. However, he was smart enough to know that wasn't a viable option. The near destruction of their relationship that had preceded Melody's mission to Zachary Wharton and the Soldiers of Jordan warned him he would get nowhere good if he simply issued orders. Worse, despite his talent for inventing credible lies, Melody always saw through them, so he wasn't going to be able to lie his way into confining her to a safer work environment. With Melody, only the truth seemed to work.

In most circumstances Nick would still rather face down rabid skunks than talk honestly about how he felt, but in the interest of persuading Melody to limit herself to desk assignments until they discovered who was behind this attempt on her life, he was prepared to submit to the torment of baring his soul. Hell, if it became absolutely necessary, he might even admit he was scared to death at the possibility of losing her. Whatever it took, he was going to see that she didn't find herself in the path of any more speeding bullets or knife-wielding assassins. He'd finally discovered the limits of his loyalty to Unit One: as far as he was concerned, there were no missions important enough to risk Melody's life.

Five

A week after the attempt on Melody's life, Melody and Nick interrogated Alejandro Garcia at the federal prison in Memphis, Tennessee, where he was incarcerated. Alejandro was brought to one of the rooms normally reserved for consultations between inmates and their lawyers. Unfortunately, he was not in pain and was considerably smarter than his cousin, Jorge. Consequently, he was in no mood to provide any useful information.

"I don't know nothing about nobody hired to kill you," he said, but the look he directed toward Melody was mocking and his voice was laced with insolence. It was as if he wanted her to know not only that he was the man responsible for almost getting her killed, but also that he was way too smart to incriminate himself after the fact.

He gave her a smile of pretended regret. "I don't like to talk bad about family, but my cousin Jorge is a stupid fuck, and that's the truth."

"Stupid because he screwed up and didn't kill me?" Melody asked.

"Nah. Stupid because he tried to pass the blame off on me. How you think I'm gonna organize a hit from inside this place? I have to wait hours in line just to make a phone call. Shit, I can't move a finger without a guard waving his nightstick at me."

Alejandro stuck his middle finger straight up, his smile even more mocking as he lifted his hand as far as the handcuffs and chains would permit. The guard outside the metal-wired window rapped his nightstick on the glass.

"See?" Alejandro said. "I can't do nothin' in this place without some guard shittin' on me."

"Plenty of inmates organize hits while they're on the inside," Nick said. "Why not you? Aren't you smart enough to beat the system, Alejandro?"

Alejandro bristled and half rose. Then he got control of himself and slouched back in his chair, which was bolted to the ground to prevent its being used as a weapon. "I'm plenty smart. That's why I've spent the past month just sitting here, minding my own business like always. No way I'm gonna get involved in any dumb-ass scheme to whack your lady." He squinted at Melody from beneath lowered lids. "Real fine piece of ass she is, too, if you go for blondes. Me, I prefer brunettes. They got more fire where it counts, if you know what I mean."

"No, I can't say that I do." Nick's face remained impassive, but Melody could feel the anger he was forcing himself to suppress.

She appreciated his outrage on her behalf, but a testosterone war between Nick and Alejandro wasn't likely to produce much useful information, so she spoke quickly. "Have you ever met a man called Wallis Beecham?" she asked. Her decision to throw out the name of her stepfather was spur of the moment. It had occurred to her as they waited for Alejandro to be brought up from his cell that she and Nick had both overlooked the obvious in trying to identify suspects who might want her dead.

"Wallis Beecham?" Alejandro's expression betrayed no hint of recognition. "Never heard of the guy. He a friend of yours?"

"What about Zachary Wharton?" she asked, ignoring his question. "That name ring any bells, Alejandro?"

Bob Spinard had run a check and found no links between Alejandro and Zachary, but absence of recorded evidence didn't mean the two had never met. Alejandro had spent a year in Detroit at the time Zachary was just establishing his first street mission, and it wasn't out of the realm of possibility for the two of them to know each other.

Melody was watching Alejandro closely, and this time she would have sworn the name provoked a tiny flicker of recognition. She leaned forward, bracing herself on the table, her body language threatening. "If Zachary ordered the hit, get smart and tell us. Because you know the sort of guy Zachary is. He's going to roll on you for sure if you don't roll on him first."

"I don't know nobody called Zachary Wharton," Alejandro said. He stood up. "I don't have to sit here and listen to this shit no more. I'm done. I'm outta here."

Nick pushed him back into the chair. "You're done when we say you're done. We know that you had dealings with Zachary Wharton back in Detroit in the early nineties."

Melody managed not to blink at Nick's lie. She quickly pressed their slight advantage. "Make life easier for yourself, Alejandro. Tell us how Zachary made contact with you to order the hit."

"He didn't make contact with me. I haven't seen him in years."

"A couple of minutes ago you said you didn't know him," Nick pointed out.

Alejandro shrugged. "I'd forgotten the creepy shit even existed. I didn't place the name until you mentioned Detroit. Hell, I been inside for the past six years and I got better things to worry about than Zachary Wharton. He ain't got nothin' to do with this." He quickly corrected himself. "Ain't *nobody* got nothin' to do with this, because I didn't arrange nothin'." He met Melody's gaze with every appearance of wide-eyed candor. "Far as I'm concerned, if you got shot at in Cancún, you're one hell of an unlucky lady, but it ain't got jack shit to do with me."

"So how do you know Jorge attempted to shoot her?" Nick demanded. "We never told you that."

Alejandro showed a split second of fear, but he quickly recovered his cool. He gave them a bland smile. "Just guessing. Jorge, he likes to pretend he's a big man with guns. Besides, how else would you expect a hit to go down?" He nodded his head toward Melody. "I'm glad my cousin messed up and didn't manage to kill you, ma'am." His mock courtesy changed to a leer. "Wouldn't like to spoil a fine pair of titties like yours. That would be a real shame."

They questioned Alejandro for another frustrating hour, and got absolutely nowhere. "I guess we'll have to go to Florence and question Zachary Wharton," Nick said, once they were outside the prison and heading back toward the airport. "Although I'm not persuaded he's the person behind Jorge's attempt to kill you. What's your take on what we just heard?"

"That Alejandro ordered the hit just as Jorge claimed and that Zachary may or may not be involved. I'm pretty sure Alejandro didn't intend to admit he knew Zachary. That just sort of slipped out because he was startled by your statement that we had proof of a connection. But once he'd made the mistake, he didn't seem too worried."

"I agree. I'd have expected him to be a bit more nervous if Zachary really was the person who ordered the hit." Nick took the highway exit signposted for the airport. "Anyway, we should get a better feel for the situation once we've questioned Zachary."

"Not *we*," Melody said quietly. "I need to go alone to question Zachary. Whether or not he's the person hiring Alejandro, you know he's going to be easier to read if I deal with him one-on-one."

She could see Nick struggling with the urge to snap out an order not to be ridiculous, that of course he was coming with her. She swallowed a laugh when he drew in a deep breath and turned to her with an expression that was practically cross-eyed with his determination to be mellow.

"Okay. I'll get Mac to organize the necessary access for you." He drew in another deep breath. "Do you want to fly to Colorado directly from here while I go back to New York?"

She smiled at him, touched by his efforts not to control her. "Thank you, Nick. I know that cost you. And yes, I would like to fly directly to Colorado. If possible, I should question Zachary before Alejandro has time to warn him we're coming. Are we sure Zachary's been sent to the federal prison in Florence? Sometimes changes in assignments get made at the last minute."

"We had word on his assignment just a couple of weeks ago, but we should confirm with Mac before you get on the plane." Nick scowled at her. "And stop managing me. I liked it better in the old days when you found me inscrutable."

She kissed him. "No, you didn't."

"No, I guess I didn't. Smart-ass." He sighed and headed toward the car rental return. "Take care, please. God knows, if Zachary wasn't behind this hit, we don't want to give him ideas for future jailhouse activities."

With that, Melody was in one-hundred-percent agreement.

Six months ago, when she last encountered Zachary Wharton, Melody had been looking at him through a haze of drug-induced nausea and hallucination. He had been trying to rape her and she had been trying to escape. Despite the fact that she had succeeded in her escape attempt and Zachary had ended up in FBI custody, he remained an intimidating figure in her memories. Consequently, it took her a couple of seconds to fully register that the hunched, skinny man shuffling into the conference room at the federal penitentiary in Florence, Colorado, was indeed Zachary Wharton. She searched hard, but could detect few remaining traces of the handsome, confident man whose charisma had convinced hundreds of people to give up their normal everyday lives, turn their finances over to him and relocate to an isolated community in rural Idaho.

The guard who'd accompanied Zachary into the interview room finished latching the prisoner's handcuffs to the steel chair. "Do you want me to stay with you, miss?"

"No, thank you. I'll be fine."

The guard appeared dubious, deceived by Melody's slender figure into assuming she was incapable of defending herself. "He hasn't caused any trouble so far, but you never can tell. Don't let him get too close, miss."

"I won't." Melody waited until the door shut behind the guard before speaking to Zachary. He looked so forlorn and defeated that for a moment she felt a flash of sympathy. Then she reminded herself that this was the man who had tried to set off a religious war; the man who had hoped that killing Johnston Yates, as well as Bashir al-Hassan, one of the Middle East's few moderate Muslim leaders, would be the trigger for plunging the world into a nightmare era of sectarian violence from which Zachary and his followers would emerge triumphant.

Melody had come here not really expecting to find that Zachary was the man behind Jorge Morrero's attempt to kill her. However, seeing him in person, and given his past willingness to hire surrogate killers, it suddenly struck her as quite likely that he was the one who'd ordered the hit. His disdain for uneducated immigrants like Alejandro might well have taken a distant second place to his desire to have her dead.

She spoke coolly, trying to strike a balance between maintaining her dominance and suggesting that she had his best interests at heart. "Hello, Zachary."

He raised his head and met her gaze. The hatred that blazed in his eyes was all the more shocking in contrast to his shrunken pallor. He didn't speak, but he didn't need to. His message of defiance had been conveyed in one burning glance.

Melody forced herself not to recoil, although Zachary's hatred was powerful enough to pack an almost physical punch. With the ever-helpful clarity of hindsight, she realized how arrogant she'd been to assume Zachary would be more likely to respond to her than to Nick; it had been even more arrogant to assume there might be some lingering physical attraction she would be able to exploit. If the man hated her enough to try to get her killed, there wasn't any remaining goodwill or mutual understanding to serve as a platform on which to build a constructive dialogue. Now that she was face-to-face with him, it seemed glaringly obvious that she should have expected a negative reception.

She decided to dispense with asking how he was, which was likely to come off sounding provocative rather than caring. "I've just flown in from a meeting with Alejandro Garcia at the federal correctional institute in Memphis," she said.

Melody detected no reaction to Alejandro's name. Zachary returned his gaze to his lap and started to play with the chain of his handcuffs. She took a moment to make sure he was just fiddling with the chain and not trying to break loose, then continued. "The government is aware of the fact that you and Alejandro Garcia met each other in Detroit in the nineties. We're searching prison records now to see if there's been any contact between the two of you in the past six months since you were taken into custody."

She paused. Zachary didn't even glance up.

Melody doggedly pushed on. "You've been trained as a lawyer, so you must know that every visitor and every piece of mail you've received has been recorded by the prison authorities. The same applies to Alejandro Garcia. If you've contacted him, or vice versa, we'll find out quite soon."

Zachary's only response was to click his handcuff chains in a rhythm vaguely reminiscent of an old-fashioned revivalist hymn.

Melody drew in a deep breath. "I also don't need to tell you that the plea bargain that saved your life will be null and void if it's discovered that you've engaged in a conspiracy with another inmate. If you contracted to have me killed, you're looking at the death penalty, Zachary. I'm doing you a big favor by coming to talk with you before the FBI completes its official investigation of the murder attempt in Mexico. The only thing that might save you from a death sentence is a full confession. That's not bullshit from an investigator trying to make a case. That's good advice."

Zachary lifted his gaze once more and stared at her. Far from looking worried, a faint glimmer of satisfaction mingled with the still-burning hatred. He wasn't going to talk, Melody realized, not even to utter a denial. It was possible that he found prison life so intolerable that he didn't care whether he lived or died, in which case she had absolutely no leverage in trying to squeeze information out of him. He knew as well as she did that the Fifth Amendment guaranteed his right not to incriminate himself and, unfortunately, he was far too smart to be tricked or manipulated into giving away information that he wanted to keep secret.

She tried to play his game, waiting out the silence, but it stretched on endlessly. Zachary leaned back in his chair, his faint smile gradually widening to a full-blown grin. He was taunting her with his refusal to speak, subtly reversing the balance of power between the two of them. In the space of a few minutes, she had become the supplicant, and Zachary wasn't even rewarding her with a verbal denial of his complicity.

She understood his hatred and his desire to thwart her by any means within his grasp. Even so, given his past behavior, she had expected him at least to pretend to cooperate and she'd hoped to be able to read between the lies of whatever story he concocted. Did his silence suggest that he was guilty, or did it just mean he relished the opportunity to piss her off? He must know that defiance carried the danger of retribution on her part. Was the pleasure of defying her potent enough to make possible reprisals irrelevant now that his life was so circumscribed?

"If you don't talk, Zachary, I'll be forced to draw the conclusion that you're guilty. The most powerful law enforcement organization in the country is devoting major resources to looking for evidence that you and Alejandro have conspired to commit murder. Silence isn't going to save you. It's going to hurt you, big-time."

His expression added scorn to hatred. Either he had never been in touch with Alejandro and so had nothing to fear, or else he was confident she wasn't going to uncover any trace of their communications. In truth, it wouldn't have been all that difficult for him to beat the system. Zachary was smart, and he'd already had six months of incarceration to scope out how to manipulate the rules. Alejandro wasn't anywhere near as smart, but he was a long-term inmate with powerful connections inside and outside the walls of the prison. It would be simple enough for him to pass a message to one of his drug-cartel cronies on visiting day. The crony would then pass the message to an inmate in the Florence penitentiary, who in turn would pass the message to Zachary in the prison yard. Such a three-tier system would be virtually impossible for investigators to track down or penetrate because there would never have been direct contact between Alejandro and Zachary.

No wonder Zachary was smirking, Melody thought. All he had to do was remain silent and he could pretty much guarantee that her trip to Colorado would be a total waste of time.

She forced herself to return his gaze without displaying her frustration. "I hope you're having lots of fun playing dumb-ass, Zachary, because your lack of cooperation is going to come back to haunt you. Maybe you don't care about ending up on a gurney, with poison dripping into your veins, but the death penalty isn't the worst that can happen to you. Is it worth risking months of solitary just to annoy me?"

She saw the flicker of alarm before he looked away, so she pressed the small advantage. "Or if the idea of solitary doesn't scare the hell out of you, how about a transfer to Marion, where you can find out firsthand what it's like to do really hard time? There are cell blocks in Marion that make your current residence look like summer camp for the Boy Scouts. And the best thing about Marion from my point of view is that nobody has to drop a hint to the guards to give you a hard time. Marion's loaded with inmates who'll make sure you never sleep easy. Hell, if they have their way, you'll never sleep."

Zachary made a small sound and then clamped his lips into a tight line, not yet ready to give up the advantage of refusing to speak. Melody leaned across the desk, jerking his head around so that he was forced to look at her.

"Let's try this one more time while you're pondering the idea of life in Cell Block D at Marion. Have you put out a contract on me, Zachary? Are you trying to get me killed?"

He finally spoke, his words searing into her, acid with the force of his hatred. "There is nothing left in this world that would make me happier than to know you are dead."

His statement carried extra impact because of the silence that had preceded it. Melody's stomach lurched, but she refused to let him see the effect he was having on her. By an effort of will, she kept her voice steady. "Okay, so you want me dead, but you didn't answer my question. Did you order the hit in Cancún, Zachary?"

"Wouldn't you like to know."

"Yes, I would." There was no way to sugarcoat that particular truth, although she realized that at this stage she had almost zero hope of getting an honest answer out of him.

Very deliberately, Zachary twisted his face in her grasp and before she could snatch her hand away, he stuck his tongue, wet and hot, into her palm, getting in two revolting licks before she jumped back. This time she couldn't conceal a shudder, and he gave her a smile that was rich with mocking satisfaction.

He was sufficiently gratified by her involuntary reaction to speak again without being prompted. "No, of course I didn't order the hit. I'm a man of God and I leave vengeance to the Lord as the Bible commands us." He laughed derisively.

Before she could even shape another question, much less ask it, he leaned back and used his elbow to push the buzzer that summoned the guard.

"Get me out of here," he said, rising to his feet as the guard came in. "This interview is over."

"Are you done with this prisoner, miss?" the guard asked.

"Yes, we're done," Melody said. There wasn't much point in staying to listen to silence and insults, and it was clear that Zachary would give her nothing else.

As soon as Zachary was unlocked from the seat, he shuffled out, disappearing through the steel-barred gate that led to the cell blocks. He never once looked back, not even to deliver a final triumphant smile.

The interview had been useless, Melody concluded grimly. In fact, Zachary had managed to confuse the issue. She was leaving Florence with no idea whether he was the man who had hired Alejandro to kill her.

Six

The ride in from LaGuardia airport took almost two traffic-jammed hours, and when Melody finally walked into the condo, Nick still wasn't home. That figured. What else would she expect at the end of a thoroughly miserable day? Her mood sank to somewhere between grouchy and totally cantankerous. She went straight into the bathroom and took a steaming hot shower, slathering her skin with imported lemon-scented soap. She even used a pumice stone in a less-than-successful effort to scrub away the lingering taint of Zachary's touch. Those two Hannibal Lecter licks he'd managed to land on her palm were really grossing her out.

Nick returned while she was blow-drying her hair, and she didn't hear him until he came into the bedroom. He put his arms around her, lifting her still-damp hair so that he could drop a kiss on the back of her neck.

He already knew from a brief phone report that the interview with Zachary hadn't gone well, but he was getting quite good at separating work from the rest of their relationship and he didn't immediately probe for more details. Or perhaps he was sensitive enough to her moods by now to realize that she really needed a break from obsessing over who might be trying to murder her.

"You look especially gorgeous tonight," he said, running his hand up and down the deep-rose silk of her pajamas.

The action sent little ripples of pleasure cascading over her skin.

"This is a new outfit, isn't it? I'm sure I'd remember if I'd seen something this sexy before."

"Yes, the outfit is new." She was grateful for the lighthearted topic. "It was on sale at Saks a couple of months ago, reduced to a price that was merely outlandish instead of insane, and I grabbed it. I've been saving it for a special occasion and I decided tonight was the night."

"Uh-oh." He pretended alarm. "I may be in trouble here. Is today some important anniversary that I've forgotten?"

"I'll give you a clue. It's Friday, December tenth…."

"One of my favorite days." He gave her a charming smile that didn't quite conceal the fact that he was doing a quick mental calendar search and coming up empty.

She put the hair dryer away in the drawer, hiding a grin. "Now that I've jogged your memory, I'm sure you remember what we have to celebrate, right?"

"Er…yes. Of course. Big day for us. Big, big day."

The anniversary had nothing to do with their personal relationship, but she played along. "Exactly what's so big about it?" She tilted her head back, barely able to suppress her laughter.

"I'll tell you in just a minute." Nick slipped his hands under her pajama top, cupping her breasts as he kissed the hollow at the base of her neck.

"Great diversionary tactics, but I'm on to you." Her voice sounded soft, breathy and already borderline aroused, even to her own ears.

"Actually, honey, it seems to me that I'm on to you." He moved his hands suggestively. "You think I don't remember what happened a year ago today, but you're wrong."

"Liar." The last of the tension caused by the miserable prison visit to Zachary Wharton seeped out of her, replaced by desire. "It's confession time, Nick. You haven't a clue what happened this time last year, have you?" Her laughter ended in an involuntary gasp as his thumbs brushed over her nipples, stroking enticingly.

"On the contrary. I remember exactly what happened."

"So tell me."

Nick scooped her up into his arms and carried her over to the bed. He looked down at her, his eyes gleaming. "It's exactly one year tonight since we first had oral sex."

She tried hard to keep a straight face. "Wrong. That's not it—"

"Of course it is. You can't remember something that important in our relationship? I'm shocked and saddened." Nick dropped her onto the bed, kicked off his shoes, shed his shirt and unzipped his slacks at record-breaking speed. He lay down beside her, pillowed by the comforter, his face alight with laughter and desire. "I promise you, a year ago tonight we had sex that was out of this world, even by our spectacular standards. And trust me, honey, I plan to make this an anniversary to remember."

Melody's laughter faded, overcome by rapidly escalating desire. She opened her arms and gathered him close. "I'll hold you to that."

She was drowsy, sated with sex, when Nick returned to the bedroom carrying two glasses of chilled white wine. "Is it really the anniversary of something?" he asked, handing her one of the glasses. "If so, I plead guilty. I don't remember what."

"It wasn't an anniversary I expected you to remember. Wallis Beecham was arraigned on December tenth last year. At the time, that struck me as a very important event."

"But this year it doesn't seem so important?" Nick asked.

"Only marginally, and I guess that's the real cause for celebration." She sipped the wine. "It's odd how intimately involved I felt in his fate then, compared to how little I feel now. Wallis Beecham seems a ghost figure, completely in my past."

"He *is* in your past. He's incarcerated, his attempt to overturn the plea bargain was laughed out of court, and he's lost all power to hurt you."

"He's lost all power to inflict emotional damage," Melody amended. "But he might still have the ability to cause physical hurt."

"You're thinking of Jorge's attack and wondering if Wallis might have been behind it?"

She nodded. "Alejandro gave no sign that he recognized Wallis's name, but he could be a better actor than we give him credit for. Wallis is a logical suspect, after all. Just because I rarely think about him these days doesn't mean he's equally indifferent to me. On the plane this afternoon, it occurred to me that if Zachary Wharton could contract a murder from behind bars, it must be equally easy for Wallis Beecham to do the same thing, and Wallis's motivation is at least as strong as Zachary's. Maybe stronger."

Nick took a sip of wine before answering her. "I think it's pretty unlikely that Wallis Beecham is involved," he said finally.

"Why do you think that? There's compelling evidence that Wallis bears a deep, personal grudge against me."

"That's true, but these days he lacks the physical ability to have organized the attack against you—"

"We've talked about that before," Melody said quickly. "I don't agree that because Wallis is confined behind bars, he's incapable of getting messages to the outside world. He still consults regularly with his lawyers, I'm sure. It would be the easiest thing in the world for him to pay one of them enough money to take a message to Alejandro."

Nick shook his head. "I don't think even Wallis Beecham could slip a secret message to his lawyers these days. The fact is, he's in a prison health-care facility."

She looked up, shocked. "What happened? Was he attacked by another prisoner?"

"No, he had a heart attack at the end of October.

While he was in the hospital recuperating from surgery, he had a stroke. I doubt if he's been arranging any contract killings for the simple reason that he can't speak anymore. These days, his communication is limited to what he can write with his left hand on a chalkboard. Using one of his lawyers to set up a hit with Alejandro would be just about impossible for him."

Melody put down her wine and swung her legs off the bed to sit on the edge of the mattress, her back turned toward Nick. An array of emotions assaulted her. However, one strand among the confusion was readily identifiable: irritation that Nick still seemed so willing to make important decisions about her life without consulting her. He must have known of Wallis Beecham's failing health for several weeks, months even, and yet he'd never mentioned it to her.

"Why didn't you tell me?" She heard the ice that edged her voice. Nick was a naturally strong and dominating man, a stereotypical alpha male, and if she didn't want to end up buried beneath his misplaced protective instincts, she needed to make clear that when he concealed important truths about her personal life, she got angry. Justifiably angry.

"It took a couple of weeks for the news of his condition to percolate from the prison authorities, through the FBI and on to Mac," Nick said. "By the time I heard the news, you were in the operating room at Gary Methodist Hospital, waiting for the surgeon to dig a bullet out of your gut. Afterward, to be honest, with your life hanging in the balance for a couple of days, I simply forgot about it."

"That explains your silence during the month of November. But when I suggested Wallis's name to Alejandro as a possible murder suspect, didn't that jog your memory?" Her voice remained cool, but the hard edge of her anger softened. She had probably been too quick to condemn, which tended to be a habit of hers.

"Yes, you're right, I should have told you then," Nick acknowledged. "But we were on the way to the airport, you were preparing to question Zachary Wharton, and it didn't seem a topic to shoehorn in between discussions of flight schedules and hotel bookings." He paused for a moment and when he spoke again, his voice was strained. "There's another factor, too. I'm never quite sure how to handle the subject of parents, even when we're talking about a lousy stepfather like Wallis Beecham. Ever since my family was murdered, the topic of mothers and fathers has been pretty much radioactive as far as I'm concerned. You have to cut me some slack, Melody. I've spent the past seventeen years not doing emotion. Our relationship is a whole new world for me, and I'm going to screw up every now and then, you can count on it. If this is one of those times, I'm sorry."

"In a lot of ways, it's a new world for me, too," Melody admitted. "With Roz for a mother, I got to be really good at protecting my own feelings. I'm not so good at considering other people's vulnerabilities."

"I think you underestimate your skills. You're an exceptionally empathetic person."

"Perhaps in work situations, where I'm standing back and making a rational analysis of other people's behavior. My empathy vibes don't seem to work so well when I'm dealing with people I care about."

He smiled faintly. "I guess that's the good news, then. You care about me enough to be irrational."

She gulped in a fortifying breath. "I don't just care about you. I love you." It was never easy for her to say the words. They'd been thrown at her too often and too casually by Roz, usually accompanied by a careless hug and kiss as she was dropping Melody off at boarding school, or at the home of any relative who would take her in for the school holidays.

"I love you, too." Nick leaned across the bed and tugged until she fell backward into his arms. He kissed her, then propped himself up on his elbow and looked down at her. "It's a weird feeling, isn't it."

"Very weird." He'd succeeded in making her smile again. She moved closer to him, her head resting on his chest, her hand splayed across the hard muscles of his abdomen. "But a nice kind of weird most of the time."

"Did you ever love Wallis Beecham?" Nick asked.

"When I was very little, I guess I did, but after he divorced Roz, we were together so infrequently that I barely knew him. Even though the custody arrangement required me to spend every summer in one of his houses, Wallis was almost never there. Still, I remember how much he loathed being dependent on other people for anything, and I can't help feeling sorry for him now. Having a stroke and being left helpless in a prison environment must be close to his worst nightmare."

"Your sympathy is misplaced. If it gets out of hand, remind yourself that the guy kidnapped you and would have murdered you if he could. That should restore your sense of perspective."

She tried to laugh but didn't quite make it. "When you start to think, there are an excessively large number of people who have either tried to kill me, or might be willing to make the attempt sometime in the near future."

Nick's arm tightened around her shoulders. "It goes with the job, honey. It's not personal."

"But it feels personal." She gave an involuntary shiver. "Zachary's hatred for me this morning was so intense I could feel it pressing on me like a boulder. I had to exert every ounce of my strength to prevent it from crushing me."

"Sometimes the backwash from a mission does feel personal," he agreed quietly. "But you need to remind yourself that Zachary hates you because you thwarted his plans to set off a religious war in this country. That's not cause for a soul-searching analysis of why people dislike you. There's nothing in your character that provokes the dislike, except your desire for justice. The problem is with Zachary, and other twisted people like him, not with you."

"Thank you for that," she said.

"You're welcome. But while we're on the subject of bad people meeting the fates they deserve—"

"Is that the subject we were on?"

"More or less. Anyway, I have another piece of news. Just before I left headquarters, we heard from the police in Cancún that Jorge Morrero is dead."

"What?" Melody shot up in bed. "Good grief. Who killed him?"

Nick shrugged. "Nobody's talking. Somebody in the

Cancún prison yard who has enough clout that none of the other prisoners is willing to point the finger. Apparently, one minute Jorge was walking around the perimeter of the yard. The next time a guard checked, he was stretched out on the concrete with a homemade knife sticking out of his back."

"You think Alejandro ordered the hit?"

"I'm almost positive Alejandro ordered the hit."

"Because he was afraid that Jorge might talk," Melody said.

Nick shook his head. "I don't think Jorge had anything more he could tell us, so I'm guessing he wasn't killed to keep him quiet."

"Then why?"

"As a punishment for messing up, and as a warning to other small-time criminals hoping to work for the drug cartel. Jorge broke the rule of silence and pointed the finger straight back to Alejandro. We caught a break when Jorge fingered his cousin. If Jorge had been smarter, he'd have kept his mouth shut tight. Alejandro didn't strike me as the sort of employer likely to give his cousin a free pass because he was family."

The news of Jorge's death bothered Melody on several different levels. "If there was any doubt as to whether Jorge was telling the truth about who hired him to kill me, I guess that's eliminated. He wouldn't have been killed unless he'd betrayed the truth."

"I agree. Unfortunately, the trail stops right there, with Alejandro Garcia."

"Is it worth questioning Alejandro again?" Melody asked.

"Confronting him with his cousin Jorge's death, you mean?"

"Yes."

Nick shook his head. "To what purpose? So that he can lie to us some more? You saw the type of man Alejandro is. There isn't a chance in hell we're going to break him. Apart from anything else, if he fingered the next person in the chain, he'd soon be a dead man himself. Criminals don't appreciate fellow criminals who shop them to the authorities. As Jorge found out."

Melody couldn't dispute his logic. "If we can't shake any names loose from Alejandro, what's the next step? I admit to being fresh out of ideas."

"Bob Spinard is running cross-checks between Alejandro and every bad guy you've crossed paths with since your first mission for Unit One. He's also rerunning all the data he can dredge up on Zachary Wharton, trying to find some definitive and recent links to Alejandro. Bob is hoping to find some evidence that points to a third party, somebody who might be easier to question than either Zachary or Alejandro. He expects to get back to us in a couple of days. Sooner if he runs across an intersection between Alejandro and anybody in your professional past."

Melody had great faith in Bob Spinard's skills as an analyst and as a collector of data. Even so, she doubted he would be able to find computerized records that would link Zachary to Alejandro, or anyone else who might have hired him. Alejandro was a drug dealer, which suggested that most of his life would have been lived off the grid, in the shadows of an undocumented netherworld. She wished she could come up with a brilliant alternative suggestion as to how they might extract the name of his employer from him, but she couldn't. If pushed to the wall, Alejandro would undoubtedly give them a name. Unfortunately, the name might or might not be that of the person who had really hired him.

She sighed. "I guess realistically there's nothing for me to do while Bob is completing his research, but get back to work."

Nick nodded. "I've arranged for you to start strength training with Sam. It's going to take you at least a couple of weeks to get back up to a level where it's safe to send you out on assignment. Double that for you to be up to speed." Nick paused. "Sam has assigned a new guy to help you brush up your combat training, and I cleared the assignment. The guy's name is Josh Straiker."

There was a slight edge to Nick's voice when he mentioned Straiker's name.

"I assume he's good or you wouldn't have assigned him?" Melody queried.

"He's good." Nick grimaced. "In fact, he's almost as good as he thinks he is. And that's sure as hell saying something."

Seven

Josh Straiker had transferred from the CIA to Unit One in September, barely three months ago, but the rumor mill already had him tagged as a potentially brilliant operative, with impressive investigative skills and even more impressive physical abilities. According to Sam, who acted as the human clearinghouse for Unit One's juiciest gossip, Josh was especially good at hand-to-hand combat. A couple of nights ago, over dinner in the cafeteria, Sam had told Melody that he thought Josh might be as good a fighter as Nick. Sam's expression had turned momentarily bleak when he made that comment and Melody hadn't needed to ask why. The only other operative who'd ever come close to Nick's level of fighting ability had been Dave Ramsdell, and the memory of Dave's double treachery still hurt.

On Christmas Eve, Melody was jumping rope, muttering curses at Sam, people who aimed bullets at her and the world in general, when Josh came into the gym.

"Hey, Josh, glad you could make it." Sam flashed the newcomer a smile that was a lot friendlier than recruits usually received from him. "I called because I knew you were here and Nick has requested that you go a coupla rounds on the mat with Melody. She's almost back in shape but she needs a combat challenge and nobody's been around for the past week to take her on."

"Sure. Be glad to help out." Josh grinned. "I love throwing beautiful women around." He shook Melody's hand, openly admiring. He was very good-looking in a Brad Pitt sort of way, with piercing blue eyes and the muscled, super-fit body typical of all Unit One operatives. "I've heard a lot of stories about your success in the field," he said. "It's good to meet you, finally."

Melody returned his smile. "I've heard rumors about you, too. Among others, that nobody can stay upright on the mat with you for more than three minutes."

"That's an exaggeration." Josh paused for a beat. "I'm sure it's never taken me as long as three minutes to defeat an opponent."

"So far you haven't gone up against Nick," Sam interjected.

"No." Josh didn't say anything, but his attitude conveyed the message that Nick was unlikely to prove an exception to the rule.

The guy might be cute, but he was in serious need of being taken down not just a peg or two, but several dozen pegs, Melody thought. Pity that hand-to-hand combat wasn't her strong suit, and that she wasn't likely to be the person to cut him down to size. Still, she'd give it her best shot, and might get lucky. She tossed the jump rope onto a bench and walked to the center of the mat.

Josh followed her, his stride slow and easy. They were both wearing shorts and sleeveless athletic shirts—not ideal clothing, since it offered too many loose straps and bands that could be grabbed. However, they were training for self-defense in the real world, as opposed to victory in a competition, and the disadvantages of their clothing helped to make the situation more realistic.

"You can start anytime," Sam said.

Melody and Josh faced off. She knew enough not to rush headlong into an attack. If Josh was half as good as everyone claimed, the only way to beat him would be to outfox him, not outfight him. On the plus side, she had the advantage of being warmed up, and arrogant macho men had a tendency to underestimate the physical agility and strength of a female opponent. She would definitely need to exploit any hint of carelessness or overconfidence on Josh's part if she hoped to catch him off guard.

She waited, her stance deceptively relaxed, and was ready for the swift lateral thrust of his right arm and the accompanying swing of his left leg, aimed to hook behind her knee and topple her. She parried by bringing her knee up to his groin—and ended flat on her back on the mat. Josh had anticipated her move, sidestepping and tossing her over his thigh in a single synchronized move.

He didn't speak as she pushed herself into a sitting position, just politely extended his hand to assist her back to her feet.

Melody resisted the urge to reject his offer of help. Gritting her teeth, she took his hand. She realized what her mistake had been and silently acknowledged that it had been a problem of attitude as much as technical skill: she'd opened herself to Josh's counterattack because she'd been too focused on hitting him right where his masculine pride was likely to take the biggest blow. Next time, she'd be less vindictive—and hopefully smarter.

They circled each other, each seeking an opportunity to attack. Josh made another lateral thrust with his right arm, a thrust that seemed identical to his previous opening strike.

In the split second available for her to react, Melody realized that he was too accomplished a fighter to make such an obvious repeat move. She countered, guessing that he planned to turn at the last minute and throw her over his back. She guessed correctly, parried and found herself once again with the chance to aim a hard knee kick to his groin. No way, buster. She wasn't going to make that mistake again. She feinted, planning to hook her foot around his ankle and use his forward momentum to send him toppling backward. Her foot connected and she experienced a brief burst of triumph.

The next thing she knew, she was lying on the mat, staring at the ceiling.

She sat up, not saying a word. Josh politely extended his hand to help her back to her feet. Seething inwardly, Melody took his hand and stood up. He was, maddening man, not even breathing deeply, whereas she was already panting. So much for having the advantage of being warmed up.

Josh at least didn't add insult to injury by telling her how well she had fought, or how good her technique was. They both knew that in the netherworld where Unit One operated, fighting well or having good technique didn't count. The only thing that mattered was being the last person standing when the fight was over.

Melody tried three more times to take Josh down. Three more times, she ended up on the mat. The clock on the gym wall indicated that the five bouts had consumed a grand total of eight minutes and forty-five seconds. She wasn't even lasting two minutes against him, much less three.

Once again Josh extended his hand to help her up. His manner remained polite, not in the least gloating, as if he had expected no other outcome than for Melody to end up on her butt, swallowing her pride, five times in a row. His confidence was all the more infuriating because it was entirely justified.

She took his hand as meekly as on the five previous occasions, but her temper was flaring. With all the speed and power she could muster, she sprang to her feet, not waiting for Sam's signal to begin another bout. Instead, the instant she was upright, she back-flipped, spun around and used the momentum of her leap to push hard against his chest with her feet.

She finally managed to catch him off guard, but she still didn't succeed in taking him down. At least his countermove was a fraction less coordinated than usual—merely excellent instead of perfect—giving her the opening she needed to leap again and use her full body weight to propel him to the ground. Okay, so she'd cheated, and her winning move had been desperate as opposed to elegant, but Josh was on the mat and she was standing. With a cuttingly polite smile, she extended her hand to help him up.

She should have quit while she was ahead. He grabbed her wrist, pulled her toward him and used his superior upper-body strength to drag her down onto the mat. She landed on top of him and he quickly rolled her over, straddling her and holding her pinned down, his arm across her neck. She could barely breathe, let alone speak, and executing a countermove was far in the land of fantasy. She slapped the palm of her hand on the mat to indicate surrender.

"You should have cheated sooner," Sam said to her, walking over to the mat and signaling for them to get up. "Two rounds should have been more than enough for you to realize there was no way you could beat Josh fair and square."

Sam was right, Melody realized, reaching for a bottle of water. She'd been fighting Josh as if they were engaged in an Olympic sporting event, instead of a no-holds-barred struggle with potentially life-threatening consequences. Her instinctive tendency to play by the rules was the curse of her boarding school background, where cheating had been one of the few crimes her schoolmates wouldn't tolerate.

"You look mad at yourself," Josh said. "Don't be. You fought well considering you're still getting back into shape. You have strong legs and you use them to good advantage. Great elevation in the jumps, too."

At least his tone of voice wasn't condescending,

Melody reflected. He was merely giving her his honest opinion, which carried a lot of weight considering his obvious expertise.

"Being marginally out of shape had nothing to do with the fact that I lost," she admitted. "You'd have taken me down just as fast even if I'd been in peak physical condition."

Josh didn't patronize her with a denial. "I've been taking classes in various forms of unarmed combat since I was in the fifth grade," he said. "I'm guessing that gives me the advantage of about twenty years' more experience than you."

"I only had a couple of years of training before I joined Unit One," Melody acknowledged.

"Maybe we could help each other out," Josh said. "I've heard that you're the fastest and most accurate shot in Unit One. Whereas me... Well, let's just say I'm somewhere between lousy and barely adequate. If we could find a few hours when we're both free, maybe I could teach you a couple of interesting combat moves, and you could teach me to shoot straight."

"That sounds like a better deal for me than for you," Melody said. "Despite all the macho mystique about guns, there isn't much skill involved. Any klutz can shoot reasonably straight with a few hours of instruction."

Josh gave a rueful laugh. "Wait till you've watched me miss the target a couple of dozen times and you'll reconsider that statement."

She found herself warming to him, despite the bruises on her rear end and the sizable dents to her pride. "I have three more days of training before I'm off the injured list. Are you on assignment right now?"

"No, I'm waiting to be assigned." Josh's expression indicated that he wasn't happy with his state of idleness.

"Then let's get together the Monday after Christmas. How about eight-thirty here in the gym? We can compare schedules and block out some time."

"Works for me," Josh said.

"Hey, Nick, I didn't notice you standing in the doorway." Sam called out a cheerful greeting. "It's been a while since I saw you."

"I just got back from California."

Nick strolled into the gym and Melody's heart raced into immediate overdrive. The reaction was so familiar, virtually automatic at the sight of him, that she'd almost reached the point where she could ignore it. Almost. Nick had been gone for ten days, and their phone contacts had been brief and infrequent, which meant that it was even more difficult than usual to restrain herself from falling into his arms.

"We're having more trouble wrapping up one of our ops than we should be," Nick said. His gaze raked the gym and stopped briefly not on her, but on Josh. "Hopefully, things are back on track now."

He nodded toward Melody, maintaining the formal distance between them. Given his role as director of operations and the fact that he was Melody's boss, they made a concerted effort to keep their personal relationship out of the workplace. Not surprisingly, few people were deceived, least of all old-timers like Sam, who watched their sidelong glances with visible amusement.

Melody sometimes thought her relationship with Nick would provoke less interested scrutiny if they simply hung a banner in the cafeteria announcing that yes, Nikolai Anwar and Melody Beecham were not only involved, but actually living together, long-term plans not yet finalized.

"Straiker." Nick gave a curt nod in Josh's direction. "I read your debrief on the Vergoni case. Your team did good work."

"Thank you, sir." Josh's stance was easy, but the atmosphere between the two men was thick with tension.

"Melody just went a few rounds against Josh," Sam said with deceptive casualness.

Nick glanced from Josh to Melody. "How did it go?" he asked her. "As I told you a couple of weeks ago, Straiker has the reputation of being very good."

"Unfortunately, I'm living proof that his reputation doesn't lie," Melody said. "I landed flat on my back five times in less than ten minutes."

"If you have the time, Nick, you should go a couple of rounds against Josh," Sam suggested.

His tone seemed light but Melody was beginning to pick up on undertones that she didn't understand.

"Do you want to fight me?" Nick asked Josh.

Melody found the way he phrased the question odd. There was definitely more going on here than mere tension between a new recruit and his boss, even if the two of them were males with a natural tendency to jockey for dominance.

"Yes, let's fight." Josh made no attempt to expand on

his answer, and the half-joking nature of his responses to Melody had entirely vanished, converted into a tense, hard-edged challenge.

Nick stripped off his jacket. Like Melody and Josh, he was wearing lightweight leather athletic shoes. Unlike them, he was also wearing tailored slacks and a dark gray knit shirt, a definite disadvantage in comparison to Josh's less cumbersome outfit. After a moment's hesitation, Nick took off his shirt, too, leaving the top half of his body bare.

The two men squared off in the center of the mat and immediately began to circle each other. Josh made the opening move, a stunning leap into the air that looked as if it had been filmed in slow motion for a scene from *The Matrix*. Nick responded with a leap of his own, vaulting past Josh's left side and lashing out with his right arm in a blow that would surely have inflicted serious injury if it had actually connected with Josh's neck. Instead, Josh blocked the blow and swung inward with an upward thrust of his right hand that connected—hard—with Nick's chin.

The bout degenerated from hard-hitting to brutal in less than ten seconds. Despite the brutality, there was a hypnotic, choreographed beauty to the violence of their moves. The fighting was so intense that by the time the three-minute mark was reached both men were sweating profusely, and their breathing sounded loud in the quiet of the gym. They circled each other again, and Nick landed a blow that caused blood to gush from Josh's nose. Melody looked quickly to Sam, expecting him to call a halt before either man, or both, ended up seriously hurt. But Sam avoided her gaze, his expression as close to impenetrable as she'd ever seen it.

The moves that ended the bout followed too quickly for Melody to discern the exact sequence. Josh lashed out with another of his stunning high kicks, but Nick must have countered successfully because he slid beneath Josh's legs and emerged on the other side. At one moment Nick appeared to be slumped on his knees, his spine hunched, his head hanging toward the mat. The next moment, he had launched himself backward, cannoning into Josh and knocking him to the ground with a thud that sounded heavy enough to be seriously damaging. Josh fell, limbs splayed. He made no move to get up.

Nick straightened, but said nothing. He bent down and touched his finger to the pulse in Josh's neck, then ran his hands swiftly down Josh's body, apparently feeling for broken bones. Reassured that his opponent was merely stunned as opposed to seriously wounded, Nick moved to the side of the mat and waited for Josh to stand up. The idea of extending a helping hand seemingly failed to cross his mind.

Melody looked again at Sam, who normally took full command of his gym regardless of who was in there, or what rank within Unit One they might hold. On this occasion, however, Sam seemed at pains to fade into the background. Melody discovered she was holding her breath, as if anticipating a disaster of major proportions.

Just as she was about to break the almost paralyzing silence, Josh pushed himself to a sitting position, and then stood up. Once on his feet, he held his spine ramrod straight, his hands balled into fists at his side. His gaze locked with Nick's, his face and eyes wiped clean of expression. He swayed once, but otherwise didn't move, not even to wipe away the blood that still dripped from his nose.

Nick spoke, his voice as blank as Josh's expression. "Come to my office in half an hour. I have an assignment for you." He turned and left the gym without saying a word to either Sam or Melody.

As soon as Nick left, Melody wet a small towel with bottled water and handed it to Josh. "I suppose it's useless for me to ask what just happened between you two."

"Yes, it's useless." Josh took the towel with a brief word of thanks, shoved it against his face and left the gym without saying another word.

"Okay," Melody said, wincing as he slammed the door behind him. "I'll try again. Sam, you know everything that goes on in this place. What the heck was that all about? For a moment there, I thought the two of them might kill each other."

"I was hopin' you could tell me what happened," Sam said. "Your guess is as good as mine."

"I don't believe that. I'm never clued in on any of the gossip, whereas you're Mr. All-Knowing."

"Not this time."

"You were the one who encouraged them to fight. And you must have done that for a reason."

"Yeah, and it looks like I stuck my nose in where I should've kept it out. I realized the two of them struck sparks whenever they were in a room together and I thought a friendly go-round on the mat might help some. Ease the tension, you know? But that fight wasn't friendly, and it was about something a hell of a lot more personal than two guys trying to work out who's leader of the wolf pack." He sent her a quizzical look. "Anyway, why are you asking me what's up with those two? You're the woman who's seeing the boss. Ask him what's goin' on."

Melody was silent for a moment. "Does everyone at headquarters know that Nick and I are…involved?" she asked.

"There may be a clerk in the filing department who hasn't heard," Sam said dryly, tossing used towels into a hamper. "But somehow I doubt it. You and Nick kinda raise the temperature in a room every time you look at each other."

"Do you think the other operatives are offended by our relationship?" Melody asked. "Be honest, Sam."

"I haven't heard any complaints, and I guess I would've if people were really pissed off."

That was a relief in several ways, not least because Nick would be less effective in his position as chief of operations if too many of the people who reported to him resented that the boss was sleeping with a recruit who had barely a year's tenure.

"What about you?" Melody asked. "Do you disapprove of our relationship, Sam? I know you had doubts about us in the beginning."

"I don't have doubts anymore," he said. "Nick's always been a good friend, but he took life pretty damn seriously until you came along. Since you're askin', I decided after you came back from Idaho that you're about the best thing to have happened to Nick in a long while. He isn't wound so damn tight anymore, and a person doesn't have to poke so hard to get through his shell. Bottom line—you make him happy."

Melody was astonished to feel a lump in her throat. "Thank you for that, Sam."

"You're welcome. Now get the hell out of here and go home. Have you forgotten it's Christmas tomorrow?"

She laughed, although the intensity of the scene between Nick and Josh still nagged at her. "I'm cooking Christmas dinner for six, which is a first for me. How could I possibly forget?"

"Whoever your guests are, bet your holiday won't be as weird as mine. My two ex-wives got together and they've invited me over to one of their houses in Larchmont. So I'm gonna be greeting Santa along with their new husbands and seven kids from various marriages." He shook his head. "I dunno. Seems to me it was easier in the old days, when people were allowed to hate their ex-spouses. Except for the impact on the kids, of course."

"Two of the children are yours, right?"

"Yeah. Samantha and Aaron. Don't know how their mothers and I managed to produce such great kids. They're proof that genes aren't destiny." Sam grinned. "I'll take pictures with my new digital camera and you can tell me how cute my kids are when I see you on Monday."

"It's a deal." Melody gave him a hug. "Have a merry Christmas, Sam."

"You, too. Now get the hell out of here, before I decide to have you jump rope again. Or maybe climb the wall. You haven't done that in a while."

Melody ran for the door.

Eight

For people who had so few relatives living within a thousand miles of Manhattan, Christmas had turned out to be a complicated holiday for Nick and Melody. Nick's uncle and aunt in Chicago had invited them for a long weekend, but Nick assured Melody they extended the invitation every year and didn't expect him to accept. In fact, he claimed, they would be horrified if he did. They also received invitations to spend the day with Jasper Fowles and his mother, Prudence, and a similar request from Johnston and Cynthia Yates.

In an effort to avoid hurt feelings, Melody had compromised by inviting both couples to dinner at the apartment. To her surprise, they all accepted. Nick, on hearing the news, pretended horror and announced that he would be taking off for Vegas until the holiday was over.

Despite his bluster, Melody had the impression that Nick was secretly rather pleased to be hosting a real, honest-to-God Christmas party. He entertained frequently in his role as Nikolai Anwar, international wheeler-dealer, but almost never on a personal basis. Still, his contacts made the preparations easy. He phoned his usual caterer to order a platter of fancy hors d'oeuvres along with enough rich desserts to satisfy even Jasper's sweet tooth, and Melody volunteered to cook the main course.

She discovered that she retained more of a sentimental streak than she'd realized. For the first time since her mother died, she experienced a burst of nostalgia for snowy Christmases spent with her grandparents and cousins on the High Ridgefield estate in Wiltshire. A whiff of fresh pine from a vendor selling Christmas trees on a Manhattan street corner carried her straight back to her childhood. She could almost smell the mince pies baking in the old-fashioned, cast-iron ovens of her grandparents' kitchens, and remembered how she had shivered with excitement when she and her cousins crept downstairs to the small family drawing room where Father Christmas left their overstuffed stockings on Christmas morning. Father Christmas always used separate chairs so that there would be no confusion about which gifts were for which cousin, and the stockings were topped with individual notes from Mr. and Mrs. Claus, which none of the kids ever seemed to notice were written in their grandfather's handwriting. Even Roz had often mellowed around the Christmas season, and would sometimes put in a brief appearance, bearing dazzlingly unsuitable gifts and entertaining them all with fascinating tales of the glamorous world in which she moved.

Feeling pleasantly domestic, Melody spent Christmas day roasting a turkey British-style, stuffed with chestnut puree, and accompanied by potatoes cooked around the bird until they were a crispy golden brown. Aided by several glasses of sherry and frequent phone calls to her grandmother in England for cooking instructions, she managed to have everything prepared and a festive table set in time for their guests' arrivals. Nick renewed his threat that he would be on the next flight to Vegas if she served her family's traditional brussels sprouts and bread sauce, so she compromised with an elegant spinach gratinée, and cheated by buying port wine gravy from the corner deli.

Their guests were lavish in their praise of her culinary efforts, Prudence Fowles going so far as to say that she couldn't remember the last Christmas she'd so much enjoyed the annual ritual of overeating. Best of all, as far as Melody was concerned, was the quiet enjoyment that she sensed in Nick. Given that his parents and sister had been murdered when he was a freshman in college, she assumed the holiday season since then had been less than ho-ho-ho jolly for him, and the brusque uncle and aunt in Chicago didn't seem the types to have swept him into the bosom of their family and smothered him with warm fuzzies.

Melody had also worried that their two sets of guests might not be compatible. Prudence and Jasper were on the flamboyant side, and Cynthia's taste was notoriously conservative. However, it turned out that the two women had served together on several charitable committees, most recently for the Guggenheim Museum, and the pair had a grand time gossiping about mutual acquaintances. They were especially worked up over the fate of an assistant curator at the museum whom they believed had been wrongly dismissed for criticizing Picasso.

Jasper and Melody exchanged amused glances as the elderly ladies expressed their outrage at museum boards that continued to pay millions of dollars for works by Picasso and his imitators. "These modern painters slap a few geometric shapes and squiggly lines onto a piece of canvas and call it art," Cynthia said. "Appalling that they can get away with it."

"Of course the Guggenheim had to fire that young man," Prudence said, her orange hair seeming to glow with righteous indignation. "He was brave enough to point out that the emperor had no clothes, and the museum couldn't allow that."

"And if Picasso's overrated, what do you think about Jackson Pollock?" Cynthia asked with grim satisfaction. "There's another overrated artist for you. The man flings paint around on the floor of his garage, and we're supposed to believe it's great art! The inflated prices people pay for his nonsense would come tumbling down to earth if a few more so-called experts had the courage to tell the truth."

The aura of harmony established by their disparagement of two of the twentieth century's most admired artists spilled over into general cordiality and merriment. After the desserts had been cleared away, the three couples lingered over a final cup of coffee before exchanging gifts.

The gifts were as successful as the rest of the dinner.

Nick and Melody gave the men specialty vodka that came from a distillery in Russia that had once catered to the czars, and that came bottled in wonderful crystal decanters. For Prudence and Cynthia, Melody had settled on pashmina shawls: a deep emerald green for Prudence, a soft dove gray for Cynthia. Prudence was extravagant in her cries of appreciation, and Cynthia seemed equally pleased, albeit more subdued, draping the shawl around her shoulders and admiring the tantalizing softness of the wool.

The Yateses gave everyone books, and Jasper gave the Yateses a carved antique inkstand, for which they expressed much admiration. For Melody, Jasper had found a nineteenth-century watercolor of an English cottage garden.

"It was painted by the vicar's wife in the village of Batheaton in Gloucestershire," he said. "It's dated 1837, the year of Queen Victoria's coronation, and I thought you might enjoy it." He grinned. "I know you have a secret passion for kitsch, especially if it's kitsch with flowers."

"This painting isn't kitsch and I love it to pieces," she said, kissing his cheek. "Thank you, Jasper. It's just lovely." Without thinking, she reached up to ruffle his hair, smoothing it back over his bald spot, the first time she'd made the affectionate gesture since discovering the role Jasper played as commander of Unit One. When she realized what she was doing, she flushed and quickly stepped away, but Jasper caught her hand and squeezed it lightly.

"I'm glad you like the painting," he said. "As soon as I saw it, I thought of you."

She kissed him again, then gave them both a moment to recover their poise by walking into the living room and propping the picture in a prominent position above the fireplace.

When she returned, Johnston Yates reached inside the breast pocket of his suit jacket and brought out a small package, elegantly wrapped in silver tissue paper. "Merry Christmas, Melody," he said, handing it to her. "Cynthia and I hope you'll like this little extra gift, although I'm sure you'll find the style rather old-fashioned."

"It's a brooch," Cynthia interjected. "You should probably mention that, Johnston."

"Oh, yes, of course. As Cynthia says, this is a brooch. My father—your grandfather—bought it for my mother on their honeymoon in 1935, and I thought you might enjoy having something that your grandmother loved to wear. The stones aren't real, of course, and the gold is only a thin veneer, so I'm afraid there's no commercial value to our gift. My parents were schoolteachers, and they married during the Depression, so they had no money to spare for buying real jewels. However, my mother treasured this little trinket until the day she died."

"You couldn't have thought of anything I would like more." Melody was surprised and touched that Johnston was willing to present her with a gift that so clearly identified her as his daughter, even though the witnesses were few and already knew of the relationship. She stole a glance at Cynthia as she tore off the tissue-paper wrapping, and was relieved to see that Johnston's wife was showing no signs of embarrassment or chagrin. Even though Johnston's infidelity was by now more than thirty years old, Melody never underestimated how much forbearance Cynthia showed at times such as this, when her husband's lack of faithfulness was exposed to scrutiny by people who moved in her own social circle.

Melody opened the battered leather jewelry box quickly, not wanting to prolong the tense moment. Inside, nestled against a pad of worn brown velvet, was a large brooch fashioned in the shape of a cluster of violets. The purple and green crystals that formed the blossoms and leaves were outlined in gold that had a much deeper coppery tinge than contemporary jewelry. The gold-colored stems were tied with a mauve bow, fashioned out of painted metal mesh. The style of the brooch would have been old-fashioned even in the thirties, Melody thought. If asked her professional opinion, she would have dated it to the early nineteen hundreds.

She stroked the flowers, overwhelmed by the sensation of contact with the paternal grandparents she had never known. She had to clear her throat before she could speak. "Thank you. It's beautiful, and I'll treasure it just as my grandmother did."

Johnston coughed and muttered something barely audible about his mother having been a remarkable woman.

"I'm so glad you like it, my dear." Cynthia smiled. "I warned Johnston that it's a little unsophisticated by today's standards and that you'll probably never be able to wear it, so please don't feel obligated."

Melody started to nod, simply to be polite. Then she changed her mind. The fact that Cynthia rarely wore any jewelry except pearls and tiny gold pins didn't mean that she had to pretend her taste was equally bland.

"I'm sure I'll find occasions to wear it," she said, smiling. "It would look stunning on a plain black dress. Actually, I like these flowers better than the abstract style of pins and brooches most people were buying in the thirties. I'm not really a fan of art deco, even though it's very much in vogue right now, so my grandmother made the perfect choice from my point of view."

Johnston looked pleased by her comment. He'd obviously accepted his wife's edict that the brooch was unwearable, and seemed delighted that his gift was going to be worn, not just placed in a drawer and honored for sentimental value. He harrumphed when Melody kissed his cheek, but gave her a hug, too. Given his difficulty in expressing his emotions, the quick hug was the equivalent of most fathers waltzing their child around the room. She remembered just in time to kiss Cynthia's cheek, too, and Cynthia squeezed her hand and told her she was a dear girl, a totally unexpected accolade.

Their guests lingered for another half hour and then left, repeating their profuse thanks for a lovely afternoon and evening. After they'd gone, Melody surveyed the kitchen, which looked pretty much like the wreckage of bears who had been feasting at the municipal garbage dump.

"Leave everything," Nick said, coming up behind her and slipping his arms around her waist. "I've already arranged for the cleaning service to come in tomorrow morning."

"And they agreed? But it's Sunday, as well as the day after Christmas."

"I know, but it's amazing what you can achieve if you offer giant sums of money. Which I did."

"Thank you, you're a wonderful man." She turned within the circle of his arms and kissed him. "I'll avoid asking what you consider giant sums of money, in case I faint."

"Wise woman." He grinned. "Naturally, I expect to be suitably rewarded for my extravagance."

"And you shall be. But we at least need to put the food away or it will spoil."

"Later." He tugged at her hand, leading her out of the kitchen.

She expected him to head for the bedroom, so he didn't have to tug very hard. Instead, he surprised her by taking her into the living room and pulling her down to sit next to him on the sofa.

"I think our first dinner party was very successful, don't you?"

She nodded. "Everyone seemed to have a really good time." She smothered a yawn. "However, I think I may have eaten one profiterole too many—"

"Only one?" Nick asked, laughing.

She threw a cushion at him, which he caught one-handed and tucked behind him. Then, instead of stretching out his arm and inviting her to rest her head against his chest, he sprang up and disappeared into the bedroom, returning with a gift-wrapped package the size of a large book.

"I have another Christmas present for you," he said,

handing it to her. "I didn't want to give it to you when there were people around."

"Let me guess." She laughed up at him. "You've been enjoying yourself researching the Victoria's Secret catalogue and were afraid Cynthia Yates would have a heart attack when she saw what you'd chosen."

"I can see I missed an opportunity there, but no, this didn't come from Victoria's Secret." He fiddled with the gold cuff links that she'd given him that morning, and stuck his hands into the pocket of his slacks, trying to appear casual, and failing. "Go ahead. Open it."

She ripped into the scarlet wrapping paper and encountered thick layers of tissue protecting a glass surface. Unfolding the tissue, she found herself looking at a silver-framed color photo of a couple laughing into the camera, with snow-capped mountains looming in the background. The shot was of her mother and Johnston Yates, she realized, taken at least thirty years ago. Judging from the size of the mountain range, as well as the brilliant sun and cloudless sky, the photo had been snapped when they were visiting one of the western ski resorts, perhaps during the trip to Vail that Johnston had mentioned to her. Roz's head was tilted back so that she could look up at Johnston, and the camera had caught a moment of unguarded sexual hunger in Johnston's expression. Lady Roz appeared almost luminous, and Melody was struck anew by how stunningly beautiful her mother had been as a young woman.

"Thank you," she said to Nick, her voice husky. "It's a wonderful picture of my parents. How in the world did you find it?"

"I begged Bob Spinard for some time at the central computer and whizzed through what seemed like a thousand newspaper and magazine archives. Eventually I came up with this. It appeared in Life magazine thirty-two years ago."

Her eyes widened in surprise. "It did? According to Johnston, he and Roz were always super-careful never to be photographed together. I wonder how this one slipped past their guard."

"The picture you're looking at is cropped," Nick said. "Actually, both Cynthia Yates and Wallis Beecham were also in the shot, standing one on either side of your parents. I simply cut them out with photo-editing software and reprinted."

Melody traced her forefinger around her mother's smiling mouth. "Even if you'd left Cynthia and Wallis in, that wouldn't disguise the intensity of the attraction between Johnston and my mother. I can't believe a photographer captured this shot and didn't immediately realize that the vice president of the United States was involved with a woman who wasn't his wife."

Nick leaned over so that he could view the picture again. "It was a more innocent time, I guess. Or perhaps the editor and photographer both noticed what they'd recorded, but they adhered to the conventions of the era and said nothing. Because you're right—to anyone paying the slightest bit of attention, Roz and Johnston are obviously lovers."

Melody touched the picture again. "There's a softness about my mother's expression as she looks at Johnston."

"And real affection in his expression, too, along with the desire. I noticed that myself."

"When we first spoke about the fact that he's my father, Johnston told me he'd been genuinely in love with my mother, not just sexually attracted, although I suppose that's what he'd *have* to tell me."

"Not necessarily." Nick shook his head. "Based on this photo, I'd say he was being honest."

"Poor Cynthia," Melody said. "It must be dreadful to live with the knowledge that your husband wasn't simply unfaithful, but that he was madly in love with the Other Woman."

"But *does* Cynthia know that?" Nick asked. "After all, Johnston didn't divorce her even though Roz was pregnant. On the contrary, he stayed in the marriage and Cynthia didn't learn about his affair with Roz until years after it was over. For all practical purposes, if Johnston was the prize, Cynthia won and Roz lost."

"You're right. On top of that, my mother is dead, so she's no threat to anyone. I'm going to stop feeling sorry for Cynthia." Melody smiled down at the photo. "Thank you so much for this, Nick. It's a wonderful gift."

She kissed him, but he must have sensed that her heart wasn't quite in it, and after a moment or two, he broke away, holding her at arm's length and searching her face. "What's up? Something's bothering you. Is it the picture of your parents? Did I goof in giving it to you?"

"No, the opposite. I love the photo. I plan to keep it on the dresser so that I can see it as soon as I wake up in the morning."

"Then what's the problem?"

She pulled a face. "I have another gift for you, too. I've been debating all day whether to give it to you or not, and whether Christmas is the right time to do this…."

He tilted her chin up and held her face, so that she couldn't look away from him. "In the movies, a spiel like that usually means the heroine is about to tell some poor, unsuspecting guy that she's pregnant with his baby."

She laughed, as he'd intended. "Don't worry. I'm not pregnant." She couldn't resist asking, "Would it be so bad if I was?"

His gaze held hers. "It wouldn't be bad at all."

She had the impression he was about to say something more, but he abruptly broke eye contact, dragging her hard against his chest and kissing her urgently on the lips. At the start of their relationship he'd often used passion to avoid genuine closeness, but it was a device neither of them employed much nowadays, since they were no longer quite so scared by the idea of intimacy. She and Nick had come a long way in terms of being honest with each other about their feelings, but her uncertainty about the gift she still hadn't given him, and his unwillingness to pursue a discussion about how he would feel if she became pregnant, reminded her how far still remained to be traveled.

In view of their stormy pasts, she supposed it wasn't surprising that they both tended to barricade their deepest emotions. Until recently, she'd respected his need for space, but these days she found the artificial boundaries frustrating, and the gift she had stashed in her underwear drawer intruded into areas Nick had clearly designated as No Go zones. In fact, if she handed over her gift, she'd be climbing right to the top of his highest and most fiercely protected wall. She could only hope he would invite her in, not push her off.

Enough debating, Melody decided, getting up from the sofa with the excuse of taking the picture of her parents into the bedroom. She would give Nick the photograph she'd had framed for him. It was ironic that they'd both come up with the same idea regarding Christmas gifts, she reflected, extracting her gold-wrapped package from beneath a pile of camisoles. At some level, Nick must recognize as clearly as she did that their relationship couldn't move any farther forward until they tended to the wounds inflicted by their pasts. The pictures they'd selected were more than nostalgic Christmas gifts; they were gateways to forbidden territory.

Returning to the living room, she handed Nick the package and waited, stomach knotted and heart racing, as he undid the festive wrapping. He stared in total silence at the picture of himself, his sister and his parents at a summer barbecue. His eyes remained blank and his face devoid of expression as he stared. For a moment Melody wondered if he had closed his mind so completely to the past that he no longer recognized his own family. Then he made a raw sound deep in his throat.

"I'd forgotten we had a dog," he said, his voice strangled. "His name was Pete, short for Peter the Great. Mom named him after the Russian emperor." He paused. "How strange. I've no idea what happened to Pete."

The fact that Nick didn't know what had happened to the family pet was no surprise. As far as Melody could tell, he'd coped with the death of his family by cutting himself off from every link to his past. She had never met anyone who was so completely deprived of physical connections to his own childhood. Nick had no treasured high school football jersey, no dog-eared copy of a favorite book, no battered piece of furniture from his childhood home, and not a single picture from his childhood—not even a snapshot. She'd begged the photo she'd just given him from Mac, who'd been a close friend and colleague of Nick's father. Mac had snapped this shot at a Fourth of July picnic following Nick's senior year in high school.

Melody could understand that a relentless focus on the future might have been a useful coping mechanism for Nick in the immediate aftermath of his family's murder, but seventeen years had passed since they were killed. Surely the time had now come when he needed to integrate his past into his current life.

"We were so happy the day this shot was taken," he said, tracing his forefinger over the dog, a black Lab. He skirted the images of his parents and sister as if touching them was still too hurtful a gesture for him to make. "We were so goddamn, naively happy."

Melody risked putting her hand over his. At least he didn't push her away. "You still have the memory of that happy day," she said. "Nobody can take that from you."

"Yeah, I have the memory." He shrugged, his expression bitter. "How can memories be pleasant or happy when I know we were living in a fool's paradise? The

happiness was all cut off before it could go anywhere."
Nick finally touched his sister's face, then immediately
pulled his finger away as if burned. "If she hadn't been
murdered, Gwynnyth would most likely have been married with children by now. I hate that I'll never get to
complain that her husband's a pain in the ass. I hate that
I'll never get to see her kids."

Melody wanted to point out that refusing to remember the happy times he'd shared with his sister wouldn't
bring her back, and consigning Gwynnyth to oblivion
was no way to honor her memory, but he spoke before
she could find the right words to express her thoughts
without hurting him.

"Gwynnyth was thirteen years old when Mac took
this picture. It was the summer right before I went away
to college and she had less than a year left to live."

"She looks as if she was very proud of her older
brother," Melody ventured.

"I was almost five years older. It was a big enough
gap that we didn't fight much."

Melody risked lightening the tone of her remarks. "I
can't help noticing that you were disgustingly handsome, even back in those days, when you were just a
skinny kid with way too long hair."

Nick didn't smile. He stared into the distance, lost
in a long-ago nightmare. "I was supposed to be in the
car with them, you know. They'd come to the college
campus to spend a long weekend, but I blew them off
because I had a hot date. I lied. I told them I had an ap-
pointment with the dean and that I'd meet them later,
back in town."

Melody didn't want to scoff at Nick's feelings, but he needed to hear the truth. "You feel guilty because you didn't die, so you're determined to rewrite the past and turn yourself into a villain. You weren't a villain, Nick. You were just a typical eighteen-year-old guy. If your family hadn't been murdered that day, the fact that you once ditched them for a hot date would be completely forgotten. Or at most be something you laughed over together."

"But they *did* die."

"Yes, and if your parents had time to think anything at all in the split second before they were gone, I'd bet anything they were thanking God that you weren't with them. That you, at least, had been saved."

He said nothing, and she leaned her head against his arm. His muscles felt stiff and unyielding. "It's been almost two decades, Nick, and you've spent that time working to make the world a better place. You've earned the right to forgive yourself for being alive."

He stared at the picture of his family, then looked away. She saw that his eyes were blind with unshed tears.

"Let your parents and sister back into your life," she pleaded. "Your best revenge against the people who murdered your family is to lead a full life. Don't let the murderers who killed your family cripple you as well. Don't give them that much of a victory."

He drew in a ragged breath. "I'm afraid," he said, avoiding her gaze. "I don't trust normal everyday happiness anymore. I want to have kids. I want you to be their mother, but I don't believe I could survive losing one of my children." He stared down at the picture and his voice lowered. "I *know* I couldn't survive losing you."

"You're not going to lose me," she said.

"How do you know?" he demanded.

She didn't know, of course, but she gave him the comfort of a lie. "Because I'm notoriously stubborn and I plan to stay by your side while I grow old and grouchy—*very* old and *very* grouchy. So be warned."

"You can't imagine how much I want that to be true."

"I can imagine quite well because I want the same thing."

Nick frowned at the picture of his parents, then looked back up at her. "You make faith in the future sound easy."

"Because life isn't worth living if you wake up each morning anticipating disaster." Melody took the picture from him and set it on the coffee table. "There are no guarantees in life for anyone," she said softly. "You want a promise that nothing terrible is ever going to happen to you again, but nobody can give you that promise. The fact that your family was murdered doesn't give you a free ride for the rest of your life, but it doesn't make it any more likely that you'll suffer another tragedy, either."

"I don't trust the odds anymore," Nick said. "Most people cope with uncertainty by pretending they can control the risk in their lives. The murder of my family made me realize that we have no control over our destinies. None."

"I don't agree. You can't predict when there's going

to be a forest fire, but you can sure as hell decide not to build your new home in the middle of a forest. And on the flip side, only a fool would decide never to build a house because sometimes, in some places, there are forest fires. Right now, what you're doing with your life is the equivalent of refusing ever to build a house."

"I think you just called me a fool." Nick almost managed a smile.

"But very politely." She took his hands and held them tight. "You can decide your loss was so horrifying that you're going to turn your back on everything we might be able to build together. Or you can find the courage to risk living your life. It's your choice to make, Nick, unless you want to surrender it to the murderers who wiped out your family."

He was silent for long enough to make her scared.

"I choose you," he said at last. "I choose you, and a house built somewhere safe, with two kids, and a family dog that's as goofy as Peter the Great."

Relief poured through her that they'd been able to confront the specter of his past head-on and emerge relatively unscathed. She smiled, although she suspected it quivered a bit at the edges. "Sounds like a plan to me."

"At least the start of a plan." He drew in a long breath, his gaze locked with hers. "Will you marry me, Melody? Will you live with me until we both grow old and wrinkled and our grandchildren have to say everything twice before we hear what they're trying to tell us?"

"Absolutely, I'll marry you," she said. "Although I might break down and buy a hearing aid."

His eyes were almost free of any lurking shadow. He

grinned. "Bet you'll be the sexiest grandma ever." He took her into his arms and kissed her with all the passion that had been theirs from the beginning, and with a tenderness that seemed to grow stronger with the passing of each day.

Melody responded to the passion, and returned the tenderness, but she was painfully aware that they'd untangled no more than a few threads of the complications choking their relationship. The idea of marriage and long-term commitment was new to Nick and he hadn't thought through the practicalities of his proposal. If he had, he would realize that working for Unit One was hardly the best way to guarantee a peaceful old age. The unpleasant truth was that their positions as field agents for Unit One left almost no room for marriage, and no room at all for the dream of starting a family.

But it was Christmas, the season of hope, the season when dreams come true. For this one night, Melody nestled in Nick's arms and allowed herself to live the fantasy of happily ever after.

Nine

Mac brewed himself a double espresso, his first in sixty-seven days, and downed it in a single ecstatic gulp. Nectar of the gods, he thought, closing his eyes to savor the aroma. He began the ritual of making himself another cup, pausing to hitch every now and again at his pants, which had become alarmingly loose since the last time he'd worn them. What the hell. Okay, he was losing weight, but he felt fine, so screw the doctors and their dire predictions about his health. If he was destined to have a second stroke—the massive one they kept threatening—why not go out with an ambrosial brew in his hand?

He waved vaguely in the direction of the espresso machine, his way of inviting Josh Straiker to make himself coffee. Josh declined on the grounds that he'd just finished a soda. Mac exercised significant restraint and didn't point out that having soda was entirely irrelevant to the question of whether you wanted a cup of espresso.

"Nick had to leave for D.C.," he said. "He's interviewing people in connection with a mission. Asked me to brief you regarding the same mission. The window of opportunity is time-sensitive, so the planning is urgent. Nick would normally lead this operation himself, but he's assigned you because he's had previous dealings with one of the principals in the case."

"What's the mission?" Josh leaned forward, hands clasped loosely in his lap, but intensely focused. This was a man who wore his self-confidence with the same casual ease that he wore his clothes, and Mac was immediately reminded of Nick, whose demons affected only his emotions, not his professional expertise. Personally, Mac did okay in the self-confidence department, he thought ruefully, it was the clothes that defeated him. Still, he held no grudge against Josh for being able to put on Wal-Mart jeans and an Armani jacket and make the outfit appear perfectly coordinated. In fact, apart from Josh's abysmal lack of appreciation for fine coffee, Mac really couldn't find much to complain about where Unit One's latest recruit was concerned.

"In essence, it's a custody battle." Mac cradled his hands around his cup. "The father in the case is Prince Abdullah Faisal of Saudi Arabia. And that's what poses the problem for Nick. He's been involved in a couple of oil deals with the prince in his role as Nikolai Anwar. Can't afford to put that connection to the Russian oil cartel at risk."

"I understand. Who's the mother in the case?"

"The mother is Elspeth Bryant, only daughter of Thomasson Bryant."

Josh whistled beneath his breath. "The attorney general of the United States?" he queried. "*That* Thomasson Bryant?"

"Yep. Although Bryant wasn't attorney general when his daughter married the prince—"

"Bryant was governor of Wyoming before he became attorney general, wasn't he?" Josh asked.

"For six years," Mac confirmed. "That's how the prince happened to meet Elspeth. Abdullah went to Yellowstone, bought up a couple of failing hotels, and the governor invited him to dinner. Governor's daughter was present at the dinner. Daughter's a good-looking woman, petite but luscious. Exactly the prince's type. No real surprise when the prince fell in love, which he does with great frequency. Usually there's a whirlwind courtship, filled with extravagant gifts. Then he gets tired of the woman. His pattern is to take the about-to-be-ex-mistress on a trip somewhere fancy—Paris, Hong Kong—and buy her jewels. Then he kisses her sadly and says *sayonara*. But this time he made the mistake of buying a ring instead of a necklace and offering marriage instead of saying goodbye. Elspeth made the even bigger mistake of taking the ring and saying yes. The wedding was ten years ago. Their kid is almost nine." Mac gave another hitch to his pants.

"Is their child a boy or a girl?" Josh asked.

"Boy," Mac said. "That's probably why there's a problem. Abdullah doesn't seem to give a damn about his daughters. Of which he has several by other wives."

"What's the little boy's name?"

Mac gave a bark of laughter. "Like everything else

in this relationship, that's in dispute. Depends who you talk to. He's called Tommy, short for Thomasson Edward, according to his mother. Farouk according to his father. Elspeth wanted him baptized. Abdullah refused to allow it, which was maybe when the problems in the marriage really began to spiral out of control. Elspeth filed for divorce when the kid was four. That was after an argument over whether the kid should go to a regular preschool, which was Elspeth's choice, or stay home with a tutor, which was the prince's choice."

Josh rocked back on his chair. "Where did she file for divorce? In the States, I assume?"

Mac nodded. "They were living in the D.C. area, but Elspeth was smart enough to file her divorce petition when she was on a trip home to Wyoming. She was staying with her dad at the governor's mansion and I guess they overcame the residency requirement by pleading special circumstances. Court papers state she filed there because the prince never let her out of his sight without an escort when she was in D.C. She claimed he beat her and threatened that if she ever dared to file for divorce, he would take Tommy away and never let her see him again."

"It sounds as if being Mrs. Prince Abdullah wasn't too much fun," Josh said.

"Sounds as if it was hell," Mac said bluntly. "The fact that her father was governor of Wyoming gave Elspeth just about the only protection she had. Governor Bryant insisted on having her come visit with Tommy, and Abdullah couldn't find a way to say no. Abdullah came, too, but he couldn't control her movements once she was in her father's house. Plus she had state troopers available at the touch of a button if the prince got too feisty. That finally altered the power equation in her favor. Enough for her to consult a lawyer and get the divorce papers filed. As expected, the prince demanded custody of their son, and offered to make a generous financial settlement if Elspeth would agree to him flying the boy back to Saudi Arabia. Elspeth wouldn't hear of it. She told the prince to take the money he'd offered and use it to buy jewels for the other women in his life. Told him he'd been unfaithful often enough that a diamond necklace for each of his mistresses would take care of all the several million dollars he was offering her."

Josh gave a crack of laughter. "I'll bet that went over well."

"Like a radioactive balloon. Prince Abdullah stormed off in a rage, and Elspeth added a clause to her divorce petition to deny Abdullah visitation rights, citing the extreme danger that the prince would take the child back to Saudi Arabia."

Josh pulled a face. "Given my sister's experience in trying to get sole custody of her kids during her divorce last year, I'm guessing that Elspeth didn't have much luck. Family court judges seem to assume kids need both parents, even if one of them is a certified asshole."

"Elspeth won half the battle," Mac said. "The judge awarded custody to her. Justified his decision on the grounds that the kid was born here, which makes him a U.S. citizen, and that he should live in the country of his citizenship. Unfortunately, he couldn't deny the father the right to see his child. The prince wasn't abusive toward Tommy. Far from it, he doted on his son. So there were no grounds to deny visitation. But the judge ordered that all visits with the dad should take place in the States, and Elspeth or one of her legal representatives was always entitled to be present. He wrote right into the final decree that Saudi Arabian customs concerning custody differed from the laws in the United States, and that the prince needed to be compelled to abide by the provisions of the divorce decree."

"Let me guess," Josh said. "The prince immediately brought in a retinue of attack lawyers and appealed to a higher court."

"Nope. The prince was smart enough to appear to agree with the judge's rulings. Promised he'd maintain his home in Maryland, and that Elspeth was welcome to stay in the house during Tommy's visits."

"Why was he so accommodating?" Then Josh answered his own question. "Oh, of course. Because he planned all along to kidnap his son and was trying to allay suspicions."

"Exactly. Part of the problem is that the prince doesn't consider that he's done anything wrong. How can a loving father be accused of kidnapping his own son?"

"Tough question."

"With no really good answers." Mac scowled. "Anyway, Abdullah took Tommy back to Riyadh almost before the ink was dry on the judge's ruling. The very first time Elspeth took the kid to the prince's home for a visit, Tommy was hustled onto one of the royal family's private jets and flown out of the country. The flight record suggests the kid traveled on one of his cousin's passports. Tommy has at least nine male cousins more or less his age, so it would have been easy enough to do. Elspeth hasn't been allowed to see her kid since."

"For five whole years?" Josh didn't attempt to hide his disgust.

"Yep. Five whole years. Like I said, the kid's nine now. Probably barely remembers his mother."

"What happened to the concept of no visits with his father unless they were supervised?" Josh demanded. "Where was Elspeth while her son was being bundled onto the prince's private jet?"

"Unconscious in a parking lot."

"How? Why?"

"The prince drugged her." Mac shook his head. "Elspeth did her best, but the truth is, her ex outfoxed her. According to Saudi law, he was divorced from Elspeth months before the decree was finalized here in the States. That was easy enough for Abdullah to arrange. All he needed to do was declare in front of witnesses that he divorced his wife, and that was the end of it as far as the Saudis were concerned. In fact, the wife is so irrelevant to the process that Elspeth didn't even hear about the divorce until weeks after it happened."

"And presumably she didn't fight it," Josh said. "After all, she wanted the same thing."

"Precisely. She didn't care if she was divorced under Saudi Arabian law as well as American. The more people who agreed the marriage was over, the better from her point of view. Later she heard not only that the prince had married again, but that his new wife—who was all of eighteen years old—was pregnant. Elspeth was even more relieved. By the time the final decree was handed down in the States, she calculated the new wife was only weeks away from giving birth."

"If the prince wanted to calm Elspeth's fears regarding Tommy, I guess having a new pregnant wife would work pretty well," Josh commented.

Mac grunted. "It was a real smart move on Abdullah's part. Elspeth hoped that the prince would write off reclaiming Tommy as more trouble than it was worth, especially since the kid was tainted by having an American mother. Abdullah had once expressed disapproval of the fact that Tommy looked so much like his mother. That gave her hope. On top of all that, the prince never paid his child support, and Elspeth didn't haul him back into court demanding payment. She hoped if she just let sleeping dogs lie, then the prince would forget about her.

"Does Tommy look like his mother?" Josh asked.

Mac pulled a picture out of the file. "Here, judge for yourself. That's what the kid looked like when he was four. The woman holding him is Elspeth."

Josh studied the studio portrait. "She's pretty. He's a stunner. Big brown eyes, brown wavy hair, oval face, wide forehead. I guess he got his father's coloring, but his bone structure is his mother's."

"I agree." Mac handed across another glossy sheet. "And here's the computer's guess of what Tommy might look like now."

"He's still a good-looking kid."

"Yeah, he is. Anyway, in the wake of their divorce,

the prince was doing a great imitation of a man in love with his new wife, and Elspeth had reached the point where she didn't really believe her ex would pull a kidnapping stunt, but she'd seen the Sally Field movie same as the rest of us—"

"That was about Iran during their revolution, not Saudi Arabia," Josh said. "Although I guess the status of women and the laws concerning child custody are the same throughout most of the Middle East. The father always gets to keep his kids, especially if it's a boy, and double especially if the mom's an infidel."

"You've nailed it," Mac said. "Elspeth was fully aware of the cultural differences and so she took precautions, on the outside chance that the prince might be planning to whisk the kid off to Arabia. On that first visit after the divorce, she personally escorted Tommy to the prince's house and took along a hired baby-sitter."

"Another woman?"

Mac shook his head. "A grad student, male, in his twenties, with plenty of muscle power. She figured there was safety in numbers, and the two of them planned to stay for the entire visit."

"What happened?"

Mac stared into his cup, more angry than he cared to show. "Seems Elspeth seriously underestimated how pissed off the prince was at being told by an American judge that he couldn't do just exactly what the hell he pleased with his own son. Worse—and this is what Elspeth didn't know—the prince's new wife had just given birth to a daughter the week before Tommy's visit. Abdullah already had four daughters from earlier marriages, and now he'd been presented with another daughter from this one. The prince didn't want daughters, who just cost him money to get married off. He wanted his son, and he didn't give a damn what American laws he broke to get the boy."

"The political climate changed, too," Josh pointed out. "A dozen years ago, the U.S. and Saudi Arabia were bosom buddies in the wake of the Gulf War. By the time Tommy was four, that relationship was beginning to sour. There was much more resentment of American cultural influence all over the Middle East."

"I've thought of that. Even allowed myself to consider how different this situation must look from the point of view of the prince's family." Mac tightened his belt a notch, frustration simmering. "This is one of those stories I'd love to watch on American TV, followed by the same story filmed by a crew for the Aljazeera network. You'd probably see a complete reversal of who's the hero and who's the villain in the two programs. There's a cultural divide operating in all this that we just can't seem to bridge."

Josh nodded. "As far as we're concerned, Abdullah is a cruel monster who abused his wife. As far as the prince's family is concerned, Elspeth is a wicked woman who's being totally unreasonable in denying her son his heritage. And they would say that if she didn't understand the cultural system she was marrying into, then that's her problem, not theirs."

Mac's mouth turned down. "Bet Elspeth wonders how she was ever naive enough to imagine that love conquers all." He realized he was heading toward the espresso machine and reluctantly abandoned the idea of another cup. He turned back to Josh.

"Anyway, back to Tommy's kidnapping. Elspeth reported that she and the baby-sitter were both drugged within moments of entering the prince's house. One minute she's in his living room drinking extremely sweet mint tea, the next time she's able to move, she's slumped behind the wheel of her car in the parking lot of the Potomac Mills Outlet Mall in Virginia, with the baby-sitter snoring in the back seat. Later Elspeth realizes her son must have been flown out of the country while she was drugged."

"And you say there hasn't been any contact between the two of them since then?" Josh asked. "Not even phone calls? Photos? Letters? For God's sake, the prince must let the kid sign his name on the occasional card to his mother."

"There've been no contacts of any sort." Mac heard the grimness in his voice. "In fact, Prince Abdullah denies ever taking the child. Insists Tommy's post-divorce visit proceeded according to plan and that Elspeth must have lost the kid somewhere between his house in Maryland and Potomac Mills Mall in Virginia. At one point, he even threatened to sue Elspeth for parental neglect—for losing his son."

Josh's mouth tightened with contempt. "That's downright cruel. It means Elspeth can't even be completely sure her son's alive."

"That might be the case, except for one small flaw in the execution of the prince's plan. Elspeth was supposed to be unconscious when the kid was taken, but she wasn't. The prince didn't know that Elspeth has an unusual reaction to sodium pentothal, which is what we believe he used to render her unconscious. She's one of a rare group of people who remain conscious even though they demonstrate the typical reaction of bodily paralysis. She couldn't move or speak, but she could hear and feel. Happens occasionally to patients having surgery and creates nightmares in hospital operating rooms. Imagine feeling every cut of the surgeon's knife but not being able to do a damn thing to tell the doctors you're awake. That would be Elspeth. Anyway, the net result is, she knew what was going on that day and is aware that Tommy was taken upstairs by the prince's mother and sister. She also knows she and the baby-sitter were driven to Potomac Mills by the prince's regular driver, although she appeared dead to the world during the entire journey."

Josh grimaced. "That makes me even sorrier for the poor woman. To know your child is being kidnapped and be absolutely powerless to prevent it. What a nightmare."

"Yep. Not a pretty scene. In the wake of the kidnapping, Elspeth suffered from severe depression, not surprisingly. Cheered herself up by deciding she was going to get her kid back or die in the attempt. Set about very methodically tracking the prince's movements. She knew when Prince Abdullah took the whole family to Paris three years ago, and also knew that he'd brought Tommy with him. Elspeth almost managed to grab the kid back, right near the Eiffel Tower, but she and her hired help were knocked unconscious by the prince's bodyguards and the Paris police wouldn't interfere. The prince and his retinue were all traveling on diplomatic passports, so they were basically immune from arrest, let alone prosecution."

Josh shook his head, visibly frustrated. "Elspeth's father is the attorney general of the United States—chief law enforcement officer of our country, in other words. Can't he send a strongly worded letter to the Saudi Arabian ambassador, demanding the return of his grandson?"

"Bryant has done that, of course. The ambassador denies all knowledge of the case. Says Prince Abdullah has never returned to Saudi Arabia in the past five years, and that his government has no idea where Tommy is, and so on. All lies, of course. The prince has been living openly in Riyadh. However, you're not allowed to tell an ambassador from a foreign country that he's a big fat liar even if you are the attorney general."

"I'd say *especially* if you're the attorney general," Josh commented dryly. "Is that where the prince is now? In Riyadh? Hell, Mac, this isn't a good time for a Unit One team to be infiltrating Saudi Arabia and attempting to snatch back a son born to a member of the ruling family. If the Saudi secret police don't take us out as soon as we get there, al-Qaeda is quite likely to choose that week to blow up the hotel where we're staying."

"Don't worry, you don't have to go to Riyadh. The prince and Tommy are currently in the United States. That's why I said this mission is time-sensitive."

"Thank God. Where are they?"

"Right this moment, in the official residence of the

Saudi Arabian ambassador. We've had visual confirmation of that."

"Son of a bitch." Josh's mouth thinned into an angry line. "Here's a novel idea—how about we break the diplomatic rules and tell the ambassador he's lying through his teeth? Followed by the suggestion that he can either turn over Tommy, or we plan to send in a company of marines to bring the kid out by force?"

Mac gave a laugh that sounded more like a snarl. "Satisfying as that might be, you know it's impossible. Hell, Josh, you were with the CIA for fourteen years. You know the rules about interfering with a foreign embassy. The ambassador's residence, legally speaking, is Saudi Arabian territory. Our laws don't apply. Theirs do. Hauling the kid out by force would be the equivalent of a declaration of war on Saudi Arabia."

Josh sighed. "Okay, so sending in the marines would be illegal. But damn, it would feel good."

"Only until all the governments in the Middle East started to retaliate and the Europeans started drawing up pissy resolutions at the United Nations. Not to mention the terrorists deciding to avenge the insult. Anyway, the attorney general has no intention of calling in the marines. He's called in Unit One instead."

"What does he want us to do?"

Mac's smile took on a tinge of genuine amusement. "His plan extended as far as dumping the problem into our laps. The rest of the planning is ours and he'd prefer to hear nothing about it. Naturally, if by any chance our plan fails, the attorney general will express his outrage and horror to the Saudi Arabians. And your team, if you're not dead already, will be toast. Deep-fried toast."

Josh's breath expelled in a sharp hiss. "Since the attorney general needs deniability, we have to get in and out of the embassy without being seen." He got to his feet and started pacing. "Do we at least have some decent intel about Tommy's routine? About which precise room he's sleeping in at the ambassador's residence? Why is he here, anyway? It seems an unnecessary risk for the prince to flaunt him right under our noses."

"Prince Abdullah appears to have a fatal attraction to American women. He's currently attempting to persuade Jacyntha Ramon to become Mrs. Prince Abdullah Faisal the Fourth. Or fifth, or twentieth, depending on how many wives and ex-wives the prince already has tucked away in Riyadh."

The name Jacyntha Ramon stopped Josh dead in his tracks, as Mac had expected. Jacyntha was the kind of movie star who tended to leave men openmouthed and panting, even when her name was tossed into the middle of a mission briefing.

Josh recovered his poise and shook his head. "Somebody needs to slip Ms. Ramon a warning that she should revise her plans. She may be all boobs and no brains, but she doesn't deserve to end up on the wrong side of a divorce battle with the prince." He paused for a moment, thinking out loud. "Or is she doing it for the publicity? Maybe right before the wedding, she's planning to dump him? In which case, more power to her. I hope she takes a huge bite out of the guy's ego."

"She's going to dump him quite soon," Mac confirmed. "But she isn't romancing him for the publicity. She's doing it to help out a friend. She and Elspeth met when Jacyntha was doing a photo shoot in Wyoming, before Jacyntha hit it big in the movies. They've stayed in touch ever since. In fact, it's thanks to Jacyntha that we have any chance at all of rescuing Tommy. You know as well as I do that a mission aimed at extracting Tommy from the ambassador's residence would have almost zero chance of success. But Jacyntha has done a fantastic job of convincing the prince that he wants to go skiing, and persuading him to bring his eldest son, Farouk—"

"You mean Tommy?"

"Of course, but Jacyntha isn't supposed to know that Farouk's mother is an American woman and that the kid used to be known as Tommy. The prince and Jacyntha are planning to celebrate the arrival of the new year in a penthouse suite atop the Ritz-Carlton in Beaver Creek. Jacyntha promises to keep him occupied with sex, skiing and more sex. That leaves you and the team you select free to rescue Tommy and get him out of Colorado before Prince Abdullah wakes up from his erotic dreams and realizes that his son has been taken."

"A hotel in Beaver Creek is easier to penetrate than storming the royal family compound in Riyadh, or the Saudi Arabian embassy in Washington." Josh ran his fingers through his hair, leaving it standing up in blond spikes. "But it's Tuesday already, and New Year's Eve is on Friday. That leaves us less than three days to get organized. How the hell am I going to pull a team together in that length of time, much less work out a rescue plan?"

"You're with Unit One now, Josh, not working to push the bureaucracy at Langley into making a major decision like changing paper clip suppliers. Three days is more time than we often have to put together a mission. Video-conference with Nick in D.C. He's with Elspeth as we speak, getting all the background information out of her that he can, about both the prince and Tommy. Bob Spinard already has detailed floor plans for the hotel, together with a schematic of all the security devices. We've booked you a suite on the same floor as the prince. I've assigned Melody Beecham as your second team member. Sam just took her off the injured list and Nick agreed to put her back on active status. Melody is good at thinking on her feet, and sexy enough to distract most men who come anywhere near her. I've already authorized Anthony to take the Gulfstream jet and fly you into Eagle County airport, which is less than forty miles west of Beaver Creek. That'll ensure you have transportation out as soon as you grab the kid—"

"Barring a blizzard," Josh said.

"The weather people aren't forecasting any major storms. Work on the details of a cover story with Melody, and decide whether you want to make yourselves known to the prince under some name or another—or whether you plan to go in and snatch the kid without ever letting the prince know you're around. The penthouse rooms are cleaned at least twice a day, which gives you plenty of opportunities to put on a service uniform and enter the suite to scope it out. Or you might want to ambush the kid on the slopes. It's your mission, and your call."

"Subject to Nick's approval, of course." There was more than a trace of irony in Josh's comment.

Mac pretended not to notice. "Nick is director of operations. Naturally his approval is required for any field op. Is that a problem?"

"No."

It probably was, Mac reflected wryly. Josh had first tried to transfer from the CIA to Unit One four years ago, within days of discovering the existence of the organization—and the crucial fact that Nikolai Anwar was director of operations. Nick had turned him down. Josh had reapplied at six-month intervals ever since. Four months ago, Nick had signed off on Josh's recruitment. Mac had asked Nick point-blank if working with Josh was going to pose any major problems. Nick's response had been a single word: No.

Despite the curt answer, Mac and Jasper had both anticipated friction between the two men—their personal history made that inevitable—but they'd decided it was worth riding out the potential storms as the two wrestled with their personal demons. If the murky world of black ops had stars, then Josh and Nick were leading contenders for the title of supreme superstar.

So far, Nick had assigned Josh to missions that barely scratched the surface of Josh's talents, and made scant use of his past experience and skills. This was the first mission in which Mac was going to have a real chance to judge if Josh lived up to his glowing reputation for operational brilliance. He was also curious to see if Nick could stand aside and watch Josh work with Melody without generating so much friction that the mission ignited.

All things considered, it was going to be an interesting few days.

Ten

The hotel bellman led Josh and Melody to a room facing straight out onto the mountain. Stowing their suitcases, he drew back the drapes to their fullest extent and gestured to indicate the spectacular vista of silvery aspen, blue spruce and dark green pine trees. The groomed ski slopes glistened, wedding-cake white, beneath a sun shining out of a sky so high and cloudless that Melody's eyes watered at the sheer brilliance of the light.

"It's a great view, isn't it?" The bellman spoke with proprietary pride, as if he had personally decorated the mountains for maximum viewing pleasure of the hotel's guests.

"It's breathtaking," Josh said. "The ski runs look in great shape, too."

"We had four inches of fresh powder yesterday. Perfect timing for the new year."

"My wife and I can't wait to get out on the slopes." Josh gestured toward Melody and she smiled her agreement.

The bellman glanced at his watch. "The last ride up on the lifts is three-fifteen, so I guess you won't make it today. But the runs open again tomorrow morning at eight, and you can ski right out from the lower level of the hotel." The bellman pointed to a brass-trimmed ice bucket. "Would you like me to get you some ice?"

Melody's cell phone rang. Knowing the call had to come from headquarters, she walked onto the snow-covered balcony to answer it, sliding the heavy glass door shut behind her. The air was so dry and thin it snatched the breath from her lungs, but the sun was bright enough to create at least the illusion of warmth. She burrowed into the collar of her coat and flipped open her phone.

"Yes." Her cell phone was new and prepaid, with no registered owner, so the chances of the call being intentionally monitored were close to zero. Nevertheless she didn't identify herself.

"Our friend and his son are no longer staying at the Ritz," Nick said.

Melody drew in a sharp breath, the only outward sign of frustration she allowed herself. "Do we have a location where our friends have moved to?"

"They're at a private ski lodge, owned by a fellow countryman of our good friend."

"Is the lodge in the Vail Valley?" she asked.

"Yes, about ten miles west of your current location. If you call me back, I'll explain more fully." Nick cut the connection, a precaution against the remote chance that their call was being audited.

Josh had paid off the bellhop by the time Melody returned to their room. She only realized just how cold she was when a blast of heat from the fake-log fireplace enveloped her in welcome warmth.

"Nick needs us to return his call," she said to Josh, stretching out her hands to the glowing logs. "Apparently the prince and Tommy aren't staying at this hotel after all."

"Damn! Where have they gone? Not back to Riyadh, I hope?"

"No, thank goodness. They're still in the Vail Valley, according to Nick—"

"With Jacyntha Ramon?"

"Presumably, although Nick didn't say. The prince has moved to a private ski lodge owned by one of his friends. We need to call back on your phone and get the precise location."

Josh unzipped a small pocket on the side of his carry-on bag and took out his phone. "As long as the lodge isn't fortified, that shouldn't pose any insurmountable problems." He dialed Nick's number, putting the phone on speaker mode so that Melody could hear what was said. Like Melody, he spoke without identifying himself. "I understand our friend and his son have moved to a new location."

"Correct." Nick's response was brusque.

"And his playmate? Where is she?"

"Still with him. Our intel regarding the move came from her. New information and schematics for the lodge have already been faxed to the plane. Anthony is en route, bringing the material to you. Obviously, you'll have to completely rethink the mission profile. Anthony will report your new operational plans back to me."

"Understood." Josh disconnected the call, exchanging rueful grimaces with Melody. "Well, now we hang around and wait for Anthony. I guess we shouldn't complain. There could be a lot worse places for us to be stuck than a fancy hotel room at a famous ski resort."

Melody flopped onto one of the beds and sighed. The plaid comforter instantly wrapped her in downy softness, but she was in no mood to appreciate the luxury of her surroundings.

She scowled. "I should have known our original mission profile would never hold up. It was too simple, not to mention way too much fun. I even fantasized about squeezing in a couple hours of skiing."

Josh rolled his eyes. "You should have known better. That sort of fantasy was tempting fate."

"Apparently." She punched the pillow and pushed it behind her back. "Want to bet the new plan will have us both clambering up onto the roof of the ski lodge, and then rappelling down a frayed rope into Tommy's bedroom? In the dark, of course, with a blizzard howling all around us to add an extra dollop of misery."

Josh laughed. "Not if I have anything to do with planning the mission. What the hell is the point of freezing your butt off on a roof, when you could cut the cable TV connection, or the electric power or the phone, and get yourself inside the house posing as a repair person? Half the hassle and twice the likelihood of success."

Melody gave him an approving glance. "You're my man, Josh. Nick, for some reason, always manages to invent reasons why there is no way to complete the mission without me dangling fifty feet above ground, desperately hanging on to some fragile outcropping with my frozen fingers."

Josh looked at her, then glanced away.

"What is it?" Melody asked. "What did I say?"

"Nothing. It's hot in here, don't you think?" Josh walked over to the fireplace and adjusted the level of the flames, taking longer than the simple task required. "The bellman was way too enthusiastic with the thermostat."

Melody crossed to his side, positioning herself so that he was forced to acknowledge her presence. "Don't change the subject, Josh. What did I say just now that bothered you?"

"Nothing at all. You misread my reaction."

She shook her head in frustration. "Stop it! You need to be honest with me or we have no chance of working together effectively. This is the first field mission I've been assigned with any partner other than Nick. The truth is, I'm already more on edge than I ought to be. You're probably no better off, despite all your experience with the CIA. You've only worked a couple of missions for Unit One, and you don't know me at all. We have to establish a basic level of trust or we'll be doing more than putting ourselves at risk—we'll endanger Tommy. So I'll ask one more time, what did I say just now that troubled you? And don't come back with another bullshit answer about how I misread you. I didn't."

"Okay, okay. But you're making too much of something trivial. It wasn't what you said, it was the way you spoke about Nick. Your whole face softened when you said his name." Josh stripped off his sweater and tossed it onto the bed, a convenient way to avoid meeting her gaze. "The rumors at headquarters are obviously correct. You're in love with him, aren't you?"

Melody's first instinct was to deny it. Then she realized that she could hardly demand honesty from Josh if she lied the first time he asked her a direct question.

"Why do you care how I feel toward Nick?" she asked.

"Because I'm attracted to you." Josh spoke coolly, but there was a faint tension to his body language that suggested the admission had not come easily.

Melody realized that her sexual and romantic feelings had been wrapped up in Nick for so long that her antennae, normally geared to picking up sexual interest from the opposite sex, had tuned out. Despite her boast about being able to read Josh's body language, apparently she'd glossed right over the indications that he was physically attracted to her.

"I'm flattered," she said. "You're an interesting man, Josh, not to mention good-looking and sexy—"

"But you're in love with Nick."

"I fell in love with Nick the second time I met him," Melody admitted, smiling faintly at the memory. "We confronted each other across the recently dead corpse of a man whose house I was attempting to burgle. I tried to run away. Nick caught up with me and tossed me to the ground, taking approximately ten seconds to disarm me—"

"And you knew he was the man for you?"

"Yep. Right away."

Josh gave a faint smile. "I'll have to remember the winning technique—chase, toss, conquer."

She returned his smile. "Based on my recent experience with you in the gym, I'd say you already have the toss-and-conquer part taken care of. Now you just need to find a woman worth chasing. Anyway, that encounter was over a year ago and for months, I kept waiting for the attraction to go away. It didn't, so now I'm resigned that I'm probably not going to get over Nick anytime soon."

"Is Nick in love with you, too?"

Melody hesitated for a moment. She and Nick had decided to wait a couple of weeks before broadcasting the news that they planned to get married. The idea of making a long-term commitment was extraordinary for both of them and they needed more time to get accustomed to the notion before facing up to all the practical problems that would be precipitated by an announcement. The fact that Nick was her boss as well as Josh's complicated things even more.

"You would have to ask Nick that question," she said finally.

Josh gave a short laugh. "Yeah, that's going to happen sometime real soon. Nick is more likely to stick red-hot needles under his fingernails than discuss his personal life with me."

"Why?"

"History." He walked over to the window and stared out at the mountain, where the winter sun was rapidly setting and the pines were casting sinister shadows on the snow. "Interesting how quickly the sun goes down here, isn't it?"

Melody brushed aside his remark with an impatient wave of her hand. "Why can't you talk to Nick?" she said. "What is it between the two of you? Anytime you're in the same room there's enough tension generated to fuel a shuttle launch."

"Ask Nick what's up between the two of us." Josh didn't turn around as he flung her own answer back at her.

"I did already. That was right after I'd checked with Sam and everyone else I could think of without success. There's a lot of gossip about you and Nick swirling around headquarters, but no facts."

"What did Nick say when you asked about me? I'm guessing it was a polite version of mind your own damn business."

"You're wrong. He said that the two of you had once been friends and that it was up to you whether you chose to explain why the friendship ended. That it wasn't his story to tell."

Josh swung around, clearly surprised. "I'm astonished he even acknowledged that we'd ever met, much less been friends."

"So where did you meet? When?"

"We were roommates in college our freshman year." Even that mundane admission seemed torn from Josh.

Melody's eyes widened. "That means you knew Nick before his family was assassinated. Did you ever meet his parents? His sister?"

"Yes, I did. They were great people. Gwynnyth was studying to be a dancer, already attending a special school, and she was probably the most graceful teenager

I'd ever met. She just about worshiped Nick, and since I was his best friend, she included me on the fringes of her hero worship." Josh attempted a casual shrug and failed. "You know how they say that time heals all wounds? Don't believe it. There's no way what happened between me and Nick will ever get any better. The years just fossilize it into a more agonizing scar. I thought joining Unit One might force a resolution of issues that Nick and I have allowed to fester for way too long. Over the past couple of months, I've come to the conclusion that resolution between us probably isn't possible. We'll just have to learn to live with the wounds."

He didn't sound happy at the prospect, Melody reflected. "Is what happened between the two of you connected in some way to the murder of his family?"

"Yes." He returned to his inspection of the setting sun.

"Tell me what happened, Josh. Nothing could be worse than what I'm imagining right now, so you've nothing to lose."

He was quiet for so long that Melody thought he would refuse to answer, but in the end he turned to her, his eyes clouded with painful memories. "Here's the short version. In the spring of my freshman year in college, I met this grad student who had supposedly just transferred in from Ohio State. Jenna Varrett was the name she went by. She was absolutely gorgeous and I couldn't believe my luck when she agreed to date me. Hell, I was barely nineteen and she claimed to be twenty-four, although I found out later that she was at least thirty. I convinced myself I was a real stud to be getting it on with a woman reportedly five years older than I was. And, man, was she ever fantastic in the sack! I walked around for an entire month in a daze of sexual gratification."

"That happens when you're eighteen."

"Yeah, especially when you're all dick and no brain." Josh's mouth turned down. "Cut to the chase. Turned out that Jenna, my luscious grad student, was really a Soviet agent, and the only reason she went out with me was that she'd tried to hook Nick and he'd been smart enough to turn her down flat. So she picked me as second best."

"Second best for what?" Melody asked, her stomach tightening with anticipatory dread.

"You know about Nick's parents, right? That his mother was a KGB agent, and his father was with the CIA. They met somewhere in Eastern Europe, fell in love, and his mother defected to the West in order to marry Nick's dad."

Melody nodded. "Yes, I knew. And also that the Soviet intelligence services finally uncovered the location of Nick's mother just a short while before the Berlin Wall was torn down. If the KGB had taken even a few more weeks to find his mother's whereabouts, then his family would probably be alive to this day."

"The timing made the tragedy of their deaths worse," Josh agreed. "There was so much relief that the Cold War was behind us, and the death of Nick's family was a jarring reminder that the KGB wasn't going to give up power easily. Although I'm not convinced that a few extra weeks would have saved the Anwars. Bottom line, in any intelligence service, you need to be able to rely on the loyalty of all your agents, and if you discover someone has betrayed you, you take them out. Once Soviet intelligence located Nick's mother, she was doomed."

"But the KGB didn't just take out a rogue agent. They deliberately set out to murder an entire family. The brutality of it is sickening."

"The Soviets were of the opinion that you accomplish nothing by showing mercy." Josh's voice was harsh, although Melody sensed that a lot of his anger was directed toward himself rather than the KGB. "Anyway, you asked me about Jenna and why she chose to date me. It was for information, of course. With Nick in college, there were a limited number of occasions when his entire family was together in one convenient spot for an assassination. The KGB had decided that Parents' Weekend was the perfect opportunity to detonate a car bomb and wipe out the Anwar family in one fell swoop. That meant they needed to find out exactly what Nick's plans were for getting together with his family."

Melody's breath caught. "Jenna was supposed to keep tabs on Nick by seducing him."

"That was the original plan." Josh's expression was grim. "Fortunately for the KGB, even when Nick turned her down, Jenna didn't have any problem finding out the most intimate details of the Anwar family schedule. Because Josh Straiker, conceited asshole with a brain half the size of his dick, was too dumb to notice that Jenna was a hell of a lot more interested in Nick's schedule than she was in anything else I might have to offer. Once Jenna had the Anwar family schedule down pat—courtesy of me—she attached plastique to the underbelly of the Anwars' car, set a timer and made sure she was far away when the car exploded right in the middle of the parking lot—"

"Except Nick wasn't with his family," Melody said, dry-mouthed.

"Yeah, Jenna didn't quite score a perfect ten. But she managed to blow up three people, injure half a dozen bystanders and still escape from campus before anyone wised up to who and what she was. I understand she's director of training these days in the new and supposedly more benign Russian foreign intelligence service that replaced the KGB."

"That must be hard for you to live with—knowing that the woman who betrayed you so badly has escaped punishment."

"I'm guessing it isn't exactly peachy keen with Nick, either." Josh's smile was bitter. "Anyway, now you know the sordid truth about why your good friend Nick can't stand to look at me. I'd like to say he's a jerk, but if I were Nick, I wouldn't speak to me, either."

Melody wished that Josh, who obviously suffered from the same overdeveloped sense of personal responsibility as Nick, had found some more productive way to cope with the bombing that wiped out three members of the Anwar family than blaming himself for the tragedy. Like Nick, it seemed to her that Josh had tried to make sense of the senseless by piling blame on himself and ignoring the major guilt that belonged to other people. Again like Nick, he'd probably spent far too much time over the past several years attempting to atone for an act of violence that was basically none of his making.

"Thank you for explaining what happened," she said quietly.

"Hey, you're welcome."

Melody responded to the underlying pain, as opposed to the superficial sarcasm. "Do you really need me to tell you that the death of Nick's family wasn't your fault? And that if Jenna hadn't latched on to you, she'd have found some other way to ferret out the details of the Anwar family's schedule? You were an eighteen-year-old kid, and you couldn't possibly have suspected that a sophisticated, highly trained KGB agent was setting you up."

"Nick was eighteen, too. He wasn't fooled by Jenna," Josh said tersely.

"Nick wasn't attracted to her," Melody responded. "He turned Jenna down because she wasn't his type and he didn't especially want to have sex with her. He didn't turn her down because he suspected she was a Soviet agent, for God's sake. Do you honestly think Nick would have stood by while you got involved with Jenna if he'd harbored the slightest suspicion of what she was up to? Obviously he had no more of a clue about her real motives than you did."

"Various psychologists and counselors have said the same thing. Somehow, the image of Josh Straiker, moronic dickhead, still clings. Reinforced by the fact that Nick didn't speak to me from the day of his family's fu-

neral until the day I joined Unit One and he was forced
to acknowledge my existence."

"Have you ever considered that Nick might not be
talking to you because you remind him of a tragedy he's
desperate to put behind him? Or that he carries more
than his share of survivor's guilt? Or how about the fact
that he has the same ridiculous sense of responsibility
as you do, and he blames himself for not being in the
car with the rest of his family?"

"Nick?" Josh stared at her, expression blank with
astonishment. "How can he possibly blame himself for
that?"

She gave him a pointed stare. "I wonder."

"I'm sure he grieves for his family, but he's moved
on from the tragedy." Josh spoke half to himself. "Nick
Anwar seems totally together to me."

"How about sharing a beer with him after work one
night, and talking about what happened the day his
family was murdered? You might be surprised to discover that Nick has plenty of baggage that haunts him
in connection with that terrible weekend." Melody
hoped she wasn't breaking Nick's confidence in sharing this much, but it struck her that he and Josh had both
spent seventeen years nursing their emotional wounds
in solitude and it was about time they got together and
pooled their burdens of excessive guilt.

"You want us to be friends again." Josh gave a laugh
that contained no trace of mirth. "You must be the
world's greatest optimist."

"No, I just think the two of you have a lot in common, and neither of you needs to be hauling around so

much old baggage about deaths you had no way to prevent."

Josh smiled at her, although his eyes were still shadowed. "You know something, Melody? For such an amazingly beautiful woman, you're very kind. How did that happen?"

"I guess there's nothing like a little parental neglect to instill sympathy for the underdog in a child," Melody said lightly.

Over the last year, she'd finally emerged from the shadow of Roz's obsessive selfishness, and she could look back on her childhood with almost none of her old pain. In retrospect, she'd had a pretty good time of it. Her grandparents had showered her with love, and she'd had all the benefits of spending vacations with her boisterous cousins on the High Ridgefield estate. The fact that Wallis Beecham had been a cold and indifferent stepfather and that Roz had been a less-than-perfect mother seemed trivial in comparison to all the happy memories that made up the rest of her childhood.

A knock at the door signaling Anthony's arrival put an end to any further exchange of confidences with Josh, but their conversation had cleared the air, and Melody felt more comfortable around him than she had earlier. Ironically, given how strongly Josh despised his own youthful behavior, she felt much more ready to trust him.

Anthony spread out the stack of faxes he'd received from headquarters on one of the beds. "Nick wanted me to alert you that he's suspicious of Prince Abdullah's change of plan. He wonders if the prince might be anticipating some attempt to snatch Tommy on the part of Elspeth's family. If so, the move to the ski lodge could be defensive, or an attempt to set a trap. In either case, Tommy is likely to be well guarded. Jacyntha couldn't talk for long when she called in to headquarters, but she apparently believes the prince had planned all along to stay in his friend's lodge, and that the hotel booking was simply to throw pursuers off the track."

"The prince is still registered at the hotel, isn't he?" Josh asked.

Anthony nodded. "He is, so if we didn't have Jacyntha as an inside contact, we'd have no clue that he'd transferred to the ski lodge."

Melody's previous encounter with Jacyntha Ramon had been dramatically unpleasant, and she was still working on adjusting her mental image of the woman. She bit her tongue, resisting the urge to make a snide remark. "Do we have a plan of the lodge's layout?"

Anthony riffled through the faxes and pulled out four sheets of paper. "These are copies of the architectural drawings on file with the county," he said. "Front elevation, interior layout and so on. The lodge is eight thousand square feet, so it's big, but not enormous. There's also an attached four-car garage."

He unrolled a set of pages that had been taped together. "This is another copy of the interior layout, enlarged. According to Jacyntha, Tommy sleeps in a corner room on the second floor. Here." He pointed to the drawing. "As you can see, there are doors from Tommy's room that lead out to a raised wooden deck. The house is built into a hill, so it has walkouts on two levels, and decks on all the main bedrooms, which are located on the third level. The deck outside Tommy's room is about eighteen feet above ground level."

"It's not a very safe location for Tommy if the prince is anticipating a kidnapping attempt," Josh commented. "Have the doors from the bedrooms to the decks been fortified?"

"There are alarms on every exterior door and window," Anthony said. "Remember this is a friend's villa, not one of the prince's own homes, so the security system is pretty standard, designed chiefly as a defense against burglars. For the protection of his son, Prince Abdullah relies on bodyguards who have been with his family for years."

"Do we have the security schematics?" Josh asked, rummaging through the faxes.

"Here." Anthony unfurled another set of faxes. "I wish these were transparencies, then we could just lay them over the architectural drawings of each floor. Bob Spinard did the best he could and superimposed an outline of the architectural footprint on each security printout. The system is a Marconi. Bob says the equipment is high quality for a private residence, but nothing spectacular."

"Perimeter motion detectors, key code access, strobe lights and blaring horns if a window or door is breached." Melody traced her finger over the various symbols on the plan and Bob Spinard's attached summation of what they were likely to encounter.

"What about guard dogs?" Josh asked.

"None. No dogs, not even a pet. The prince is a Muslim, remember, and he considers dogs unclean."

"One small blessing at least," Josh said.

"If we take out the electrical supply, do we deactivate the alarm system?" Melody didn't have much hope that Anthony's answer would be affirmative.

He shook his head regretfully. "You would deactivate the perimeter fence, but the alarms and interior security lighting are designed to switch over to battery power if the electrical supply is cut. In addition, there's a backup generator. Apparently electrical storms take out the power fairly often up here, and you need a backup generator to run the heating system. Otherwise you could freeze to death waiting for the power company to dig through the icy ground to find the faulty cable."

Josh scowled at the schematics. "So even if we cut the power, the interior security lighting will still be operational, and the generator is going to kick in within five minutes or so."

"Exactly."

"That's not enough time," Josh said. "We need at least ten minutes of total darkness."

"Where's the backup generator located?" Melody asked. "In the garage?"

Anthony shook his head. "In the basement utility room. So is the control panel for the security system."

"Which means we have to be inside to sabotage them." Josh tugged at his lower lip. "That's tough."

"Should we reconsider the possibility of grabbing Tommy while he's out skiing?" Melody asked.

"Too difficult," Josh said at once. "We know Tommy has at least two bodyguards with him all the time when he's outside. Inside the house, he has only his so-called tutor. Besides, how do we find out where they plan to ski tomorrow?"

"Jacyntha?" Anthony suggested.

"It's possible. But even if we managed to locate him on one of the slopes, how are we going to get him off the mountain and back to a car?" Josh asked. "We have no way of positioning a getaway vehicle except in one of the official parking lots. We could easily end up skiing across miles of mountain, dragging a struggling ten-year-old. If his bodyguards don't catch up with us, the Ski Patrol probably would. And we're no help to Tommy if we've been arrested."

"Then we have no choice but to disable the generator and sabotage the control panel for the security system," Melody said.

Josh nodded. "Once we're sure the generator isn't working, we cut the main electric power to the house and grab Tommy in the dark."

"Do we already know where the switch to cut off electrical current to the lodge is located?" Melody asked.

"Yes." Anthony pulled another sheet of paper. "Here it is. It's a junction box and you'll actually be cutting power to three houses, but hopefully the other two homes have generators."

Josh went back to studying the security schematics. "We'll have to use Jacyntha to gain access to the house," he said. "Otherwise I don't see how we can pull this off."

"Even with Jacyntha's help, it's going to be difficult." Anthony stroked his mustache, a sure sign of nervous tension. "What excuse are you going to use to gain access?"

"I'll pretend to be her agent," Josh said. "I'll claim that she needs to sign off on a hot movie deal. Once I'm inside the house, we'll make an excuse to go down to the basement—"

"You and Jacyntha?" Melody interjected. "The two of you alone?" She shook her head. "Jacyntha's supposed to have the hots for the prince, so that's not going to work."

"Why not?"

"Because you're too damn sexy and good-looking. Abdullah would never let the two of you go anywhere alone. Sorry, Josh, but it's much better to send me. The prince is less likely to hover if Jacyntha is tripping down to the basement with a woman."

Anthony cut across Josh's protests. "Melody's right."

"I disagree." Josh's mouth set in a stubborn line. "The prince has been dating starlets and models for years. Unless he's been walking through Hollywood asleep, he'll know that Jacyntha's agent is a man. All the power brokers in Hollywood are men."

"Then I'll pose as an assistant to Jacyntha's agent," Melody said.

"Jacyntha's A-list," Josh said. " Or at least A minus. She doesn't deal with assistants."

"All the better for us," Melody said. "Jacyntha can be pissy with me because the great man hasn't come himself. The more irritated she acts, the better. It makes my intrusion seem more credible, as opposed to something planned by her."

"Right," Anthony said decisively. "Melody should go. The prince is much less likely to suspect a woman."

Josh ceded the point without any more protests. Melody liked the way he'd fought for his point of view, and then surrendered as soon as logical reasons were provided for doing something different.

"Obviously before I go in, we need to find out the name of Jacyntha's agent and a couple of facts about him so that I don't make a complete fool of myself," she said.

"Are you sure you know how to disable the generator once you've gained access?" Josh asked.

Melody turned slowly and gave him a witheringly polite smile. "You're new to Unit One, Josh. So instead of cutting off your balls, I'll pretend I didn't hear that remark."

Anthony smothered a laugh. "Okay, folks, it's already four o'clock. It's going to take me fifty minutes to get back to the plane and run your plans by Nick. Then Nick has to be in touch with Jacyntha. Assuming he can reach her and get a meeting set up, can you be ready to leave here by six-thirty, Melody? That will get you to the ski lodge by seven-fifteen, which should be before Jacyntha and the prince sit down to dinner."

"How much time will you need to disable the generator?" Josh asked.

Melody was amused to note that he sounded wary asking the question.

"I'll need five minutes to disable the generator and another couple of minutes to take out the control panel for the security system. That's assuming Bob Spinard can tell me exactly how to disarm the system without setting off any alarms. I'll call him from here, while we're waiting, and get instructions. However, I can't walk into the lodge and immediately suggest taking a stroll through the basement. Jacyntha and I will have to get rid of the prince first." She thought for a moment. "All in all, I'd say you need to allow me a minimum of half an hour."

"Okay, so here's our schedule," Josh said. "Melody enters the lodge at seven-fifteen. By seven forty-five, she's made her way to the basement and deactivated the generator and security system control panel. I need confirmation that's happened before I cut the main power line. Our body mikes aren't going to have sufficient range for you to talk to me. Can you call me, Melody?"

"I don't see why not." She turned to Anthony. "Can you think of any reason why I shouldn't call?"

He shook his head. "Jacyntha has called from the lodge without problems. You should be okay."

"I'll wait to hear from you, then." Josh made some measurements on the map, using a scrap of paper. "It's a quarter of a mile from the switching box to the ski lodge, give or take a few yards. However, it's going to be dark and there's frozen, packed snow on the ground. I'll wear night-vision goggles, which means I can travel a bit faster. Estimate no more than three minutes for me to get to the house after your call. As soon as I'm outside the house, our body mikes should be operational."

"How are you going to get inside?" Melody asked.

"It will be pitch-dark and—we hope—there will be mass confusion as people run around trying to find flashlights and candles. I'll head straight for Tommy's room—"

"How are you going to do that?" Melody demanded. "Even in the dark, the prince's bodyguards will surely notice an intruder."

"There's a deck, remember?" Josh pointed to the plan of the lodge. "I'll throw a line and climb up—"

"Climb up?" Melody exclaimed. "Eighteen feet in the freezing cold?"

"As you've just pointed out, it's a lot safer than going through the house."

She rolled her eyes. "So you claim. Good grief, you're no better than Nick! So much for *I'm not freezing my butt off climbing on the roof when I can walk up and ring the front doorbell.*"

"Sorry. At least there isn't a raging blizzard." He gave her a grin. "Although I'm not sure why I'm apologizing. You're not doing the climbing, I am."

"Just wait," Melody said gloomily. "You haven't got to the bit yet where we escape from the lodge, with the two of us cradling Tommy as we climb back down the rope you left hanging from the balcony."

Josh had the audacity to laugh out loud. "Sounds like an excellent plan," he said. "In fact, now you mention it, I don't see any other way to do it. We'd run into too much opposition going through the house."

"I knew it." Melody's melancholy wasn't faked. "Jeez, what is it with you men and ropes?"

"Make your way up to the corridor outside Tommy's room as quickly as you can, but don't go in until I'm there," Josh said. "We don't know how many bodyguards there are in the house, and how many of them are assigned to take care of the kid in an emergency. But you'll be able to hear what's going on with the body mikes, so choose your moment to come in."

"I'll wait with the Land Rover at the utility switching box," Anthony said. "That way, if for any reason you can't access Melody's car, you'll have backup transportation. We'll drive straight to the airport, and Josh can have the plane cleared for takeoff before we get there."

"Sounds like a plan," Josh said.

"Wait!" Melody said. "What about Jacyntha? How's she going to explain that her agent's assistant has suddenly disappeared, taking the prince's son with her?"

"Shit." Josh looked at her, brow furrowed. "We can't leave Jacyntha behind. If the prince suspects her role, he might be mad enough to kill her first and worry about the consequences afterwards."

"In the dark, he could claim the bodyguards shot her by accident," Anthony said. "So he's not even facing much of a consequence."

"She'll most likely be wearing high heels and some sort of cocktail outfit," Melody said. "All part of her plan to keep the prince dazzled. She can't rappel down a rope and run through a quarter mile of frozen snow wearing that." She frowned, rapidly assessing and discarding ideas.

"Jacyntha's an actress," she said finally. "She's got a Golden Globe to prove it. We should use her talents. I'll tie her up in the basement, and she'll just have to pretend outrage at having been tricked by an impostor. She has the skill to pull it off."

"Works for me." Anthony stood up. "I'll leave you two to work out the fine points," he said. "I'm going back to the plane. I'll call you as soon as I have operational approval from Nick."

Eleven

Melody stopped her rented Cadillac Escalade at the rough-hewn wooden gates that marked the entrance to the ski lodge in Cordillera where Prince Abdullah Faisal and his son were staying. Two moose-head skulls, complete with antlers, perched atop the gate's support pillars, shone with appropriate ghostliness in the light of the rising moon. Despite the cow country decorative theme, the gate was backed by slick, no-nonsense steel bars that even a Hummer would have trouble crashing. She sincerely hoped the rest of the security wasn't equally formidable.

Icy air blasted her face and nipped at her ears as Melody leaned through the open window to depress the intercom button. Her leather gloves, chosen for suppleness rather than warmth, barely protected her fingertips from the freezing metal of the touch pad.

"Yes? Who is it?" The questioner, a man, spoke with a guttural accent that the crackle of the intercom didn't hide.

"I'm Eve Nightingale, executive assistant to Ms. Ramon's agent. I've just flown in from the West Coast. Ms. Ramon is expecting me."

"Yes, they tell us. Pleez to park in front of main door, away from entrance to garage."

The gate began to swing open before the man finished his parking instructions. Melody drove slowly down the steeply sloped driveway, on the lookout for black ice, and parked in the plowed courtyard area as instructed. Her soft leather briefcase, which was crammed with the tools of her trade, felt reassuringly heavy when she shouldered it. Wrapping her scarf over her nose and mouth, she quickly walked up the steps that led to the covered portico. Now that the sun had gone down, the temperature was falling rapidly into the low teens. The absence of humidity was supposed to make the cold more bearable, but right at this moment, Melody wouldn't have bet money on the proposition.

Gate security had been under the supervision of a man—presumably one of the bodyguards—but the door was opened by a woman who appeared to be in her early sixties. She wore a plain sweater, a woolen skirt reaching to her ankles, and a black, lace-trimmed headscarf.

"My name is Aliya," she said, with a slight bow. "I am the housekeeper here. Please enter."

The lodge was owned by Sheikh Ibrahim Al-Nassar, a wealthy Saudi businessman who was currently in his native country. Jacyntha had reported that there were a total of six employees living in the house at the moment, including two professional bodyguards. The sheikh's cook and housekeeper were of Middle Eastern descent, but they were long-time American residents and spoke excellent English. According to Jacyntha, the prince was traveling with only two personal servants: Tommy's tutor and the prince's own secretary. Both men were Saudi Arabian, and neither had ever spoken English in Jacyntha's hearing. The two additional bodyguards were also of Middle Eastern heritage and kept very much to themselves. Jacyntha hadn't been clear whether they were permanent employees of Sheikh Ibrahim, or temporary hires of Prince Abdullah Faisal, reporting directly to him. Whatever the case, Melody hoped that neither bodyguard felt fierce family or tribal loyalty toward his employer, or she and Josh could find themselves confronting two men who were prepared to die to keep Tommy safe.

"May I take your scarf and gloves?" the housekeeper asked.

"Thanks, but I'll just put them in here." Melody stuffed the scarf and gloves into the side pouch of her briefcase, not wanting to find herself braving the bitter cold outside with bare hands and nothing around her neck.

"What about your coat, miss? Shall I hang it up?"

"No, thanks." Melody softened her refusal with a smile. "I'll keep it on until I've warmed up a bit. It's incredible how cold it is out there in comparison to California. I'm still shivering." She unsnapped her ski jacket and brushed the snow off her boots on the large coir doormat. As she started to walk into the house, a horrified exclamation from the maid stopped her.

Melody turned around and saw Aliya gesticulating frantically toward her feet. "Your shoes, miss. Please to leave them here."

Melody quickly reversed tracks to the safety of the doormat, apologizing as she went. *Bloody hell.* How could she and Josh and Anthony all three have forgotten that in a Muslim home, outdoor shoes were invariably left at the door? She unlaced her four-hundred-dollar Mephisto boots, carefully selected to give maximum flexibility and speed, combined with protection from the snow, and stashed them neatly on the mat, hoping like hell that the maid wouldn't whisk them off to some even-less-accessible spot the moment Melody's back was turned.

The housekeeper opened a narrow cupboard to the right of the front door and removed a pair of backless cloth slippers from a collection of at least two dozen assorted sizes. "For you, miss, if you would prefer not to walk in your socks."

"Thank you." Melody put on the slippers, which were too big, and shuffled awkwardly in Aliya's wake. As soon as the lights were out, she would have to make her way back up to the front door and retrieve her boots. Fortunately, she had night-vision equipment in her briefcase, but putting on and lacing up boots was an extra task she would much prefer to do without.

She had the layout of the lodge memorized, and followed the housekeeper into a room that she recalled was designated as the gathering room in the architectural drawings. The walls were finished in brick, the floor was oak plank, and the ceiling was supported by huge, rough-hewn logs the size of small tree trunks. Lights and fixtures were hammered iron, interspersed with the occasional gleam of polished stainless steel. This much fake simplicity must have cost the owner a fortune, Melody thought, hiding a grin.

A tall, slender man sat in a low-backed leather armchair drawn up close to the fire, which was burning real wood, a banned luxury in most of Vail Valley. His hair was dark, his eyes smoldering and his features perfectly proportioned, giving him the appearance of a middle-aged Rudolph Valentino. He wore tailored slacks and a cashmere knit shirt that shrieked European designer. Only his embroidered black silk slippers hinted at his Arabian heritage. If this was the prince, Melody thought, no wonder Elspeth Bryant had fallen for him. He was incredibly handsome, with the magnetism that came from a lifetime of wealth, privilege and all the power that money could buy.

Jacyntha Ramon was curled up on a huge scarlet cushion set next to the prince's feet, her hand resting possessively on his knee. She was every bit as petite, vivacious and gorgeous as Melody remembered: the sex kitten personified. If anything, the aura of sexuality that glowed almost visibly around her was even stronger than it had been on their last ill-fated meeting.

Melody's stomach knotted with an emotion she was embarrassed to recognize as jealousy. Six months ago she'd walked in on Jacyntha and Nick when they were supposedly in the throes of making love. The scene had been staged, but the image of Jacyntha slathered against Nick's body was engraved indelibly on Melody's psyche and leaped out from time to time to take a snarling bite out of her self-confidence.

Tonight Jacyntha wore black satin harem pants, and a diaphanous top with long sleeves and a high neck. Gold sequins were sewn strategically to conceal her nipples. Or perhaps sewn strategically to remind the prince of the nipples that couldn't be seen. The effect of the blatant transparency combined with the modestly high neck and long sleeves was erotic in the extreme. Her perfectly shaped feet were bare, and her toenails glittered with gold polish shot through with iridescent spangles. If Jacyntha had gone out of her way to make Melody feel like an undersexed, overdressed beanpole, she couldn't possibly have been more successful.

Melody strode with a great deal more confidence than she felt toward the pair. Hollywood agents, even junior assistants to Hollywood agents, weren't known for their shyness. She flashed a smile that bordered on the brash. "Excuse me for intruding, Jacyntha. And you must be Prince Abdullah Faisal. How are you, sir?"

The prince gave a bored nod. Jacyntha didn't even demonstrate that much interest. Melody hoped like hell that at least Jacyntha was acting.

"I'm Eve Nightingale, Sol Fairstein's executive assistant," she said. "Sol's just closed the deal for the Paramount project you've been so enthusiastic about, Jacyntha, and I've brought the preliminary contract for you to sign."

Melody held out her hand. Her cheery smile slipped without any need for acting as Jacyntha uncoiled herself and slowly rose to her full height of five foot three. Jacyntha not only ignored Melody's outstretched hand, she somehow managed to create the illusion of looking down her nose at her. Quite an achievement, since Melody was a good five inches taller.

"Yes, I'm Ms. Ramon." Jacyntha wasn't subtle about correcting Melody's use of her first name. "What did you say your name is?"

"Eve. Eve Nightingale."

Jacyntha's body language was so hostile that Melody had to remind herself that the actress was on their side, and that she herself had been the one to suggest that Jacyntha should pretend to be cold and unwelcoming.

Jacyntha gave an irritable shrug. "I don't understand why Sol needs these papers signed tonight. And I certainly don't understand why he's sent you. Where's Rosemary if Sol is too busy to come himself? In fact, how can he be too busy to handle my affairs in person, since I was responsible for more than half his income last year? How, exactly, does he think he's earning his fifteen percent by sending you? I've never even met you, for Christ's sake."

Rosemary was Sol Fairstein's executive assistant. "Rosemary is sick," Melody lied, having no trouble at all sounding placating. Jacyntha's act was convincing enough to provoke an automatic appeasing response. "And Sol's daughter just had a baby boy. He and his wife flew out to Chicago as soon as he'd closed the deal on your behalf."

Jacyntha came as close to scowling as was possible without actively wrinkling her forehead. "Presumably the new baby's going to be around for the next eighty years or so, whereas this deal is only on the table if I agree to sign it. It's not like Sol to delegate. I hope he hasn't fucked—" She pulled herself up, presumably because she didn't want the prince to hear her swear. "I trust Sol remembered all the points I told him to negotiate."

Melody shot a nervous glance toward the prince. His silence was clearly meant to be intimidating, so she provided him with the reaction he wanted, although in reality she found his attitude faintly amusing. Having grown up as the granddaughter of a British earl, she'd been snubbed plenty of times by people who'd been practicing the art of putting upstarts in their place for twenty generations. Abdullah would be mortified to hear he wasn't in the same league.

"There are a few items that Sol has asked me to bring to your attention, Ms. Ramon." Melody cleared her throat. "Perhaps there's some place…er, private where we could discuss the clauses in question?"

"You may conduct your business here." Prince Abdullah Faisal finally spoke, although he didn't go as far as actually looking at Melody.

Jacyntha turned to the prince and gave him a smile so laden with sexual promise that Melody felt her cheeks flush with heat.

Then, in the blink of an eye, Jacyntha's features hardened into an expression barely removed from contempt as she turned back to look at Melody. "You can discuss anything in front of the prince. I have no secrets from him."

Great. The request to speak in private was supposed to be Jacyntha's cue to suggest a trip to the basement level, deserted at this time of night since nobody was playing billiards or watching movies in the media room. Melody reminded herself that the woman was known as one of Hollywood's smartest actors, and that her failure to pick up on the cue was neither willfulness nor stupidity. Jacyntha was merely behaving in the way best calculated to conceal her complicity in Tommy's upcoming disappearance.

So what was she supposed to say now? Melody wondered. She needed something that would persuade the seemingly hostile Jacyntha to change her mind about continuing the discussion in private.

Inspiration struck. "Ms. Ramon…" Melody let her gaze flick once again toward the prince, who had relapsed into hostile silence, although she had a feeling that he was casting plenty of slimy glances her way— and mentally stripping her with each one.

"Ms. Ramon…there are clauses even in this preliminary contract that refer to the love scenes in the movie," Melody said.

"Which love scenes?" Jacyntha demanded.

"The…um, the lesbian love scenes. With the nun and the psychiatrist."

"Oh, those scenes." For a split second, Melody thought she detected a flash of laughter in Jacyntha's eyes.

"Yes. There are nudity requirements that the director feels strongly about. He feels it reflects on the integrity of his vision and he won't accept a body double—"

"We'll see about that," Jacyntha snapped.

"Ms. Ramon, I'm sorry, but an insistence on your part concerning the use of a body double might be a deal breaker. The director was adamant—"

"I can see why Sol chickened out and sent you." Jacyntha paced angrily. "He's scared of what I might say to him, and he damn well should be. He *knows* I won't do the love scenes. I *demand* a body double—"

"If we could, um, just discuss this in private? I think you'll be pleased with the protections that Sol has had built into the contract. And the money's great."

Jacyntha's eyes narrowed, gleaming with avarice. "How much?"

Melody hadn't a clue how much Jacyntha might hope to command for a movie. A million bucks? Ten million? "What you asked for, Ms. Ramon. Sol has negotiated your top figure."

Jacyntha tossed her mane of luscious dark-auburn hair. "All right. I guess I'll have to find ten minutes to speak with you." She leaned down and murmured something in the prince's ear. Whatever she said made him laugh. He reached out to cup her breast, utterly indifferent to Melody's presence. The prince ignoring the peasant, Melody thought, more amused than offended. His behavior was rude enough to be ridiculous.

Jacyntha gave a little sigh of pleasure as the prince kneaded her breast. Then she kissed his forehead, her left hand stroking his jaw. Melody would have sworn that Jacyntha was relishing every moment of the exchange, if not for the fact that she had positioned her right hand behind her back where the prince couldn't see it, and was sticking her middle finger straight up.

"Darling, I'll be right back," Jacyntha told the prince, kissing the finger she'd just stuck in the air and resting it with a flourish against his mouth.

"Stay here." The prince finally spoke again. "Why do you need to speak with this woman? Refuse to sign the contract. I don't want you to appear in a movie with such a disgusting theme. It sounds very Western and decadent." He scowled at Melody. "Tell her that you're not signing. Tell her to leave."

"Darling, you can be sure that when I sign, it will be on my terms. This part is made for me once I've tweaked the contract terms a little. I just don't want you to be forced to listen while I explain to this dimwit of a girl exactly why I pay my agent. Trust me, it sure as hell isn't to hear that the director is expecting me to cavort on a bed with another woman playing the part of a nun."

Jacyntha stalked from the room and Melody hurried after her, slippers flapping.

"Where are you going?" the prince called out.

"The media room, darling." Jacyntha turned and gave him a little wave. "Doesn't that seem like just the perfect place to discuss a movie contract?"

"Don't be long." The prince bared his teeth in a smile that scarcely managed to conceal the fact that he was giving an order.

"No more than fifteen minutes, but I have to take care of business. There are several million dollars at stake here."

Prince Abdullah grunted. Presumably several million dollars didn't strike him as especially important given the size of his own fortune. With a final blown kiss, Jacyntha walked into the hallway and turned toward the stairs without bothering to check that Melody was following.

They proceeded down the basement stairs in silence. When they reached the lower level, Jacyntha spoke quite loudly. "Here. The media room is to your left. Take a seat. I don't have all night, you know."

Jacyntha didn't turn into the media room, however. "Nude love scenes with a nun *and* a psychiatrist?" she murmured, eyebrow raised.

"I was improvising," Melody said.

Jacyntha bit back a laugh. Finger pressed to her lips to indicate that they needed to be quiet, she switched on an overhead light and quickly walked through the main basement area, throwing open doors to a bathroom and a storage closet packed with ski equipment. Satisfied that there were no unexpected bodyguards, or servants working on a late-night chore, she finally opened the door to a cement-floored utility room.

"Electrical panels," Jacyntha said softly, pointing to three gray metal boxes on the wall. She checked off the various pieces of equipment. "Water heaters, furnace for the central heating system, cable box for the media room, and there's the generator." She swung around, indicating a cupboard with Perspex doors set into the wall. "That's the security system control panel. It's armed twenty-four/seven. I've had no luck finding out the codes, although I tried."

"That's not a problem. I'm used to deactivating security systems." Melody was already unwinding a length of thin cord from around her waist. "First things first. I'm going to tie you up, so that if anyone comes down unexpectedly, you don't have to invent explanations as to what you're doing. I'll have to tape your mouth shut, too, to explain why you couldn't scream, but the tape is perforated, so it shouldn't be as unpleasant as it sounds. Remember, if we're caught, just tell everyone that as soon as we got downstairs, I attacked you and tied you up."

"Not a chance, babe." Jacyntha still spoke softly, but there was absolute determination in her voice. "When you leave tonight, I'm coming with you."

"Sorry, but you can't—"

"There is no way on God's earth that I'm spending ten seconds with that pig once Tommy's been rescued, let alone another three days. He makes my flesh crawl. His manners in the bedroom suck the big one. And that's a very polite way to describe it."

There was no time to be tactful, and even less time to marvel at the powerful illusion of sexual attraction Jacyntha had created upstairs. The Golden Globe she'd won was clearly no fluke.

"I sympathize," Melody said. "I truly sympathize. But you can't come with us. It's at least twenty-five degrees below freezing out there and you're the next best thing to naked. Besides, the escape route is via a rope from Tommy's balcony. Without gloves, in this weather, you would rip the flesh from your hands."

Jacyntha pulled a face. "Trust me, skinned hands would be preferable to spending another night with

Prince Creepy Crawly. However, you don't have to worry about clothes. I'm prepared."

"How?" Melody glanced at her watch. Four minutes since they left the prince. They didn't have time for this discussion.

Jacyntha disappeared into the storage closet that held ski equipment and came out twenty seconds later zipping up a pair of waterproof snowpants, with a pair of Gore-Tex ankle boots and a down parka tucked under her arm.

"I stashed these yesterday. They should provide sufficient protection to get me off the balcony and into the getaway car. Agreed?"

Melody gave a reluctant nod. "Agreed." In truth, she was surprised at the efficiency and forethought of Jacyntha's planning.

Jacyntha laid the parka and boots on a packing case near the door. "Okay, let's get ready to rescue Tommy. I'll take out the generator, if you'll loan me a screwdriver. I was raised on a farm in Iowa, so I know what I'm doing. I managed to sneak a look at the generator yesterday. Abdullah fell asleep watching a movie and I slipped in here. It's a single-phase, gasoline-powered unit, with electronic controls. I can permanently disable the control panel by opening it up and ripping out the low-voltage wires. Then I'll knock out the igniter to be doubly sure. The igniter's made of plastic. It would be easy enough to break it by accident, let alone on purpose."

Jacyntha did sound as if she knew what she was talking about. It would be a big help if she could disable the generator, since it would shave three or four minutes from their time. Melody wasn't reassured by the tale of growing up on an Iowa farm, though. She remembered reading an article in which Jacyntha claimed to have been raised in Acapulco by a rich uncle and aunt. In any event, since the generator wasn't alarmed, Melody decided there was no risk to letting her loose on it.

Unzipping her briefcase and laying it on the ground, Melody indicated the small stock of tools, packed along with a flashlight and night-vision equipment. "One of these screwdrivers should be the right size for taking off the control panel."

Jacyntha got busy on the generator and Melody double-checked that the utility room door was firmly shut. She wished the door boasted a lock, but at least she would hear anybody coming downstairs, and that would give her a few seconds of warning if the prince came searching. It was already almost six minutes since she and Jacyntha had left him sulking in the gathering room, and their window of opportunity was closing fast.

Attention focused, Melody examined the control panel for the security system, pushing worries about Jacyntha and what the prince might be doing to the back of her mind. She had written out the exact sequence in which Bob Spinard had instructed her to disarm the system functions. It wasn't an especially difficult task. In a practice situation, she'd have had everything disconnected in less than a minute. However, the stakes were high tonight. The doors and windows all had electronic locks in addition to the regular ones, and if she couldn't deactivate the system, Josh would be seriously delayed getting off the balcony and into Tommy's bedroom, losing him the element of surprise. Even worse, if she screwed up and set off an alarm, the whole mission would have to be aborted. Brow furrowed, she took her time, checking the sheet of schematics each time before she moved on to the next step.

She allowed herself a soft whoop of satisfaction when the activation lights on the alarm system turned first to red, and then died without any accompanying screech. She glanced at her watch: eight minutes and thirty seconds elapsed time. How long was the prince likely to sit upstairs, twiddling his thumbs, while his playmate supposedly discussed lesbian love scenes?

"Need any help with the generator?" she asked Jacyntha.

"No, I just finished. It's disabled." Jacyntha slotted the screwdrivers back into their pouch, then shoved her feet into the Gore-Tex boots and began to lace them. "What happens now?"

"I call Josh, my partner, and tell him to go ahead and cut the power to the house. Then we'll make our way upstairs to Tommy's room. We'll have to move fast if we want to avoid people coming down to check why the generator hasn't kicked in."

"It's going to be very dark," Jacyntha said.

"Yes." Melody wondered why Jacyntha bothered to state the obvious. "Here, you'd better take the flashlight, but stay close to me." She froze in the act of zipping up her jacket.

"What is it?" Jacyntha asked.

"Someone's coming downstairs." Melody kept her voice low, but made an urgent slashing motion with her hand. "Hide!"

Jacyntha, thank goodness, didn't waste time asking questions. She quickly squeezed in between the generator and the wall, disappearing from view. Taking her Glock from its holster, Melody slipped behind the door.

It was a single set of footsteps coming downstairs, she decided. That, at least, was a minor blessing.

"Jacyntha? Where are you? What's going on?" Prince Abdullah's voice floated through the door, barely muffled by the plywood panels. He must have glanced into the media room and found it empty. Unfortunately, he knew they hadn't gone upstairs, and it wouldn't take him many seconds to figure out that if they weren't in the media room, there were a limited number of other options.

"Jacyntha? Are you all right?" The prince sounded more annoyed then worried.

Melody heard the prince open one door, and then another. Presumably he now knew they weren't in the bathroom, or the ski closet. She fixed her attention on the utility room door. She needed to knock the prince out the moment he stepped through. She couldn't afford to have him shout for help.

The door handle rattled. "Jacyntha? Are you in here? What on earth is going on?" Prince Faisal strode into the utility room, banging the door toward the wall.

Melody caught the door on its backward swing and stepped out in the prince's wake. Before he had a clue that anyone was behind him, she brought the butt of her gun down on the back of his head in a swift, hard, chopping motion. He tumbled onto his hands and knees, and then crumpled facedown on the cement. She poked him with her toe to make sure he wasn't faking. He didn't stir.

She holstered her Glock, letting out a tight breath. Fortunately, she had the rope, originally intended to tie up Jacyntha. She pulled the prince's arms behind his back, preparing to bind his wrists, and as she did so, a palm-size electronic gadget fell from his hand.

Jacyntha emerged from behind the generator. "That's the prince's portable intercom. He uses it to summon his assistant. His secretary, Omar." Her voice cracked with tension.

Had Abdullah summoned help already? Melody tied the final knot on the prince's makeshift handcuffs and sliced off a length of cord to tie his feet, as well. But there was no time to complete the job. She heard the sound of more footsteps pounding down the stairs. Apparently, the prince had indeed summoned Omar.

No time to hide the prince's body. She pushed the door shut once again and flipped off the lights just as the footsteps reached the bottom of the stairs.

Jacyntha was still standing by the prince's unconscious body, transfixed. Melody grabbed Jacyntha's arm, pulling her behind the door and shoving her behind her own body for protection. Jacyntha jumped when the assistant called out in Arabic, and Melody put her hand on the actress's arm, reassuring her and simultaneously warning her not to make any sound.

Doors were opened and banged shut. Melody visualized the assistant checking out the media room, the bathroom, the ski closet. All too soon, there was nowhere left for him to look except the utility room. Melody braced for him to walk in and discover Abdullah.

The utility room door was pushed open and light from the ceiling fixtures in the family room instantly streamed in. The prince's motionless body, spread-eagled on the bare cement, was spotlighted with distressing clarity. Exclaiming over and over again in Arabic, Omar rushed to his employer's side.

He was carrying a revolver, a businesslike Walther P-99 revolver, standard issue for James Bond movies and many European police forces. Melody brought her Glock down on the back of the assistant's skull before he could remember what he was holding and decide to use it. He staggered, but didn't fall. He swung around, but fortunately his arms were flailing. She kicked the revolver from his hand, following up with a hard, double-fisted blow to his chin. The Glock ripped open a gash that spurted blood, but the man still wasn't quite out, and she had to hit him on the temple before he finally swayed and tumbled to the ground.

Jacyntha edged out from behind the door. "Do you recognize him?" Melody asked, once again holstering her weapon. "Is it the prince's assistant?"

Jacyntha nodded. "Yes, it's Omar."

Melody pulled a face. "I was hoping against hope he might be a bodyguard. That would have been a gift, since he couldn't fight worth a damn."

"He looked pretty convincing to me." Jacyntha's

voice was noticeably shaky. "And anything he lacked in fighting skills, his gun more than made up for."

Melody shook her head. "Not really. He still had the safety on."

"Didn't you?"

Jacyntha looked nervous enough that Melody decided not to mention that her Glock didn't come equipped with a safety. "Tie Omar's hands behind his back, could you?" she asked, changing the subject. She tossed Jacyntha the length of cord she'd originally cut to tie up Abdullah's legs. "Make the knots really tight. And pat him down to make sure he doesn't have another weapon."

As she spoke, the prince started to stir. Melody quickly found one of her plastic vials of chloroform, tore open the twist-off cap, and emptied the contents onto a washcloth she'd filched from the hotel specifically for the purpose. She pressed the cloth over the prince's nose and mouth, held it there for about thirty seconds and watched his body relax into limpness.

"Jesus!" Jacyntha winced. "I know the guy's a total pain in the ass, but is he going to be okay?"

"Yes, it's only chloroform. And before you waste too much sympathy, remember this is the man who's been tormenting Elspeth for the past five years. He didn't just kidnap her son, he actually tried to set it up so that Elspeth wouldn't know for sure whether Tommy was alive or dead. Half an hour facedown on cement, followed by a really bad headache, doesn't seem too much punishment to me."

"He's going to lose his son, too. That's the real punishment."

Melody drained the dregs from the vial onto the washcloth and held it over Omar's nose and mouth. "Abdullah has nobody to blame except himself. He could have seen Tommy regularly if he'd been willing to play by the rules."

"I know," Jacyntha acknowledged. "But the only redeeming feature the asshole has is the fact that he really loves his son."

"Elspeth loves her son, too." Melody realized that eighteen months with Unit One had changed her view of the world. Before her mother died and she learned that Wallis Beecham wasn't her father, she'd seen the world in myriad shades of subtle gray. These days, courtesy of Unit One, her world was painted in much starker black and white. She wondered if that was progress, or a giant step in the wrong direction.

She made sure that nothing blocked Abdullah's and Omar's air passages, and that they were breathing steadily. Then she retrieved her night-vision goggles from her briefcase and slung them over her wrist before pulling out her phone and punching in the speed-dial code to reach Josh.

He answered with welcome promptness. "You're late calling. Everything okay?"

"We ran into a couple of minor problems," Melody said. "But they're stretched out on the utility room floor. The security system is now disabled, and the generator is no longer functional. The sooner you cut the power to the house, the better."

"Should be less than a minute to blackout. Who did you take out?"

"The prince and his secretary."

"That leaves two bodyguards and Tommy's tutor still to go. See you at the lodge in about four minutes."

Melody closed the phone and turned to Jacyntha. "Okay, as soon as the lights go out, we'll make our way upstairs to the main level. We're planning a total removal of power to the area, so it's going to be much darker than you're accustomed to. Stay close to me."

"Are you kidding? Honey, they'll have to pry my cold, dead fingers from your arm if they want to separate us."

Melody smiled. "You're doing really well, Jacyntha."

She shook her head. "Nice of you to say so, but I know when I'm out of my depth. This is much too strong a dose of reality for my taste. I do better when I'm on a set and I know the guns are only shooting blanks."

"If I do my job right, nobody's going to fire any bullets tonight." Melody zipped up her briefcase and slung it over her shoulder, holding out the night-vision goggles to show Jacyntha. "These only work if there's a certain minimum amount of ambient light, but there should be—"

Jacyntha gave a little yelp as the lights suddenly went out, plunging the utility room into utter blackness. Melody switched on the flashlight and Jacyntha gave an audible sigh of relief.

"Sorry," she said. "The truth is, I'm not wild about the darkness. My stepmother probably locked me in the broom closet one too many times when I was a kid."

There was no time to pursue the unexpected confidence or even to question whether it was true. "Hang on to me. You'll be fine," Melody said softly.

She felt Jacyntha's hand reach out and clutch her arm and she gave a quick, reassuring pat. "Okay, let's get out of here before somebody comes down to inquire why the generator isn't working."

They glided up the basement stairs, keeping close to the wall, where they would be almost invisible in the surrounding blackness. The sounds of confusion got louder as they approached the main level, and Melody knew she would have to find safe passage through that confusion. What the hell was she going to do with Jacyntha? A woman who was scared of the dark would be a major drag given the mission profile she and Josh had developed, which depended on darkness. In fact, their attempt to rescue Tommy would be compromised if she tried to keep Jacyntha with her. Melody gave a tiny sigh of relief when she remembered that she'd arrived at the lodge in a rental car—a safe haven for Jacyntha.

"Here are the keys to my SUV," she said when she and Jacyntha reached the main level, which appeared temporarily deserted. "Take them."

"I can't leave you alone with these jerk-offs—"

"Sure you can. It's my job to be alone with jerk-offs. In fact, I get off on thwarting jerk-offs."

Jacyntha's teeth flashed white in the surrounding darkness. "Time to consider a career change, babe."

Melody answered her smile. "I'll consider your advice. Anyway, my car's a rented Cadillac Escalade and it's parked right outside the front door. Don't turn on the headlights—we need darkness outside, too. But you can turn on the engine to stay warm. That down jacket you're wearing is going to feel mighty thin once the night air hits."

They had reached the front door, and Jacyntha was still protesting. Melody reclaimed her boots, relieved that they hadn't been moved. She let Jacyntha rattle on while she finished lacing them. Then she put her hand across Jacyntha's mouth.

"I know you're scared, but it's time to shut up and listen. There's a remote chance that Josh and I might need a backup getaway vehicle. That means you shouldn't drive off unless you think you're in danger. On the other hand, don't try to play the heroine. If you feel threatened in any way, get the hell out of here as fast as you can. Now, I'm going to take my hand away. Please don't waste time vowing to stay with me through thick and thin, okay? I want you in the car. Please go."

Jacyntha nodded. As soon as Melody lifted her hand, she let out a harsh breath. "Shit! I hate this darkness. I can't think straight."

"You don't have to think. Just sit in the car and be ready to drive off as soon as you see Josh and me coming over the balcony with Tommy. In fact, you're doing me a favor if you hide out in the car. It's easier for me if I don't have to worry about your safety."

"Good luck, then. Rescue Tommy before he turns into Prince Creepy Crawly Junior. The women of the world will be in your debt."

Melody opened the door, almost pushing Jacyntha out. Immediately, she heard the sound of light, cautious footsteps slowly making their way across the hallway. Definitely feminine, which meant it had to be Aliya or the cook.

Jacyntha progressed a couple of yards across the portico, then swung back, staring at Melody in the moonlight. "You're an interesting woman, Melody Beecham. Not to mention quite disgustingly beautiful. Despite my best intentions, I can't help liking you."

Melody smiled. "Funny. I came to precisely the same conclusion about you."

Twelve

"Where is the prince?" the housekeeper demanded. "And why is Miss Ramon leaving? That *was* Miss Ramon, wasn't it?"

Melody debated how she was going to disable the housekeeper. Knocking the poor woman unconscious would be dangerously brutal. She snatched off her night-vision goggles, trying to think. It was one thing to bash the prince and his secretary over the head, but she drew the line at battering little old ladies.

She swung around to face the housekeeper, using her foot to close the front door behind her. With the door shut, there was only enough moonlight filtering through the skylight to discern the general outline of the housekeeper's body, and her face was no more than a shadowy oval with two dark spots for eyes. Good. Aliya would be having just as much difficulty seeing what Melody was up to.

Chloroform shouldn't do any lasting damage, Melody decided, even to a woman of Aliya's age. She slipped her hand into the small pocket on the side of her briefcase. Her fingers encountered the slim, cylindrical shape of another vial of chloroform and the folded washcloth, tucked inside its plastic carrying bag.

"I haven't seen the prince," she said, responding to the least difficult of Aliya's questions. "I was downstairs with Ms. Ramon. Isn't the prince in his bedroom?"

"I don't know. I thought he was waiting for the actress down here." The way Aliya said "the actress" suggested that Jacyntha came somewhere slightly lower than rat droppings on the housekeeper's scale of approval. "Anyway, why has she gone outside?"

Truth came to Melody's rescue. "Ms. Ramon is frightened of the dark. She was feeling very claustrophobic. She's gone to sit in my car."

Melody had managed to snap the twist-top off the vial of chloroform and tip the contents onto the washcloth. She needed to act fast, or the potency would dissipate.

Aliya nodded. "Perhaps it would be safest if you joined her, miss."

"You're right. It would be a lot safer." Melody grabbed the woman and pressed the chloroform-soaked cloth over her mouth and nose. "Sorry, Aliya," she murmured. "I'm really sorry."

The housekeeper had time for no more than one astonished moan of protest before her body slumped. Melody caught her as she began to fall and laid her down neatly on the floor, making sure that her skirt was pulled down over her legs and that her veil still covered her head and shoulders. Could you show respect to somebody you'd just chloroformed against her will? she wondered.

Three down and four to go. The cook was another older lady, so presumably didn't pose too much threat, but Tommy's tutor and the two professional bodyguards remained potentially formidable obstacles. A man's voice called out in Arabic, and another masculine voice responded, immediately followed by the sound of running feet, still all on the second level where the bedrooms were located. It was frustrating not to be able to understand what they were saying. It was also strange that nobody had thought to check the generator. On the other hand, if the bodyguards had been hired by Prince Faisal, not the sheikh, it was possible that neither of them knew of the existence of an emergency generator, much less where it was located.

Melody put her night-vision equipment back on and ducked into a narrow corridor that led off the main foyer, heading toward the kitchen. She'd heard too much activity in the vicinity of the main staircase for her to risk using it to access Tommy's bedroom. She knew from the architectural drawings that a second staircase at the rear of the house led from the kitchen up to the second floor. The staircase serviced a small separate wing of the house that Jacyntha had said was used exclusively by the domestic help. A door connected the servants' wing to the main section of the house on the second level, so it provided perfect access to Tommy's bedroom. She would still have to brave the stretch of corridor where the bodyguards seemed to be running so energetically, but right now using the back stairs seemed to present fewer dangers than the front of the house.

She found the kitchen with no difficulty. Sadly, it was occupied by another veiled lady, at least a decade older than Aliya. The old woman was clucking mournfully as she carried a huge covered Pyrex dish from the counter and took it toward the back door, pausing to slip her feet into heavy ankle boots before taking the dish outside and burying it in a nearby snowbank.

Taking advantage of the cook's momentary absence, Melody hurriedly bent down and tugged off her own boots, pushing them under the counter where she hoped they wouldn't be noticed.

When the old woman returned to the kitchen, she introduced herself at once to avoid any danger of the woman screaming for help. "Hi, I'm Eve Nightingale. I work for Jacyntha Ramon. I just flew in from the Coast and I hadn't even been here an hour when the power went out."

"It happens all the time, but usually when there's a storm. I am Daria, and I have been cook to Sheikh Ibrahim for thirty years." Barely pausing to draw breath she added, "I believe working for the actress must be a hard job."

Melody stifled a laugh. Jacyntha had obviously been playing her role of spoiled movie star to the hilt. "Ms. Ramon is very talented," she said, avoiding the question. "Did you just take a dish of food outside? Aren't you afraid of attracting bears, or at least coyotes?" Melody was determined to do nothing to arouse the cook's suspicions. She was really anxious to avoid chloroforming yet another innocent bystander.

"Yes, you're right." The cook sighed. "But I finished simmering my special casserole of beef with cinnamon only an hour ago, and the dish is still warm. If I don't cool it, the beef will be rancid by morning. I can think of no other way to keep it fresh. I dare not take ice from the freezer, or that food will be ruined, too."

"How about piling snow in the sink?" Melody suggested. "You could pack the snow around the dish and that should keep it cool. I can scoop up some snow for you, if you like."

"That's a very good idea." The cook looked at her approvingly. "Here, you can take this pail, if you would be so kind. It's clean. And those boots by the door should be big enough to fit you."

The boots fit, and Melody used a plastic flour scoop to shovel snow into the pail. Two loads were more than enough to fill the sink and—hopefully—to save the casserole.

"I am most grateful for your help," the old lady said. "Could I offer you a drink of juice? Or perhaps a fruit ice?"

"Thank you, but I'm on an errand. I was on my way upstairs and got lost in the dark. Ms. Ramon needs something from her bedroom right away. May I take these stairs here?"

"Of course." Thankfully, the cook didn't question how Melody had managed to miss the giant staircase in the middle of the main vestibule. "Here, I have a spare flashlight. Do you need it?"

"Thanks, it would be a big help." Melody took the flashlight, partly because it would have been ungrateful to refuse, and partly because it made one less source of available light for Tommy's protectors. She slid behind the counter and picked up her boots. "Are you coming upstairs, too, now that you've rescued the casserole?"

Thank God, Daria shook her head. "I have to think what I can prepare for breakfast tomorrow if the power doesn't come on. The prince can't face the day without his hot tea, so that is a problem right away."

Melody gave an encouraging smile. "Let's hope the power is back on very soon."

"Ins'allah." The cook bowed her head respectfully. "Watch the bend in the stairs. It's a bad angle, especially without light to guide your steps."

The servants' corridor was empty. No real surprise, since Omar was snoozing in the utility room, Aliya was dozing by the front door and Daria was inventing a breakfast menu in the kitchen. The tutor and the bodyguards must all be with Tommy, which meant she and Josh would be fighting two against three, with a child to keep out of danger. Still, with Josh on her side, that didn't seem like insurmountable odds.

Melody stopped to lace up her boots for the second time. Just as she pushed open the door dividing servants from employers, she finally heard one of the bodyguards call out in English.

"I agree," he said, dashing toward the main staircase. "I will check the basement."

A second man replied—but in Arabic, which didn't help Melody. She flattened herself against the wall, allowing the connecting door to the servants' corridor to close very slowly. Adrenaline set her heart pumping when she realized that if she'd been twenty seconds earlier, she'd have stepped through the door just as the bodyguards came out of Tommy's bedroom. And what story she'd have invented to explain herself, she couldn't begin to imagine.

She was trying to decide if she was in the very best place to remain hidden and yet close to Tommy's room, when Josh's voice spoke in her ear. "Melody?"

"Yes." Her response was barely more than a murmur, although the door to Tommy's room was closed and the bodyguard and the tutor were both inside.

"I'm at the corner of the house, about twenty feet from the support struts for the deck outside Tommy's room. What's the situation inside the lodge?"

"The prince, his secretary and the housekeeper are all unconscious. The cook, who must be at least seventy, is in the kitchen. One bodyguard has just gone into Tommy's bedroom. The other one has finally gone downstairs, presumably to check on the generator. So far, everyone seems to be treating this blackout as nothing more suspicious than an annoying power failure."

"Good. Where's Jacyntha?"

"Jacyntha is sitting in my rental car, outside the front door."

"What the hell is she doing there? She was supposed to be your prisoner and left tied up in the basement."

"Jacyntha didn't like that plan. She's coming with us."

"What the hell?"

"She refuses—quote—to spend ten seconds in Prince Abdullah's company once Tommy is rescued."

"She'd better not have screwed things up," Josh muttered. "Have you confirmed that Tommy is in his room?"

"No. But he's not on either of the other two levels, so it seems certain that he's in his bedroom, guarded by his tutor and a bodyguard."

"The odds are never going to be any better than that. Okay, I've moving in. I'm leaving my mike open, so you can hear exactly what's going on."

"Good luck."

Josh didn't respond. He traveled so quietly on the snow that Melody couldn't hear his footsteps despite the powerful amplifying capacity of their body mikes. She paralleled his silent movement, gliding along the upstairs hallway. After half a minute, she heard a faint rattle when the hook of Josh's climbing rope hit the deck railing. She held her breath, waiting for a reaction from the people inside Tommy's room, but there was no break in the low murmur of their voices.

With his rope in place, Josh must have made quick work of the eighteen-foot climb. She didn't hear the thud of his landing on the balcony, but she heard the ear-shattering crash as he smashed the glass of the slider and hurtled into the bedroom.

Thank God his entry wasn't followed by the sounds of gunfire, only the heavy thud of men fighting. Josh must have disarmed the bodyguard before he could squeeze off a shot. The fight seemed to be raging hard, which meant the bodyguard had to be really good at hand-to-hand combat, given Josh's stellar level of expertise.

Melody dropped her briefcase in the hallway and shucked her jacket for greater flexibility. At least she could tackle the tutor and prevent him coming to the bodyguard's aid. She was on the point of entering the bedroom, when a man and a young boy suddenly ran out of the room.

Melody acted almost before the thought had crystallized at a conscious level and long before the agitated tutor became aware of a potential attacker waiting in the pitch-dark corridor. She kicked the tutor's arm with all the force she could muster. He gasped in pain, reflexively loosening his grip on Tommy and lunging toward her in automatic self-defense. She grabbed his thrust-out arm and twisted it behind his back in a half nelson that had to be excruciatingly painful.

To his credit, the tutor's concern was for his charge. He groaned out a command in Arabic and Tommy started to run. Melody finished off the tutor by the effective but inelegant method of banging his head against the wall, then took off down the corridor in pursuit of the boy.

He'd fled in the direction he happened to be facing when the tutor ordered him to run, which was toward the servants' staircase. Melody sprinted, determined not to let him reach the kitchen and the cook. If the old woman saw Tommy struggling, she would attempt a rescue. There was no way Daria could prevail, and Melody wanted to avoid useless violence if she could.

"The bodyguard's disarmed and disabled but I've lost the kid and his tutor!" Josh's voice spoke in her ear, worry breaking through his attempt to sound coolly professional.

"The tutor's neutralized and I have a visual on Tommy," Melody reassured him. "I'm in pursuit."

She caught up with the terrified child ten feet past the service entrance. "I'm a friend of your mother's," she said, hauling him close. She knelt down so that the two of them were eye-to-eye. She tried to sound nonthreatening, but her actions belied her words. He started to fight and she was forced to lock his arms against his body. He was squirming so desperately that she was afraid he'd do himself an injury.

"I won't hurt you, Tommy." She kept her voice low. "Everything's going to be all right. Nobody has been seriously injured. Your father is safe. I'm going to take you to your mother."

Even if Tommy understood what she was saying, there was no reason for him to believe her. He spat out some furiously angry Arabic. She was reluctant to hold him with too much force and he managed to break loose just long enough to scratch her face.

She caught his hands, wishing there had been a better way to rescue him. "I'm sorry, Tommy. I know this must be really frightening, but everything will be all right soon, I promise."

"Bring him back to the bedroom," Josh said, stepping out into the corridor. "It's safe. The bodyguard's neutralized."

Melody swung Tommy into her arms and carried him back toward Josh and the bedroom. The poor kid was shaking, she wasn't sure whether from cold, anger, fear, or a combination of all three.

Josh preceded them into the bedroom and shook out

a shiny silver thermal wrap. He zipped it around Tommy like a long, tightly fitting cloak, pulling the attached hood over the boy's head.

"Okay, I'm taking Tommy back to the Jeep," he said. He wasted no more time, but stepped out onto the balcony and prepared to slide down the rope.

Melody hoped the balustrades, made brittle by the cold, would support their combined weight.

"I'll follow." Melody buried her chin in her scarf and avoided looking over the balcony. No need to confirm how many looming, empty feet she had to traverse before hitting solid ground. No need to listen to the ominous creek of the metal balustrades. Much as she would have preferred to use the stairs and exit via the front door, there was still one bodyguard unaccounted for, not to mention the possibility that Prince Faisal and Omar might have regained consciousness. The balcony was the only logical way to safety.

Josh was already sliding down the rope, Tommy suspended from a harness on his back. He landed with a soft thud and almost immediately started running.

"I'll pick up Jacyntha and the rental car, and meet you at the rendezvous point," Melody said.

"See you in about five minutes?" Josh's voice was fainter as he moved out of range of the body mikes, running astonishingly fast given that he was carrying Tommy across snow whose surface had melted during the sunny day, leaving behind a lethal glaze of ice.

"Five minutes or less. Call in to the pilot and tell him I'm dreaming about hot chocolate waiting for us on the plane." Melody climbed over the balcony ledge and grasped the rope. Wind soughed and she heard the mournful howl of a hungry coyote. "Hey, you're no more miserable than I am," she muttered.

She climbed down with grim determination, her heart pounding and her legs shaking. She kept hoping that constant exposure to heights would help her to overcome her phobia. So far, no such luck.

When she reached the ground, she wasn't sure whether to give a whoop of joy or recite a prayer of thankfulness, so she did both, although Nick's training had been effective enough that she ran as she thanked.

By the time she reached the front of the house, euphoria was beginning to set in despite the difficulty of running across ice, with no light beyond the moon to illumine her path. Melody tamped down on the euphoria. There were still obstacles to overcome before she could fully relax. She needed to reach the rendezvous point as quickly as possible, so that Josh wasn't delayed, and then they needed to ensure that Tommy made it safely to the plane.

Still, she was grinning as she sprinted the final twenty yards from the corner of the house to the place where she'd parked her Escalade what felt like several hours earlier. In reality, only fifty minutes had passed since she first drove through the moose-head entrance gates.

The Escalade was dark and Jacyntha didn't react by switching on the headlamps even though Melody ventured a quick wave. Jacyntha might not have spotted her, or else she was obeying instructions to the letter, Melody decided. Even as the thought formed, a premonition of disaster followed. Heart pounding with fear as well as exertion, she ripped open the driver-side door of the SUV.

Jacyntha was slumped over the steering wheel, not moving. In fact, she didn't appear to be breathing. Stomach churning, Melody leaned into the car and gently lifted Jacyntha's head off the steering wheel. Nausea welled in her throat when she saw the beaten and brutalized condition of Jacyntha's once-beautiful face. Holy God. Who had done this to her?

She almost cried with relief when Jacyntha gave a faint moan. "It's Melody," she said softly. "I'm going to take you to a doctor right now. You're going to be all right."

Jacyntha didn't reply.

Melody climbed onto the running board, working grimly to slide Jacyntha out of the driver's seat without causing her further injury. Bad as the battering to her face was, she feared the damage to Jacyntha's body might be worse. Jacyntha was ice cold, possibly suffering from hypothermia. As she leaned deeper into the car, Melody realized not only that the car engine was not running, but that the keys weren't in the ignition.

The bastard who'd done this to Jacyntha had probably thrown them in the snow. But at least in this one small thing, Melody had the last laugh. She had a duplicate set of keys zipped into her pants pocket, a standard precaution when vehicles were used during a mission.

A narrow but powerful beam of light shone out from the front door. Melody didn't waste time looking around to check the source. Light coming from the house was a threat. There was no more time for careful levering of Jacyntha into the passenger seat, and no time to strap her into a seat belt, even though she badly needed one in her unconscious state. Melody rolled Jacyntha out of the way, shutting her ears when the poor woman moaned without regaining consciousness, and gritting her teeth when she had to shove Jacyntha's legs past the center console without paying any heed to gentleness or comfort.

The noise of gunfire added the final spice of urgency. It was only one gun, though, and it was fired by a lousy shot. Probably the prince. Any hired bodyguard would surely have a better aim.

Keeping her head low, Melody shoved the key into the ignition. A couple of bullets ricocheted off the hood, but the windshield wasn't shattered and she didn't lose a tire. She turned the key and the engine coughed only once before roaring to life. She shifted into low gear and roared up the driveway.

She was afraid to check if Jacyntha was still breathing.

Thirteen

"You must be waitin' for somebody real special," the woman said to Nick. They were both penned by security barriers into the same area of LaGuardia, near the exit from Baggage Claim, so there was no escaping her chatter. The woman had already informed him that she was waiting for her son to arrive back in New York after a six-month assignment to a military base in Wyoming.

"You just about wore out that strip of carpet, you been pacing so long." She gave a cheerful laugh to let Nick know that she was only trying to be friendly. "And I reckoned *I* was anxious to see *my* boy!"

"I'm waiting for my fiancée." Nick tested the word— the first time he'd used it in public to describe his relationship with Melody. He decided it sounded pretty damn fine, so he used it again. "My fiancée went away on a business trip that was supposed to last two days, but ended up lasting more than a week."

"You'll be glad to see her, then. Me, I'm just glad my boy wasn't sent to Iraq. Oh, look, there he is! I swear he's two inches taller and ten pounds skinnier since I last laid eyes on him."

The woman dashed off as fast as her plump legs would carry her. She hugged a young man in khakis who looked as if he hadn't been shaving for more than a couple of years, let alone training to defend the nation from enemy attack.

Melody came out of the baggage claim area five minutes later. She appeared tired, but her eyes lit up when she saw Nick, and her face softened into a smile that damn near melted his insides. She went into his arms, her body automatically in perfect alignment with his. The ache of loneliness that had been his constant companion since the moment she left for Beaver Creek instantly vanished.

"What a wonderful surprise!" Her smile widened. "What are you doing here?"

"I missed you." He tossed the words out with a casualness that belied their truth. "I decided I couldn't wait the extra two hours for you to get home." Nick kissed her, and felt his body heat with the unique combination of desire and well-being that having Melody around inspired.

They drew apart, breathless. "I'm glad you came," Melody said. "It's good to see a friendly face."

He heard the almost imperceptible catch in her voice, and knew that he'd been correct to assume she found the outcome of their latest mission hard to deal with. He put his arm around her waist, offering silent comfort.

She laid her head against his chest while he dialed the limo service and gave his reservation number to the dispatcher. Unfortunately, the man's command of the English language seemed to have been lost somewhere between Ulan Bator and Kabul, making for a very difficult conversation.

"Colorado is spectacularly beautiful, but it's wonderful to be home," she said when he hung up, having finally managed to convince the dispatcher that he and Melody were ready to be picked up.

Nick took her suitcase and headed toward the airport exit. "Rough few days?" he asked, although he already knew the answer. Jacyntha's life had hung in the balance for several hours after Melody drove her to Vail Valley hospital, and she'd undergone two surgeries since then, although both relatively minor. Melody was undoubtedly blaming herself for failing to offer Jacyntha better protection.

"More than rough." Melody's expression darkened. "Nick, you can't imagine what that son-of-a-bitch prince did to Jax's face. Not to mention what he did to the rest of her. Faisal was so out of control, it's lucky he didn't decide to shoot her. I spent a lot of time in the hospital wondering why he didn't just kill her, then wait in the car and kill me, too. I can only assume it was because he had trouble finding a gun, given that it was almost pitch-black inside the ski lodge."

Nick's opinion was that Abdullah hadn't been out of control at all, at least not in the sense of being incapable of calculating risk. The prince had been infuriated by Jacyntha's betrayal, and he'd punished her by beating her up and pummeling her face so that she would be unable to return to work for weeks, perhaps months. He'd drawn the line at killing her, not out of moderation but because of potential consequences to himself. Nick suspected that even the prince's hopelessly inaccurate potshots as Melody drove off had been another deliberate expression of rage, rather than an abortive attempt to kill.

"You're giving Faisal credit for way too much honest emotion," Nick said. "He's a man who calculates his every move. The whole history of his dealings with Tommy proves that. But at least the news about Jacyntha's medical condition has finally turned positive. I saw the latest hospital bulletin before I came to pick you up. The doctors are planning to release her tomorrow morning."

"That's why I felt able to leave," Melody said, following Nick through the automatic doors. "Plus Jax's assistant, Cathy, arrived from L.A. yesterday and she seems super-efficient, which is a good thing, since Jacyntha is going to need plastic surgery to reconstruct her nose. Did you already hear about that?"

"No. *Damn.*" Nick shook his head. "At least a nose job isn't life-threatening."

"But it isn't a trivial problem, since Jacyntha's face tends to get plastered all over the planet in giant Technicolor close-ups." Melody's eyes flashed with angry fire. "Meanwhile, Mac tells me Prince Abdullah skipped the country on one of the royal family's private jets before anyone could question him. Presumably, he's relaxing back in Saudi Arabia, surrounded by an assortment of meek and adoring local wives."

"Worse than that. We had a report that he was enjoying the nightlife in Hong Kong with an Italian TV starlet in tow," Nick said.

Melody shook her head in wonderment. "How does he attract all these women, for heaven's sake?"

"Money. Power. Good looks," Nick said dryly. "He doesn't come with a warning notice tattooed on his forehead, you know."

"I was naive enough to assume he'd have the decency to hole up in Riyadh and keep a low profile for a while. Still, at least he doesn't have Tommy anymore." Melody spoke with grim satisfaction. "Elspeth has her son back, and that's worth a lot."

"It sure is." Nick smiled. "Josh reported that Elspeth was incoherent with happiness when they handed Tommy over to her. I expect he told you, too?"

She nodded. "I wish I could have been there to see the reunion."

Melody sounded regretful and Nick gave her arm a quick squeeze. "Jacyntha needed you in Vail."

"You're right, and I was glad to be there. I like her a lot." Melody smiled ruefully. "And I never thought I'd live long enough to feel that way about her, much less admit it to you, of all people."

Nick was smart enough not to revisit the outsized can of worms that was his supposed relationship with Jacyntha, and he turned with relief to point out to Melody that their limo was pulling up to the curb at last.

It was 6:00 p.m. by the time they got into the car, and

the traffic heading into Manhattan was bumper to bumper, with the added complication of an accident right at the exit from the airport onto the highway.

"I have some news for you from Bob Spinard," Nick said, watching their driver inch past the sideswiped Honda blocking their lane. "It's about Alejandro Garcia." His preferred choice of activity right now would have been making love to Melody, but since this was a hired car and there was no screen between the driver and passengers, he had regretfully decided that hot sex wasn't an option. As an alternative, he might as well get some unpleasant business out of the way.

Melody turned quickly. "Has Bob found a link between Alejandro and Zachary Wharton?"

Nick shook his head. "Bob has run their names through every database he can think of, and there are no intersections."

Melody's face showed only mild frustration. "I'm not sure I expected anything else. Did you?"

Nick shrugged. "Expected? No. Hoped? Yes."

"Despite the absence of a paper trail, I still think it's quite likely that Zachary Wharton is the person who paid Alejandro to have me killed."

"I agree it's a possibility. We'll continue to check it out." Nick paused. "Bob did turn up one unexpected link to Alejandro, however, and it wasn't to Zachary Wharton."

"Who was it to?"

Nick grimaced. "You won't be as surprised as the rest of us were. The link was to Wallis Beecham."

"I knew it," Melody said softly. Her hands clenched

around her briefcase. "Okay, I admit to being paranoid about the man, but this is one more example of the fact that sometimes paranoid people really do have enemies. Okay, how are they linked?"

"Pretty directly," Nick conceded. "Do you remember that your stepfather owned a road-paving company? Well, it turns out that Alejandro was on the payroll of Beecham Paving for almost eight months. What's more, he was employed there during the time that Christopher Beecham was running the company on behalf of his father."

"I knew it!" Melody repeated, and gave a satisfied sigh, then shot him a taunting glance. "Because I'm a mature adult, I'll resist saying I told you so."

"Thank you, because I really dislike a smart-ass." Nick was relieved that Melody's attitude reflected pleasure in being proved right, rather than despair at the idea that her stepfather and stepbrother might still be trying to murder her. "So far, there's only a paper link between Alejandro and Christopher. There's no evidence they actually met during the time they both worked for Beecham Paving."

"It isn't a big company," Melody said. "Just a small subsidiary of Wallis's empire, in fact. It would have been hard for them to avoid each other."

"If they'd both worked in management, maybe. But Alejandro wasn't working in the office. He headed up a road repair crew and had no real reason to come into contact with Christopher."

"With the two of them working in the same small company, at the same time, on the same project, it's no stretch to believe they met," Melody retorted. "Especially since Christopher has always liked cocaine and Alejandro's criminal records suggest that he's been dealing coke since he was in high school. Now there's a connection that isn't likely to make it onto any databases." She leaned forward, visibly energized by the new lead. "Where's Christopher right now, do we know? Can we spring a surprise visit and question him?"

"He's in Freeport—"

"In the Bahamas?"

Nick nodded. "Bob and I are working on a scheme to get him back to New York, so that we can question him without having to make a trip to Freeport."

"Because, gee whiz, flying to the Bahamas would be such a rotten idea at this time of year. I mean, who wants to loll around on sunny beaches, when we have Manhattan's glorious concrete canyons and icy winds for our leisure-time enjoyment?"

Nick grinned, pleased to see more evidence that she could joke about the situation. When you got right down to it, there wasn't much amusing in the fact that Wallis Beecham still hated his stepdaughter enough that he might be plotting to have her killed, more than a year after the events that had landed him in federal prison.

They made it back to the apartment by seven-thirty, having taken a mere hour and a half to cover a journey from LaGuardia that could sometimes be completed in twenty-five minutes. Nick relished the contented sigh Melody gave as they walked into the apartment, a sigh that told him more clearly than words that she was happy to be back.

She smiled at the bouquet of yellow roses he'd bought for the console table in the entrance and gently touched the photo of Roz and Johnston Yates that held a place of honor on her dresser. When she saw that he'd put the picture of his own family on the nightstand on his side of their bed, her smile deepened, but she didn't say anything. She didn't need to; they both understood what a huge step it was for him.

After the photos, the first thing she noticed in the bedroom were the paper horn tooters, emblazoned "Happy New Year" in pink glitter, and the silly hats with silver tassels that he'd put on the bed. She picked up one of the horns and blew it a couple of times before giving him a quick, apologetic kiss. "I'm sorry I missed the New Year's party at Sam's. I hope you had fun. Did Mac actually attend this year, or did he make another of his lame excuses?"

She turned away, starting to unpack her suitcase without waiting for him to reply, but Nick stepped in front of her, arms crossed, brows drawn together in an exaggerated frown.

"You can't possibly imagine that you're going to get away with that feeble attempt at an apology?"

She pressed her fingertips to his frown, smoothing it out. "I'm *very* sorry I missed Sam's party. Is that better?"

He shook his head. "It was pitiful. I had important plans for New Year's Eve and I expect a truly abject apology."

"Ah, I'm beginning to understand." She started to

laugh. "Would you by any chance expect this apology to take place in bed?"

"Where else?" he asked.

"And does my apology involve full-frontal nudity, as Jacyntha and her friends in the film biz would say?"

"Lots of full-frontal nudity," Nick confirmed. "And rear nudity, as well. In fact, utter and total nakedness." To underline his point, he began stripping off his shirt.

Melody began, very slowly, to unfasten the buttons of her sweater. "Just so you know, contact with Prince Faisal has given me an aversion to the idea of abject apologies and submissive women. I've decided to adopt a more aggressive attitude in bed from now on."

At the rate she was unbuttoning her sweater, he'd be dead from anticipation before he finally got her naked. "Honey, if aggression is what turns you on, I say go for it. In fact, as a sign of goodwill, for your birthday I'll buy you a whip and chain. But for now, could you please just take off the damn sweater?"

She unfastened the final button, letting it slip from her shoulders to the floor. Underneath, she was wearing a lace-trimmed camisole, but no bra.

"Take it off," he breathed, stroking the black satin straps.

She kept a poker face, but her incredible blue eyes gleamed with laughter. "I'm trying to decide if taking off my clothes on command fits into my new aggressive approach to sexual relations."

"That's clearly an important philosophical issue. While you're making up your mind, I'm happy to help out with the practicalities." Nick swept her into his arms and deposited her in the middle of their king-size bed. He grabbed her wrists and held them over her head, releasing them only to pull off the camisole. Then he unzipped her slacks, pushing them down her legs, kissing as he went.

She pretended to resist for a few seconds, then turned to him, wrapping her arms tightly around him. "I missed you," she whispered. "I missed this."

To say that he'd missed her didn't begin to describe what he'd experienced, sending her off on a mission with only Josh and Anthony for protection. As for the torment Nick had endured during the eighty-four minutes between her entry into the sheikh's ski lodge and her report from the Vail Valley hospital where she'd delivered Jacyntha to the ER, just remembering it made him shudder. He'd maintained operational control well enough to deceive Josh and Anthony, who were two thousand miles away at the end of their cell phones, but Mac hadn't been deceived for five seconds, let alone eighty-four minutes.

Mac, however, hadn't said anything, either at the time or since, leaving Nick to wrestle alone with the problem of what the hell he was going to do about the fact that he was in love with a woman who put her life on the line on a regular basis.

In the end, he responded to Melody's comment the only way he could. "I missed you, too," he said, and hoped that his actions would make up for the hopeless inadequacy of his words.

Their lovemaking had the sweetness of familiarity, mixed with the piquancy of their recent separation, the pleasure intensified for Nick by the relief of having Melody back safely. Afterward, they lay with arms and legs haphazardly entwined while he filled her in on the details of Sam's New Year's Eve party, and she told him about the hotel in Beaver Creek and why it would be a great place to go for a vacation.

"How did you like working with Josh Straiker?" he asked eventually.

She knew, of course, that the question was nowhere near as casual as he tried to make it sound. "Josh was a good partner," she said. "He's competent, innovative and willing to work as part of a team. Best of all, he's experienced enough from his time at Langley that he doesn't need to prove himself by playing Mr. Macho Superhero. Didn't you get the report I e-mailed you? My comments were ninety-nine-percent positive."

"I got the report. I just wanted to hear your assessment as well as reading the official version." He hesitated. "Josh invited me out for a beer last night."

Nick heard the slight intake of her breath.

"Did you go?" she asked.

"I went." He stroked his hand down her side, loving the smooth, muscled feel of her hips and thighs. "He told me that he'd talked to you about his affair with Jenna Varrett."

"Yes, he did," Melody said.

"What did you think of his story?"

"To be honest, I felt sorry for him. Josh strikes me as an honorable person, with a sense of responsibility that's as outsized as yours. The bottom line is that he was tricked by a well-trained Soviet agent, and he's been carrying a load of undeserved guilt ever since. It's past time for him to get rid of some of the burden, and you can help him do that, Nick." ·

Nick realized he'd turned automatically to look at the photo of his family. "I always recognized that Josh wasn't responsible for their deaths," he said. "Mac told me right after the murders that Jenna was one of the KGB's most talented agents and I realized even then that if she hadn't seduced Josh, she'd have found some other way to get the information she needed."·

"So why could you never tell Josh that?" Melody asked. "It would have meant so much to him."

She had a habit of asking the obvious questions that he'd successfully spent eighteen years avoiding, Nick reflected. These days, all that mental ducking and weaving felt tiring instead of life-saving.

"I guess I needed to blame somebody closer at hand than the KGB," he said. "Somebody with a face. Somebody I could get really mad at. Josh was right there, almost begging to be held responsible, and I was only too happy to oblige. I was busy nursing this huge load of guilt and self-pity, and it was a lot easier to blame him than to talk rationally about what had happened. So I refused to clear the air right after the murder, and discussing my family's death with him became more impossible as each year passed. The wound just festered and wouldn't heal."

"But now you've talked to each other?" Melody asked. "Really talked, I mean, not just agreed to adopt a more sophisticated version of that squaring-off, male-dog-bristling thing you've been doing ever since Josh joined Unit One?"

He smiled at the image she conjured up, albeit rue-fully. "Yes, we've really talked to each other. I'm not quite ready to say Josh is a good guy, but I guess I'm heading in that direction."

"I'm very glad, because he *is* a good guy."

Nick leaned over and kissed her briefly on the mouth. "Thank you for pushing us both to act a little smarter than we have been for the past eighteen years. I owe you one, Melody. Or maybe a lot more than one, if we're reckoning up accounts."

"You're welcome." She yawned and scowled in the direction of her suitcase. "I didn't realize how tired I was. I'm so not in the mood to start unpacking, and sort-ing out dirty laundry."

"Then don't. I'll order stroganoff and blintzes from the Russian restaurant on Third Avenue, and you can have a lazy evening. What's left of it."

He called in their order, then came back and sat on the edge of the bed. "The food will be here in twenty-five minutes."

"That's quicker than room service at a hotel." Mel-ody stretched lazily. "It feels so good to be back in my own bed."

"Stay there, if you like."

"In pursuit of dinner, I guess I'm willing to move." She got out of bed in search of a robe.

Nick used the belt of the robe to twist her around to face him. "What's your schedule for the rest of the week? Are you going to ride into headquarters with me tomorrow?"

She shook her head. "Wish I could, but I have to go into the gallery. We're bound to be backed up on administrative stuff after the Christmas rush and I ought to be there. Jasper's already handling two jobs, each of which could easily fill a minimum fifty-hour week, so he really needs me to be on top of my workload there."

Melody's comment crystallized the idea that had been fomenting in Nick's subconscious ever since he'd asked her to marry him. The trouble was, having originally used blackmail, bribes and threats to convince Melody that she was ideally suited for life as a Unit One field operative, he was all too aware that he was likely to end up living the rest of his life as a eunuch if he now suggested to her that she should simply quit.

They were interrupted by the arrival of the delivery from the restaurant, and by the time they had the food set out on the dining room table, with a bottle of chardonnay opened for good measure, he was able to return to the subject of her resigning from Unit One without seeming to.

"Have you noticed that Mac isn't drinking coffee anymore?" he asked, helping himself to rice.

She nodded, spooning cream sauce over her mushrooms. "He looked really tired the other day, too. And he's losing weight." Her gaze was troubled when she looked up. "Is he ill, Nick?"

"He needs to slow down," Nick said. "That's for sure."

"Because he's tired? Stressed? Or something more specific? Don't tell me if it's breaking a confidence."

"He had a mild heart attack when you were in the Caribbean with the Yateses," Nick acknowledged. "He also had a ministroke a month ago. It wasn't severe enough to affect his speech, but I noticed the other day that his left hand isn't quite functional."

Melody winced. "I can't believe I didn't notice that. It's impossible to imagine Unit One without Mac in charge, but it's even worse to imagine him stubbornly staying on as director until he keels over from another heart attack."

"That just about sums up the problem," Nick agreed.

"He has this supposedly fabulous house on the New Jersey shore. Isn't there any way to convince him to actually go live there?"

"Sure," Nick said wryly. "We could lock him inside, install steel grids over the doors and windows, and post Unit One guards on the property. Short of that, I'm not optimistic."

"I was hoping for a slightly more humane solution than incarceration."

"Jasper may have come up with one," Nick said. "He plans to ask Mac to take over a new position as director of training for our recruits. It's a job that Mac himself has pushed to get established, and it would be a lot less stressful than his current assignment."

Melody looked dubious. "Is there even a remote chance Mac would accept the position?" Her mouth tilted up in a grin. "Somehow, I don't think he views himself as an educator, or a mentor to the young and clueless."

"If the alternative is compulsory retirement, he might be persuaded. And Jasper told me he was ready to put the suggestion to Mac in those terms. Take the job as training director, and sleep at home at least four nights out of seven, or you're fired."

"I guess Mac would consider any job at Unit One a better option than being forced into compulsory retirement." Melody pushed beef and mushrooms around on her plate, clearly deep in thought. When she glanced up, the look she directed toward Nick was openly speculative.

"So if Mac becomes director of training, who will take over his current job as director of Unit One?"

Nick held her gaze. "Jasper asked me if I would be interested."

He saw a flash of hope in her eyes, but she looked away, pretending a renewed fascination with her food, and when she spoke, she was careful to keep her voice neutral. "You're very good in the field, Nick, and you're a superb chief of operations. And I say that despite having suffered on frequent occasions when you've been dishing out your pain-in-the-ass orders. Given how much you love your current position, why would you ever consider taking on a desk job?"

He was able to answer her with complete honesty. "A year ago, I'd never have considered taking Mac's job. But my goals have changed over the past few months." He reached out to put his hand on hers, preventing her from inflicting any more damage to the shredded remains of her stroganoff.

"I want to marry you, Melody. Not five years down the road, but soon. I want us to buy a house somewhere in the New Jersey suburbs, not too far from headquarters, so that we can have a life outside Unit One. I want us to have at least one child, maybe two. But we couldn't care for a child if we're both running all over the country, putting our lives on the line on a regular basis. That means I have to make some changes."

"I want all of that," she said, her expression wistful. "But much as I would like to marry you and live the suburban dream, I know we'll never be happy together if you're secretly yearning for a job that you sacrificed because of me."

"If I take Mac's job, I wouldn't be giving up anything that's important to me nowadays," he said. "In fact, I'd be pretty much reclaiming my life after eighteen years of substituting adrenaline highs for almost every other form of emotion. I realized at Christmas that I want to marry you a lot more than I want to continue working as chief of operations for Unit One."

Given the mess he'd made of a similar decision right before the Soldiers of Jordan mission last spring, it was a major admission on his part, and Melody recognized it as such. Her eyes, always hypnotic in their allure, were brighter than usual with unshed tears.

"Thanks for that, Nick. When you asked me to marry you, I wasn't sure if you'd considered how many changes it would demand in your way of life. Now I realize you're so far ahead of me that I'll have to run fast to catch up with all your plans!"

He smiled. "My plans for the next few years are simple. Marry you. Buy a house. Work hard on making a baby. Precise order of the above three line items open to debate."

"The current order sounds pretty good to me." She looked away from him, and then with visible effort forced herself to turn back. "Nick, the last time we discussed the possibility of me resigning from Unit One, it nearly ended our relationship. Is it safe for me to raise the subject again?"

"It's safe," he said, not bothering to hide a sigh of relief. Thank God, Melody had finally broached the subject he'd been dancing around in all his grand plans. "Do you still want to resign from Unit One?" His attempt not to sound too eager was a dismal failure.

The look she sent him was part irritation, part affection. "God knows, it's tempting to pretend you've converted me into a gung-ho field agent, and that I'm looking forward to cracking safes and shimmying down rope ladders until I'm too old and arthritic to hang on."

He held his breath.

"But that isn't what I really want," she said, releasing him from his misery. "I'll admit that the adrenaline rush of a mission is addictive, as is the thrill of achievement when everything turns out the way it should. But the truth is that I've always wanted to make my career in the art world."

Nick felt hope blossom, but the memory of his past manipulations of her life left him wary of coming on too strong. "Does that mean you're considering a return to working full time at the gallery?"

She nodded. "But with a twist. I'd like to propose to Jasper that I take over the complete running of the gallery in all but name and legal reality. That would free him up to spend many more hours each week on Unit One business. Quite apart from how much I'd enjoy being in charge of the gallery, I'm probably more use to Unit One easing the burden on Jasper than doing anything else."

Nick's professional judgment kicked in and wouldn't let him remain silent. "I don't agree. You're not just a good field agent, Melody. You're exceptional."

She shrugged, dismissing the compliment. "I'm sure there are plenty of people who can be recruited and trained to take my place as a field agent. But I'm in a unique position to run the Van der Meer Gallery. Once Jasper has passed his current workload off to me, he can devote almost all of his attention to Unit One affairs without damaging a business that's been in his family for three generations. Plus he would never have to worry about his staff catching him out in a lie, because I'd be protecting him."

She leaned back, as if realizing how intense she sounded. "Anyway, that's the plan I've been kicking around in my head for the past ten days or so. Do you approve? Do you think Jasper might approve?"

"I think it's a great idea, and I'm fairly sure Jasper will, too," Nick said. Melody's suggestion meshed so perfectly with his own wishes that he laughed out loud for sheer happiness. Then his laughter died, burned away by a flicker of superstitious alarm. When two people with such strong personalities and baggage-laden pasts agreed so easily about their future plans, it was hard to avoid wondering what tricks fate was preparing to play. Life, in his experience, was never this easy.

He pushed the worry aside. As Melody kept advising him, he needed to have more faith in the future. He needed to remind himself every now and again that the past wasn't the sole predictor of the future.

He picked up his wineglass and held it out to her. "I

propose a toast. Here's to us. To desk jobs, and a quiet life in the suburbs."

Melody smiled and clinked her glass against his. "To us, and our plans to become the most boring, stay-at-home couple in the neighborhood."

It was amazing, Nick thought, how appealing that humdrum lifestyle sounded.

Fourteen

Melody spent much of the morning at the gallery meeting with the vice president of a hotel chain who wanted to buy eight statues—no nudes—for his company's new corporate headquarters. He insisted on telling her at length how well informed he was about the art market, and then managed to undercut his own claim every time he opened his mouth.

Melody smiled a lot and said very little. Either her smiles or her silence inspired the VP to inform her that he was impressed by her wide-ranging knowledge of nineteenth-century art. There was absolutely nothing like letting a braggart listen to himself talk for clinching a sale, Melody reflected wryly.

When she finally managed to break free and return to her office, Ellen Peyton, her assistant, came in at once. "You'll never guess who came into the gallery while you were busy with the insurance guy."

"No, I probably won't. So why don't you tell me?"

"Johnston Yates," Ellen said. "He wanted to speak to you, but he wouldn't let me interrupt your meeting."

"Did he mention what he wanted?"

Ellen, despite her efficiency in other areas, rarely felt hampered by the need to answer questions concisely. "I've never spoken to a vice president before, even an ex-vice president," she said. "Usually big-shot politicians won't talk to the hired help, but Mr. Yates acted quite friendly. Anyway, he wants you to call him back ASAP. Something about a collection of paintings he plans to sell?"

"That sounds promising," Melody answered, deliberately crisp. Johnston Yates had made no special effort over the past six months to conceal his relationship to her. On the other hand, he'd made no effort to publicize it either, and she wasn't going to be the one who trumpeted the news. "Thanks, Ellen. I'll put him at the top of my to-do list."

"Here's his phone number." Ellen handed over a slip of paper.

Melody noticed that her father had given Ellen the number of his direct personal line.

When she finally found a spare five minutes after lunch to return the call, he picked up himself on the second ring.

"How are you, Johnston? It's Melody. My assistant told me you needed to speak with me." Despite the time spent cruising on his yacht and their holiday get-together, she still didn't feel free just to pick up the phone and chat for no special reason. She was surprised at how pleased she was to have an excuse to talk to him.

"I'm well," he said. "And all the better for hearing your voice. I called after Christmas to thank you for the lovely dinner at your apartment, but I got your answering machine."

"I've been out of town," Melody said. "I just returned last night."

"Ah." Johnston paused. "I'm glad you're back safely. Very glad."

Unit One had first started operating during the years Johnston was vice president, so he was aware of its existence, despite its deeply covert nature. However, Johnston was very much of the old school, and he took his security clearances seriously. Six months earlier, when Melody saved his life, he had been made aware of her connection to Unit One, but he had never asked for details of her role in the organization.

His failure to ask any questions about where she had been since Christmas meant that he understood she had been away on a mission. Melody appreciated his tactful silence, which allowed her to avoid lying to him. Given the duplicitous nature of the first thirty-two years of their relationship, avoiding more lies seemed a desirable goal.

"I called because Cynthia and I have decided to sell our cottage on Cape Cod," Johnston said. "We almost never get out there anymore, and somebody who's going to enjoy it might as well buy the place."

"Cynthia mentioned that you were thinking of selling the cottage when I was with you in the Caribbean. She said that both of you like to swim and fish somewhere warmer than the North Atlantic these days."

Johnston gave a rueful chuckle. "She's entirely right, I'm afraid. A comfortable cruise on the yacht is much more our style now that our blood is thin, and our bones on the elderly side. Anyway, we put the cottage on the market last week. We're offering it furnished—but not including five wonderful nineteenth-century marine paintings. My father-in-law bought them during the fifties, when he was first elected to the Senate, but leaving them at the cottage has been an insurance nightmare for the past few years. There's no resident housekeeper, you see, only a maintenance company that checks the property on a weekly basis."

"I'm surprised any insurance company even agreed to provide coverage," Melody said. "Who are the artists? Do you have an approximate idea of the value of the paintings?"

"Four of them are late-nineteenth century, painted by some of the lesser American Impressionists. The insurance company assessed their worth at between ten and fifteen thousand dollars each. Nothing spectacular by today's standards. However, the best of the bunch is a view of Newport Harbor by Fitz Hugh Lane. He painted it in 1868, and it is very lovely, to my untrained eye."

Fitz Hugh Lane was considered among the finest marine painters ever to have worked in America. The subject of his paintings was as much the mood evoked by the crystalline light as the ships and the calm seas on which they were anchored. Melody wondered if her father had any idea just how valuable Lane's painting of Newport Harbor might be.

"Did you know that one of Fitz Hugh Lane's oils

from the 1850s was auctioned not too long ago for three and a half million dollars? I believe I'm remembering the amount correctly."

"Good God," Johnston exclaimed. "Three and a half *million?*"

"Give or take a hundred thousand," Melody said.

"Good heavens." Johnston was clearly flabbergasted. "Cynthia and I had no idea! And for all the fuss the insurance company's been making, they never suggested the painting might be truly valuable."

Melody could almost see Johnston shaking his head at the other end of the phone.

"My father-in-law bought the painting for nine thousand dollars, if you can imagine."

"I think you can safely say your father-in-law made an excellent investment." Melody gave a wry smile. "I also agree with the insurance company. You probably shouldn't have an original Fitz Hugh Lane oil hanging on the wall of a summer cottage that only gets visited a few weeks a year."

"Thank goodness Cynthia and I had all five paintings shipped here early in December. Otherwise I'd be planning a midwinter dash to the Cape!"

"Much as I'd love to offer the Fitz Hugh Lane through our gallery, you're likely to get a better price if you arrange for it to be auctioned by one of the big houses. But why don't I come and take a look at the paintings before you finally commit to selling them?"

"That's an excellent idea," Johnston said. "Cynthia has just joined me in my office and she suggests that perhaps you could check the paintings one night after work, and then stay for dinner. What's your schedule like for the next few days?"

"As it happens, Nick is meeting a business acquaintance for cocktails tonight, so I'd planned to stay late at the gallery anyway. But I'd much prefer to come and look at your marine paintings, if this evening is convenient for you."

"It works well for me—" Johnston broke off for a moment. "But not for Cynthia," he said regretfully. "She has one of her board meetings starting at seven, a joint task force on homelessness among former prison inmates. She's worked like a demon to get various volunteer organizations and state agencies to cooperate on a new housing initiative, and now, as far as I can tell, she's keeping the whole project afloat by injections of sheer willpower. She always tells me that you've never seen real feuding until you've seen charitable organizations carving up turf. Makes us politicians look as harmonious as a church choir by comparison."

Melody laughed. "I can't imagine how Cynthia keeps her patience. Except that fighting homelessness is such a worthy cause."

"Especially since ex-convicts don't have many champions," Johnston said.

Melody had known that Cynthia was active in the vast network of charitable activity that helped to keep New York City functioning, but she hadn't realized that Cynthia's interests extended to problems of poverty and homelessness, as well as the more elite causes of art exhibits and the New York Symphony. Perhaps Cynthia had exerted a mellowing influence over her husband's politics, too. Johnston Yates had been considered one of the most right-wing politicians ever to hold the position of vice president, but Melody had noticed several occasions recently when his opinions on various social issues seemed to have wandered close to the middle of the road.

She had no intention of telling him that, of course. The poor man considered the word *liberal* an obscene epithet, and would probably die of shock if she suggested he was inching leftward in his old age.

"Since tonight doesn't work, how about later in the week?" Johnston said, cutting into her thoughts. "Cynthia and I are both home the day after tomorrow. Would Friday evening be convenient for you?"

"Friday would work well. I'll look forward to seeing you as soon as I can get away from the gallery. About six?"

"I'm making a note as we speak. And why don't you ask Nikolai to join us for dinner?"

"If Nick is free, I'm sure he'd like that."

They talked a while longer before saying goodbye.

The rest of the afternoon sped by in a blur of meetings, phone calls and client visits, and it was four-fifteen before Melody could begin to make a dent in the pile of pending acquisitions. Checking the provenance of works of art was an important enough task that she and Jasper always undertook it themselves. It was also a task that could eat up hours of precious time, since nothing could be purchased for the gallery until they were sure they weren't dealing in stolen property or forged works of art.

The first two files Melody looked at were easy to authenticate, giving rise to a spurt of optimism. Perhaps she'd get lucky tonight, and the verification process would be swift and painless in every case.

Ellen left promptly at five o'clock, dashing off to a hot date in the eternal hope that tonight's man was somehow going to prove perfect, despite the fifty or so losers that she'd managed to hook up with in the three years Melody had known her. The rest of the staff soon followed Ellen into the sleet and winter darkness. The gallery was already quiet when Jasper came into her office at five-thirty, the steel window grids having locked into place automatically, and the city noises muffled by the soundproofing so necessary to the peaceful ambience of the gallery.

"What's up, sweetie?" he asked, perching on the corner of her desk. "You're scowling."

"Checking provenance always makes me scowl." Melody looked up from her scrutiny of a document signed by the owner of a Parisian gallery in June 1946, certifying the sale of a painting by Andre Derain, a friend and colleague of Matisse.

For any major piece of art that had changed hands during the Second World War or immediately afterward, there was always the lingering suspicion that it might have been stolen. This was especially true of sales that had taken place in Paris, because that city had been a center for the distribution of art looted by the Nazis.

Melody swiveled the invoice around on her desk so that Jasper could see what she was reading. The Derain painting had never been offered for sale after 1946, so the documents had gone unchallenged—and unchecked—for almost sixty years.

Jasper wrinkled his nose when he saw what she was working on, instantly understanding the problem. "I don't think you have to worry. The date raises a red flag, but the painting was sold by the Galerie Philippe Fournier. They've been in business for a hundred and fifty years, and their reputation is impeccable. Plus this invoice is signed by Maurice Abelard, who was the managing director of the gallery from the late 1930s onward. The provenance looks solid to me."

"Abelard was never accused of being a front for the Nazis, was he?" Melody had memorized the names of the dealers who had been the most notorious Nazi collaborators, and Abelard's name wasn't on the list.

Jasper shook his head. "On the contrary, he was arrested twice by the Gestapo on charges of being a member of the French Resistance, so I seriously doubt that he ever dealt in works of art looted by the occupying forces."

He studied the bill of sale one more time, then closed the file with a decisive snap. "In the thirty-five years I've been involved in this business, there have been no questions raised about the ethics of the Galerie Philippe Fournier, or the integrity of Maurice Abelard. As far as I'm concerned, his signature guarantees that the sale was legitimate."

She smiled at him. "Thanks, Jasper. You just saved me hours of research. And the painting will be easy to sell, so it's a great acquisition for us."

"I'm delighted to have been of service. However, I actually came in not to discuss gallery matters, but to pass on some interesting news about Prince Abdullah. He was involved in an accident last night."

Melody's head jerked up. "What sort of an accident?"

"He was—and I swear I'm not making this up—run over by a bus. He slipped off the curb as he came out of a nightclub in Hong Kong, with his drunken Italian starlet in tow, and the bus backed up over him. He was rushed to the hospital, but he was pronounced dead on arrival. The actress survived, by the way."

Melody swallowed. "Did we—?"

"No, my dear. *We* absolutely did not. Sometimes— nowhere near often enough in my opinion—the universe decides to serve up justice. Prince Abdullah met the fate he deserves. It strikes me as especially appropriate that he was killed by a lowly form of public transportation that I'm certain he had never used or thought about in his entire life."

"Does Elspeth know her ex-husband is dead?"

"The attorney general knows and I assume he's informed his daughter." Jasper looked at her consideringly. "You look less happy than I would have expected, given your rage over what the prince did to Jacyntha Ramon."

"I feel sorry for Tommy," Melody admitted. "First the poor kid is thrust into a completely new environment with a family he barely remembers. Now he's about to learn that his father is dead. That much loss and change has to be hard for a little boy to handle."

"You're too softhearted for your own good, Melody."

Jasper smiled affectionately, their relationship sufficiently restored to its old footing that he gave her an encouraging hug. "I realize that Tommy will grieve for his
father. However, in my opinion, the prince's death
makes it more likely that Tommy will grow up without
feeling torn between two cultures that currently don't
seem able to get along very well. And that has to be a
major positive to balance against the loss of his father."

"I'm sure you're right."

"I usually am. I'd offer to take you out for a drink to
reinforce that positive opinion of my wisdom, but my
driver is already complaining that I'm late for an ap-
pointment downtown and you know how he harasses
me if I keep him waiting."

Melody grinned, the temperament of Jasper's Unit
One-supplied bodyguard-driver being a frequent topic
of wry jokes between the two of them. "It's just as well
Mike is cracking the whip," she said. "It prevents temptation. And I need to clear at least one more acquisition
file before I leave anyway."

Jasper slid off her desk. "Don't stay too late. I can't
remember when you last left here before six. You work
too hard."

She laughed. "Funny, I was saying the same thing
about you just the other day." She was tempted to tell
him right then and there of her decision to leave Unit
One and return to working full time at the gallery, but
she knew it would be better to have the discussion at
headquarters, rather than here, so she held her peace.

Jasper stepped out of her office and made his way
around one of the cleaning crew, who was buffing the

marble-tiled floor of the main display area with a very large and noisy polishing machine.

"*Buenas noches, señor.*" The man nodded politely, dragging the cord for his machine out of Jasper's way.

"*Buenas noches,*" Jasper replied. He waved a final goodbye to Melody and then backtracked to close her office door, shutting out some of the din.

Opening a bottle of water, Melody took a couple of sips and pulled another file out of her in-tray. One more provenance check and she was going to call it a night. This file was for another painting from the estate of the recently deceased French woman, also accompanied by a bill of sale from the Galerie Philippe Fournier. This invoice was dated August 1946, and was once again signed by Maurice Abelard.

Melody stared at Monsieur Abelard's signature. If she had examined the two bills of sale even an hour apart, she would probably have noticed nothing wrong. But she was looking at these two invoices within a few minutes of each other, and she felt a pricking at the base of her neck.

She reached for the previous file, removing it from the top of the stack she'd approved for acquisition. Pulling the invoice dated June 1946 and laying it directly beneath the invoice for August of the same year, she made a letter-by-letter comparison of the two signatures. Supposedly written two months apart, they appeared identical in every dot, quiver and flourish.

Far from being reassuring, the similarity set off major alarm bells. Authentic signatures varied in the tiny details, even in documents signed one immediately after the other. Two signatures showing zero variation, and supposedly written months apart, suggested that she was looking at the work of a forger.

If a wartime looter wanted to conceal his crime, what better way than to provide documents from a gallery with an impeccable reputation? More intrigued than upset by the possibility that she'd uncovered a sixty-year-old theft, Melody pulled open her desk drawer and fumbled for her magnifying glass, her gaze still fixed on the two signatures. Her hand rooted in vain until she remembered that Ellen had borrowed the magnifier earlier that afternoon. With an irritated click of her tongue, Melody got up and walked out of her office to her assistant's desk.

Melody was so focused on the signatures that it took her a moment to realize the floor-polishing machine was producing a high-pitched whine instead of a contented roar. She looked in the direction of the noise and saw that the machine had been abandoned. It was propped up against the wall, immobilized but not switched off.

Had the cleaner gone to the restroom? Taken ill? Come to think of it, she'd been here with the cleaners on many other occasions and they always worked in a four-person crew. So where were the other three members of the team? She'd neither seen nor heard them. Even as the question formed, a man wearing uniform coveralls emerged from the narrow corridor that led to the restrooms and storage area at the rear of the gallery.

He was dark-haired and stocky, and she thought he was the same man who'd spoken earlier to Jasper, although she hadn't really paid much attention and couldn't be sure. He appeared ill at ease when he saw her, so she gave him a friendly nod.

She remembered that he'd greeted Jasper in Spanish. *"Buenas noches,"* she said, picking up the magnifying glass from Ellen's desk. He didn't respond, but those two words more or less exhausted her Spanish vocabulary, so she turned to walk back into her office without saying anything more.

As she turned, she saw the cleaner reflected in the glass of a gilt-framed etching hanging on the partition that separated Ellen's workstation from her own office. In the blurred reflection, he seemed to be staring at her with almost hypnotic fascination, and his right hand was reaching inside his coveralls, just above the level of his waist.

What the *hell* was he doing?

Fifteen

The blurred image shrieked a warning. Instinct provoked a physical reaction before her brain had processed any reasoned threat of danger. Melody swung around, flinging the steel-handled magnifying glass straight at the man's face. The second she'd thrown it, she dived for cover behind Ellen's desk.

She heard the sound of a gun firing as she hit the floor, accompanied by the almost simultaneous explosion of glass shattering. A shard of glass speared the bottom drawer of Ellen's desk, propelled with sufficient force to penetrate the wood and lodge there. The projectile had missed her left eye by less than an inch. The bullet, she realized, had destroyed the etching that had been right behind her head a moment earlier.

The pounding of rubber-soled shoes on the marble floor warned her that the gunman was coming to find her. Hunched double to keep below the level of the desk, she scuttled back into her office. The gunman must have spotted her moving—not a difficult task—and he pumped out another couple of shots in her direction. Thank God, his aim was off and neither shot hit her.

He can't be much of a marksman, she thought, straightening to her full height as she covered the final yard and scooted into the relative safety of her office. She started to slam the door behind her, wishing that it locked, but the gunman was hard on her heels.

Too hard. Too close.

She quelled a moment of panic as he shoved his shoulder against the door, preventing it shutting. Should she keep trying to close the door, or jump away out of firing range? Why the hell didn't he just spray bullets into the plywood panels? He surely wouldn't be crazy enough to follow her into the office, knowing she was behind the door? He must realize that such a move would be setting him up for disaster.

Incredibly, it seemed that he didn't. He ran into the room, gun extended in front of him, providing Melody with a textbook-simple opportunity to reach out from behind the door and kick the weapon from his grasp. She kicked full-throttle hard, connected with his wrist and heard the reassuring sound of the gun clattering onto the porcelain floor tiles of her office. She followed through by swinging around and using her other leg to deliver a wickedly hard blow to his kidneys.

The gunman grunted in pain. "What the fuck?"

He looked and sounded bemused, and there was no lilt of Spanish in his all-American obscenity. Astonishingly, he stopped to rub the small of his back, in the spot where she'd kicked him, seeming to forget for a crucial moment that his gun was now lying on the floor, up for grabs.

Melody didn't waste any time wondering why in the world he was leaving himself so defenseless against her attack. She was tired of people trying to kill her, and anger momentarily climbed right to the top of her tangled emotions, defeating fear, and leaving compassion withering by the wayside. She seized the gun, aimed and fired.

Fortunately, even when she was angry she was capable of extreme precision. She aimed for his kneecap, the favored spot for movie villains and IRA terrorists. She knew the pain would be excruciating, but the injury wouldn't be life threatening. The combination suited her perfectly.

The bullet found its target with unerring precision. The gunman shrieked, then stared at her in silence, his face twisting into a cartoon-like expression of disbelief that would have been comic in other circumstances. After a moment or two, he collapsed onto the floor, his anguished cry fading once more into silence.

She hoped to God the stupid asshole hadn't died of a heart attack.

Melody collapsed against the desk, panting as if she'd run a race. She was shaking, from reaction to the adrenaline rush rather than fear, she realized. She gulped air, steadying herself. First things first. Even before she checked that the guy wasn't faking unconsciousness, she needed to ensure he couldn't seize back a functioning weapon. He might be injured, but he had at least a fifty-pound weight advantage over her, and sometimes brute force could defeat agility.

She removed the bullet clip from his gun, a cheap Saturday night special, shoving the clip into her jacket pocket before putting the defanged weapon on her desk. Avoiding his hands, she knelt behind the fallen gunman's head and felt for the pulse in his neck. He made no attempt to seize her, but he stirred slightly when she touched him, providing reassuring proof that he was alive. Good. Not only because she was glad to have avoided the role of executioner, but also because she sure as hell planned to question the bastard until she'd found out every single damn thing he knew about who had hired him to kill her.

She performed a quick body search and discovered a small dagger tucked into a wrist sheath, and an illegal switchblade knife strapped to his uninjured left leg. He had no more guns, however. His right knee was bleeding, although not with dangerous profusion, but she turned distinctly queasy at the sight of the messy wound she'd inflicted. Then she stiffened her spine. He'd been trying to kill her, dammit! This was not time to start feeling guilty because she'd lost her temper and hadn't defended herself by some less gruesome method than shattering his kneecap.

The shakes returned with debilitating force. Three serious brushes with death within three months was enough to give anyone an attack of the wobblies. She gripped the edge of the desk, steadying herself. She didn't have time right now to drown in self-pity.

Unfortunately, her teeth refused to stop chattering. Melody clamped her jaw shut. You are not going to go to pieces, she told herself.

Then what the hell am I going to do? My knees are shaking so hard I can barely stand.

You're going to call Nick.

Of course. Call Nick.

She seized the idea as the lifeline it was. Sitting down at her desk, she dialed Nick's cell phone number. When the asshole gunman woke up, he would be temporarily vulnerable, and she needed to be sure that they asked the right questions during that brief window of opportunity. That meant she needed somebody calmer than herself to help out with the questioning.

She'd called Nick on his work phone, the choice of number instinctive. He answered at once, without any of the friendly chitchat that would have been inevitable if she'd used his regular number. "Yes."

"I need you to come to the gallery right away. There's been another attempt on my life."

"Sorry, I can't quite hear you. Let me move away from the bar. Give me a minute, please." There was a thirty-second pause. "I'm alone now. Are you injured?"

"No. But I shot the man who tried to kill me."

"Is he dead?"

"No. I kneecapped him. He's unconscious."

"I'll be there in fifteen minutes or less. Don't notify the police." Nick cut the connection.

Melody found the curtness of their exchange oddly calming, as if Nick's expectation that she would react with professional detachment made it easier for that professionalism to kick in. Okay, so if this were a mission, what would she do while she waited for Nick? As soon as she viewed the situation in those terms, she re-

alized that the gunman needed to be tied up before he
regained consciousness. The fact that it had taken several minutes to recognize something so fundamental
suggested that she had not been functioning anywhere
near peak efficiency.

She found heavy-duty package-strapping tape in Ellen's desk and used it to bind the gunman's wrists in
makeshift handcuffs. Then she bound his uninjured leg
to the leg of her desk, using up almost the entire roll of
tape to ensure that he was immobilized. Not only did
she want to avoid being injured by him, she also wanted
to avoid the need to wound him again in self-defense.
Inflicting pain was definitely not her thing.

The gunman regained consciousness as she finished
taping his leg to the desk. He was visibly hurting and
she had to fight the impulse to call for medical help. She
did offer him a wad of paper towels, soaked in some of
her bottled water, to press against the jagged cut in his
cheek that must have been opened by the magnifying
glass she'd hurled at his head.

He tried to heave himself into a sitting position, an
impossible task with one kneecap shattered and the
other leg immobilized. The effort had him groaning
until he briefly passed out again. Melody relented
enough to push a small cushion beneath his head.

"I need a doctor," he whined, when he came to for
the second time. "Shit, look at all the goddamn blood!
You gotta take me to the hospital."

"First we talk, then I'll arrange for you to go to the
hospital. Maybe. If I like what you're telling me." She
kept his own gun trained on him. No need for him to

know that it was no longer loaded. "What's your name?" she asked.

He tried for a sneer. "Wouldn't you like to know?"

"Not especially." She shrugged. "I'll give you a nickname, just so you know when I'm talking to you and when you need to answer. How about Stupid?"

"I'm not stupid."

"If I were you, I'd get a second opinion on that." Melody leaned back against the edge of her desk, arms folded, gun dangling from her hand. She hoped her body language conveyed contempt. "Do you know somebody called Alejandro Garcia? Did he hire you to kill me?"

"Alejandro Garcia? Never heard of him." Unfortunately, the man looked and sounded as if he might be telling the truth.

"What's *my* name?"

"Bitch," he spat out. "Fuckin' bitch."

"Nope," she said, spinning the gun around by the trigger mechanism, so that it was pointing at him again. "Hey, you weren't even close." She angled the empty gun straight at his uninjured knee. "Try again. You only get one more guess and then I pull the trigger."

"Melody Beecham," he said quickly. "You're Melody Beecham."

"And who sent you to kill me? I want the name."

"Nobody sent me. I wasn't gonna kill you. You attacked me for no reason."

Melody laughed. "Yeah, the cops will believe that for sure."

"I'm gonna sue. You've crippled me."

"Yes, I have." Melody spoke with sudden seriousness.

The gunman looked up at her, then down at his knee, realizing for the first time that this was an injury that would have lifetime consequences. His eyes narrowed with hatred. Then he dropped his chin on his chest and sank into surly silence.

"How much were you paid to kill me?"

"Not enough." He sounded bitterly resentful. "He shoulda warned me you was gonna make like one of Charlie's fuckin' Angels. Nobody said nothin' about that."

"How did you know I'd be here at the gallery tonight?" she asked. "And where's the rest of the cleaning crew?" A sudden chill ran down her spine. "Have you killed them?"

"'Course not. I'm not a murderer." He sounded outraged by her suggestion. Astonishingly, he also appeared to believe his claim. "The rest of the crew stayed home."

"Why? How did you persuade them to let you come here tonight alone?"

He treated her to another silent glower, and she realized that she'd asked too many scattershot questions, too quickly, and had expressed far too much ignorance to tempt him into talking. He might be a man who ate dumbflakes for breakfast, but even he could figure out that the less he said, the better.

Her cell phone rang at just the right moment to hide the fact that she hadn't a clue what to ask him next, or how to force him to talk without resorting to torture. She flipped her phone open. "Yes."

"I'm at the front entrance," Nick said. "Can you let me in?"

"I'm coming now." She snapped the phone shut and

walked out of her office without saying anything to the gunman.

"Hey, where are you goin'? You can't leave me here! I'm bleedin' to death."

Melody stopped and once again looked pointedly at his shattered knee. "Yes, you quite possibly are. If you want to save your leg, you should consider finding better answers to some of my questions. I'll be back in a couple of minutes."

At the main entrance, she keyed in a manual override to the electronic door lock, waiting through the thirty-second delay before the lock disarmed. The gallery security system was state of the art, which was part of the reason she had always felt safe working alone in the building.

The door locking system on the front and back entrances came into automatic operation at five-thirty each night. The rest of the security system activated itself at seven o'clock, unless Jasper or Melody turned it off. The ninety-minute delay between the two activations allowed just enough time for a four-person cleaning crew to complete their chores without setting off alarms every time they traversed a motion detector or broke an infrared security beam.

Whoever devised the murder plan, Melody reflected, had been smart enough to choose one of the very few disguises that would gain a would-be killer unsupervised access to the gallery, and they'd chosen the precise time when witnesses were unlikely. What's more, the person contracting the murder—Christopher Beecham acting on behalf of his father?—had either been incredibly lucky when planning the shooting, or he'd known about the ninety-minute window between the locking of the door and the activation of the rest of the security system. Those ninety minutes had allowed the gunman to shoot at her with no record of his action recorded on camera, and no alarms going off at the police station.

The indicator light flashed green, telling her the lock was disarmed. The moment she opened the door, Nick strode in, his expression ferocious, his body radiating barely controlled anger. He'd obviously decided to sublimate his fear for her safety in action. He held her briefly in his arms, maintaining a grim silence as he inspected her for signs of injury.

"Can you hold up for another few minutes?" he asked, when he was satisfied that she hadn't been lying about being safe and sustaining no injuries.

"I'm fine." Now that Nick was here, it wasn't a lie. Anger returned in a giant wave, powerful enough to sweep away the lingering remnants of shock and self-pity. "I just want some answers from the bastard who shot me."

"Where is he?" Nick asked.

"In my office."

"What's his name?"

"So far, he's not saying."

Nick took his gun from his shoulder holster and marched through the main showroom. He was barely inside her office when he pulled the trigger. A bullet plowed into the porcelain tile a quarter of an inch from the wounded man's chin. Chips of pressed stone flew up and hit his face. Not surprisingly, the man screamed.

"My next bullet takes out the cartilage in your shoulder," Nick said. "Then you'll have a lifelong bum shoulder to go along with your bum knee. If you want to avoid that, tell me your name."

Beads of sweat stood out on the gunman's forehead, and his complexion had taken on a sickly gray tinge. Perhaps he was the sort of chauvinist who responded better to men than to women, or perhaps he recognized that Nick would do precisely what he threatened, whereas Melody's warnings had been undercut by her own uncertainty. In any event, he hesitated for no more than a moment before responding. "Bud, short for Bruno."

"Last name, Bud?"

He closed his eyes on a wave of pain. "Silveira."

"Okay, Bud, next question. Another easy one, so make sure you don't screw up and earn that bullet in your shoulder before we even get to any of the hard questions. How did you get the uniform for Alpha Cleaning Services?"

"I work for them, that's how. Look, you gotta get me a doctor. I'm dyin' here."

"How long have you worked for them?"

"Since I got outta—" He corrected himself quickly. "Since the week before Christmas."

"So you were in prison," Nick said. "Where were you incarcerated? How long for?"

"Green Haven," he admitted reluctantly. "Three years."

Melody and Nick exchanged glances. Green Haven

was a state prison, one of New York's maximum security facilities, located about a hundred miles north of the city. If Bud had been shut up there for the past three years, it seemed unlikely that he and Alejandro had ever met in person, since federal and state prisoners didn't cross paths.

Significantly, however, Wallis Beecham had been briefly incarcerated in Green Haven soon after he was arrested. The State of New York and the federal government had waged a full-scale turf battle about who had jurisdiction over his case, and whether Wallis should be prosecuted on federal charges of kidnapping and murder, or by the state for criminal conduct in connection with the Bonita Partnership. The Feds had won, and Wallis had been transferred to federal custody. Wallis had been locked up in Green Haven for no more than six weeks while the battle over jurisdiction raged, so he certainly couldn't know Bud well. Fortunately, if the two men had ever met, if they'd been housed in the same cell block for example, it would be a snap for Bob Spinard to find out.

"Is Wallis Beecham a friend of yours?" Melody asked.

"Nope," Bud responded quickly. Too quickly? "Never heard of the man."

Melody was fairly sure that Bud had genuinely failed to recognize Alejandro Garcia's name. She was almost equally certain that he recognized the name of Wallis Beecham.

Nick obviously shared her opinion, because he didn't

let the subject drop. "Did you meet Wallis Beecham in prison?" he asked.

"No. I already told you. I don't know nothin' about him."

Nick pretended to accept Bud's denial. They could always confront him with proof that he'd lied if Bob Spinard turned up a connection.

"What were the charges that put you away?" he asked, changing the subject.

"My ex-wife turned me in to the cops on a fuckin' domestic violence charge. Stupid bitch."

"Why in the world did she pick on a gentle, fun-loving guy like you, I wonder?" Nick shook his head in mock sorrow.

Bud grunted. "Because she's a bitch, that's why. She didn't need no other reason."

"And now the cops are going to come and pick you up any minute, and you'll be charged with carrying an illegal concealed weapon, with intent to commit murder, while out on parole. Seems you're up to your ass in alligators, Bud."

"Jesus, I'm the one who got shot! You can't make no murder charges stick to me!"

Nick laughed. "Want to watch me? The judge is going to toss you back in jail so fast your head will spin. He's going to lock you up, throw away the key and add fifteen years of hard time to your sentence."

"But I didn't do nothin'," Bud bleated.

Nick's moment of amusement faded. He grabbed Bud by the shoulders and lifted him up, ignoring the man's howls of pain. "Let's be clear what we're talking about, okay? You're not an innocent victim, Bud. You're a piece of shit who tried to kill Melody Beecham. You can either tell me everything you know about who hired you, and precisely what your instructions were, or I'm going to blow you away, body part by body part. For your sake, I really hope you don't kid yourself that I'm making empty threats here. Trust me, you don't want to die that way."

He let go of Bud's shoulders, and the man collapsed back onto the floor, gasping. "Who hired you?" Nick demanded, indifferent to Bud's moans of pain.

Bud's gaze was dark with resentment. "Guess what? He didn't introduce himself."

"What does he look like?"

"I never seen him. He hired me by phone. Called me at my apartment the day I got outta prison." Bud looked up at Melody as if hopeful she would instantly forgive him once he provided his excuses. "I didn't want to kill her. It's nothin' personal, you understand, but I needed money."

"Why?" Nick asked.

"I owe people," he replied vaguely. "They was comin' after me right from the moment I got sprung. And they sure ain't people to mess around with."

"Okay, let's talk money. How much were you offered for the job? And how did you get paid if you never saw who hired you?"

"He left the money in a coffee shop near where I live. In the men's room, taped under the top of the toilet tank, all wrapped in plastic."

"And how much did you get?"

"Fifteen thousand up front. He promised me another fifteen when she was dead. Told me to lie low for a coupla days after the killin' and then he'd pay me."

"Was the extra money going to be delivered in the same way?"

"No. There's this Internet chat room I gotta go into. Then he'll tell me where to go to pick up the money." Bud jerked his bound hands toward Melody, his expression regretful. "What does it matter, anyways? I ain't gonna get that extra fifteen now."

"That's true. But where you're going, Buddy boy, you won't need it. If I were you, and if I knew anything at all about who hired me for this job, I'd sure as hell share the information. Otherwise, you're going to end up doing the time for somebody else's crime."

Bud sounded genuinely regretful when he replied. "Man, I don't know nothin' about who hired me, and that's God's own truth. Don't even have a phone number. Only the chat room address."

It apparently cost quite a bit more to hire a killer in the States than it did in Mexico, Melody reflected. Bud had been offered twice as much as Jorge had been paid for his attempt in Cancún. Still, she couldn't help thinking that even thirty thousand was a bargain-basement price for ending her life. If Christopher Beecham was recruiting these killers on behalf of Wallis Beecham, why in the world did he keep hiring such obvious losers?

Admittedly Christopher wasn't the brightest glowworm in the meadow, but even he ought to have noticed that while Bud might be the type to perform well in a barroom brawl, he was seriously short of the skills necessary to take out a trained operative from a government agency that specialized in covert operations. Christopher and Wallis had both seen her in action. They knew she was capable of defending herself. Once Jorge failed in his attempt, wouldn't it have been logical for Christopher to make sure that the second killer he hired at least had sufficient smarts not to walk into a room where he *knew* the target was behind the door, waiting to kick his weapon out of his hand?

Could Wallis Beecham conceivably be so short of money that he was reduced to getting her killed for the lowest possible price? The government had stepped in and confiscated all of his assets arising from the Bonita Partnership, but Melody had always assumed that left Christopher and his mother with at least a few million bucks to cushion the blow of their public humiliation. Wallis Beecham's finances were another area for Bob Spinard to research, she decided.

Nick's research, meanwhile, was focused on Bud's job history. He had just asked Bud who got him the job with Alpha.

"My parole officer," Bud mumbled.

"What's your parole officer's name?"

"Warren Harding."

"Stop bullshitting me," Nick said, his mouth thinning with anger.

"Whatcha mean? What did I do? What did I say?"

"Warren Harding was the twenty-ninth president of the United States."

"Never heard of him. He's a dead president, right?"

"Yes. For eighty years or so."

"See? You shoulda known I wasn't talkin' about no dead president. My parole officer is alive." Bud looked nervously at Nick's finger slowly squeezing the gun trigger. "Jesus Christ, man, you need to watch that finger of yours. Are you gonna waste me because of a dead president with the same name as my parole officer? Me, I know a bunch of guys called Bud, but that don't mean I'm itchin' to go around shootin' them."

Perhaps even Bud realized that he was in no position to be claiming the moral high ground, or perhaps the pain of his wound silenced him. He closed his eyes, ignoring Nick's questions. A minute later, he slid back into unconsciousness.

"We have to get him to the hospital," Melody said, kneeling beside Bud and pressing her fingertips against his neck. "His pulse is thready and I'm sure he's not faking unconsciousness."

Nick shook his head. "If we call EMS, he'll be taken into police custody. That would be disastrous because they'd be in charge of the investigation, and they'd control our access to Bud."

"Then what are we going to do? He needs medical attention, sooner rather than later."

"He'll be okay. I already called headquarters when I was on my way over here. They're sending two of our most experienced paramedics and an ambulance. They told me they'd be here within thirty-five minutes." He looked at his watch. "That was twenty-five minutes ago."

"Let's hope traffic doesn't hold them up."

"They can always use their siren." He handed her a bottle of water from the mini-fridge in the corner of her office. "In the meantime, let's try to bring Bud around. Now that he's really hurting, we might finally get some useful information out of him."

Bud, however, had passed beyond the stage of coherent conversation. His breathing was alarmingly shallow and the cold water Melody sprinkled on his forehead barely revived him. He muttered something incomprehensible about the money he was never gonna get before passing out completely.

"Stop looking so damn guilty," Nick said, putting his arm around her, his voice softening. "Take a leaf out of Bud's book. He's a hell of a lot more troubled by the fact that he's not going to get his extra fifteen thousand than he is by the fact that he tried to kill you."

"I know." Melody rested her head on Nick's shoulder, allowing herself to relax for a couple of seconds. Her mind stopped its frantic spinning, and an idea that had been tickling the edges of her thoughts, jostling to be acknowledged, jumped into her awareness.

She interrupted Nick in midsentence as he started to outline his plans for keeping her safe, and how she would have to stay permanently at headquarters until they caught the killer.

"Oh my God."

Nick grabbed her hands. "What? What is it?"

"I just had an idea. It's so outrageous, it might work."

"Tell me."

She shook her head. "Some questions first, in case I'm way off base. Do you think the person who hired Bud would really have come through with that fifteen K bonus he promised?"

"I imagine so," Nick said. "Fifteen thousand isn't a great deal of money. Better to keep Bud happy than to have him angry enough that he spills his guts to the cops."

"That's what I thought. Presumably the killer was planning to make the second payment to Bud the same way as the first time—a package of hundred-dollar bills left in some public place where the murderer can hide the money without much risk of being spotted."

"That's what Bud indicated." Nick stroked her hair, and his expression grew dark as if he were visualizing how differently the night's events might have turned out. "Your death would have made the local TV news, and maybe even the front page of some of the tabloids. With all the publicity, whoever contracted the killing would know you were dead even before Bud called and demanded his bonus."

"That's part of what I'm counting on to make my plan work," Melody said. "You suggested taking me back to headquarters so that I can be safe. But locking me up is merely a defensive move on our part, and not even a very good defensive move. Besides, attack is always a better option than climbing into a hole and trying to hide. What happens if three months go by and we haven't found the killer? A year? Five years? Am I going to live at headquarters forever? I really have no desire to turn into Mac."

"I agree. Confining you to headquarters isn't a great plan even short-term. Unfortunately, I see no way to launch an attack against a killer whose identity is completely unknown."

"I may have come up with a way to smoke him out,"

Melody said. "What if we let the person who hired Bud believe he's been successful?"

Nick let out a short, sharp breath. "You mean—pretend you're dead?"

She nodded. "Someone seems mighty anxious to have me dead. Why don't we grant his wish? We could make it appear as if I was killed tonight, right here in my office. That way, Bud can claim his fifteen thousand bucks bonus—"

"And we have a chance to trap the killer when he drops off the bonus payment." Nick's voice was hoarse with sudden excitement, and he swung her around to deliver a smacking kiss. "My God, Melody, you're a genius. A certifiable genius."

"Thank you—"

"We still have to whisk you off to headquarters, and the logistics of getting you out of here will be difficult, but as long as absolutely nobody sees you, it could work."

"Fortunately, we didn't notify EMS or the cops."

"Yes, that makes everything easier." He frowned, thoughts almost visibly racing. "I need to call Mac right away. Jasper, too. They'll have to get this cleared at the highest levels of the NYPD. In effect, the cops will be conducting a phony investigation into your murder, so they have to agree to come on board. Maybe if they're told it's a national security issue, which it may well be depending on who's trying to kill you…"

"I have to tell my grandparents the truth before word gets out that I'm dead," Melody said quickly. "My grandfather isn't in the best of health, and I'm not willing to put him through even a few days of imagining that I've been murdered."

Nick gave a decisive shake of his head. "I'm sorry, I know it's going to be difficult for them, but if this is going to work, you can't tell anyone." He opened his phone and started to dial. "If we go through with faking your death, every detail has to be convincing—"

"My grandparents have to know the truth." Melody put her hand over Nick's, preventing him from making his call. On this point she wasn't prepared to compromise. "Before you bring Mac and Jasper in on the deal, you need to agree to that."

"Honey, it's too difficult for people without special training to fake grief—"

"For heaven's sake, my grandparents can fake stuff that's a hell of a lot more complicated than pretending to be sad because I'm dead! They were parachuted behind enemy lines during the Second World War. My grandfather was captured and imprisoned by the Waffen SS until some fighters in the French Resistance managed to free him. During the time he was held captive, he never revealed a single name, or any other secret. You can't possibly imagine that he would put my life at risk by betraying the fact that Bud didn't kill me?"

"The war ended sixty years ago, honey. Your grandparents are in their eighties now, and they're frail. Of course I don't imagine that they would *deliberately* reveal the secret to anyone—"

"Not deliberately, and not by mistake," Melody said quietly but with absolute conviction. "My grandfather managed to convince the Nazis that he was both a Frenchman and the village baker for a period of fifteen months. My grandmother convinced them she was the village midwife, a young woman afflicted with a speech impediment because her French wasn't quite good enough to pass for native. And the only babies she'd ever seen born before she landed in Normandy were the foals and calves delivered on her father's estate! My grandparents may be old, but they're still smart. With their background, I'm positive they're capable of convincing the media for a few days that my death has left them devastated. Anyway, bottom line—either they're told the truth, or I'm not prepared to play dead. It's a deal-breaker, Nick."

Nick spread his hands in a gesture of surrender. "If you're sure they can pull it off, I have to trust your judgment. But please, Melody, make sure your grandparents understand they're not to drop the faintest hint to your cousins, and aunts and uncles. Your life is literally going to be in their hands."

"That's a very safe place for it to be." She thought of old friends and family members who would be shocked and saddened by her death. And Johnston Yates, too. Her relationship with her father was still so new and fragile. Still, better that everyone should grieve unnecessarily for a few days than that they should grieve for her genuine death if the killer tried again—and succeeded.

A phone call announced the arrival of the Unit One emergency medical team at the entrance to the gallery and Nick let them in. Since their story was going to be that Melody had been mortally wounded by an unknown assailant, they couldn't afford to have any pedestrians see her alive and well and opening gallery doors for the paramedics.

"This is Angela and Chad," Nick said, gesturing to Unit One's paramedic team, who were already unwrapping equipment from the stretcher they'd parked outside her office door. "I've explained to them that Bud tried to kill you, and that we plan to let the world believe he succeeded."

Melody gave the paramedics a friendly nod. "I'm really glad you're here. I shot out Bud's kneecap almost an hour ago. I know he's hurting and I'm afraid he might be going into shock."

"We'll take care of him," Angela said, unwrapping a blood-pressure cuff as she spoke. "Put a few fluids back into him, give him a shot of painkiller, and he'll be a new man."

"Were there any photographers around when the ambulance drew up?" Melody asked Nick, stepping aside to give the paramedics room to work.

"No, not yet, but a crowd of rubberneckers gathered as if by magic, so some freelance journalist or cameraperson is bound to materialize soon. This is a famous gallery and we now have an ambulance that supposedly comes from New York's Emergency Medical Services drawn up right in front of the main entrance. I'm betting that when we try to leave, there's going to be at least one camera to record the scene."

"Then I'll have to go out on the stretcher," Melody said.

"Exactly." Nick gave a quick nod. "We'll wrap a

bloody bandage around your head, tape an IV line to the back of your hand and cover you neck to chin. Then we'll rush you into the back of the ambulance—"

"And hope that a camera person has arrived in time to record the scene." Melody gave a slight grin. "I never thought I'd be so anxious for a head-on collision with the paparazzi."

Nick returned her smile. His mood, like Melody's, had lightened considerably now that they'd come up with a plan that offered real hope of tracking down the person who wanted her dead.

"While the paramedics are working on Bud, I'm going to call Mac and Jasper," he said. "We have to warn off the New York Police Department right now, before a cop on the beat files an incident report."

"We also have to find a way to get Bud out of here," Melody said. "How the blazes are we going to do that?"

"Can you work on that problem while I call Mac and Jasper?" Nick was already punching in the code for headquarters on his cell phone. "We're hurting for time here."

Melody walked back to the paramedics, who had cut away the leg of Bud's pants and injected a local anesthetic into the swollen and bloody mess that was his knee. An IV drip was already delivering electrolytes and antibiotics, and Bud had regained both color in his cheeks and enough energy to curse out the medics in a steady, blasphemous stream.

"How long before he's ready to leave?" Melody asked.

"He can go now," Chad said. "The sooner the better, from a medical perspective."

"Is there any way he's going to be able to walk?"

"Eventually?" Chad asked. "Sure."

"I meant tonight."

Chad frowned. "He shouldn't put any weight on that injured leg. He really needs to go out of here on a stretcher."

"Damn!" Melody paced the office, her mind so empty of ideas that she became gloomily convinced that her plan was going to come unraveled over the practical problem of getting Bud out of the gallery without his being seen. Could they flag down a taxi? No, the cab-driver would be certain to talk. A Unit One operative could come with a car, but the distance from head-quarters meant at least another forty-minute delay, more likely an hour. They couldn't afford that amount of time.

Nick came back into the office, closing his cell phone. "Mac is on board," he told Melody. "He's call-ing the police commissioner now, and he'll follow up with a call to New York hospital. Unit One saved the medical center's collective ass eighteen months ago, and he's confident he'll be able to get the director to issue a bulletin announcing that you were transported there and pronounced dead on arrival."

"That takes care of me, but we still need a plan for getting Bud out of here," Melody said. "I seem to have used up all my creativity deciding to play dead. Chad and Angela say Bud should be transported on a stretcher. Problem is, I'm going to be on the stretcher."

Nick took Melody's hand. "Excuse us for a mo-ment," he said to the paramedics, leading her out of the office.

"Jasper is on his way here," he said, when they were too far away to be overheard by Chad or Angela. "He's in his limo, and his bodyguard is driving. Mike will take the limo into the parking garage beneath the gallery. With luck, nobody will notice their arrival since the entrance is at the rear of the gallery and any media people are likely to be clustered out front."

"But what if somebody from the press does chance to spot the limo—and goes to the trouble of checking the license plate and identifying Jasper as the owner?"

"It's not a disaster," Nick said. "There's a valid excuse for his being here. Jasper owns the gallery, and his most senior employee has been shot. End of story from the point of view of the press. Once Jasper is safely inside the parking garage, Mike will come up and help Chad carry Bud into the elevator and down to the limo."

Melody grimaced. "Do you think Bud will be okay? His leg ought to be immobilized—"

"I think Bud is being treated a whole hell of a lot better than he deserves. He'll do just fine stretched out on the back seat of Jasper's limo, and Chad can travel with them to make sure there are no medical surprises. Angela and I will come in the ambulance with you."

"How are we going to explain Jasper's helpfulness to Chad and Angela? I assume they have no idea of his role as chief of Unit One?"

"We'll use the same story with them that we're going to use with the media. Jasper is the owner of the gallery, your boss and an old friend. That's all the explanation Chad and Angela will get. They'll suspect more, of course, especially when Mike drives Jasper's limo straight to headquarters, but they're trained not to ask questions unless they're medically related."

Melody heaved a sigh of relief. "Okay, that's Bud taken care of. Now it's my turn. Let's hope Angela and Chad have a few tricks up their sleeves that can make me look like the victim of a shooting attack who isn't going to survive the night. The ambulance has been standing outside too long. We need to get this show on the road."

Nick caught her as she walked past. He dragged her close, kissing her passionately, his body tense with the fear he refused to show in any other way. "We have to make this plan succeed," he said when they finally broke apart. He tried to smile. "Even if you survived another attempt on your life, I'm pretty sure I wouldn't."

Melody was all too aware that these attacks played into every one of Nick's worst nightmares about the capriciousness of fate and the danger of allowing oneself to love. "We're going to catch the killer," she said. As she spoke, she realized her confidence wasn't feigned.

She took his hands, holding them tight. "I really believe it, Nick. We're setting a powerful trap, loading up the bait, and the killer is going to walk right in."

Sixteen

The dank cold of the January night nipped at Melody's face as soon as Angela wheeled her out of the gallery and onto the crowded sidewalk. The blood they had pricked from her fingers and smeared on her cheeks to disguise their healthy pink glow began to freeze. The icy streaks made her skin itch and she had to fight the urge to reach up and scratch.

She heard the immediate murmur that went up from the crowd, and even though she kept her eyes closed, she sensed the flash of at least two cameras coming at her from different directions. Nick squeezed her hand, a silent signal confirming that there were journalists recording the scene. She concentrated on looking as lifeless as possible for the cameras.

"Keep back, please! Make way!" Angela called as Melody felt the stretcher being maneuvered off the sidewalk.

"For God's sake, keep back! We have to get her to

the emergency room!" Nick's voice was convincingly pitched somewhere between anger and desperation.

A female voice called out. "What happened? Was it a robbery?"

Neither Nick nor Angela answered.

"Here, let me help." It was a new masculine voice. From the fact that Angela thanked him, Melody concluded this was the ambulance driver, a Unit One employee.

Nick finally released Melody's hand—hanging over her had been the best way to prevent anyone from getting close enough for a good look—and she felt the stretcher being stowed in the back of the ambulance, the front wheels collapsing automatically as Angela and the driver pushed her inside.

Nick jumped into the ambulance with her, and she realized that carrying civilian passengers was something a regular paramedic team would never have allowed. Too late to worry about that now. She could only hope that nobody would pick up on the botched detail. Angela followed Nick inside and the doors slammed shut. The driver turned on his siren, and Melody felt the ambulance pull away from the curb, speeding east toward the river and the hospital.

She opened her eyes. "Is it safe to sit up?"

"It sure is." Angela removed the medical tape that strapped an IV line to the back of her hand. The tape had concealed the fact that there was no needle. She handed Melody a baby wipe. "For your face," she said, smiling slightly. "You kinda look as if you've been in a war zone."

Then she looked pretty much the way she felt, Melody reflected.

Nick had been peering out of the narrow window in the rear doors but he finally turned away. "Nobody is following us," he said.

"Thank goodness," Melody said. "It would have been disastrous if we'd been forced to shake a trail of ambulance chasers."

Nick sat next to Angela, across from Melody and the stretcher. "At the moment, the story probably doesn't seem worth much of an effort."

"Did anybody take pictures as I was being loaded into the ambulance?" Melody asked. "I thought I sensed more than one flashbulb go off."

"There were two people with cameras," Nick confirmed. "I didn't have much chance to check them out, but I think one of the photographers was just a ghoulish bystander. Luckily, the other guy seemed to have professional equipment."

The Unit One operative driving the ambulance turned off the siren, apparently deciding that they were far enough away from the gallery that it was better if they now tried to avoid attention instead of attracting it.

Nick opened his cell phone. "I'll let Mac know that Bud was locked up in Green Haven for three years, and that his stay overlapped with Wallis Beecham's. Bob Spinard shouldn't take long to find records that would confirm or deny the possibility that the two men knew each other there."

Nick's conversation lasted several minutes more than

Melody would have expected and he kept his expression so carefully blank that she knew Mac was telling him something important. After he finished the call, he sent Angela to sit in front next to the driver. Before passing on Mac's news to Melody, he closed the partition so that they couldn't be overheard.

"Mac has Christopher Beecham at headquarters," he said. "I knew Sam and Tony were going after him, but it's a huge break for us that they managed to bring him in this evening."

Melody's eyes widened. "It sure is. When did Chris arrive in New York? Last I heard, you and Bob Spinard were still working on a scheme to lure him back from the Bahamas."

"He flew back three days ago, as we discovered when we started making serious efforts to track him down."

"I'd say it's a good possibility that he flew back to New York to supervise the attempt on my life."

Nick nodded. "I agree. Bob Spinard was tracking his credit card purchases, but we caught a break when he hung around the bar in his hotel long enough for Tony and Sam to catch up with him, without mounting a full-scale extraction operation. Mac has him stashed in an interrogation room, waiting for our arrival. There's a viewing window, so you'll be able to see for yourself what Christopher's reaction is when we tell him you're dead."

Melody grimaced. "Wild enthusiasm, I imagine, even if by some slim chance he has nothing to do with the attacks against me." She thought for a moment.

"You'll have to walk a thin line when you question him. Otherwise he might get sufficiently spooked to leave town instead of paying Bud his bonus. And there would go all our hope of proving he and Wallis are behind the attacks."

"Mac made the same point." Nick's brows drew together in a worried scowl. "We could have left him on the loose, but what if he has another killer lined up, ready and waiting to take you out?"

"We could hope that Chris would be dumb enough to hire another hit man as incompetent as the last two."

"That's too slim a hope as far as I'm concerned." Nick's scowl deepened. "Besides, Jorge and Bud weren't really incompetent—you were just better equipped to protect yourself than they expected."

Something important tickled at the edges of Melody's thoughts, then slid away before she could capture it. "Plus I got lucky," she said. "In Acapulco, you happened to arrive just when Jorge was winning the fight. Tonight, I happened to walk out of my office at the crucial moment. If I'd been sitting at my desk another minute or two, Bud would have walked in and shot me before I could move."

Nick did not look happy at the reminders of how narrowly she'd escaped with her life. He reached for her hand, as if needing physical contact to reassure himself that she was truly okay. "Having you pretend to be dead is the best shot we have of catching the killer, but it's a thousand miles away from foolproof," he said, his voice grim.

The ambulance drove out of the Holland Tunnel,

meaning they were less than fifteen minutes away from Unit One's headquarters. Melody glanced at her watch and saw that it was only a few minutes after seven o'clock. She felt as if ninety hours rather than minutes had passed since Bud shot her. Even though she knew how capable Unit One was of acting fast, and how much power they had when it was really needed, she was still surprised at how quickly they had managed to bring together the basic elements necessary for faking her death.

"How long do you think it will be before reports filter out that I've been murdered?" she asked.

"A few hours, no more. You need to phone your grandparents the minute we reach headquarters. Mac personally called in an anonymous tip to New York's Channel 9, telling them there had been a shooting at the Van der Meer Gallery and the rumor was that Melody Beecham had been killed. People still remember that you were the most successful Infinity Woman in the history of Infinity Cosmetics, so they're certain to follow up on the story. I expect they'll have pictures in time for the eleven-o'clock news. With the time difference, that means the Brits will be seeing the story on their breakfast shows tomorrow morning."

"The media will rehash all the stories about my mother's death, won't they?" She was just beginning to grasp the consequences flowing from the idea she'd tossed out so casually. The ripples were already big. Quite soon, they would be enormous.

"I'm afraid so. By noon, you can expect to hear a dozen different conspiracy theories linking Lady Roz's death and yours." Nick's mouth twisted ruefully. "The bloggers are going to have a field day."

"Oh Lord, I'd forgotten about the bloggers! There's already a Web site run by some anti-royal family nut who claims Lady Roz was murdered on orders from Buckingham Palace. I wonder how he'll squeeze me into his theory?"

Nick quirked an eyebrow. "And the palace's motive for eliminating Lady Roz was what?"

"To cover up the fact that Lady Roz had an affair with Prince Philip."

Nick grinned. "Did she?"

Melody smiled faintly. "As far as I know, Prince Philip was one of the few really famous men in England that my mother *didn't* have an affair with."

Nick peered out of the window again. "We're almost to headquarters. Mac has already rounded up half a dozen Unit One agents and dispatched them to the gallery. A couple of them will be outfitted in police uniforms. The rest are pretending to be detectives or forensic experts. Our guys on the scene will direct reporters to New York hospital, where the spokesperson will report that you were dead on arrival." He paused for a moment, then gathered her into his arms. "I'm so goddamn grateful that this is all pretense, instead of for real."

Melody's smile was wry. "And so am I."

The phone call to her grandparents took more than an hour. They understood immediately why they couldn't tell the truth to her aunts, uncles and cousins, but they were worried for her safety and wanted to hear more than once that she was in a safe place and would stay there until the would-be killer was caught.

It was her grandmother's parting comment that shocked Melody the most. She'd learned to dismiss conspiracy theories from tabloids and bloggers. She hadn't expected to hear one from her grandmother. "I never believed that Roz's death was an accident," the countess said, her voice more angry than sad. "You mark my words, Melody. Somebody wanted your mother eliminated, and now they're coming after you. Be very careful, my dear. Your grandfather and I simply couldn't bear to lose you, as well as our daughter."

Melody had made the call from Mac's office, on a secure phone line. She knew that the whole conversation would have been recorded, but she repeated her grandmother's final comment to him anyway.

Mac tugged thoughtfully at his lower lip. "You always did suspect your mother's death was something other than accidental. Interesting that your grandmother shares your view."

"She didn't actually mention Wallis Beecham by name," Melody said. "But he certainly has strong motives for getting rid of both of us."

"Christopher may be the man with the answers," Mac said, tapping numbers on an internal phone. "Let's go and watch what happens. Nick was waiting for you to finish your conversation before starting—"

He broke off and spoke into the phone. "Yes, Nick. Melody's finished her call to England. We're coming down now. Give us three minutes to get there."

He hung up and hustled Melody from the room, his short legs moving so fast that Melody was almost running to keep up. They arrived at a heavy steel door, and Mac punched in a code to activate the retinal scanner. When both he and Melody had been scanned, an electronic buzz indicated that the door had unlocked and they walked into a corridor Melody had never visited before.

Mac waved her into a chair and sat down next to her. The interrogation room was built at a lower level than the viewing corridor, so that the window they were looking through would appear almost at ceiling height to the occupants of the room. Unlike many police stations, where grunge was often the prevailing decorative theme, this room was painted white, with a pristine white linoleum floor and white molded plastic furniture. There was nothing to relieve the starkness, except a jug made of unbreakable plastic, along with some paper cups.

Melody would have found the stark cleanliness more intimidating than squalor and she wondered if Christopher felt the same. He certainly looked uneasy. He was alone in the room and he shifted in his chair, disconsolately poking at the ice in his cup.

Thirty seconds after Mac and Melody had seated themselves at the viewing window, Nick and Sam walked into the interrogation room. Nick appeared wild-eyed, with blood smears on his shirt and his tie hanging unfastened around his neck. He paced the room, apparently unable to keep still even for a moment.

He was really a damn good actor, Melody thought, not sure whether to be amused or impressed.

"Hello, Christopher," Sam said. "How are you doing?"

"Miserable. How the fuck do you think I am? Why did you pick me up this time? I'd threaten to call my lawyers, except I know it's a joke to expect you people to obey the law. What the hell am I supposed to have done now?"

"You know damn well what you've done—" Nick lunged across the table, and Sam grabbed him, frog-marching him over to a corner of the room and murmuring something inaudible. As soon as Sam released his hold, Nick turned and slammed his fist into the wall.

"What's with the Russian mafioso?" Christopher asked, momentarily forgetting his own problems as he stared at Nick. "Who's been stomping on his dick?"

"Melody Beecham has been murdered," Sam said.

"Murdered? Melody? *Murdered?*" Christopher stared blankly, first at Sam and then at Nick, who had turned around and was leaning against the wall, arms hanging limp and aimless at his side. His gaze, however, was anything but aimless; it was intense and fixed on Christopher.

"Are you telling me that—Melody's dead?" Christopher rubbed his hand across his forehead, back and forth in a pointless movement.

"Yes," Sam said. "She was shot at the art gallery earlier this evening."

"Son of a bitch." Christopher slumped back in his plastic chair. He gave a laugh that contained no amusement whatsoever. "Son of a bitch," he said again.

"How do you feel about Melody being dead?" Sam asked.

Christopher gave another cough of humorless laughter. "Nowhere near as good as I thought I would."

Nick lunged for him again. "What does that mean, you little prick? Did you and your father arrange to have her killed?"

Christopher jerked up straight. "Hell, no!" He blinked, comprehension dawning. "Oh, is that what this is about? You think I hired the person who killed her?"

Sam stepped in front of Nick, who looked about ready to tear Christopher apart bone from bone. And this time Melody wasn't at all sure the simmering rage was feigned.

"You and your father have plenty of reasons to want her dead," Sam said.

"What reasons?"

"Wallis is in prison because of Melody. She caused you to lose a great deal of money. Almost as bad, you and your mother were publicly humiliated. She claims that she genuinely didn't know Wallis wasn't her father, but I'm sure you don't believe her—"

"You know what's really funny?" Christopher interrupted, his voice absent, as if he were talking to himself. "The whole time I was growing up, I hated her. It seemed as if every time I turned around, there was another person pointing out to me how goddamn beautiful she was, and how hard she worked, and if she was so smart, how come I was such a fucking loser?"

Sam frowned. "But you were always your father's favorite, weren't you?"

"My father's favorite?" Christopher's mouth twisted as if he'd eaten something unbearably bitter. "He was the worst of the lot. He rubbed my nose in her success the whole damn time. Asked me every time he saw me why I couldn't be more like my sister." Christopher choked out another laugh. "Happiest day of my goddamn life when I heard she wasn't my father's kid."

"Until today." Nick braced himself on the table across from Christopher, his body looming with menace. "Let's be accurate, Chris. It was the happiest day of your life until just now when you heard that Melody is dead."

"I'm not happy she's dead," Christopher said. "And that's probably a bigger surprise to me than it is to you."

"It isn't a surprise to us," Nick said. "Because we don't believe you."

Christopher shrugged. "You can believe me or not, I don't give a shit. But I'm telling you, I didn't kill my sister—" He cut himself off. "I had nothing to do with killing Melody Beecham. If you want to find out who did, go talk to my father. You're right, he hates her. But mostly because he wishes like hell that she was his kid."

Melody was so involved in the scene taking place in the interrogation room that she jumped in her seat at the sound of Mac's internal communicator buzzing. He answered curtly his name, then listened in silence. After a couple of minutes, he gave a grunt of acknowledgment and hung up.

"That was Bob Spinard," he told Melody. "He's finished cross-checking the prison records of Bruno Silveira, alias Bud, against the prison records of Wallis Beecham."

Melody's mouth was so dry she had to swallow before she could speak. Witnessing Christopher's reaction to her death had not only been a strange experience, it had been unexpectedly painful. She should have realized long ago that in a family as dysfunctional as hers, she wouldn't have been the only child to suffer. Empathy for Christopher Beecham was about the last emotion she'd ever expected to feel.

"What did Bob find out?" she asked Mac.

"He hit the jackpot. Bud and Wallis were in Green Haven at the same time, and they were in the same cell block, on the same floor, the entire six weeks Wallis was incarcerated there."

Melody had expected all along to hear there was a link between the man she'd believed to be her father and the man who had tried his best to kill her less than three hours earlier. Nevertheless, the confirmation of her suspicions produced a sick feeling in the pit of her stomach. Her glance flicked instinctively toward the interrogation room and Christopher, who was slumped in his chair, refusing to answer any more questions.

Despite the news from Bob Spinard, she couldn't shake the impression that Christopher's body language suggested sadness and genuine regret. She expressed some of her confusion to Mac. "If we hadn't just heard about the link between Wallis and Bud, I'd be convinced Christopher knew nothing about tonight's attack until Sam told him. I would never have expected him to be such an outstanding actor, that's for sure."

Mac was frowning so hard that his face, always faintly gnomish, looked like a plaster model for one of the Seven Dwarfs. "Christopher Beecham's got as much acting ability as a rock," he said. "And that's insulting the rock."

Melody wanted to be sure she'd understood Mac's meaning. "Are you suggesting Christopher is so messed up that he's sad I'm dead, even though he and Wallis hired the killer?"

Mac shrugged. "Plenty of killers are devastated when their victim dies."

"Do you think Christopher's one of them?"

"Not likely, based on his reactions tonight. My conclusion? There's no way Christopher knew you were going to be killed."

Apparently Sam and Nick felt the same way, because they left the interrogation room. A minute later, they entered the viewing area.

"You saw the whole interview?" Nick asked them.

"Yep. What's your take on Christopher?" Mac asked. "Was he involved in plotting Melody's death? Not involved?"

Nick responded first. "I can't believe I'm saying this, but the guy seemed genuinely shocked and upset."

Sam nodded. "I was lookin' straight into Christopher's eyes when I told him Melody was dead. If he was faking surprise, the man's missed his calling. He should be in Hollywood, linin' up to receive his Oscar."

Mac repeated his earlier opinion. "Hasn't got the smarts."

"I agree Christopher doesn't appear to be involved," Melody said. "But that doesn't let Wallis off the hook. Especially now that we know Bud and Wallis were in Green Haven at the same time."

Nick's head shot up. "Bob Spinard's reported back?"

"Wallis and Bruno Silveira were in the same cell block," Mac confirmed.

"Not just the same cell block," Melody said. "The two of them were on the same floor, as well."

"So who the hell did Beecham use to do the deed, if not his son?" Sam muttered.

"Bob can run another check on the log of Wallis Beecham's visitors," Nick said. "Last time, we just asked him to check that Christopher had visited his father. We never asked for a complete list of everyone who paid a visit."

"In the meantime, we need a decision about what to do with Christopher Beecham," Mac said. "Nick? Sam?"

"Let him go," Sam said. "It's what we planned to do anyway."

"We'll keep him under surveillance," Nick said. "Melody's confined to headquarters, so she's not at risk if he turns out to be the killer despite all our doubts. Plus we've implanted a microchip, so we don't have to devote massive amounts of manpower to following him."

"His hotel room is bugged?" Mac asked.

"Yes," Nick confirmed. "That means we'll have audio coverage at least until Christopher moves out of the hotel."

Mac hitched his wayward pants. "How much chance he'll find the tracking chip?"

"We planted it in his left buttock when he was unconscious," Sam said. "We used Rohypnol to put him out, and he shouldn't remember even being unconscious."

"Melody, what's your take?" Mac turned to her. "You

heard the safety precautions. You okay with letting Christopher go free?"

She nodded, barely hesitating. "As Sam said, it's what we planned to do anyway, even if we thought he was guilty. He's more use to the investigation if he's out there, doing his thing, with us keeping tabs on his activities."

"Okay, let's get moving." Mac pointed to Nick. "As far as Christopher is concerned, you're supposed to be half crazed with grief over Melody's death. You should go check with Bob Spinard and get a report from the surgeon who's operating on Bud. See how long it'll be before he's coherent enough to answer some more questions. Sam, you drive Christopher back to his hotel. Blindfolds, of course. Melody, you stick with me. Sorry, but I'm not even going to give you the full run of headquarters. The fewer people who know you're alive, the better."

Sam had just left when Mac's communicator buzzed again. Nick turned to leave also, but Mac gestured for him to come back into the viewing area. Mac listened without interrupting, and spoke only to thank his caller for the update before closing the device.

"That was Jasper," he told Melody and Nick. "Three local TV stations have already run a breaking-news flash, reporting your death. They're promising pictures at eleven. And Jasper wants to see all three of us in his office. Right now."

Seventeen

Jasper greeted Melody with a long and searching look, but he'd already hugged her at the gallery, and he made no overt gesture to emphasize their years of friendship outside Unit One. He motioned for them to sit in the chairs already pulled up in front of his desk.

"Bud parted with some interesting information during our limo ride," he said. "Right away, it struck me that he was facing a dilemma. It was essential for him to be alone with Melody in order for his murder plan to work, but he couldn't afford to let his teammates know that he was the only man who'd gone to the gallery tonight. It's possible that the other three members of the crew would have agreed to keep quiet about a robbery, but surely they wouldn't all keep silent about a murder where they had no reason to want the victim dead."

"So how did Bud finesse it?" Nick asked.

Jasper's mouth thinned. "I'm sure *Bud* didn't. His *employer* fixed it with smart planning, and inside knowledge of gallery operations. The owner of Alpha Cleaning Services received a phone call around two this afternoon. Supposedly this call was made by me. I don't believe I've ever spoken to Alpha, so they had no reason to question whether it was my voice."

"I was the one who hired Alpha nine months ago," Melody said. "I can't think of any reason you would have had to call them since then. They provide very reliable service."

"Precisely." Jasper took off his rimless glasses and folded the gold earpieces with excessive care. "The man pretending to be me informed Alpha that a pipe had burst in one of the gallery walls and the entire showroom floor was under a half-inch of water. Alpha was told that a plumbing company was at work fixing the broken pipes and there was no point in sending in the cleaning crew that night. The fake Jasper promised to call again as soon as the wall damage had been repaired and the pipes fixed. At that point, he promised Alpha would be asked to send in a crew to take care of refinishing the ruined marble tiles as well as general maintenance. So there was going to be no loss of income for Alpha. The caller said it would be at least another two days before this final cleanup could begin. Bud told me some of this story, and I've already confirmed the rest of it with Mr. Martinez, Alpha's owner."

Mac shoved his hands under the baggy sleeves of his sweater and scratched his forearms, a nervous tic that indicated rapid thinking on his part. "Want to confirm I have this straight. Around two, the boss of Alpha Cleaning receives a phone call saying, don't send in your crew tonight. Mr. Martinez immediately notifies all four cleaners to stay home because the gallery floor is flooded."

Unable to sit still any longer, Mac jumped up and began to pace. "Three of the team stay home, as ordered. Bud, on the other hand, knows this is his signal to kill Melody. He comes into the gallery at five-fifteen, as per usual. He checks out the gallery to make sure he and Melody are alone, and then he shoots her. Except he misses, and she shoots him right back."

"That seems to be what happened," Jasper agreed. "Bud also mentioned that he'd smuggled the murder weapon in days ago, and it was stashed above the ceiling panel in the janitor's closet. I don't know if he told you that earlier. Anyway, the main conclusion to draw from all of this is that whoever hired Bud didn't expect us to have the chance to question him. It's coming up for nine o'clock. At this point, Melody's body wasn't even supposed to have been discovered. Instead of which, it's less than four hours after the attack and we already have the outline of the murder plan."

The narrowness of her escape struck Melody with renewed force. "In fact, if Bud had succeeded in killing me, nobody would have known I was dead until Nick raised the alarm that I hadn't returned home."

"That could have been as late as midnight," Nick said. "And by then, Bud would be long gone from the gallery. Five hours gone."

"Leaving behind no evidence," Mac pointed out. "The beauty of Bud having worked for Alpha is that even if his fingerprints or traces of his DNA were found in

Melody's office, it wouldn't prove he was there at the time of the murder, much less that he was the guy doing the killing. Only thing it proves is that he was there at some time or another—probably in the course of his job."

"So there would be no reason to suspect him, much less to pin the crime on him," Nick said.

"Sophisticated planning has gone into this murder," Mac said, tugging at his chin. "Intricate pieces all have to fall into place."

"I agree." Jasper refolded the earpieces of his glasses and when he looked up again, his expression was bleak. "You've seen Bud. You've talked to him. We all know he would never have been capable of working out a murder plan with this degree of complexity. We're dealing with somebody doing the planning who's a hell of a lot smarter than the killer he hired to do the deed. That person has managed to acquire a significant amount of information about the gallery and its operations without any of us suspecting that we're being studied. The killer knows the details of the security system. He knows that Melody is almost the only gallery employee who works late—the other staff members prefer to come in early and catch up on paperwork before the gallery opens at ten. The killer knew that one day Melody would be alone in the gallery after office hours—"

"Because the killer's plan has one vital requirement if it's going to succeed," Nick said. "He has to know when Melody is working late."

Jasper nodded. "And given her erratic schedule, that isn't easy information to come by."

"I work late most nights," Melody protested.

"You work late on the days that you come in," Jasper corrected. "To an outsider, those days wouldn't be predictable. In fact, those days wouldn't be predictable to any gallery employees except Ellen, who's usually warned in advance. And to me, of course."

Nick's expression was one of almost ferocious concentration. "That suggests the killer was in touch with someone at the gallery today. Possibly Ellen. Possibly you, Jasper. Or else Melody herself."

"I didn't discuss Melody's schedule with anyone today," Jasper said. He let his response hang in the air.

Melody made a small, involuntary sound of protest. She saw the direction in which Jasper's comments were heading, and she wanted to change directions immediately before he marched them all down the road to a conclusion she didn't like.

Jasper turned to her, his gaze sympathetic. The sympathy worried her. "Did Ellen give out details of your schedule today, do you know?" he asked.

"I don't think so, but we need to check with her directly." Melody realized she was knotting and unknotting her fingers, so she tucked her hands under her thighs, where they couldn't betray her inner tension.

Nick had no reason to fear where Jasper's arguments were leading, and Melody sensed the excitement building in him as they homed in on their quarry. "The fact that Bud gave us details of how the murder was set up limits the pool of suspects in a way the murderer wouldn't have anticipated," he said. "We have a huge jump on him."

Mac snorted. "He's an arrogant bastard. You can tell from his plan. He's confident we're not going to catch him."

"That's good. It means he won't hesitate to make arrangements to pay Bud his bonus." Nick swung around to face Melody, so relieved that he was smiling. "The person trying to kill you must be somebody who knew you were staying late at the gallery tonight. That's a very small pool of suspects!"

Melody didn't respond.

Jasper leaned forward, hands clasped, albeit lightly. Only someone who knew him well would have recognized his tension. "Nick's right," he said to her. "The question for us now is quite simple. Who knew you were staying late at the gallery tonight, Melody?"

She felt a sharp stabbing sensation that began in the pit of her stomach and swelled upward, until she was consumed by pain that spread from the inside out in a burning lava flow of hurt and betrayal. She needed a few more seconds to come to terms with the horrible, sickening suspicion that had been growing for the past several minutes, and so she didn't answer Jasper's question. Instead, she asked one of her own. One she didn't care about.

"If Bud wanted to avoid being questioned in connection with the killing, why did he let you see him on your way out of the gallery?"

Jasper's response surprised her enough to offer a split-second respite from the pain of her suspicions. "What does Bud look like?" he asked.

She blinked, trying to focus through the fog of hurt.

"Long black hair. Dark brown skin. Brown eyes. Maybe slightly less than average height."

"You describe him exactly as I would have," Jasper said. "Except that Bud's hair is light brown and his skin is fair, rather than dark—as the medics discovered when they prepped him for surgery."

Nick exclaimed in surprise, "He was wearing a wig and skin dye? I can't believe he fooled us!"

"Because you were busy worrying about a hundred other things. As I was when I walked out of the gallery and almost tripped over his polishing machine." Despite the digression, Jasper wasn't about to lose track of the question Melody hadn't answered. He looked at her again, and she was sure he had already guessed what she was going to tell him. Or at the very least that she didn't like her own answer.

"So who knew that you were going to be working late tonight, Melody? Half a dozen people? Less? More?"

"Ellen knew, of course, as we already mentioned." Melody's mouth was drier than the Sahara Desert and swallowing provided no relief.

Jasper silently poured a glass of ice water and offered it to her.

"Thank you." She sipped, which cured the dryness but not the pain. "I'm sure a couple of other staff people at the gallery knew, and I suppose they might have told somebody."

"Easy enough to check that out tomorrow," Mac said.

"Who else might have known?" Jasper prompted patiently. "Did you yourself tell anyone you would be working late?"

She stared at her glass of water, which felt very cold even though her fingers were themselves icy. The molten lava flow of pain seemed to have frozen into jagged chunks of ice that chilled her from the marrow out.

"There was only one person I told myself."

"Who?" Nick demanded.

"Johnston Yates." The name echoed inside her head as well as in the sudden intense silence of the room. Johnston Yates, her biological father. The man who had been an enthusiastic partner to Wallis Beecham. The man who hadn't acknowledged her existence for almost thirty-two years. The man on whose yacht her mother had been sailing when she mysteriously tumbled overboard. It seemed she'd been right to suspect her father of wanting to kill her, Melody thought with bitter mirth. Unfortunately, in suspecting Wallis Beecham, she'd been focusing on the wrong father.

She had stunned her listeners into silence, not an easy feat with these three men. She cleared the huskiness from her throat. "Johnston called me this morning about some paintings he wants to sell. We discussed the possibility of my going around to his house tonight for a preliminary viewing of the paintings, but that turned out not to be convenient." Her voice died away, but she gulped in air and forced herself to continue. "I told him that I would be working late."

"What's his motive?" Mac demanded. "It's not enough for him to have the opportunity. He needs a motive."

"Revenge?" Melody suggested. "Maybe he lost enough money on the Bonita Partnership that Wallis Beecham persuaded him that I deserved to die." She paused. "My grandmother thinks the attacks on me are linked to my mother's death. Maybe she's right. Maybe Roz was blackmailing Johnston and he killed her. After all, she was on board his yacht when she went overboard."

Melody fell silent, chiefly because her throat had closed up so tight that she couldn't talk. All three men understood at least something of what she was feeling, but the rush of sympathy that she sensed barely scratched the surface of her ice-encased emotions. She'd grown up neglected by Roz and ignored by Wallis Beecham. Apparently she'd invested a lot more in her relationship with Johnston Yates than she'd realized, and the possibility that he'd been trying to kill her was devastating.

Nick came and knelt beside her chair. Whatever he'd planned to say remained unspoken. One look at her was enough to warn him that this was not the moment for words, or even for rational expressions of sympathy—or doubt about her conclusions. He just stood up, pulling her with him, and took her into his arms, indifferent to the presence of Mac and Jasper. He held her close, angling her head onto his chest and murmuring soothing words.

Melody was sure she would have felt grateful to Nick if she'd been able to feel anything at all. As it was, she stood within the circle of his arms, vaguely aware of his physical presence but unable to derive any comfort from it.

Jasper finally spoke. Thank God he didn't express his sympathy. In fact, he said nothing remotely personal.

He didn't even comment on her theories about why Johnston might want to kill her. Instead, he reeled off a brisk list of things for Mac and Nick to do. Melody heard various items. Others slid past her, not registering. Check on exactly how Bud was supposed to make contact with his employer. Get Nick interviewed on at least one TV station, so that he could inform the world how devastated he was by Melody's death. Run yet another cross-check of Wallis Beecham's visitors, this time to see if Johnston Yates had visited his former business partner in the months since Wallis was imprisoned.

That would be the ultimate alliance, Melody thought hysterically—the stepfather who loathed her and the biological father who had ignored her, plotting together to get rid of her. How amazing it was that she had managed to inspire so much hatred by the simple act of having been born.

"I'm really tired," she said, interrupting a discussion between Jasper and Nick as to whether he should try to get a brief spot on tonight's local news, or whether he should wait until tomorrow and arrange an interview on one of the cable networks.

Nick immediately broke off his discussion and escorted her back to the sleeping quarters that had been assigned to her. The eight-by-twelve room had its own attached bathroom, which was pure luxury by the Spartan standards of headquarters. He pointed out to her that the bathroom cabinet held basic toiletries, and the chest of drawers next to the bed was stocked with an assortment of the gray cotton knit sweatsuits that were routinely supplied to new recruits.

She murmured an acknowledgment before sitting down on the bed. Nick joined her there. When she didn't even turn her head, he framed her face in his hands, tipping her head so that she was compelled to look at him.

"Don't leap to conclusions," he said. "We haven't questioned any of the gallery staff. For all we know, Ellen or one of the sales staff could have mentioned to half a dozen people that you were planning to work late tonight. It doesn't have to be Johnston Yates. In fact, I still see no motive for him to kill you. It's not as if he needed to keep the secret that you're his daughter. That cat jumped out of the bag a long time ago."

"I know." She appreciated Nick's efforts to make her feel better, but she didn't have the energy to explain to him that she didn't actually feel bad anymore. She simply didn't feel anything at all.

He kissed her slowly and tenderly. She was aware of the brush of his lips against hers, the softness of his tongue briefly touching her teeth, and the roughness of his unshaven chin rasping against her cheek. The sensations were achingly familiar, but there was no accompanying flutter of desire, no urge to return his kiss. Just—emptiness.

He drew away from her, and she recognized that his features were drawn tight with worry.

Speaking was an effort, but if she could identify any want at all, it was to be alone. "I'm fine," she told him. "Really."

It wasn't exactly a lie. Since she felt nothing, it was

as true to say that she was fine as it would have been to say that she felt terrible.

"Would you like me to rustle up a sleeping pill?" His voice was husky with concern. His hands stroked her gently, trying to soothe, to heal the hurt.

"Thanks, but I'm sure I'll be able to sleep." That was an outright lie, but she needed to be alone so that she could lie down, pull the covers over her head and sink into darkness. The thought of waiting for Nick to come back with a sleeping pill was more than she could bear.

He gave her another worried look. Then he pushed her hair away from her forehead and kissed her one more time. "Josh is going to stand guard outside your room tonight," he said. "You don't have to worry. You're totally safe here."

She would have laughed at that, but she didn't have the energy. How could she be safe when it was a toss-up whether her father or her stepfather was trying harder to kill her? "Thank you," she said. "Good night."

"Good night, sweetheart."

She waited until Nick left the room. Then she slid down on the bed and turned her face into the pillow. She didn't cry. She'd learned when she was very small that tears couldn't make your parents love you.

Eighteen

At midnight, when Nick got back to the apartment, the blinking light on his answering machine informed him that he had four messages. One was from Ellen, Melody's assistant. The second was from Prudence Fowles, Jasper's mother. The other two were from Johnston Yates.

"Nick, I can't believe the news," Ellen said shakily. "I'm really, really sorry, Nick. This is awful. Tell me what I can do to help. Anything you need—anything, just let me know."

It was harder to deal with Ellen's sympathy than Nick would have expected, either because he felt guilty for her unnecessary sadness, or because it made the pretense of Melody's death seem too real for comfort. He wished that it wasn't necessary to deceive Melody's friends, but there was nothing he could do to relieve Ellen's grief, so he gritted his teeth and pressed the button to listen to the next message.

"Nikolai, my dear boy, I'm so very sorry." Prudence's voice shook with emotion. She was notorious for the passion with which she embraced causes, and her voice normally vibrated with the cheerful conviction that she had sorted through the muddle of other people's uncertainties and arrived at the only possible conclusion. Tonight, however, she sounded like any other frail, elderly lady.

"I can't believe that Melody is gone. She was such a shining star moving through our lives. I've no idea how Jasper will cope. She was his emotional anchor. If there's anything I can do—anything at all—you have only to say the word. You and Melody are in my prayers." She hung up, forgetting to say goodbye.

If it had been difficult to deal with Ellen's grief, it was impossible to dwell on how badly they were hurting Prudence. Telling himself that she would understand the need for the deception when she learned the truth, he clicked quickly on the next message.

"I just heard the most extraordinary report about Melody," Johnston Yates said, his tone of voice nowhere near as forceful as his words. The tape hissed through a moment of silence. "It isn't true, is it? It can't be true. No, I won't believe it. Please call me as soon as you get this message. Here's my number."

The second message from Yates had been left ten minutes later. "I didn't give you the number of my direct line the last time I called. Here it is." He repeated the number twice. "I see that CNN is also reporting that Melody has been...has been murdered. That she's dead." There was a significant pause before Yates spoke again. "Whenever you get home, Nikolai, call me. Whatever the hour, I'll be waiting."

Nick played the messages three times, trying to decide if Melody was right to be suspicious of her father. Yates sounded convincingly upset—his reluctance on the first message to come right out and say that he'd heard Melody was dead was exactly the sort of denial to be expected from a grieving father. However, the fact that Yates could fake worry and sadness didn't mean too much. They already knew he was a good actor, or he would never have managed to conceal an adulterous affair with Lady Roz while he was vice president of the United States. Clearly this was a man capable of high-level deception.

Should he call Yates back, or ignore him? If Yates was behind the attempts on Melody's life, he wanted to do nothing that would give the man cause to wonder if there was anything hokey about the news reports. How would he cope if Melody were truly dead? Nick wondered. He imagined he would be nonfunctional, close to catatonic. However, Melody's father might be among the small group of people he would summon the energy to speak with. On balance, Nick decided there would be nothing suspicious about responding to Yates's messages and that it might even be useful to hear exactly what the man had to say for himself.

He dialed the number Yates had left for him. The phone was snatched up before it completed its first ring. "Yes."

"This is Nick Anwar." He kept his voice level and drained of emotion, as if exhausted from the strain of processing too much horror in too short a period. He sounded pretty much the way Melody had sounded when he left her, Nick realized, tamping down a flash of renewed rage.

"What happened tonight?" Yates asked. "For God's sake, what happened? Was this an undercover op that went wrong?" He sounded as if he was perched on the very edge of control, ready to tumble into the abyss at any moment.

"Melody wasn't working on any undercover ops," Nick said flatly.

"Then what happened, for Christ's sake?"

"I don't know." Nick faked a choking noise, deep in his throat. "There are two valuable statues missing from the gallery—"

"You mean she was killed in the course of a burglary?"

"I don't know. Maybe."

"How…how did she die?"

"She was shot through the heart and in the stomach. Either shot could have been fatal." Nick mentioned the wounds that had been agreed upon between Mac and the director of the hospital.

"Why was she shot? Why didn't she defend herself? I don't understand." Yates was doing a great job of sounding like a distraught father trying to wrap his mind around the unimaginable. "Do the police know who did it?"

"Not yet. Melody was working late at the gallery and she was by herself. There don't seem to be any witnesses. Nobody is reporting seeing anything out of the ordinary." Nick waited for Yates to make some heart-broken comment to the effect that he had spoken to Melody only that afternoon, but he said nothing at all about his phone conversation with his daughter. Was that indicative of his guilt, or did it simply indicate the depths of his misery?

"Did she die instantly?" Yates asked. His question sounded fearful.

Because he was afraid Melody had suffered? Or because he was afraid she'd said something incriminating before she died?

Let the guy sweat a little, Nick thought. "No, she didn't die instantly. We managed to transport her to the hospital, but she died before they could get her into surgery."

"I hope she didn't...suffer. Was she unconscious when you found her?"

Nick was sorely tempted to say that Melody had been talking right up until a couple of minutes before she died, and that she'd described her murderer with exquisite clarity. But the official story was that he'd found Melody near death and that the killer had vanished before Nick arrived on the scene. Nick couldn't meddle with that story. If Yates were behind the attacks, the last thing Nick wanted was to raise doubts in the man's mind about whether Bud had earned his bonus.

"The doctors said she didn't suffer—" Nick said, allowing his voice to break. "They think she must have been unconscious from the moment the second bullet hit her heart."

"Dear God." Yates drew in a breath that ended in a muffled sob. There was another pause before he said anything more, and this time it sounded as if he spoke as much to himself as to Nick. "How could I have wasted all those years without admitting she was my daughter? What a fool I was. How utterly misplaced my concerns and values were."

Nick started to reply, and then realized he was talking to empty air. Yates had already cut the connection. Nick hung up the phone, aware that he was shaking with suppressed rage. *Hypocritical bastard.* Yates had talked just long enough to reassure himself that Melody hadn't been able to provide any useful clues about her killer, and then he'd wasted no time before hanging up.

Nick stormed into the kitchen and used his thumbs to pop the cap on a bottle of beer, then took a long, cold swallow, and another. The beer brought his emotional temperature down enough for him to realize that he needed to do a better job of maintaining at least a modicum of professional detachment. Melody's feeling of betrayal was excruciating for him to watch, but he would be no help to her if he empathized too much. He would be doing her a disservice if he fell into the trap of sharing her suspicions about Yates before they had adequate proof that her father was indeed the man behind the attempted killings.

Nick reported his phone conversation to Mac late the next morning as they walked together from the elevator to the infirmary, where Bud was recuperating from his knee surgery.

"Yates is clever," Nick conceded grudgingly. "Everything he said could have been the natural reaction of a father beside himself with shock. Or it could have been the calculated ploy of a killer, probing for information."

"I don't think there's any way to judge whether the man is acting or grieving," Mac said. "Best thing is to work with Bud and get hard proof of who's behind the attempts to kill Melody. With any luck, we'll get to the bottom of this within the next forty-eight hours. By the way, we tracked Christopher Beecham to the airport at the crack of dawn this morning. He caught the first flight out to Bermuda."

"So he's either reneging on his agreement to pay Bud an extra fifteen K, or he had nothing to do with hiring him."

"We'll soon find out which," Mac said. He cocked his head. "From your perspective, how's Melody doing this morning? Called and asked her if she wanted to have breakfast with me, but she said she preferred to eat in her room. Didn't sound like a good idea to me, but she wouldn't change her mind."

"The possibility that Yates is the person trying to kill her has hit her really hard," Nick said. "She feels so badly betrayed that she isn't even angry. She's completely flattened."

"Are you surprised?" Mac asked. "Shouldn't be."

"Not surprised, but worried," Nick admitted. "Melody is usually so strong—"

"Strong, yes, but she's human, not superwoman. Life's been a bitch for her these past couple of years. Her mother dies in mysterious circumstances. Her stepfather and stepbrother kidnap her, then try to kill her. She finds out that Jasper, the man she trusts most in the world, is chief of Unit One and has been deceiving her for years. There've been three attempts on her life in the past three months. Six months ago she learned Yates is her biological father. Now it seems possible Yates is the person who's been trying to kill her. That's heavy stuff, man."

Mac scratched his head, leaving tufts of white hair sticking up in a serrated halo. "My opinion? It's a miracle she's even semi-functional at this point. Good thing she's got you to rely on."

Nick had known and admired his boss for too many years not to understand that Mac's final casual comment hadn't been casual at all. He was sufficiently amused by Mac's snooping to summon a faint grin. "I assume that's a question, Mac, and the answer is yes. Melody and I are going to be married as soon as this mess is over."

Mac snorted, but looked delighted. "About goddamn time. Can't think why she said yes, but that's women for you. No accounting for their strange taste in men."

They'd reached the infirmary and Mac gave the day's pass code to the security guard stationed outside Bud's room. They discovered Bud sitting up in bed, watching cartoons on a TV set mounted on the wall. He greeted them with a scowl and immediately turned his gaze back to *The Simpsons*.

"How's your leg?" Mac asked.

"Lousy." Bud didn't bother to look away from the TV. "I've been butchered. I want a lawyer."

"Right, and you can have one in a couple of weeks when we turn you over to law enforcement." Mac smiled amiably. "Right now, my associate and I need to ask you some questions."

"Ask away. I ain't answering."

"Your choice." Mac didn't sound in the least put out, which clearly made Bud nervous.

He sneaked a covert glance in Mac's direction, visibly disconcerted when Mac gave him another cheery smile.

"Well, let's get down to business, shall we?" Mac perched on the end of Bud's bed, as if they were best pals. "I just need to know what arrangements you have for contacting the guy who hired you to kill Melody Beecham. Give us the details, and we'll leave you to enjoy your show."

Bud responded with a string of obscenities.

Ignoring the cussing, Mac hopped off the bed, stuck his head around the door and spoke to the guard posted outside. "Get Dr. Franks to come in here, would you? Tell him to bring the truth serum. And let him know we're in a big hurry."

"Yessir. I'm on it." The guard left at once.

Nick spoke to Mac in a low voice, although he made sure Bud could hear what he was saying. "Do we have to go straight to the truth serum, Mac? That's so extreme. Maybe we could try something else first. Something that doesn't have such drastic consequences."

Mac shook his head. "No time. We need this information. Bud won't talk, so it has to be the truth serum."

"Truth serum?" Bud said scornfully. He might not have an overly large vocabulary, but that caught his attention. He looked at Mac, his expression dismissive. "There ain't no such thing as truth serum. Ain't nothin' can make me talk if I don't wanna."

"Sure there is." Mac bounced around the room, jingling the change in his pants pocket. "You've probably noticed, Bud, that we're not an organization that pays too much attention to the law. We have a truth serum that works. And, trust me, we're not talking about using a wussy drug like sodium pentothal."

"Whatcha talkin' about, then?"

"Anthocyanine," Mac said promptly.

"What's that? Never heard of it."

"I'm sure you haven't. It's a top-secret derivative of LSD that they developed over at the CIA for use on terrorists. You want to see an al-Qaeda operative whimper, all you have to do is say anthocyanine. Its effects are real interesting. As soon as it's injected into your bloodstream, you start tripping, just as if you were on regular acid. Except you're not quite off in la-la land. You're just about halfway there, and any questions we ask, you give us the answers. From our point of view, it's a great drug. From your point of view, however, it's not so great. Not only do you spill everything you know, but this is a drug with *real* interesting aftereffects."

"What's that mean? Whatcha talkin' about?"

Nick leaned forward and spoke softly, as if confiding a truth too embarrassing to speak out loud. "It leaves you impotent, Buddy-boy. One shot of this drug, and you're totally and completely impotent. For life."

"Impotent?" Bud looked appalled.

"Yep," Mac said. "Once we inject you with this drug, your sex life's finished. You'll never be able to get it up again. And I mean never."

"I don't believe you." Bud, however, looked as if he believed every word.

With impeccable timing, Dr. Franks came into the room carrying a stainless-steel tray loaded with several items, of which the most visible was a very large syringe. He gave the occupants of the room a cheerful salute. "Morning, Mac. Nick. You need me to inject truth serum into the patient?"

"Afraid so," Mac replied. "He's not willing to cooperate."

The doctor picked up the syringe and stuck the needle into a small bottle filled with an ominous-looking dark purple liquid. "Has he been warned of the consequences?"

"We told him," Nick said.

Dr. Frank looked at Bud, who was by now cowering under the covers. "Before I inject you, I want to be sure you understand that the consequences will be lifelong sexual dysfunction, and complete inability to attain orgasm—"

Nick interrupted. "What the doc's trying to tell you, Bud, is the same as we told you already. You're never going to get it up again. The minute that needle hits your vein, it's all over."

"You can't do that. I have rights."

Nick laughed. "Yeah, tell me about 'em. Mac, you strap his right arm to the bed. I'll take his left—"

"No! Don't stick that needle into me!" Bud squirmed in panic.

"Then answer our questions," Nick said, keeping hold of Bud's arm. "If you don't want the needle, then talk to us."

Bud looked at Nick with real hatred. "What do you want to know?"

"How are you supposed to get in touch with the guy who hired you to kill Melody Beecham?" Nick asked. "That's all, Bud. Nothing difficult."

It took a few more threats, but Bud eventually repeated his earlier story that he was supposed to contact the man who'd hired him by meeting online in a chat room. His employer would be in a chat room for fly fishermen for ten minutes starting at 3:00 p.m. each afternoon for the next four days. Bud had the exact URL of the chat room written down in a notebook that he kept in his lodging house, but he swore he didn't remember the details except that he was to use the online name of PurpleBassPopper and his contact would use the name HummerWoolyWorm.

"Those are flies for catchin' fish," Bud said. "In case you didn't know."

Mac and Nick ended the interview moments later, leaving Dr. Frank to remove his syringe and vial of anthocyanine, otherwise known as grape juice, while they hurried back to Mac's office. Nick dispatched Josh to Bud's lodging house to retrieve the notebook containing the address of the chat room. Mac, meanwhile, was caught up fielding an irate phone call from New York's chief of police, followed by an even more irate phone call from the director of the hospital, whose panic was mounting in direct proportion to the number of inquiries about Melody's death that he'd received from journalists.

Nick left Mac to soothe officialdom and made his

way to Melody's room. He found her dressed and sitting cross-legged on the bed. She had a copy of *The New Yorker* open on her lap, but it was all too obvious that she wasn't reading it.

He took the magazine from her lap and sat down next to her, telling her about Bud, and the impotence drug, and almost making her smile. But then she remembered why it was that they were questioning Bud and her smile died.

"Why does my father want to kill me?" she asked. "There's no good reason for him to want me dead. It's not as if he's planning to run for president, or any other public office."

"You're jumping to conclusions," he said, hoping to God that was true. "We have no proof that Johnston Yates is responsible for the attacks on you. And he has no real motive."

She nodded in polite acknowledgment, but he knew he wasn't getting through to her. Unfortunately, she knew as well as he did that murderers often killed for reasons that seemed inadequate or even bizarre to normal people. He tried again to reassure her, hating the resignation in her eyes and the defeated slump of her shoulders.

"Jasper questioned the gallery staff this morning, and it turns out that several of them knew you planned to work late last night," he said. "Don't give up, Melody. We haven't had a chance to unravel the threads of all the people who might have been in a position to organize Bud's attack on you."

He needed all his powers of persuasion to convince her

to eat lunch with him in Mac's office, but she perked up when Josh called in from Bud's lodging house in Queens to give them the URL for the chat room, and by the time they all congregated in Bob Spinard's office for the three o'clock cyber meeting with HummerWoolyWorm, she had shaken off her lethargy. She asked Mac if she could be the one to impersonate Bud, and he agreed.

"What are the chances that you'll be able to track this HummerWoolyWorm person's physical location?" she asked Bob, sitting down at a monitor across the desk from his.

"It depends how sophisticated his cover is and how long he stays online," Bob said. "If he's using a wireless connection, it's going to be almost impossible. If he suggests going into a private chat room, say yes. That'll give me more time to catch up with him."

Melody entered the chat room at one minute to three. There were sixteen cyber occupants when she entered, but HummerWoolyWorm wasn't one of them. However, two minutes later, his name showed up on the list of participants.

Melody typed in her message, and Nick could see that her fingers shook a little on the keys. Since Bud wasn't a man who seemed likely to go for the subtle approach, they'd decided on something direct, simple and lacking in punctuation.

I did it, she wrote. *Youve seen the news now you owe me.*

Hopefully, the other participants in the chat room would assume PurpleBassPopper was talking about catching a big fish, and collecting on a bet.

HummerWoolyWorm responded within seconds, instructing Bud to follow him into a private chat room. Once there, he wasted no time.

Go to Chat-a-Latte Internet Café at the intersection of Columbus and West Ninety-sixth in Manhattan. Be there at three tomorrow afternoon. Access this same chat room from one of the café's computers. I'll give you precise directions at that time on where to pick up your money.

Melody quickly keyed in *Tell me now* but there was no response from HummerWoolyWorm and Bob confirmed that he had gone offline.

"Did you trace WoolyWorm's location?" Mac asked as Melody regretfully signed out of the empty chat room.

Bob nodded. "It was a snap to locate him. He didn't have any security protocols in place, and he made no attempt to disguise the routing of his signal. He was communicating from a computer located at the intersection of Columbus and West Ninety-sixth. In other words, most likely from the cyber café where he told Bud to go tomorrow."

"Then we can eliminate Christopher Beecham as a suspect," Nick said. "We have confirmation that he's back in Bermuda."

"We should go to the café right now." Melody was on her feet. "We'll take a picture of Johnston Yates and show it around. We'll ask if anyone recognizes him—"

"Sorry, Melody. No can do." Mac gently pushed her back into her seat, saving Nick the task. "In the first place, there's a good chance we'd go bounding into the café and nobody would recognize Johnston's picture even if he is the man behind the attempted killings. Let's face it, patrons of a cyber café aren't usually the types known for nurturing a burning interest in their fellow human beings. Secondly, why on earth would we do anything that might give WoolyWorm cold feet? We don't know for sure that WoolyWorm is actually Johnston Yates. That means we could go in there while the real murderer is sitting in a corner of the café watching us make our inquiries. He'd realize at once that we're closing in on him and he'd run like hell. At a minimum Bud could kiss his bonus payment goodbye. Talk about blowing our best chance of getting the evidence we need to put him away!"

Nick could see Melody struggling to adjust to the fact that she would have to wait an entire twenty-four hours before they could identify the person who had been trying to kill her. Some of her punch had come back as she sat at the computer, though, and she won the battle.

"Come to my office and I'll bring you up-to-date on the investigation," he said. "Among other things, we have a video clip of your grandmother talking to reporters in England. You were right. She handles them brilliantly."

Melody produced her first real smile of the day. "Told you so," she said.

Nineteen

The task force assigned to effect the identification and capture of WoolyWorm consisted of Unit One's four most skilled field agents and three more technical analysts working back at headquarters under Bob Spinard's supervision. Intense planning had filled much of the previous twenty-three hours, and despite their years of accumulated experience, all four agents were on edge. WoolyWorm had tried twice to kill one of their own, and they were determined to bring him down.

By two-thirty in the afternoon, Sam and Josh, in separate cars, were each circling a different ten-block radius around Chat-a-Latte Internet Café, ready to rush to whatever location WoolyWorm indicated in his next message. Tony, whose height and body build resembled Bud's more closely than did any of Unit One's other agents, waited with Nick in a parked panel truck bearing the phone company logo. Tony wore a thin latex mask, made from a mold of Bud's face, and his light brown hair had been buzz-cut to imitate Bud's natural hairstyle.

At two forty-five, Tony would be the person to enter Chat-a-Latte's and make contact with WoolyWorm and he needed to look as much as possible like the real Bud Silveira. It seemed unlikely that WoolyWorm would also be in the café, but they needed to be prepared for that possibility. Bob Spinard had already established a link with the café's computer network and he would be able to monitor everything Tony wrote and everything WoolyWorm replied. In addition, Bob hoped to get a physical location fix on WoolyWorm in case he was far away from the drop-off site for Bud's payoff.

Nick was also disguised with a latex face mask and a blond wig, since anybody wanting to murder Melody was likely to know Nick at least by sight. All four agents were wired for sound. They had microchip implants that enabled Bob Spinard's team to keep track of their movements, and all four carried networked communicators, designed to look like cell phones. One of the advantages of the explosion in cell phone use by the general population was that field agents no longer had to huddle in corners and talk into their sleeves like FBI agents in bad movies. These days they could pull out a cell phone and chatter away without raising anyone's suspicions.

Melody, to her major frustration, had been left at headquarters, stationed in Mac's office so that she would be at the center of the communications hub. Much as she yearned to be actively involved in Wooly-Worm's capture, she understood that there was no disguise good enough to ensure that her presence wouldn't blow the entire operation. Condemned to inactivity, she paced the floor—for once, more fidgety than Mac, and drinking as much coffee as he used to in the old days.

She wasn't at all sure that WoolyWorm was going to show, despite yesterday's positive cyber message. From WoolyWorm's perspective, there were obvious advantages to dangling the offer of a reward in front of Bud. However, that didn't mean he intended to fulfill his promise. Bud's insistence on claiming his bonus left WoolyWorm facing a set of nasty choices. If he didn't pay up, he ran the risk of angering Bud, who might talk to the police or even make a focused effort to discover WoolyWorm's true identity. But paying the money as promised carried its own inherent set of problems. If WoolyWorm hid the money too early, or too far from the cyber café, it might be stolen, or at least discovered, before Bud arrived to collect it. If he hid it only moments before Bud arrived for the pickup, then there was a chance he might be spotted by Bud.

But would Bud recognize his employer even if the two men met face-to-face? Melody wondered. More to the point, would Bud care enough to look? As Mac pointed out, WoolyWorm must realize by now that Bud wasn't gifted with an inquiring mind. Melody's fear was that Bud's lack of curiosity might encourage WoolyWorm to renege on his debt. Why pay Bud fifteen thousand dollars when there seemed so little chance that Bud would ever be able to identify the person who'd hired him?

Nick, Mac and Sam took the opposite view. Since

there was so little chance of being recognized, Wooly-Worm was likely to hover at the drop site to make sure that Bud collected his payoff. Fifteen thousand wasn't all that much money to a man like Johnston Yates—assuming he was the killer—and watching Bud pick up the money would reassure him that the final thread in Melody's murder had been tied off.

At two forty-five, Mac gave the word to start the operation. Tony went into Chat-a-Latte four minutes ahead of Nick, and was already settled at a computer station when Nick walked in. Nick bought half an hour of computer time, and followed Tony into the fly-fishing chat room. HummerWoolyWorm was not yet online, and Nick spent a few minutes covertly studying the other people in the café.

Three men, all of them in their twenties, and each one more geekish than the last, sat at terminals along the wall. He knew firsthand the miraculous transformations that could be achieved with clever makeup, and it was possible that their grunge look was an artful disguise. Age, however, could only be faked upward, or a very few years downward. There was no chance at all that any of the men were Johnston Yates, and he could think of few reasons why a twenty-year-old computer nerd would want to murder Melody.

The only other occupant of the café was a young woman seated at the prime corner table. She looked as if she might be as old as thirty, but no more. Quite apart from the fact that she was the wrong sex to be a suspect, nothing about her struck Nick as offering the least cause for alarm. He and Mac had decided during their brainstorming sessions that WoolyWorm was unlikely to risk sitting in Chat-a-Latte at the same time as Bud. None of the computer users in the café provided him with a reason to change that opinion.

Keeping half an eye on the other occupants of the café, in case he was underestimating their murderous potential, he turned his attention back to the chat room. HummerWoolyWorm still wasn't listed as present. To a man who had never understood the joy of standing hip deep in icy water without any certainty that you were actually going to catch your dinner, the passion with which the chat room occupants discussed the white fly hatch on Pennsylvania's Susquehanna River was astonishing. And who knew that the south fork of the Snake River was the best place to catch cutthroats? Which, Nick could only assume, were fish rather than criminals.

HummerWoolyWorm entered the chat room.

Nick's spine gave an involuntary jerk. Trying not to make his interest too obvious, he watched Tony type in his message. He knew exactly what it said, because the wording had been agreed on beforehand.

Its Bud Im here.

Once again, HummerWoolyWorm invited Bud into a private chat room. Nick didn't dare to follow. According to Bob Spinard's analysis, nothing about yesterday's cyber-encounter with WoolyWorm suggested that the man was a sophisticated tech nerd, but it didn't require much expertise to detect a lurker in a private chat room. Nick tried to look as if he was fascinated by the screen in front of him, but his tension rose exponentially as Tony continued to type. Melody had literally staked her life on this single chance to identify the man attempting to kill her, and he couldn't bear to contemplate the possibility that their high-stakes gamble might not work.

It was an agonizingly long three minutes before Tony took his scarf from the back of his chair and placed it on the right side of the computer monitor—their agreed signal to show that he had been successful in getting directions. Nick immediately logged out of the chat room and exited the café.

He picked up the traffic cones that they'd placed around the truck and tossed them into the back. Tony came running up just as he was climbing behind the wheel.

"I have the directions," Tony said. "The money's going to be in a prayer book on the third pew from the back, left hand side, in Our Lady of Lourdes Church on 106th Street and Broadway."

"He's paying you off in a church?" Nick was shocked, although he didn't quite know why. If a person had a sufficiently warped mind or blunted moral sense that he was willing to arrange for the murder of a fellow human being, presumably his conscience wasn't going to trouble him if the transaction was finalized in a sacred building.

"Yeah," Tony said. "He thinks I'm getting there on foot, so if you drive fast, we might catch him in the act. Obviously, he can't leave the money lying around for too long. That's not the best of neighborhoods and it's likely to get found—and stolen."

"Sam or Josh might be closer to the church." Nick

was already heading north. "Give them the directions but tell them whatever they do, don't scare off Wooly-Worm. That's the number one priority. Oh, and tell Mac where we're headed."

Out of consideration for his boss's lovesick state, Tony was charitable enough to refrain from pointing out that Sam and Josh, being experienced field agents, both grasped the concept that the purpose of the operation was to arrest WoolyWorm, not send him running. He bit off a sarcastic comment and called in to Mac to report that they were headed to 106th Street and Broadway.

Bob Spinard had successfully monitored the online communication between Tony and WoolyWorm, so Mac already knew that Bud's final payoff was going to be hidden in Our Lady of Lourdes Church. Mac, in turn, was able to pass on the information that Wooly-Worm had been physically located at 106th Street during his cyber chat with Tony. This was a big relief to everyone, since there had always been the fear that WoolyWorm would stash the money hours in advance of Bud's supposed arrival and be long gone by the time the Unit One team arrived to make the pickup.

"Open your communication link," Tony said to Nick when Mac signed off. "Melody wants to say something to all four of us." He buzzed Sam and Josh, so that they would know to access their devices.

When Melody came on the line, Nick was relieved to hear that she sounded much more cheerful. "I'll be quick as I can, guys, because I know you're rushing to the drop-off site. But ever since Bud tried to kill me, I've had this niggling sensation that I was missing something significant. Everything we know about WoolyWorm suggests he's a detail-oriented person, right? His arrangements for being in touch with Bud after my death are not only complicated, they're painstaking. He obviously wants every last loophole closed off without any clue leading back to him.

"I checked with Mac, and he agreed with my assessment. I realized how odd it is that WoolyWorm has paid two people to kill me, neither of whom had any significant skills as marksmen. And even less in hand-to-hand combat."

"It is odd," Nick agreed, fingers drumming on the steering wheel as a traffic light forced the van to a halt. "But I'm not sure it means anything."

"I think it means a lot. I survived Jorge's attack in Mexico in part because you turned up unexpectedly, Nick, and at just the right moment. But if Jorge had been a better fighter, I'd have been dead before you arrived.

"It's almost the same story with Bud. Yes, I got lucky and happened to walk out of my office just as he was planning to launch his attack, but I had the combat skills to take advantage of my luck. It was easy for me because Unit One has spent hours and hours training me, and Bud wasn't expecting me to fight back. He said as much when we were questioning him, remember? Something like *nobody warned me you were going to make like one of Charlie's Angels.*"

"I agree that Bud is a thug, pure and simple, with no combat training," Nick said. "Unless you count brawls in the prison exercise yard, where victory depends more on hitting first and having backup thugs on your side."

"Exactly. Bottom line, Bud wasn't prepared for the situation he found himself in. When I fought back, he had no plan B. Why not? Because the murder plan was designed by WoolyWorm, and WoolyWorm had no idea that I have experience and training to defend myself against killers. Bud was caught totally off guard."

Nick drew in a sharp breath, belatedly grasping the significance of Melody's insight. "You think Wooly-Worm is unaware of the fact that you're an operative for Unit One. He can't know that, or he would have hired a different type of killer."

"Bingo!" Melody said. "We've been searching for WoolyWorm's identity in all the wrong places. Every single person we've considered as a suspect knows that I work for Unit One. But it's obvious WoolyWorm doesn't know that. He hasn't a clue that I can be counted on to fight back when I'm threatened. Or that I'm trained to anticipate attacks at unlikely times in unlikely places."

"In other words, WoolyWorm can't be Johnston Yates," Nick said, suddenly understanding why Melody sounded so happy. "Yates has not only seen you in action, he's alive today because you shot two professional assassins before they could kill him. He's intimately aware of your skills. If he wanted you dead, he would send brains and talent to kill you, not brawn and muscle. WoolyWorm did the opposite."

"Yes. If my father had wanted to kill me, he'd have known that he needed to hire the best marksmen his money could buy. I can't believe that it took me all this time to figure out something so simple."

"You did have a few other things on your mind, like the trivial fact that you'd just dodged your third set of bullets in three months."

She laughed. "I guess that many bullets whizzing past your head does tend to cloud your thought processes."

The sound of her laughter rippled over Nick like a balm. "When it seemed that Johnston was one of the few people who had the knowledge necessary to kill you, you faced your worst fear and decided you had no choice but to embrace it."

"Not quite my worst fear," she said, not caring that Mac, Sam, Tony and Josh were all listening to the conversation. "Losing you is my worst fear."

"Not going to happen, honey. I'm planning to hang around for at least the next seventy years." Nick suppressed a growing sensation of exuberance. Worry about her father's guilt had been devastating to Melody's psyche, and he was relieved that she had freed herself of her doubts. Her reasoning about WoolyWorm made absolute sense. However, just as professional caution had required him to doubt Johnston Yates's guilt, that same caution now required him to consider the possibility, however slight, that the man wasn't innocent.

He didn't mention his tiny, lingering doubt to Melody. "We appreciate the tip," he said. "We would have gone into the church looking for somebody trying to disguise the fact that he was a six foot-two inch, sixty-six-year-old man. Now we'll be more open-minded. Or clueless as to what we're looking for is another way of expressing it."

"We've arrived," Tony said. "Gotta go, Melody. We'll report in as soon as we have your killer under arrest."

Nick sincerely hoped that Tony's optimism would prove justified. He drove through the intersection and parked the van halfway down the next block, circling the vehicle with cones to ensure that the traffic cops didn't tow it away. He and Tony jogged back toward the church, dodging around clusters of teenagers and quite a few adults. There was a school right next door to the church, Nick realized, his stomach knotting as he surveyed the crowds.

"School just let out," Tony said. "Holy shit! How are we supposed to spot WoolyWorm in this mob scene?"

"With difficulty," Nick said. "Time for us to split up. We don't want WoolyWorm to see us together." Quite apart from the difficulty of recognizing their target in the crowd, he worried about avoiding injuries to innocent bystanders if the guy started shooting. His admiration for WoolyWorm increased, albeit reluctantly. Arranging for Bud to collect his fifteen K bonus at the precise time school let out was yet another example of clever planning. Still, what worked to conceal Wooly-Worm's identity also made Nick and the other Unit One agents less noticeable. They would just have to make sure that they apprehended WoolyWorm inside the church, he decided, and not allow him to escape onto the crowded sidewalk.

Nick climbed the steps that led to the covered portico of the church, aware that Tony was following a few yards behind. Bud would certainly have entered the church alone to claim his killing bonus, so Tony would do the same.

By fortunate coincidence, a couple of teenage girls were hanging around the imposing entrance doors engrossed in conversation, but when Nick stepped inside, they chose to enter. He kept as close to the pair as he could without freaking them out. If WoolyWorm noticed him, Nick hoped that he might appear to be a teacher with two of his students.

Once inside the nave, Nick skirted the baptismal font, then cast a quick, comprehensive glance around the expansive interior. This was a huge church, probably at least a hundred years old, with a soaring, arched ceiling and pillars leading to side chapels, very much in the European style. Wall niches housed statues of saints, some stone, some painted plaster, and there were a hundred nooks and crannies in which WoolyWorm could hide.

And that was before he took into account the choir and organ loft that occupied a second level directly over the entrance.

Josh was nowhere to be seen, but Sam was already inside the church and he looked right at home, lighting a candle in front of a statue of the Virgin Mary. Sam had been raised a Catholic, and despite two divorces and a thousand other violations of doctrine, he retained an emotional connection to the church of his childhood. Clearly at ease with the ritual, he genuflected and stepped back from the bank of candles, sliding into a side pew that, Nick realized, provided him with as close to a panoramic view as was possible without standing at the altar and looking back into the nave.

He spoke quietly into his communicator, careful not to look in Sam's direction. "Where's Josh?"

"In the choir loft," Josh's voice replied. "There's nobody up here but me. I'll come down now and guard the exit. We don't want WoolyWorm escaping into that mob of high school kids."

"Good plan," Nick murmured. "Sam, you scope out the left side of the church, I'll take the right."

The church was nowhere near as crowded as the sidewalk. Nick counted only five people in the echoing building, apart from himself, Sam and Josh. A nun was removing dead blooms from a giant vase of flowers that decorated the carpeted steps leading up to the altar. A middle-aged and muscular priest was walking from pew to pew, tidying missals and gathering up mass cards. On the right of the church, in a side aisle, an elderly woman was seated near the confession box, apparently waiting for a priest to arrive.

The two teenagers who had entered the church at the same time as Nick made their way to the confession box, and took seats behind the elderly woman. Nick slipped into a seat across from the trio and studied the woman at close quarters, just in case she might be WoolyWorm wearing a clever disguise. There was nothing like dressing up as a member of the opposite sex to confuse pursuers. But this woman was really a woman, Nick concluded. Her sparse gray hair showed tiny patches of pink scalp, and her hands were delicate and utterly feminine. Not his quarry, he decided.

He sat back and scanned the church again. Of the half-dozen choices, the priest tidying up the pews seemed far and away the most likely candidate to be WoolyWorm—more especially since he was steadily working his way toward the rear of the church and the designated pew. His muscular build suggested that he either worked out more frequently than most parish priests could find time for, or he wasn't really a priest. Next to dressing up as a member of the opposite sex, donning a uniform—as a priest, or fireman or airline pilot—came close in terms of effectiveness for disguise. People instinctively looked at the uniform, not the person wearing it.

Tony finally entered the church, and Nick moved quietly toward the main aisle. He had deliberately stayed away from the rear pews until now because he didn't want to draw the priest's attention. Concealed behind a fat stone pillar, Nick watched as Tony sat down in the third pew and opened one of the prayer books. He flipped through the pages, found nothing, and set it back in the rack. He took the next prayer book and repeated the search. Fifteen thousand in hundred-dollar bills was going to be a tight fit even if the interior of the book was hollowed out. Tony was riffling through the pages in order to give Sam and Nick more time to identify WoolyWorm, not because he really expected to find the money there.

The priest was definitely watching Tony. His pretense of tidying up the pews and collecting Mass cards was becoming less convincing with every second that passed. He appeared to be poised to approach Tony and speak to him. Tony was probably having a hard time right now calculating how the real Bud would behave. Would Bud try to find the money as quickly and inconspicuously as possible? Or would bravado get the better of him and would he attempt to lure the priest into talking to him?

Very quietly, Nick stood up. At the far left side of the church, he saw Sam also rise to his feet. Clearly, he was suspicious of the priest, too, and was getting ready to move in. Timing was a delicate matter here. Unit One didn't have to abide by the evidentiary rules of more orthodox law enforcement agencies such as the FBI. On the other hand, just from the point of view of pressuring a confession out of WoolyWorm, it would be helpful if the priest could be tricked into displaying some knowledge of what Bud was searching for.

Tony opened another prayer book. Even from where he was standing, Nick could see that the inside had been hollowed out, and money had been stashed into the hollow. There was no longer any excuse for Tony to stay in the church, and the priest still hadn't approached him.

Maybe he should move in and pretend to steal the money, Nick thought. That ought to provoke a reaction from the priest. He started to cross the central aisle. In his peripheral vision he saw that the nun had stopped fussing with the altar flowers and was now marching briskly toward the exit. He didn't want to involve her in a robbery, even a fake one, so he stopped to let her pass.

She smiled at him and murmured a word of thanks. For a split second, Nick thought that his heart had stopped beating before it raced forward again in triple time.

The woman wearing the nun's simple gray dress and short black veil was none other than Cynthia Yates.

Twenty

It took Nick a moment to recall that he was wearing a face mask and that, although he had recognized Cynthia Yates, she hadn't recognized him. Yet another moment ticked past before he remembered that neither Sam nor Tony had ever met Cynthia and that they would have no idea why he was standing in the middle of the church, staring at an elderly nun, no doubt looking as if he'd been poleaxed.

Cynthia might not have recognized him, but she picked up on the intensity of his shock. Her smile froze and she started to run. Nick's instinctive reluctance to manhandle an elderly woman burned away in a cascading wave of white-hot anger. This was the person who had tried to kill Melody, and he was seized by a primitive desire to retaliate.

Battling to keep his rage from rampaging out of control, he grabbed Cynthia as she tried to dodge past him. He used almost no force, but she stumbled and would have fallen if he hadn't caught her. The arm he clamped around her upper body acted half as a support and half as a restraint. Her knees kept buckling, making him aware of how frail she was physically despite the havoc she had wreaked on Melody's life.

"Let me go!" she shrieked. "Monster! Rapist!"

"Behind you! Look out!" Sam's shout from across the church provided Nick with just enough warning for him to swing around and avoid the worst of the blow aimed at him by the priest. Thanks to Sam's shout, the double-handed hit landed hard on Nick's shoulder instead of on the back of his neck. Judging by the force behind the swing, the priest's muscles were very much for real. Pain shot down Nick's arm, paralyzing him for a crucial second.

If Cynthia had been stronger or more agile she would easily have shaken off his grip. As it was, Nick managed to hold onto her with one hand and ward off the priest's second blow with the other. He was aided by the fact that Cynthia wasted a lot of energy screaming for help.

"Run, Sister! Run! Call the police!" The priest sounded breathless but determined as he attempted to move in close enough to pry Nick's restraining arm away from Cynthia's shoulders. The poor guy obviously thought he was saving a helpless innocent from vicious attack, Nick thought in frustration.

There was no choice but to be ruthless. Without turning around, Nick shoved his elbow into the priest's midriff with brutal force and simultaneously hooked his foot around the priest's ankle. The priest toppled to the ground with a heavy thud, retching as he fell.

Nick winced. "Sorry, Father." His sympathy didn't extend to the point of allowing the priest any chance to recover. He planted his foot squarely on the man's heaving stomach, simultaneously lunging forward to grab Cynthia as she attempted to flee for the second time. He caught her left arm, but he was off balance because of the need to hold the priest pinned to the ground, and she was able to twist around, although his grip on her never loosened.

Cynthia made a last desperate attempt to free herself by scratching his eyes. Nick jerked his head out of reach and her nails raked down his cheeks, tearing off strips of the face mask and even scraping his underlying skin. When the latex started to peel off, she recoiled with a convulsive jerk.

Nick grabbed Cynthia's clawing hands and reeled her in, his patience exhausted. He dragged her arms behind her back, indifferent to her mewling and her trembling. As he ripped off her veil to tie her wrists, he noticed that Tony and Sam were both standing nearby, watching him in silent approval.

"Feel free to join in and help anytime," he said.

"You seem to have everything under control," Sam replied. "I take it that the woman you're tying up is WoolyWorm. How the hell did you identify her?"

"I recognized her," Nick said. He swung her around to face Tony and Sam. "This is Cynthia Yates."

Sam's eyes widened. "As in—the wife of Johnston Yates?"

"That's the one."

"I'll be damned."

"Yes, you probably will," Nick said. "In the meantime, there's an elderly priest, a terrified old lady and two teenagers cowering by the confessional box. You could try to earn a few points toward salvation by reassuring them that they're not about to be robbed, raped or murdered."

"Sure." Sam gave a mock salute. "I have some FBI identification with me. That always seems to reassure people."

"Go for it," Nick said. He looked down at the priest, still pinned to the ground by the pressure of his foot. The poor man had landed hard on the stone floor. He was sufficiently recovered to be squirming, but not yet capable of breaking free.

"I'm sorry to have been so rough, Father, but the nun isn't a nun, despite her veil. She's a killer, and we're law enforcement officials."

"Show me...your...ID," the priest panted.

"Tony, you take care of the explanations. Josh, can you hear me?"

"Yessir." Josh's voice reverberated clearly in Nick's ear mike.

"Help me escort Cynthia to the van. Tony, I'll meet you back there in a few minutes when you've finished up in here."

Tony took over guarding the priest, and Nick propelled a newly quiescent Cynthia to the carved oak doors that marked the exit from the nave. He discovered Josh trying to persuade a pair of parishioners that the church building would reopen for its regularly scheduled activities in half an hour.

The couple had been arguing with Josh, but they stopped to stare at Nick in slack-jawed horror before beating a hasty retreat. Nick was too anxious to get Cynthia locked up in the van to waste time wondering why he had inspired such fear.

"Okay," he said to Josh. "Let's move it. I want to attract as little attention as possible getting Cynthia back to the van."

"In that case I'm going to rip off some of those strips of latex you have hanging from your cheeks," Josh said, tugging as he spoke. "Even for blasé Manhattan, you look gruesome enough to turn heads." He worked for a moment or two, and then stepped back. "Okay, that's better. Now you merely look weird as opposed to certifiably nuts."

Cynthia had started moaning again, but her moans stopped as Josh finished ripping off the mask. Tossing her head back, she glared at Nick, her eyes coming alive with hatred as recognition dawned. "I know who you are. You're Nick, Melody's Nick."

Nick met her gaze. "Yes, I am. And you're Cynthia Yates, the murdering bitch who tried to kill her."

"*Tried* to kill her?" Cynthia's mouth twisted into a gloating smile. "I didn't just try. I succeeded. Melody Beecham is dead, shot through the heart and the stomach."

Nick didn't correct Cynthia's mistake. "I'm surprised you sound so pleased with yourself," he said. "You're about to be charged with soliciting murder, which means you're likely to spend the rest of your life in prison."

She gave an incongruous giggle, her expression still gloating. "You seem to have forgotten that I'm the wife of Johnston Yates. Have you any idea how powerful he still is? How many connections he has to the highest levels of government?"

"I'm sure his connections aren't powerful enough to get you off a murder charge."

"Then you're a lot more naive than I would have expected for a man who's reputed to have connections to the Russian mafia. Money and political power are an unbeatable combination, as you must know." She shrugged, giving him no chance to reply. "Besides, I'm rich enough to hire the world's best lawyers. On top of which, I'm seventy years old and I look like everyone's little old grandmother. I'm not likely to see the inside of a prison for more than a couple of hours, much less spend the rest of my life there."

"You could be right about that," Nick said. He was almost more astonished by Cynthia's cold appraisal of her chances for evading punishment than he had been by the discovery that she was the person behind the attempts on Melody's life. She sounded rational, and yet she hadn't demanded a lawyer, and she'd raised no questions about being taken into custody by a man she believed to be an international oil broker. Or was she simply assuming that he'd come in pursuit of her as a private citizen, because he was Melody's lover?

Whatever the case, Nick felt a surge of almost vicious pleasure at the prospect of informing her that one major element in her calculation was far off base. With an exercise of considerable will, he resisted the temptation to break the news of Melody's survival. He didn't want to silence Cynthia's flow of triumphant admissions.

"I assume you're going to plead insanity," he said to her. "Personally, I'm not sure that an asylum for the criminally insane is going to be any more fun than prison."

"Maybe not." Cynthia tossed her head, the gesture as much impatient as defiant. "I don't care what happens to me now. I've won. Melody Beecham and her whore of a mother are both roasting in hell. Johnny has lost his precious daughter, and my beautiful little baby boy is avenged at last. I've won!"

Her beautiful little baby? Nick had never heard any mention that Cynthia had given birth. Was she delusional? "You waited a long time to avenge your baby's death," he said. It seemed a safe comment. Cynthia was in her seventies, so any baby of hers must surely have been born at least thirty years earlier.

Her gaze slid toward the oncoming traffic. Nick and Josh both tightened their hold on her arms. No way either one of them was going to allow Cynthia to evade punishment by killing herself.

Cynthia looked at Nick again, becoming almost introspective. "For the last thirty years, I've had Johnny all to myself, and totally in my power. There was no reason for me to kill Roz as long as she was willing to let the world believe that Wallis Beecham was Melody's father. For twenty-eight years, Roz not only kept up the pretense, she forbade Johnny to go anywhere near Melody. That was just fine and dandy with me. All those years the two of them kept the secret—and then Roz had to ruin everything. Just like she always ruined everything. If Roz had stuck to her agreement with Johnny, she'd be alive to this day. As it was, she left me no choice. I had to kill her."

Cynthia's casual confession that she'd killed Lady Roz hit Nick with the force of a kick aimed straight at his gut. Melody had been so right to suspect that her mother's death was murder, not suicide or an accident. And Melody's grandmother had been spot-on with her assertion that the person trying to kill Melody was likely to be the same person who had murdered Roz. He wondered what distorted piece of logic had Cynthia transferring her murderous rage to Melody once Lady Roz died.

"Is that why you invited Lady Roz to sail with you in the Caribbean?" he asked Cynthia. "So that it would be easier for you to kill her and make it look like an accident?"

"Why else would I have allowed Johnny to invite that not-so-high-class whore to join a party on *my* yacht? If I hadn't planned to get rid of her, I never would have dreamed of it." Cynthia sniffed, genuinely insulted by Nick's question. "Good God, I have some respect for the institution of holy matrimony, even if nobody else does these days. With Roz on board, my yacht was the next best thing to a floating brothel."

"How long had you been planning to kill Lady Roz?" Nick asked, confident that his colleagues back at Unit One were hearing every word of Cynthia's confession. "Pushing her overboard couldn't have been a spur-of-the-moment thing."

"I planned for a couple of months. I'm good at planning. I drugged the wine, and put an emetic in Roz's birthday cake so that everyone was puking like crazy. The storm came up and they thought it was seasickness. The storm was a sign from God that Roz deserved to die." Cynthia's mouth puckered with bitter disdain. "She was threatening Johnny. Ordering him to acknowledge that he was Melody's father or she would go public with her lying and twisted version of how Melody was conceived."

"And what version was that?"

"She threatened to accuse my husband of rape unless he paid her off." Cynthia's voice thickened with hatred. "Roz had no conscience. She ruined my life, she killed my baby, and then she had the gall to try to extort more money from my husband! She said she would make her announcement right before the elections when it was guaranteed to bring the most embarrassment to the people in our party who are trying to maintain some standards of public decency. Johnny refused to give her any money and told her to do her worst. Roz lost her temper. She said it was about time she provided the world with another reminder that it's always the politicians who make the most noise about the sanctity of the family who are screwing everything that isn't nailed down."

Unfortunately, Nick had very little difficulty believing that Roz had threatened Johnston exactly as Cynthia claimed. Not that Roz's attempted blackmail justified Cynthia's decision to kill her, and it certainly didn't begin to excuse Cynthia's decision to kill Melody.

"I understand why you decided to kill Lady Roz," Nick said, with some measure of truth. "But why Melody? What had she ever done to you?"

Cynthia turned to look at him, her eyes wild with hatred. "She lived, when my poor little baby died. And then she started to take Johnny from me. He's always been crazy about her, but at least they never spent time together. Have you any idea how many hours a day I've had to sit and listen to Johnny talking about her for the past six months? His beautiful, talented, smart daughter." Cynthia spat out the words. "He even rewrote his will. His parents were schoolteachers, for God's sake. When he married me, he barely had enough money to buy the black-tie outfit for our wedding. Four months ago, he told me he was planning to leave most of his estate to *Melody*. My parents' money—millions of their hard-earned dollars—were going to end up in the bank account of Melody Beecham. The daughter of the whore who killed my baby! I don't think so."

"So you decided to kill Melody."

"Of course." Cynthia's laugh spiraled upward. "I took care of that situation pretty damn fast. Now I know all Daddy's money will go just where he would have wanted—because Melody Beecham is dead. *She's dead.* Totally and completely dead, like my poor baby. And now Johnny will devote all his attention to me because his daughter is gone and he has nobody else left to love."

Nick's control over his temper snapped. They had arrived back at the van, and he slammed open the sliding door to the rear seats with a brutal force that did nothing to relieve the pressure of his simmering emotions.

"You might have to rethink some of those calculations about your future, Cynthia. There's something important I want to tell you before we take you back to headquarters for questioning."

"What's that?"

"Melody Beecham isn't dead."

The blood drained from Cynthia's cheeks, leaving them a sickly gray, but she soon recovered. "Of course she's dead. I saw the hospital director announce it on television. Jasper Fowles came and gave the news personally to Johnny. Her grandfather has begun to make funeral arrangements. Johnny plans to fly to England to give a eulogy—"

"All those things are true," Nick agreed. "But I can assure you, Melody is very much alive. Bud Silveira screwed up on his assignment, just as Jorge Morrero screwed up back in Cancún. Melody shot Bud, not the other way around. She's been hiding in deep protective custody for the past two days, waiting for us to smoke out the person who's been trying to kill her. Now that we've found you, there's no reason to keep up the pretense anymore. Melody Beecham is alive, and completely unharmed. You failed, Cynthia. Your husband's daughter is alive and very well."

She looked at him without saying a word, her gaze searching. Apparently she decided he was telling the truth. "No," she said, her voice hoarse with anguish. "No, she can't be alive. It's not fair. I won't let her take my Johnny away from me! Johnny is all I have left."

"Melody is alive," Nick repeated. "I'm taking you to see her right now."

"No!" Cynthia's scream rose to a wild, agonized crescendo. Her eyes rolled up, her body convulsed, and she would have fallen to the ground if Nick and Josh hadn't been holding her.

"Jesus Christ!" Josh ripped open the neck of her dress. "She's having a heart attack."

"Or a stroke," Nick said, grabbing the first-aid kit. "Damn it to hell! She's no use to us dead."

Tony arrived at that moment and took in the scene at a glance. "Get her into the back of the truck," he said. "I'll drive."

"Where are we taking her?" Josh asked. "Headquarters?"

"The nearest emergency room," Nick said grimly, putting an oxygen mask over Cynthia's face as he and Josh placed her in the back of the van. "And drive fast. I don't want this woman to be lucky enough to die."

Twenty-One

Heart pounding at the prospect of what lay ahead, Melody walked into the small reception room reserved for visitors to Unit One headquarters. She found Johnston Yates pacing the worn linoleum floor with the frantic intensity of a caged lion. His mane of silver-gray hair, usually immaculate, stuck out around his head in a wild halo, increasing his resemblance to a captive animal. His clothes had obviously been thrown on at random, with no regard for matching colors or styles.

He seemed not to hear her come in. "Johnston? Nick told me you were here—"

"Melody! Oh, thank God." He rushed to her, arms outstretched, clearly intending to hug her. But he pulled himself up short, relief at finding her alive swamped by the knowledge that his wife of forty years was guilty of trying to murder her. His hands dropped limply to his sides, awkward appendages for which he could find no place.

"I've just come from the hospital," he said. "Cynthia is still unconscious. Did you know that?" He didn't wait for an answer, but rushed right on. "I'm not sure right at this moment whether I'm standing on my head or my heels. It's so good to see you, but I can't bear to think about what you've suffered at Cynthia's hands. The doctors aren't sure if she'll ever recover normal brain function. I can't believe she paid two people to kill you! How could I have been so oblivious to what was going on?"

Johnston, usually so eloquent, followed his rambling burst of words with abrupt silence. He resumed his restless pacing, as if the pounding of his feet on the floor might somehow force his chaotic thoughts into order.

"I'm sorry that we had to deceive you," Melody said. "But there didn't seem to be any other way to flush out the killer."

"The killer—who just happens to be my wife." Johnston stopped pacing and swung around to face her, his expression haunted. "I don't know what to say or how to apologize. I told Nick that I needed to talk to you just this one time, but I'll understand if you decide never to see me again after tonight."

"I don't blame you for what happened. How could you have known what Cynthia was trying to do? She went to such lengths to hide her feelings." Melody wished she could run to Johnston and sublimate explanations and apologies in a warm hug and floods of emotional tears. Unfortunately, she could never entirely put the logical side of her personality to rest, and the tiny part of her that wondered how Johnston could have been so blind to his wife's hatred kept her glued to the spot.

Johnston didn't appear comforted by her attempt at reassurance. "It's true that Cynthia was careful never to let me see the truth of her feelings about you, but I was aware of what had happened in the past, and I should have realized her friendly attitude was nothing more than an act. I should have questioned her more." His voice rose harshly. "Dammit, I should have known!"

"You're assigning too much blame to yourself and nowhere near enough to other people."

"I wish that were the case, but there's more than enough blame to spread around." Johnston's austere features twisted into an expression of self-loathing. "Despite the horror of what Cynthia has done to you and your mother, she was a good woman when I first met her. As for Roz, she was clearly a woman with the potential to become something special, until I intervened and set her running fast in the wrong direction."

It was tempting to let Johnston take the blame for her mother's failures. Tempting, but unfair. "You may have hurt my mother badly, but in the end, she chose the lessons that she learned from your relationship. After all, Roz was married to Wallis Beecham when she started the affair with you. You weren't the only person breaking promises and hurting your spouse."

"That's true, although I was years older than Roz, and I should have been wiser. But the heaviest weight on my conscience is the way I've treated you. You're my daughter, and instead of making your life easier, I've made it a hundred times more difficult. From the moment of your conception, it seems that I've let you down in every way that matters."

"Not in every way," Melody said. "We got a late start, but for the past six months we've both tried hard to build something meaningful out of the mess of the past. I think we're succeeding, don't you? Cynthia wouldn't have been so jealous and angry unless she'd felt threatened by our relationship."

"I hope so much that we've succeeded," Johnston said. "I know I've cherished every moment we've spent together since the day you saved my life. For the past six months, you've been the sun that warms and brightens my days."

He gave a mocking laugh, the mockery directed entirely at himself. "Have you any idea how difficult it is for me to make even that simple admission? It's as if when I broke up with Roz all those years ago, I squeezed every drop of emotion and passion out of my life and there was nothing left to share with anyone until you came along. It was only when you shot Dave Ramsdell and saved my life that my rusting emotional system began to clank and clatter back into action."

"I'm very glad that it did—and that we were given a chance to get to know one another."

"And so am I. You have no idea how much I've cherished these past few months." He let out a ragged breath. "God, Melody, when I heard you were dead I realized just how much I regretted all those *stupid* lost years. I still can't believe you're here. That you were saved and that I've been given yet another chance to play some sort of a role in your life. It's too much happiness to take in after the sadness of the past couple of days, and the horror of Cynthia's involvement in the attacks on you."

Johnston swung away from her, his shoulders shaking. Melody realized he was crying, although he made no sound. The silent weeping made her heart ache, and for once she acted instinctively, without policing her own actions or thinking up twenty-five rational excuses to behave some other way.

"Don't cry, Dad." She put her arms around his waist, resting her cheek against his back. "Hey, the good news is that we're both alive. And speaking for myself, I plan to stay that way for many years to come."

Johnston took a monogrammed linen handkerchief from his pocket and gave a fierce blow before turning around to face her, one hand resting lightly on her shoulder. "You called me Dad."

"It sort of slipped out in the heat of the moment. I can stick with Johnston if you prefer."

"I definitely prefer Dad." A flush of color heated his cheeks at the admission, but he gave her another hug before stepping away and glancing behind him. "Are those chairs over there as uncomfortable as they look?"

"Probably. Unit One doesn't encourage visitors to hang out and relax."

"Well, I guess we'll have to make the best of them, because I have a lot to tell you, and I want to get it off my chest now before the media find out that you're alive and all hell breaks loose."

"If you know why Cynthia was angry enough with me to make two attempts at killing me off, I definitely want to hear what you have to say." Melody hesitated for a moment and then decided to state the obvious. "According to the doctors, it doesn't seem likely that Cynthia will ever recover sufficiently to tell us anything."

"No, she's unlikely to recover, although she could live for months or even years in a semi-vegetative state." Johnston's mouth trembled, but he quickly reasserted control. "We've been together more than forty years. I'm not even sure whether to feel relieved that Cynthia is unaware of her surroundings, or angry that she'll never be required to take responsibility for what she's done."

"Perhaps it's okay to feel both?" Melody suggested.

Johnston's mouth turned down. "Once again, you're too generous." He sat down in one of the armchairs that looked slightly sturdier than its thrift-store companions. "Secrets, silence and lies—that's the story of my life for the past thirty years. With those three ingredients thrown into the pot, you can almost guarantee an explosion. I wonder why that's always so easy to see in retrospect, and so hard to see when you're one of the people plotting the lies and covering up the secrets? That's a rhetorical question. I know there's no rational answer."

"Except that you're a human being, and by definition human beings make mistakes." Melody sat cross-legged in the chair next to her father, wondering if there was really any explanation he could provide that would make Cynthia's murderous rage seem comprehensible.

"I married Cynthia for money and the political power her father could give me," Johnston said. "It was a marriage of convenience for me, not a love match, but we were both happy enough at first. I was running for the Senate and we both enjoyed the hectic pace. Cynthia was a couple of years older than me, she'd been involved in politics all her life, and she was completely at ease on the campaign trail. We got along really well for the first year of our marriage. Our problems began when the election was over and I'd won. We tried to start a family, without success. Cynthia desperately wanted a baby, and although there were already some fairly good infertility treatments thirty-five years ago, they were nothing like the range of options available today, and nothing worked for us."

"I've heard that infertility is one of the major stresses on any marriage," Melody said. "I can only imagine how difficult it must be when you're in the public spotlight at the same time as you're wrestling with all the emotional and physical problems of trying to get pregnant."

Johnston nodded. "I can vouch for that. We struggled on for years, trying everything known to medical science in those days. Nothing worked, although nobody was ever able to tell us why not. Cynthia was approaching forty when I became vice president, and our marriage was soon in really big trouble, in part because I no sooner took the oath of office than I was consumed with ambition to become president. I had very little time to pay attention to her grief and even less time to sympathize with her continued longing for a baby. From my perspective, it was time to move on. We had a fascinating life and there was a great political future ahead. I couldn't understand why she wasn't satisfied."

Johnston fell silent, staring straight ahead, seeing scenes from the past that clearly disturbed him. "I failed Cynthia in the worst way," he said quietly. "I not only refused to understand the depths of her longing for a baby, I was drunk with the power of being one of the youngest and most successful vice presidents ever. And then, on top of all our other problems, I met Roz."

His voice softened, and his mouth tilted into a small smile. "In those days, Roz was everything that Cynthia wasn't. She was smart as a whip, but bored senseless by politics. The power struggles, far from impressing her, simply made her laugh. She would do wicked imitations of various politicians and their wives and, being the daughter of an earl, she'd grown up with enough pomp and ceremony that she wasn't impressed by any of the names I dropped. Before I met Roz, I'd had plenty of women suggest that they'd be thrilled to have an affair with me—except they weren't really interested in me. They were interested in adding Vice President of the United States to their list of conquests. But with Roz, she was so indifferent to politics, especially American politics, that I knew she was in love with *me,* the man, not the office. Before I knew what had happened, I realized I not only returned Roz's feelings, I was head over heels in love with her."

"You mentioned once before that you loved my mother. And yet, I have the impression that by the time I was born, the two of you almost hated each other."

"You're right," Johnston admitted. "There was a lot of anger and hurt when our affair ended, on both sides. When love goes as badly wrong as ours did, friendship is impossible and indifference unlikely. That only leaves hatred." He grimaced ruefully. "It turned out that Roz and I did hatred really well."

"Why was she so angry?" Melody asked. "Because she felt that you'd betrayed her?"

"Yes. And in a way, I had. When I started the affair with Roz, I never seriously considered that it might lead to marriage. Not to put too pretty a gloss on it, we were both married to other people, and in our set, adultery was winked at whereas divorce was frowned on. More importantly, Cynthia's father was one of the most powerful senators in the country and he enjoyed a closer relationship with the president than I did. My political career depended on having my father-in-law's support. If he turned against me in the wake of a messy divorce from his daughter, I knew there would be no chance of getting my party's presidential nomination."

"Why didn't my mother understand that you had no intention of marrying her?" Melody asked. "After all, she must have known the conventions of the circles she was moving in."

"You know, I'm not sure that she did. As I said, she was not only young and from a foreign country, in some ways she was naive as well. We rarely discussed politics, but I assumed she knew that my hopes of becoming president would vanish overnight if I divorced Cynthia. In retrospect, I suspect that she romanticized our affair to the point that she had blotted out the practical demands of a presidential campaign. Then, six months into our relationship, your mother came to me and told me that she was pregnant. I was astonished by how happy I was to know that Roz was carrying my child, and how much I wanted to be with her and raise our child together. So much so that I began to imagine ways in which I could divorce Cynthia and still run for president."

Johnston's mouth twisted as if he'd tasted something bitter. "You'll notice that I never considered the possibility of giving up my presidential ambitions in order to marry your mother. That was never in the cards as far as I was concerned."

He fell silent again. After a moment, he stood up and walked a few steps across the room, his back to Melody. "This is obviously a difficult subject for me to discuss with my daughter. Unfortunately, there's no way to sugarcoat the fact that I was committing adultery, and that I was sleeping not only with your mother but also with my wife—"

Melody felt her cheeks burn. "You don't have to explain—"

"Yes, I do." He drew in an audible breath and swung around to face her. "Exactly five days after Roz told me she was pregnant, Cynthia told me she was pregnant, too."

"Oh my God." Melody's heart began to race, almost as if the news of Cynthia's pregnancy were fresh, instead of more than thirty years old.

"That barely begins to describe my feelings at the time," Johnston said wryly. "After ten years of failure, Cynthia was already fourteen weeks pregnant."

"She waited three months to tell you?" Melody was incredulous. "I would have expected her to be so happy that she would have told you five minutes after she found out."

"She hadn't realized she was pregnant until that very day. She'd been feeling tired and listless and generally out of sorts, so finally she consulted her ob-gyn, to see if it was a hormonal problem. He gave her the news that she was pregnant." Johnston shook his head. "I don't know if you can imagine how ecstatically happy she was, or how guilty I felt. I realized I'd not only put myself in an impossible position, but I'd also inflicted harm on the two women I cared about most in the world. Because at that point, I did still care about Cynthia, despite being unfaithful. Not as a lover, or a soul mate, you understand, but as a companion who deserved my loyalty. I was paralyzed with indecision for the next week, and then tragedy struck. I lied to my Secret Service detail—I told them I planned to spend the night at home, and then slipped away to have dinner with Roz at an out-of-the-way restaurant in the suburbs. Needless to say, our conversation wasn't going anywhere very productive because there was no good place for it to go. I suggested an abortion. Your mother refused. We finally parted company without making any decisions. That was the last time Roz and I ever spent time together that could be considered reasonably pleasant and cordial. When I got home, I found Cynthia lying on the bedroom floor in a pool of blood, half conscious."

Melody's stomach lurched. "She miscarried?"

Johnston nodded. "She'd started to hemorrhage two hours earlier, but when she couldn't find me, she simply lay down on the bedroom floor and cried. We rushed her to the naval hospital in Bethesda, but of course it was too late, and she lost the baby."

Melody would have sworn there was nothing in Cynthia's past that could make her feel sympathy for the woman who'd spent three months trying to murder her. But she had been wrong. She had to swallow hard before she could speak. "Could the baby have been saved if Cynthia had arrived at the hospital earlier?"

"Not according to the doctors. They told me that the placenta wasn't attached properly to Cynthia's uterus, and that the fetus had probably been dead for at least forty-eight hours before the hemorrhage." Johnston's face was gray with remembered misery. "Of course, Cynthia never believed that. She believes to this day that if I had been home, where I was supposed to be, our baby son would have been born strong and healthy. In addition to ignoring the doctors' verdict, she also ignores the fact that there were at least half a dozen people in the house who could have driven her to the ER despite the fact that I wasn't there."

Melody still felt her stomach roiling with sympathy. "Did Cynthia know that you were with my mother?"

"Not then." Johnston's expression darkened with self-loathing. "I lied and told her that I'd been dealing with a national emergency. She believed me. Not that it comforted her particularly."

"I can imagine that it wouldn't."

"The final irony was that Roz considered Cynthia's miscarriage a miraculous solution to all our problems. Now that my wife wasn't pregnant anymore, there was no reason in Roz's mind why I couldn't divorce Cynthia and marry her. The fact that Cynthia was almost beside herself with grief struck Roz as supremely irrelevant. It was the first glimpse I'd had of Roz's ability to be self-centered to the point that she was utterly blind to the needs of another person."

It was painful for Melody to acknowledge, even to herself, that Roz's behavior in the wake of Cynthia's miscarriage was entirely typical of everything she had observed about her mother in later years.

"Roz must have been desperately worried," she said, wondering why the need to defend her mother was still so strong. "After all, she was pregnant, too."

"You're right," Johnston said wearily. "Roz was frantic with worry. The truth is, I'd created a situation where there could be only losers. I chose to stay with my wife, but I'm not sure my reasons were noble. Cynthia was literally sick with grief after she lost the baby and I felt unable to abandon her. But I also wanted to become president of the United States, and sticking with Cynthia made that dream possible, whereas divorcing her and marrying Roz meant accepting that I would never be president."

"But this is what I've never understood about your political career," Melody said. "You remained married to Cynthia. No whisper of your affair with my mother ever reached the public. And yet you never even campaigned for the Republican nomination, much less the presidency. What happened?"

It was a long time before Johnston replied. "I've been a rotten father, but the truth is, I've avoided talking about the past because I wanted to avoid hurting you. I hoped it would never be necessary to tell you this part of the story. However, I can't explain Cynthia's murderous feelings toward your mother and then toward you without giving you this last piece of the puzzle."

Did she want to know the truth? Melody wondered. The answer came swiftly. Of course she did. Johnston himself had started out this conversation by saying that secrets and lies had led to literally murderous unhappiness. How could any useful purpose be served by asking her father to remain silent?

"I want to hear what happened," she said. "I'm assuming that somehow my mother is involved in the explanation of why you never ran for the presidency?"

"Roz is the only reason I didn't run," Johnston said simply. "When I told Roz that our affair had to end because I'd decided to stay with Cynthia, she was hurt and bewildered. She couldn't—wouldn't—understand why I chose loyalty toward Cynthia over love for her. She wasn't just hurt, she was furiously angry."

He made a defeated gesture. "You know the decisions she made once I abandoned her. Wallis Beecham was already a wealthy man and she had no intention of losing his financial support. She convinced him that you were his child, and for a couple of years, I'm sure she went out of her way to play the loving and faithful wife, just so that he would never harbor any suspicions about your paternity."

Johnston must have seen her squirming, because he reached across and patted her knee. "Roz's motives in going back to Wallis weren't entirely selfish, you know. She wanted you to grow up with a father, and with enough money to provide you with some of the luxuries of life."

For a woman who professed to believe that love was the answer to everything, Roz unfortunately seemed to have left that vital factor out of the equation when planning for her daughter's life, Melody reflected. "Nothing you've told me explains why you didn't run for the presidency," she said. "It doesn't explain why Cynthia killed my mother, either."

"Your mother made it impossible for me to run for president," Johnston said. "On the day you were born, she sent me a message, inviting me to come to the hospital to see you. I ignored her message. I never visited you or Roz."

Melody's mouth was so dry she couldn't even swallow. She licked her lips. "Why not?"

Johnston didn't turn away, but she could see that it was costing him significant effort to continue to meet her gaze. "Because I couldn't afford to start any rumors. Because my marriage to Cynthia was rapidly descending from loveless into unbearable. Because becoming president of the United States suddenly seemed to be the only goal left to me that might—just possibly—make sense of the nightmare my life had become. Most of all, I didn't go to see you because I wasn't sure I wanted to meet a daughter I could never claim as my own."

"Roz could have asked you to be my godfather. That would have given you a legitimate excuse to see me now and again."

Johnston smiled grimly. "I don't think Roz was looking for solutions at that point. She was already looking for vengeance. She took you back to England so that you could be christened in the family chapel, in the three-hundred-year-old gown worn by generations of Ridgefield babies. Then she sent me a slew of newspaper and magazine photos of the event, just to make sure I knew what I was missing."

"What did you do with the pictures?"

"I kept them. They were the start of the scrapbooks I made about your life. I carefully snipped Wallis Beecham out of any shots where he appeared, and imagined what it would have been like if I'd been there with you. When Roz came back from England, she sent one last message, asking me to meet her. I refused."

Johnston made no attempt to excuse his behavior. "I might have been sentimental about your baby pictures, but I still planned to be president of the United States. Two days after my refusal to visit you, I walked into my office and found Roz there, chatting amiably to my secretary and flashing photos of you. In your pram, this time. My secretary made the comment that you looked just like Roz. Roz smiled sweetly and said, 'Oh no, my baby looks exactly like her father.'"

"I think Roz was right," Melody said softly.

Johnston's smile lost some of its grimness. "Thank you. Anyway, to cut a long and painful story short, Roz followed me into my office and covered my desk with compromising material. There were Polaroids of me that she'd taken in various hotel bedrooms. She had kept hotel receipts, handwritten notes, literally dozens of pieces of memorabilia that she'd collected during the months of our affair. She'd originally saved everything because she treasured them as mementos of our time together. But that day when she confronted me in my office, she turned her treasures into weapons. She said that if I ever tried to see you or contact you, she would send the entire file of our liaison to Cynthia. And if I ever tried to run for president, she would make sure that every tabloid in the country had copies of the photos, and that she'd shout the news from the rooftops that you were my child and that my wife had miscarried a longed-for baby while I was out wining and dining my mistress."

Johnston shrugged, the gesture carrying a world of dashed hopes. "No presidential candidate could withstand revelations like that, even today. Thirty years ago, they would have been the kiss of death. If Roz had forced me to drink a cup of poison, she couldn't have put a more effective end to my presidential ambitions."

Unfortunately, Melody could visualize her mother making such threats with crystal clarity. But for the first time, she understood that perhaps Roz's vengeful attitude toward the men in her life sprang out of pain caused by the devastating failure of her only true love affair. Perhaps her need always to have the upper hand in a relationship had roots in the lack of power she must have felt in the face of Johnston's rejection.

"I understand why my mother's threats made it impossible for you to run for president," she said. "And I understand how angry you must have been with her, and how resentful you must have felt at the way she'd thwarted your political ambitions. But I still don't understand why Cynthia waited almost twenty-eight years to kill my mother and another eighteen months before she tried to kill me."

"Cynthia never knew you were my child," Johnston said. "Roz kept her side of the bargain, perhaps because it suited her financial needs to convince Wallis Beecham that you were his daughter. You looked absolutely nothing like him, so there was a lot of pressure on Roz to make sure Wallis never started to wonder or to ask questions. And if she told Cynthia the truth, how could she be sure Cynthia wouldn't tell Wallis? Then two years ago, I think Roz must have been in financial difficulties. She came to me and claimed that she wanted me to get to know my daughter, that she regretted having kept us apart. Most of all, she regretted having allowed you to believe that Wallis Beecham was your father. She suggested that she was going to tell everyone the truth, starting with Cynthia, unless I felt motivated to contribute a couple of hundred thousand dollars to her income each year."

Melody felt sick. It had been bad enough to find out after Roz's death that her mother had made her living through blackmail and extortion. It was even worse to discover that she herself had been the fulcrum of Roz's blackmail attempts, at least on this occasion.

"I'm sorry," Johnston said softly, covering her hand with his. "But I think the time for glossing over the hard parts of the story is well and truly over."

"Yes," Melody agreed, despite the nausea still churning in her stomach. "You were right earlier on when you said that it's dangerous to let secrets fester. How did you respond to my mother's threats?"

"In a way that I should have done years before," he said. "I told Roz that she should go ahead and let the world know the truth. That I had a lot to gain and absolutely nothing to lose by the revelation that I was fortunate enough to be the father of a young woman as talented and successful as you. I told her—truthfully—that I'd wanted to make contact with you for several years and had held off only out of consideration for our respective partners. I guessed that Wallis Beecham provided most of your mother's income, and I was pretty sure that the last thing she would want was for him to learn the truth. I must have guessed correctly, because she backed down immediately. But it was in the wake of those extortion attempts on Roz's part that I decided to tell Cynthia the truth. I realized the truth was ultimately the only way to defang your mother. Unfortunately, I came to the realization thirty years too late."

Melody winced at the words *extortion* and *defang*, but she couldn't deny their accuracy. "I was going to ask how Cynthia reacted to the news, but I guess I don't need to. We know that she was furious enough to kill my mother and try to kill me."

"We know that now, but I completely misread her reaction at the time." Johnston resumed his frantic pacing until Melody blocked his path.

"We all misread Cynthia," she said, reaching out to take his hand. "It was almost guaranteed that we would. Adultery is treated so casually nowadays that it's hard to grasp the magnitude of what flowed from the fact that you and my mother had an extramarital affair."

Johnston tugged her toward him and wrapped her in a tight, hard hug. "But together we produced you Thank God there was at least one thing the two of us managed to get absolutely right."

Epilogue

Malmesbury, England
April 2005

The April sun shed warmth and clear light over thatched roofs and daffodils dancing in the window boxes of the houses that lined the cobbled streets of the picturesque town of Malmesbury. A soft breeze carried the smell of fertile earth and leaves unfurling on apple trees into the heart of the market square. To complete the idyllic setting, the grass surrounding the famous abbey was the intense springtime green celebrated by generations of poets, providing a startlingly lovely background for the soaring stone buttresses of the abbey itself.

The beauties of nature and architecture were entirely wasted on the jostling crowd of spectators, photographers, journalists and TV crews gathered behind the rope barricades that marked off the entrance to the eleven-hundred-year-old church. The spectators had made the ninety mile trek out of London to ogle the glittering assortment of guests scheduled to attend the wedding of Melody Rosalind Beecham to Nikolai David Anwar, and they weren't about to get distracted by mundane details like church architecture or English horticulture. It wasn't every day that a person came back from the dead...and then announced that her father was actually a former vice president of the United States.

Celebrity spotters had already been rewarded by a steady stream of rich and famous guests arriving at the abbey. Jacyntha Ramon, whose latest movie was reputed to be Oscar-bound, had been escorted into the church by a Belgian prince—real royalty, since his family had managed to hang on to their throne.

The Earl and Countess of Ridgefield, grandparents of the bride, arrived shortly after Jacyntha. Managing to ignore the spectators with such completeness that even the most hardened paparazzi felt invisible, the earl and countess walked into the abbey, accompanied by their two sons, their daughters-in-law and the bride's four cousins.

The earl and countess were followed by a steady stream of the famous and near famous, including the Russian ambassador to the United Nations and his American counterpart.

Nikolai Anwar, the groom himself, arrived fifteen minutes before the scheduled start of the ceremony, looking so incredibly handsome in his morning suit that the crowd almost forgave him for capturing Melody Beecham's heart without being either a movie star or a prince.

Nikolai's best man, identified by London's most famous gossip columnist as a college friend by the name of Josh Straiker, was accompanied by two other groomsmen. One of the groomsmen, a distinguished-looking older man, was recognized by several paparazzi as Jasper Fowles, owner of the Van der Meer Gallery. Jasper was also Melody's boss, and the man who had originally pronounced her dead. The third groomsman, who looked like a cross between a leprechaun and a house elf from Harry Potter, was unknown to everyone. He walked along the flagstone path, tugging at the knot of his gray silk cravat, which already resided neatly beneath his left ear.

Finally a silver Rolls-Royce drew up to the curb. A collective sigh escaped from the crowd as a tall, silver-haired man stepped out onto the pavement. Johnston Yates, former vice president of the United States, held out his hand and turned to help his daughter out of the car. Her dress, a shimmering confection of white organdy embroidered with silver thread, brought gasps of pleasure from the women watching.

Melody stepped out of the car and smiled at her father, oblivious to the pop of flashbulbs and the friendly applause from the crowd. Brides were supposed to be nervous, but she couldn't remember an occasion in her life when she had been so certain that she was doing the right thing.

She stepped out of the sunshine into the soft, filtered light of the abbey, her father's arm providing strong support. Her flower girls, the children of her cousins, and none older than eight, clustered around her, full of self-importance and delight in their roles. The organist began to play Purcell's Trumpet Voluntary and the congregation rose to its feet.

Melody saw only Nick. He waited for her in front of the altar, so handsome and solemn that her heart suddenly seemed as if it needed to be twice as big in order to accommodate all the love she felt for him. She reached his side and smiled up at him, barely able to contain her joy.

Nick met her gaze, his expression awestruck. "You're so beautiful, I can't breathe. I can't believe you're about to marry me."

She laughed. She couldn't help it. "You're rather magnificent yourself. You shouldn't be in the least surprised that I want to marry you."

The bishop coughed. "If we could begin the ceremony…"

Melody and Nick turned to him and spoke together. "Yes, please."

Outside, the photographers began to pack away their gear, mentally captioning their pictures of the bride as they worked. *Radiant amidst the love of her extended family,* one decided as they all traipsed off to the distant car park.

They weren't a sentimental bunch either by profession or by nature, but some of them actually felt a slight quiver of emotion as they remembered the last time they'd waited outside Malmesbury Abbey, which had been on the occasion of the memorial service to Lady Rosalind, Melody's mother. Weddings were better than funerals, they decided. One of them even offered a silent toast, though he would have undergone torture before admitting to it.

Here's to you, Melody and Nikolai. Live long and prosper.

JASMINE CRESSWELL

32066 FULL PURSUIT	___ $6.50 U.S.	___ $7.99 CAN.
32012 DECOY	___ $6.50 U.S.	___ $7.99 CAN.
66931 THE THIRD WIFE	___ $6.50 U.S.	___ $7.99 CAN.
66838 THE CONSPIRACY	___ $6.50 U.S.	___ $7.99 CAN.
66712 DEAD RINGER	___ $6.50 U.S.	___ $7.99 CAN.

(limited quantities available)

TOTAL AMOUNT	$ _____
POSTAGE & HANDLING	$ _____
($1.00 FOR 1 BOOK, 50¢ for each additional)	
APPLICABLE TAXES*	$ _____
TOTAL PAYABLE	$ _____

(check or money order—please do not send cash)

To order, complete this form and send it, along with a check or money order for the total above, payable to MIRA Books, to: **In the U.S.:** 3010 Walden Avenue, P.O. Box 9077, Buffalo, NY 14269-9077; **In Canada:** P.O. Box 636, Fort Erie, Ontario, L2A 5X3.

Name: _____

Address: _____ City: _____

State/Prov.: _____ Zip/Postal Code: _____

Account Number (if applicable): _____

075 CSAS

*New York residents remit applicable sales taxes.
*Canadian residents remit applicable GST and provincial taxes.

MIRA®

www.MIRABooks.com

MJC0505BL

written from his gut with the compassion that Dostoevski called the chief law of human existence. An articulate literary renegade, Selby has created more than he has seen, exploding remembered violence and depravity in a Rorschach of living savagery."

—Webster Schott, *The Nation*

"Without a doubt one of the most extraordinary writers alive. The impact of this book will be immediate and profound. Its influence will be felt for decades."

—Alfred Chester

"His style is the most arrestingly original since *Naked Lunch* and *One Hundred Dollar Misunderstanding*. Also, like Burroughs, Selby is one of the really strong moralists—with a classic sense of the Absurd, a foolproof ear and a great heart."

—Terry Southern

"A book that ought to shock us, not because of this word or that, but because a sound craftsman has shown us so much of what we prefer to ignore . . . No author that I can think of has presented so impressive . . . an account of the life of people at the bottom of the heap . . . So far as the literary future is concerned, my money is on Selby."

—Granville Hicks, *Saturday Review*

LAST EXIT TO BROOKLYN

LAST EXIT
TO
BROOKLYN

---

by Hubert Selby, Jr.

GROVE PRESS, INC.

NEW YORK

Some of the sections of this book have appeared in *Black Mountain Review, New Directions #17, Provincetown Review* and *Swank.*

Thirteenth Printing

MANUFACTURED IN THE UNITED STATES OF AMERICA

DISTRIBUTED BY RANDOM HOUSE, INC., NEW YORK

This book is dedicated,
with love, to Gil.

PART I

ANOTHER DAY ANOTHER DOLLAR

For that which befalleth the sons of men befalleth beasts; even one thing befalleth them: as the one dieth, so dieth the other; yea, they have all one breath; so that a man hath no preeminence above a beast: for all is vanity.

Ecclesiastes 3:19

THEY SPRAWLED ALONG the counter and on the chairs.
Another night. Another drag of a night in the Greeks, a
beatup all night diner near the Brooklyn Armybase. Once
in a while a doggie or seaman came in for a hamburger
and played the jukebox. But they usually played some
goddam hillbilly record. They tried to get the Greek to
take those records off, but hed tell them no. They come in
and spend money. You sit all night and buy notting. Are
yakiddin me Alex? Ya could retire on the money we spend
in here. Scatah. You dont pay my carfare . . .

24 records
on the jukebox. They could have any 12 they wanted, but
the others were for the customers from the Base. If somebody played a Lefty Frizzell record or some other shit-
kicker they moaned, made motions with their hands
(man! what a fuckin square) and walked out to the street. 2
jokers were throwing quarters in so they leaned against the
lamppost and carfenders. A warm clear night and they
walked in small circles, dragging the right foot slowly in the
hip Coxsackie shuffle, cigarettes hanging from mouths, collars of sportshirts turned up in the back, down and rolled in
front. Squinting. Spitting. Watching cars roll by. Identifying them. Make. Model. Year. Horse power. Overhead

13

valve. V-8. 6, 8, a hundred cylinders. Lots a horses. Lots a chrome. Red and Amber grill lights. Yasee the grill on the new Pontiac? Man, thats real sharp. Yeah, but a lousy pickup. Cant beat a Plymouth fora pickup. Shit. Cant hold the road like a Buick. Outrun any cop in the city with a Roadmaster. If ya get started. Straightaways. Turns. Outrun the law. Dynaflows. Hydramatics. Cant get started. Theyd be all overya before ya got a block. Not in the new 88. Ya hit the gas and it throwsya outta the seat. Great car. Aint stealin nothin else anymore. Greatest for a job. Still like the Pontiac. If I was *buyin* a car. Put fender skirts on it, grill lights, a set a Caddy hubcaps and a bigass aerial in the rear. . . . shit, thats the sharpest job on the road. Your ass. Nothin can touch the 47 Continental convertible. Theyre the end. We saw one uptown the other day. What-a-fuckin-load. Man!!! The shitkickers still wailed and they talked and walked, talked and walked, adjusting their shirts and slacks, cigarettes flipped into the street—ya shoulda seen this load. Chartreuse with white walls. Cruise around in a load like that with the top down and a pair of shades and some sharp clothes and ya haveta beat the snatch off witha club—spitting after every other word, aiming for a crack in the sidewalk; smoothing their hair lightly with the palms of their hands, pushing their d a/s gently and patting them in place, feeling with their fingertips for a stray hair that may be out of place and not hanging with the proper effect— ya should see the sharp shirts they got in Obies. That real great gabadine. Hey, did yadig that sharp silverblue sharkskin suit in the window? Yeah, yeah. The onebutton single breasted job with the big lapels—and whats to do on a night like this. Just a few drops of gas in the tank and no loot to fill it up. And anyway, wheres to go— but yagotta have a onebutton lounge. Ya wardrobe aint complete without one. Yeah, but I dig that new shawl

14

job. Its real sharp even as a sports jacket—the con rolled
on and no one noticed that the same guys were saying the
same things and somebody found a new tailor who could
make the greatest pants for 14 skins; and how about the
shockabsorbers in the Lincoln; and they watched the cars
pass, giving hardlooks and spitting; and who laid this
broad and who laid that one; and someone took a small
brush from his pocket and cleaned his suede shoes then
rubbed his hands and adjusted his clothing and someone
else flipped a coin and when it dropped a foot stamped on
it before it could be picked up and as he moved the leg
from the coin his hair was mussed and he called him a
fuck and whipped out his comb and when his hair was
once more neatly in place it was mussed again and he got
salty as hell and the other guys laughed and someone elses
hair was mussed and they shoved each other and someone
else shoved and then someone suggested a game of mum
and said Vinnie should start and they yelled yeah and
Vinnie said whatthefuck, hed start, and they formed a
circle around him and he turned slowly jerking his head
quickly trying to catch the one punching him so he would
replace him in the center and he was hit in the side and
when he turned he got hit again and as he spun around 2
fists hit him in the back then another in the kidney and he
buckled and they laughed and he jerked around and
caught a shot in the stomach and fell but he pointed and
he left the center and just stood for a minute in the circle
catching his wind then started punching and felt better
when he hit Tony a good shot in the kidney without being
seen and Tony slowed down and got pelted for a few
minutes then finally pointed and Harry said he was fulla-
shit, he didn't really see him hitim. But he was thrown in
the center anyway and Tony waited and hooked him hard
in the ribs and the game continued for another 5 minutes
or so and Harry was still in the center, panting and almost

15

on his knees and they were rapping him pretty much as they pleased, but they got bored and the game broke up and they went back in the Greeks, Harry still bent and panting, the others laughing, and went to the lavatory to wash.

They washed and threw cold water on their necks and hair then fought for a clean spot on the dirty apron that served as a towel, yelling through the door that Alex was a no good fuck for not havin a towel forem, then jockeyed for a place in front of the mirror. Eventually they went to the large mirror at the front of the diner and finished combing their hair and fixing their clothes, laughing and still kidding Harry, then sprawled and leaned.

The shitkickers left and they yelled to Alex to get some music on the radio. Why dont you put money in the jukebox? Then you hear what you want. Comeon man. Dont be a drag. Why dont you get a job. Then you have money. Hey, watch ya language. Yeah, no cursin Alex. Go get a job you no good bums. Whos a bum. Yeah, who? They laughed and yelled at Alex and he sat, smiling, on a small stool at the end of the counter and someone leaned over the counter and turned the radio on and spun the dial until a sax wailed and someone yelled for service and Alex told him to go to hell, and he pounded on the counter for service and Alex asked if he wanted ham and eggs and he told Alex he wouldnt eat an egg here unless he saw it hatched and Alex laughed, Scatah, and walked slowly to the coffee urn and filled a cup and asked if he was going to buy everybody coffee and they laughed and Alex told them to get a job, you all the time hang around like bums. Someday you be sorry. You get caught and you wont be able to drink this good coffee. COFFEE!!! Man this is worse than piss. The dishwater upstate tastes betteran this. Pretty soon maybe you be drinking it again. Yourass I will. I should report

16

you. Then Id have some peace and quiet. Youd die without us Alex. Whod protect ya from the drunks? Look at all the trouble we saveya. You boys are going to get in trouble. You see. All the time fuckaround. Ah Alex. Dont talk like that. Ya make us feel bad. Yeah man. Ya hurt our feelings. . . .

Alex sat on his stool smoking and smiling and they smoked and laughed. Cars passed and some tried to identify them by the sound of the motor then looked to see if they were right, raising their shoulders and swaggering back to their seats if they were. Occasionally a drunk came in and they would yell to Alex to get up off his ass and serve the customer or tell the guy ta getthehell out before he was poisoned with Alexs horsemeat and coffee and Alex would pick up the dirty rag and wipe off the spot in front of the drunk and say yes sir, what you want, and theyd want to know why he didnt call them sir and Alex would smile and sit on his stool until the drunk finished and then walk slowly back, take the money, ring it up then back to his stool and tell them they should be quiet, you want to scare good customers away, and Alex would laugh with them and spit the cigarette butt out of his mouth and turn his shoe on it; and the cars still passed and the drunks still passed and the sky was clear and bright with stars and moon and a light breeze was blowing and you could hear the tugs in the harbor chugging and the deep ooooo from their whistles floated across the bay and rolled down 2nd avenue and even the ferrys mooring winch could be heard, when it was quiet and still, clanging a ferry into the slip . . . and it was a drag of a night, beat for loot and they flipped their cigarettes out the doors and walked to the mirror and adjusted and combed and someone turned up the volume of the radio and a few of the girls came in and the guys smoothed the waist of their shirts as they walked over to their table and Rosie grabbed

Freddy, a girl he laid occasionally, and asked him for a halfabuck and he told her to go fuckerself and walked away and sat on a stool. She sat beside him. He talked with the guys and every few minutes she would say something, but he ignored her. When he moved slightly on his stool she started to get up and when he sat down she sat. Freddy stood, adjusted his pants, put his hands in his pockets and slowly walked out the door and strolled to the corner. Rosie walked 6 inches to his right and 6 inches to his rear. He leaned against the lampost and spit past her face. Youre worse than a leech. A leech yacan get rid of. You dont go for nothin. Dont bullshit me ya bastard. I know yascored for a few bucks last night. Whats that to you? and anyway its gone. I aint even got a pack of cigarettes. Dont tell me. I aint ya father. Ya cheap motherfucka! Go tell ya troubles to jesus and stop breakin my balls. I/ll break ya balls ya rotten bastard, trying to kick him in the groin, but Freddy turned and lifted his leg then slapped her across the face.

Three drunken rebel soldiers were going back to the Base after buying drinks for a couple of whores in a neighborhood bar and were thrown out when they started a fight after the whores left them for a couple of seamen. They stopped when they heard Rosie shout and watched as she staggered back from the slap, Freddy grabbing her by the neck. Go giter little boy. Hey, dont chuall know youre not to fuck girls on the street. . . . They laughed and yelled and Freddy let go of Rosie and turned and looked at them for a second then yelled at them to go fuck their mothers, ya cottonpickin bastards. I hear shes good hump. The soldiers stopped laughing and started crossing the street toward Freddy. We/ll cut yur niggerlovin heart out. Freddy yelled and the others ran out of the Greeks. When the doggies saw them they stopped then turned and ran

18

toward the gate to the Base. Freddy ran to his car and the others jumped in and on the fenders or held on to the open doors, and Freddy chased the doggies down the street. Two of them continued running toward the gate, but the third panicked and tried to climb over the fence and Freddy tried to squash him against it with the car but the doggie pulled his legs up just before the car bumped the fence. The guys jumped off the fender and leaped on the doggies back and yanked him down and he fell on the edge of the hood and then to the ground. They formed a circle and kicked. He tried to roll over on his stomach and cover his face with his arms, but as he got to his side he was kicked in the groin and stomped on the ear and he screamed, cried, started pleading then just cried as a foot cracked his mouth, Ya fuckin cottonpickin punk, and a hard kick in the ribs turned him slightly and he tried to raise himself on one knee and someone took a short step forward and kicked him in the solarplexus and he fell on his side, his knees up, arms folded across his abdomen, gasping for air and the blood in his mouth gurgled as he tried to scream, rolled down his chin then spumed forth as he vomited violently and someone stomped his face into the pool of vomit and the blood whirled slightly in arcs and a few bubbles gurgled in the puke as he panted and gasped and their shoes thudded into the shiteatinbastards kidneys and ribs and he groaned and his head rolled in the puke breaking the arching patterns of blood and he gasped as a kick broke his nose then coughed and retched as his gasping sucked some of the vomit back in his mouth and he cried and tried to yell but it was muffled by the pool and the guys yells and Freddy kicked him in the temple and the yellowbastards eyes rolled back and his head lolled for a moment and he passed out and his head splashed and thumped to the ground and someone yelled the cops and they jammed back into and on the car and

Freddy started to turn but the prowl car stopped in front of them and the cops got out with their guns drawn so Freddy stopped the car and the guys got out and off the car and slowly walked across the street. The cops lined them against the wall. The guys stood with their hands in their pockets, their shoulders rounded and heads slumped forward, straightening up and raising their arms while being frisked, then resuming their previous positions and attitudes.

Heads popped from windows, people occurred in doorways and from bars asking what happened and the cops yelled for everybody to shutup then asked what was going on. The guys shrugged and murmured. One of the cops started yelling the question again when an MP and the 2 doggies who had continued running, holding the third one suspended between them, head hanging limply, his toes dragging along the ground, came up to them. The cop turned to them and asked what this was all about. Those goddam yankees like takill our buddy heuh, nodding to the soldier between them, his head rolling from side to side, face and front of his uniform covered with blood and puke, blood dribbling from his head. Freddy pointed at him and stepped toward the cop and told him theres nothin wrong with him. Hes only foolin. The guys raised their heads slightly and looked at Freddy and chuckled and someone murmured hes got some pair of balls. The cop looked at the soldier and told Freddy if hes fooling hes one hell of an actor. The chuckling grew louder and a few in the crowd of onlookers laughed. The cops told them to shut up. Now, what in the hell is this all about. The doggies started to speak but Freddy outshouted them. They insulted my wife. Someone said o jésus and Freddy stared at the doggies waiting for them to say something so he could call them a goddam liar. The cop asked him where his wife was and he told him right over there. Hey Rosie! Comere! She wentover, her blouse hanging out, her hair hanging in lumps, lipstick smeared from Freddy's slap, her eyelashes matted and the heads of pimples shining through many layers of old dirty makeup. We was standin on the corner talkin when these three creeps started makin obscene remarks to my wife and when I toldem ta shutup they came after me. Aint that right? Yeah. They insulted me, the god—Yuh dirty hoarrr. How could yawl be insulted??? Freddy started toward him but the cop rapped him in the gut with his club and told him to take it easy. And youd better watch your mouth soldier. All yuhgoddamn yankees are the same. A buncha no good niggerlovin bastards. Thats all yuare. The cop stepped over to the soldier and told him if he didnt shut up right now hed lock him up, and your friend along with you. He stared at the soldier until the doggie lowered his eyes, then turned to the crowd and asked if anyone had seen what had happened and they yelled that they saw the whole thing that the drunken rebels had started it, they insulted the boys wife and tried to beat him up and the cop told them ok, ok, shut up. He turned back to the soldiers and told them to get back to the base and have someone look after their friend, then turned to Freddy and the others and told them to beat it and if I see any of you punks in a fight again I/ll personally split your skulls and—Hey wait a minute. The cop turned as the MP walked up to him. This aint going to be the end of this officer. These men have rights and its my duty to remind them of them. They might want to prefer charges against these hoodlums. What in hell are you? a Philadelphia lawyer? No sir. I'm just doing my duty and reminding these men of their rights. Alright, you reminded them now go back to the base and leave well enough alone. You know these neighborhood bars are off limits. Yes sir, thats true, but—but nothing. The MP started stammering something, then looked to the three soldiers for support, but they had already started back to the Base, the two dragging the third, blood splattering on the street as it fell from his head.

The bodies went back in the doors and bars and the heads in the windows. The cops drove away and Freddy and the guys went back into the Greeks and the street was quiet, just the sound of a tug and an occasional car; and even the blood couldnt be seen from a few feet away. They slammed around the lavatory washing, laughing, nudging each other, roaring at Freddy, splashing water, inspecting their shoes for scratches, ripping the dirty apron, pulling the toiletpaper off by the yard, throwing the wet wads at each other, slapping each other on the back, smoothing their shirts, going to the mirror up front, combing their hair, turning their collars up in the back and rolling them down in front, adjusting their slacks on their hips. Hey, didya see the look on the bastards face when we threwim off the fence? Yeah. The sonofabitch was scared shitless. A buncha punks. Hey Freddy, hows ya gut. That was some rap that bastard giveya. Shit. I fuck cops where they eat . . .

Someday you boys going to get in trouble. All the time fighting. Whatayamean Alex. We was just defendin Freddys wife. Yeah, they insulted Rosie. They roared, stamped, and banged their fists on the counter and tables. Alex grinned and said Scatah. Someday you be sorry. You should get a job. Hey, watch yalanguage Alex. Yeah. No cursin in fronna married women. They laughed and sprawled along the counter and on the chairs. All the time fuckaround. Someday you get in trouble. Ah Alex, dont talk like that. Ya makus feel bad. Yeh, man, ya hurt our feelings. . .

PART II

THE QUEEN IS DEAD

*So God created man in his own image,
in the image of God created he him;
male and female created he them.*

Genesis 1:27

GEORGETTE WAS A HIP queer. She (he) didnt try to disguise or conceal it with marriage and mans talk, satisfying her homosexuality with the keeping of a secret scrapbook of pictures of favorite male actors or athletes or by supervising the activities of young boys or visiting turkish baths or mens locker rooms, leering sidely while seeking protection behind a carefully guarded guise of virility (fearing that moment at a cocktail party or in a bar when this front may start crumbling from alcohol and be completely disintegrated with an attempted kiss or groping of an attractive young man and being repelled with a punch and—rotten fairy—followed with hysteria and incoherent apologies and excuses and running from the room) but, took a pride in being a homosexual by feeling intellectually and esthetically superior to those (especially women) who werent gay (look at all the great artists who were fairies!); and with the wearing of womens panties, lipstick, eye makeup (this including occasionally gold and silver—stardust—on the lids), long marcelled hair, manicured and polished fingernails, the wearing of womens clothes complete with padded bra, high heels and wig (one of her biggest thrills was going to BOP CITY dressed as a tall stately blond (she was 6'4" in

25

heels) in the company of a negro (He was a big beautiful black bastard and when he floated in all the cats in the place jumped and the squares bugged. We were at a crazy pad before going and were blasting like crazy and were up so high that I just didn't give a shit for anyone honey, let me tell you!)); and the occasional wearing of a menstrual napkin.

She was in love with Vinnie and rarely came home while he was in jail, but stayed uptown with her girl friends, high most of the time on benzedrine and marijuana. She had come home one morning with one of her friends after a three day tea party with her makeup still on and her older brother slapped her across the face and told her that if he ever came home like that again hed kill him. She and her friend ran screaming from the house calling her brother a dirty fairy. After that she always called to see if her brother was in before going home.

Her life didnt revolve, but spun centrifugally, around stimulants, opiates, johns (who paid her to dance for them in womens panties then ripped them off her; bisexuals who told their wives they were going out with the boys and spent the night with Georgette (she trying to imagine they were Vinnie)), the freakish precipitate coming to the top.

When she heard that Vinnie had been paroled she went to Brooklyn (first buying 10 dozen benzedrine tablets) and sat in the Greeks all night following Vinnie everywhere and trying to get him alone. She bought him coffeand, sat on his lap and asked him to go for a walk. He would refuse and tell her theres plenty of time sweetheart. Maybe later. Georgette would wiggle on his lap, play with his earlobes feeling like a young girl on her first date. She looked at him coquettishly. Let me do you Vinnie, forcing herself to refrain from trying to kiss him,

26

from embracing him, from caressing his thighs, dreaming of the warmth of his groin, seeing him nude, holding her head (not too gently), pressing close to him, watching his muscles contract running her fingertips gently along the tightened thigh muscles (he might even groan at the climax); the feel, taste, smell. . . . Please Vinnie, the dream almost carrying over to consciousness, the benzedrine making it even more difficult not to try to animate the dream *now*.

It wasnt fear of being rebuked or hit by him (that could be developed in her mind into a lovers quarrel ending in a beautiful reconciliation) that restrained her, but she knew if done in the presence of his friends (who tolerated more than accepted her, or used her as a means to get high when broke or for amusement when bored) his pride would force him to abjure her completely and then there would not only be no hope, but, perhaps no dream. She put her hand tentatively on the back of his neck twisting the short hairs. She jumped up as he pushed her, and giggled as he patted her on the buttox. She strutted over to the counter. May I please have another cup of coffee Alex? you big Greek fairy. She put another benzedrine tablet in her mouth and swallowed it with the coffee; put a nickel in the jukebox and started wiggling as a tenor sax wailed a blues number Some of the others in the Greeks clapped in time to the music and yelled, Go Georgette, Go! She put her hands behind her head, ellipsed her pelvis slowly and- bumped—up to one of the girls who was laughing *at* her and *threw* her hip in her face. Heres one for you, you big bitch. When the music stopped she sat on a stool at the counter, finished her coffee, spun around a few times on the stool, stopped, stood up holding her hands delicately in front of her in the dramatic manner of a concert singer and sang *un bel di* in a wavering falsetto. Someone laughed and said she should go on the stage. You have a nice voice Georgie. Yeah, from the same girl, fa callin hogs. Georgette turned, put her hands on her hips, leaned her head to one side and looked at her disdainfully. What would you know about opera Miss Cocksucker? She *threw* her head back and sauntered out to the street in her finest regal fashion.

Vinnie was 12 the first time he was arrested. He had stolen a hearse. He was so short that he had to slide down in the seat so far to reach the pedals that a cop standing on a corner looking at the hearse, stopped for a redlight, thought the cab was empty. The cop was so surprised when he opened the door and saw Vinnie behind the wheel that he had almost shifted the gears and started moving before the cop realized what was happening and pulled him out. The judge was just as surprised as the arresting officer and had some difficulty suppressing a laugh while reprimanding Vinnie and making him promise never to do such a bad thing again. Go home and be a good boy.

Two days later he stole another car. This time with friends who were older and better able to drive a car without attracting too much attention. They would keep a car, driving to school when they went, until it ran out of gas then leave it and steal another. They were caught many times, but Vinnie was always released after promising not to do it again. He was so young, looking even younger, and innocent looking that it was impossible for a judge to think of him as a criminal and they were hesitant about sending him to an institution where he might learn to be a thief rather than just a mischievous boy. When he was 15 and arrested for the 11th time he was sent to a correctional institution for boys. When he was released a representative of a social organization talked with him and asked him to visit their boys club in the neighborhood. Vinnie had grown during the last year and took great pride in his ability to fight better than other kids his age and better than most who were older. After starting a few fights at the boys club for kicks he stopped going and another invitation was never extended.

He was sent up for his first real bit when he was 16. He had stolen a car and was speeding along Ocean Parkway (he wanted to see how fast the car could go in case he had to outrun the law) and crackedup. His only injury was a gash in his head. An ambulance and the police were called The ambulance attendant bandaged his head and told the policemen he was well enough to be taken to the police station. Vinnie still wasnt fully aware of what had happened as the 2 policemen helped him up the steps of the stationhouse, but he knew they were cops. He pushed one down the steps, punched the other knocking him down, and ran. Possibly he might have gotten away, but he went to the Greeks and displayed the gash in his head to his friends telling them how he dumped the two cops.

He was permitted to plead guilty to a misdemeanor and was sentenced to 1 to 3 years.

He seemed to enjoy the time he spent in jail. While there he tattooed his number on his wrist with a pin and ink and displayed it to everyone when he came home. He went straight to the Greeks when he was paroled, sitting there all night telling stories about the things he did while doing time. Many of the others in the Greeks had been in the same prison and they talked about the guards, the work, the yard and their cells. The day after his release 3 gunmen were shot attempting to stickup a store. One died instantly and the other 2 were in the hospital in critical condition. When he heard about it he bought a paper, cut the story and pictures out and carried them with him for days, until they finally fell apart from handling, telling everyone that they were friends of his. I did time with them guys. Yaknow this guy Steve who got killed? He was my boy. He was on the same bench with me. Me and him was real tight man. We ran the yard up there. We was the *gees* on the first bench and what we said was law. We even got sent to the hole tagether. A couplea creeps wouldnt giveus the packages they got from home so we dumpedem. Im tellinya, we was real tight man.

The glory of having known someone killed by the police during a stickup was the greatest event of his life and a memory he cherished as would an aging invalid, at the end of a disappointing life, a winning touchdown made at the end of the final game of the season.

Vinnie got kicks from refusing Georgette when she tried to get him to take a walk with her, and from patting her on the ass and telling her not now sweetheart. Maybe later. He felt good having someone hot forim like that. Even if it is a fag. He followed her over to the counter where she was sitting and, wetting his finger and sticking it in her ear, laughed as she squirmed and giggled. Too bad I didn't haveya upstate. I had a couple of sweet kids but they didnt have chips like this, patting her again on the ass and looking at the others, smiling, and waiting for them to smile in appreciation of his witticisms. It cost loot ta do me now sweetchips, turning once more to the others wanting to be certain that they understood that Georgette was in love with him and that he could have her anytime he wanted to, but, he was playing it cool, waiting for her to give him loot before he condescended to allow her to do him; feeling superior to the others because he knew

Steve who had been killed by the bulls, and because Georgette was smart and could snow them under with words (at the same time hating anyone else who might use polysyllabic words and thinking anyone who went to school was a creep, but (mistaking in his dull, never to be matured mind, her loneliness for respect of his strength and virility) she would never try that with him.

He followed Georgette out to the street turning to laugh at the girl Georgette had insulted, sitting, trying desperately to think of something to say, her rage manifest on her face and thickening her tongue. She spit and called him a goddam faggot bastard Georgette turned, holding a cigarette between middle and forefinger of the right hand, hand inverted and outstretched, left hand on her hip and looking disdainfully at the flushed face, Whats your excuse churl? did you leave your nature in the outer ring or in a cesspool?

Vinnie laughed trying to give the impression he dug Georgettes remark (only vaguely aware that there *may* be something in the remark he didnt understand) and pushed the girl back into her chair as she started toward the door, and walked out and pinched Georgette on the cheek, then took a cigarette from her pocket. Whattayasay we take a walk? I might even letya do me. Oh, aren't you the one though, hoping he was serious, trying in her finest effeminate manner to act coy. I/ll only chargeya a fin, leaning against the fender of a parked car looking through the open door into the Greeks at the others, wanting to be certain they saw and heard. Your generosity overwhelms me Vincent, smiling at his, My name is Vinnie and can that Vincent shit, and wanting to have him even if she did have to pay, but not wanting him on a business basis. She would give him money if he wanted it, but not at *that* time; if she did it would not only kill, or at least blur, the dream, but it

31

would make her his john and that would be unbearable, especially after having waited so long. She knew he wouldnt go with her while the others were there, fearing the jeers of queerbait, so was forced to wait and hope the others might leave. Reasoning thus, yet hoping, in her benzedrined mind, that she may be wrong and he would take her by the arm and walk away with her, she continued the little game. I/ll have you know that I have dozens of johns who pay me, and not a paltry five dollars either.

I wont charge ya nothin Georgie, grabbing one of her ears. Dont touch me Harry, you big freak, pushing his hand away and slapping at it. Im not about to have sex with *you*. Harry took his pushbutton knife from his pocket, opened it, locked the blade in the open position, felt the blade and tip and walked toward Georgette as she backed away shaking limp wristed hands at him. Stand still and I/ll makeya a real woman without goin ta Denmark. He and Vinnie laughed as Georgette continued to back away, her hands limply extended. You dont want that big sazeech gettin in yaway Georgie boy. Let me cut it off. It is *not* big Miss *Pinky,* trying to suppress her fears by thinking herself a heroine, and get away from me.

Harry flipped the knife underhand at her and yelled think fast! She lifted her left leg slightly, covered her face with her hands, turned away and shrilled an OOOOOOO as the knife hit the sidewalk, bouncing off the wall behind her and skipping a few feet away. Harry and Vinnie were laughing, Vinnie walking over to the knife and picking it up, Georgette walking away still screeching at Harry. You big freak! You Neanderthal fairy! You—Vinnie threw the knife yelling think fast. Georgette leaping, pirouetting away from the knife screaming at them to stop (only the benzedrine preventing hysteria now), but they laughed, their daring growing with her fear; throwing the knife harder and closer to her feet; the knife skipping and billiarding away, picked up and thrown again at the dancing feet (the scene resembling one in a grade B western); the laughing, leaping and pirouetting stopping suddenly as the blade of the knife stuck in the calf of her leg (had it been a board, not flesh, the blade would have vibrated and twanged). Georgette looked quizzically at the small portion of the blade visible, and handle sticking from her leg, too surprised to feel the blood rolling down her leg to think of the wound or the danger, but just staring at the knife trying to understand what had happened. Vinnie and Harry just looked. Harry muttered something about that being a good shot and Vinnie smiled. Georgette looked up, saw Vinnie smiling at her, looked back at the knife and screamed that her new slacks were ruined. The others, watching from the Greeks, laughed and Harry asked her what she was growin from her leg. Georgette simply called him a fuck and hopped over to the step leading to the side door of the Greeks and sat down slowly, carefully keeping the leg stiff and extended in front of her. Harry asked her if she wanted him to yank the knife out and she screamed at him to go to hell. Leaning down and gently holding the handle in her fingertips and closing her eyes she tugged tentatively, then slowly pulled the knife from her leg. She sighed and dropped the knife, then leaned back against the door jamb, flexed her leg slightly and reached down and pulled her shoe off. It was filled with blood. The effects of the benzedrine were almost completely worn off and she shivered as she poured the blood from her shoe, the blood splattering as it hit the sidewalk, the small puddle flowing off in rills in to cracks in the pavement, mixing with the dirt in the cracks and disappearing. . . . She screamed and cursed Harry.

Whats the matta Georgie? Has the poor little girl got a Booboo? She screeched. You brought me down! You rotten freaks, you brought me down! She looked at Vinnie with pleading in her eyes trying to regain her composure (the effects of the benzedrine completely gone now and panic starting to take its place), hoping to gain his sympathy, looking tenderly as a lover taking irrevocable leave, and Vinnie laughed thinking how much she looked like a dog beggin for a bone. Whats the matta? Ya hurt or somethin?

She almost fainted from fear and anger as the others roared with laughter. She looked at the blur of faces wanting to kick them, spit into them, slap them, scratch them, but, when she tried to move the pain in her leg stopped her and she leaned back against the jamb, now fully conscious of her leg and, for the first time, thinking of the wound. She lifted her pant leg up to her knee and trembled as she felt the blood soaked pant leg and looked at the wound, blood still oozing out, her blood soaked sock and the small pool of blood under her foot, trying to ignore the whistles and, Atta girl, take it off.

Vinnie had gone into the Greeks and got a bottle of iodine from Alex and came out and told Georgette not taworry about it. I/ll fix it up. He lifted her leg and poured the iodine into the wound and laughed, with the others, when Georgette screamed and jumped up, holding the injured leg with both hands, hopping up and down on the other. They whistled, clapped their hands and someone started singing, Dance Ballerina Dance. Georgette fell to the ground, still clutching her leg frantically, and sat in the middle of the sidewalk spotted by the light from the Greeks, one leg curved under her, the other up and bent at the knee, her head bowed and between her legs, like a clown imitating a dancer.

34

When the pain subsided she got up and hopped back to the step, sat down and asked for a handkerchief to wrap around her leg. Whatta yacrazy? I dont want my hankerchief all messed up. The laughter again. Vinnie stepped gallantly forward and pulled the handkerchief from his pocket and helped her tie it around her leg. There yaare Georgie. All fixed up. She said nothing but stared at the blood; the wound growing larger and larger; blood poisoning streaking her leg, the streak widening and almost to her heart; the stench of gangrene from her rotting leg. . . .

Well, comeon, give. What? What did you say Vinnie? I said give me some loot and I/ll getya a cab so you can go home. I cant go home Vinnie. Why not? My brothers home. Well, whereya gonna go? Ya cant sit here all night. I/ll go to the hospital. They can fix my leg and then I/ll go uptown to Marys. Areya crazy or somethin. Ya cant go to the hospital. When they see that leg of yours theyll wanna know what happened and the next thing yaknow the lawll be knockin on my door and I/ll be back in the can. I wont tell them anything Vinnie. You know that. Honestly. Inna pigs ass. They getya up there and shoot somethin inya and youll talk ya ass off, vague memories of radio programs heard and movies seen. I/ll getya a cab and takeya home. No Vinnie, please! I wont tell them anything. I promise. I/ll tell them some spick kids did it, holding her leg tightly with both hands, rocking back and forth with a steady hypnotical rhythm and trying with desperation not to get hysterical and to ignore the throbbing pain in her leg. Please! My brothers home. I cant go home now! Look, I dont know what yabrother will do and I dont give a shit, but I know what Im gonna do if ya dont shut the hellup.

35

Georgette called to him as he walked toward the avenue to hail a cab, pleading and promising anything. She didnt want to argue with Vinnie; she didnt want him to dislike her; she didn't want to provoke him; but she knew what would happen when she got home. Her Mother would cry and call the doctor; and if her brother didnt find the bennie (she couldn't throw them away and there was too much to take at once) the doctor would know she had been taking something and tell them. She knew they would take her clothes off and see the red spangled G string she was wearing. Her brother might ignore the makeup (when he saw her leg and all the blood; and when her Mother started worrying about her and telling the brother to leave him alone) but, he would never ignore the bennie and the G string.

Yet this was not what she really feared; it wasn't being slapped by her brother that brought back the fear that almost caused her to faint; that made her think (only briefly) of praying; that pushed from her mind the smell of gangrene. It was knowing that she would have to stay in the house for a few days, maybe even a week. The doctor would tell her to stay off the leg until it healed properly and her Mother and brother would enforce the doctors order; and she knew they wouldnt allow any of her girl friends to visit her and she had nothing except the benzedrine which would probably be found and thrown away. There was nothing hidden in the house; no way she could get it. In the house a week or more with nothing. I/d crack. I cant stay down that long. Theyll bug me. Bug me. O jesus jesus jesus. . . .

A cab stopped in front of the Greeks and Vinnie got out and he and Harry helped (forced) Georgette into the rear of the cab. She continued to plead, to beg; she told them she had a john who was a Wallstreet Broker and she was

36

going to see him this weekend and he was good for 20, maybe more. I/ll give it to you. I/ll give you more. I know where you can get hundreds without any trouble at all. I know a few fairies who own an Arts & Crafts Shoppee in the Village. You can stick them up. They always have a lot of money around; it wont be any trouble— Vinnie slapped her face and told her ta shut the hell up, trying to see if the cab driver was paying any attention to what she was saying and telling him something, almost incoherently, about his friend just having a accident and was still kindda shook.

It took less than 3 minutes to drive the few blocks to Georgettes house. When the cab stopped in front of her house Vinnie took the change from her pocket and the 3 singles from her wallet. Is that all yagot? I/ll give you more in a few days if you take me to the hospital. Look, if ya dont walk in, we/ll carryya in and tell ya brother ya tried ta pick up a couplea sailors and they dumpedya. Will you come over to the house tomorrow and see me, alone? Yeah, sure. I/ll seeya tomorrow, winking at Harry. Georgette tried to believe him and for a moment forgot her previous fears and the old dream flashed briefly across her mind and she could see her room, the bed, Vinnie. . . .

She limped toward the door and stopped in the vestibule, put a handful of bennie in her mouth, chewed then swallowed them. Before knocking on her door she turned and yelled to Vinnie not to forget about tomorrow. Vinnie laughed at her.

Vinnie and Harry waited in the cab until they saw the door open and Georgette go inside, her Mother closing the door behind her, before they paid the driver. They left the cab, walked down the street to the avenue, turned the corner and walked back to the Greeks.

The door closed. A hundred times. Closed. Even as it
swung open she heard it bang shut. Closed. Closed. Dozens of doors like many pictures jerkily animated by a
thumb, tumbling mistily like shadows. . . . and the click,
click, the goddamn click click click of the latch and it
banged shut. SHUT. Again and again and again it
BANGED SHUT. A thousand miserable times. BANG
BANG. BANG. Always banging shut. Never a knock.
Think it. Force it. A knock. A knock. Please, please. O
Jesus a knock. Make it a knock. Make it someone knocking. To come in. Why cant it be a knock. Goldie with
bennie. Anything. Anybody. Closed. Closed. Bang.
BANG. BANG! SHUT!!! O Jesus SHUT! And I cant
get out. Only roll in bed. This dirty freak of a bed (VIN-
NIE!!!) and that rotten fairy of a doctor wouldnt give me
anything. Not even a little codeine. And it throbs. It
does. It does. It throbs and pains. I can feel it squeezing
up my leg and it hurts. It hurts dreadfully. It does. It really
does. I need something for the pain. O Jesus I cant stay
down. And I cant get out. Not even Soakie. She might
have *something*. Let her in. I cant get out. Out. Up—(the
door banged and her Mother looked up and noticed first
the strange look on her sons face, the staring eyes; then
the blood on his slacks and as she ran to him she collapsed on Mothers shoulder, crying, wanting to cry on
Mothers shoulder and have her listen and stroke her hair
(I love him Mother. I love him and want him.); and
knowing that she must scare her Mother so she would be
protected by her sympathy, and perhaps Mother would
get her to bed (she wanted to run to the bed, but she
knew she had to hobble to impress her), get her to bed
before her brother came in the room. She might be able
to hide the bennie. She had to try! Her mother staggered
and they hobbled toward the bed (mustnt run), wanting
her Mother near, wanting the comfort; and feeling calmer,

safer, as her Mothers face paled and her hands shook;
yet calculating just how far she could go with the scene
so Mother would be properly concerned yet still capable of protecting her from Arthur . . . and she may
yet be able to hide the bennie) . . .

Why couldnt he be out.
Why did he have to be home. If only he were dead.
You sonofabitch die. DIE (Whats the matter with mommys little girl. Did ooo stub oo little toesywoesy Georgie-
worgie? Dont touch me you fairy. Dont touch me. Look
whos calling someone a fairy. Aint that a laugh. Ha! You
freak. Freak FREAK FREAK FREAK! Why you rotten
punk—Georgette leaned more heavily upon Mother and
swung the injured leg from side to side, groaning. Please
Arthur. Please. Leave your brother alone. Hes hurt. Hes
passing out from loss of blood. Brother? Thats a goodone.
Please—Georgette groaned louder and started sliding
from Mothers neck (if only she could get to the bed and
hide the bennie. Hide the bennie. Hide the bennie);
please, not again. Not now. Just call the doctor. For me.
Please.) If he had stayed out. Or had just gone to the
kitchen . . . Georgie porgie puddin n pie . . . Why do they
do this to me? Why wont they leave me alone??? (Arthur
looked at his brother and grunted with disgust then went
to the phone and Georgette tried frantically to get the
bennie out of her pocket but her slacks were so tight she
couldnt get her hand in and she was afraid to move away
from her Mother so she could get her hand in her pocket.
She fell on the bed and rolled on her side and tried to get
them out and under the mattress or even the pillow (yes,
the pillow) but her Mother thought she was rolling with
pain and held her hands trying to comfort and soothe her
son, telling him to try to relax, the doctor will be here
soon and you will be alright. Dont worry darling. Youll
see. Everything will be alright . . . and then her brother

39

came back, looked at his Mother then the ripped slacks
and blood and said they had better take the pants off and
put a little mercurochrome on the leg and Georgette tried
to yank her hands free, but her Mother gripped tighter,
trying to absorb her sons pain, and Georgette fought furiously, trying to hold her slacks and keep her brother from
pulling them off. She screamed and kicked, but when she
did the pain really throbbed through her leg, and she tried
biting her Mothers hands but her brother pushed her head
down (the G string! The bennie!!!). Stop. Stop! Go away.
Dont let him. Please dont let him. It will be alright son.
The doctor will be here soon. Nobody wants to hurt you.
You rotten fairy, stop. Stop! You queer sonofabitch.
STOP, but her brother loosened the belt and grabbed her
pants by the cuffs and Georgette screeched and her
Mothers tears fell on her face, begging Arthur to be
careful; and Arthur pulled them slowly yet still tore loose
the clot from the wound and blood started oozing, then
flowing down the leg and Georgette fell back crying and
screaming, and Arthur let the pants fall to the floor and
stared at his brother . . . watching the blood roll to the
sheet, the leg jerk . . . listening to his brother crying and
wanting to laugh with satisfaction, and even happy to see
the misery on his Mothers face as she looked at Georgette
and lifted his head in her arms and stroked his head,
humming, shaking tears from her face . . . Arthur wanting to lean over and punch his face, that goddamn face
covered with makeup, wanting to tear at the leg and
listen to his fairy brother wail . . . He straightened up and
stood silently at the foot of the bed for a moment half-
hearing the sobs and his thoughts, then stepped around
to the side and started yanking at the Red Spangled G
String. You disgusting degenerate. In front of my Mother
you have the nerve to lay here with this thing on. He
yanked, and slapped Georgette across the face, Mother

pleading, crying, soothing, and Georgette rolled and clawed as the tight G String scraped along her leg, and Mother begged Arthur to leave his brother alone— BROTHER?—but he tugged and yanked, yelling above them until it was off and he flung it from him into another room. How can you hold him like that. Hes nothing but a filthy homosexual. You should throw him out in the street. Hes your brother son. You should help him. Hes my son (hes my baby. My baby) and I love him and you should love him. She rocked with Georgettes head cradled in her arms and Arthur stormed out of the house and Georgette rolled over on her back trying to reach the slacks and the bennie, but her Mother held her, continuing to tell her son that it would be alright. Everything will be alright.)

        O please, please, please, please . . . why are you torturing me? The bitches. The dirty bitches. O let me out. Let someone come in. I dont want to be alone. Please let them come. Anything. Im down. Let them come. For christs sake. Im down. DOWN! I cant stay in this room. This dirty room. Let Vinnie in. Let him take me away. Vinnie. O Vinnie, my darling. Take me away. Its ugly in here. Ugly. And I loved the carousel. Puddin n pie. Vinnie—(the doctor looked at her eyes, said nothing, then examined her leg. He washed the wound, probed gently, and Georgette groaned, hoping hed write a prescription, and rolled on the bed trying to hang over the side and reach the slacks and the doctor mumbled; her Mother watched, shaking, and Georgette looked pleadingly at her, wanting her caresses and protection, but she couldnt reach the slacks. Jesus, why cant I reach them? She stopped rolling and cried. Her Mother stroked her forehead and the doctor bandaged the leg and told her to stay off it for a few days and come in to see him when she felt better. He closed his bag (shut. Shut. It banged Shut!),

41

smiled and told Mrs. Hanson it would be better if George didnt have any visitors for a few days. She nodded (Georgette leaned slowly to the edge of the bed—when they go to the door) and thanked him. Dont bother to walk me to the door. I can find my way out))—not even a little codeine. Nothing. If that fucking Harry wasnt there. That freak. And those rotten bitches. Two cent cunt. Not even a nebbie. He could have given me one at least. Not much of a cut. Just stay in bed a few days. Days. Days. Days . . . DAYS. DAYS!!! The walls will fall. Theyll crush me. Mother? O Mother. Mother? Give me something. Please. Anything. Try to relax son. Your leg will be better soon. My leg?—(Stop. Arthur, for the love of God stop. Stop? You see these? You see them? More of those goddamn dopepills. Thats what they are. Dopepills. Well, you will never see these again dear sweet *brother!* Give them to me. Give me them. Mother, make him give them to me. Shut up or I/ll kill you. Do you hear me? I swear I will kill you. Always crying. Mommy this and Mommy that. Every time you get a little scratch—Arthur. Stop! He stood shaking, clutching the end of the bed watching brother crawl and squirm on the bed, hiding behind his Mommy, wanting Mommys love and kisses . . . then shoved the pills in his pocket, spun around and dragged out the boxes in the back of the closet and dumped them on the floor—Mommy this and Mommy that—ripping and tearing Georgettes drag clothes, her lovely dresses and silks, stamping on her shoes . . . You see these Mother? You see them? Look. Look at these disgusting pictures. O Arthur—Look at them. Just LOOK! Men making love to each other. It isnt pretty is it? Arthur, please. Well? is it? Are they? ARE THEY??? Filth. Thats what they are. FILTH!!! Why dont you die Geor*gie!* Why dont you go away and die. Stop. STOP! For the love of god Arthur, stop. I cant stand it anymore. Well, neither

can I. You saw those pictures. Now you should know what
he *really* is. A degenerate. A filthy degenerate! Arthur,
please, for my sake. I know. I know. Leave your brother
alone. Please. *Brother???*)—O god, theyll bug me. They
know I cant stay down. They know it. Nothing to see. To
look at. Why me? Why wont somebody help me. I dont
want to be alone. I cant stand it. Please help me. At least
Goldie has bennie. I cant stay down. Always alone. O
jesus, jesus, jesus . . . why me??? Mommy? Mommy? O
god I need something. Those sick johns. Always? I dont
want to be straight. I just need something. I/ll go crazy.
Theyre keeping me down. Down. Why do they want to kill
me? and the near shadowless room continued shrinking
and she looked for dark corners, but there were none,
just a penumbra as the closet door partially blocked the
light from the living room. Georgette called . . . looked
around the room. At the bed. Sat up and called again . . .
then slowly swung her legs over the side and tentatively
touched the floor . . . stood . . . hobbled to the door and
looked at Mother sleeping in a chair. She dressed, took
money from Mothers pocketbook and left. When she
stood on the stoop she realized she didnt know the day
or time. But the sun had set. Leaning against parked cars
she limped to the corner and hailed a cab, praying that
Goldie was home. She gave the driver the address and
thought of Goldies and bennie.

       When she got to Goldies
one of the girls helped her upstairs and to a chair. She
asked for someone to light her a cigarette and leaned
back in the chair, closed her eyes, allowing her hand
and body to shake, extending her leg stiffly in front of her
and groaning. The girls stood around, asking, wondering,
thrilling to the scene and exulting over the sudden breaking of the monotony; the monotony of the last few days
that dragged them even with bennie and pot and forced

them to sit, just sit, and bitch about the heat like tired johns, and remember beatings by punks, and stares of squares; but Georgette twisted her face with pain, not too much though, and they wondered and thrilled. Goldie handed her half a dozen bennie and she swallowed them, gulped hot coffee and sat silent . . . trying to think the bennie into her mind (and her room and the past few days out); not wanting to wait for it to dissolve and be absorbed by the blood and pumped through her body; wanting her heart to pound *now;* wanting the chills *now;* wanting the lie *now;* Now!!! The others jabbered and squealed as she opened her eyes, shaking her head tragically, her arms hanging limply . . . speaking in whispers and shaking away questions, nodding and slowly raising her cigarette to her lips and taking shallow asthmatic puffs. They gave her more coffee and then the tingle, the pounding of the heart and she lit another cigarette and straightened slightly in the chair. Goldie asked her if she was feeling better and she said yes. A little thanks. Would you like some pot? O, do you have any? Of course honey. Goldie gave her a stick and Georgette sucked the smoke refusing, absolutely refusing to cough; and they watched and waited until Georgette had chewed the roach & put her makeup on before bubbling forth with their questions. Well, I must say you look much better now. You looked simply frightful when you came in. I have been down for days. Days? What happened. Yes, dishus honey. Do you have another stick Goldie. Of course. Well for gods sake, you just going to sit there all night or are you going to tell us what happened. O really Miss Lee. Cant you see the poor girl is overwrought. You don't have to yell Miss Thing. Im simply dying to know what happened, thats all. Thats alright honey—O thank you Goldie—I understand. Just let me get myself together and I/ll tell you the whole story. She smoked the second

44

stick and told them how she was stabbed; how the freak Harry started the whole thing; how the doctor wouldnt give her anything, not even one little nebbie; and how they kept her locked in her room not allowing her to have one visitor, and I heard Vinnie at the door a couple of times and they wouldn't let him in; and how she defied her brother, the freak, and how she laid him out and walked right out of the house. And I mean right past him honey, right past him, and you should have seen his face! he was agog, simply agog. O I laid him out but good. O how wonderful. How simply wonderful. O how I wish I had been there. I would have adored seeing you lay that big freak out. I/ll never forget that atrocious scene he pulled on us. Never. All those straight creeps are like that. They clapped their hands, twittered and aaad and decided to have a party in honor of Georgette and the laying out of Arthur.

Goldie sent Rosie, a demented female who acted as sortofa housemaid, for gin, cigarettes and another gross of bennie. They made a small pot of bouillon and danced around it dropping tablets in and chanting *ben*nie in the *bouil*lon, *ben*nie in the *bouil*lon, whirling away the fear and boredom, giggling, popping bennie, drinking gin, toasting Georgette: Long Live THE QUEEN, and the laying out of Arthur. He should be laid out, but I mean really, the freak, each in her mind and turn laying out every rough or straight sonofabitch that ever hit them or pointed and laughed; dancing through the apartment until they fell into chairs trying to catch their breath, fanning themselves; and Rosie brought bouillon, ice and gin and they spoke more quietly, still laughing, asking Georgette again and again to tell them how she laid her brother out . . . then gradually they quieted. too spent to shout, stretching in their seats, getting higher and higher as they sat quietly and becoming

conscious of the absence of men, their high spirits and
overflowing joy making the absence of love known. So her
subjects petitioned the Queen to summon forth her dashing husband and his rough trade friends, for tonight they
were daring and even Camille, a frail queen from a small
town in Jersey, longed for rough arms, there being no
room, but absolutely no room, for johns. So Georgette,
flying in her world of junk, called the Greeks and flushed
(O, my libido is twitching) when she heard Vinnies voice
and fluttered her lids when he said hello sweetchips,
whereya been? O, Ive been balling it loverman, smiling
at her friends and too high to be bothered by, Ive got ya
loverman shit. Itll still costya. She asked him to come
over with some of the boys, giggling yes when he asked if
she was high, telling him they had loads of gin and not
to worry about gold for gas to get back, and Vinnie said
maybe they would (for kicks) and Georgette continued
to talk after Vinnie hungup, rolling her hips as she sighed,
O Vinnie baby, and sighing as she slowly lowered the
phone. They asked her if they were coming, how many,
when—and Georgette played it cool and to the hilt;
regally walking back to her throne, telling the girls to be
quiet. Really! One would think it was years since you had
a real man. They may be here in an hour or so, if they
dont pull a job, so just keep your legs crossed, flaunting
her arms, smiling graciously and secretly. They drank
more bouillon, popped more bennie and dished the dirt.
Camille was nervous, never having met an excon before.
You just never meet that sort back home. As a matter of
fact Goldie was the first hip queen she had ever met. All
the fairies in her town were closet queens or pinkteas, so
she was all a dither, jumping up, jerking around the room,
asking question after question, Georgette telling her
stories about broken noses, cut throats and Camille ooood
and squealed, loving the tightness in her stomach and the

apprehension in her bowels. She said she felt faint and that she simply must take a bath. The others laughed and chided, Georgette waving off the how could you/s as Camille filled one of the tubs in the kitchen and laid out her brushes: One for her back, one for her stomach, one for her chest, one for her arms, one for her legs, one for her feet, one for her toenails, one for her hands, one for her fingernails, and a special jar of cream for her face. She lined them up, handles facing her, and started from the left with the back brush. They told her to hurry or she would be attacked while bathing and O she was frightened, they should know better than to talk of such things. She was so upset she almost broke wind.

Camille had finished her bath, collected her brushes and was primping in the bathroom when the bell rang. Georgette almost jumped to the door, but contained herself, sat back, leaning her head to one side hoping the light was falling on her face properly, and waited for someone to open the door. She held her cigarette daintily and tried to hide her excitement. Over an hour since the call and though Miss Camille, while in the tub, had afforded Georgette an opportunity to appear relaxed and carefree, during the time that elapsed since Camille finished Georgette was forced to retain her position, and the center of attraction, by amusing the others with stories, laying this one and that one out, the girls laughing at her wit; continually talking and hoping the bell would ring before too many seconds of silence forced her to think of what to say next or allowed the others to become conscious of time and ask about Vinnie (VINNIE!!! Vinnie had to come) or allowed her fears to come back to the surface . . . but the bell rang and she swallowed another bennie, finished her bouillon and once again adjusted herself on her throne.

47

Goldie
opened the door and the boys strolled in, looked around,
stood in the kitchen, looking, until Vinnie led the way into
the living room. Whatayasay Georgie? Hows the leg? O,
just fine, thank you, tilting her head to the side just a wee
bit more and taking a quick Bette Davis like drag on her
cigarette. The other guys strolled around the room, eventually flopping here and there. Harrys eyes bugged when
he saw Lee. She looked like one of the show girls you see
in some of the magazines (her hair was shoulder length
and golden blond and she was always smartly in drag), a
real doll. Harry kept staring, not digging the score. He had
never been to Goldies before and he thought maybe she
was Rosie the freak he had heard the guys talk about, but
man, she didnt look like no freak. She looked like a
real fine piecea ass. Goldie prepared drinks, putting a
bennie in each, and stepped lightly through the rooms
dispensing them, smiling and simply brimming over with
joy. Lee told Rosie to bring her another pack of cigarettes
and when Rosie simpered and said no Lee pointed a
finger at her and told her to bring them here at once or
you will be out on the street with the other freaks, Miss
Cocksucker. (Harry looked at Lee, still puzzled, then
figured she must be one of the queens. But shes still a fine
piecea ass.) Rosie threw the cigarettes to Lee and ran to
the bathroom and pounded on the door until Camille unlocked it, then stepped around her and sat on the floor
between the sink and the toiletbowl. O really Rosie. I
mean! Camille sniffed, primped her hair again, peeked
out, walked to the kitchen and slowly inched her way to
the living room hoping her makeup was on properly
(that light over the mirror is simply terrible) and glided
into the room and slowly lowered herself beside Goldie
and, as did the other girls, surveyed the prospective
suitors. Her eyes almost blurred with excitement. They

48

had such hard looks. Why their eyes went right through you as if you were naked. She squirmed slightly. But it is wonderful. But what should she do? Of course she had never even so much as hinted the truth to the other girls, but she was a virgin. She had talked with a few of the queens back home and they told her how to go about *do*ing it, always cautioning her never, but never to take it out of her mouth when he was coming because it might just get all over you and in your eyes and you know honey, you can go blind from that, and anyway thats the moment when everything just explodes and you wont want to take it out . . . But how do you start? what do you say??? O, I hope everything will be alright.

Goldie inquired if they were ready for another drink and they said yeah, but not so much of that sodashit. Thats o k for you girls, but I like somethin with a kick, so Goldie swished lightly to the kitchen, lowering her eyes at Malfie, fixed another drink with just a drop of mixer and another bennie, distributed the drinks and asked them if they would like a bennie. Sure, why not. So she pased the box around, telling them to take two, then sat down glancing coyly from time to time, at Malfie.

Georgette no longer tried to control the conversation, but concentrated on Vinnie, trying, of course, to give a disinterested impression, wanting to let her friends see that he was hers. She tried toying with Harry, hoping to arouse a sense of jealousy in Vinnie, but Harry continually grabbed her by the ears and rubbed his crotch and tolder he got a nice fat lob forer ta suck, and Georgette sat back on her throne and threw her head to the side and told him she wasnt interested in boys, Miss Pinkie, then leaned toward Vinnie when she saw him staring at Lee. Vinnie was hip to Lee, but she still looked like a lovely doll and he thought of her as a

dame. Lee enjoyed the idea of them staring at her, but
turned her head and spoke to Goldie or Camille or the
room in general. After all, she had worked in some of the
best drag joints and had been featured in the professional
magazines and it certainly would be beneath her dignity to
openly fraternize with roughtrade (admittedly though she
did enjoy them within the safety of the apartment). That
may be alright for Georgette, and the others, but someone in her position couldnt afford to be seen with scum,
and their manners are far too repulsive . . . but it might
be fun to play with them . . . Camille continued to look,
worry and hope.

      Goldie asked Malfie if he would like an-
other drink and he said sure sweetheart, fillerup and
Goldie filled the glass with gin, just a bit of mixer, no
bennie (too much might kill his nature), yelled for Rosie
to get more gin like a good girl. Rosie smiled, you like me
Goldie? and Goldie patted her head, of course Rosie. Now
run along like a good girl and get the gin. When Goldie
handed the drink to Malfie she brushed lightly against
his leg and smiled. Malfie raised his eyes slightly and
Goldie twittered and asked if he would like some pot.
Yamean weed? Of course darling. Yeah. She rushed into
the bedroom (he didn't move his leg), came out with a
small cookie tin and passed the joints around. Georgette
blasted with a flourish, letting the ash get long and loose
then dragging hard and sucking the ash in with the smoke.
She laughed loudly, turning and pointing to be certain
that everyone was aware why she was laughing, and
watched Harry as he struggled with the stick and ranked
him as he covered his nose and mouth trying to suppress a
cough. You should have asked us to show you how
Harold. Theres no sense in wasting good pot on amateurs.
Georgette enjoyed the light laughter and sat back sucking
hard on her joint, pointing at Harry as he continued to

struggle, feeling her eyes cloud slightly . . . She rolled her shoulders and looked at her Vinnie then turned back to Harry as he finally stopped choking and tolder ta shuter mout, ya cocksucker. I am an expert in my field honey. No body can suck a cock better than I. But you!!! why youre not even a good thief. Youre just rank, and she sucked the joint down to an ⅛th of an inch then dropped the roach in her mouth and, smiling disdainfully, leaned over and took the partially smoked stick from Harry. His body was as sluggish as his imagination and he only got partway to his feet then sat down, trying to ignore the smiles of the guys and the twittering of the queens, straining to think of something to say, but only mumbling, fag. Shutup and take your dope pills, ya hophead. Lee burst out with a roar and told Georgette she was surprised that her friends were so square. Not all of them honey, and she flourished her wrist and tapped Vinnie on the knee. Lee continued to rank Harry, but he was getting frightfully nasty and Lee started getting nervous and asked Goldie to turn on the radio and get some music. Goldie tuned in a jazz program and they slowly relaxed with the tea and the music. Harry wanted to open a window, but the guys said nothing and the queens frowned so he sat still, sipping his drink and watching Lee. Goldie watched Malfies eyes fog, then stared at his chest as it swelled with the beating of his heart, told him he may as well take his shirt off as having it hanging open like that, then watched his flesh move and shine with sweat, loving the small mat of hair between his breasts and the sweat rolling down and into the mat. Rosie had been knocking on the door for almost a minute before Lee, annoyed with the manner in which Miss Goldie was ogling Malfie, got up in a huff and opened the door. She took the gin from Rosie, put it on the table in the living room, took four more bennie and a glass of hot bouillon and sat down, disgusted, and tried to withdraw as far as possible from the sordid party. Cant even take a few bennie and a little pot without simply drifting off. How ridiculous. I must say Georgette that I dont think much of these *men* friends of yours. I thought they were hip. Goldie heard, but didnt bother to look at her and continued to stare at Malfie, thinking of how wonderful it was that they *werent* used to bennie (getting kicks too from turning them (him) on), and waiting for the time to fly, as it does when youre up on bennie, and stop with her and Malfie. Georgette went to the kitchen, brought back a bowl of ice and a bottle of mixer, and filled hers and Vinnies glasses. There is no need to worry Miss Lee. They dont want to have anything to do with the likes of you. Vinnie was digging the conversation, but was goofed with the tea and didnt bother to say anything, and just took the drink from Georgette and looked over his glass at Lee, letting the smoke come slowly from his nose, and gave her a *gee* look until Lee turned her head then Vinnie pursed his lips at Camille and smiled, glowing inside at the fear in her eyes. Don't worry chippy, nobodys gonna hurtya. Maybe fuckya a little—Georgette asked him for a cigarette and he told her ta smoke her own and she fumbled for a moment until she was certain he was finished speaking to Camille, then found them.

Rosie sucked at a glass of gin, sitting at Goldies feet, and Georgette worried about Vinnie going with one of the other girls and what they would say if he did . . . then stopped worrying about what they might say but simply about keeping them away from him. She wanted them to think he was her lover, but more than that she wanted him as her lover. Even if only once. If only that. She took another bennie with her gin and listened to the music. The Bird was playing. She tilted her head toward the radio and listened to the hard sounds piling up on each other, yet not touching, wanting to hold Vinnies hand, the strange beautiful sounds (bennie, tea and gin too) moving her to a strange romance where love was born of affection, not sex; wanting to share just this, just these three minutes of the Bird with Vinnie, these three minutes out of space and time and just stand together, perhaps their hands touching, not speaking, yet knowing . . . just stand complete with and for each other not as man and woman or two men, not as friends or lovers, but as two who love . . . these three minutes together in a world of beauty, a world where there wasnt even a memory of johns or punks, butch queens or Arthurs, just the now of love . . .

and the strange rhythms of the Bird ripped to her, the piling patterns of sound all falling properly and articulately into place, and there was no wonderment at the Bird blowing love.

Then it was over and the background music came in and Georgette looked up and her eyes cleared as she saw the sick look in Harrys eyes as he looked at Rosies snatch. Her legs were raised and she rested her head on her knees staring at a spot on the rug, waiting, as always, for Goldie to speak and she would jump. Georgette turned her head and tried to think the Bird back into her mind, but she slowly turned her head back, unable to ignore Rosie, or avoid thinking about her. Rosie had always been more than taken for granted—she had never been thought of. Not even as a demented human, but as a scooper: someone to scoop up the empties; to buy the bennie; to meet the connection . . . Georgette looked at the spot on the rug, then back at Rosies face. Who was Rosie? What? Did she think? What did she feel? She must feel something or why would she stay with Goldie? Had she ever loved? Was she ever loved? Could she love? Georgette looked at the leer on Harrys face, the lust breaking through the

junk facade. If Rosie were to move Harry would jump up
and lay her right there—hold her arms, bend over her
with his leering face next to hers (spit dribbling from his
mouth) and shove it in if he had to fight for—Georgette
lifted her head so she couldnt see his face. If Harry did
have sex with her would she enjoy it? Would Rosie feel
anything? Did she ever think of it? Did she ever long
for love??? An analogy started to form and Georgette
had to fight it, she had to fight before it defined itself or
she would not be able to ignore or deny it. She popped
more bennie and gulped gin. She almost puked from the
gin and in panic lit a cigarette and sat still, smoking, until
the nausea passed (the analogy becoming fainter) then
turned up the radio and concentrated on the music, snapping her fingers, looking at Vinnie and hoping the bennie
would soon overtake the tea and Vinnie would get with it.
                                                    Camille
asked Georgette what the name of the number was that
was being played, saying she liked it very much, and
Georgette told her, and who was blowing and Camille
started moving slightly in time with the music and Lee
turned to her and told her not to wiggle like a slut in
heat. And I really dont see how you can listen to that
trashy music Georgette. You who love Opera so much.
O really Miss Thing—Camille moved back and sat still
—take the icecube out of your ass. Vinnie laughed and
Georgette turned to him, coyly, turning the volume up a
little more and marked one up on Lee, took a drink of gin
and when the record ended and another came on she asked
Camille if she liked it, digging the glance she directed at
Lee—well dont look at me honey. Its your bad taste not
mine—and Camille wished she knew what to say, if she
liked it or not (did she like it?), looked at Sal and
shivered again. Its alright, I guess (would he be as rough
as looks?).

The phone rang and Goldie tapped Rosie on the head and she jumped up and answered it, then turned to Goldie and said it was Sheila. Goldie listened, said yes and hung up. Shes coming home with an all night John so we will have to go down to Miss Tonys. O that place is loathsome. Well *Lee,* you can always go home, if you have one. Rosie, heat up the bouillon. O I think youre awful, living with a woman. O youre just jealous Lee. Why dont you just go about your own business Georgette. Honestly Goldie, I really dont see how you do it, even if she does support you and keep you in bennie. I think that that is my business Miss Lee. Hey, whats all this bullshit about? Were going downstairs to someone elses apartment. That is if its alright with you Harold. I honestly dont see how you can have sex with her Goldie. Or do you only eat it? O O OOO. Goldie flew from the room and Rosie spit at Lee and ran after her. O for heavens sake, dont be so touchy. The guys started stirring and digging the scene, but didnt know from nothin, so they just shrugged and Georgette looked after Goldie and inquired if she was alright and Camille was much taken aback, after all this is not the way ladies should act. And Lee is supposed to be so elegant. This sort of thing never happened back home. But it is exciting and he is *so* manly; and Lee said she was terribly sorry, I didnt mean to upset you dear. Its just that Tonys place is so dreary, with the electricity turned off and everything, and I guess I just have the rag on tonight anyway, so they kissed and made up, and they all helped finish the bouillon (with a few more bennie) gathered the gin and bennie and went downstairs, the guys stumbling behind, not sure exactly what was happening but having kicks and too high to care, and walked into Tonys apartment.

She was sleeping so Goldie lit a few candles and told her Sheila was turning a trick so they

had to come down here and Im sure you dont mind
honey, handing her some bennie, and told Rosie to make
coffee. Rosie lit the small kerosene stove in the kitchen
and put on a pot of coffee. When it was ready she passed
out paper cups of coffee then went back to the kitchen
and made another pot, continuing to make pot after pot
of coffee, coming in inbetween to sit at Goldies feet. The
guys slowly snapped out of the tea goof and soon the
bennie got to their tongues too and everybody yakked.
Goldie said she felt ever so much better. I guess I needed
a good cry and she passed around the bennie again and
they all popped bennie and sipped hot coffee and Goldie
sat next to Malfie and asked him if he was enjoying himself, and he said yeah, Im having a ball; and Goldie just
floated along on a soft purple cloud, feeling luxurious and
slightly smug: a handsome piece of trade beside her;
wonderful girl friends; and a beautiful bennie connection
in the corner drugstore where she could get a dozen 10
grain tablets for 50¢. O this is divine. I mean the candle-
light and everything . . . it brings to mind Genet. Genet?
I fail to see how *this* reminds you of her. Whose this
junay? A french writer Vinnie. I am certain you would
not know about such things—I really dont see how all this
gloom reminds you of Genet (Georgette looked at Lee
as she talked and glanced at Vinnie and sighed. Vinnie
will never have anything to do with her after that remark). I mean she is so beautiful. Well that is exactly
what I mean darling. She creates such beauty out of the
tortured darkness of our souls—O well, yes. That is true
enough—and I feel so beautiful. Hey! wheres the shit-
house. Georgette jumped up (Camille was shocked and
looked askance) and said it is outside. I will show you.
Vinnie walked past her, patted her on the ass. Thats o k
sweetchips, I can find it. Georgette whirled slightly and
sat down, smiling and chalking another one up. O it will

be so wonderful . . . later. Rosie was passing more coffee around and Harry asked her if she blew cock and she fell back spilling some of the coffee. Goldie told her to be more careful, you might have burned someone, and Rosie wailed and buried her head in Goldies lap and Goldie told her it was alright. Nobody was hurt. You can continue serving the coffee, and Rosie smiled a smile of salvation and stepped over the feet and passed out the coffee; and Georgette looked at the tears slowly streaking Rosies face and glistening in the sepia room; and Harry thought it might be kicks ta sloff it inna weird dame like that. Whattsa matta Rosie? afraida my lob? Rosie backed out of the room and Harry laughed and asked the guys if they saw the look oner face. Man, shes a real weirdy. Whered yapick that up? Goldie said she found her somewhere and Camille went out to the kitchen to see if Rosie was alright, thinking Harry was terribly cruel and Goldie should not let them do that to her. She did not see Rosie immediately and stared at the low blue flame of the kerosene stove, the perking coffee looking like a witches brew. Then she saw Rosie sitting in the corner, her head resting on her knees. Camille was nervous, but felt she should try to comfort her. She called softly, tentatively, then stood silent for a moment listening to the coffee perking, the strong rhythm broken every third or fourth beat with a double beat, then she looked back in the living room and everyone was talking, drinking (Georgette seemed to have been watching her), and when she caught Sals eye she blushed and turned back to Rosie and called her again. Rosie sat in the corner with her head on her knees. Camille walked over to her, carefully avoiding the stove, asked if she was alright. Why dont you come back inside Rosie, lightly touching her shoulder. Rosie jerked her head around, bit Camilles hand, looked at her for a moment then put her head back on her knees. Camille screeched and ran back to the living room clutching her injured hand, extending it before her. She bit me, she bit me, that crazy little thing. She turned in a circle, arms still stiffly extended, jumping up and down. What thefucks wrong wit you? O she bit me. O for heavens sake Camille sit down. Sit down. O she bit me. Shaddup. Harry pushed her and she fell on Lee and they screeched and tried to right themselves, but Camille kept falling down as she tried to push herself up then remembered her hand and halfway up she would try to clutch it and fall again, her arms whirling in the air and she rolled off Lee and Lee fought frantically to keep her skirts down, all the time yelling at Camille to get off her and Camille finally raised herself to her knees and grabbed the elusive hand and searched for the teeth marks. Dont worry little girl yawont get the rabyz. Lee sat up and smoothed her skirt and threw Camille a vicious glance, O really Miss Thing, and took a mirror from her pocketbook. examined her face then dove in her pocketbook and extracted her comb, cosmetics and hurredly fixed her face. Camille finally sat down and continued to examine her finger, completely ignoring the laughter. O it was terrible. All I did was try to speak to her and she bit me. She bit me like—— like some kind of animal. O it was terrible. Why didntya biter back? She/d get the crud. Here, dipit in the hot coffee. Goldie was laughing as hard as the rest but managed to lean over and offer solace and bennie. O yes, please. She brought me down something dreadful. O . . . she scooped up the bennie and dropped them in her mouth (with her good hand) then picked up her coffee (with her good hand) and took a few tiny sips until the bennie were down. Hey, what time does the next show start? They were all laughing, except Camille, and Lee only sneered at first, but when she finished putting her face on she too relaxed and joined the party, each new remark bringing forth a loud guffaw and refined laughter; Camille sitting with a peevish look on her face; but the boys were having a ball, not too sure what they were laughing about, but really digging the bennie scene, enjoying the cold chills and the strange feeling in their jaws as they clenched and ground their teeth (Harry wondering if maybe he oughtta go out to the kitchen and straighten Rosie out); Georgette content to relax and laugh (she was 3 up on Lee) yet still watchful for an opportunity to regain the center of attraction; and Goldie was ethereal . . . things were going so well and she was atingle with anticipation; but poor Camille felt ashamed and tried to relax and laugh it off but O it was so terribly embarrassing. She had carried on so; and Lee was determined to maintain her aloofness (yet she did not want to estrange herself from Goldie), the aloofness that her beauty and position demanded. The laughter continued even after they were too breathless from laughing to continue dropping remarks, and Goldie called for more coffee and Rosie made the rounds once more and retired to the kitchen and started a new pot and sat in the corner with her head on her knees. Goldie counted the bennie determining that there would be enough left for a few rounds (and by then the drugstore would be open) and handed more out. Vinnie asked for some gin (spurts of giggling still coming forth) and Georgette offered her glass but Vinnie refused (the code forbids drinking from the same glass as a fag) so she filled a paper cup for him, hoping this would not alter the score and glanced at Lee but she did not seem to notice; and Tony said thank you after taking a bennie and wondered if they would share their trade with her and trying desperately to think of something to say or do that would draw everyones attention to her and make them aware of her presence and perhaps Goldie would be grateful and one of the men would find her attractive. She looked around the room, smiling and rapidly blinking her eyes . . . then jumped up and jerked open a drawer and took out a new candle. She slammed the drawer closed and tripped lightly to the candle that was burned to the bottom, lit the new one and placed it carefully over the old one. There, that is much better, then sat down happily and beaming at Goldie certain she would appreciate the act.

Everyone stared at the new candle and the shadows the jerking flame created, still speaking softly, still smoking, still sipping coffee and gin; watching the top soften and the first little drop of wax seep to the edge and stagger down the side of the candle, the wick glowing brighter and redder in the middle of the flame . . . then another drop rolled to the first; and another started a new stream as the flame bent and the edge sloped away and soon many little drops were rolling down and piling up and flowing down the side of the candle and everyone relaxed even more, calmed by the new flame and slightly enervated by the laughing, and they sat deeper in their seats and the guys stretched their legs even more and the girls became softer and more coy; and their eyes eventually strayed from the flame and everything seemed softer and even Lee felt she was a part of the group and turned in her seat and faced the others and started telling little tidbits about backstage life and soon they all joined in and when someone was not talking they were listening to two or three stories being told at once. Lee told them about how almost all actors are gay (and even most of the church officials—and you know who honey), and how the cast of one of the revues she was starring in were pickedup and the club closed because they were all blasting backstage—and their hands fluttered about and the guys flipped their ashes—and I am telling you it was a scream. Caldonia was just so high—I mean she had been

60

drinking like crazy for hours and she struts around Broadway and 45th st. crowing like a rooster, COCKadoodledo COCKadoodledo—Im not shittinya, he was caught fuckin a stiff. He was in the El witme. He worked inna hospital, you know, in the morgue, and this nice lookin young head croaks so he throws a hump inner—Rosie refilled all the cups and ran back to the kitchen when Harry lunged for her snatch, and sat in the corner with her head on her knees—well, you think you have weird johns . . . well, I have one that makes me beat him with his belt—O that is just masochism honey—O I know that, but I have to be wearing a bra—ice blue with lace and panties to match, and stockings and a garter belt and he rubs his hands up and down my legs and snaps the garters until I am just black and blue and by the time he comes I can hardly move my arm—we got a weirdy like that in the neighborhood. He owns a beauty shop in the 80s on third and comes around a couple a nights a week—yeah, yeah, I know the guy. Hes got a new Dodge. Green. Yeah. And he picks up somea the kids and takesem for a ride and paysem a quarter ta fart—Tony kept leaning forward more and more, listening, laughing, making certain that each one was aware that she was listening to their story and enjoying it; trying to think of some little anecdote she could tell, some funny little thing that had happened or she had seen . . . or even something in a movie . . . she refilled her glass with gin, smiling at Goldie; nodded, smiled, laughed, still trying to think of something funny, even slightly humorous, thumbing through years of memories and finding nothing—Well how about Leslie?—O!!! that filthy thing—she goes through Central Park about 5 in the morning looking for used condoms and sucks them. Holy Krist. Well I have a john who makes me throw golfballs—we had a kid upstate who stuck a life magazine up his ass and couldnt get it out. The—O

I love the ones who almost cry when they are finished and start telling you about how much they love their wife and kiddies. And when they take out the pic—O I hate those freaks—Hey, how about that guy the Spook met in the Village that night who gaveim 10 bucks for his left shoe. The Spook toldim he could havem both for 10 bucks and his socks too—Goldie kept looking at Malfie and the way his hair waved back into a thick d a; and Georgette leaned closer to Vinnie and everyone seemed so close, as if they belonged to and with each other and everything was wonderful—Did Francene ever tell you about that Arab she met one night? Well honey, he just fucked her until she thought she would turn insideout. O, that must have been divine.—Camille looked nervously at Sal—It is so refreshing to meet a man who will give you a good fucking. Yes honey, but she almost had to have a hysterectomy. O was she—We had this here guy—

The door banged open and a young woman with a bruised face and an enormous belly stumbled in and called to Tony. Tony looked at the others apologetically then crossed the room to her sister, led her into the kitchen and helped her lie down, took the pot off the stove and turned up the flame. Rosie looked at them, at the pot, but when Goldie said nothing she lowered her head to her knees. Tony knelt beside her sister, embarrassed because she knew Goldie and the others didnt like Mary, and asked her what was wrong. She raised her head slightly then let it fall back and it seemed to bounce on the floor (Goldie and Lee turned their heads, disgusted. Camille stared and shook), then rolled it from side to side, moaning, jerking up with a scream, clutching her moundish abdomen, banging her head and arms on the floor, jerking her legs up then jutting and spreading them out, grabbing Tony by the shoulders as another pain ripped her and Tony clawed

at her hands. Let go! Let go! O youre hurting me, and the
hands finally fell and she lay still and Tony looked into
the other room, hoping they wouldnt hold her responsible
for all this; and the queens turned their heads and the
guys looked blankly, taking another drag or another
drink, a little curious, and Tony asked if she should call
the police so they could take her to a hospital. You aint
callin no cops. Not with us here—What am I going to do?
Why dont you just throw her out, the dirty slut. Shes going
to have a baby—O is she? I thought perhaps it was gas.
They roared with laughter (Rosie opened her eyes, her
head on her knees, then closed them) and Tony almost
cried. (O why did she pick now of all times? They would
have asked me upstairs and we could have been friends)
Why dont you get the slob shes living with? After all, he
is the father, not us. I assure you. They roared again—
how do you know he is. It could be almost anybody.
(Camille still felt a little nauseous but she was determined
to ignore it and be one of the girls.) Hey, did she swolla
a watermelon seed. Even Harrys belching brought forth
laughter, but everyone was becoming tense, especially the
queens. This could ruin a perfectly delightful evening.
If this were prolonged much longer it would bring everybody down and all the plans—Mary bolted up! Screaming! Not just one short scream, but one after another after
another. Her face darkened and threatened to burst. The
welts on her face oozed and she sat as if propped from behind, screaming, screeching, wailing, screaming . . . Tony
leaned back and banged into the wall (Rosie still sat with
her head on her knees) and Camille covered her face
with her hands. The screams scraped through their ears
and her eyes bulged, her arms still lifted toward Tony, her
face becoming darker . . . then she stopped and fell back,
her head smashing on the floor and the screams and the
sound of her head hitting the floor resounded through the

room and jammed in everyones ear and wouldnt leave like the sound of the sea in a shell . . . O O OOO!!! She broke water. She broke her water. The queens jumped up and Harry stared at the spreading moisture. Get her out of here. Get her out Get her out! Comeon yafuck, geter outta here before the law comes. O shes bringing me down. That dirty slut. That filthy whore. Rosie ROSIE! Get her out. Get her out! Rosie grabbed an arm, but it was wet with perspiration and it slipped from her grip. She pulled Marys skirt up and wiped her hands and Marys arms, then noticing her face wiped it too and told Tony to get the other arm. She tugged and Tony kept falling under the weight and looking pleadingly at Goldie and Rosie screamed at Tony to pull, pull, and Rosie yanked and Marys body jerked with each yank and shuddered with each shock of pain and the sweat burned her eyes and blinded her and all she could do was moan and moan and Harry got up and walked over to them and said hed help. He got behind her and put his hands over her tits, smiling at the guys, and lifted her up and Rosie yanked again almost pulling them over, and they slowly raised the mountainous Mary and dragged her to the door. Harry told Tony to get a cab and he and Rosie would get her to the door. Tony left, and Rosie held on to the arm, watching Harry, and they dragged her along the hallway, water and blood dripping down her legs, to the door. Harry asked Rosie how she was doin and she didnt move. Just held on to the arm and watched Harry. He laughed and dropped Mary on the floor and waited for the cab.

When Harry and Rosie came back everyone was silent, shadows jumping on the walls, and Harry asked what was wrong, this a morgue or somethin, and sat down and lit a cigarette. Man, shes some ton of a dame. She had a nice pair though. Couldnt get my hand aroundem they were so big . . . The others remained silent, not even smoking, and Rosie put the pot back on the stove and waited. Lee was simply repulsed at the entire scene—thats a real drag though man. Whatta yamean Sal? You know, havin a kid and some guy lumps yaup. Camille still frightfully upset —the others agreed with Sal that it was a real drag to be havin a kid like that and a guy lumps yaup. A guy like that should be dumped, the sonofabitch, even if she is a pig- -and Goldie and Georgette were anxious. They had been planning and anticipating all evening and things were going so well that it just wasnt right that everything should crumble now . . . now when it was coming close to the time . . . and Georgette frantically searched for something to say or do . . . something that would not only save the moment and the night, but something that would make it her moment and night . . . something that would once more make her the nucleus of the night. She looked around the room . . . thought . . . then remembered a book and yes, it was still there. She picked it up, opened it, looked at it for a moment then decided to say nothing but to start to read

> *Once upon a midnight dreary, while I pondered, weak and weary, . . .*

The first few words were low, tentative, but hearing her voice above the breathing of the others, ringing through the room, thrilled her and she read louder, each word clear and true

> *As of some one gently rapping, rapping at my chamber door.*
> *" 'Tis some visitor," I muttered, "tapping at my chamber door . . .*

and the others hushed and Vinnie turned his face toward
her

> *Ah, distinctly I remember it was in the bleak De-*
> *cember;*
> *And each separate dying ember wrought its ghost*
> *upon the floor.*
> *Eagerly I wished the morrow;—vainly I had sought*
> *to borrow . . .*

they were all watching her now (could Rosie be watching
too?). They were all looking at her. At HER!

> *Deep into that darkness peering, long I stood there*
> *wondering, fearing,*
> *Doubting, dreaming dreams no mortal ever dared*
> *to dream before;*
> *But the silence was unbroken, and the stillness gave*
> *no token, . . .*

the drama of the moment swelled her breast and the poem
came forth with beauty and feeling and the waves from
her mouth caused the candle flames to flicker and she
knew that everyone saw a Raven in the shadows

> *Let me see, then, what thereat is, and this mystery*
> *explore—*
> *Let my heart be still a moment and this mystery*
> *explore;—*
> *'Tis the wind and nothing more!" . . .*

and she was no longer merely reading a poem, but she
was the poem and every word was coming from her soul
and all the wonderful shadows whirled around her

*Then this ebony bird beguiling my sad fancy into
  smiling,*
*By the grave and stern decorum of the countenance
  it wore,*
*"Though thy crest be shorn and shaven, thou," I
  said, "art sure no craven,*
*Ghastly grim and ancient Raven wandering from
  the Nightly shore . . .*

The guys were staring and Vinnie seemed so close she
could feel the sweat on his face and even Lee was listening
and watching her read and they all knew she was there;
they all knew she was THE QUEEN.

*Nothing farther then he uttered—not a feather then
  he fluttered—*
*Till I scarcely more than muttered, "Other friends
  have flown before—*
*On the morrow he will leave me, as my hopes have
  flown before."*
       Then the bird said "Nevermore." . . .

Vinnie was staring at Georgette and the shadows that
highlighted her eyes, then her cheeks, then her eyes . . .
thinking it was a shame she was gay. Hes a good lookin
guy and real great, especially for a queen . . . being
honestly moved by Georgettes reading, but even with the
bennie stimulating his imagination it was impossible for
him to get beyond the weirdness and the kick

*Fancy unto fancy, thinking what this ominous bird
  of yore—*
*What this grim, ungainly, ghastly, gaunt, and omi-
  nous bird of yore*
      Meant in croaking "Nevermore."

This I sat engaged in guessing, but no syllable expressing
To the fowl whose fiery eyes now burned into my bosom's core;
This and more I sat divining, with my head at ease reclining
On the cushion's velvet lining that the lamp-light gloated o'er, . . .
> *She, shall press, ah, nevermore! . . .*

and the Bird was blowing (can you hear him Vinnie? Listen Listen Its the Bird. Can you hear him? Hes blowing love. Blowing love for us) and the incongruent rhythms of the Birds whirled and rang . . . then reconciled and O God it is beautiful

> *". . . Quaff, oh quaff this kind nepenthe and forget this lost Lenore!"*
> *Quoth the Raven "Nevermore."*

"Prophet!" said I, "thing of evil! prophet still, if bird or devil!—
Whether Tempter sent, or whether tempest tossed thee here ashore,
Desolate yet all undaunted, on this desert land enchanted . . .

and through a rip in the black shade she saw dancing points of gray and soon light would streak the sky and the shadows would soften and dance and the soft early morning light would seep through the room pushing the shadows from the now darkened corners and the candles soon would be out

> *And the Raven, never flitting, still is sitting, still is sitting*

*On the pallid bust of Pallas just above my chamber
    door;
And his eyes have all the seeming of a demon's that
    is dreaming,
And the lamp-light o'er him streaming throws his
    shadow on the floor;
And my soul from out that shadow that lies floating
    on the floor
        Shall be lifted—nevermore!*

and the Bird was blowing a final chorus, high, and the
set wouldnt end, but the Bird would slowly fade and you
would never know when he really stopped and the sounds
would hang and roll in your ear and all would be love—
Quoth the Bird Evermore—and the flames bowed and
licked the edge of the candles and even Harry didnt fight
his lethargy and try to break the spell and Georgette
lowered the book to her lap with full dramatic presence
and the final words still whirled with the light and stayed
in the ear as the sea in a shell and Georgette sat on a
wondrous throne in a wondrous land where people loved
and kissed and sat silent together, holding hands and
walking through magic nights and Goldie got up and
kissed the Queen and told her it was beautiful, simply
beautiful and the guys mumbled and smiled and Vinnie
struggled with the softness he felt, trying honestly, for a
second, to understand it, then let it slide and slapped
Georgette on her thigh, gently, as one does a friend, and
smiled, at her—Georgette almost crying seeing the flash
of tenderness in his eyes—he smiled and groped for
words, battling with his boundaries then saying, Hey, that
was alright Georgie boy, then the knowledge of his friends
being there, especially Harry, forced its way through the
bennie and the mood and he sat back quickly, took a
drink and grubbed a smoke from Harry.

The light forced itself through the many holes in the shades . . . the candles slowly becoming anonymous. Goldie opened the box of bennie slowly and proffered it to Georgette. She took two, just two thank you, smiled and laid them on her tongue and sipped her gin They spoke quietly, smiling, sipping their drinks, at peace with all and Georgette leaned back in her chair speaking softly with Vinnie, and the others when addressed. all her movements: smoking, drinking, nodding, soft and regal; feeling extremely human; looking upon her world (kingdom) with kindness, softness; waiting, excitedly yet not nervously, for the time, soon, for her to nod to her lover . . . but the sun continued to rise and the room became brighter and the girls became conscious of the perspiration streaks in their makeup, hoping the boys would not notice it before they got upstairs and had a chance to fix their faces. Goldie kept glancing at her watch and listening to hear Sheila and her john leaving, wanting to get out of this ugly room and upstairs with the boys before the light brought them down and they lost what Georgette had given them; afraid if a bennie depression set in that the boys would simply become rough and not trade. She watched the room becoming brighter, too bright, and listened, listened . . . then she heard some(one) rushing through the hallway and Tony opened the door—Goldies heart was pounding and she tried to ignore Tony and listen for steps (four) on the stairs—and started apologizing. looking hopefully at Goldie, before the door closed and Goldie finally turned to her and told her to shut up. Tony obeyed immediately (she had dropped her sister off at the hospital and stayed in the cab and came right back, wanting to get back before Goldie left; hoping to be invited to join them; she didnt want to sit alone in that evil apartment and she

wanted so much to be a friend of Goldies, to get high with
them and have other girls to talk with) she obeyed immediately and stopped in the middle of a syllable and
looked around the room but they all ignored her—Goldie
jumped up and went to the door, listened then opened it
slightly—so Tony walked across the room (between them
. . . between them. Theyre watching me. I know they are.
It wasnt my fault) and sat—Goldie turned and said they
left. Rosie, gather our things. They left. Tony sat, then
got up and walked around the room (not even a bennie
. . . not one); went to the kitchen, poured a cup of coffee
(maybe I should have stayed with her. Might just as well
have) and walked back to her chair.

Goldie ran to the bathroom to fix her face. Georgette
picked up the half filled bottle of Scotch that the john
had left and poured Vinnie a drink, on the rocks, then
turned on the radio. She could see that Vinnie and the
boys were getting higher and higher and by the time the
Scotch would be finished (and there was still gin and a
fresh supply of bennie forthcoming) they would be searching for the floor when they walked. O what a wonderful
day. (She went to the windows and fixed the blinds so
too much light would not come in.) Just simply too much.
She visited different parts of the room, talking, smiling,
fixing drinks, singing (Vinnie, Vinnie), dancing; even
laughing with Lee. Camille ran to the bathroom, when
Goldie came out, with her hair brush, nail brush, finger
brush and hand brush. Goldie gave Rosie money for
bennie then called Georgette aside and asked her to be
intermediary between she and Malfie and she told her,
Of course; and Goldie told her she had a box of syrettes
and in a few minutes when things are a little more settled
we will go inside and turn on. Georgette kissed her and
really started swinging. A little morphine now would be

just perfect. O yes, just perfect. O Lordy . . . MS and Vinnie!!! She filled a glass with gin and sat next to Vinnie (should I offer him a shot too?) talking with him and the boys (No. Might ruin him) and even Harry and his absurd remarks were palatable (O God! I hope the bennie didnt kill his nature), but of course she did her utmost to avoid any dissertation with *him* (If only the others would leave we could sit together and he would kiss me and I would caress his neck and kiss the lobe of his ear and we would undress each other and lie on the bed with our arms around each other and I would run the tips of my fingers along his thighs and his muscles would tighten and we would both squirm slightly and I would kiss his chest and feel his back and smell the sweat and put my legs around his hips—Whatta yasay sweetchips? Georgette turned and started opening her arms and Vinnie pinched her cheek, how about taking this inside and ringing it out, standing up slowly his hand clutching his crotch. Georgette lowered one hand (not now . . . later) and let the other one slide along his leg. Wanna help me empty this? wavering slightly then spreading his legs further apart and laughing as he bounced his balls with his hand. She leaned forward slightly (no no no!!! You will ruin everything) and he turned, still laughing, and went to the bathroom (his eyes are bugging out of his head. O Christ he is high. It will be beautiful!!!!) and roared as Camille leaped from the bathroom when he goosed her, dropping her brushes then carefully stooping, watching the bathroom door, picking them up and dashing to the living room.

Georgette sat back and sipped her gin for many seconds. Harry got up and chirped at Georgette, stoned out of his head, and plopped down beside Lee. Georgette followed him with her eyes, still sipping gin and still fighting for control of herself. She could not fuck it up now. It wont be long. It wont be long. Vinnie and MS. Yes. She picked up the bottle of gin and refilled Malfies glass and asked him if he would let Goldie do him. Malfie closed his eyes slightly and smiled, took the glass from her hand. Got more bennie? She patted his cheek and got two more for him and went to tell Goldie that everything was arranged. O everything is just so wonderful. Vinnie and his boys are stoned out of their heads and soon she would have Vinnie. Goldie took her into the bedroom and gave her a syrette. Arent you going to take one? Not now honey. I/ll wait until after that big cocked guinea has fucked me. So Georgette shot up and waited for the first wave to pass then went back to her throne, next to Vinnie. He was yakking with Malfie and Harry—Lee and Camille joining in, Goldie just watching Malfie and occasionally laughing—and tugged Georgettes ear when she sat down. She smiled and did a rolling bump before sitting down, nodding modestly to the applause. Georgette whirled digging the scene and everybody was swinging. Even Harry and Lee were making it and the sounds came from the radio and Camille was snapping her fingers (a little too demonstratively if you ask me, but its alright because we/re (Vinnie and MS—VINNIE) swinging) and everything fell into its proper place, all words fitted; and Goldie sat beside Malfie and he grinned, *aspet . . . una moment*; and Camille felt real bitchy and daring and winked at Sal and he tried to speak but he couldnt stop grinding his teeth and his head just lolled back and forth, droplets of scotch dribbling down his chin, but he was so strong and handsome—O what a marvelous chin—and she giggled thinking of the letter she would write to the pinkteas back home: O honey, do you know from nothing. What a gorgeous way to lose ones virginity! Sal laughed and blurted, I gotit swingin bitch HAARRR; and Malfie emptied his glass, refilled it and followed Goldie into the bedroom and Georgette watched, floating around their heads bopping SALT PEAnuts, SALT PEAnuts—quoth the Diz evermore—Vinnie and MS—VINNie and MS—and Lee moved a few inches and Harry grabbed her by the arm and yanked her back, Where doya think ya goin, queeny, grabbing her wrist and forcing it between his legs. I gotta nice hunkka meat forya and Vinnie yelled, Is she tryin ta get fresh witya man? and they both roared and Lee started to panic, trying to free her arm, but Harry squeezed tighter and twisted until she screeched, Stop, Stop! Youre hurting me you vile fairy (wonderful, wonderful. This should teach you a lesson you evil queen. *He* is what you deserve. VINNie and MS—VINNie and MS—cause we/re having a party and the people are nice, and the people are nice . . .) and Harrys eyes bugged even more and he stood up and pulled Lee off the couch, comon motherfucka. You wanna look like a broad ya gonna get fucked like one (Camille shoved her fingers in her mouth, rose halfway then fell back onto the couch and inched her way to the other end (but hes not like *that* (?)))—Hey Vinnie, comeon. Lets throw a hump intaer. Shit man, Im down. Letsgo. He grabbed her other arm and they started dragging her to the bedroom, screaming, screeching, crying, pleading and they roared and twisted her arms then Harry grabbed her by her hair, her precious golden shoulder length hair, and slapped her face. Comeon ya cocksucker. Stop theshit. Hey Malfie, open the door. Malfie opened the door and grinned as they dragged Lee in, and Goldie shrieked and ran from the room, the door slamming behind her. She listened to Lee screaming and the guys slapping her and cursing as they ripped her dress off . . . then Goldie swallowed a half dozen bennies; Camille looked at Georgette, who hadnt moved (No, No! No you fucking bitch. VINNie VINNie . . . VINNIE!!! Not with Lee. I love you Vinnie.

74

I love you. He will see my red spangled G string. Please Vinnie. Vinnie . . .), Camille looked at Georgette then at Sal as he wobbled across the room toward her. No room in there. He opened his fly and yanked out his cock (Its so big. And red. Be careful of your eyes. Put your arms around his ass) O???? O . . . Sal? Sal dont. Sal? Please. Ple—I got a big lob forya. Sa—he shoved it in her mouth and grabbed her long-shining-wavy-auburn-hair—Lee stopped squirming as Vinnie and Malfie held her and Harry mounted her. Vaseline. Vaseline! Please, not without vaseline. Vinnie handed her the jar, then Lee said alright then closed her eyes and cringed as Harry lunged viciously then put her arms around him and her legs around his waist. Vinnie and Malfie leaned against the wall and Harrys sweat fell on Lees face and she smiled and sucked his neck and groaned, hoping he would never come, that he would continue to lunge and lunge and lunge . . .—Thats the way Camille. Thats it HAHA OOOOO Hey, take it easy with yatongue, and Camille clutched at his belt hoping she was doing it properly; and Goldie took the syrette from her pocket, calmer now that the screaming had stopped, and though she did not approve of Camille having public sex like that she had to admit that she did not have much choice in the matter, and they did so seem to enjoy each other (I hope Malfie wont be completely useless after this), and turned on. Everything seems to have developed beautifully—He had to help his friends. Of course. Why shouldnt he help Harry fuck her. Cause we/re having a party and the people are nice, and the people are nice . . .—Harry took a slip from a drawer and wiped his cock. I bet yaknow youve been fucked! Harry and Malfie laughed and Lee watched Vinnie as he mounted her then closed her eyes and wrapped her legs around his hips—Goldie went back to the living room and sat on the couch, ignoring Camille and Sal, watched the smoke drift from her mouth and the sound waves from the radio; and Sals legs shook and he bent at the knees and Camille grunted and gurgled, moving her head fantastically, digging her nails into his ass, trying to get every inch of his cock in her mouth—Soon. Soon . . . (Quaff, oh, quaff this kind nepenthe); and we will hear tugboat whistles blowing high . . .—Sal put his pants over the back of a chair and stretched out with a new cigarette and drink; Camille went to the bathroom with her nail brush, finger brush, hand brush, hair brush and toothbrush—The guys came out of the bedroom, sweat pouring from their faces, and filled glasses with gin and ice. Lee called to Miss Goldie and asked her if she could borrow a dress, and she told her, Of course. The gorgeous blue number I wore to the DRAG BALL last year is in the closet if you want it. Thank you, but I think it would be better if I wore something simple, an afternoon dress will do. Something I can slip out of easily. Yeah! HAHAHAHARRR The guys took a few more bennie each and sauntered back into the living room. Hey Sal, whatta yadoin? posin fa holy pictures? They all roared and Goldie looked with pride at Malfie. Vinnie sat next to Georgette and stuck a wet finger in her ear. How yadoin Georgie? O Vincent (of course he did not) dont do that, squirming and trying to giggle but she couldnt fight the momentum of the centrifuge and her face only twisted. Whats the matta? got a booboo? You like the Bird? Bird? Hey whats withya sweetchips, pinching her cheek and turning to the others, ya been eatin birdseed? laughing and looking around the room. O snapping his fingers, yamean the Raven thing. Yeah. Yeah, sure. Take me inside Vinnie (?) dropping her hand on his leg. Whatsa matta? ya hungry? rubbing her hand in his crotch. It takes loot tado me sweetchips, looking around the room lifting his glass to his mouth, the gin slobbering down his chin, how much yagot? I have love, I have love—(Camille came back from the bathroom, fresh and clean, her hair so neatly brushed, the highlights gleaming, swishing ever so gaily across the room. O really Miss Thing, one would think it was the first cock you ever sucked. Camille fluttered a few fingers at Goldie and sat beside Sal)—I have love and the Bird. (O god not after *her*. Vinnie. O Vinnie. Please. That was so long ago. So long ago. When? When? It was my brother and the G string)—Lee stepped from the bedroom and hurried to the bathroom. I dont know why she doesnt keep at least a hair brush in there—(Goldies not half as attractive as I) still silent and trying, trying to smile coquettishly, but it wouldnt come, it wouldnt come. And the Bird was gone. Gone! Only a Raven. Nevermore . . . and she whirled and whirled and whirled and sounds whirled and smoke whirled and Vinnie laughed, he laughed. Vinnie laughed and soon he would pick her up and carry her to the bedroom . . . A voice A Voice. O God, not his john. I cant. Not now. Not after—Lee clicked into the room wearing a pair of Sheilas stockings and best shoes and sat daintily and looked at Harrys wet, dirty, smug, leering face . . . happy, O so happy that she wasnt a degenerate freak like that pervert; but loving his vicious prick and the next time we will be alone and he can be as freaky as he wants, and suck my tongue, and he will come around many times . . . if I want him to. She looked at Georgette and lifted an eyebrow. What are you on honey? (bitch! Evil Bitch! Leave me alone!) Well common Georgie. Getup somea those chips. Ya dont want yadinner taget cold, doya?

She rose with dignity—come and get it Sweetchips—and they walked hand in hand through the softness and he gave her a rose and she laid it across her hand like a scepter and gently raised it to her lips and its fragrance was en-

chanting and she smiled the smile of a rose, so soft, delicate, so lovely and the Bird was there oncemore, blowing,
and she placed the rose on its satin cushion and let the
robes slip from her body—Whatta yadoin?—and they
folded softly at her feet—ya just gonna suckit. Here yaare sweetchips, and make sure ya dont biteit, haha—A
rose. Rose! No. It was Harry. Nevermore! Evermore.
EVERMORE EVERMORE!!! O Vinnie, Vinnie my love
my love—Stop the shit man and start suckin. (my love,
love) He flicked his ashes, laughing, and took a drink.
Will he groan? Make him groan, and she opened his belt
and pulled his pants down and slid her hands along his
sweaty ass (love, love) and he grabbed her ears and
laughed, and she ran her fingers gently along his tightened
thigh muscles (now, brother, now!) felt the hairs on his
ass . . . the feeling, the feeling . . .—no. NO. O JESUS
NO!!! Its just a smell from the bed—Watch the balls fa
chrissake—from Harry. Harry. Its not shit. Please. He
didnt fuck her. Dont let it be shit—the feel, taste, smell—
SMELL! Vinnie picked up the slip from the floor. Youre
alright Georgie, patting the kneeling queen on the head.
Yacan do me anytime. Too bad I didnt haveya upstate.
We couldda had a ball. She looked up at him and smiled.
Vinnie? He looked into her face, bent and patted her
cheek gently. Comeon Georgie, Lets havea drink.

She sat

amongst her robes and watched him leave. Why didnt he
kiss me? If he would only let me kiss him. She looked at
her slacks and the small hole in one leg, running her
finger tips over the scab on her calf. Dance Ballerina
Dance. Dreams? Now? When? When? I had him. I *did*
have him. He didn't fuck her. Smell, feel, taste . . . It
was on the bed. From Harry. It was right. It is beautiful.
It was what I wanted. It is . . . is . . . I had him. Vinnie.
Again. She tried to scrape the scab off the wound, sticking

her fingernail under the edge, but only a tiny piece broke loose; she felt the slime of pus and tried to tear the scab loose with one quick rip . . . her hand wouldnt move. It hurt. Pained . . . She covered the wound with her hand and took a syrette from the drawer, found a vein in her arm then put her hand back on her leg. And it was now. Now. It wasnt yesterday and it isnt tomorrow . . . but there will be a tomorrow and there will be dreams . . . fulfilled . . . fulfilled . . . no it wasnt . . . It was Harry. Vinnie has me. Anytime . . . yes anytime . . . But Rosie is different . . . its not the same . . . She took another syrette, toyed with it for a few moments, hit a vein in her leg then placed it on the bed and rushed from the apartment. The others watched her leave and Camille asked where she was going. O her libido is probably twitching so madly shes going to run around the block 3 times. Yeah. She wishes she had one.

> The door banged shut and she leaned against the banister until the nausea subsided then stumbled down the stairs (Tony watching her) and out to the street. The sun was hot and bright and light rammed and slashed her from windows, windshields, hoods of cars, from tin signs, shirt buttons, bottle caps and slips of paper lying in the street. Her gut glowed and she bumped against parked cars, but she was moving, moving, and everything got brighter, whiter, hotter. She clutched the railing and stumbled down the stairs to the subway, the beautiful dark subway. Only a few people. No one near her. She folded her arms and rested her head on the seat in front of her. Cool. It cooled. Yes, it was cooler and her head was beautifully warm and she would have Vinnie again and the next time, some time, he would kiss her. And they would go out together. A movie and holdhands or go for walks and he would light her cigarette . . . yes, he would cup his hands around the

match, his cigarette hanging from the corner of his mouth, and I will put my hands around his and he will blow out the match and toss it away . . . but we dont have to go dancing. I know he doesnt like to dance. I will wear a smart print dress. Something simple. Something trim and neat. Vinnie? It *was* Harry . . . No. No, I wont have to go in drag. We will defy them all, and love . . . Love. And we will be loved. And I will be loved. And the Bird will come in high blowing love and we will fly . . . O that evil bitch. I am a far more convincing woman in drag than Lee. She looks like Chaplin. And I will dance like Melissa. If only I were a little shorter. Well we showed Miss Lee up, didnt we Vincent- -(Georgette danced around the room humming tunes, in her silk panties and padded bra, and a john sat naked, on the edge of the bed, sweat sliding down his greasy body, touching the silk as Georgette whirled by, playing with his genitals, licking his lips, spit hanging from his lips; then she stepped out of her panties and he grabbed them, buried his face in them and fell on the bed groaning, groveling . . .)—No. No. Its now. Tomorrow. Vinnie . . . yes, yes. Vincennti. Vincennti d/Amore. *Che gelida mania* . . . yes, yes. Cold, O my beloved. *Sì me chiamano Mimì* . . . Si, A candle. Soft candle light . . . and I will read to you. And we will drink wine. No. Its not cold. Not really. Just the breeze from the Lake. Its so lovely. Peaceful. See, just the slightest ripple on the surface. And willows. Yes. Si. Majestic bowing willows looking at themselves in the waters; nodding, saying yes to us. Yes, yes, yes . . . O Vincennti, hold me. Tighter. Vincennti. d/Amore. *O soave fanciulla.*— (Georgie is a friend of mine, he will blow me anytime, for a nickle or a)—The Lake. The Lake. And a moon . . . Yes . . . Look. Look. Do you see there? A swan. O how beautiful. How serene. The moon follows her. See how it lights her. O such grace. O yes yes yes I do

Vinnie, I do . . . Vincennti . . . See. See, she glides to us. Us. For us. O how white. Yes. She is. Whiter than the snows on the mountains. And they are but shadows now. But she glistens, shimmers. The queen of birds. Yes. O yes, yes, Cellos. Hundreds of cellos and we will glide in the moonlight, pirouetting to THE SWAN and kiss her head and nod to the Willows and bow to the night and they will grace us . . . they will grace us and the Lake will grace us and smile and the moon will grace us and the mountains will grace us and the breeze will grace us and the sun will gently rise and its rays will stretch and spread and even the willows will lift their heads ever so slightly and the snow will grow whiter and the shadows will rise from the mountains and it will be warm . . . yes, it will be warm . . . the shadows will stay, but the moonlight will be warm (Dance Ballerina Dance) Vinnie??? the moonlight will be warm. It will get warmer. Hold me Vincennti. Love me. Just love me. But fields of flowers are so lovely in the sun. In the bright flooding sunlight. Warm and brilliant. And the tall grasses flow and part and the colors burst and small drops of dew glisten and it is all red and violet and purple and green and white . . . yes white, and gold and blue and pink, soft pink and see the fireflies . . . like flowers of night . . . o yes, yes, flowers of night. Soft little lights. Lovely little lights. O, Im so cold. *La commèdia è finita.* No! NO! Vincennti. Yes, yes my darling. *Sì me chiamano Mimi.* Georgie-porgie puddin n pie. The Bird. Listen Vinnie. Bird. O yes my darling, I do I do. I love you. Love you. O Vinnie. Vincennti. Your mouth, lips, are so warm. d/Amore. O see how the stars soften the sky. Yes, like jewels. O Vinnie, im so cold. Come, let us walk. *Sone Andati.* Yes my love, I hear him. Yes. He is blowing love. Love Vinnie . . . blowing love . . . no NO! O God no!!! Vinnie loves me. He loves me. It.

Wasn/t.

Shit

PART III

AND BABY MAKES THREE

Thou shalt know also that thy seed shall be great, and thine offspring as the grass of the earth.

Job 5:25

THE BABY WAS CHRISTENED 4 hours after the wedding. Well, whatthehell, they got married first anyway. But I/ll tellya man, it was a ball! I mean after. Her old man threw a great party. And Spook with his damn motorcycle. Tommy had a 76 Indian. Hes the guy who got married. He had this Indian—you know, one of those small jobs. Not a onelunger. Nonea the boys would have one a those. They can really move and all that, but they're small. Yawant somethin that can be fixed up. Yaknow, made real sharp—streamers and things and a bigass buddyseat with chrome. Man, the snatch really comes runnin. Its real crazy! Anyway, he had this 76 and Tommys long and kinda skinny and he sorta looked like the bike was growin outtaim; like he had a bike between his legs instead of a pecka. And when he kicked it over he just sat there like he was restin or somethin and gave a little push on the peddle and BaROOOOM. All the other guysd be standin with their bikes leanin and kickin and kickin and the goddamn bike coughin and fartin and Tommyd sit on this pecka with wheels gunnin the motor and retadin the spark soundin like a gun battle and then hed ride around, slow, in circles and wait forem to get their bikes started.

But Tommy was a great guy. Sorta quiet. Especially compared with the other guys. And he worked. Mosta the time anyway. He used ta go out with Suzy once inawhile. Hed taker ridin on the bike and a few movies (I think) and they usually went to the neighborhood beerrackets together. But we didnt know she was knockedup until she was about 7 months gone. Maybe more. She was a bighipped Polack and even her oldman didnt know she was knockedup until she was in the hospital. I suppose he didnt look very hard. Yaknow, he was a bit ofa lush anyway. So when the oldlady toldim why Suzy was in the hospital he flipped. But afta stayin juiced for a few days he went slobberin up to the hospital cryin how he was gonna do everythin for his little girl (she was only a inch or 2 shorter than Tommy and outweighedim by 40 pounds); and why didnt she tellim she was in trouble and she just sorta looked and askedim for a smoke and toldim she wasnt in any trouble and a week or so later the oldman was like always studyin the scratchsheet and sippin beer until a liveone came in. But I gotta hand it toim. He really threw a ball after the christenin. It started after the weddin, but things really moved after the christenin. Thats when Spook had a few beers and hadta go ridin. Spook had the hots for a bike for months. 6 months before he even got one he was wearing a motorcycle hat. Of course all the boys with bikes woreem. No boots or jackets with eagles or anya that shit, but yagotta have a hat ta keep ya hair outta ya eyes. Anyway, Spook had this hat and he didnt have no bike. Hed sit in the Greeks all nite and wouldnt part with that hat for nothin. Man, you try and get that thing off his head and hed go outta his mind. Well, anyway, once inawhile Tommyd let Spook ride his bike and Spookd be bugged outta his mind. Hed spark the damn thing and bang it and blast it and yell and scream and fix that damn hat of his and go rollin along 2nd avenue making all kindsa goddamn noise. Then Tommyd waveim back and Spookd make a slow turn and come backfirin up to Tommy, gun the motor a few times, push the kick stand down, turn the motor off, and get off real careful and sorta pat the seat and tank and tell him itsa great bike. Real great. And the next day Spookd make the rounds of all the bike shops downtown and stare at the jobs in the window, droolin, and go in and pricem and the guyed tellim its still 1500 dollars just like two days ago and Spookd ask if he got any new second hand jobs and the guyd shake his head and go about his business and Spookd look around at the lights, seats, streamers, windshields and boots and go half out of his mind and hed come back to the Greeks and tellus about the great Harley-Davidson machine he saw—a brand new model and he knew every goddamn strip of chrome and every bolt and nut on the sonofabitch and everybodyd laugh and someone would sneak up behind him through the side door and take his hat off and toss it around and Spookd go ape tryin ta get it back and then someoned plop it on his head and we/d laugh and hed tellus that we didnt know what it was ta want a bike. Fifty times a day the same thing. You dont know what it is ta want a bike. Then somebodyd tellim he could ride withim if he bought coffee-and, so Spookd breakdown and part with a dime (it was pretty hard ta getim to part with anything, especially money. I guess he stashed his loot in a piggybank tryin ta save for a bike.) and hed fix his hat and theyd take off and hed yell GEROOOOni-mOOOOO and theyd hit the Belt Parkway and weave between traffic and Spookd be flipped off his ass yellin and screamin and theyd get back ta the Greeks and hed say, Christ! I gotta get a bike. Man, you dont know what it is ta want a bike, and off hed go the next day, downtown.

Well, anyway, when Suzy told Tommy she was on the hill I guess he was a little surprised. I dont know. He didnt say nothin, but I guess he was. So she toldim and they went for a ride along the Belt and on the way back they stopped at Coney Island and had some hotdogs at Nathans and he was workin at the time and I guess he tolder hed marryer. Anyway I dont think he said he wouldnt. It really didnt make too much difference. I mean he had his bike. All paid for an fixedup like he wanted it and they could move in with her oldman and oldlady. Downstairs. So whatthehell. And I think she sorta wanted to get married anyway. You know. But I dont know if she even askedim. I mean, she coulda dumped the kid without too much trouble. Theres all kinds of agencies. But Tommy was alright. He never bothered nobody and hed never beaterup or anythin so I guess she wanted ta get married. And like this she wouldnt haveta work. Just feed the kid and that sorta stuff. So actually it worked out pretty good. So anyway, Tommy comes into the Greeks one nite and tellsus hes gonna be a father and Alex gives-im a cupa coffee on the house and Tommy lets Spook go for a ride.

So when her oldman dries out a little he tellser (when she comes home from the hospital with the baby and she says, thats grandpa, and the oldman starts slobberin again) that hes gonna giver a real party and he goes and sees Murphy in the bar and tellsim he wants ta rent upstairs for a weddin reception. And when Murphy asks when he says he dont know, but itll be soon and Murphy tellsim that the Raven S.A.C. is goin ta throw a racket soon so the oldman tellsim two weeks and he leaves a deposit and goes home and tellsem and they get a holda Tommy and he says OK and finishes shining his bike so they set the wedding date and make arrangements for the christenin. Of course they lied a little at the christenin, you know, but the oldlady figured it was better forem ta lie a little than not have the poor little tyke christened at all. So they got the papers and a few of the boys went withem and it was over in a few minutes and then we went ta Murphys ta wait until it was time for the christenin and ta figureout who was gonna be godparents. I think they finally got some aunt and uncle, I dont know, but anyway that was when things started swingin. Murphys Hall is a big room above the bar and he had bottles of whisky on a small bar in the corner and kegs abeer and a big long table stacked with all kindsa sandwiches. So we each grabbed a pitcher a beer and started scoffin the sandwiches and Spook comes in and tellsus he got a bike. Ya shoulda seenim. His eyes was bugged outta his head. I thought he was up on tea or somethin, but he was just high with a bike. He picked up a old police bike for a few bucks and fixed it up. You know, threw some paint on it and stole a wildass buddyseat all covered with fur and chrome, and was all fulla piss and vinegar ta go. We toldim ta play it cool and relax and celebrate Tommys marriage. So someone pushed a beer in his hand, but he flipped when someone tried ta get that goddamn hat off his head so we said OK, wed go down stairs and look at his bike. So we looked. Big deal. Yaknow, when the cops is finished with a bike, man, its had it. But it was a bike and it moved. I think that sonofabitch woulda used it even if he had ta push it or pedal it like a kiddy car. So he kicks it over after 5 minutes and we listen to it cough and miss and Spook went puttin off with a shiteatin grin on his face and we went back up stairs and a few minutes later he comes back. Smilin all over the goddamn place and the strap of his hat under his chin. I tellya man, it was a pissa. But whatthehell, we were havin a ball and we didnt know what it was ta want a bike and pretty soon he was talkin ta Suzys old lady about this bike and she

89

was throwin the booze down like crazy and soon she
starts weepin about her poor little girl and tellin Spook
how she looked when she was born and it seems like only
yesterday and now here she is all grownup and married
and a mother and Spook kept noddin and said yeah, but
all he really has ta do is clean the sparks and maybe giver
a carbon job—which he could do himself at nite and it
wont cost nothin—and itll run as good as any bike on the
road and when ya figure it only cost a yard its a damn
good deal . . . and long since Suzy had cut from the oldman and oldlady and was shovin salami sandwiches down
likemad and things was really movin. Of course some a
the skells from the bar worked their way up and con-
gratulated and grabbed what they could and when the
christenin was over and they came back with the kid
everybody was tellin the oldman and oldlady that it looked
just likem (and man, the oldladys some dog!) and they
sniff and pound backs and tellem ta drinkup and somebody had a camera and flashbulbs was poppin then
smashed against the wall. Of course the kid started yappin
but they took care of it and the party really started. They
had a phonograph and a lot of real great records like
Illinois Jacquet and Kenton; and Roberta, a real hip
queer from the neighborhood, cameup and started dancin
and wigglin and somea the boys was stoned and was
dancin wither and she was havin a ball! Of course she was
up on bennie, like always (unless she got some pot) and
onea the guys askeder if she was the bride and she said
no, she practices birthcontrol and then she started dancin
with Suzys oldlady and oldman. That was a real gassa!
She was still all snots and tears and her big lardass was
wigglin and we were pissin in our pants. Man, it was a
ball!

Of course Tommy didnt drink much. I mean, not because he got married. That didnt make any difference now.

90

He just never drank much. A couple a beers now and then was about all. Ya know. But he was sorta ballin. For Tommy anyway. The oldlady almost put a drag on the party by diggin up a record with some dame singin Because, and then she goes staggerin over ta Suzy and starts huggin and kissener and Suzys tryin ta stuff a salami sandwich in her mouth and she cant chew because the oldladys all overer. But Roberta really broke usup. She was standin in a corner makin like she was singin and man, it was a gas. You know, flutterin her eyelids (she had that shiny stardust stuff glued to her eyelids) and doin a few bumps and grinds and that sorta stuff. But the oldlady didnt seeer (I dont think she could see much by that time) and she wanted to dance with Suzy and starts waltzin around, stumblin all over and Suzy still holdin that salami sandwich, but the record ended and Roberta threw a Dinah Washington side on real quick and Suzy got ridda the oldlady and we all started ballin again. Pretty soon the oldlady passed out and they stretched her out on a cot in the back and we ended up in a corner jumpin with the music and doin some real juicin and even Spook was a little high. Tony got real stoned and goosed some dame and there was a bit of rumble with her husband, but it didnt amount ta much so we just pushed Tony in the corner and letim sleep. Of course a few of the old Irishmen started throwin blows at each other, but they didnt do any real damage and as long as they didnt get too close ta the bar they letim fight until they passed out. But

Spook couldnt sit still for long. He wanted ta go ridin. Everybody toldim ta go, but he didnt want ta go alone and everybody, but Tommy, was too stoned ta ride a goddamn bike. So Suzy tells Tommy ta go. Whatthehell. Cant do anythin tonite anyway. You know, too soon. And she figured shed look around for the kid and takeim home and go ta bed. She said her ass was draggin anyway. It was only two weeks or so since she had the kid. And it was a pretty good size one. Eight pounds somethin. I dont know exactly, but somethin like that. She said it was like shittin a watermelon. Havin a kid. So she hunted around and found the kid and cutout. So Tommy figured hed take a spin with Spook. It was a real nice nite. Just right for ridin. And probably be in the house all day tomorra fixin things. You know, puttin this here and that there and takin care of the kid and that kinda stuff. So when Roberta sees Tommy gettin ready ta cut she comes hustlin over and starts cooin at Tommy ta takeer for a ride, shes feelin so depressed watchin somebody else with a baby and gettin ready for a honeymoon, and she flutters her lids and everybody cracksup, so Tommy laughs and says OK and Roberta giggles and waves bye bye and Spook is halfway down the stairs his hat all tied under his chin and they cut.

       Of course we stayed until they kicked us out the next morning. I mean, whatthehell. The oldman paid good money for the joint and everything. No sense in lettin it go ta waste.

92

PART IV

TRALALA

I will rise now, and go about the city in the streets, and in the broad ways I will seek him whom my soul loveth: I sought him, but I found him not.

The watchmen that go about the city found me: to whom I said, Saw ye him whom my soul loveth?

Song of Solomon 3:2, 3

TRALALA WAS 15 the first time time she was laid. There was no real passion. Just diversion. She hungout in the Greeks with the other neighborhood kids. Nothin to do. Sit and talk. Listen to the jukebox. Drink coffee. Bum cigarettes. Everything a drag. She said yes. In the park. 3 or 4 couples finding their own tree and grass. Actually she didnt say yes. She said nothing. Tony or Vinnie or whoever it was just continued. They all met later at the exit. They grinned at each other. The guys felt real sharp. The girls walked in front and talked about it. They giggled and alluded. Tralala shrugged her shoulders. Getting laid was getting laid. Why all the bullshit? She went to the park often. She always had her pick. The other girls were as willing, but played games. They liked to tease. And giggle. Tralala didn't fuckaround. Nobody likes a cock-teaser. Either you put out or you dont. Thats all. And she had big tits. She was built like a woman. Not like some kid. They preferred her. And even before the first summer was over she played games. Different ones though. She didnt tease the guys. No sense in that. No money either. Some of the girls bugged her and she broke their balls. If a girl liked one of the guys or tried to get him for any reason Tralala cut in. For kicks. The girls

95

hated her. So what. Who needs them. The guys had what she wanted. Especially when they lushed a drunk. Or pulled a job. She always got something out of it. Theyd take her to the movies. Buy cigarettes. Go to a PIZZERIA for a pie. There was no end of drunks. Everybody had money during the war. The waterfront was filled with drunken seamen. And of course the base was filled with doggies. And they were always good for a few bucks at least. Sometimes more. And Tralala always got her share. No tricks. All very simple. The guys had a ball and she got a few bucks. If there was no room to go to there was always the Wolffe Building cellar. Miles and miles of cellar. One screwed and the others played chick. Sometimes for hours. But she got what she wanted. All she had to do was putout. It was kicks too. Sometimes. If not, so what? It made no difference. Lay on your back. Or bend over a garbage can. Better than working. And its kicks. For a while anyway. But time always passes. They grew older. Werent satisfied with the few bucks they got from drunks. Why wait for a drunk to passout. After theyve spent most of their loot. Drop them on their way back to the Army-base. Every night dozens left Willies, a bar across the street from the Greeks. Theyd get them on their way back to the base or the docks. They usually let the doggies go. They didn't have too much. But the seamen were usually loaded. If they were too big or too sober theyd hit them over the head with a brick. If they looked easy one would hold him and the other(s) would lump him. A few times they got one in the lot on 57th street. That was a ball. It was real dark back by the fence. Theyd hit him until their arms were tired. Good kicks. Then a pie and beer. And Tralala. She was always there. As more time passed they acquired valuable experience. They were more selective. And stronger. They didn't need bricks anymore. Theyd make the rounds of the bars and spot some guy with a roll.

96

When he left theyd lush him. Sometimes Tralala would set him up. Walk him to a doorway. Sometimes through the lot. It worked beautifully. They all had new clothes. Tralala dressed well. She wore a clean sweater every few days. They had no trouble. Just stick to the seamen. They come and go and who knows the difference. Who gives a shit. They have more than they need anyway. And whats a few lumps. They might get killed so whats the difference. They stayed away from doggies. Usually. They played it smart and nobody bothered them. But Tralala wanted more than the small share she was getting. It was about time she got something on her own. If she was going to get laid by a couple of guys for a few bucks she figured it would be smarter to get laid by one guy and get it all. All the drunks gave her the eye. And stared at her tits. It would be a slopeout. Just be sure to pick a liveone. Not some bum with a few lousy bucks. None of that shit. She waited, alone, in the Greeks. A doggie came in and ordered coffee and a hamburger. He asked her if she wanted something. Why not. He smiled. He pulled a bill from a thick roll and dropped it on the counter. She pushed her chest out. He told her about his ribbons. And medals. Bronze Star. And a Purpleheart with 2 Oakleaf Clusters. Been overseas 2 years. Going home. He talked and slobbered and she smiled. She hoped he didnt have all ones. She wanted to get him out before anybody else came. They got in a cab and drove to a downtown hotel. He bought a bottle of whiskey and they sat and drank and he talked. She kept filling his glass. He kept talking. About the war. How he was shot up. About home: What he was going to do. About the months in the hospital and all the operations. She kept pouring but he wouldnt pass out. The bastard. He said he just wanted to be near her for a while. Talk to her and have a few drinks. She waited. Cursed him and his goddamn mother. And who gives a shit about your leg gettin all shotup. She had been there over an hour. If hed fucker maybe she could get the money out of his pocket. But he just talked. The hell with it. She hit him over the head with the bottle. She emptied his pockets and left. She took the money out of his wallet and threw the wallet away. She counted it on the subway. 50 bucks. Not bad. Never had this much at once before. Shouldve gotten more though Listenin to all that bullshit. Yeah. That sonofabitch. I shoulda hitim again. A lousy 50 bucks and hes talkin like a wheel or somethin. She kept 10 and stashed the rest and hurried back to the Greeks. Tony and Al were there and asked her where she was. Alex says ya cutout with a drunken doggie a couple a hours ago. Yeah. Some creep. I thought he was loaded. Didju score? Yeah. How much? 10 bucks. He kept bullshittin how much he had and alls he had was a lousy 10. Yeah? Lets see. She showed them the money. Yasure thats all yagot? Ya wanna search me? Yathink I got somethin stashed up my ass or somethin? We/ll take a look later. Yeah. How about you? Score? We got a few. But you dont have ta worry aboutit. You got enough. She said nothing and shrugged her shoulders. She smiled and offered to buy them coffee. And? Krist. What a bunch of bloodsuckers. OK Hey Alex . . . They were still sitting at the counter when the doggie came in. He was holding a bloodied handkerchief to his head and blood had caked on his wrist and cheek. He grabbed Tralala by the arm and pulled her from the stool. Give me my wallet you goddamn whore. She spit in his face and told him ta go fuckhimself. Al and Tony pushed him against the wall and asked him who he thought he was. Look, I dont know you and you dont know me. I got no call to fight with you boys. All I want is my wallet. I need my ID Card or I cant get back in the Base. You can keep the goddamn money. I dont care. Tralala screamed in his face that he was a no

good mothafuckin sonofabitch and then started kicking
him, afraid he might say how much she had taken. Ya
lousy fuckin hero. Go peddle a couple of medals if yaneed
money so fuckin bad. She spit in his face again, no longer
afraid he might say something, but mad. Goddamn mad.
A lousy 50 bucks and he was cryin. And anyway, he
shouldve had more. Ya lousy fuckin creep. She kicked
him in the balls. He grabbed her again. He was crying
and bent over struggling to breathe from the pain of the
kick. If I don't have the pass I cant get in the Base. I
have to get back. Theyre going to fly me home tomorrow.
I havent been home for almost 3 years. Ive been all shot
up. Please, PLEASE. Just the wallet. Thats all I want.
Just the ID Card. PLEASE PLEASE!!! The tears streaked
the caked blood and he hung on Tonys and Als grip and
Tralala swung at his face, spitting, cursing and kicking.
Alex yelled to stop and get out. I dont want trouble in
here. Tony grabbed the doggie around the neck and Al
shoved the bloodied handkerchief in his mouth and they
dragged him outside and into a darkened doorway. He was
still crying and begging for his ID Card and trying to tell
them he wanted to go home when Tony pulled his head
up by his hair and Al punched him a few times in the
stomach and then in the face, then held him up while
Tony hit him a few times; but they soon stopped, not
afraid that the cops might come, but they knew he didn't
have any money and they were tired from hitting the seaman they had lushed earlier, so they dropped him and he
fell to the ground on his back. Before they left Tralala
stomped on his face until both eyes were bleeding and his
nose was split and broken then kicked him a few times
in the balls. Ya rotten scumbag, then they left and walked
slowly to 4th avenue and took a subway to manhattan.
Just in case somebody might put up a stink. In a day or
two he/ll be shipped out and nobodyll know the differ-

ence. Just another fuckin doggie. And anyway he deserved it. They ate in a cafeteria and went to an allnight movie. They next day they got a couple of rooms in a hotel on the east side and stayed in manhattan until the following night. When they went back to the Greeks Alex told them some MPs and a detective were in asking about the guys who beat up a soldier the other night. They said he was in bad shape. Had to operate on him and he may go blind in one eye. Ain't that just too bad. The MPs said if they get ahold of the guys who did it theyd killem. Those fuckin punks. Whad the law say. Nottin. You know. Yeah. Killus! The creeps. We oughtta dumpem on general principles. Tralala laughed. I shoulda pressed charges fa rape. I wont be 18 for a week. He raped me the dirty freaky sonofabitch. They laughed and ordered coffeeand. When they finished Al and Tony figured theyd better make the rounds of a few of the bars and see what was doin. In one of the bars they noticed the bartender slip an envelope in a tin box behind the bar. It looked like a pile of bills on the bottom of the box. They checked the window in the MENS ROOM and the alley behind it then left the bar and went back to the Greeks. They told Tralala what they were going to do and went to a furnished room they had rented over one of the bars on 1st avenue. When the bars closed they took a heavy duty screwdriver and walked to the bar. Tralala stood outside and watched the street while they broke in. It only took a few minutes to force open the window, drop inside, crawl to the bar, pickup the box and climb out the window and drop to the alley. They pried open the box in the alley and started to count. They almost panicked when they finished counting. They had almost 2 thousand dollars. They stared at it for a moment then jammed it into their pockets. Then Tony took a few hundred and put it into another pocket and told Al theyd tell Tralala that that was all they got. They smiled and almost laughed then calmed themselves before leaving the alley and meeting Tralala. They took the box with them and dropped it into a sewer then walked back to the room. When they stepped from the alley Tralala ran over to them asking them how they made out and how much they got and Tony told her to keep quiet that they got a couple a hundred and to play it cool until they got back to the room. When they got back to the room Al started telling her what a snap it was and how they just climbed in and took the box but Tralala ignored him and kept asking how much they got. Tony took the lump of money from his pocket and they counted it. Not bad eh Tral? 250 clams. Yeah. How about giving my 50 now. What for? You aint going no where now. She shrugged and they went to bed. The next afternoon they went to the Greeks for coffee and two detectives came in and told them to come outside. They searched them, took the money from their pockets and pushed them into their car. The detectives waved the money in front of their faces and shook their heads. Dont you know better than to knock over a bookie drop? Huh? Huh, Huh! Real clever arent you. The detectives laughed and actually felt a professional amazement as they looked at their dumb expressions and realized that they really didnt know who they had robbed. Tony slowly started to come out of the coma and started to protest that they didnt do nothin. One of the detectives slapped his face and told him to shutup. For Christs sake dont give us any of that horseshit. I suppose you just found a couple of grand lying in an empty lot? Tralala screeched, a what? The detectives looked at her briefly then turned back to Tony and Al. You can lush a few drunken seamen now and then and get away with it, but when you start taking money from my pocket youre going too far sonny. What a pair of stupid punks . . . OK sister, beat it. Unless you want to

come along for the ride? She automatically backed away
from the car, still staring at Tony and Al. The doors
slammed shut and they drove away. Tralala went back
to the Greeks and sat at the counter cursing Tony and Al
and then the bulls for pickinem up before she could get
hers. Didn't even spend a penny of it. The goddamn bastards. The rotten stinkin sonsofbitches. Those thievin flat-
footed bastards. She sat drinking coffee all afternoon then
left and went across the street to Willies. She walked to
the end of the bar and started talking with Ruthy, the
barmaid, telling her what happened, stopping every few
minutes to curse Tony, Al, the bulls and lousy luck. The
bar was slowly filling and Ruthy left her every few minutes
to pour a drink and when she came back Tralala would
repeat the story from the beginning, yelling about the 2
grand and they never even got a chance to spend a
penny. With the repeating of the story she forget about
Tony and Al and just cursed the bulls and her luck and an
occasional seaman or doggie who passed by and asked
her if she wanted a drink or just looked at her. Ruthy
kept filling Tralalas glass as soon as she emptied it and
told her to forget about it. Thats the breaks. No sense in
beatin yahead against the wall about it. Theres plenty
more. Maybe not that much, but enough. Tralala snarled,
finished her drink and told Ruthy to fill it up. Eventually
she absorbed her anger and quieted down and when a
young seaman staggered over to her she glanced at him
and said yes. Ruthy brought them two drinks and smiled.
Tralala watched him take the money out of his pocket
and figured it might be worthwhile. She told him there
were better places to drink than this crummy dump. Well,
lez go baby. He gulped his drink and Tralala left hers on
the bar and they left. They got into a cab and the seaman
asked her whereto and she said she didnt care, anywhere.
OK. Takeus to Times Square. He offered her a cigarette

and started telling her about everything. His name was
Harry. He came from Idaho. He just got back from Italy.
He was going to—she didnt bother smiling but watched
him, trying to figure out how soon he would pass out.
Sometimes they last allnight. Cant really tell. She relaxed
and gave it thought. Cant konkim here. Just have ta wait
until he passes out or maybe just ask for some money.
The way they throw it around. Just gotta getim in a
room alone. If he dont pass out I/ll just rapim with somethin—and you should see what we did to that little ol . . .
He talked on and Tralala smoked and the lampposts
flicked by and the meter ticked. He stopped talking when
the cab stopped in front of the Crossroads. They got out
and tried to get in the Crossroads but the bartender looked
at the drunken seaman and shook his head no. So they
crossed the street and went to another bar. The bar was
jammed, but they found a small table in the rear and sat
down. They ordered drinks and Tralala sipped hers then
pushed her unfinished drink across the table to him when
he finished his. He started talking again but the lights and
the music slowly affected him and the subject matter was
changed and he started telling Tralala what a good
lookin girl she was and what a good time he was going to
show her; and she told him that she would show him the
time of his life and didnt bother to hide a yawn. He
beamed and drank faster and Tralala asked him if he
would give her some money. She was broke and had to
have some money or she/d be locked out of her room. He
told her not to worry that hed find a place for her to stay
tonight and he winked and Tralala wanted to shove her
cigarette in his face, the cheap sonofabitch, but figured
she/d better wait and get his money before she did anything. He toyed with her hand and she looked around
the bar and noticed an Army Officer staring at her. He
had a lot of ribbons just like the one she had rolled and

she figured hed have more money than Harry. Officers are usually loaded. She got up from the table telling Harry she was going to the ladies room. The Officer swayed slightly as she walked up to him and smiled. He took her arm and asked her where she was going. Nowhere. O, we cant have a pretty girl like you going nowhere. I have a place thats all empty and a sack of whiskey. Well . . . She told him to wait and went back to the table. Harry was almost asleep and she tried to get the money from his pocket and he started to stir. When his eyes opened she started shaking him, taking her hand out of his pocket, and telling him to wakeup. I thought yawere goin to show me a good time. You bet. He nodded his head and it slowly descended toward the table. Hey Harry, wakeup. The waiter wants to know if yahave any money. Showem ya money so I wont have to pay. He slowly took the crumpled mess of bills from his pocket and Tralala grabbed it from his hand and said I toldya he had money. She picked up the cigarettes from the table, put the money in her pocketbook and walked back to the bar. My friend is sleeping so I dont think he/ll mind, but I think we/d better leave. They left the bar and walked to his hotel. Tralala hoped she didnt make a mistake. Harry mightta had more money stashed somewhere. The Officer should have more though and anyway she probably got everything Harry had and she could get more from this jerk if he has any. She looked at him trying to determine how much he could have, but all Officers look the same. Thats the trouble with a goddamn uniform. And then she wondered how much she had gotten from Harry and how long she would have to wait to count it. When they got to his room she went right into the bathroom, smoothed out the bills a little and counted them. 45. Shit. Fuckit. She folded the money, left the bathroom and stuffed the money in a coat pocket. He poured two small drinks and they sat and talked for a few minutes then put the light out. Tralala figured there was no sense in trying anything now, so she relaxed and enjoyed herself. They were having a smoke and another drink when he turned and kissed her and told her she had the most beautiful pair of tits he had ever seen. He continued talking for a few minutes, but she didnt pay any attention. She thought about her tits and what he had said and how she could get anybody with her tits and the hell with Willies and those slobs, she/d hang around here for a while and do alright. They put out their cigarettes and for the rest of the night she didn't wonder how much money he had. At breakfast the next morning he tried to remember everything that had happened in the bar, but Harry was only vaguely remembered and he didn't want to ask her. A few times he tried speaking, but when he looked at her he started feeling vaguely guilty. When they had finished eating he lit her cigarette, smiled, and asked her if he could buy her something. A dress or something like that. I mean, well you know . . . Id like to buy you a little present. He tried not to sound maudlin or look sheepish, but'he found it hard to say what he felt, now, in the morning, with a slight hangover, and she looked to him pretty and even a little innocent. Primarily he didnt want her to think he was offering to pay her or think he was insulting her by insinuating that she was just another prostitute; but much of his loneliness was gone and he wanted to thank her. You see, I only have a few days leave left before I go back and I thought perhaps we could—that is I thought we could spend some more time together . . . he stammered on apologetically hoping she understood what he was trying to say but the words bounced off her and when she noticed that he had finished talking she said sure. What thefuck. This is much better than wresslin with a drunk and she felt good this morning, much better

than yesterday (briefly remembering the bulls and th
money they took from her) and he might even give he
his money before he went back overseas (what could
he do with it) and with her tits she could always makeout
and whatthehell, it was the best screwin she ever had . . .
They went shopping and she bought a dress, a couple
of sweaters (2 sizes too small), shoes, stockings, a pocketbook and an overnight bag to put her clothes in. She protested slightly when he told her to buy a cosmetic case
(not knowing what it was when he handed it to her and
she saw no sense in spending money on that when he
could as well give her cash), and he enjoyed her modesty
in not wanting to spend too much of his money; and he
chuckled at her childlike excitement at being in the stores,
looking and buying. They took all the packages back to
the hotel and Tralala put on her new dress and shoes and
they went out to eat and then to a movie. For the next few
days they went to movies, restaurants (Tralala trying to
make a mental note of the ones where the Officers hung
out), a few more stores and back to the hotel. When they
woke on the 4th day he told her he had to leave and asked
her if she would come with him to the station. She went
thinking he might give her his money and she stood awkwardly on the station with him, their bags around them,
waiting for him to go on the train and leave. Finally the
time came for him to leave and he handed her an envelope
as she lifted her face slightly so he could kiss her. It was
thin and she figured it might be a check. She put it in her
pocketbook, picked up her bag and went to the waiting
room and sat on a bench and opened the envelope. She
opened the paper and started reading: Dear Tral: There
are many things I would like to say and should have said,
but — A letter. A goddamn LETTER. She ripped the
envelope apart and turned the letter over a few times.
Not a cent. I hope you understand what I mean and am

unable to say—she looked at the words—if you do feel as
I hope you do Im writing my address at the bottom. I dont
know if I/ll live through this war, but—Shit. Not vehe-
mently but factually. She dropped the letter and rode the
subway to Brooklyn. She went to Willies to display her
finery. Ruthy was behind the bar and Waterman Annie
was sitting in a booth with a seaman. She stood at the bar
talking with Ruthy for a few minutes answering her questions about the clothes and telling her about the rich john
she was living with and how much money he gave her and
where they went. Ruthy left occasionally to pour a drink
and when she came back Tralala continued her story, but
soon Ruthy tired of listening to her bullshit as Tralalas
short imagination bogged down. Tralala turned and
looked at Annie and asked her when they leter out.
Annie told her ta go screw herself. Youre the only one
who would. Annie laughed and Tralala told her ta keep
her shiteatin mouth shut. The seaman got up from the
booth and staggered toward Tralala. You shouldnt talk to
my girl friend like that. That douchebag? You should be
able ta do betteran that. She smiled and pushed her chest
out. The seaman laughed and leaned on the bar and asked
her if she would like a drink. Sure. But not in this crummy
place. Lets go ta some place thats not crawlin with stinkin
whores. The seaman roared, walked back to the table,
finished his drink and left with Tralala. Annie screamed
at them and tried to throw a glass at Tralala but someone
grabbed her arm. Tralala and Jack (he was an oiler and
he . . .) got into a cab and drove downtown. Tralala
thought of ditching him rightaway (she only wanted to
break Annies balls), but figured she ought to wait and
see. She stayed with him and they went to a hotel and
when he passedout she took what he had and went back
uptown. She went to a bar in Times Square and sat at the
bar. It was filled with servicemen and a few drunken

sailors smiled at her as she looked around, but she ignored
them and the others in the bar ignored her. She wanted
to be sure she picked up a liveone. No drunken twobit
sailor or doggie for her. O no. Ya bet ya sweetass no.
With her clothes and tits? Who inthehell do those punks
think they are. I oughtta go spit in their stinkin faces. Shit!
They couldnt kiss my ass. She jammed her cigarette out
and took a short sip of her drink. She waited. She smiled
at a few Officers she thought might have loot, but they
were with women. She cursed the dames under her breath,
pulled the top of her dress down, looked around and
sipped her drink. Even with sipping the drink was soon
gone and she had to order another. The bartender refilled
her glass and marked her for an amateur. He smiled and
was almost tempted to tell her that she was trying the
wrong place, but didnt. He just refilled her glass thinking
she would be better off in one of the 8th avenue bars.
She sipped the new drink and lit another cigarette. Why
was she still alone? What was with this joint? Everybody
with a few bucks had a dame. Goddamn pigs. Not one
ofem had a pair half as big as hers. She could have any
sonofabitch in Willies or any bum stumbling into the
Greeks. Whats with the creeps in here. They should be
all around her. She shouldnt be sitting alone. She/d
been there 2 hours already. She felt like standing up and
yelling fuck you to everybody in the joint. Youre all a
bunch of goddamn creeps. She snarled at the women who
passed. She pulled her dress tight and forced her shoulders
back. Time still passed. She still ignored the drunks figuring somebody with gelt would popup. She didnt touch her
third drink, but sat looking around, cursing every sonofabitch in the joint and growing more defiant and desperate. Soon she was screaming in her mind and wishing
takrist she had a blade, she/d cut their goddamn balls off.
A CPO came up to her and asked her if she wanted a

drink and she damn near spit in his face, but just mumbled as she looked at the clock and said shit. Yeah, yeah, lets go. She gulped down her drink and they left. Her mind was still such a fury of screechings (and that sonofabitch gives me nothin but a fuckin letter) that she just lay in bed staring at the ceiling and ignored the sailor as he screwed her and when he finally rolled off for the last time and fell asleep she continued staring and cursing for hours before falling asleep. The next afternoon she demanded that he giver some money and he laughed. She tried to hit him but he grabbed her arm, slapped her across the face and told her she was out of her mind. He laughed and told her to take it easy. He had a few days leave and he had enough money for both of them. They could have a good time. She cursed him and spit and he told her to grab her gear and shove off. She stopped in a cafeteria and went to the ladies room and threw some water on her face and bought a cup of coffee and a bun. She left and went back to the same bar. It was not very crowded being filled mostly with servicemen trying to drink away hangovers, and she sat and sipped a few drinks until the bar started filling. She tried looking for a liveone, but after an hour or so, and a few drinks, she ignored everyone and waited. A couple of sailors asked her if she wanted a drink and she said whatthefuck and left with them. They roamed around for hours drinking and then she went to a room with two of them and they gave her a few bucks in the morning so she stayed with them for a few days, 2 or 3, staying drunk most of the time and going back to the room now and then with them and their friends. And then they left or went somewhere and she went back to the bar to look for another one or a whole damn ship. Whats the difference. She pulled her dress tight but didnt think of washing. She hadnt reached the bar when someone grabbed her arm, walked her to the side door and told her to leave.

She stood on the corner of 42nd & Broadway cursing them and wanting to know why they let those scabby whores in but kick a nice young girl out, ya lousy bunch apricks. She turned and crossed the street, still mumbling to herself, and went in another bar. It was jammed and she worked her way to the back near the jukebox and looked. When someone came back to play a number she smiled, threw her shoulder back and pushed the hair from her face. She stood there drinking and smiling and eventually left with a drunken soldier. They screwed most of the night, slept for a short time then awoke and started drinking and screwing again. She stayed with him for a day or two, perhaps longer, she wasnt sure and it didnt make any difference anyway, then he was gone and she was back in a bar looking. She bounced from one bar to another still pulling her dress tight and occasionally throwing some water on her face before leaving a hotel room, slobbering drinks and soon not looking but just saying yeah, yeah, whatthefuck and pushing an empty glass toward the bartender and sometimes never seeing the face of the drunk buying her drinks and rolling on and off her belly and slobbering over her tits; just drinking then pulling off her clothes and spreading her legs and drifting off to sleep or a drunken stupor with the first lunge. Time passed—months, maybe years, who knows, and the dress was gone and just a beatup skirt and sweater and the Broadway bars were 8th avenue bars, but soon even these joints with their hustlers, pushers, pimps, queens and wouldbe thugs kicked her out and the inlaid linoleum turned to wood and then was covered with sawdust and she hung over a beer in a dump on the waterfront, snarling and cursing every sonofabitch who fucked herup and left with anyone who looked at her or had a place to flop. The honeymoon was over and still she pulled the sweater tight but there was no one there to look. When she crawled out of a flophouse she fell in the nearest bar and stayed until another offer of a flop was made. But each night she would shove her tits out and look around for a liveone, not wanting any goddamn wino but the bums only looked at their beers and she waited for the liveone who had an extra 50¢ he didnt mind spending on beer for a piece of ass and she flopped from one joint to another growing dirtier and scabbier. She was in a South street bar and a seaman bought her a beer and his friends who depended on him for their drinks got panicky fearing he would leave them and spend their beer money on her so when he went to the head they took the beer from her and threw her out into the street. She sat on the curb yelling until a cop came along and kicked her and told her to move. She sprawled to her feet cursing every sonofabitch and his brother and told them they could stick their fuckin beer up their ass. She didnt need any goddamn skell to buy her a drink. She could get anything she wanted in Willies. She had her kicks. She/d go back to Willies where what she said goes. That was the joint. There was always somebody in there with money. No bums like these cruds. Did they think she/d let any goddamn bum in her pants and play with her tits just for a few bucks. Shit! She could get a seamans whole payoff just sittin in Willies. People knew who she was in Willies. You bet yasweet ass they did. She stumbled down the subway and rode to Brooklyn, muttering and cursing, sweat streaking the dirt on her face. She walked up the 3 steps to the door and was briefly disappointed that the door wasnt closed so she could throw it open. She stood for just a second in the doorway looking around then walked to the rear where Waterman Annie, Ruthy and a seaman were sitting. She stood beside the seaman, leaned in front of him and smiled at Annie and Ruthy then ordered a drink. The bartender looked at her and asked her if she had any money. She told him it was none of his goddamn business. My friend here is going to pay for it. Wontya honey. The seaman laughed and pushed a bill forward and she got her drink and sneered at the ignorant sonofabitchin bartender. The rotten scumbag. Annie pulled her aside and told her if she tried cuttin her throat she/d dump her guts on the floor. Mean Ruthys gonna leave as soon as Jacks friend comes and if ya screw it up youll be a sorry sonofabitch. Tralala yanked her arm away and went back to the bar and leaned against the seaman and rubbed her tits against his arm. He laughed and told her to drinkup. Ruthy told Annie not ta botha witha, Fredll be here soon and we/ll go, and they talked with Jack and Tralala leaned over and interrupted their conversation and snarled at Annie hoping she burns like hell when Jack left with *her* and Jack laughed at everything and pounded the bar and bought drinks and Tralala smiled and drank and the jukebox blared hillbilly songs and an occasional blues song, and the red and blue neon lights around the mirror behind the bar sputtered and winked and the soldiers seamen and whores in the booths and hanging on the bar yelled and laughed and Tralala lifted her drink and said chugalug and banged her glass on the bar and she rubbed her tits against Jacks arm and he looked at her wondering how many blackheads she had on her face and if that large pimple on her cheek would burst and ooze and he said something to Annie then roared and slapped her leg and Annie smiled and wrote Tralala off and the cash register kachanged and the smoke just hung and Fred came and joined the party and Tralala yelled for another drink and asked Fred how he liked her tits and he poked them with a finger and said I guess theyre real and Jack pounded the bar and laughed and Annie cursed Tralala and tried to get them to leave and they said lets stay for a while, we/re having fun and Fred winked and some-

one rapped a table and roared and a glass fell to the floor
and the smoke fell when it reached the door and Tralala
opened Jacks fly and smiled and he closed it 5 6 7 times
laughing and stared at the pimple and the lights blinked
and the cashregister crooned kachang kachang and Tralala told Jack she had big tits and he pounded the bar
and laughed and Fred winked and laughed and Ruthy and
Annie wanted to leave before something screwed up their
deal and wondered how much money they had and hating
to see them spend it on Tralala and Tralala gulped her
drinks and yelled for more and Fred and Jack laughed and
winked and pounded the bar and another glass fell to the
floor and someone bemoaned the loss of a beer and two
hands fought their way up a skirt under a table and she
blew smoke in their faces and someone passedout and
his head fell on the table and a beer was grabbed before
it fell and Tralala glowed she had it made and she/d
shove it up Annies ass or anybody elses and she gulped
another drink and it spilled down her chin and she hung
on Jacks neck and rubbed her chest against his cheek and
he reached up and turned them like knobs and roared and
Tralala smiled and O she had it made now and piss on all
those mothafuckas and someone walked a mile for a
smile and someone pulled the drunk out of the booth and
dropped him out the back door and Tralala pulled her
sweater up and bounced her tits on the palms of her
hands and grinned and grinned and grinned and Jack
and Fred whooped and roared and the bartender told
her to put those goddamn things away and get thehellouta-
here and Ruthy and Annie winked and Tralala slowly
turned around bouncing them hard on her hands exhibiting her pride to the bar and she smiled and bounced the
biggest most beautiful pair of tits in the world on her
hands and someone yelled is that for real and Tralala
shoved them in his face and everyone laughed and an-

other glass fell from a table and guys stood and looked and the hands came out from under the skirt and beer was poured on Tralalas tits and someone yelled that she had been christened and the beer ran down her stomach and dripped from her nipples and she slapped his face with her tits and someone yelled youll smotherim ta death —what a way to die- -hey, whats for desert—I said taput those goddamn things away ya fuckin hippopotamus and Tralala told him she had the prettiest tits in the world and she fell against the jukebox and the needle scraped along the record sounding like a long belch and someone yelled all tits and no cunt and Tralala told him to comeon and find out and a drunken soldier banged out of a booth and said comeon and glasses fell and Jack knocked over his stool and fell on Fred and they hung over the bar nearing hysteria and Ruthy hoped she wouldnt get fired because this was a good deal and Annie closed her eyes and laughed relieved that they wouldnt have to worry about Tralala and they didnt spend too much money and Tralala still bounced her tits on the palms of her hands turning to everyone as she was dragged out the door by the arm by 2 or 3 and she yelled to Jack to comeon and she/d fuckim blind not like that fuckin douchebag he was with and someone yelled we/re coming and she was dragged down the steps tripping over someones feet and scraping her ankles on the stone steps and yelling but the mob not slowing their pace dragged her by an arm and Jack and Fred still hung on the bar roaring and Ruthy took off her apron getting ready to leave before something happened to louse up their deal and the 10 or 15 drunks dragged Tralala to a wrecked car in the lot on the corner of 57th street and yanked her clothes off and pushed her inside and a few guys fought to see who would be first and finally a sort of line was formed everyone yelling and laughing and someone yelled to the guys on the end to go get some beer and they left and came back with cans of beer which were passed around the daisychain and the guys from the Greeks cameover and some of the other kids from the neighborhood stood around watching and waiting and Tralala yelled and shoved her tits into the faces as they occurred before her and beers were passed around and the empties dropped or thrown and guys left the car and went back on line and had a few beers and waited their turn again and more guys came from Willies and a phone call to the Armybase brought more seamen and doggies and more beer was brought from Willies and Tralala drank beer while being laid and someone asked if anyone was keeping score and someone yelled who can count that far and Tralalas back was streaked with dirt and sweat and her ankles stung from the sweat and dirt in the scrapes from the steps and sweat and beer dripped from the faces onto hers but she kept yelling she had the biggest goddamn pair of tits in the world and someone answered ya bet ya sweet ass yado and more came 40 maybe 50 and they screwed her and went back on line and had a beer and yelled and laughed and someone yelled that the car stunk of cunt so Tralala and the seat were taken out of the car and laid in the lot and she lay there naked on the seat and their shadows hid her pimples and scabs and she drank flipping her tits with the other hand and somebody shoved the beer can against her mouth and they all laughed and Tralala cursed and spit out a piece of tooth and someone shoved it again and they laughed and yelled and the next one mounted her and her lips were split this time and the blood trickled to her chin and someone mopped her brow with a beer soaked handkerchief and another can of beer was handed to her and she drank and yelled about her tits and another tooth was chipped and the split in her lips was widened and everyone laughed and she laughed and she drank more and more and soon

she passedout and they slapped her a few times and she
mumbled and turned her head but they couldnt revive her
so they continued to fuck her as she lay unconscious on
the seat in the lot and soon they tired of the dead piece
and the daisychain brokeup and they went back to Willies
the Greeks and the base and the kids who were watching
and waiting to take a turn took out their disappointment
on Tralala and tore her clothes to small scraps put out
a few cigarettes on her nipples pissed on her jerkedoff on
her jammed a broomstick up her snatch then bored they
left her lying amongst the broken bottles rusty cans and
rubble of the lot and Jack and Fred and Ruthy and Annie
stumbled into a cab still laughing and they leaned toward
the window as they passed the lot and got a good look at
Tralala lying naked covered with blood urine and semen
and a small blot forming on the seat between her legs as
blood seeped from her crotch and Ruthy and Annie happy
and completely relaxed now that they were on their way
downtown and their deal wasnt lousedup and they would
have plenty of money and Fred looking through the rear
window and Jack pounding his leg and roaring with
laughter . . .

PART V

STRIKE

I went by the field of the slothful, and by the vineyard of the man void of understanding;

And, lo, it was all grown over with thorns, and nettles had covered the face thereof, and the stone wall thereof was broken down.

Proverbs 24: 30, 31

HARRY LOOKED AT HIS SON as he lay on the table playing with a diaper. He covered his head with it and giggled. Harry watched him wave the diaper for a few seconds. He looked at his sons penis. He stared at it then touched it. He wondered if an 8 month old kid could feel anything different there. Maybe it felt the same no matter where you touched him. It got hard sometimes when he had to piss, but he didnt think that meant anything. His hand was still on his sons penis when he heard his wife walking into the room. He pulled his hand away. He stood back. Mary took the clean diaper from the babys hand and kissed his stomach. Harry watched her rub the babys stomach with her cheek, her neck brushing his penis occasionally. It looked as if she were going to put it in her mouth. He turned away. His stomach knotted, a slight nausea starting. He went into the living room. Mary dressed the baby and put him in the crib. Harry heard her jostling the crib. Heard the baby sucking on his bottle. The muscles and nerves of Harrys body twisted and vibrated. He wished to krist he could take the sounds and shove them up her ass. Take the goddamn kid and jam it back up her snatch. He picked up the tv guide, looked at his watch, slid his finger down the column of numbers, twice, then

119

turned on the set and twirled the dials. In a few minutes his wife came into the room, stood alongside Harry and rubbed the back of his neck. What show you watchin? I dont know, twisting his head and leaning away from her hand. She walked over to the coffee table, took a cigarette from the pack on the table and sat on the couch. When Harry shook her hand from his neck she felt disappointed for a second, but it passed. She understood. Harry was funny sometimes. Probably worrying about the job, what with the chance of there being a strike and everything. Thats probably what it is.

Harry tried to ignore the presence of his wife but no matter how he stared at the tv, or covered the side of his head with his hand, he was still conscious of her being there. There! Sitting on the couch. Looking at him. Smiling. For krists sake, what thefuck she smilin at? Got hot fuckin pants again. Always breakin my balls. Wish takrist there was somethin good on tv. Why cant they have fights on Tuesday nights. They think people only wanna look at fights on Fridays? What the fuck ya smilin at?

Harry yawned, turning his head and trying to hide his face with his hand—Mary said nothing, just smiled—trying to interest himself in the show, whatever it was; trying to stay awake until she went to sleep. If only the fuckin bitch would go tabed. Married over a year and you could count the times she went to sleep first. He looked at the tv; smoked, and ignored Mary. He yawned again unable to hide it it came so quickly. He tried to swallow it in the middle, tried to cough or some damn thing, but all he could do was let his mouth hang open and groan. Its gettin kindda late Harry, why dont we go tabed? You go. Im gonna have anotha cigarette. She thought for a moment of having another one too, but figured she/d better not. Harry got very aggravated, when he was like this, if you bothered him too much. She got up, stroking the back of his neck as she passed— Harry jerking his head forward—and went into the bedroom.

Harry knew she would still be awake when he went to bed. The tv was still on but Harry wasnt watching it. Eventually the cigarette was too short to allow him to take another drag. He dropped it in the ashtray.

Mary rolled over onto her back when Harry came into the room. She said nothing, but watched him undress—Harry turning his back toward her and piling his clothes on the chair by the bed—Mary looking at the hair on the base of his spine, thinking of the dirt ingrained in the callouses on his hands and under his finger nails. Harry sat on the edge of the bed for a moment. but it was inevitable: he would have to lie down next to her. He lowered his head to the pillow then lifted his legs onto the bed, Mary holding the covers up so he could slide his legs under. She pulled the covers up to his chest and leaned on her side facing him. Harry turned on his side facing away from her. Mary rubbed his neck, his shoulders, then his back. Harry wished takrist she/d go to sleep and leave him alone. He felt her hand going lower down his back, hoping nothing would happen; hoping he could fall asleep (he had thought that after he got married he would get used to it); wishing he could turn over and slap her across the goddamn face and tell her to stop—krist, how many times had he thought of smashing her head. He tried thinking of something so he could ignore her and what she was doing and what was happening. He tried to concentrate on the fight he saw on tv last friday where Pete Laughlin beat the shit out of some fuckin nigga and had him bleedin all over the face and the ref finally stopped the fight in the, 6th and Harry was madashell that he stopped it . . .

but still he was conscious of her hand on his thigh. He tried remembering how the boss looked last week when he told him off again—he smiled twistedly—that bastard, he cant shove me around. I tellim right to his face. Vice President. Shit. He knows he cant fuck with me. Id have the whole plant shut down in 5 minutes—the caressing hand still there. He could control nothing. The fuckin bitch. Why cant she just leave me alone. Why dont she goaway somewhere with that fuckin kid. Id like ta rip her cunt right the fuck outta her.

He squeezed his eyes shut so hard they pained then suddenly rolled over on Mary, hitting her on the head with his elbow, squeezing her hand between his legs as he turned, almost breaking her wrist—Mary stunned for a moment, hearing more than feeling his elbow hit her; struggling to free her hand; seeing his body on hers; feeling his weight, his hand groping for her crotch . . . then she relaxed and put her arms around him. Harry fumbled at her crotch anxious and clumsy with anger; wanting to pile drive his cock into her, but when he tried he scratched and burned the head and he instinctively stopped for a second, but his anger and hatred started him lunging and lunging until he finally was all the way in—Mary wincing slightly then sighing— and Harry shoved and pounded as hard as he could, wanting to drive the fucking thing out of the top of her head; wishing he could put on a rubber dipped in iron filings or ground glass and rip her guts out—Mary wrapping her legs around his and tightening her arms around his back, biting his neck, rolling from side to side with excitement as she felt all of his cock going in her again and again—Harry physically numb, feeling neither pain nor pleasure, but moving with the force and automation of a machine; unable now to even formulate a vague thought, the attempt at thought being jumbled by his

anger and hatred; not even capable of trying to determine
if he was hurting her, completely unaware of the pleasure
he was giving his wife; his mind not allowing him to reach
the quick climax he wanted so he could roll off and over;
unaware that his brutality in bed was the one thing that
kept his wife clinging to him and the harder he tried to
drive her away, to split her guts with his cock, the closer
and tighter she clung to him——and Mary rolled from side
to side half faint with excitement, enjoying one orgasm,
another, while Harry continued driving and pounding
until eventually the semen flowed, Harry continuing with
the same rhythm and force, feeling nothing, until his
energy drained with the semen and he stopped suddenly,
suddenly nauseous with disgust. He quickly rolled off his
wife and lay on his side, his back toward her, and gripped
the pillow with his hands, almost tearing it, his face buried
in it, almost crying; his stomach crawling with nausea; his
disgust seeming to wrap itself around him as a snake
slowly, methodically and painfully squeezing the life from
him, but each time it reached the point where just the
slightest more pressure would bring an end to everything:
life, misery, pain, it stopped tightening, retained the pressure and Harry just hung there his body alive with pain,
his mind sick with disgust. He moaned and Mary reached
over and touched his shoulder, her body still tingling. She
closed her eyes, her body relaxing, and soon went to sleep,
her hand slowly sliding from Harrys shoulder.

Harry could
do nothing but endure the nausea and slimy disgust. He
wanted to smoke a cigarette, but was afraid, afraid that
the slightest movement, even the taking of a deep breath,
would cause him to heave his guts up; afraid even to
swallow. So he just lay there, a sour taste in his throat;
his stomach seeming to be pressuring against his palate;
his face still buried in the pillow; his eyes tightly squeezed

shut; concentrating on his stomach, trying to think the pressure and foul taste away or, if not, at least control it. He knew, after years of fighting it, losing each time and ending up hanging over a bowl or sink if he was lucky enough to make it there, that this was all he could do. Nothing else would help. Except crying. And he was no longer able to cry. He had many times, locked in a bathroom or on the street after running from the woman he had been with, but now the tears no longer rilled from his eyes, even if he tried relaxing and allowing them to, his eyes just ached, feeling swollen and damp, unrelieved, just as the pressure at his throat remained constant and un-relieved. He just lay there . . . if only something would happen. He clutched harder at the pillow; clenched his jaw tighter until a piercing pain in his ear and a spasm in his neck muscles forced him to relax. His body jerked slightly, involuntarily. Nothing broke through or even slightly grayed the darkness; his eyes were shut and his head was jammed in the hemispherical blackness, the boundaries unseen, unfelt, to Harry nonexistent. It was just black.

He tightened the muscles in his toes until they cramped, the pain increasing; trying to concentrate on the pain enough to forget everything else. His toes felt as if they would shatter and his feet started to cramp, then the calves of his legs, and still he didnt relax his muscles until the pain became unbearable and he wanted to scream and only then he relaxed but the muscles remained tightened and he had to direct all his energy to the relaxing of the muscles before the pain killed him. His calves still ached, though they started to loosen slightly, but his feet felt as if they were going to twist and bend back upon themselves and his toes felt as if they were going to snap. His ears and neck started paining again from the clenching of his jaw —one thing though accomplished, he was no longer aware of the nausea and disgust, of the pressure against his throat and the taste of bile—his ears and neck pained though he was only vaguely aware of it. His calves loosened a little more and slowly the muscles relaxed until his feet and then his toes started to straighten and he then became aware of the ache in his jaw, then that too started slowly to lessen and eventually the cramps and pains disappeared and he loosened his grip slightly on the pillow and lay there, enervated, sweating, feeling for a moment nothing but weakness, then slowly aware of his throat and stomach, the disgust and nausea forcing themselves upon his consciousness again. If something would happen . . . tears pounded against his eyes but couldnt force their way through. Something . . . anything . . . krist. jesus fuckin krist. He allowed his eyes to open—the tears still pounding behind his eyes. His eyes focused on the bureau: there were two large knobs, a smaller one above, another large one to the side; a wall. His eyes started to smart from sweat. He wiped his face against the pillow. He turned his head slightly until he could see the ceiling. Now his vision reached to an end. The ceiling was there. The walls were there. No mysteries. Nothing hidden. There was something to be seen. It had an order. His eyes felt better. No longer felt pinched. No longer afraid to look. Now he had to move. The pressure must have gone down. It was still there, but it must have lessened. It must have. Should be able to move. He swallowed . . . again . . . his throat burned with the bitterness. He lay completely immobile. Not breathing. Stomach bubbling, trying to erupt. Throat pulsating. Burning. He swallowed again . . . breathed. Shallowly. Eruption subsiding slightly. Throat quieting. Still burning. Swallowed . . . breathed . . . slowly pulled his legs up . . . let them slide over the side of the bed. Sat up slowly. Not breathing. Contracting his nostrils. Sucking air gently between his teeth . . . he stood. Rubbed his face . . . went slowly to the parlor. Sat down and lit a cigarette and stared out the window. Smoked. Nothing on the street. No one. Car parked across the street. empty. Lit a second cigarette from the first. Throat burned, but stomach relaxing. Nausea no longer critical. Still there though. Foul. Mouth tasted foul. He sat and smoked. Stared. Eyes damp. Aching. No tears. Dropped the cigarette in the ashtray. Rubbed his face. Went back to bed. Stared at the ceiling until his eyes started to close. If something would happen. What? What? What could happen?? For what? About what? His eyes burned and watered. Couldn't keep them open. His body started to loosen. His head rolled slightly to one side. He adjusted his body. Still hadnt looked at Mary. Hadnt thought of *her*. His body twitched. He brushed his face against the pillow. He moaned in his halfsleep. Soon he slept.

                                            The Harpies swooped down on Harry and in the darkness under their wings he could see nothing but their eyes: small, and filled with hatred, their eyes laughing at him, mocking him as he tried to evade them, knowing he couldnt and that they could toy with him before they slowly destroyed him. He tried turning his head but it wouldnt move. He tried and tried until it rolled back and forth but still the eyes glared and mocked and the gigantic wings beat faster and faster and the wind whirled around Harry and his body chilled and he could sense their large sharp beaks and feel the tips of feathers as they brushed his face. He tried to slide down the rock but no matter how often he did he was still on the top with the wind whirling and the Harpies screeching, screeching and above the roar of the wind and the screeching he could hear his flesh being ripped from his belly, could hear the sharp tearing sound prick its way into his ears and then he heard his screams and the Harpies slowly, very slowly tore bits of flesh from his belly then slowly tugged as the long strips of flesh were pulled from his body and he yelled and rolled over and over and leaped up and ran, tripped and tumbled down the rock yet he was still on top of the rock and the Harpies still mocked him as they tore the flesh from his belly, his chest, and scraped their beaks on his ribs and suddenly thrust their beaks into his eyes and plucked them from their sockets and he heard the plop, plop of his eyes leaving his head and the screeching of the Harpies increased until he no longer could hear his own screams and he kicked and punched at them yet his body refused to move and all he could do was lie still as they once again, and again, over and over started ripping the flesh from his belly and chest, scraping his ribs and once more plucking the eyes from his head

and he was alone on a street looking, turning slowly around in a circle, looking, looking at nothing. Everything was endless in every direction until there were walls that seemed to be moving on an eccentric rod and the walls came closer together, still rolling in half circles and Harry still turned in a circle and the walls came closer together and Harry yelled and started crying yet it was silent not even the walls making a sound as they approached each other and Harry ran until he hit a wall and was in the middle of the diminishing room and he could feel the slate smoothness of the walls as they touched his arms, the back of his head, his nose, and the wall slowly crushed him

and his eyes rolled and bounced up the hill and Harry stumbled after them trying to find them, picking up stones, pebbles and burrs and trying to force them in the empty sockets and he spit out the stones and yelled as the burrs tore the already bleeding sockets and he continued to stumble up the hill and occasionally the eyes would stop and they would look at each other with a gigantic stare and wait until Harry almost touched them then continued to roll up the hill and Harry jammed two more burrs into the sockets and screamed as they ripped the lids and he screamed louder and louder as he twisted the burrs trying to get them out, his bloodied hands preventing him from getting a firm grip on them and his screams were louder and louder until he finally did scream and he sprang up in bed and opened his eyes waiting years for the wall and the chest of drawers to be recognized.

Mary stirred slightly and Harry held his head with his hands and moaned. The nightmare wasnt always exactly the same but after it was over it always seemed as if it had been. Year after year Harry would bolt up in bed occasionally, near dead with terror, trying to shove the weight off his chest so he could breathe and then slowly some familiar object would be seen and he would know he was finally awake. Again his eyes swelled but no tears flowed. He sat for many minutes then slowly lowered his head back to the pillow, wiping his face and head with his hand then covering his eyes with his arm.

Harry moved along the few blocks from his house to the factory, punched his time card, changed his clothes and went to his bench. He was the worst lathe operator of the more than 1,000 men working in the factory. He started shortly before the war and remained there all during the war. Soon after the war started the shop steward was drafted and Harry took his place and devoted more time to the activities of the union than he did his job. From the beginning he hounded and haunted the bosses and soon he was part of the outer clique of the union. During the war the company was powerless to fire him and when they tried after the war the union threatened to call a strike so Harry still stood in front of the same lathe.

Harry
worked for 30 minutes or so each morning then turned
off his lathe and made the rounds of the factory reminding those who were behind in their dues that they had to
pay by a certain date; asking others why they hadnt been
to the last union meeting; or simply telling others not to
work so fast, it aint gonna get ya nothin. Youre only
makin money for the company and they got enough. And
though he had been doing this for years and the foremen
had learned to ignore him, many of the executives, especially cost estimators, production engineers, and the General Manager of the plant who was also a Vice-President
of the Company, were still incensed whenever they saw
him walking around the factory in defiance of all the
rules and regulations. Usually they stormed off in another
direction, but occasionally they would demand to know
what he was doing and he would tell them he was doin
his job, and if they persisted in questioning him he would
tell them to go fuckthemselves, and if they did their job
as good as he did his everybody would be better off and
what the fuck do they know about work, all they do is sit
on their fat asses all day breakin balls . . . and he would
be sure to walk away smiling his sneering smile, looking
at everyone, letting them know by his attitude that he
wasnt afraid of any bigass boss, but they damn sure were
afraid of him, convinced that what he had said was true
and that he was right in doing and saying what he had.
His
morning round usually took an hour and a half to 2 hours.
Then he would go back to his bench and work until lunch
time. Harry never went home for lunch, but went across
the street to the bar and ate with the boys. He always
started with a couple a quick shots and a beer, then a few
beers with a sandwich and a few more after. He talked
with some of the men, listening to their jokes, their stories

of dames fucked, following each story with one of his own about how he bagged some dame and threw a fuck intoer and how she thought he was so great and wanted to seeim again and the others would listen, tolerating him, relieved when he would finally leave their group to go to another; and Harry would continue making the rounds of the bar, listening briefly then telling his stories or a joke about a queer who had his ears pulled off; occasionally sticking a finger in someones stomach and farting; or asking someone when they were going to buy him a drink, laughing, slapping the guy on the shoulder, and leaving when he said right after you do; or if they were new on the job he would put his empty glass on the bar and wait for the bartender to fill it up and take the money from their change on the bar.

   During the middle of the afternoon Harry reached the part of a job that required resetting the lathe and doing a small amount of figuring to set the job up properly so he decided to take a little walk. If he got too far behind in the work the foreman would have to set the job up. He slowly roamed around the factory asking some of the men how it was going, but mostly saying nothing and just smiling his smile, looking and roaming. He was walking around the 6th floor when he suddenly stopped and frowned, thought hard for a few minutes, took the small union booklet from his pocket describing the duties of different classifications, checked it then went over to one of the benches, turned off the lathe and asked the man working there what inthehell he thought he was doin. The man just stood there, trying to understand what had happened and trying to understand what Harry was talking about. Harry stood in front of him waving the booklet in the air, yelling over the noise of the factory. A few of the men near by turned to look and the foreman came running over, yelling at the operator, still standing in front of Harry trying to understand what was going on, and yelled, whys that goddamn machine off? Harry turned to the foreman and asked him if he told him to do this job. Whointhehell do you think toldim to do it. Im the foreman aint I. Well what the fucks the idea of havinim cut heavy stainless, eh? What the fucks the idea? Whattayamean whats the idea? This guys a A man. Hes been cuttin stainless for years. Why shouldnt he cut it. Cause hes a new man thats why. He only been here a couple a months. He doesnt even have a full union book yet. Aint that right, eh? Aint it? yellin in the operators face, waving the booklet. Yeah, but Ive been in the business 20 years. I can cut anything. Harry stepped closer to him, turning his back to the foreman and yelling louder. I dont give a fuck what ya can cut, ya hear me? The union says ya gotta have a full book or been here 6 months before ya can cut heavy stainless, and ya betta do like I tellya or youll find yaself blackballed, yelling even louder, his face swollen—the operator staring, not understanding, wanting only to do his work and be left alone—ya hear me? The foreman finally forced himself into the line of Harrys vision and yelled at him ta shut up. Fa krists sake, what thefuck ya yellin about? Im yellin cause I wanna yell. And youd betta get this guy off the job or youll find your ass inna sling too. Fa krists sake Harry, this jobs gotta be done and hes the only guy whos not workin a job that can do it. I dont give a fuck if ya havta wait ten fuckin years ta get it done, and I dont giveashit how much it costs the boss. Comeon Harry be reasonable, you—I can cut stainless or any other damn thing you got around here. Look buddy, youd better shut yafuckinmouth or youll be out on your ass. The operators face turned red and he started to reach for a wrench and the foreman quickly stepped in front of him, grabbed him by the shoulders and told him to go take a

break, I/ll getya when we settle this. He left and the foreman took a deep breath and closed his eyes for a second
before turning back to Harry. Look Harry, theres no sense
in making a issue of this. You know I never break any
union rules, but this jobs gotta be done and he can do it
so whats the harm? Dont try and brownnose me Mike.
He aint cuttin no stainless. OK, OK, let me call upstairs
and see what we can do. He walked back to his desk to
call and Harry leaned against the idle lathe. The foreman
hung up the phone and came back. Wilsonll be right
down and maybe we can get this straightened out. I dont
give a fuck whos comin down.

          In a few minutes Wilson, a
production manager, came rushing across the floor. He
smiled, put his arms around Mikes and Harrys shoulders.
What seems to be the problem boys, smiling at Harry and
giving Mikes shoulder a reassuring and knowing squeeze.
Harry scowled, turned slightly so that Wilsons hand fell
from his shoulder and barely opened his mouth when he
spoke. The man at this machine aint cuttin no stainless.
I tried to tellim Mr. Wilson that the job had ta be done
—thats OK Mike, patting his shoulder and smiling even
broader at both of them Im sure we can straighten this
thing out. Harrys a reasonable man. Nothin ta straighten
out. He aint cuttin stainless. Mike started to throw his
arms up in disgust, but Wilson put an arm around him
and held his arms for a second, smiled then patted him
again on the back. Why dont we go into the lounge and
have a smoke and talk this over? How about it boys?
Mike said OK and started walking toward the smoking
room. Harry grunted and stood still as Wilson motioned
him on, waiting until Wilson started walking behind Mike
before he too followed, a foot or so behind Wilson. When
they got to the smoking room Wilson took out a pack of
cigarettes and offered them. Mike took one and stuck it

132

in his mouth. Harry said nothing, but took one out of his own pack, ignored Wilsons lighter, lighting his own cigarette. Wilson asked them if they would like a coke and they both declined. The operator, who had been sitting in the corner, came over to Mike and asked him if he could go back to work. Harry started to yell something, but Mike told the man to go out to his bench, but not to turn his machine on. Just wait there. We/ll be out in a minute. The man left and Wilson turned immediately to Harry, smiling, trying to appear relaxed and trying to hide his hatred for him.

Wilson looked at Harry and decided that it wouldnt do to try the arm around the shoulder routine again. Now look Harry, I understand and respect your position. I have known and have had the pleasure of working with you for quite a few years now and I know, just as Mike here knows, and everyone in the plant knows, that youre a good and honest worker, and that you always have the interest of the organization and the men at heart. Isnt that right Mike? Mike nodded automatically. Like I say Harry, we all know you are a good man and that no one else could have done the job you have in keeping the union affairs of this plant functioning as they have been and we all respect and admire you for this. And we all respect and admire your intelligence and ability. And believe me when I say this, because I say this not as an executive of the organization, but as a man who works with the other men here, I say this as a fellow worker: I would be the last person in the world to ask anyone to make even the slightest breach in the union rules and regulations. To me a contract is a sacred instrument and I will stand by it come hell or high water . . . but, and I say this as a worker and an executive . . . look, its like this: its just like in the union itself. You have your constitution and bylaws. Right? I am certain you are familiar with them. And I am also certain that you follow them to the letter, but there are times when you might have to make a slight exception. Now wait a minute—Harry leaning forward and starting to speak—just hear me out. Now look, suppose the rules say a meeting should start at 8 oclock, but suddenly theres a big snow storm and it takes the men 30 minutes or an hour longer to get to the meeting. Now, you either will have to wait and start the meeting late or you will have to start it on time without the proper number of members present. Wilson smiled, relaxed and took a drag of his cigarette, satisfied with his cleverness, thinking that Harrys position was untenable. Harry took a drag of his cigarette, blew the smoke in Wilsons direction, dropped the butt on the floor and squashed it under his shoe What we do at the union meetins is none of your business unless we want ta tellya about it. O, I know that Harry, I certainly didnt mean to imply otherwise. All I am trying to say is that this organization, like your union, is like any other organization in that it is a team and everyone connected with the organization from the President to the elevator operators are a member of that team and we all have to pull together. Everyones job is equally important. The Presidents job is no more important than yours in that if you dont cooperate, just as he must cooperate, we can not get the job done. That is what I am trying to say. We all have to get behind the wheel, just like in the union. Now, we have a job that must be done and it must be done now. This new man is the only man available to do it at this time. That is the only reason he is doing it. We certainly had no intention of being instrumental in asking anyone to do anything that might even be considered a breach of union rules, but the job has to be done—look, this guys a new man and aint cuttin no stainless so just stop the shit. If ya put him back on the job I/ll call the whole goddamn plant out, Harrys face becoming redder, his eyes glaring, ya get that? I/ll stand by that fuckin bench all day if I have ta and if ya try to putim back on that job I swear ta krist the whole fuckin plantll be out on the street in two fuckin seconds and you and no ballbreakin fuck in the jointll stop me. Ya getit? If ya want a strike I/ll giveya one. He walked out of the room, slammed the door and walked back to the bench. He said nothing to the man who was leaning impatiently against the bench, but simply stood at the other end.

Mike and Wilson looked at the door for a moment then Mike asked Wilson if he wanted him to put the man back anyway. No Mike, you had better not. I do not want any trouble. You just go back to your desk. I/ll see Mr. Harrington.

Wilson was disconcerted about having to see Mr. Harrington, but he didn't know what else to do. He certainly did not want the responsibility of precipitating a strike. Mr. Harrington waved him toward a chair and asked Wilson what was on his mind. Wilson sat down and told him the story. As soon as he heard Harrys name Mr. Harrington frowned, then banged his desk with his fist when Wilson started relating the details. He listened becoming more and more infuriated and insulted not only because Harry had the audacity to defy him, one of the Vice-Presidents, and the Corporation, but also because he knew he would have to compromise and not break Harry as he would like to, but would have to avoid any trouble; that particular job had to be done according to schedule. He could not afford a delay. But there would be a strike soon and then he would get rid of Harry. He had hated Harry for years and had never been able to get rid of him, but he was hopeful he could use the strike to get rid of him. As head of the Corporations negotiating committee he knew he could persuade the other members to

135

continue to reject the unions demands even if those demands became reasonable. He knew the Corporation could let the men stay on strike for the remainder of the year with only a slight loss in net earnings. He assumed that when the strike was 6 months old the union would gladly settle the strike if he gave in to most of their demands on the condition that he could discharge Harry. It was worth a try. He had nothing to lose.

By the time Wilson had finished telling him what had happened he had decided what to do He stared directly into Wilsons eyes. Well, you certainly made a mess of it didnt you? The corners of Wilsons mouth sagged a little more. He said nothing. It seems as if I have to do everything around here or the entire organization starts to crumble. I did the —never mind that now. The important thing is to get the job done. Now . . . we simply have to get someone else to do that job. How many men do you have working on the Kearny job? 6. Fine. Take one of the men off that job and have him change with the man working on the Collins job. The Kearny job is all brass if I remember correctly. Yes, it is. But it will take an hour or so to go over the job with the man and I was trying to save all the time I could. Save time! You have already wasted over an hour trying to save time. Now get back and do as I told you.

Wilson got up immediately and left the office. He went directly to the foreman of the Kearny job, and explained the situation. The foreman took one of his men off the job and the man went with Wilson to the 6th floor. Wilson explained to Mike and Harry what was going to be done then told the new man who to report to upstairs. When Harry saw him leave, and Mike and the man who had come down with Wilson go over to the lathe with the stainless steel stock, he left.

When he got back to his own bench his foreman was just finishing setting up the job for Harry. Think you can finish this job by tomorrow morning Harry? Its a rush. Yeah, sure. I wouldve finished it today, but that wise punk Wilson tried to pull a fast one and I had to straightenim out. He thought he could push me around, but I fixed hisass. Harry turned slightly toward his bench and the foreman left. He was a few feet away when Harry noticed he had gone and he sneered and muttered, chickenshit. Afraid the boss might see him with me. Harry jabbed at the button that turned his lathe on and started working. Fuckim.

Harry worked as slowly as possible, moving the cutting tool almost imperceptibly, and when the time came to go home he still had another hours or so work before the job would be finished.

Harry was in high spirits when he got home. As he washed his hands and splashed water on his face he told his wife what had happened and when she would tell him he ought to be careful, he might lose his job, he would laugh his evil laugh and tell her, they wouldn't fire me. If they tried that Id have the whole joint on strike and they know it. They cant fuck me around. When he finished eating he went up to the bar and yelled to the guys at the bar how he told the punk ballbreaker off at work, punctuating his story with his laugh.

Mary had already gone to bed by the time Harry got home, but it didnt make any difference to him one way or the other whether or not she was awake, she wouldnt bother him for awhile anyway. He undressed and plopped into bed and looked at Mary to see if she would wake up, but she uttered a low grunting noise and pulled her knees up closer to her chin. Harry stayed on his side, facing Mary, and fell asleep.

The next morning Harry went up to the 6th floor before going to his own bench. He checked to make sure the new man wasnt working on the stainless job. He smiled when he saw that he wasnt at his bench and stayed around for a while just to be sure they werent trying to pull a fast one; and before he left he went over to the foreman and told him he would see him later. He made his rounds throughout the rest of the plant and when he got back to his bench more than 2 hours had passed. He jabbed the start button and began working. The foreman came over and asked him when the job would be ready, the rest of the job is finished and we/re just waiting for this piece. He sneered at the foreman and told him it would be ready when he finished. The foreman took a quick glance at the job, estimating how long it would be before Harry finished, and left. Harry stared at him for a few minutes, wise fuck, then turned back to the job.

When Harry came back from lunch he went back to the 6th floor and checked again, then strolled around the plant. He got back to his bench eventually and finished the job then went back to the 6th floor. The new man was back at his bench, but a piece of brass was in his machine. Harry went over to him. Thats betta. You come close ta losin your book yesterday mac. He just glanced at Harry, wanting to tell him what he thought of him, but said nothing, having been told that morning about Harry and how he had had more than one book pulled, for no reason at all, from more than one guy. Harry sneered and walked away. He went back to his work, still glowing and feeling omnipotent. He didnt particularly care about the new guy, but he was glad he had shoved it up the boss/s ass and broke it off. He stayed at his work the rest of the day thinking occasionally of yesterday and of the fact that the union contract with the company expired in two weeks and the negotiating committees had not reached an agreement for a new contract and it was a sure thing that there would be a strike. Harry was so happy about going on strike—of closing down the entire shop, of setting up picket lines and watching the few bosses going into the empty factory and sitting at their desks and thinking and worrying about all the money they were losing while he got his every week from the union—that he laughed every now and then to himself and at times felt like shouting as loud as he could, fuck all you company bastards, all ya ball breakin pricks. We/ll showya. We/ll makeya get on yaknees and begus ta come back tawork. We/ll breakya ya fat fucks.

With each day Harry felt bigger. He walked around the plant waving at the guys, yelling to them above the noise; thinking that soon it would be silent. The whole fuckin shop/d be quiet. And he had cartoon like images in his mind of dollar bills with wings flying out the window, out of the pocket and pocketbook of a fat baldheaded cigar smoking boss; and punks with white shirts and ties and expensive suits sitting at an empty desk and opening empty pay envelopes. There were images of gigantic concrete buildings crumbling and pieces flying out of the middle and himself suspended in air smashing the buildings to pieces. He could see himself crushing heads and bodies and heaving them from the windows and watching them splatter on the sidewalks below and he roared with laughter as he watched the bodies floating in pools of blood and drifting toward the sewers and he, Harry Black, age 33, shop steward of local 392 watched and roared with laughter.

At night, after supper, he went to the empty store the union was fixing up to use as a strike headquarters. He did little and talked a lot.

Harry slept better, deep and without dreams; but before sleeping he would lie on his side and let the various images of empty shops, crumbling buildings and splattering bodies drift through his mind, more real, more vivid, the features and images more sharply defined, the flesh more pulpy, more flaccid; the cigar tips glowing, the smell of cigar smoke and after shave lotion resented and enjoyed. Then slowly the images would start overlapping each other, become entangled and whirl together in one amorphous multiexposure picture and Harry would smile, the sneer almost disappearing, then he slept.

The last day of the contract Harry whistled as he worked. Not really a whistle, but a flat hissing sound that at times approached a whistle. A new contract had not as yet been signed and there was to be a union meeting that night. When the working day was over Harry walked happily from the shop, slapping many of the men on the back with as deep a feeling of comradeship as he was capable of feeling, telling them not to forget the meeting and he would see them at the hall. Some of the men stopped in the bar before going home and slowly drank a few beers, talking about the strike, wondering how long it would last and what they would get. Harry bought a beer and walked around the bar slapping a back or squeezing a shoulder, not saying much, simply a this is it, or tonights the night. He hung around for half an hour or so then went home.

The officers were already on the platform when Harry got to the hall. He walked away from the steps on the side of the platform and walked around to the front and vaulted up onto the platform. He shook hands with everyone there, smiling his smile, and listened for a few minutes to each group huddling on the platform, continuing to go from one to the other, as the hall slowly filled, until it was 10 minutes past the official time for the meeting to start and the President of the local indicated that he would start the meeting soon and the groups broke up and the men took their seats, Harry sitting in the second row on the end, adjusting his chair so he could be seen between the two men in front of him.

The President sat, taking papers from his attache case, looking them over, occasionally passing one to some one else, a brief and hushed discussion following. Eventually he had the papers sorted as he wanted and he rose, remaining behind the small desk in front of him. The men in the hall quieted and the President called the meeting to order and called on the Secretary to read the minutes of the last meeting. They were read, voted upon and officially accepted by the rank and file. Next the Treasurer read his report consisting of many figures and explanations of expenditures, of how much was in the treasury and how much in the strike fund, the strike fund figure read last, slowly and loudly and the non-official members of the clique scattered throughout the hall applauded, as planned, and whistled, many others joining them. This report was voted upon and accepted by the rank and file.

Then the President got down to the business at hand and informed all the members that they knew what they were really here for tonight. More applause and whistles from the clique and others. The President raised his hands, solemnly, for silence. Your negotiating committee has been working hard for a long time trying to get a fair contract and wage for you men. Applause. We/re not asking for much, just what we work for. But the company wants you to do all the work while they keep all the money. Boos and the stamping of feet. Let me just read their last offer. He yanked papers from the desk, crumpled the edges in his hand and looked at them scornfully. They want us to keep a 35 hour week— a loud no—give us a lousy 12 holidays—another no— the President continued to read through the noise that followed. No holiday for birthdays, keep time and a half for overtime—another roar—a stinking 25c an hour raise, and only a small increase in their contributions to the welfare plan and they want it to be controlled by a independent trustee—a look of contempt on his face as he looked at the men and read—and a lot of double talk that amounts to nothing and they have the nerve to offer us this—hoots and catcalls. But we showed them, pounding on the table and yelling defiantly, we showed them what kind of stuff union men are made of: we told them to go to hell. He sipped water then wiped his face and lowered his head slightly and waited for the men to quiet down. Now, we all know how hard we work—dont forget I sweated for 20 years myself over a lathe and that was before the union when they was really sweat shops— applause—the President raised his hands. And the company knows how hard you men work but do they care —a NOOOOO from the clique and a few others, then a roar from the men—but we care, dont we—a roaring YEEEEES—youre damn right we do, and by jesus theres not a man one of us whos going to allow them to get away with this—a roar—and you can bet your life they know it. He paused, took a sip of water, cleared his throat. All we/re asking for is an honest wage for an honest days work and decent working conditions, and thats something that every American as a free man is entitled to, pounding on the desk emphasizing the words american, free, entitled, and leaning slightly toward the men as they roared and stamped their feet. Now we all know what we/re asking for—the men in the hall looked quizzically at each other, trying to remember just what

142

they were asking for—but I/ll read them as they were presented to the company. A 30 hour week—cheers—a $1 an hour raise—cheers—a 25% increase in the companys contributions to our welfare plan to be supervised by the union, looking up from the paper, leaning forward and pounding on the table, I said supervised by the union so those goddamn company lawyers and accountants cant cheat you out of what you should get—whistling and stamping of feet—16 paid holidays, including every members birthday, or double time if he has to work on any of those holidays—applause. He straightened. Now . . . your negotiating committee met with theirs and after 2 weeks of head to head bargaining—and theres not a man one of us who doesnt know that you deserve everything weve asked for—and after 2 weeks the Vice-President told us that the Company couldn't afford to meet our demands—roars and boos . . . We/re going to meet with them again but, I want everyman here to understand that we never have and never will have any intention of allowing them to bulldoze us into accepting a contract thats not fair for the rank and file of this union—whistles, roars, stamping —and no matter how many of their slick or conniving tricks they try or no matter how long the strike lasts theyre not going to get away with it—a roar—and if they think theyre dealing with jerks they got another guess coming . . .

The President of Local 392 continued for another 30 minutes, interrupted with cheers, the stamping of feet, whistling, explaining that if they gave in to the company now theyd grind their faces in the mud for the rest of their lives; and how every union member in the country was behind them, pledged to give all assistance and aid—and that means money—as long as the strike lasts; of how the union was completely ready and geared for the strike—an empty store had been rented as a temporary strike headquarters, signs have already been painted and instructions have been printed telling each brother when he has to walk the picket line—denouncing and promising . . .

When he finished he introduced other members of the board who talked about what they were doing to help the strike and their union brothers. When they finished the President introduced brother Harry Black, shop steward and militant union brother, who was to be in charge of the strike headquarters. Harry tried to look over the heads of the men in the hall as he spoke, but was unable to keep from seeing their faces so he lowered his head and closed his eyes until they were open just enough to see his shoes and the edge of the platform. Like Brother Jones toldya the unions rented a store for a strike headquarters, you all know the place its next ta Willies bar and a free $10 bag of groceries will be given ta everybody every saturday morning for as long as the strike lasts and the place is big enough for everything so that we dont have ta worry about it and before we/re through with this strike the bossesll be on their knees begginus ta come back. Harry turned, opened his eyes and tried to find his seat but was unable to focus his eyes and he shook his head from side to side trying to orient himself and the President came over to him and tapped him on the shoulder and pushed him toward his seat. Harry stumbled, knocked into one of the members sitting near him and finally found his seat and sat down, sweat dripping from his armpits, his shirt stuck to his chest and back. He lowered his head, closed his eyes for a few moments and heard nothing until he finally raised his head and saw the President once more speaking to the men.

Now you have some idea of how hard we have been working for you to get everything in order for the strike and have

it setup so we can take care of everything no matter how
long the strike lasts. He sipped water then wiped his face
with his handkerchief. He just stood there for a few
minutes, head slightly bowed, listening to the men roar
and when he noticed that it was starting to subside he
turned once again toward the men and raised his hands,
looking humble and worn, for silence. The men quieted
and he looked around the hall, slowly, still keeping the
humble expression, then once more started speaking. He
reviewed the preparations that had been made; told them
that everyman had to put in a couple of hours a week on
the picket line and that his book would be stamped after
every turn on the line and if anyone didnt have his book
stamped that he had better be able to prove he couldnt
walk or his book would be yanked, we/re not going to
allow any scabbing—yells and cheers—and coffee and
sandwiches will be given to all the men on the line and
explained a few more details of how they would conduct
the strike before putting up to the rank and file whether or
not they wanted to accept the companys offer or go on
strike. Just as he finished speaking one of the nonofficial
members of the clique made a motion that they tell the
company ta go tahell and go on strike. Another member
seconded the motion and the President yelled that a
motion has been made and duly seconded. All in favor
say aye and a roar went up as some men murmured, a
few looked around confused, but almost everyone remained in the current of the evening and added their
voice to the roar after the initial aye. The President
banged on the desk, the motion has been accepted by
acclamation, banged the desk again and another roar went
up along with the scraping of chair legs on the floor as
the men got up and started pounding each other on the
back. The meeting was over. The strike was official.

Although the picketing wouldnt start until 8 oclock, the beginning of the normal working day, Harry was in the strike headquarters at 6:30. It was a small store that had been vacant for many years and a telephone had been installed as well as a small refrigerator, stove and large coffee urn. There were many folding chairs around the room and an old desk in the corner. Against the rear wall were dozens of picket signs. Harry sat behind the desk and looked at the phone for a few minutes hoping it would ring and he could answer it, local 392 strike headquarters, Brother Black, Shop Steward talkin. It probably wouldnt be long before the phoned be ringin all the time and hed be talkin ta the President and all the other officers all the time about how he was runnin the strike. He wished he knew somebody he could call so he could tellem how he was there and what was goin on. It wouldnt be long before the menll be showin up for the picket line. He leaned back in the chair and it moved slightly. He looked down at the legs and noticed they had wheels so he pushed himself back and forth a few times. He stopped and looked at the phone again for a few minutes, then pushed hard against the desk and the chair rolled back to the wall.

                             The first few men came a little before 8. Harry got up, rolling back his chair, slapped them on the back and told them everything was all set. The signs are over there. Ya can each take one and start picketing the front of the building. Harry rushed over to the pile of signs and selected three, giving one to each man, trying to remember what else there was to do. The men started to leave, then one of them asked when they got their book stamped. Harry stared for a minute. book stamped. stamp. His jaw started to quiver slightly. Ya gonna stampem now or after we finish walking. uuuuuuhhh . . . They gonna be stamped after? A few more men came in and started talking—book, stamp—

with the men who were ready to leave with their signs. No one was looking at Harry. He managed to turn and move toward the desk. The books were to be stamped. Yes. He pulled out a few drawers then he knew definitely what it was he was looking for. A rubber stamp and a stamp pad. He pulled the big drawer all the way out. Looked. Yeah, there it was. He took them out. I guess I might as well do it now. Bring your books over here. The men with the signs went over and Harry stamped their books. Any sonofabitch that dont get this stamped is gonna get his ass inna sling. One of the men who had just come in asked what was going on. Ya gotta get ya book stamped before ya go out. He came over to the desk with his book out. Ya gotta get a sign first, and Harry went back to the pile of signs and handed one to each of the men. OK, now I/ll stamp ya books. Ya oughta put a sign up so the guysll know. I was just gonna do that, and Harry stamped their books and the men put the signs on and looked at each other, smiling and joking. OK you guys, hit the concrete. Its afta 8. And dont all you guys stay in one spot. Spread out and keep moving. No standin still.

The men left and Harry went back to his desk and stamp pad. He ripped a piece of paper off a pad and printed a sign, get book stamped before going, and stuck it over the pile of signs. Men continued to come in and Harry handed out signs and stamped books; told some of them to go to the rear of the plant, and keep movin, no standin still; and when the men came in or back from picketing they poured themselves cups of coffee and stood around the store, or out in front, and talked and joked. In a few hours Harry started to panic with so many men around. Something inside his arms, his stomach, legs, seemed to be tightening and caused him to grind his teeth. He told one of the men to take over for a while, telling him to make sure he stamped the books, and went to Willies next door. He went to the end of the bar and had a couple of drinks and started to relax. He stayed for a while, drinking, until the tenseness faded. He left the bar and walked over to the picket line to see how things were going. He looked scornfully at the cops who were there in case of trouble and waved to the men as he walked around to the side to see how things were going there. He asked one of the men if anybody was around back and he said he thought so and Harry figured he might just as well take a look anyway. He walked the block to the rear of the factory and spoke to the men for a few minutes, reminding them to keep movin so the fuckin cops couldnt have nothin ta say, then went back to the office. He went back to the desk and resumed stamping.

The office wasnt as crowded now, many of the men standing outside in the warm May sun talking, joking, enjoying having a day off with nothing to do but hang around and drink beer and talk with the boys; and others used the time to wash and polish their cars, a steady stream of men walking through the office to fill buckets with water.

During the day Harry made a few more trips to the bar, staying outside after each trip to talk with the men and tell them how they was gonna show these ball breakers who was boss. During the afternoon one of the Union Officials came in and asked Harry how everything was going. He told him he had everything under control. I keep the guys movin. The cops aint got nothin ta bitch about; and you can bet nobodys gettin in the shop except a few pencil stiffs. Youre a good man Harry. Harry smiled his smile. And dont forget, if you need anything just charge it to the union and put it on your expense voucher. And dont forget to send your voucher in each week. Harry was glowing. He nodded. Dont worry about nothin. We/ll break their backs. The official left and Harry stretched out in his chair and smoked for a while, talking occasionally to one of the men, then slowly once more started to feel squeezed. He got up from the chair and walked to the back and stood in the yard for a while and started to feel better, but soon some of the men came back too, some bringing chairs, others cards, and in a few minutes a card game had started and Harry went back into the office. He figured hed go for a drink, then asked one of the men if he knew of a joint that delivered beer around there. Yeah, theres a guy down a ways on 2nd avenue. Harry called and an hour later the truck pulled up and a keg of beer was rolled in, tapped and Harry drew the first glass. Before the end of the day the keg was empty and Harry called to have another one delivered, but was told it couldnt be delivered before 5 so Harry said to bring it the first thing in the morning.

By the time the picketing day ended Harry was relaxed and joking with the men as they came in with their signs. When all the signs had been piled against the wall, and everyone gone, Harry stayed to have one last smoke while sitting in his chair behind his desk. The tension that made him feel as if his body was going to split was forgotten now. All the signs were back; the books were stamped; the big boys liked the way he was handling the strike and he had a nice whisky glow. Everything was going along just fine. The men kept moving like they was supposed to and everybody was really workin ta break the bosses backs. Nothin to it. Alls we gotta do is keep that picket line movin and the shop closed and theyll be on their knees beggin us please come back on our terms. The first day of the strike was over.

Harry flopped at the kitchen table and tried to ignore his wife as she served supper and asked questions about how the strike went and how long would it be . . . She put the food on the plates and sat down and started eating, still asking questions, Harry mumbling answers. He glanced at his wife from time to time and soon his body started to tighten and it continued until his body was once more one gigantic knot. He felt like rapping her across the face. He looked at her. She continued to ask questions. He dropped his fork on the plate and got up from the table. Where you going? Back to the office, I think I forgot something. He rushed from the house before she could say anything and went to the bar. He went to the end of the bar and stayed there, alone, drinking, saying nothing. After an hour or so he once more started to feel better and soon became conscious of a few of the neighborhood guys standing a few feet away. Actually what attracted him to them was a high pitched feminine voice. It took a moment or two for him to realize that one of the guys standing near him was a fairy. He looked at him, trying not to be too obvious, lowering his eyes everytime somebody moved his head toward him, slowly raising them again to stare at the fairy. Harry couldnt hear everything he was saying, but he watched the delicate way in which he emphasized what he said with his hands, and the way his neck seemed to move in a hypnotic slowmotioned manner as he talked and gestured. He seemed to be telling the guys about a party, a drag ball, that had taken place last Thanksgiving at a place called Charlie Blacks. Harry continued to stare and listen, fascinated.

They stayed there for more than an hour, Harry listening and ignoring his beer. When they left he watched them leave hoping they were going across the street to the Greeks so he could follow them in a few minutes, but they got into a car and drove away. Harry continued to stare out the door after they drove away and only the sudden blaring of music from the jukebox caused him to blink his eyes and turn back to the bar. He lifted his glass automatically and finished his beer.

He stayed at the bar until about midnight, the image of the fairys face and hands still in his mind, his voice still in his ear. When he finished his last beer and left for home he was unaware of his body: partly from his preoccupation with the image and sound, partly from the beer. The fresh air clouded the image slightly, but it was still there. It was still there when he undressed and fell into bed. He lay on his side away from Mary, but soon Marys groping hand and voice forced the image to dissolve. When she first started caressing him it was still with him and excitement shocked through him. Then he became aware of her and there was nothing but her and anger, the anger keeping alive the excitement. He bolted around immediately and pounded on her trying desperately to evoke the image and sound but it was irrevocably gone for now and Mary groaned and scratched . . .

He rolled over, lay awake for a while, once more almost crying, the confusion blinding him, but he was so exhausted from all that had happened that day that he soon fell asleep.

The next morning he awoke early and left before Mary had a chance to speak to him. He went to the Greeks and had coffee and cake, glancing at the clock every now and then, but still it wasnt even 6:30 yet. He had another cup of coffee, another cake, gulping them down, still looking at the clock every few minutes feeling a need to rush, no thought from what or to where, but only a vague yet crushing pressure of time, time that seemed to wrap itself around him like a python. He dropped money on the counter and went across the street to his office. He went immediately to his desk and sat down, looking at the desk for many minutes—the serpent not loosening its grip—unable to feel the air around his body. He lit a cigarette and looked around the office. He went over to the beer keg and pumped for a while but nothing came out. Not even a hint of foam. It was empty. Theyll be here with another one soon though.

The python continued to crush him and time seemed motionless. The hands on the clock were stuck. The urgency now was not only for him to move, but for time to move too; for the men to come, to take their signs, to walk, to joke, to drink coffee and beer; for him to stamp books, to listen, to tell, to watch. They had to come soon. A cigarette only takes a certain amount of time to smoke and though this takes time it seems to take less and less with each one and you can only smoke so many, there comes a time when you have to stop. when you just cant light the next one . . . at least not for a while.

He opened the rear door and looked around not really seeing anything. Nothing seemed to really exist. The objects in the office were there, they could be seen each in its place, yet still there was confusion. He knew what each object was, what it was for yet there was no real definition. He sat at his desk for a while, walked around for a while . . . sat . . . walked . . . sat . . . walked . . . looked . . . sat . . . walked . . . the only important thing was that the men get there. They had to. The day had to start. He walked . . . sat . . smoked . . . the python still there. Were there no hands on the clock? He smoked . . . Drew a cup of coffee . . . It was strong, bitter, yet it passed his mouth and throat without leaving a taste. Only a film. Dont clocks tick anymore?

Is even the sun motionless. The water is boiled, poured
over the coffee and it drips through and time passes . . .
even if it only drips it passes . . . through. How long does
it take his chair to get from the desk to the wall a few
feet behind him when he pushes and the chair rolls on its
little wheels? Even that takes time: time enough for a
man to walk from the door to the signs, or from the urn
to the door; enough time to stamp three books one right
after the other: 1,2,3 . . . and yet there was not a de-
finable thought in his mind. Only a terrifying effort to get
from one side of a match box to another . . . the door
opened and three men came in. Harry jumped up. The
python slithered into the match box. The day had begun.
Whattayasay,
bumping into the corner of the desk and stumbling toward
the men. Bright and early, eh? Thats the way. Cant be too
early for those bastards. Theres some coffee left. Have
some new coffee soon. Gonna have some beer soon too.
The men stood looking at him for a moment hearing his
rambling voice, then started moving toward the urn. Guess
I/ll order some cake an buns and stuff from some baker.
Cant go all day without eatin, eh? and the union wants ta
take care of its men. Cant hit the concrete without somethin. The men looked at the coffee, poured it out and
started putting on signs. Dont forget to get ya book
stamped, adjusting the sign on one of the men then
rushing back to his desk, yanking open the drawer and
plunging his hand in and bulldozing it back and forth
until he found the stamp and ink pad. Gotta get yabook
stamped. Anybody who dont have a stamp is gonna get
his ass ina sling. The first crew who walked yesterday did
a good job. Ya just gotta keep movin or the copsll break
ya balls. The men put their books on the table, looking
at each other as Harry pounded the books with the stamp,
still rambling. The fuckin copsed just love ta try and

break the picket line. The men started moving toward
the door. Dont stay in a mob, but stay apart and keep
movin. You guys can take the front. I/ll send the other
guys around back and on the sides and if anybody gives
ya any trouble just yell, aint nobody gonna break this
strike. The men left and started across the street to the
factory, Harry yelling after them ta keep movin and make
sure only the punk pencil pushers get in. The men shook
their heads and continued walking. They had a little time
to put in and then the day was theirs. Strikes can be ok
sometimes. It was a nice day.

Harry hustled around the
office. The beer should be there soon. He looked at the
signs. They were ok. A few more men came in and Harry
said ta grab a sign and he stamped their books and told
them where to walk, and ta keep movin, and more men
came in and grabbed signs and the day was really there
now and soon the man came with the beer and Harry told
him to come back with two more kegs later and Harry
called for boxes of cakes and buns and signed all the bills
spreading his signature across the bottom of the paper
and putting his title, shop steward local 392, under it and
Harry kept his glass filled with beer all through the day
and the men came and went, took signs, returned them,
had their books stamped; washed and polished their cars,
played cards or just stood around talking and joking, enjoying the clear sky and warm weather; leaving when
they finished their tour of duty and joking about the three
day weekend and about this being the first Friday theyve
had off since they cant remember when and not many of
them took the strike seriously. Theyd have to picket for a
while, a few days maybe even a week or two, but in
weather like this who cares (if it gets a little warmer we
can even go to the beach after walking) and theyll make
the money back in no time with the raise and the unions

going to give them food next Saturday so theres really nothing to worry about. It was an early vacation.

The keg of beer was empty almost an hour before the other two were delivered and Harry and a few others who had been drinking steadily were slightly drunk. When the two kegs were set up Harry told the guy to bring four more Monday morning. That should lastus, and he laughed his laugh.

During the afternoon Harry sat in the yard, in the back, drinking and talking with some of the men as they played cards or just sat around. When some one took a sign he yelled at them to come in the back and get their book stamped and they kidded him about what a hard job he had and he slapped them on the back and laughed his laugh and the men laughed and put on their signs and walked up and down around the factory, talking with the cops, kidding them about having to be there longer than they did and the cops smiled telling them they wished they could strike and maybe then theyd get a break and that they hoped the men got what they wanted without being out of work too long and occasionally one of the men would stand still for a moment and look at the cops and smile and someone else would yell, laughingly, to keep moving and the teams of pickets changed every hour or so and the conversation would start from the beginning between themselves and the cops, only an occasional word changing and then the cops too got a relief and the ones leaving waved to the men, happy that their day had ended and their weekend started and the new cops stood silent for a while, but they too, soon started talking with the pickets and everyone enjoyed the weather and the novelty and the day moved along as logically as the sun.

Harry was drunk by the time the last sign was piled against the wall. He put his stamp and pad back in the drawer and he and a couple of others stayed and finished the beer, hanging over the keg, pumping and pumping until nothing came out of the tap but a hiss. Harry put his arms around the shoulders of the two near him and told them they would show those sonsofbitches. And especially that punk Wilson. I/ll show that fuckin fairy, that queer punk. They all laughed.

Harry went across the street to the Greeks after locking his office. Some of the neighborhood guys were there, among them the ones who were in the bar last night, and Harry sat at the counter and ordered something to eat and occasionally spoke to the guys about the strike, they asking him how it was going and he telling them they hadem by the balls and they should come over and have a drink. He hung around the Greeks for a few hours until the guys left then he too left and went home.

The next day he slept late and left the house right after eating and went to the Greeks, but it was too early for any of the guys to be there. He sat around for a while then went over to his office and sat at his desk. He smoked a few cigarettes then called the Secretary of local 392 and told him that he was in the office just checkin on things and the Secretary told him he was doing a good job and Harry hung up the phone and tried to think of someone else to call but he couldnt think of another except the beer distributors number. He called them. He told them who he was and said that they might as well send over the four kegs now as wait for Monday. He sat around for a while, filled out his expense sheet then walked around the office until the beer was delivered and the kegs set up then he filled a pitcher and sat at his desk with it and a glass drinking and watching the street.

156

Sometime in the middle of the afternoon he saw a car park in front of the Greeks and a few of the guys get out so he locked the office and went to the Greeks. He asked the guys how they were doing and they nodded and he sat for a while with them, but no one else came in. Eventually he asked them if they would like some beer, I got four fuckin kegs in the office, and they said yeah, so they left, the guys leaving word with the counterman where they would be and went to the office. Harry got them glasses and he and Vinnie, Sal and Malfie sat around drinking beer. Harry told them how he was in charge of the office and the entire strike, but they didnt pay too much attention to him, figuring him for a creep from the first time he spoke to them, and just yeahd him and drank the beer and looked around the office. Malfie told him he should have a radio so they could listen to some music and Vinnie and Sal agreed and Harry said he didnt have one, but maybe he should get one. Yeah, sure yashould. The union oughtta give yaone so yawont go nuts just sittin around here doin nothin. Yeah. Why not. Harry told them he had a lot to do takin care of the strike. Ya dont know all the—if the unionll pay for the beer they should pay for a radio Yeah. If you toldem yaneeded one they couldn't say nothin. Yeah. Yeah, they wouldnt say nothin if I got one. Yeah, and afta the strike ya could take it home. Who would know the difference. Yeah, why not? We can gettya a good one for 20, 30 bucks. Krist, thats a lotta money. A lotta money? Whats 30 bucks to the union. They got millions. We/ll getya a good radio and yacan giveus the money and get it from the union. Dont worry about it, they wont say nothin. As soon as we see a good one we/ll pick it up forya. The guys looked at each other and smiled thinking of the radio in the window of the new store on 5th avenue. We should be able ta get yaone by tomorrow. Yeah, a real nice job.

They continued drinking and talking, Harry telling them about the union and what he was doing. From time to time he picked up the empty pitcher and refilled it and set it on his desk, being sure to push his chair back and let it roll to the wall before getting up. After a few hours a few more of the guys came in and by the time the sun set Harry was getting drunk and entertaining about a dozen of the neighborhood guys, feeling like a patriarch because he was in charge of the strike. The guys drank the beer and ignored Harry, talking to him only when necessary; yet Harry was happy, enjoying having them around him and excited with anticipation. He asked Vinnie, laughing and slapping him on the shoulder, who that fruit was that was with them the othernight and Vinnie told him she was just one of the queens from uptown, onea Georgettes friends. Why, ya wanna meeter? Naw, slapping Vinnies knee, what the fuck I wanna meet a fuckin fruit for. I dont know, maybe ya go for that stuff, laughing and peering at Harry. Haha, leaning back in his chair, pushing with his hands against the desk, the chair rolling back to the wall. I was just wonderin what ya guys were doing with a fruit. I didnt think yahung around with those kindda fucks. Theyre ok sometimes. Theyre always good for loot when they got it and they getya high when yawanna. Stick around. She may be around later, smiling. Hahaha, rolling the chair back to the desk. I dont go for that shit. Im strickly a cunt man myself. I was just wonderin how come he hung around with you guys is all. I got more cunt than ya could fuck in a year. Shit, last night I had ta chase one away, a good lookin bitch too, but I promised the old lady Id throw a fuck inner, you know how it is. Ya gotta—Vinnie turned his head and started talking to Sal and some of the other guys, but Harry couldnt stop: he soliloquized about the babe who picked him up a few weeks ago and took him home and she had a new car and the blond and how many more women who damned near fucked the ass offim, but they couldnt do that, he could put fuck any woman around and he never did like queers, everytime he saw one he wanted ta rapim in his mouth and whenever he throws a fuck inta the old lady she creams all over the place and Vinnie and the guys got up and walked away and Harry leaned toward a few of the other guys near by, his voice still working, the words still spilling, his laugh blurting out occasionally and he stopped for a second, drank his beer, filled the glass again and continued talking, lower, walking around telling the guys he could fixem up anytime they wanted ta get a good piece a tail and a few nodded, one or two even smiled, and soon Harry was able to stop talking and he went back to his desk and drank beer, more rapidly, keeping all the pitchers full, telling the guys ta drinkup, theres plenty more, the unions gonna keep the beer flowin, hahaha, and he emptied another glass, refilled it and soon was unable to move without staggering and he sat at his desk, pushing his chair back and forth from time to time, spilled a glass of beer on his desk and laughed as it trickled off the edge, someone yelling that it was a good strike and a few others yelled, yeah, and Harry laughed his laugh and pushed the beer off the desk with the palm of his hand and said theres plenty more and the guys laughed and soon tired of hanging around with Harry and told him goodbye, we/ll seeya, keep the beer cold, and Harry asked them not to go, hang around a while. We/ll getus some pussy later, but the guys said they had business and left.

Harry looked at his desk, the glass and pitcher of beer. haha. No work tomorrow. Gotta piss. He stood, bumped against the desk, shoved his chair back and laughed when it banged against the wall, leaned on the desk looking at the beer then staggered to the yard and pissed, sighing. Thats what I needed. A good piss. haha. Nothin like a good piss. Maybe the guysll come back tomorrow. ahh . . . thats betta. He turned off the lights and went home.

He left the house the next morning as soon as he dressed and went to his office. He filled a pitcher with beer and sat at his desk. He leaned back and put his feet on the desk. It was kindda nice to sit alone and drink beer for a while. He could use the relaxation. Hed been working hard on the strike and tomorrow would be another busy day. It was kindda nice to sit alone in his office. He really liked it. It really wasnt so bad. He picked up the pitcher to refill his glass. It was empty. Didnt think hed been there that long, but I guess maybe I have. He laughed and got up and refilled the pitcher and then his glass. Somea the guys should be around soon. Must be late enough. He sat back and put his feet up on the desk. It wasnt bad being alone though. For a while.

A car stopped in front of the Greeks and he got up from his desk and went to the door and yelled across to the guys going into the Greeks. They looked and strolled across the street, Vinnie carrying a package. Harry stood at the door as they walked in and the guys flopped around after filling glasses with beer. Vinnie put the package on the desk and tore the paper off. Here yaare Harry. We toldya we/d getya a radio. Hows this? pretty good, eh? If we wasnt so desperate for loot youd never get it. Harry walked over to the desk and looked at the radio, turned the knobs and watched the needle move along the dial. Youre lucky we/re beat man or we/d never giveit toya for a lousy 30 skins. Now at least we can have some music around here. This joints

like a morgue, unwinding the cord and plugging it in.
It even has short wave man, turning the dial and stopping when a voice singing in a foreign language came from
the radio. See. I wish ta fuck I could keep the thing. Yeah,
it sounds pretty good, turning the dial again, stopping as
the sound of different languages reached them. Hey Vin,
get some music, yeah? Vinnie switched it back to the
standard band and Harry reached over and started toying
with the dial. He watched the needle move slowly across the
lighted numbers and when a screeching sax wailed someone yelled, thats it man, and a hand pushed Harrys from
the knob and tuned in the sax. The volume was turned
up and someone told Harry ta fill up the pichas and
someone slapped him on the back, great set, eh man?
and Harry nodded and picked up a pitcher and refilled it
and he watched and listened to the guys snap their fingers
and yell with the music and Harry felt their friendship
and felt too, again, spasms of expectation and everything
seemed sortofright and Harry felt comfortable.

When
Vinnie told him to give him the money now Harry took
the thirty dollars from his wallet and handed it to him
and told the guys ta drink up, the brewery needs the bar-
rels and laughed and toldem theres plenty more and once
more started blithering and babbling about the union
and women and the guys just ignored him and continued
to drink until they got bored and left Harry with his beer
and radio. Harry sat alone for a while listening to his
radio, toying with the dials, drinking the beer, laughing
his laugh, gripping the knobs tighter and twirling them
fast then slow, moving the dial where and as he pleased,
listening to a station for a few minutes, changing it,
tuning in shortwave and feeling that he could drag the
foreign countries in as he pleased.

He stayed at his desk drinking beer and listening to his radio until his head started to hang toward his chest. He emptied his glass, unplugged the radio, put it under his desk, and put out the lights, locked the door and started walking the few blocks, which would only take a few minutes and and was only a short distance away, home.

Harry was sick the next morning but dragged himself from the house to his office. His entire body was twitching and Harry forced down a few beers to straighten himself out before the men came. He got a couple of glasses down and a half dozen aspirin, his headache slowly leaving and the turmoil in his stomach subsiding, yet he still felt a tension, an apprehension, and he cursed the bars for not being open yet so he could get a shot and get rid of his hangover. When the men started coming, a little before 8, their joking and laughter, as they grabbed signs and had their books stamped, annoyed Harry. When all the signs had been distributed and fresh coffee made, Harry went to the bar for a couple of fast shots and came back convinced he felt better. When he got back to the office he turned the radio on and sat behind his desk drinking beer and joking with the men. When one of the officials called Harry told him he had bought a radio for the office, figured the men/d like a little music or maybe hear a ballgame when they come off the line, and the official told him to send a bill to the union and he would be reimbursed. Harry hung up the phone and sat back in his chair feeling very official and important, and although the morning passed slowly for Harry until he got over his hangover, the afternoon passed rapidly, especially after his phone conversation (strike headquarters, local 392, Brother Black talkin) with the union official.

When the last of the men left that night Harry sat

at his desk drinking for a while then went across the street to the Greeks. He ate slowly until a few of the guys came in and then ate rapidly, talking and laughing. When he finished they went back to the office and drank and listened to the radio, the guys ignoring Harry as usual, just nodding or mumbling an occasional answer. A few more of the guys came in but they didnt stay too long and once again Harry was sitting behind his desk alone with a pitcher of beer and a glass. The sun had set and the street was quiet and cool and though Harry had been drinking beer all day, and had been feeling relaxed for hours, the butterflies in his stomach started again as he walked home.

The baby was asleep when he got there and Mary was watching tv, waiting for him. She called him in the living room and Harry sat in a chair, Mary leaning over to rub his ear, Harry too confused and not drunk enough to shove her hand away. After rubbing his ear for a few minutes without Harry twisting his head away Mary sat on the arm of the chair and put an arm around his neck. A short time later she coaxed him into the bedroom and Harry undressed and lay beside her until she pulled him on her. Harry continued to drift, as he had through the day, only silently and lethargically, still experiencing the sharp depression that overcame him when the guys left and he was alone with his radio, beer, desk and chair, the depression of disappointment after a long wait. When Mary pulled him over on her he allowed his body to move in the directed direction and she put her arms around him, breathing on his neck, rolling under him. Harry just lay on her until he became conscious of her voice then rolled off, lit a cigarette and lay on his side smoking. Mary rubbed his back, kissed his neck and Harry continued to smoke, still immobile, still silent and Mary rubbed his ear and rubbed his arms until Harry eventually shook her hands off. Mary lay on her back for a while, mumbling and rolling slightly from side to side, Harry still silent, until Harry finally put his cigarette out and adjusted himself to go to sleep. Mary looked at his back for a while then rolled over on her side, pulled her knees up toward her chin and eventually fell asleep.

Mary told Harry tagotahell when he told her to fix breakfast. He told her again to fix breakfast or hed break her fuckin head. Do it yourself and dont botha me. Harry called her a fuckin slut and left the house. Harry couldnt remember how he had felt the night before, but he did know he felt different this morning, the usual resentment against Mary filling his thoughts. She was once more responsible for his misery as were the bosses for the fact that he didnt make much money. Between them they tried to make his life miserable; they tried ta fuckim everytime he moved; if it wasnt for them things would be different.

Harry slowed down in his bustling around the office as the days passed until, after a few weeks, he just sat, most of the time, behind his desk except for an occasional walk to the line to relieve the tension of just sitting in the small office. The men too slowed and while on the picket line moved just enough not to be standing still. When they spoke with each other it was with comparatively quiet voices and when they spoke with the police it was just a word or two, or, more usually, a nod. There was no desperation in their appearance or action, but the novelty of being on strike was over and now it was just a job like any other job only they werent getting paid for this. What little lightheartedness remained after the first full week of picketing slowly vanished with the forming of each Saturday food line and when the men went home with $10 worth of groceries. They had to report to the meeting hall and before the food was distributed the President gave a speech and the first

Saturday he told them what a fine job they were doing on the line and especially praised brother Harry Black for the way in which he carried out his duties as organizer and administrator of the strike field office. He told the men that they had met with the companys negotiating committee each day the past week, but they were offering starvation wages and that their committee refused to give in to them even if they had to stay on strike a year. When he finished speaking the clique stamped, cheered and whistled and soon most of the men were applauding the President as he jumped from the platform and walked among the men slapping them on their back and shaking their hands. Then the men lined up for their food bags. There were many comments, jokes and laughter as the lines slowly moved forward and each man was handed his bag, but when they were alone the bag looked small. The second Saturday the Presidents speech was even shorter, the applause quieter, the men more silent as they stood on line. Only a few could think of something funny to say. And so each week ended.

When the men first started picketing the plant they would make jokes about the few executives who were going to work, greeting them occasionally with jeers and boos, but soon they cursed them each morning and each night, the police telling them to shut up and keep moving. After the first few weeks had passed the men stood still as the executives entered the building and started threatening them, the police waving their clubs in their faces and telling them to be quiet and keep the lines moving or they would pull them in. Each day the voices, curses and threats of men were more vehement and after a few weeks more police were stationed at the entrance of the building in the morning and evening; and when they told the men to watch themselves and keep moving the men spit in front of the cops or mumbled something about goons; and each day the routine was the same except that it grew more intense and the men were continually looking for an excuse to hit someone, anyone; and the police were just waiting for someone to start something so they too could find relief from the boredom by cracking someones skull. And as the boredom increased so did the resentment: the resentment of the men toward the cops for being there and trying to prevent them from winning the strike; and the police toward the strikers for making it necessary for them to stand around like this for hours each day when they werent even allowed to go on strike if they wanted more money. The men moved as slowly as possible, sneering at the police when they passed them; and the police stood facing them all day swinging their clubs by the leather thong and telling the men to keep moving if they stopped even for a second; and the men would stand still for a moment, staring, hoping someone would say fuckyou to one of the cops so they could wrap their signs around their heads, but no one said anything and as a cop took a step forward the men started moving again and the strike and the game continued.

When the men came back to the office now they dropped their signs on the floor, Harry telling them at first to take it easy then, after being told to go fuckhimself a few times, said nothing and picked the signs up when they left. Soon new signs had to be painted and each time the men saw newly painted signs they became more bitter and cursed the fucks in the company who were keeping them out of work, and cursed the cops for helping those fuckinbellyrobbers.

The company had been preparing for the strike many months before it started and so, when the first pickets donned their signs and started parading jubilantly up and down in front of the factory, the existing orders had been filled and work transferred to other plants throughout the country or subcontracted to other firms and the primary, and almost only, concern of the executives in the Brooklyn factory was coordinating the transferring and shipping of work and finished products between the various plants and subcontractors. The first few days of the strike were hectic and, at times, slightly chaotic for those executives responsible for coordinating work between the various firms, but after that everything proceeded routinely with only an occasional emergency that would be met with long distance calls and soon enough the situation would once more be under control.

When the strike was months old a call came from one of the factories located in the northern part of New York State where the final assembling of large units was being done. The contract was a time penalizing one and if all the units werent delivered by the specified date a $1,000 per day, for each day over the time, would have to be defaulted by the company. The work had already been delayed for three days because of various failures and breakdowns, but the assembly line had finally been set up and half the factory and personnel were geared to complete the work by the specified time. The work had proceeded smoothly, and it was determined that the work would be completed on time, when it was discovered that one of the final elements, made in the Brooklyn plant, was missing. A call went in immediately to the Brooklyn plant and a quick check of the records indicated that the entire lot had been finished the day before the strike started but, for some reason, had never been shipped. The shipping department was almost empty so the crates containing the needed parts were found quickly. A call was made to the upstate plant and the information relayed along with a promise that they would go out tonight.

Mr. Harrington cursed the men with him, but only for a moment, then started calling small neighborhood trucking firms to find one that would cross ihe picket line and deliver the material. He finally found one who said he would do it and quoted a fantastic price, but the manager had no choice but to agree and made out a check for half the amount, the other half to be paid when the delivery was made.

The men on the picket line were startled when the trucks turned into the runway leading to the loading platform, but only for a second. They yelled at the drivers of the trucks that they were on strike and the drivers yelled fuck you. A few of the men tried to jump on the hoods of the trucks, but fell; a few others picked up stones and tin cans and threw them at the drivers but they just bounced off the cabs. When the men tried to follow the trucks to the platform the police grabbed them and held them back. The yelling of the men on the picket line was heard by the others hanging around the office and they came running; and a call was made from one of the police cars for additional men. Some of the police formed a line across the runway while others pushed the men back. Soon there were hundreds of men yelling and pushing; those in the rear shouting to shove the fuckin cops outta the way and get those fuckinscabs; the men in front screaming in the faces of the cops and being shoved by the mob behind them into the line of police that was slowly weakening. For many minutes the amoeba like mass flowed forward, backward and around, arms and signs bobbing up and down over heads; white gloves and clubs raised; red infuriated faces almost pressed together, words and spit bouncing off faces; anger clouding and watering eyes. Then more police arrived by the carsful. Then a firetruck. Men leaped from the cars and were assimilated by the mass. A fire hose was quickly unraveled and connected; a loudspeaker screeched and told the men to breakitup. FUCKYOU FLATFOOT GO AND FUCKYASELF YASONOFABITCH IF YOU MEN DONT BREAKITUP WE/LL RUN YOU ALL IN NOW GET BACK FROM THAT RUNWAY YEAH, SURE, AFTA WE BREAK THOSE FUCKIN-SCABSHEADS DERE TAKIN THE BREAD FROM OUR MOUTHS IM TELLING YOU FOR THE LAST TIME, BREAKITUP OR I/LL TURN THE HOSE ON YOU WHO PAID YAOFF YASONOFABITCH The line of police had been extended and was pushing as hard as it could against the mob, but the men became more incensed as more cops fought them and the voice threatened them and they felt the power of their numbers and the frustration and lost hope of fruitless months on the picket and food lines finally found the release it had been looking for. Now there was something tangible to strike at. And the police who had been standing, bored, for months as the men walked up and down, telling them to keep moving, envying them because they at least could do something tangible to get more money while all they could do was put in a request to the mayor and be turned down by the rotten politicians, finally found the outlet they too had been waiting for and soon the line became absorbed by the mass and two and three went down to their knees and then others too, strikers and cops, and a sign swooped through the air and thudded against a head and a white gloved hand went up and then a club thudded and hands, clubs, signs, rocks, bottles were lifted and thrown as if governed by a runaway eccentric rod and the mass spread out, some falling over others and heads popped out of windows and doorways and peered and a few cars parked cautiously or slowed and observed for a moment and the mass continued to wallow along and across 2nd avenue as a galaxy through the heavens with the swooshing of comets and meteors and the voice that screeched now directed itself to the firemen and they walked slowly toward the grinding mass and a white glove clutched at a head and the glove turned red and occasionally a bloody body would be exuded from the mass and roll a foot or two and just lie there or perhaps wriggle slightly and four or five beaten and bloodied cops managed to work their way free from the gravity of the mass and stood side by side and walked back to the mass swinging their clubs and screaming and a sign was broken over one of their heads but the cop only screamed louder and continued to swing, still walking, until his club was broken over a head and he picked up the broken sign without breaking rank and continued and the thudding of the clubs on heads was only slightly audible and the sound not at all unpleasant as it was muted by the screams and curses and they stepped over a few bodies until a line of strikers was somehow formed and they charged the cops not stopping as the clubs were methodically pounded on their heads and the two lines formed a whirling heated nebula that spun off from the galaxy to disintegrate as the strikers overwhelmed them and kicked the cops as they tried to regain their feet or roll away and sirens screeched but were unheard and more police jumped from cars and trucks and another fire hose was unraveled and aimed the order given to open the hydrants and not wait until the police who were whirling with the strikers could extricate themselves and a few of the strikers noticed the second hose being readied and then noticed the first hose and charged the firemen but the water leaped forth in an overpowering gush and one of the men took the full force in his abdomen and his mouth jutted open but if a sound came out it was unheard and he doubled over and spun like a gyroscope runamuck bouncing off the men behind him and bouncing to the curb and those who were behind him were knocked and spun and a few policemen ran frantically to the various street corners trying to direct and divert traffic but all of the cars moved slowly no matter how urgently the police waved them on not wanting to miss any of the excitement and the voice screeched again giving directions and the two powered battering rams were directed with knowledge and precision and soon the mass was a chaos of colliding particles that bounced tumbled and whirled around against and over each other and soon it was quiet enough to hear the ambulance sirens and the louder moans that spewed from the mass and soon the street was clear of the smaller debris and even the blood had been washed away.

The fire hoses were shut off and those who were injured too seriously to move unaided were helped to the sidewalk where they sat down and leaned against the buildings or were helped into one of the waiting ambulances or patrol cars and taken to the hospital. The street was still congested with men, cars, trucks, ambulances and onlookers. There were still hundreds of strikers standing in small groups talking, helping injured strikers, looking at the cops and waiting for the trucks to come out. Harry, who had carefully avoided the fight, moved from group to group, his shirt hanging out, hair mussed and face dirtied, cursing the bosses, the cops and those fuckin scabs, asking the men how they were and slapping them on the back.

The police too were concerned about the trucks. Additional men had arrived and a barricade was setup to keep the strikers away from the runway and the hoses were placed in strategic positions. Again the voice told the strikers to breakitup and again the men said FUCKYOU and remained where they were: eyeing the cops, who stood behind the barricade, and the firemen with their hoses. The voice told them they didnt want to use force but, if they didnt disperse immediately, that force would be used. The men yelled and cursed and started spreading out getting ready to charge the barricade as soon as the trucks came up the runway. The voice told them they had exactly 60 seconds before the hoses would be turned on again and started counting. There were still 30 seconds left when the first truck was heard coming up the runway. The counting was stopped and the hoses were ordered turned on. The men had yet to take their first forward step when the water hit them. The hoses were used expertly and none of the strikers reached the barricade until the trucks were almost a block away and then they just stood yelling and cursing.

When the trucks were out of sight the men backed away from the barricade, stood looking at the cops for a few minutes then slowly walked away, going home or back to the office. The police and firemen slowly gathered up their equipment and went back to their various stationhouses. 83 men were hospitalized.

Some of the strikers going back to the office carried the remnants of signs, some helped others still bleeding or still dazed from the fight. The injured men were driven home, Harry telling them hed see that their books were marked that they got hurt; the others crowded into the office or hung around outside.

The men in the office were still yelling and cursing, Harry passing out beer, telling them how he clobbered a cop—hoping no one had noticed he avoided the fight—or how he just missed getting hit with a club, but everyone was too angry to pay any attention to him just as they had been too busy to remember who was where during the fight. Harry eventually worked his way over to his desk and sat down with a beer, extremely conscious of the noise and wondering if there was something he could do. He leaned on the desk, sipped his beer, wishing a thought would pop into his head. It wasn't until he saw the President and a few other officials forcing their way through the crowd that he realized he should have called the union office. He leaped up and stumbled around his desk shouting that he had been trying to reach the office and everyone was yelling and crowding around the officials and they stood still and yelled for the men to be quiet, for krists sake. How can we find out what happened with everybody yelling. They all started yelling again and the officials waved their hands and the men started to quiet and Harry tried to force his way forward but one of the men placed himself in front of the President and told him hed tellem what happened. I was on the line when the trucks came in. What trucks? All the men started answering and yelling and officials waved their arms again and the man who had started talking yelled ta shuttup. I/ll tellem what happened. We was on the line when all ofasudden these 4 trucks come down 2nd avenue and turned down the runway to the loadin platform . . . When the entire story hdd been told the President asked if anyone saw the name of the trucking company and one of the men said he knewem. Ive seen those trucks in the neighborhood, and he gave the officials the name and told them where they were usually parked. Then the President told the men that everything would be taken care of and that no more trucks would pass the line and that they should go home and take it easy and that from now on there would be someone watching the street at all times and when anything, I mean anything and I dont give a fuck what it is, tries to pass the line that everybody was to haulass over to the line and block the joint. The men yelled, yeah, we/ll show the fucks. But dont hang around the plant or the copsll only start again. The law says you can only have so

many men on the picket line and theyll use any excuse
they can to split your skulls so dont givem the chance. Try
and stay off the street as much as possible when youre not
on the line and they cant do a thing.

The President went
over to the desk and made a phone call while the other
officials shook hands with the men and patted them on the
back as they walked them toward the door. The President was on the phone for some time, making arrangements to have more signs printed and making certain that
they would definitely be in the strike office by 8 oclock
in the morning; then spoke to a few other people in the
union office and by the time he finished the office was
empty except for the other officials and Harry, who
had been standing behind him ever since he first picked
up the phone.

Harry offered him a cigarette then fumbled
for a match, the President finally taking one out of his
own pocket. Harry tried to tell him how he had tried to
stop the trucks, but was interrupted by the other officials
who started talking to the President. They formed a small
huddle, talking low, Harry standing on the fringe, and
Vinnie and Sal came in. Whattaysay Harry? I hear yahad
a little trouble. Yeah man, I hear we missed a good
rumble. They filled a couple of glasses with beer then
rejoined Harry. Ya not gonna letem getaway with that
shit, areya? Yabet yasweet ass we/re not. Dont worry,
itll never happen again. If it wasnt for the fuckin cops
they never wouldve got pastus. Shitman, theres other
ways ta stopem. Yeah, smiling at each other and drinking
their beer. Whattayamean? Shit, all yagotta do—the
President came over and asked Harry who they were.
Harry told him their names and said they were a couple
of the guys from the neighborhood. This is the President
of the union. Whattayasay. Had a little trouble, eh? Not

174

too much. You boys have something on your minds? Just
a little business proposition, eh Sal? Yeah. Like what?
Like gettin ridda the trucks. Is it worth 200 taya ta get
riddathem? Do you think you can do it without any
trouble? Yeah. If theyre parked where that guy says
they are itll be a slopeout. The President turned his back
to the others, gave them $200, said goodbye to Harry
and left with the other officials. Sal and Vinnie split the
money, finished their beers and left. Another day of the
strike had ended.

       The next day there were hundreds of
men at the office by a few minutes after 8. By 8:30 they
were spread throughout the office and the street drinking
coffee, eating cake and drinking beer. The signs had been
delivered a few minutes after Harry opened the office and
the men rushed with firstdayofthestrike eagerness to grab
them and set up the picket line. They joked, laughed and
slapped each other on the back energetically, as they did
that first day, but they werent relaxed as they were then,
but were tensed and hopeful, hopeful of another fight but
this time they would be expecting it and would be ready
and each man could animate the dreams and thoughts of
the night before where they stopped the trucks, pulled the
drivers from the cabs and beat their skulls in, each man
doing it singlehandedly or, at the most, with the help of
a few friends; and when the cops tried to stop them they
took their clubs from them and bashed their fuckinskulls-
toapulp then took the fire hoses and washed the rotten
bastards down the fuckin sewer. They drank beer and
coffee, continually looking toward the factory, slapping
each other on the shoulder but, as they did they tensed
their muscles wishing, and hoping takrist, that it was the
face of one of the shiteatin cops or one of the scabbastard
drivers that they were shovin their fist in . . . or maybe

one of the punk executives would givem some shit and they could beat his ass.

But no one came to work that day and no trucks came within two blocks of the factory. Mr. Harrington told the others to stay home, it was Friday and one day would not do any harm. The shipment went out and there was nothing left that they had to do; and by Monday the strikers would have gotten over their anger and everything would settle back into the routine of the days, months, preceding the fight. The men stayed all day, greeting each newcomer loudly, slapping briskly, but as the day moved and nothing happened they became tired of commenting on all the cops they had there now, must be over a hundred ofem, and how theyd like to break their fuckin skulls; and as the day slowly passed so did their enthusiasm, their frustration and anger increasing. Their cursing was more vehement but it not only lacked organization it also lacked direction. The cops were just standing there, saying nothing; there were no trucks trying to break the line and no wiseyoungpunkofapencilpusher trying to take the bread from their mouths.

The sky re-mained cloudless all day and the sun bright. It was hot. Very hot. A perfect day for the beach, but none of them were in a mood to enjoy the beach yet they cursed those bastards, if it wasn't for them they could be down the beach now or sittin home with a can of beer watching the ballgame on tv. And they cursed those bastards to each other and by mid afternoon the 4 kegs of beer were empty and Harry ordered a few more and they were delivered rightaway, but some of the men were tired of drinking beer and they drifted, in small groups, into the bar next door to get something stronger, something more satisfying and by the time 5 oclock came, and the sun still had a few hours before it set, their anger was simply anger, no longer even attempting to direct it but just letting it grow until they went home and passed out or got in a fight in a neighborhood bar. When the men left Harry told them to be back bright and early Monday.

Harry felt good sitting at his desk drinking beer and smoking. He had spent the day telling the men how the union wouldnt let them get away with that kindda shit, and wishing he could tell them what he had planned to do to the trucks. If only he could tell them. Then theyd really know how important he is. But whatthefuck, theyd know how important he was anyway. Yeah. He put his feet up on the desk and emptied his glass and leaned back thinking of how soon all the men would nod and say hello when he came by and hed really be respected and maybe he could get rid of the bitchofawife who was always breakin his balls and gettinhim so nervous he could hardly work sometimes and then that fuckinpencilpushinpunk wilson would shit when Harry Black came around and his smile almost became a smile and he refilled his glass, lit a cigarette, closed his eyes and watched wilson and some of the other punks cowering in fear.

Sal and Vinnie left the Greeks a little after 11, stole a car, got a few cans of gasoline and drove to the small lot where the trucks were parked. They stopped for a moment, looked around, then drove around the block a few times, then the neighborhood for about 10 minutes or so making sure there were no streets closed for any reason or cops in the vicinity, then drove back to the lot and parked the car. The trucks were old models with gas tanks on the side. They tossed gasoline over the trucks, opened the gas tanks, soaked rags in gasoline and put them in the tank openings letting them hang to the ground, then poured a line of gasoline from one rag to the other, all the lines connecting and leading toward the exit. They put the empty gas cans back in the car then lit the stream of gas and ran to the car. They waited until they saw the first trucks catch fire then drove away, turning left on 3rd avenue and speeding as fast as they could for a few blocks then turned down to 2nd avenue which was completely deserted. About a minute after they left the lot they heard an explosion and saw a red glow in the sky. There goes the first one Vin. Yeah. Looks kindda pretty, eh? Yeah. Itll look even better when the others go too. Yeah, and they laughed. They were half way back to the Greeks when they heard more explosions, muffled but still identifiable, and the glow in the sky was brighter. Pretty good job, eh? Yeah. I guess we gavem their moneys worth. You know Sal, we could go in business if the strike lasts long enough. Yeah, laughing. They ditched the car, first dumping the gas cans, and went back to the Greeks.

Harry was standing on the sidewalk looking down 2nd avenue toward the glow in the sky. Harry laughed his laugh when he saw Sal and Vinnie. Whaddayause a hand grenade? hahaha. Whattayasay Harry? Whattayadoin here? I came ta watch the fireworks, haha. Ya guys sure know how ta blow things up, haha. Take it easy, eh man. Yeah, dont talk so fuckin loud. Dont worry. We/re not, but youd betta get home. If the law comes around they'll drag yaass in. Yeah, turning away from the creep and going into the Greeks. I/ll seeya, laughing his laugh and going home.

Harry had a long lovely sleep. When he awoke, late in the morning, he lit a cigarette and looked at the ceiling, closing his eyes from time to time, hearing, but not paying attention to, the sounds Mary made, as she walked around the apartment, and his son, as he played on the living room floor. He thought of that lovely red glow in the sky and how hed like to go up to wilson and the boss and tell them ta watch out or theyd get their asses blown up too, just like those fuckin scab trucks ya sent out. Ya may think youre a big wheel or somethin, but dont fuck with me or youll be sorry, yahear? Dont fuck with Harry Black, Shop Steward of Local 392 so watch it buddy, youre not fuckin with a nobody. Im on the union payroll now and dontya forget it because I pull weight around here and I get my money every week no matter how long the strike lasts and what Mary dont know wont hurt her, I could use the extra money myself anyway, Im the fuckin boss around here and she/d betta not fuck with me either or I/ll throw her ass out in the street. Id be betta off withouter the way shes always breakin my balls . . .

Harry stayed in bed for a couple of hours, looking at the ceiling, closing his eyes, smoking, his face twisting occasionally into an almost smile. When he got up he dressed and went up to the Greeks. He had a couple of cups of coffee and something to eat and sat around for a while then told the counterman to tell Sal and Vinnie, or any of the guys that come in, that he was across the street in his office.

He filled a pitcher with beer, grabbed a glass and sat at his desk, rolling the chair back and forth a few times. He sat at the desk for a few minutes then jumped up and went next door to the bar and asked the bartender if he had todays paper. Yeah, theres one on the table in the back. Takeit if yawant. Harry took the paper and left the bar waving to the bartender. Seeya lateta. He spread the paper out on his desk, after looking at the front page, and looked at the centerfold. There was a small picture of a few trucks burning. The caption said that the trucks were parked in the lot for the night and had mysteriously burst into flames and exploded. No one was injured. Harry guzzled some beer, licked his lips and stared at the picture, almost smiling, for many minutes, then called the union office. I see in the paper that a couplea trucks got burned last night, hahaha. Yes, the police have been here already. No shit? what happened? Nothing. They asked some questions and we told them that we knew nothing about it. Fuckem, the pricks. Right, and the conversation was ended.

Harry had almost finished his second pitcher of beer when Sal, Vinnie, a few of the other guys and the fairy that had been in the bar, came in. Harry got up and waved to the guys, whattayasay, looking at the fairy, watching her walk daintily across the floor toward him. The guys grabbed glasses. Howd yalike that little job we did? Not bad, eh? and someone handed the fairy a glass. She eyed it disdainfully, I hope you dont expect me to drink from this filthy thing . . . really! Theres a sink in the back. Go washit. What the fuck ya bitchin about? youve had worse than that in ya mouth, and the guys laughed. Any meat I put in my mouth honey has the government stamp of approval, and she sauntered to the sink and carefully washed the glass. Harry watching her until she came back then he turned to Vinnie. Yeah, that was a good job. Theres a picha in the paper. Here. They looked at the picture and laughed. Man, whatta night. What a fuckin ball. Yeah. Weve been gobblin bennies all night and we/re highern a motherfucka. Hey, how about some music, and the radio was turned on. Hey, this kegs almost empty man. That one over theres full. Tapit. Hey Harry, this heres Ginger, a real sweet kid, chuckling, but dont fuck witer man. She use ta be a brick layer. Yeah, now shes a prick layer. The guys laughed and Harry leered at her. Hey, dont yaknow how ta tap a fuckin keg? the fuckin beers goin all over. Whattaya want from me? its warm as piss. Harry said hello and Ginger curtsied. Go next door and get some ice from Al. Its too fuckin hot ta drink warm beer. No shitman, she really use ta be a bricklayer. Yeah, shoim ya muscle Ginger. She smiled and rolled up her sleeve and exhibited a large appleshaped muscle. Aint that some shit? But she got chips, snapping his fingers and making a chirping sound. You can look but dont touch. Thats it man, pack the sonofabitch with ice. I like cold beer. Tell me Harold, are you in charge of this establishment. Hey, watch yalanguage. Harry sat down, pushed his chair back and drank some beer. Yeah. Im in charge a the strike, wiping his mouth with his hand, still staring. Ginger smiled and almost told him he looked ludicrous, but could not be bothered putting the freak down. My, that must be quite a task. Yeah, its a bitch of a job, but I get it done. Im pretty big in the union yaknow. Yes, I can well imagine, her stomach twitching from swallowed giggles. Whattayamean its not cold enough yet. Im dyin a thirst. How inthefuck can yadrink warm beer. Wit my mouth, what thefuck yathink. You know, I'm hungry. Why dont one of you gentlemen get me something to eat. Here, I got ya suppa, swingin, and they laughed. Im sorry honey, but I don't like moldy worm eaten meat. Save it for your Mother . . . if you have one. Hahaha, youre my motha, come an getit. Hey Harry, how about callin up some joint and havin some food sent down here. Ya can sign the bill. O, can you do that Harold? Sure. I can get anythin yawant. I just send the bills to the union. I got a expense sheet. Id just love a barbecued chicken. How the fuck canya eat afta all those bennies. I couldn't go near any food. All I wanna do is drink. Im driernhell. O you novices. Really! Order me a barbecued chicken Harold and get a chocolate layer cake, waving her hand majestically and nodding her head to indicate that she had given an irrevocable order. Yeah, get some chickens, a couplea cakes—and a gallon a ice cream. Man could I go for some ice cream. And how about some potato salad and pickles? Yeah, and—call up Kramers delicatessen on 5th avenue. They got all that shit up there. Harry got on the phone and they continued to shout orders at him and he relayed them to Mr. Kramer. When he finished ordering he sat back and took another gulp of beer and watched Ginger as she danced lightly around the room, the excitement that had started when he awoke and increased as he looked at the picture and continued to grow when he called the union office and when the guys and Ginger came in, continued to increase and he leaned forward in his chair slightly as Ginger whirled around the room shaking the tight cheeks of her ass and Harry caressed his beer glass and licked his lips not knowing exactly what he was doing, his body reacting and tingling, aware of nothing but a lightness, almost a giddiness, and a fascination. And a feeling of power and strength. Things would be different now. He was Harry Black. On the payroll of local 392.

When the food came Ginger accepted Harrys gracious offer and sat in his chair and well manneredly ate a chicken, a few helpings of potato salad and cole slaw and cake, then, tired of drinking unladylike beer, told Harry he should get a few bottles of gin, some tonic water and a few limes which Harry did, adding the bills to the pile in the drawer, and the party continued. Harry was getting very drunk and Ginger, who was in an even more bitchy mood than usual, thought it would be fun to toy with him. She got up from the chair and told Harry to sit then sat on his lap, put her finger in his ear and played with his hair. Harry leered, his eyes rolling slightly. He was drunk but still able to fee' the tingling in his thighs yet unaware of the spasmodic jerking of his fingers, the moisture in his mouth. Ginger leaned her face closer to Harrys, tenderly caressing his neck and she watched Harrys lips quiver, felt the trembling in his legs and saw his eyes unfocusing and rolling back. Ginger roared hysterically inside herself and leaned closer to Harry, smiling, until she could feel his slimy breath on her cheek, then jumped up and tapped him playfully on the nose. O you naughty man, getting a nice young girl like me all excited, posing provocatively in front of him. She took a few short dainty steps backward, smiling at him coquettishly, and wriggled in time to the music from the radio, glancing over her shoulder at Harry occasionally, leaning her head to one side and winking. Harry continued to lean forward until he fell from the chair, spilling his drink, and kneeling on the floor behind his desk. He dropped the glass and pulled himself up, tiny droplets of saliva hanging from his lips and chin. He pulled himself up and leaned forward. Comeon, lets dansh. Ginger put her hands on her hips and watched him lumber toward her, feeling the power she had over him and despising him. She put her arms around him and started dragging him around the floor, stamping heavily on his toes and lifting her knee up into his groin from time to time, Harry wincing but still trying to smile and drunkenly trying to get closer to her. Ginger pinched his neck fiercely with her fingernails and laughed as Harrys eyes closed, then patted him on the cheek and rubbed his head. Thats a good dog. Do you know how to beg for a bone, lifting her knee into his crotch, Harrys face twisting. Its a shame we/re not in Marys now. You could buy me drinks and we would have a wonderful time, pinching him again. Harrys eyes closed again. Watch Marys? O, a lovely club I know on 72nd street thats just filled with freaks like you. Youd love it, stepping on his foot and grinding her heel into it. Harrys eyes watered. Letsgo, sliding his hand down Gingers arm, Ginger flexing her hard muscle, bending her arm and squeezing Harrys hand in the crotch of her elbow until he stopped dancing and tugged to loosen it, Ginger squeezing harder, her face set in a smile, putting all her strength, hatred and loathing into the squeezing of Harrys hand, wallowing in the joy of holding Harry immobile with the bending of her arm, feeling like David, not killing Goliath with one stone from his sling, but slowly twisting him down and down and down with the simple twisting of one massive finger with her small dainty ladylike hand. Ginger applied as much pressure as she could, the pressure now hurting her too, but she continued to squeeze Harrys hand as he tugged to loosen it, his face becoming whiter, his eyes bulging, too startled and in too much pain to yell, his mouth hanging open, saliva dripping, spreading his legs for balance and leverage, pushing her arm with his other hand, looking at her in complete bewilderment, not understanding what was happening, too drunk to comprehend the incongruity of the situation: the little faggot conquering the giant with the crotch of her arm; his eyes asking why but no question formed in his mind, just instinctively trying to free himself of the pain. Ginger stared directly into his face, smiling still, wanting to crush him, to force him to his knees. He bent his arm to one side, still not using his other hand against Harry, his face stiffening as Harrys body started to lean with the pressure, Ginger wanting to yell IM MORE OF A MAN THAN YOU, then suddenly she opened her arm, spun around and left Harry standing there, looking after her as she mixed herself another drink, holding his hand and rubbing it.

Ginger strolled around the room, gulping at her drink, talking with the guys and looking at Harry occasionally and smiling. Harry made his way back to his chair, filled his glass and sat, rubbing his hand, wondering just what had happened, slowly becoming conscious of the noise from the guys and the radio. Somebody

slapped him on the back, whattayasay Harry, laughed and
staggered away, Harry looking at him dumbly and nodding. Ginger came up behind him and twirled his hair
with her fingers and slowly moved around in front of him
and leaned against the desk. I like your party. I hope the
strike lasts for a while, we can have a ball. Harry nodded
his head as he weaved back and forth in his chair, almost
falling off again. Ginger patted his cheek, Youre cute. I
like you, smiling and giggling inside as Harrys eyes once
more showed his bewilderment. Its too bad we cant be
alone, we would have such fun. Harry put his hand on her
leg and Ginger lifted it gently. Fresh. My, but you get a
girl all aquiver, crossing her arms against her breast.
Harry leaned toward her, licking his lips, mumbling
something, and Ginger patted his cheek, then turned
away, tired of her little game, turned the radio off and
announced that they should go back uptown. I find staying in Brooklyn too long very oppressive. Yeah, letsgo.
Maybe therell be some action tanight. Harry tried to grab
Gingers arm as she picked up the gin bottle, but she
twirled away from him and strutted out of the office.
Harry leaned forward in his chair holding onto the edge
of the desk and watched her leave, not noticing the guys
as they picked up the other gin bottles and food and left.
                                                      Harry
leaned against the desk staring at the door in a semi-
catatonic state, his head slowly drooping to one side until
his head finally bumped against the desk. He jerked it up,
blinked his eyes then stared again at the door, slowly sliding from his chair until he was on the floor. Harry curled
up under the desk and slept.
                          Harry slept, curled cozily un-
der his desk, until late morning. The sun was bright and
shone through the office window, lighting the entire office
except for Harrys snug little cove. Harry sat in the dark-

ness under his desk with his knees under his chin fighting
to squint his eyes open, peering up at his chair, and its
barred shadow on the wall, conscious only of the pain in
his eyes. He attempted nothing, not even closing his eyes
against the brightness of the sun shining on the wall, a
brightness that reflected only on his eyes and not into the
darkness of his cubicle. He sat there for hours not thinking of challenging his lethargy until the demand to urinate
became so intense he was forced to crawl from his niche.
After he urinated he leaned over the sink and let cold
water pour on his head for many minutes then found his
way back to his chair and sat smoking and staring until
the pain in his head prodded him from his chair and he
locked the office and went next door to the bar. He sat
alone and silent at the end of the bar drinking, not thinking or glowing over the fact that he could spend as much
as he wanted then get it back from the union as he had
been doing since the strike started; not even aware that
his head stopped aching after an hour or so. For a short
time, after drinking for a few hours, he started thinking
of the previous day and he felt an excitement in his body
but he could not fight through the haze that obscured the
night and soon he was just drunk. It was still early evening when he left the bar and stumbled home and into
bed, still fully clothed, and curled up in a corner and slept.

Monday morning the men had regained some of their
former enthusiasm with the possibility of another truck
trying to cross the picket line, a truck that they would be
prepared to stop. The incident of the trucks took on
added importance to the men during the weekend. They
had talked about it continually on Friday and by the time
they drank their last beer Sunday night they were convinced that the fact that the company had to break the
line with trucks meant that they were hardup to fill orders

and that soon they couldnt afford to keep the shop closed. Some even thought, briefly, of going down to the office Sunday night or early Monday morning to see if the company would try to sneak trucks in before the men started picketing, but soon convinced themselves that it wasnt necessary. So, Monday they were slightly elated as they knew the strike would soon be over and they could stop haggling with the wife about money. They were convinced too that the company would try again to break the line before giving in to the strikers and so everyone, even those who stayed in the office drinking, were ready to run down 2nd avenue when the word was given that more trucks were coming and when they did and were stopped, then the company would have to accept the unions demands. And so they waited and hoped.

Everytime Harry stamped a book during the morning he asked the men if they saw the picture in the paper of the trucks burning, and intimated in every way that he was completely responsible for burning the trucks. By late morning even Harry was a little tired of hearing the same thing for hours so he stopped talking about the trucks and soon, after a pitcher of beer or so, a few memories and images of Saturday night returned and he remembered the guys coming in the office, he remembered the music, the gin and Ginger dancing. He had felt good Saturday night, that he definitely remembered, and too he remembered how the guys seemed to respect him because of his position in the union and because he could order any thing he wanted and have the union pay for it; and he remembered how Ginger admired him for his strength and how she liked to talk with him and feel the muscles in his arms and legs. There were still a few things he could not remember, but they must have been unimportant and soon the thought that they existed was absorbed and they had never happened.

The men rejuvenated their hope through the day but, as the picketing day approached an end, the effect of all the hopeful efforts was almost negligible. The trucks that were to prelude the ending of the strike never arrived and though they tried at first to think that they would not come until later and that it was natural that the company should wait a day or so before trying again, the men could not accept these explanations no matter how hard they tried. They had started the day expecting a deus ex machina and with its appearance their troubles and the strike would be over; and though they tried to convince themselves, and each other, with many arguments, that the company would have to give in soon they found it impossible to maintain any optimism and when the day came to an end they put their signs away quietly, nodded to each other and left. The day had been long and hot. It had been many hours since anyone had looked up at the clear blue sky. It was still summertime and there were many more hot days to come.

The union and management met regularly to arbitrate their dispute. Each side was more arrogant and noisy than usual the first meeting after the incident of the trucks, but the result of the meeting was the same as all the previous ones. The union could not allow anyone to administer the welfare plan but, even if their books had been in order it was far too late now for them to concede to the companys demands. After being on strike this long they could not settle for the same contract that had been offered before they started the strike. There was still ample money in the strike fund, enough to continue to give the men their 10 dollars bag of food each week, to last a year if necessary; and other unions throughout the country had pledged assistance any time it was needed.

The union officials were indignant about the companys attitude in being so rigid and in sending trucks through the line and left Mondays meeting declaring they would not meet with them for a few weeks, not until the company reconsidered its arbitrary stand and realized that the men were willing to stay on strike for a year if necessary in order to get a decent contract. The recording secretary remained in the city and the other officials went to Canada for a rest. They needed a rest from the pressures of the strike and the oppressive heat.

Mr. Harrington told the other company representatives that they had to remain firm. Except for the oversight that necessitated their hiring a freight forwarding firm to cross the picket line and deliver the much needed parts to the upstate plant, everything had been running smoothly. Their other plants, and subcontractors, throughout the country had been geared in ample time to handle all existing orders and any that might come in during the immediate future. All their government contracts were being fulfilled and no new ones would be forthcoming before February of the following year. At least none of any quantity. And too, the manner in which the contracts had been distributed to other plants, and the manner in which the transfers had been noted on the books, meant a substantial tax saving would be effected. Of course a few of the younger executives had a burdensome amount of work to do because of the strike, but a substantial bonus at Christmas and a pat on the back would not only satisfy them but would encourage them to work even harder in the future. And the cost of the bonuses would only amount to a minute percentage of the money saved in unpaid wages. Perhaps they would be prevented from taking a vacation now, but Mr. Harrington did not care if no one went on vacation for years, he was determined to try and get rid of Harry Black. After all, what did he have to lose.

Harry did not notice the change in the men as they carefully leaned their signs against the wall and left. A few minutes after five he was the only one in the office so he just hung around for a while, drinking beer, his mind wandering over what had happened lately, and he remembered Ginger mentioning Marys on 72nd street. He thought about it for a while then decided to go. He got a cab and when they got to 72nd street he told the driver to go down the street and when he saw Marys he told the driver to stop at the next corner and he walked back.

It wasnt until he approached the door that he started to feel uneasy, that he became conscious of being in a strange neighborhood, outside a strange bar. He went in and moved immediately to the side and tried to melt in with the others standing at the bar. There were so many people in Marys and so much noise—the jukebox in the rear clashing with the one at the bar—that Harry was able to lose himself in the chaos and his selfconsciousness faded before he finished his first drink. Eventually he was able to work his way into a spot at the bar where he could see the rest of the bar and most of the back room. At first he was surprised at the way in which the women acted, but after listening to them talk and watching them move he eventually realized that most of them were men dressed as women. He stared at everyone as they moved and talked, never certain of their sex, but enjoying watching them and enjoying too the thrill and excitement he felt at being in such a weird place. The people in the back room fascinated him more than the others as he imagined what they were doing with their hands under the table, and was particularly amazed when he saw a big, muscled,

truckdriver looking guy lean over and kiss the guy sitting
next to him. The kiss seemed to last for many minutes and
Harry could almost feel their tongues touching. He stared.
He noticed the tattoos on the big guys arms. He looked
quickly at his own dirty fingernails then back at the lovers
in the booth. Their mouths slowly separated and they
looked at each other for a moment then reached for their
drinks, the big guys arms still around his lovers shoulder.
Harry continued to stare until his uneasiness forced him
to lower his eyes and he picked up his drink and gulped
it down. He ordered another, sipped at it, lit a cigarette
and continued to lookaround.

Occasionally someone smiled
at Harry, brushed against him or spoke to him and a few
times he smiled his smile but it ended the scene rather
than continued it, so Harry stayed alone drinking and
looking until he noticed Ginger come in. She walked
quickly to the back and was out of sight before Harry
could move. He stared after her for a moment wanting
to go after her, but he knew if he did that the guys from
the Greeks would find out so he finally decided to finish
his drink and leave before she saw him.

The next morning
Mary wanted to know where Harry went last night and
where he was last Saturday night and if he was going to
be home tonight and if he thought this was a flophouse
and he could come home any fuckin time he felt like it
and ever since the strike started he was goin around like
he thought who he was and she wasnt gonna stand for
any shit like this . . .

Harry continued to throw water on
his face as she talked and ignored her as he walked past
her into the bedroom and got dressed and when he
finished and was ready to leave he told her ta shutthe-
fuckup or hed raper in the mouth. Mary stared at him

191

determined not to tolerate his complete indifference. She
looked Harry in the eye, expecting, waiting, for him to
lower his eyes or turn his head and told him she wasnt
going to stand for any more of his shit. Harry stood where
he was, still staring at her, but becoming more and more
conscious of her eyes, of her, and starting to waver inside,
starting to think of spitting in her face, of walking out of
the house, becoming more conscious of his thoughts and
indecision and almost starting to fear her when her voice
pushed these things down in his mind. It wasnt what she
said—her words undefined, only one long penetrating
sound heard—but just the movement of her lips and the
sound providing something tangible to stop his faltering.
She had just stopped talking and was still staring at him
when he slapped her across the face. Go fuck yaself.
Mary continued staring at Harry, her mouth open, touching the cheek with the tips of her fingers. Harry left the
house and walked quickly, smiling his smile, to the office
ready to start another day of the strike.

The men picked
up their signs and gave their books to Harry to be
stamped; or filled a cup with coffee, a glass with beer,
with a certain amount of resignation and a large degree
of silence. They were not completely humorless, but were
in no mood for jokes. Harry felt good, free, but was in an
introverted mood thinking about Marys and so he sat
quietly, nodding, speaking occasionally, and not slapping
backs and roaring, but seeming to share the uneasiness
and concern of the men.

Harry did not go back to Marys
until Friday night. He filled out his expense voucher as
usual, talked to the guys who had come over from the
Greeks as usual to drink beer, stayed in the office for a
while after they left, then went to Marys. He walked right
in and went to the corner of the bar, looked around to

see if Ginger was there, then ordered a drink. Marys was even more crowded than it had been the other night and there was so much noise from the jukeboxes and people screeching that he could not hear the bartender when he asked him if he wanted his drink mixed. He leaned over the bar to hear, nodded, then jerked his head back when he heard a whistle. A pretty young fairy was looking at him, smiling and shaking his head, saying something, but Harry could not hear him. Harry turned his head but glanced occasionally at him from the corner of his eye. He leaned a little more heavily against the bar, looking around the bar, into the backroom, watching people move, watching their gestures, glancing occasionally at the pretty young one still standing in the same place at the bar. Harry tried to imagine what was being done with hands under the tables in the backroom, and what was being done at the tables out of his sight.

He finished each drink in two swallows and the swallows were closer together. He felt good when the strike started. He was nervous when he had to talk to the men at the meeting when they started the strike, but he felt good then too; and he felt good a couple a times since then when the guys came around and they talked and drank and that sort of thing; and he felt real great when the trucks got blown up, yeah . . . yeah, he felt real good that night and the next day with the picture in the paper . . . yeah, thats when they started to know who he really was. They knew he was something before, but after that they really knew. Yeah, it was great gettin more money and spending all ya wanted and just fillin in a slip, just like those pricks in the company and that punk wilson who think theyre such hot shit walkin around in a white shirt and all that shit, but he was just as good as any ofem, he knew a few things and could throw a buck on the bar. Fuck

them, the ballbreakers. They couldnt shove him around
anymore . . . yeah, and fuck Mary too. Aint breakin my
balls anymore . . . thats right, aint had that dream since
the strike started. Blow a couple more trucks up and I/ll
never have it. Fuckit. Anyway its gone . . . and thingsll
be different after the strikes over too. Ya bet yasweetass
—he glanced again at the pretty fairy and when he looked
back at Harry Harry didnt turn his head. He continued
to look and his face unfolded slightly and fell into his
smile, but this time it came a little closer to being a real
smile and the pretty one smiled and winked—yeah,
thingsve been good since the strike. He wished ta krist
he could see that fuck wilson and that ballbreaker harrington—Mr. Bigshit—sweatin it out. They mustta shit
their pants when the trucks were bombed. Bet he knows
what he/ll get if he fucks with me too much—the pretty
one was standing next to him. Harry smiled down at him.
She wiggled slightly. Can I buy you a drink? Yeah. Harry
gulped the last swallow of his drink and let her buy him
one. Harry rocked a little on his feet. Guess Im a little
drunk. Ive really been throwinem down. You look like
the sort of man who can drink a great deal of hard liquor,
touching his forearm and leaning closer. I mustta put a
quart away already, not countin what I had this afternoon,
holding on to the edge of the bar and twisting his arm
slightly so his muscles would tighten. Isnt this place simply
marvelous? Yeah, trying to stand taller and straighter. I
just love men who work hard, I mean who work with
their hands. Yeah, I hate pencil pushers. Me, Im a ma-
chinist. 1st class journeyman. But I really work for the
union. O, are you a union officer too, smiling. All her
johns and trade were the same. They were all some kind
of big shot. Yeah, Im pretty big in the union. Im takin
care a the strike. O, that must be interesting, not minding
a certain amount of this sort of conversation, but hoping

it wouldnt go too far. It really is rather crowded and
noisy in here, isnt it, smiling and tilting her head back
gracefully. Yeah, but it aint bad though. Would you care
to leave? we could go to my apartment and have a few
quiet drinks. Harry stared for a moment then nodded.

When
they got to the apartment Harry sprawled on the couch.
He felt drunk. Everything was alright. My name is Alberta, handing him a drink. Whats yours? Harry. She sat
next to him. Why dont you take your shirt off. Its rather
warm in here. Yeah, sure, fumbling with the buttons.
Here, let me help you, leaning over and slowly unbuttoning Harrys shirt, glancing up at Harry, pulling the shirt
out of his trousers then sliding it off the shoulders and
arms and letting it fall behind the couch. Harry watched
her as she unbuttoned his shirt, felt the slight pressure
of her fingers. He almost thought about the guys and
what they would say if they saw him now, but the thought
was easily absorbed by the alcohol before it formed and
he closed his eyes and enjoyed the closeness of Alberta.

She
stayed close to him, resting one hand gently on his shoulder, looking up at him, sliding her hand along his shoulder
to his neck, watching his face, his eyes, for any reaction;
feeling a little uneasy with Harry, not absolutely certain
how he would react. Usually she knew how rough trade
would react before she attempted anything, but with Harry
she wasnt too certain; there was something strange in his
eyes. She thought she understood what was behind them,
but she still preferred a little caution to recklessness. And
too, this was exciting. Occasionally she just had to cruise
and bring home trade that looked dangerous; but, slowly,
as she caressed his neck and back and looked into his
face, she realized that she didnt have to fear Harry; and
she understood too that this was a new experience to

Harry. The puzzled expectant look on his face excited
her. She had a cherry. She tingled. She rubbed his chest
with the palm of her other hand. Your chest is so strong
and hairy, the tip of her tongue showing between her lips;
rubbing his back, touching gently the pimples and pock-
marks. Youre so strong, moving closer, touching his neck
with her lips, her hand moving from his chest to his
stomach, to his belt, his fly; her mouth on his chest, then
his stomach. Harry raised himself slightly as she tugged
at his pants then relaxed, then tensed as she kissed his
thighs and put his cock in her mouth. Harry pushed
against the back of the couch, squirmed with pleasure;
almost screamed with pleasure at the image of his wife
being split in two with a large cock that turned into an
enormous barbed pole, then he was there smashing her
face with his fist and laughing, laughing and spitting and
punching until the face was just a blob that oozed and
then she became an old man and he stopped punching
and then once more it was Mary, or it almost looked like
Mary but it was a woman and she screamed as a burning
white hot cock was shoved and hammered into her cunt
then slowly pulled out, pulling with it her entrails and
Harry sat watching, laughing his laugh and groaning,
groaning with pleasure and then he heard the groan,
heard it not only from inside, but heard it enter his ear
from outside and he opened his eyes and saw Albertas
head moving furiously and Harry moaned and squirmed
frantically.

      Alberta kept her head still for many minutes
before getting up and going to the bathroom. Harry
watched her walk away then looked at his prick hanging
half rigidly between his legs. It hypnotized him and he
stared at it for a moment knowing it was his yet not
recognizing it, as if he had never seen it before yet knowing he had. How many times had he held it in his hands

as he pissed; why did it seem new to him? Why did it suddenly fascinate him so? He blinked his eyes and heard the water running in the bathroom. He looked at his penis again and the strangeness disappeared. He wondered briefly about his thoughts of a moment ago. He couldnt remember them. He felt good. He looked toward the bathroom waiting to see Albertas face.

Her face had a polished wax glow and her long hair was neatly combed. She wiggled toward him, smiling. She laughed, lightly, at Harrys surprised look when he noticed she was wearing nothing but a pair of womans lace panties. She poured two more drinks and sat beside him. Harry took a gulp of his drink and touched her panties. Do you like my silks? Harrys hand jerked back. He felt Albertas hand on the back of his neck. She gently guided his hand to her leg. I love them. They're so smooth, holding his hand on her leg and kissing his neck, his mouth, sliding her tongue into his mouth, searching for his, feeling the bottom of it as Harry curled his tongue back in his mouth, caressing the base of his tongue with hers. Harrys tongue slowly unfolding and lapping against hers, his hand grabbing her cock, Alberta moving his hand away and back on her leg, letting her saliva drip from the tip of her tongue onto Harrys, squirming as he clutched her leg tightly, almost feeling the drops of spit being absorbed by Harrys mouth, feeling his tongue lunging into her mouth as if he were trying to choke her; she sucked on his tongue then let him suck on hers, rolling her head with his, moving her hand over his lumpy back; slowly moving her head back and away from his. Lets go into the bedroom, darling. Harry pulled her toward him and sucked on her lips. She slowly separated her mouth from his and tugged him from the back of his neck. Lets go to bed, slowly standing, still tugging. Harry stood, staggering slightly. Alberta looked down and laughed. You still have your shoes and socks on. Harry blinked. He was standing with legs spread, penis standing straight before him, naked except for his black socks and shoes. Alberta giggled then took his shoes and socks off. Come on lover. She grabbed him by the prick and led him to the bedroom.

Harry flopped onto the bed and rolled over and kissed her, missing her mouth and kissing her chin. She laughed and guided him to her mouth. He pushed at her side and at first Alberta was puzzled, trying to understand what he was trying to do, then realized that he was trying to turn her over. She giggled again. You silly you. You never have fucked a fairy before, have you? Harry grumbled, still fumbling and kissing her neck and chest. We make love just like anybody else honey, a little peeved at first then once more relishing the charm of having a cherry. Just relax, rolling over on her side and kissing him, whispering in his ear. When she finished the preparations she rolled back onto her back, Harry rolling over on her, and moved rhythmically with Harry, her legs and arms wrapped around him, rolling, squirming, groaning.

Harry lunged at first, then, looking at Alberta, slowed to an exciting movement; and as he moved he was conscious of his movements, of his excitement and enjoyment and not wanting it to end; and though he clenched his teeth from lust and pinched her back and bit her neck there was a comparative relaxing, the tautness and spasms being caused by pleasure and desire to be where he was and to do what he was doing. Harry could hear her and his moans blending, could feel her under him, could feel her flesh in his mouth; there were many tangible things and yet there was still a confusion, but it stemmed from inexperience, from the sudden overpowering sensations of pleasure, a pleasure he had never known, a pleasure that he, with its excitement and tenderness, had never experienced—he wanted to grab and squeeze the flesh he felt in his hands, he wanted to bite it, yet he didnt want to destroy it; he wanted it to be there, he wanted to come back to it. Harry continued to move with the same satisfying rhythm; continued to blend his moans with hers through the whirlygig of confusion; bewildered but not distracted or disturbed by these new emotions giving birth to each other in his mind, but just concentrating on the pleasure and allowing it to guide him as Alberta had. When he stopped moving he lay still for a moment hearing their heavy breathing then kissed her, caressed her arms then rolled slowly and gently onto the bed, stretched out and soon slept. Harry was happy.

Harry didnt open his eyes immediately when he awoke, but lay thinking then opened them suddenly, very wide, and turned and looked at Alberta. Harry sat up. The entire evening jammed itself into Harrys mind and his eyes clouded from his terrible anxiety and confusion. For the briefest moment he hid behind alcohol and overlapping images hung in front of him, then passed. He dropped back on the bed and fell asleep once more. When he awoke again later he no longer wanted to run. The frightening clarity felt for the moment when he first awoke assimilated itself with the usual confusion of Harrys mind and he was now able to look at Alberta and remember the night, in a general penumbrous way, and not be afraid to be there—though still fearing the consequences of having someone find out—but the fears and confusion were overshadowed by his feeling of happiness.

Actually it was this feeling of happiness that bothered Harry more than anything else at the immediate moment he sat in the bed and looked at Alberta and remembered, with

pleasure, the night before. He knew he felt good, yet he couldn't define his feeling. He couldnt say, Im happy. He had nothing with which to compare his feeling. He felt good when he was telling wilson off; he felt good when he was with the guys having a drink; at those times he told himself he was happy, but his feeling now went so much beyond that that it was incomprehensible. He didnt realize that he had never been happy, this happy, before.
He looked at Alberta again, then got out of bed and poured himself a drink. Too many things were starting to run through his mind. He couldnt take the chance of sitting there, sober, and allowing them to free themselves upon him. He lit a cigarette and drank the drink as fast as he could, then poured another. He took a little longer drinking this, then went back to the bedroom and sat on the edge of the bed with his 3rd drink.

He wanted to wake Alberta up. He didnt want to sit there alone and vulnerable; he wanted to talk with her, but he didnt know if he should call her or shake her or perhaps just bounce up and down on the bed. He took a drink, a drag of hs cigarette, then put the cigarette out, rattling the ashtray on the table. Alberta moved and Harry quickly moved his head so he wouldnt be looking at her and yawned loudly. Alberta rolled over and mumbled something and Harry quickly turned, bouncing the bed as much as possible, whatdidyasay? Alberta mumbled again and opened her eyes. Harry smiled his smile and took another drink. Another day had started.

It took Alberta a while to wake up completely, though she did get out of bed and wash and go about her usual morning routine, and so it was quite a while before she became conscious of what Harry was saying and the fact that he was following her around the apartment. He wasnt hanging over her shoulder, but he was always within a few feet of her and whenever she turned Harry was there, smiling his smile. The first word she was aware of, while they drank coffee, was strike and though she still wasnt awake enough to understand each word she understood that he was telling her how he was running a strike, or some such thing, and how he was gonna shove it up somebodys ass. She hoped that he would either stop or slow down or that she would get enough energy to say something that would at least change the subject; but after a few more drinks Harry slowed down and they enjoyed each others company. They went to a movie in the afternoon; ate when they came out; then sat for a few hours in a bar. When they got home Harry made love to Alberta then they sat drinking and listening to music. Alberta found Harry amusing and enjoyed being with him, except when he tried to convince her he was a big shot—though she didnt mind his throwing money on the bar or taking a cab when they only had a few blocks to go—but when he did she changed the subject; and, too, she liked the way Harry kissed her. Not that he kissed any better or was less freaky than the others, but she could feel his excitement from the newness of the experience. They sat for hours on the couch, drinking, vaguely aware of the music from the radio, holding hands and kissing. Alberta leaned her head on Harrys shoulder, her eyes half closed, humming, turning from time to time to glance at Harry. Harry smiled his smile and there was a slight softness about it, and even his eyes had a slight tenderness in them. He touched her hair lightly and his hand tightened on her shoulder. They spoke infrequently and when they did their voices were low, Harrys even losing some of its roughness. They just sat, cuddled on the couch, for hours, Alberta moving a foot in time to the music; Harry loving having his arm around her and feeling her

close to him. When Alberta asked Harry if he would like
to go to bed he nodded and they got up and, still holding
hands, walked slowly to the bedroom.

When Harry left
Alberta Sunday afternoon he was in a daze. He hadnt
thought of leaving. If she hadnt told him that she had to
see someone that afternoon and that he had better leave
he would have remained unaware of time and the fact
that tomorrow was Monday and there were books to be
stamped. He remembered the weekend and everything
that happened, but he couldnt believe it was Sunday. Time
just couldnt have passed that fast. The bouncing of the
cab and the noises of the streets forced reality upon him
and he knew he was going back to Brooklyn. He had
wanted to ask her if he could see her again, but he didnt
know how, no words came from his mouth, they hadnt
even completely formed in his mind. He tried hard to
think of how to ask her and to get the question out, but
then the door was closed and he was walking down the
street and now he was on his way to Brooklyn. Who was
she going to see? Hed probably see her again in Marys.
Hed be going there again.

He didnt go right home but
went to the bar for a few hours. When he got home Mary
was watching tv. He said nothing, but undressed and
went to bed, smoked and thought of Alberta, remembering many times the last kiss in the doorway. Before he
fell asleep the baby awoke and started crying and Mary
eventually came in and talked to him and bounced him in
the crib. The sound of their voices seemed to come from
a dream and didnt interfere with his thoughts or the
memory of the kiss.

The next morning Harry washed and
dressed without saying a word. Mary watched determined
to say something. She was nervous, but even a slap on the

face was better than nothing. As Harry was about to
leave she asked him if he was coming home that night.
Harry shrugged. Where wereya Friday and Satu—Harry
swung his arm in a stiff arc, fist clenched, and hit her in
the corner of her mouth with the back of his fist. He
hadnt looked or thought, but had simply closed his fist
and swung. He paid no attention to the biting sensation
he felt as his hand hit her teeth nor later did he think of
the fact that it was the first time he had punched her—
thousands of times he had thought of it, dreamed of it,
had tried—or turn to look at her after hitting her. He just
swung and turned and left the house.

                                      He rubbed his hand
as he walked. He felt good. Relieved. It had been a long
time since he had had his nightmare. It was not even a
memory.

        Harry stamped books with accuracy, retaining
the silent introspective mood he had recently acquired.
The men were quieter and more solemn as they picked up
their signs and had their books stamped, Harrys still quiet
mood allowing them to ignore him, and they walked the
picket line in the same despondent way they did everything else. Most of them had lately tried to get another
job, but because they were on strike it was impossible to
get one, the companies thinking they would leave as soon
as the strike was settled, and so they walked around the
plant, nodded to each other, took out their book, poured
a cup of coffee or a glass of beer, put away their signs,
said goodbye and left with the same air of hopelessness.
Since the incident of the trucks the police guard had been
increased and the men rotated so one officer was never
there more than 3 hours a week, the department thinking
this would prevent any personal disputes, caused by the
boredom of having to be there, doing nothing, from
erupting into a major incident; and so the policemen stood

their posts, chatted with each other, and watched the strikers in an officially alert and disinterested manner.

At the first meeting between the company and the union after vacations they spoke for a while, said nothing, then decided to meet again in two days. At that meeting a few of the problems were discussed before the meeting was adjourned with a decision to meet in two days. Three, and sometimes four, times a week they met, put their briefcases on the large conference table, sat opposite each other, took their papers out of the briefcases and started talking. Slowly, by almost infinitesimal degrees, they seriously discussed a few of the issues that were preventing a settlement of the strike. Summer was almost over. Harrington was under no pressure to end the strike, having convinced the other officers of the corporation and negotiating committee that the company could afford to allow the strike to continue for many more months without an appreciable loss in net income, and he did not think there was enough pressure on the union to attempt to dispose of Harry, and he was determined not to agree to any settlement until he had tried everything possible to rid himself of Harry Black.

            The union would have liked to have the strike settled as soon as possible, but only on their terms: they had to have complete control of the Welfare Plan. Though the strike had been in effect for many months the union officials felt no pressure on them. Everything was going smoothly and though their personal incomes had been cut because there had been no contributions to the Welfare Plan since the strike had started, there were ample funds coming in from other unions throughout the country to take the extra money they needed from these contributions. And the men were getting their bag of groceries each week. Some of them might be getting a little short of money, which was unfortunate, but the strike would continue, for months if necessary, until it was agreed that they would retain control of the Welfare Plan. And so no urgency was felt by either side.

The President, or another member of the committee, gave a short speech each Saturday before the food was distributed. They assured the men they were doing everything they could to settle the strike—they knew the men wanted to get back to work; that they couldnt afford to stay out of work for ever; that their bank accounts were running low; and that, in many cases, their wives had to go to work—but, they also told them, they knew the men wouldnt settle for anything less than a decent contract with a decent wage and that they were going to see that the men got that. They werent going to sign any sweetheart contract and let the company continue to take the bread out of their mouths . . . and the clique whistled and yelled and a few of the others joined in and the orator descended from the platform and mingled with the men, slapping them on the back, encouraging them, and nodding to each one as he accepted his bag of groceries.

Harry went to Marys every weekend and, after the first few weeks, during the week occasionally. The first time he went there after meeting Alberta she introduced him to some of her friends and during the months that followed Harry met some lovely young boys at Marys and the parties he went to with them. When he went to Marys he no longer slid to a place at the bar near the door, but walked around looking to see who was there, nodding and sitting at tables, wondering who was standing at the bar envying him as he put his arm around a young shoulder. Most of the fairies he met liked him—he was a good fuck and he spent money—but didnt like to be with him too long too often. It wasnt just his talking about the strike that caused them to shy away, though he was a boor, but a strangeness and a feeling of uncertainty that eventually made them uncomfortable. They had all seen, kissed, sucked and fucked freaks of all varieties from men who had spent most of their lives in prisons and could be satisfied only by a boy, men who were capable of cutting a throat not only without feeling, but without reason, to men who locked themselves in the bathroom when their wives went out and dressed in their wives clothes, occasionally going to a place like Marys when they had a night out. But these men were completely obvious to the fairies and they knew just how far they could go in any direction with them. Harry was different, or at least they felt he was. There was some little something that they couldnt sense, that they were uncertain about, that eventually made them nervous. It might simply be that Harry would like to dress up as a woman and go to a drag ball, or parade down Broadway; or perhaps some day he would flip and kill one of them. They didnt know.

As summer passed, and the pleasant autumn weather followed, Harry joined his new friends when they went for a drive in the country. They would jam into a car with a few bottles of gin and benzedrine, turn the radio up and slap the side of the car in rhythm to a jazz or blues song and sing along with it, snapping their fingers, wiggling in their seats—O honey, what I couldnt do to this number—passing the bottle back and forth—taking an occasional bennie—flirting with men in other cars; or, if in the mood, they would listen to an Italian opera, sighing rapturously after each aria; telling anecdotes about the gorgeous tenor or the temperamental diva, their heads moving gently with the music; taking small sips from the bottle; squealing and pointing at trees whose leaves reminded them of a Renoir and they jumped in their seats to see a new combination of colors, each one, almost by turn, pointing to a grove that was thrilling with reds, browns, orange or gold and at ones where all the colors blended and the leaves seemed to toy with the sunlight their colors were so brilliant; and in between were the greens of pines and blues of spruces and a few times they stopped by a lake or pond and giggled as they scampered around picking up acorns or chestnuts and took off their shoes and splashed their feet in the water and giggled as they watched squirrels peek at them for a moment before dashing away; and they would sit by the water or under a tree and sip the gin, take more bennie, then fill the car trunk with leaves, keeping some out to hold on their laps, to look at, to smell, to rub with a handkerchief, continually talking of how beautiful it was . . . and Harry sat in the back, saying little, not minding the music or their screeching over a bunch of leaves, not noticing much of anything, but happy to be with them.

Walking the picket line was less tiring now that the cooler weather had arrived. When the men finished their time on the line and handed their signs to their relief, or put them away at night, they werent sweaty or fatigued as they had been during the summer, yet they still started and ended each day a little more despondent than the day before. Though a few, while not on the picket line, sat around the office drinking beer, most of them sat or stood in small groups talking. The two kegs of beer that used to be ordered each day now lasted 3 or 4 days— Harry adding the extra money that had been spent on beer to his expense sheet—and were drunk mostly by Harry and the guys from the Greeks. And, as it got darker earlier each day, more of the men left after their tour of duty and went home to watch tv or cook supper and wait for the wife to come home from work; and some went to a bar, going home late to avoid the argument about who was going to cook and clean now that the wife was working.

The men no longer looked down 2nd avenue expecting to see trucks. The incident wasnt forgotten, but the hope that it had aroused—and the hatred that had revived their enthusiasm—was irrevocably lost and they performed their duties as strikers listlessly and hopelessly. A few of the men were able to get new jobs and their books were voided. When this was announced at a Saturday meeting boos and catcalls came from the clique, but the men were silent, some envying them, others no longer capable of anything but lethargy; and the men whose books had been voided were only thought of, if at all, when the strikers joined the hundreds of workers from the Army Base at five oclock walking up 58th street to the subway.

Daylight saving time was in its last week when the company made the long awaited concession: they finally agreed to consider allowing the union to continue the administration of the Welfare Fund. But there were conditions. A few were with respect to the amount of the companys contribution, certain aspects of supervision in the factory, and a few other items that they both knew could be negotiated easily; but they also wanted the right to discharge Harry Black. The union representatives immediately leaped to their feet and declared the demand unreasonable and unthinkable. It was more than just a case of Harry being a member in good standing and an able worker, but to even suggest that they would or could violate the trust and welfare of the membership was an insult to their integrity. Not only that, it was an insult to every union member and officer in the country.

They slammed their briefcases shut and the two forces stood opposite each other haggling for many minutes before the union representatives walked out.

The company and the union had had over a hundred meetings since the beginning of the strike and had been meeting every day, for many grueling hours, for over a month now. Although neither side was, as yet, in a desperate position, pressure was mounting. The union officials knew they couldnt allow the strike to continue too much longer without a good, tangible, palatable reason to give the men. There was too much grumbling; the men were obviously dissatisfied and pressure had been slowly building up from government agencies who might, eventually, investigate the reasons for the prolonging of the strike; but now they had their reason.

Harrington recognized and realized that the men with whom he was negotiating would see the plant remain closed for a year rather than relinquish their control of the Welfare Fund and he was perfectly willing, now, to buy them off—to offer a concession—by allowing them to continue to administer it, but they had to make concessions too. The pressure on the company was increasing, but Harrington was determined to try to get rid of Harry Black and he was willing to keep the plant closed for many more months in order to accomplish this. The company could go to the end of the year without losing too much, that had been definitely established by their accountants and tax experts. Pressure was building up on the company, but Harrington knew it was building up on the union too and so he decided it was time to barter. He felt they would gladly concede Harry for the fund which they obviously could not afford to have checked. Even after the union officials had walked out of the meeting he still retained this hope, knowing that they could not possibly concede immediately, but would have to take at least a month, or perhaps even longer, to devise a method to accomplish this within the legal framework of the union.

Of course each of the union officials thought, at first to himself, of a way they could get rid of Harry without making themselves open to criticism: they could dump him easily enough and give as an excuse that he was defrauding the union of money by submitting fraudulent expense vouchers, or any number of other reasons. Actually they could tell the membership anything and it wouldnt be noticed if they told them just before that the company gave in and signed the new contract. Nobody would miss Harry.

They tossed a few more ideas around, evaluated the whole setup, and decided the best thing to do was to maintain their present position: Harry was a good man and stays on the job. Harry was a nut, but that was what made him so valuable. He continually overstepped the limits of the contract with regard to working, but this, in its own little way, helped prevent the company from trying the same thing. Harry forced the company to fight so hard, and spend so much time, getting what they were allowed under the contract that they didnt have time to infringe on the limitations the contract set on them. They recognized that Harry was the best diversionary action they had. And too, this made dealing with the company easier for the officials. Although most, if not all, of the men they had to deal with at the company hated the union, so much of their hatred was personal and directed against Harry that the union officials had a much easier time talking and, under ordinary circumstances, dealing with them. Harry, in addition to all the other functions he served, was their builtin patsy. They could never find another shop steward for local 392 as willing and as capable as Harry Black. He was irreplaceable.

But of course the real reason they didnt want to allow the firing of Harry was that if they did they would be conceding a point, no matter how meaningless, to the company; and, most important of all, if they ever allowed the company the authority and privilege to fire someone they would be forfeiting a right that was theirs and theirs alone; and if they allowed it once they might, somehow, be forced to allow it again. Yet even if they were reasonably certain that the company would not try to exercise this right again they could not allow it even once. Someone might get ideas about them. It had been a long time since anyone tried to take their local away from them (that attempt being stopped easily with a few killings) and if they allowed this there would bound to be someone who thought they were too weak to keep their local. They didnt believe that anyone could actually take it away from them, but they didnt want to be forced to spend the time and money to keep what was theirs, especially now that they had, in addition to many other things, the Welfare Fund functioning so nicely for themselves. Each of them had made long term loans based on their cut from the fund and keeping the books in order required time and attention and then sometimes when theres trouble things get out of hand and there are investigations and more time and money are lost.

All these things were considered and smoked and drunk over and, now that the company obviously wasnt going to fight against their administering the fund any longer, they had no need to worry. Pressure was building up, but the company must be feeling it even more to have made the offer. And now they had something to relieve the pressure, slightly, for a while. Next Saturday, before the men received their bag of groceries, they would tell the rank and file that those sonsofbitches, those bellyrobbinbastards, were willing to concede a few points if we allowed them to fire men. And, of course, they would remind the men of this each Saturday and it should prove enough to get their hatred directed actively and completely against the company. The officials looked at each other. No one had anything to add. They agreed that that was about the size of the situation. Nothing more need be said. They would not give up their power.

The guys from the Greeks still came over almost every night after the picketers had left and sat around with Harry drinking beer and, if in the mood, ordering food. Harry putting the cost on his expense sheet. Harry gave them his usual rundown on the strike and, as usual, the guys ignored him and played the radio and drank and, as usual, Harry continued his narration.

During the week when Harry didnt go up to Marys he would lock up the office after the guys left and go home. He hadnt said more than a few words to Mary, nor she to him, since the morning he punched her. She left for a few days with the baby after that—Harry didnt notice that she was gone— but it was even worse being with her parents so, after a few days, she came back where she could at least watch tv. Harry would go right to bed and lie on his back thinking—not noticing Mary when she got into bed, thinking of her seldom, usually only when he dropped some money on the table for her to buy food. He would lie in bed thinking not only of all his friends at Marys, but hoping, as he had so many times, that tomorrow night he might meet someone who would not only ask him to take her home that night but every night; hoping he might meet someone who would want to live with him and they could make love everynight or just sit and hold hands and feel her small, soft and weak in his arms . . . not all slimy like a ballbreakin cunt.

Saturday the President spoke to the men before they were given their packages. The men, for the last few months, stayed on the side of the hall near the doors where the packages were handed out and half of the hall was empty while they jammed and shoved each other to retain or take a place near the doors; and each week the shoving and yelling increased. The officials tried to get the men to sit, but they absolutely refused to give up their places near the doors and so more than 1,000 men shoved and jostled each other as the President spoke. Men . . .

Men, we/re beating them! Theyre starting to COLLAPSE! The men quieted a little and most of them were looking at the President. Its been a long time—and krist knows weve suffered with you—but theyre comin around. They havent given in down the line yet, but its only a matter of time. Theyve agreed to most of the terms and it wont be long before they agree to the rest. The men started to move uneasily at hearing the same words again and the noises started increasing. The President raised his hands and yelled louder. We could have settled the strike this week if we wanted to, but we didnt. You want to know why? The men quieted again and stared. Because we like talking to those stuffedshirtbastards? because we like to argue with men who are trying to take the bread out of our families mouths? because we like workin 16 and 18 hours a day??? No! I/ll tell you why. Because they wanted the right to fire anybody they want, thats why. If they get a bug up their ass and decide they dont like the looks of some guy they want to be able to fire him right there and then. No questions asked, no answers given. Just kick him out on his ass and let him and his family starve. Thats why we have been fighting those bastards so hard; thats why we have been out of work so long. The men were silent, still. More than 1,000 men huddled near the doors staring at the speaker. More than once since we have been negotiating with them they have tried to buy us off in one way or another if we would let them throw men out in the cold any time they wanted to. And you know what we told them. You know what we said when they tried that shit on us. I/ll tell you what we said. We stood up and looked those bastards right in the eye and told them, right to their fat faces, FUCK YOU! The clique roared approval—thats what we told them—others joined in the yelling and whistling—thats what the elected officials of your union said and we walked out—more yelling and stamping of feet—we left those bastards standing. And you can bet your sweet ass those sonsofbitches know theres no weak link in this union—almost all the men roared and whistled—and we/ll see them dead and buried and piss on their graves before we let them throw one of our brothers to the wolves—the men continued to shout and the President leaned over the edge of the platform and yelled over and between their shouts —we let those bellyrobbinbastards know that all we want is an honest dollar for an honest days work . . . we dont want any handouts, we want to work for our money, but by krist we/re not going to let them get fat from our sweat. We/re the men who break our backs while they sit their fat asses on soft chairs in an air conditioned office and rake in the money for our work. And you know what they say? They say that the average pay for you men is $8,000 a year plus another $1,000 in fringe benefits. They say this is enough. They say that they cant afford to pay more without firing as many as they want. You know what we said? We told them to let us have all over $50,000 a year that they were getting and they shut their goddamn mouths fast enough—the men roared so loud he had to stop speaking for a moment—thats just what we told them. He stood with his head bowed then slowly raised it, his voice lower, husky with dedication. I tell you men now that no matter what happens—even if it should cost me my life—you will not have to worry about whether or not you will have a job tomorrow or the next day or the next, speaking slowly, each word seeming to be forced separately from his overworked and weakened body, this I tell you now and guarantee that when we sign a contract you will be able to go home from work each night and know that there will be a job waiting for you tomorrow. There will be no sleepless nights or empty bellies. He backed away from the edge of the platform and sat with the rest of the officials, his head bowed slightly. The men roared, slapped each other and laughed as they lined up for their $10 bag of groceries. There would be no trouble from them for a few weeks.

The next Monday the mens spirits were still raised. There wasnt the picnic atmosphere of the first days of the strike when they joked, played ball, shot crap and washed and polished their cars; but the despondency and hopelessness of the past few months had been relieved, temporarily at least. Now, as with the incident of the trucks, they had a tangible reason for hating and this allowed them to ignore the reality of the strike, of their lack of money, of the fact that they had been out of work for 6 months and did not know how much longer the strike would last; the daily arguments with the wife, and that they had to scrimp to make the payments on the house and car and, in some cases, that there no longer was a car. Now their hatred and anger was no longer spread over and around everything and everyone they came in contact with, but was directed, with energy at the company and the men who were trying to break their union. There was even a little buoyancy in their stride as they walked the picket line and a hint of optimism in their voices as they spoke to each other and occasionally laughed.

Harry walked around with the men too, patting them on the backside and telling them that theyd break those ballbreakers. Theyll find out they cant fuckus, and he would smile his smile and stamp books.

Only a slight reminder was needed the following Saturday to keep the men comparatively content, but soon the grins once more faded into scowls and the scowls into blankness and though the President gave an exuberant and loud speech before they received their $10 bag of groceries, and told them in as fatherly a manner as he could, that Thanksgiving morning they would each receive, in addition to their regular bag of groceries, a 4 lb. chicken— the clique applauding—they lined up, walked and spoke with the same sullenness and hopelessness they had not too many weeks before. And then it was Thanksgiving day. At least the wife would be home today to cook.

That night Harry went to the dragball. Hundreds of fairies were there dressed as women, some having rented expensive gowns, jewelry and fur wraps. They pranced about the huge ballroom calling to each other, hugging each other, admiring each other, sneering disdainfully as a hated queen passed. O, just look at the rags she wearing. She looks like a bowery whore. Well, lets face it, its not the clothes. She would look simply ugly in a Dior original, and they would stare contemptuously and continue prancing.

There were, too, hundreds not dressed as women: a few of them fairies who walked about with the others, but the majority were johns, trade, and bisexuals. They sat around the perimeter of the ballroom on folding chairs or stood leaning against the wall, dimly visible in the shadows of the barely lighted ballroom, squinting and leering at the queens. The entire ballroom was lit by four medium sized spotlights, one in each corner, and the light was filtered through multicolored discs so spots of colored light crawled along the ceiling and walls, fell to the floor then crawled along the floor, over a leg or back and back into the corner. The queens standing or walking around the floor were continually brushed with the colored spots and their smooth bared arms would be pocked with green, purple, red, violet, yellow, or combinations as the colors crossed each other, and flesh would be covered with brownish or bluish cores with various colored ellipses wiggling from them; or a check would be pink or white or tan with makeup then suddenly mottled with a large gangrenous spot, the rest of the face shaded with yellow and violet and then the cheek would turn purple, then red; and an occasional light scratched across the faces of the stag line along the sides of the grand ballroom, a wide staring eye or green wet lips briefly visible in the shadows; the lights crawling down the wall, rushing across their faces, then crawling along the floor to their corner and starting the journey again. A few of the shadows spoke, some even smiled, but most sat still and silent, hunched forward slightly following the movements of the lights and queens. Occasionally a flame would appear as a cigarette was lit and an orange face would be thrust forward then be completely invisible for many seconds before coming slowly from the shadows again, the eyes never once, not for a second, looking anywhere but at the queens and the roving lights.

      Harry stood at the entrance to the grand ballroom looking around then slid to the side and leaned against the wall trying to recognize his friends. He knew almost everyone from Marys would be there,

but he could not recognize them in drag. When his eyes
became accustomed to the light he looked more closely
at the queens on the floor. He was surprised, though he
knew they were men, how much they looked like women.
Beautiful women. He had never in his life seen women
look more beautiful or feminine than the queens strolling
about the floor of the ballroom. Yet, when his surprise
passed, he felt a little disappointed and looked at the fairies not in drag. He spotted a few he knew and walked over
to them. At first he felt conspicuous leaving the shadowed
edge of the room and walking across the floor with the
lights bobbing around, but as he stood and talked with his
friends he wished the lights were brighter. Occasionally
one of their friends, who was in drag, would join them
and though Harry was still surprised at how beautiful they
were he was impatient for them to leave.

Later in the eve-
ning a small band played dance music and couples glided,
bumped and twisted across the dance floor. From time to
time a couple would stand almost immobile, arms tight
around each other, kissing and an evil queen would dance
by and tap the queen on the shoulder and tell her to take
it easy. You might get a hardon honey and rip that dress
all up, and laugh and dance away; and people walked back
and forth to the bar and others stood on the stairs in the
hallway gulping at a bottle; and couples sprawled up and
down the stairs, some looking deperately for a dark
corner; and the band played a Charleston and the queens
and their johns and lovers shuffled and kicked and a few
queens lifted their dresses, squealing and screaming, each
trying to kick higher than the other, the colored spots
crawling up their legs and across their genitals; and the
walls and corners were empty now except for embracing
couples; and Harry went out and bought a couple of pints
of gin and he and his properly dressed fairy friends made

218

frequent trips to the hall and Harry, for the only time during the evening, watched the queens, but when the Charleston was over he once more ignored the couples on the dance floor of the grand ballroom.

All the queens were high now on gin and bennie and the dance floor was a chaos of giggling, flitting queens, the drooling bodies from the shadows tracking them. All during the night queens came over to Harry and his friends and talked with them and many asked Harry to dance or take a walk and he always refused and when they left he would turn and start talking to Regina, a fairy he had met many times in Marys, but, for some reason, had never taken home or thought of; and soon he was always at Reginas side, talking, drinking, smoking or just standing, and wherever she went Harry followed. She was wearing a pair of tight slacks and a sportshirt and all the whirling of skirts seemed to force Harry to her side. After the Charleston ended Harry put his arm around her and she smiled and kissed him. Harry smiled his smile and rubbed the back of her neck and they went out of the hall with the others, finished what was left of the gin, stood talking with their friends for a while then, when the others went back to the ballroom, they left and Harry took Regina home.

The weeks following Thanksgiving were lovely and exciting for Harry. He saw Regina often and though, if he thought about it, he might have wished he were with Alberta or one of the other fairies he had made love with, he liked being with her, making love with her and calling her on the phone and making a date to meet in Marys. She was a little different than the others and her attitude toward Harry was not the same as the others. She wasnt nervous with him at all. She had no doubts as to what Harry would do. She was more like Ginger when she danced with him at the office and almost crushed his hand. And Harry loved going up to Marys and walking to the tables in the rear knowing someone was waiting specifically for him. He still hung around the office after five drinking beer with the guys from the Greeks, but left shortly after they did and took a cab uptown. He went out more often with Regina than he had with any of the others and occasionally he would buy her a shirt or some little something she asked for. And so he added a few more dollars each week to his expense sheet.

For the other strikers the weeks following Thanksgiving were the beginning of winter. There were days of cold drizzling rain when the men were so cold after walking the picket line, from the weather and dejection, that the coffee, no matter how hot, did not warm them, nor did they feel alive enough to shiver. They just walked the line or waited in the office, only a few of them bothering to curse the weather and then only under their breath. And each Saturday they lined up, after being reassured by one of the officials, and collected their $10 bag of groceries, no longer interested in what was said at the last meeting of the negotiating committees, or the fact that every union in the country was sending money each week to their local so they could continue to provide their men with the staples of life.

Harry loved sitting in the back of Marys with his arm around Regina, waving to his friends, ordering drinks, inviting people to his table, even waving to Ginger one night when she walked in and keeping her at the table until he left with Regina. One night Harry took Regina home and early the next morning he was slowly awakened by something tickling his face. He opened his eyes and Regina was kneeling beside him rubbing her cock against his mouth. He stared then sat up. Whatthefuck yadoin, unable to look her in the eye for more than a second, looking at her cock and the hand around it, the manicured and redpolished nails. Regina laughed then Harry laughed too and they fell back on the bed laughing until Regina finally rolled over and kissed him.

On xmas eve the men reported to the hall for their bags of groceries. The hall was strung with decorations and over the platform was a huge sign stretched from wall to wall: MERRY XMAS AND A HAPPY NEW YEAR. Recorded xmas carols were played and the officials wished each man, individually, a merry xmas. Each man got an additional $5.00 worth of groceries, another 4 lb. chicken and an xmas stocking filled with hard candy.

At the first meeting after the xmas holidays the strike was settled. New government contracts were awarded the company and work would have to begin by the middle of January so Harrington was forced to settle the strike. He was certain that if they prolonged the strike another month he would be able to rid himself of Harry Black, but the Board of Directors informed him that the plant must be in full operation by the middle of January and so an agreement was reached.

Although the union officials had realized thousands of dollars from the strike fund and there was more money coming in every day from unions throughout the country, it was not as much as their income from the Welfare Fund and so the agreement reached was satisfying. And too, after so many years of leisure, the strain of working a few hours every few days that had been necessitated by the long strike enervated them and they were looking forward to the end of the strike and a rest. And, of course, the deposits to the Welfare Fund had been increased and its administration remained in their control.

On December 29th, at 1:30 pm, the men once again assembled in the hall and though they knew that the strike was over they remained huddled by the doors while the President made the announcement. Well men its all over. They gave in to us one-hundredpercent-right-down-the-line. The clique cheered. A few others joined in. Its been a long hard fight but we showed them what a strong union can do. A few more cheers. The President of local·392 told how hard he and the other members of the negotiating committee worked; reminded them what ratbastards the company men were; expressed his thanks and the appreciation of all the men for the fine job done by Brother Harry Black; and told them that the real credit goes to them, the rank and file of·the union, the heart of the organization, who walked the picket line in fair weather and foul, who gave their time and blood that the union could win and help secure an honorable contract. He then told them about the contract and the additional monies to the Welfare Fund and how their jobs were secure; avoiding telling them that they would be assessed $10 each month for the next year—about half of their increase in pay—to build up the now depleted strike fund. When he finished he asked for a vote on the new contract, announced the ayes had it and so the contract was ratified. The clique hootedandhollered. A few others joined them. They were to start work the next day. As the men ambled out of the hall, the officials walking among them, slapping backs and smiling, a recording of auld lang syne was played.

When the meeting was over Harry called Regina then hopped in a cab and went up to her apartment. When he paid the cabdriver and started up the stairs he realized that he could no longer afford to take cabs back and forth, that he could not spend money the way he had while there was a strike. He would no longer be on the union payroll and have an expense sheet. He realized he would not have much money for himself after the rent was paid and he gave Mary a few bucks for food. Regina opened the door and he went in. You know you awakened me from a simply *delightful* sleep. I dont know why you had to call so *early*. I just came from a meetin. The strikes over. O you and that strike. Im going to shower, dress and put a face on then we can go to Marys for a few drinks and after that you can take me to dinner and perhaps the cinema if I should happen to be in the mood. I—I . . . a dont know if I can go ta Marys—Regina strode briskly to the bathroom. The water splashed suddenly against the side of the shower stall—maybe we could just hangaround here—I cant hear a *word* youre saying—Harry still standing in the middle of the room—I thought maybe we could eat here, huh?— Regina was singing—Harry stopped talking yet remained standing in the middle of the room. 20 minutes later Regina turned the water off, opened the bathroom door and started arranging her hair. Yalook pretty Regina. She continued combing her hair, humming and occasionally singing a line or two. Be a dear and get my brush in the bedroom. Harry moved from his spot, picked up the brush from the dresser, walked to the bathroom door and handed the brush to Regina. She grabbed it and started brushing. Harry stayed in the doorway watching. O Harry, for *heavens* sake, dont stand there like that. Go away. Go on. Go. Shoo. He backed away and sat on the couch, the couch he had sat on with her many times. I know what. You can take me to Stewarts for a seafood dinner. I adore the place and they have the most divine shrimp and lobster. She went to the bedroom and Harry got up and followed her. I dont have enough money for

Stewarts. What do you mean you dont have enough money. Go get some. And please dont hang over me like that. You bug me. Harry backed away and sat on the bed. I cant get anymore. I only got a few bucks. O dont be silly Harry. Of course you can get some more. Go get my kerchief from the bathroom. Harry got it. He stood behind her for a second then grabbed her and started kissing her neck. Regina squirmed and pushed him away. Don't be such a bore. Cant we stay here tanight. I/ll go get a couple a bottles a beer. O what are you talking about. We dont have ta go out. We could stay here, huh? O Harry sometimes you are just *too much*. I have no intention of staying here tonight or any night. Now will you please leave me alone. But I dont have enough money ta go out and Id like ta stay here and we could have a few beers and nobodyd botha us and I aint so hungry and anyway we could get some sandwiches and—O for gods sake will you please stop babbling like a baby. Im going out this evening. If you have money you can meet me at Marys, if not please do not annoy me any further. Now please leave so I can dress. But we dont have ta—she shoved him in front of her toward the door. *Really* Harry. You are getting hysterical. She opened the door and shoved him out into the hall. The door slammed shut. Harry stood for a long time, feeling a swelling behind his eyes—how long since he had felt it? It almost felt new yet he knew it was not— then left the building and rode the subway to Marys.

He stood by the door for a moment looking around then walked to the back and sat at a table. The others at the table spoke to him occasionally but Harry just nodded or grunted. He ordered a drink and when the others asked if he wasnt going to buy them one he told them he didnt have much money. They kidded him, but when they realized he was serious they ignored him and Harry sat nursing his drink and watching the door. Harry still had a few drops of melted ice in his glass when Regina finally arrived. She sat and dished with the girls for a few minutes then asked Harry if he was going to take her to Stewarts. Harry mumbled and stuttered and Regina jerked her head around and disdainfully told him to forget about it. She would get someone else to escort her. Why dontya have a drink and we could talk, caressing his glass with his finger tips and hunching over the table. Theres an empty booth in the back. We could be alone and talk. And just what would we discuss? High finance? sneering at Harry then looking at the other girls who giggled. Comeon Regina. O really, getting up with many shrugs of her shoulders and going to the phone booth. When she came back she looked down at Harry, you still here? How long are you going to sit there jerking that glass off? You know its really a terrible habit. Harry looked up at her then lowered his head, his hand tightening around the glass. Harry stayed at the table glancing at Regina from time to time, but Regina and the others ignored him completely and continued to talk among themselves until Regina stood up, adjusted her clothing, my date just arrived. I am sure you girls will excuse me, and walked to the bar. The fairies laughed and Harry stared at Regina until she left with her date. Harry looked at his empty glass for many minutes then left and rode the subway back to Brooklyn. It had been a long time since Harry had ridden the subway and it seemed to be exceptionally cold and stuffy and every turn and bump seemed to be directed against his comfort and he had to fight to keep himself on the seat and not be tossed up against the roof or thrown on the floor or against the opposite side. When he got out of the subway he took a cab the 2 blocks to the bar next to the strike office then regretted it when he paid the driver, debating whether or not to tip him, finally giving him a nickel. He sat at the bar and brooded for an hour over the 35¢ he spent for the cab. Whatever it was that happened happened too suddenly. He just couldnt figure it out. But things seemed to be all loused up again. He could have taken Regina to Stewarts. He still had a little money. They could have had a good time. He looked in his wallet. A couple of bucks. Fuckit. An hour later he called Regina. The phone rang and rang and he finally hung up and went back to the bar. An hour or so later he called again. Hello. Regina? Harry. Can I seeya tomorra night we could go ta Stewarts if yalike or som—O really Harry—we could go anywhere youd wanna I— O dont bother me. I am very busy. She hung up and Harry stared at the mouthpiece. Regina? Regina?

He let the phone drop from his hand and left the bar and staggered home. Mary was in bed and he stood over her. Slowly he started leaning toward the bed. The covers were held tightly around her neck with a hand. Her hair was spread over the pillow. Ya ballbreakin cunt. Ya hearme? Youre a ballbreakin cunt ya no good sonofabitch—Mary stirred then rolled over on her back and opened her eyes—Yeah, you bitch, grabbing an arm, twisting it and yanking her up to a sitting position, ya fuckin cunt. Whats the matta with you? ya gone crazy or somethin? trying to pull her arm loose. Yeah, I'm crazy, crazy fa lettin ya break my fuckin balls—the baby rolled over and started whimpering then crying. Ya better let me go or I/ll killya. Ya aint pushin me around ya drunken slob. Drunken slob, eh? I/ll showya. I/ll showya, twisting harder and slapping her face. Drunken slob, eh? howya like that, eh? howya likeit, twisting and shaking, slapping her face. YA FILTY BASTAD. I/LL KILLYA. YA CANT SLAP ME AROUND LIKE THAT, scratching his hand. YA LOUSY CUNT, IF IT WASNT FOR YOU ITD BE

DIFFERENT. ITS ALL YAFAULT—Mary bit his hand
and he let go of her arm shaking his hand and still yelling
—the baby banged against the side of the crib still crying.
Harry went out to the bathroom and Mary sat in bed yelling after him and cursing him then lay down and covered
her head with the pillow to drown out the noise of the kid
crying. Harry let water run on his hand then sat at the
kitchen table, rested his head on his arm and, still muttering, soon fell asleep. After a while the baby started to fall
into an exhausted sleep, still whimpering.

The men felt strange and uneasy the first day back on
the job. They had been on strike so long they almost got
lost trying to find their machines. The first day of the
strike was a warm spring day and the men had joked,
cleaned their cars, drunk beer . . . now there was snow
on the ground and it was a new year. It had been months
since they were even capable of hoping. The executives
and foremen were rushing about distributing jobs, getting
them set up, getting the proper tools and supplies to the
right places; and the men stood by their machines, waiting
until they had everything necessary to start a job, then
worked without enthusiasm, stopping occasionally as the
reality of being back on the job startled them.

              Harry
fumbled around his machine doing little, looking around
at the men rushing from one bench to another, one floor
to another, watching Wilson, thinking of Harrington, hearing the noise of the machinery, the piece of stock in his
lathe and the prints on his bench annoying him. The foreman set up the job for Harry and turned the lathe on.
Harry watched the thin spiraling strip of metal unwind
from the stock. He watched the fuckin stock spin and
the shavings twirl. He thought maybe he should take a
look around, make his rounds, but didnt feel like moving.

When one cut had been made on the stock he didnt reset the machine, but just stood there until the foreman came over, reset it and left. Eventually Harry left. He didnt turn his machine off or tell anyone he was leaving. He just turned, took a step, then continued walking.

He sat in the bar all afternoon drinking whisky; called Regina a few more times, but she either didnt answer or hung up when she heard his voice. Coulda been uptown. Ballbreakin-bastards.

He left the bar a little after 8. He leaned against the wall as he walked, unable to stand, slipping on the icy ground. He leaned against the window of the empty store that had been used as the strike office. He lit a few matches trying to see inside, but he still couldnt see anything. There was nothing to see anyway. He had already taken the radio home. It was once again an empty store with a for rent sign on the door.

He walked to the corner, slipping several times, finally having to crawl to the lamp-post to help himself stand. He clutched the post for a few minutes catching his breath. A kid, about 10 years old, from his block walked over to him and laughed. Youre drunk Mr. Black. Harry touched him on the head, then stuck his hand down under the large collar of the kids jacket and rubbed the back of his neck. It was very warm. Even slightly moist. The kid laughed again. Hey, your hands cold. Quit it. Harry smiled his smile and pulled him closer. Where yagoin Joey? Up the corner to see the fellas. Harrys hand was warm now and Joey stopped squirming. Howya like a soda. You buyin? Yeah. ok. They started slowly up 57th street, Harrys hand still on the back of Joeys neck. When they had walked a few feet Harry stopped. They stood still a second then Harry started walking into the empty lot. Hey, where

228

yagoin. Over there. Comeon, I wanna show yasomethin. What yawant ta show me? Comeon. They crossed the lot and went behind the large advertising sign. Whats here? Harry leaned against the billboard for a moment then lowered himself to his knees. Joey watched him, his hands in his jacket pockets. Harry reached up and opened Joeys fly and pulled out his cock. Hey, whatta yadoin, trying to back away. Harry clutched Joey by the legs and put Joeys small warm cock in his mouth, his head being tossed from side to side by Joeys atempts to free himself, but he clung to Joeys legs, keeping his cock in his mouth and muttering please . . . please. Joey pounded him on the head and tried to kick him with his knee. LETME GO! LETME GO YA FUCKIN FREAK! Harry felt the fists on his head, the cold ground under his knees; felt the legs squirming and his hands starting to cramp from holding them so tight; and felt the warm prick in his mouth and the spittle dribbling down his chin; and Joey continued to scream, squirm and pound his head until he finally broke loose and ran from the lot, still screaming, to the Greeks. When Joey broke loose Harry fell on his face, his eyes swelling and tears starting to ooze out and roll down his cheeks. He tried to stand but kept falling to his knees then flat on his face, still muttering please. A minute later Joey, Vinnie and Sal and the rest of the guys from the Greeks came running down 2nd avenue to the lot. Harry was almost standing, holding on to the billboard, when they reached him. THERE HE IS. THERE HEIS. THE SONOFABITCH TRIED TA SUCK ME OFF. Harry let go of the billboard and started to extend his arms when Vinnie hit him on the cheek. Ya fuckin freak. Someone else hit him on the back of the neck and Harry fell to the ground and they kicked and stomped him, Joey squeezing in between to kick him too, and Harry barely moved, barely made a sound beyond a whimpering. A couple of the guys picked him up and stretched his arms across and around one of the crossbars of the sign and hung on his arms with all their weight and strength until Harrys arms were straining at the shoulder sockets, threatening to snap, and they took turns punching his stomach and chest and face until both eyes were drowned with blood, then a few of the guys joined the two pulling on his arms and they all tugged until they heard a snap and then they twisted his arms behind him almost tying them in a knot and when they let go he continued to hang from the bar then slowly started to slide down and to one side until one arm jerked around the bar and flopped back and forth like a snapped twig held only by a thin piece of bark and his shoulder jerked up until it was almost on a level with the top of his head and the guys watched Harry Black as he slowly descended from the billboard, his arms flapping back and forth until his jacket got caught on a splinter and the other arm spun around and he hung, impaled, and they hit and kicked him until the splinter snapped and Harry descended to the ground.

Harry lay still, sobbing. He cried then screamed a long loud AAAAAAAAAAAAAAAA AAAAAAAAAAA that was muffled as his face fell back into the dirt of the lot.

He tried to raise his head but could not. He could only turn it slightly so he rested on a cheek. He was able to open his eyes slightly, but was blinded by the blood. He yelled again. He heard the sound loud inside his head, GOD O GOD

he yelled but no sound came from his mouth. He heard his voice loud in his head but only a slight gurgle came from his lips. GOD   GOD
YOU SUCK COCK
The moon neither noticed nor ignored Harry as he lay

at the foot of the billboard, but continued on its unalterable journey. The guys washed up in the Greeks, drying their hands with toilet paper and tossing the wet wads at each other, laughing. It was the first real kick since blowing up the trucks. The first good rumble since they dumped that doggy. They sprawled at the counter and at the tables and ordered coffeeand.

CODA

LANDSEND

How much less in them that dwell in houses of clay, whose foundation is in the dust, which are crushed before the moth?
They are destroyed from morning to evening: they perish for ever without any regarding it.
Doth not their excellency which is in them go away? they die, even without wisdom.

Job 4:19-21

MIKE KELLY TOLD HIS WIFE ta go tahell and rolled over, covering his head with the blanket. Comeon, gutup. We need milk and bread. He said nothing. Comeon Mike, I/ll be late for work. Still silent. Aw please get up Mike, sitting on the edge of the bed and gently pushing his shoulder. Wont yago to the store while I get dressed. Comeon. Mike turned over, knocking her hand from his shoulder, and leaned on his elbow. Look, go tawork and dont bother me, willya? turning back and falling on the bed, pulling the covers back over his head. Irene jerked up and noisily walked to the chair, yanked her clothing off it and started dressing. Youre a bastard Mike. Yahear me? a bastard, slamming down into the chair and putting her socks on. Get lost bitch before I break yahead. Irene continued to mumble as she dressed then stomped off to the bathroom and banged the door shut. Ya better stop the shit Irene or I/ll rapya. She faced the closed door and stuck her tongue out then turned both water faucets on quickly, the water splashing out of the basin. She jammed the stopper into the hole, still cursing Mike (the bastard), wrenched the faucets closed and threw the face cloth into the sink. She scrubbed her face, still muttering and Helen, her 3 year old daughter, knocked on the door. Irene jerked the door open. What do *you* want? Helen put her

thumb in her mouth and stared at her mother. Well? Have
to go peepee Mommy. Well, go ahead. Helen went to the
bathroom and Irene rinsed then dried her face. Im going
to be late. I just know it. She attacked her hair with a
brush and Arthur, almost 18 months old, started crying.
O godDAMNit. She threw the hair brush into the tub
(Helens thumb was still in her mouth and she waited until
Irene left the bathroom before sliding off the seat, flush-
ing the toilet and running into the living room) and raged
into the bedroom. The least yacan do is take care of the
baby. Mike jerked up and shouted for her to get thehell-
out and leave him alone. Youre his mother, you take care
of him. Irene stamped her foot and her face flushed.
If youd go out and get a job I could take care of him. He
pulled the covers back over his head. Don't bother me.
You bastard you. You—she yanked a jacket off a hanger,
Arthur still wailing for a bottle, Helen sitting in the
corner of the living room waiting for the argument to
stop. Irene thrust her arms into the sleeves of the jacket.
Give me some money for breakfast. He threw the covers
off and reached over to his pants and took a dollar out of
his wallet. Here. Now get thehell outtahere and stop
breakin my balls. She snatched the dollar from his hand
and stomped out of the apartment, hoping Arthur would
cry louder and make Mike get up, the bastard. Every
morning the same thing. Never gives me a hand. Wont
even fix the baby a bottle. I come home from work and *I*
have to fix supper and *I* have to wash the dishes and *I*
have to wash the clothes and *I* have to take care of the
kids!!! O, the dirty bastard!!!—rushing along the street
to the store. She went in, ignoring the clerks good morning
Irene, and picked up a dozen eggs then put them back and
took a half dozen as she needed cigarettes, a quart of
milk and 2 rolls. She took the cigarettes out of the bag
and put them in her pocket so she wouldn't forget them

and leave them for Mike (the bastard). When she got
back to the apartment she kicked open the door then
slammed it shut. Arthur was still crying, Helen standing
alongside the crib talking to him, and Mike yelled out ta
shut the kid up. Why dontya take care of the kid before
yago to the store, truly and honestly indignant at the
manner in which she neglected the children. If youre
so concerned why dontya get up and take care of him,
bastard? He sat up in bed and turned toward the open
door. Youd better watch your mouth or I/ll shove a fist
init, falling back on the bed and covering his head with
the blanket. Irene shook but all she could do was stamp
a foot, still holding the bag of groceries, and OOOOOO
OOOOOOOOOOOO . . . Then she noticed the time and
put the bag on the table, put on a pot of water, ran to
the kids room and grabbed Arthurs bottle, filled it with
milk, heated it enough to take the chill off; poured some
corn flakes and milk in a bowl while the bottle was
heating, rushed back to the crib with the bottle, Arthur
taking it and stopping his crying (Mike moaning a thank
krist); then Irene called Helen to eat her corn flakes and
made herself a cup of instant coffee, buttered a roll,
dunked it, ate it and rushed to the bedroom. Give me
some money. O for krists sake, you still here? Hurry
Mike. I/ll be late. He threw her half a dollar. Hey, how
about the change from the dollar? There isnt any (at least
she got an extra dime and a pack of cigarettes). Irene
gulped the last of her coffee and rushed out. She ran to
the bus stop hoping she wouldnt have to wait too long
and still cursing Mike, the bastard. If he doesnt clean the
house today I/ll quit the job. Thats what I/ll do. Let him
get a job. She saw a bus coming and ran faster, just getting
to the bus stop in time. The bastard.

* * * * * * *

Ada opened the window. The air was still and warm. She smiled and looked at the trees; the old ones, tall, big and strong; the young ones small, springy, hopeful; sunshine lighting the new leaves and buds. Even the budding leaves on the hedges and the young thin grass and dandelion sprouts were alive with sunshine. O, it is so lovely. And Ada praised god, the being and creator of the universe who brought forth the spring with the warmth of his sun. She leaned out the window, her favorite window. From it the factory and the empty lots and junkyards were not visible; she could see only the landscaping and the playground. And everything was coming to life and it was warm with sunshine. There were dozens of shades of green and now that spring was *really* here it would get greener and life would multiply on the earth and the birds would be more plentiful and their song would wake her in the mornings. All would be beautiful. She watched the birds hopping on the ground, flying to the tree limbs still thin but soon to be thick and heavy with green leaves. Yes, the first warm day of the year. She breathed deeply. Yes, it is warm. The first warm day of the year. There were a few other days when the sun had shone and the air had been warm, but there was always the last of the winter winds to chill it or rain to wet it. But not so today. The long winter was over. The long cold bitter winter when all you could do was walk to the store and back to the apartment . . . back to the apartment to sit and stare out the window and wait . . . wait for a day such as this. There were a few days—yes a few, not many—when she had been able to sit on the bench, but even though the winds were still and the sun bright she could only sit downstairs for a few minutes and then, though she had bundled herself well in sweaters, gloves, scarf, and coat and sat where the sun was shining brightest, a chill would seep through her clothing and she would

238

have to go upstairs. And even with the sun bright you couldnt really feel it, not *really* feel it as you should, as the sun is supposed to light your body and warm it through right to your heart. No, you could feel it only a little on your face. And, there was never anyone to talk to in the winter. No one came and sat. Not even for a few minutes. And too, the winters are so long. And lonely. All alone in her 3 rooms filled with furniture, the relics saved from the old days, sitting by the window watching the bare tree limbs shiver in the wind; the birds searching the frozen, bare ground; people walking with their backs turned to the wind and the whole world with their backs to her. In the winter everyones hate was bare if you looked. She saw hate in the icicles that hung from her window; she saw it in the dirty slush on the streets; she heard it in the hail that scratched her window and bit her face; she could see it in the lowered heads hurrying to warm homes . . . yes their heads were lowered away from Ada and Ada beat her breast and pulled her hair yelling to the Lord God Jehovah to have pity and be merciful and she scratched her face until her fingernails filled with flesh and blood dribbled down her cheeks, beating her head against her window until her head was bruised and small droplets of thin blood smeared with the moisture on her wailing wall, her arms still raised in supplication to Jehovah asking why she was being punished, begging mercy, asking why the people turned against her, beating her breast and begging mercy from her God who delivered the Tablets unto Moses and guided *his* children across the burning desert; the wrathful God who parted the Red Sea for the chosen people and drowned the pursuing armies in its turbulent waters; pleading with the revengeful God who delivered a pestilence unto the Pharaoh and the children of Israel when they turned their backs to *him* . . . O God have mercy . . . and Ada stood in front of her wailing wall looking at heaven through the frost covered glass smeared with her blood, praying to the Father as did the trees with their bared limbs raised to heaven; and she beat her breast and pulled her hair and tore the flesh from her cheeks and banged her head, and she would fall against her window weeping, sobbing, slowly sinking. sinking to her knees muttering . . . and Ada would lie on the floor sobbing, crying, bleeding . . . then, after a time, sleep. When she awoke she fasted for 24 hours, sitting among her relics, reciting ancient prayers aloud, rocking back and forth in her chair as she prayed. At the end of the 24 hours she fixed a cup of broth and stood in front of her window looking at the leafless trees and frozen earth, ignoring the concrete, the cars that passed, hearing only the voice of God and thinking only of the warm days to come. For 2 more days, 3 days in all, her face remained unwashed and she stayed within her apartment, drinking only 1 cup of broth each day, praying, looking out the window, walking through her rooms, back and forth. conscious of the stiffness of the dried wounds on her face. looking in the mirror at the scabs and gently touching them with the tips of her fingers. Then at the end of the third day she would wash her face and eat a meal and go to the store and buy the few things she needed, smiling at the people. asking the clerk how he was and telling him to keep well and take care.

But winter was over and now she could sit on a bench and feel the sun, watch the birds, the children playing, and perhaps someone would sit and talk with her.

*　　*　　*　　*　　*　　*　　*

Vinnie and Mary would still be unmarried if they hadnt met. But they finally did, when he was 40 and she was 35,

and were married and both families were joyous. As soon
as they were alone the first night Vinnie dragged Mary to
bed and pounced on her, shaking the bed, the chest of
drawers, the picture of the Blessed Mother over the bed,
until her stomach was so sore she couldnt move, but could
only lie on her back groaning and SCREAMING AT
HIM TO STOP. But Vinnie continued to bangaway,
slobbering at the mouth and YELLING THAT SHE
WAS HIS WIFE AND THEY CONTINUED TO
BOUNCE ON THE BED (the Blessed Mother shaking)
BANGING, BANGING, BANGING AND YELLING. 5
years later they had two kids and were still yelling. The
kids had been sitting up in the crib yelling for half an hour
before Vinnie and Mary got up. Mary rolled to the side
of the bed and YELLED TO THE KIDS TO SHAT-
UUUUUP WHATS THEMATTA? VINNIE SLAPPED
HER BACK AND TOLD HER TA FIX A BOTTLE
AND STOP YELLIN, then sat on the side of the bed
scratching his head. They both got up and stood facing
each other, scratching, THE KIDS STILL YELLING.
GO ON. FIX THE BOTTLE. IYAM. IYAM. WHATS
THE MATTA YOU GOTTA YELL! WHATTAYA-
MEAN YELL? FIX THE BOTTLE. AW SHATUP.
Mary stepped into her slippers and slopped out to the
kitchen and fixed the bottle, standing over the stove wait-
ing for it to heat, scratching her belly and armpits. She
went back to the bedroom to get dressed after giving the
baby the bottle, but when she took her nightgown off
Vinnie came over and slapped her tits back and forth.
DEY HANG TA YAKNEES. She pushed him away.
GOWAY STUPID. He reached down and pulled her
pubic hair, WHATTA BUSH. She shoved him away, YA
CRAZY. YA NO GOOD, and grabbed her clothes and
went to the bathroom to dress, closing and locking the
door. Vinnie dressed and went to see the kids. He looked

down at them and smiled and pinched their cheeks. YA DRINK THE BOTTLE, EH? THATS GOOD. They blinked, the baby continuing to suck on the nipple of his bottle. THATS A GOOD KIDS, pinching them again before leaving the room. HEY, HURRYUP, EH? I GOTTA GO THE BATHROOM. WHATTZAMATTA, YAIN A HURRY? SHADUP AND HURRY, YEAH? Vinnie paced up and down, going out to the kitchen, back to the kids room, then pounded on the bathroom door. COMEON, COMEON. HURRYUP, YEAH? WHATS YAHURRY? WAIT, slowly putting her clothes on then slowly filling the sink with water. Vinnie banged with both fists on the door. FA KRISTS SAKE OPEN THE DOOR. I GOTTA PISS. GAWAY. WHY DONT-YA DRESS IN THE BEDROOM? CAUSE YA BODDA ME. GOWAY, YEAH? Vinnie punched and kicked the door YA DIRTY BITCH. He turned from the door and started pacing again, holding his crotch, walking faster and faster, jumping up and down. I CANT WAIT. OPEN THE DOOR. GO WAY. He punched the door again. I/LL KILLYA WHEN YA COME OUT, turning once more from the door and going to the bedroom. He opened the window and urinated, the stream hitting the open window of the bedroom below, splashing off the open window and onto the baby in the crib. Mrs. Jones stared for a moment, then called her husband and told him about the water coming from upstairs and splashing on the baby. I/ll go see about it. It must be those crazy ones upstairs. Nobody elsed do that. He marched out of the apartment and up the stairs. Mary finally opened the door and walked slowly from the bathroom. IM FINISHED. GO ON. I TOUGHT YA WAS IN A HURRY GO AHEAD, PISS. Vinnie slapped her on the head. WHATZA-MATTA, YA CRAZY BITCH. YA STUPID A SOME-THIN? EH? She slapped him back. WHO YA THINK

YA HITTIN YA MOUNTIN WOP. He swung and missed and SCREAMED AT HER and Mr. Jones pounded on the door and Mary YELLED TO VINNIE TA SHADUUUUUUP and she opened the door and Mr. Jones wanted to know what was the idea of pouring water out the window, it went all over his baby, and Mary shrugged her shoulders and said WHAAAA? WHA WATTA? WHA YA TALKIN ABOUT? and Mr. Jones said you know what Im talking about, and the baby finished his bottle and threw it out of the crib and both kids started yellin again and MARY YELLED TO VINNIE TA SHAD THE KIDS UP AND VINNIE YELLED HE WAS GETTIN DRESSED, and Mary turned back to Mr. Jones when he tapped her on the shoulder and said, well? and she said WHAAA? AND YELLED AT THE KIDS TA SHADUUUUUP and Vinnie went to the kids room, WHATZAMATTA? WHY YA CRY, EH? and picked the kids up and Mary told Mr. Jones SHE DIDNT KNOW NOTHIN ABOUT NO WATTA OUT THE WINDOW and he threw his arms up in the air and Mary turned and told the kids JUST A MINUTE, YEAH? and Mr. Jones said dont let it happen again or hed get the cops and Mary shrugged and let the door close and the kids still YELLED AND VINNIE TOLD THEM TO BE QUIET. MARY, TAKE CAREA THE KIDS, YEAH? and she changed them and Vinnie went to the bathroom to wash and YELLED OUT TO MARY TA FIX BREAKFAST AND SHE SAID TA HOLD HIS WATTA and she finished with the kids and they ran back to their room to get some toys and Vinnie splashed water on his face and Mary SLAMMED THE COFFEE POT ON THE STOVE AND VINNIE CAME OUT AND POURED HIMSELF A GLASS OF JUICE AND SHE SAID HOW ABOUT ME? AND HE TOLD HER TA POUR HER OWN JUICE AND SHE SAID

TA FIX HIS OWN BREAKFAST AND HE SLAPPED
HER HEAD AND SHE KICKED HIS LEG AND HE
KICKED HER BACK AND TOLD HER TA FIX
BREAKFAST AND GET THE KIDS READY SO
THEY COULD GET SOME FRESH AIR AND SHE
SAID PISS ONYA AND BANGED A FRYING PAN
ON THE STOVE AND FRIED TWO EGGS FOR
HERSELF AND WHEN SHE FINISHED HE FRIED
HIS AND TOLD HER SHE BETTA FEED THE KIDS
OR HED THROWER OUT THE WINDA AND SHE
SAID DONT WORRY ABOUT IT, YEAH? AND HE
DUMPED HIS EGGS ONTO A PLATE AND
BANGED THE PLATE ON THE TABLE AND BOTH
KIDS WANTED THE SAME TOY AND THEY
TUGGED AT IT AND THEY SCREAMED AT EACH
OTHER AND CRIED AND MARY SAID SHAD-
UUUUUP AND VINNIE TOLD HER TASEE WHAT
WAS WRONG AND SLURRPED AN EGG INTO HIS
MOUTH AND MARY WENT INTO THEIR ROOM
AND TOOK THE TOY AWAY FROM THEM AND
TOLD THEM TA GO OUTSIDE AND SHE FIXED
THEM BREAKFAST AND VINNIE SAT IN THE
LIVING ROOM YELLING OUT TO MARY AND
MARY YELLED BACK AND EVERY NOW AND
THEN THE KIDS WOULD YELL AND THE BOTH
OF THEM WOULD YELL AT THE KIDS AND THE
KIDS WOULD YELL LOUDER AND VINNIE AND
MARY WOULD SCREAM AND FINALLY BREAK-
FAST WAS FINISHED AND EVERYONE CON-
TINUED TO YELL AS THE KIDS RAN TO THEIR
ROOM AND MARY STARTED WASHING THE
DISHES AND THE NEIGHBORS TURNED UP
THEIR RADIOS.

*   *   *   *   *   *   *

PROJECT NEWSLETTER
AIRMAIL

Throwing garbage out of windows is referred to as AIRMAIL. We do not want any AIRMAIL from this Project. There have been many complaints lately of garbage on the street, in the halls, and even a few cases of people being hit with garbage being thrown from windows. AIRMAIL is a violation of the Health Code and a violation of the Housing Authority Regulations. Any tenant f und guilty of throwing garbage from there windows will be immediately evicted. We want this Project to be a safe and clean place to live. It is up to you to keep it this way.

*   *   *   *   *   *   *

Lucy got out of bed slowly and went to the childrens room, changed and dressed Robert, her youngest son, took him out of the crib, then dressed Johnny. She told them to play quietly (she certainly wasnt going to allow her children to run around like indians), Daddys sleeping, and went to the kitchen to fix breakfast. She filled 3 glasses with juice and softly called the children. They came running out and she hushed them and told them to be quiet, nice little boys dont run around the house making a lot of noise. They drank their juice and went back to their room to play. A few minutes later they were yelling BANG, BANG and Lucy ran to their room and told them to hush. But we/re playing guns Mommy. Johnny, how many times have I told you that nice young boys dont play guns in the house. I dont know Mommy. Lucy looked at him for a second. Well, never mind, just be quiet. OK. Then see that you do, and Lucy went back to the kitchen listening for noise from the childrens room, relieved that the children were quiet and not acting like a bunch of roughnecks. She was just about to call them when someone knocked on the door. She adjusted her bathrobe, smoothed down her hair then opened the door. The nice young white girl from downstairs smiled at her. I think there may be something wrong in your bathroom Lucy. Water is leaking down through my ceiling. Lucy OOOOO/d and rushed to the bathroom. She opened the door and the children spun around, Johnny frantically trying to turn off the faucets. She glared at them, the water on the floor——Robert starting to whine and Johnny still turning the faucets and saying 'm sorry —the water still pouring over the sides of the basin. She reached over and slapped Johnnys hands off the faucets and turned off the water. Johnny started to cry and she opened her mouth to scold him when she remembered the girl was still at the door. She rushed back to the door and told her she was terribly sorry, the kids were playing and she hoped no damage had been done. Im really awfully sorry about this Jean. No, its alright. No harm done. They smiled at each other and the girl left. Lucy almost slammed the door, but caught it in time and closed it quietly not wanting the girl to think she was angry with her. She leaned against the door mortified. Of all the people in the Project it had to be that nice white girl. Such a nice quiet family and now she probably thinks we/re just like the rest. She rushed back to the bathroom. Johnny was still standing by the sink staring at the doorway, but Robert had left and gone to their room leaving wet foot prints. Lucy grabbed Johnny by the arm and dragged him from the bathroom. O youre going to get it. Dont you know better than to do a thing like that, DONT YOU? slapping him on the backside, still dragging him to his room. Johnny crying and yelling Im sorry Mommy. Youre

sorry. YOURE SORRY, slapping him again and pushing
him onto his bed. Johnny continued crying and pleading
—Robert standing in the corner afraid he too would be
spanked—and Lucy yelling at Johnny that he would be
punished for this . . . then she realized she was yelling
and perhaps the people downstairs could hear her, or
others may have heard her . . . she listened for a moment
and then quickly closed the door, telling Johnny to be
quiet. Her teeth were clenched and she snarled at him.
If youve wakened your daddy youll be sorry, shaking
with anger and frustration, exasperated by what had happened and with the fear that someone had heard her yelling. She listened to hear if Louis had awakened, but no
sound came from the bedroom. She turned back to
Johnny, who was trying to stop crying (we didnt make
any noise in the bathroom), but tears still rolled down
his cheeks and his breath was caught with sobs. Robert
started whimpering and Lucy told him to hush, her voice
quieter and more controlled. Johnny could see that the
worst was over, so he started to control his sobbing. still
looking pleadingly at his mother. I-Im su?su-sorry Mom-
Mommy. Just be quiet and calm down and—THE OAT-
MEAL! She rushed to the kitchen and snatched the pot
off the stove. O thank goodness its not ruined. She put the
oatmeal on the childrens plates and called them. They
sat quietly at the table and started eating. Lucy went back
to her now cold cup of coffee. She poured another cup
and sat at the table with the children. She could hear
Vinnie and Mary screaming at each other. Lucy shook her
head and cursed the Project. She finished her coffee then
remembered the water on the bathroom floor and grabbed
the mop from the closet and rushed to the bathroom
and mopped the floor. just waiting for Johnny to make
a sound and she would give it to him good. She wrung out
the mop, put it away and sat back at the table. Johnny had

finished his cereal and sat quietly looking at his Mother as she fed Robert then cleared the table. She told the children to go to their room and play quietly then went to the bedroom and dressed. After dressing she got the clothes ready for the laundromat. She washed, then brushed her hair, put the laundry in the laundry cart and hustled the children from the apartment. She hurried to the elevator, opened the door and was about to step in when she noticed a pile (actually noticing the smell first) of human shit on the elevator floor. Again! She stopped and grabbed Robert as he was about to step in it, then quickly turned away before someone saw her there. Picking up Robert she started down the stairs (O God, now I/ll have to walk up two flights of stairs with the cart). Lucy flushed with embarrassment, wanting to get as far away from the elevator as possible before someone else opened the door, Johnny yelling at his Mother to wait for him. Lucy waited for Johnny at the door (already convincing herself that a spick had done it) then rushed from the building, Johnny running to keep up.

*   *   *   *   *   *   *

Abraham got up late. He stayed in bed as long as he could, but the noise the 5 kids made was too much for him. Even the closed door didnt help so he got up. He sat on the side of the bed and carefully took the hairnet off his konked and marcelled hair, lit a cigarette and started thinking about the fine, I mean *real* fine brownskinned gal that was in MELS last night. Her skin was light and real smooth and her hair was long and wavy. Not all tight and stiff, but smooth man, and long. Yeah . . . And she had on this real tight dress and when she walked her big ol ass just quivered and shook like crazy and when she danced the slop you could see the muscles of that fine

ass just rollin all ovuh. Yeah . . . that was some fine stuff.
Man, he shuh would like to bag that bitch and really lay it
oner. Sheeeit . . . Id fuck the ass right offen that bitch
man, I mean right *off*. Man, when I finish screwin that ol
broad she/d know she/d been laid and she/d damn sure
know who tu call daddyo. Ghuddamn . . . I/ll put on some
fine rags tunight and make all those cats look like bums
man. I mean this stud is gonna be the sharpest motherfucka that chick ever seed. Sheeit. This is ol Abe. Ol
honest Abe Washington, hehhehheh . . . and aint nobody,
man I mean nobody caint put no shit ovuh on *me*. This
cats hip man, and when I lay it on that chick I mean shes
gonna knowit . . . Yeah . . . He stood up and stretched,
put out his cigarette and dressed. He opened the bedroom
door and yelled to the kids tu shut up as he walked to
the bathroom. They quieted for a moment then continued
running, yelling and shooting. Abe worked the soap up to
a lather then worked the lather thoroughly into his face,
rinsing first with warm water then cold. He patted his
face dry with the towel then inspected his face in the mirror, going over every square centimeter very carefully,
pushing his nose first to one side then the other, stretching
the skin of his neck. After 5 minutes he was happy to find
only one pimple. This he carefully squeezed then wet the
corner of the towel with cold water and patted the infected
area. He brushed his teeth which were naturally white,
but he had to be certain he got off the yellow smoking
stains. Than he gargled. Next he rubbed skin cream into
his face—leaning out of the door to yell at the Ghuddamn kids tu shut up—then inspected his face once
more. He was satisfied. He rubbed some hair grease between the palms of his hands then patted it on his hair.
Then he picked up the comb and gently, tentatively at
first, combed his hair, laying down the comb from time to
time and using the soft brush, pushing each wave in place,

touching here and there, working up this wave a little more than the other, being careful a hair wasnt sticking up or out of place—why dont chuall shutup—stepping back from the mirror to admire the way his hair sparkled, adjusting a wave a little more, then picking up the small hand mirror and turning his back to the large mirror over the sink and holding the small mirror in front of him he inspected the back of his head, pushing a little here and there, then, smiling and thinking of her fine ass, wiped his hands off on the towel and went out to the kitchen. He told his wife to fix him some eggs and sat down and cleaned his nails, scraping the funk off on the edge of the table He filed away at his nails and asked his wife why she didnt get the kids dressed and send them out. They make too ghuddamn much noise runnin all ovuh. She told him she was too busy to fret about the kids. The kids had stopped for a moment again, but started running and shooting and one stepped on Abes foot and he yelled and swung his arm. The kid darted away, but knocked into his mother as she was taking the eggs from the refrigerator. She put the eggs down and yelled that she was gonna get a strap toem and then maybe theyd stop runnin around like crazy mens. The kid started whimpering that he was sorry and she took the strap from around her waist and waved it at him and he cringed and backed away until his mother relented, then he sat quietly and his sister, the oldest, scolded him for being naughty and he wanted to kick her like he usually did, but was afraid. Hed wait until they got outside. Abe wanted to know what was holdin up his eggs, he had some things to do today. She brought the eggs and he ate, Nancy telling him about how the doctor at the clinic say the kids got the maltrition and they giver some cod*liver*oil, but he say they should have some vitamins and Abe dipped his bread in the yoke and caught the yoke with his tongue as it dribbled from the bread and tolder not tu wurry him about no vitamins and she say she need some money forem and he tolder he giver 20 dollars every week and she can get the vitamins with that. But ah caint. He shrugged and tolder to givem more collard greens and he slopped up the stringy uncooked white of the egg with his bread and tolder to givem his coffee and she poured it and said Ghuddamnit, I need some more money and he said sheeit, he worked his ass off on the docks fur his money and he be Ghuddamned if hed let her throw it away, and the kids still sat in silence waiting for the father to go so they could be dressed and get out where it was safe, and Nancy cursed Abes black ass and he tolder tu shut up those blubber lips and he counted out 20 dollars and threw it on the table and said she was lucky to have all that, that he had a whole mess a bills tu pay and all she had tu do was buy food and Ghuddamnit if yu caint buy enough with that and the Ghuddamn vitamins then shame onyu. She snatched the money off the table and yelled at the kids to get dressed and get the hell out and the two older boys scampered to their room, the daughter saying, yes Mommy and walking; and Abe gulped down his coffee and left the kitchen. He put on a jacket, inspected his face and hair once more, adjusting the frontmost wave, then left the house.

* * * * * * *

THE CHASE

A group of kids, about 5 and 6 years old, stood on the steps of the entrance to one of the buildings. Another group stood huddled about a hundred feet away. The 2 groups eyed each other, spitting, cursing, staring. Some of the kids on the steps wanted to get the mothafuckas now and killem, the others wanted to wait for Jimmy. Jimmy was the biggest guy they had. When he come we/ll get the bastards. He run fasteran any ofem. Sheeit man, we/ll catchem all and killem. Yeah man, we/ll burn the mothafuckas alive. They paced on the steps impatiently, spitting and glaring at the other group. Then they heard someone running down the stairs and Jimmy came out. Jimmy yelled to them and took out a gun and said, come-on, lets kill those fuckinbastards. They all screeched wildly and followed Jimmy as he ran at the other gang. They screeched too and started running. The game of cowboys and indians had started. They ran along the streets shooting, yelling, bang, bang, yur dead mother-fucka. I gotya. Yo aiss yo did. I gotya. Bang. Bang. In, out and between the people walking, standing, sitting on the benches; running around the trees, bang, bang, look-ing behind and shooting at the pursuer; knocking into someone and spinning him around—Why dontya look where ya goin ya stupid bastard—or if they were small they simply knocked them down the pursuer jumping over the fallen kid who was now crying and yelling for his mommy. Bang, bang, through the hedges and spin-ning around the young trees; knocking over the shrubs, bang, bang. Jimmy got one cornered by the steps. He stood just in front of Jimmy on the other side of a baby carriage. The kid feinted to one side then the other. Finally Jimmy committed himself to one side and the kid whirled around the opposite side pulling over the car-riage, the baby falling out and rolling along the ground, stopping as it hit the hedge. The 2 kids looked at it for a moment, listening to it scream, then a head popped out a window and wanted to know what the fuck they was doin, and the kids hauledass and Jimmy ran through the hedge after the other kid, bang, bang, and they ran around the building out of sight. The game of cowboys and indians continued.

*   *   *   *   *   *   *

Ada hummed as she washed the dishes. She scoured the sink then made her bed, first opening the windows so the bed clothes should air out, then carefully tucking in the sheets and blanket, fluffing up the pillows (Hymie always liked his pillow thick and fluffy), then hanging up her nightgown and the pajamas she laid out on Hymies side of the bed each night. (Hymie had always liked a clean pair of pajamas every night and though he had been dead these 5 years, 6 in October, October the 23rd, she still laid out a pair of pajamas every night, though now she used the same pair each night, washing them once a month, ironing them and putting them back on the bed.) Then she tidied up the apartment, sweeping the kitchen floor and adjusting the furniture, before wiping the dishes and putting them away with the other dairy dishes. The humming evolved into light singing as she put on her sweater and coat and readied herself to go downstairs. She looked around the apartment, making certain the stove was off and all the lights out, before closing the door and going out. Near the entrance to the building was a small area bordered with benches and a few young trees. Here Ada sat whenever the weather permitted. She sat on a bench on the near side as she knew it would be in the sun longer than any of the others. This was *her* bench and here she sat and watched the children, the people passing or sitting, and enjoying the warmth of the sunshine. She closed her eyes and faced the sun, lifting her face, and sat thus for many minutes feeling the heat on her forehead, her eyelids, her cheeks, feeling the suns rays penetrating her chest, warming her heart, making her feel almost happy. She breathed deeply, sighing inaudibly, and lowered her head and opened her eyes, then raised her feet slightly and wiggled her toes in her shoes. Her poor feet had such a burden to carry and they suffered so in the winter, but now even they were alive and relieved. It would be many, many wonderfully warm and sunny months before her feet would have to be tortured with thick heavy socks and forced to feel the cold. Soon she could go one day to Coney Island and sit on the Boardwalk and watch the swimmers or maybe she could even walk in the surf, but she wasnt sure if she should. She might slip, or someone might knock her over. Anyway, the beach was nice even just sitting on a bench getting the sun. She watched a small child ride by on his tricycle then watched a group of children running after each other and yelling. Occasionally she would be able to distinguish the words they were yelling and she blushed and immediately pushed it from her mind (this too would be remembered next winter) then turned abruptly as she heard a baby crying, seeing the overturned carriage, hearing the voice from a window, seeing a blur as 2 children ran away; trying to locate the baby, getting up from the bench when she saw a woman coming out of the building. Those children really should be more careful. She watched the mother pick up the child and drop him in the carriage and shove a bottle in his mouth and go upstairs. I hope it wasnt hurt. The baby eventually stopped crying and Ada turned away and once more watched the child circling the benches on its tricycle. She saw a woman passing with her children and shopping cart. The woman smiled, nodded and said Hello. Ada returned her greeting but didnt smile. She was a nice lady but her husband was a no good. He always looked at Ada funny like he was going to hurt her. Not like her Hymie. Her Hymie was always friendly. Such a good man. They would have been married 43 years this summer, July 29th, if he was still alive. Hymie used to help her all the time. And he too loved the beach. But so seldom they could go. Only on Mondays when they closed the store and then sometimes it wouldnt be so nice. But many times they would go and she would make sandwiches and a thermos of a cold drink and Hymie always got for her a beach chair and umbrella. He always insisted. I want you should be comfortable and enjoy yourself. Thats what he said. She would always say no, dont bother. Who needs it? and they would laugh. But always Hymie insisted she should have the umbrella in case she might want to sit in the shade, but she never did and they would sit on the beach chairs getting the sun and once, maybe twice, during the day they would go down to the surf and splash around. He was so good her Hymie. And sometimes when her Ira got older he would tell them to go to the beach, he would mind the store and they would go an extra day to the beach. Her Ira was the best boy any Mother could have. (Everynight before going to bed she kissed their pictures.) Still only a boy already when they killed him. Just a boy. Not even married. Not even married when the Army took him. And he was such a good boy. When he was still just a little one he would come home from school and tell her to take a nap, hed help papa in the store and Hymie would smile so big and rub little Iras head and say yes, take a nap, Iras a big boy now and he will help me and Ira would smile up at his father and Ada would go back to the small rooms behind the candy store and lie down. And sometimes, when maybe it wasnt too busy, Hymie would fix the supper while Ira watched the store and then Ira would come back and wake her up and say suppers ready Mommy. See? And everything would be on the table and they would eat and she would go out and take care of the store while Hymie ate. And Hymie worked so hard. Opening the store at 6 in the morning and going out and getting the papers off the street. and sometimes it would be cold and raining, and he would carry in the big bundles of papers all by himself (he would never let her help him with that) and cut the cords and arrange them on the stand and she would lie in bed, pretending to be asleep, and all the years they were married Hymie got out of bed so quietly so she should sleeplonger and every morning she would wake up but she never let him know she was awake so he wouldnt worry about her. Then he would come back at 8 oclock and she would pretend to wake up when he touched her, and she would get up and fx the breakfast. For 20 years they had that store and they were so happy—the child ran his tricycle into a tree and toppled off, but got right up and started riding again— maybe they didnt always have so much, but they were happy and she could still smell the soda fountain; the sweet smell of ice cream. syrups mixed fruits, hot fudge, marshmallow, whipped cream and the fudgicles, popsicles and ices and the candy and chewing gum on the counter and the candy shelves on the opposite side of the store, the sliding glass doors smeared by the smudgy hands of thousands of children. She used to lean on the counter and watch them look at the candies pointing with their fingers pressed against the glass. Many times each day this would happen and Ada would wonder why they had to lean against the glass with their hands and why it took them so long to make up their minds what candy they wanted. And then when Ira came, late in her life, it didnt annoy her as much. They were young like her Ira. But when they get older they werent so nice and said bad things to you. But Ira was always such a good boy. And they had to kill him. And they didnt even see his body. Just a telegram and many years later a sealed coffin. My

poor Ira. So young. Not even a father and now dead.
Dead already 15 years—a few other children joined the
one with the tricycle and they took turns riding it, laughing and running around in circles. Ada smiled as she
watched them. Dead 15 years and not even children to
remember you. I dont know why they did this to me.
Even dead before Hymie, his father. And even Hymie
left me. Such a good man. Worked so hard his back bent
—someone passed and Ada smiled, but they just walked
past not noticing Ada and Ada almost yelled at them, but
stopped as she noticed that now women were coming
down and people were going to the store and children
were running and laughing and the sun was getting
brighter and warmer and a few men straddled a bench
with a checker board between them and maybe someone
would sit down next to her and they would talk.

* * * * * * *

WOMENS CHORUS I

The housewives were on a bench. They looked at Ada
and laughed. Everything comes out in this weather. Even
Ada. I guess shes airing out her clothes. Laughter. Same
shitty coat. She wears it all winter. Why dont she take it
off? She got nothin on underneath. Whattaya mean? I
bet shes wearing scabs. Laughter. Shes a filthy slob. I bet
even the fumigator is afraid to go up her house. I bet
her crotch smells like limburger cheese. Laughter. (One
picked her nose, exploring each nostril first with the
pinky, locating the choice deposits, then with the forefinger broke loose the nights accumulations, scraping with
the thumb and plucking forth, with thumb and forefinger,
a choice meaty snot, long and green, spotted with yellows,
waving it about, then rolling it in a ball, caressing it be-

tween her fingers, trying to flip it off but it clung tenaciously, adhesively to the finger until it was finally rubbed off on the bench.) And that fuckin Lucy. I saw her goin to the laundromat with another bunch of clothes. Aaaaa, who the fuck she thinks she is. Always washin clothes. Yeah, whos she tryin ta kid. You know her husbands goin ta school. Yeah. I guess he thinks hes gonna be somethin. Maybe hes gonna learn ta be a pimp. What for. Aint nobody gonna want ta fuck Lucy. I bet she thinks its ta piss through. Me, I wash my clothes when they need it, but I dont act like that. (One lifted a cheek of her ass, let go a loud gurgling fart and sighed.) Laughter. Looka Ada smilin. I think shes nuts the way she smiles all the time like that. She is. Shes got people talkin to/er in her head. Somebody oughtta call up Kings County and turner in. Laughter. Yeah, it aint safe with nuts runnin around. All she needs is a good fuckin. Maybe I should send Henry ova, hed do a good job. Laughter. I bet shes got money put away somewhere. You know those kind. Yeah. Her husband was in business for himself and you cant tell me shes gotta go on Relief. Look atter sittin alone and smilin. If I had her money you wouldnt catch me sittin here. (A scab is picked off a leg, examined from various angles then flicked away.)

*　　*　　*　　*　　*　　*　　*

PROJECT NEWSLETTER

It has been brought to the attention of the Management of this Project that certain Adolescent children are taking money from younger children, threatening to beat them up if they do not give up the money they have. They are also stopping the smaller children on there way to the store with deposit bottles and taking them away from them along with any money they might have. Any child caught taking money from younger children will be handed over to the Police Department for prosecution and the families of the children will be immediately evicted. The management recommends that mothers refrain from sending young children to the store with money or deposit bottles. We want this Project to be a safe place for everyone to live. It is up to everyone to cooperate.

*   *   *   *   *   *   *

Mike finally got up. The babys crying was faint, but he knew that as soon as he opened the door the crying would be louder and Helen would come over to him and bother him about something wanting to eat or get dressed or ask some damn stupid questions. He got dressed and sat back on the edge of the bed and smoked a cigarette, then stretched out on the bed hoping he would feel sleepy. He covered his eyes with his arm, but it didnt help. He put out the cigarette and rolled over on his side—Helen heard the movement and turned from the window, where she had been watching the kids, and waited for the door to open—but he just didnt feel tired. Still he lay there hoping he might drowse off and maybe sleep for a few more hours. At least there would be that much more time passed. I wonder what time it is? Cant be 12 yet, didnt hear the whistle. If the kids would just shut up maybe I could get ta sleep. But the sun was bright and even with the shade drawn there was plenty of light in the room and goddamnit, he might just as well get up. Might just as well. He rolled back to the edge of the bed and slowly stood. The goddamn kid was probably wet. Krist can he make noise. He went to the window and peered out, keeping the shade down. Most of the windows of the apartments were open and he looked in each one, not shifting to the next one until he was fully accustomed to the changes of light and was certain there was nothing to be seen. Once he had seen a woman, not a bad lookin head either, leaning out the window, talking to someone downstairs, and one of her tits fell out of her robe. She didnt know he was watching so she didnt hurry to stick it back. And it was a good size tit too. Things like that might happen anytime, especially when the weather was warm. That was a good day. He had felt good the whole day. It was almost as good as gettin a strange piece. He had a gigantic hardon all day and when Irene came home from work he walked her right into the bedroom and they fucked like crazy. He had her sit on it and her tits stuck way out and he buried his face in them and all the time Irene wiggled her ass and Krist did his cock twitch. Yeah, that was some day. He wished ta Krist somethin like that would happen again. A couple a times hed seen a nigga bitch walkin around with her tits hangin out, but that was different. It gotim horny, but not the way it did when he saw a white broads tits with big rosy nipples. Thats what he needed. A strange piece. Been a long time since he fucked anybody but Irene . . . Except, of course, for a couplea gangbangs at beer rackets, but that was different. Its not like really makin a broad. Its not that Irene aint a good piece—shes built real nice and got a great pair of tits—but he was gettin tired of the same old shit all the time. And lately she/d been breakin his balls about getting a job again. Fuck her. Why should he work? He dont get nothin outta it. Why should he get up in the mornin and break his balls? They was doin alright like this with Irene workin.—The baby was still crying, but he was completely accustomed to the noise now and with his mind preoccupied he didnt hear him. He continued looking carefully into each window. A young jew girl lived across from him and he watched her window for a long time. She had a nice pair of boobs and hed like ta catch her sometime. If only he could see in the bathroom window and watch her come outta the tub, man that would be somethin. Nice young stuff. Shit. Shes probably outta the house by now. He passed on to the next window. Why in the hell should I work? Break yaballs for what? Ya dont get nothin anyway. Shit. Almost 26 and whatave I got? Nothin. Why should I break my balls for some jew for a lousy couple a bucks a week and they get all the gravy. Fuckem. If I had a couple a bucks I could see somea the boys tonight and maybe we/d pick somethin up. Thats what I need ta straighten me out. Been feelin kindda crummy lately. Need ta go out with the boys is all. If I dont wanna work its my business. He finished making the rounds of the windows, but went over them again, quickly, but still there was nothing to be seen. Balls. He left the room. He ignored the now loud crying of the baby and went out to the kitchen, Helen walking behind him. I hope ta Krist Irene made a good pot of coffee this morning. He looked at the jar of instant coffee on the table and cursed Irenes lazy ass for not making a pot of coffee. He heated some water and made a cup of coffee, shaking his head yes, no, at Helen who hadnt stopped talking since he came out, agreeing, disagreeing, telling her ok, wait a minute; not today, maybe tomorrow. He lit a cigarette, turned on the radio—Helen still talking—and finally told Helen to stop bothering him. I want to go out Daddy. OK, OK, let me finish my coffee, willya? He drank his coffee and smoked a cigarette then started to dress her, tearing clothes out of drawers, looking for an undershirt and, where the hell areya pants, cursing Irene for not laying out the kids clothes before she left. How inthehell did she expect him ta know where she

kept everything and all the time Arthur was crying and
Helen stood away, her thumb in her mouth, and Mike
was goddamn mad because there was no reason why the
things couldnt be where he could find them and why
the hell didnt she dress the kid before she left and he
finally said the hell with it and Helen started crying and
he yelled to shut up and shoved her in her room. He
made himself another cup of coffee and lit another cigarette, trying to ignore Arthur, but he couldnt and knew
that sooner or later he would have to change him just as
he knew each morning when he awoke that eventually he
would have to get up and he would reach this same point
when he could no longer ignore the yellin brat and hed
have ta change the pissy diaper. Krist, how he hated ta
change the kid in the morning. He didnt mind so much
in the afternoon, the other time he changed him (when
he did), but in the morning it was disgusting. The goddamn diaper was soaked with piss and they stunk like
hell. And usually there was a pile of shit and it was
smeared all over the kids ass. He finished the coffee and
cigarette, but didnt move from the table. Maybe he should
go out and get a few bottles of beer first. Yeah, that was
a good idea. He bought a few quarts of beer and came
back feeling better. He poured a glass and went into the
kids room, looked at Arthur, why doya have ta make so
goddamn much noise. Krist, ya stink. He yanked the
rubber diaper off, then carefully took out the pins and
turned his head slightly as he slowly pulled the diaper
off. O Jesus, what a fuckin mess! He clamped his teeth
together and was so goddamn mad he wanted to slap the
kid. Arthur finally stopped crying as the wet diaper was
removed and Mike looked at him and told him hed better
shut up or hed wrap the diaper around his goddamn head.
He dumped the shit in the toilet bowl and dropped the
diaper in a bucket. The bucket was filled with dirty

diapers and he cursed Irene for not cleaning them yesterday like he told her. She knows she should wash diapers
everyday, the sonofabitch. Shit. He went back to Arthur,
put a clean diaper on him, pulled up the rubber pants,
tnen dropped a few toys in the crib before going back
to the kitchen and his beer. At least that much was over
and now he could at least sit and have a beer and listen
to the radio and maybe think of something to do.

*   *   *   *   *   *   *

The laundromat was crowded and Lucy sat on a bench
waiting. She sat the children beside her and told them to
sit still, but Robert started kicking his feet and Johnny
was sliding off the bench, Lucy grabbing his arm and pulling him back and telling him to sit still and be quiet. I
dont want you running around like those other kids. Lucy
glanced at the machines that had been assigned her by
the woman in charge, trying to determine how much
longer it would be before she could use them. She wished
she had a magazine to look at to pass the time, but if she
did she knew she wouldnt be able to concentrate because
Johnny was sure to play with some other kid if she didnt
watch him. She pulled him back to the bench and told
Robert to keep his legs still. O, how she hated waiting in
this place. Nothing to do but sit, and listen to those stupid
women giggling and talking to each other and hehehehe-
heing all over the place. Always laughing. O, she hated
this place. Johnny had slid down again and was standing
leaning against the bench watching his Mother to see if
she would pull him back. She checked the machines again.
Wont be too much longer. Johnny took a step—she hadnt
done anything yet and maybe he could walk around now.
Lucy pulled him back by the arm and sat him down. He
would have to wait. Finally the machines stopped and the

woman took her clothes out, Lucy eyeing them. They were still a little dingy. She got her clothes ready for the machines. Johnny, who had slid down again from the bench, was moping around. Robert watched his brother for a moment, then he too slid down and stood, holding on to the bench. Lucy put the soap in the machines, then added just a little more. Finished, she turned away from the machines and saw Robert pick something up from the floor and quickly took it from him, then looked around for Johnny as she put Robert back on the bench. He was playing with a little boy at the other end of the laundromat and Lucy almost yelled, but controlled herself and calmly walked over to get him. Johnny was playing with a spick boy wearing dirty dungarees and filthy ripped sneakers. Lucy wanted to yank Johnny away, but she calmly took his hand and took him back to where they were sitting. Johnny whined and wanted to know why he couldnt play with the other kid and Lucy told him that he must sit down, that he might get hurt by one of the washing machines. Johnny argued, but Lucy was firm. She smiled at him and told him to sit quietly. Then she looked at her machines and frowned as she saw that suds were above the indicated level and were actually visible on the edge of the funnel on the top of the machine where the soap was poured in. She stared at the rising mound of suds, her hand still on Johnnys leg, and watched it foam over the sides and run down the sides of the machine. She didnt know what to do and was too embarrassed to call the woman who worked there. The suds continued to billow over and a stream of water ran down between the machines. Finally someone called it to the attention of the woman and she came over, tinkered with something in the rear of the machines and the suds went down and then she asked who had the machine. Lucy got up and started apologizing and the woman told her she should be careful of how much soap powder she put in the machine then told her where she could find the mop. Lucy got it and wiped up the water self-consciously avoiding everyones eyes. She replaced the mop and started feeling a resentment and at the same time incapable of keeping from wondering if the woman thought she was no better than the spick at the other end. She went back to the bench and saw that Johnny was not there, but had once again gone to play with the little boy. She yelled at him roughly and Johnny came running and jumped up on the bench, not daring to look at her (remembering the morning), but knowing she was glaring at him. The children sat still and Lucy said nothing, but stared at the machines, burning with embarrassment and resentment. The machines finally stopped and she told the children to sit right there and she emptied the machines then sat back on the bench and waited to used the extractor. While she waited a woman came in with a cart of clothes and asked if she could use the extractor, the one in her laundromat across the way broke down. The woman in charge told her she would have to wait until all *her* people were finished, that she couldnt let people from other buildings come in here and use her extractor until her people were finished and she didnt know if theyd be finished in time, it was getting late and there were a awful lot of people waiting and she had to close soon. The woman was annoyed at having waited for an hour in the other laundromat and then the ghuddamn thing went and broke down and she was ghuddamned if shed take any lip from anybudy. She said she just wanted to use the *extractor* and she/d wait ghuddamnit, but she was gonna use it and she didnt want no argument, glaring at the whitewoman and ghuddamn mad at her for talking like that at her. Well, youll just wait until all my people are finished and *if* theres still time you can use it and dont be so damn snotty. Look, ah didnt come here to take any of yo shit, ahm just gonna use the *ex*tractor and thats all, yo hear? The woman wanted to tell her to get her black ass the hell outta her laundromat, but she didnt dare. She turned her back on her, suddenly deciding to help a woman (colored) take her clothes out of the machine, then told the intruder (the nigga bastard) that this laundromat was only for the people in this building, and anyway, the woman in the other laundromat never lets any of my people use her extractor. The other woman walked over to her and told her not to give her any of her shit, that if she wanted to use the mothafuckan *ex*tractor that she/d use it ghuddamn it. The operator stood straight, put her hands on her hips and beamed. You can just get the hell outta here sister. We have ladies here who arent used to that kind of language (you filthy nigga whore). Dont chuall tell me what to do mothafucka. This heres for usall to use an ghuddamnit Im gonna use this mothafucka if ah gotta break yo fuckin haid. Dont you swear at me you sonofa(black)bitchen scum—Lucy grabbed Robert and the cart, and rushed from the laundromat, up the ramp and out into the air, rushing from the laundromat as she did from the elevator, Johnny running to keep up with her.

* * * * * * *

Abraham opened the door of his bigass Cadillac and looked smugly around at the people sitting, the people passing and the people washing their cars, children running back and forth with clean buckets of water, before getting in and closing the door with a flourish. He stretched his legs, pushing back against the seat, and smiled. It was his. Ghuddamn right. All his. He looked at the dashboard with all its knobs and patted it. Every

ghuddamn hunk of chrome belonged to him, Abe. He
started the motor and let it idle, then turned on the radio
and opened the window on his side. He tuned in the
station he wanted, tapping his foot as a sax screeched and
wailed, took a cigarette out of the pack, placed it slowly
and carefully between his lips, pushed in the dashboard
lighter, leaned back, still tapping his foot and smiling,
until the lighter popped out then pulled it from the socket
and lit his cigarette, blowing the smoke at the windshield,
watching it drift out the window. He looked again at the
poor studs washing their cars by hand and sneered. You
didnt catch this cat washing his own car. Not ol Abe. He
rested his elbow on the door, stretched his legs again and
adjusted his genitals (I/ll fuck the lightskinned ass
ofener). Ol Abe always felt relaxed and great in his
Cadillac and today he felt betteranever. Ghuddamn if
this wasnt a real fine day and he looked at the back seat,
at the floor (seems to be a little messy, but the boys
always clean it out after theys finished washin), rubbed
his hand along the fine upholstery, patted the dashboard
again (ghuddamn if it didnt shine like a babys ass),
turned up the radio and once more dug the cats washin
their cars with buckets of water, soap and sponges. Ghuddamn if it dont look like every ass in the Projects is out
today washing his car. Thats not fo me. Ah *pays* to have
that shit done. Ah, it was great, real great man, to just
sit and dig the radio and smell the car, that special
CADILLAC smell and not have those ghuddamn house-
rats arunnin all ovuhya, and that ghuddamn bitch yellin.
Abe inhaled deeply and flipped his cigarette out the window. Betta get mah ass movin. He threw the car into
reverse and backed out, made a screeching u-turn (haha,
looka those cats diggin me) and drove to Blackies garage.
He stepped forth from his Cadillac and Blackie came over
to greet him. How yodoin man? Great Blackie. Hows mah

man? OK pops. Want the usual job? Youknow me, ah knows how to treat a Cadillac. Ahll be back afta awhile for it. Abe strolled down the block to the barber shop and when he opened the door everyone greeted him and he smiled and walked to a vacant seat, beaming at everyone and waving his hand. his popularity making him feel great, real great cause everyone knew he was a great guy, a real swingin cat. and everyone dug him the most. As soon as he sat down the bootblack came over and started shining his shoes. He wisht that chick could see him now and how everyone knew he was a great guy, but she/d know that tonight. Man, would she know it. She/d know she wasnt messin with no farm boy fresh from the south, but Ol Abe, and he was one stud who really knew the score (caressing his genitals) and she/d damn sure know it soon enough. The radio was playing and Abe sang along with the vocalist, singing much louder, and he knew he was a damn sight better than the cat on the radio, although he was good enough. The bootblack finished with Abes shoes and he flipped him a half dollar. Before Abe sat in the chair to have his hair cut he carefully combed it again, adjusting each wave until it was in precisely the proper position then he sat down and said, the usual. He crossed his legs and checked the barber in the mirror as he cut. He supervised the cutting of each and every hair, having the barber lift a mirror to the back of his head every few minutes, making certain the back was absolutely straight across and not too short, checking the length of his sideburns, watching how he shaved around the ears and telling him to cut the tips of the few hairs that were sticking out on the left side just behind the second wave. The chair was leveled and Abe was shaved, the barber working carefully so there wouldnt be any irritation or danger of a slight rash, and Abe told him which way to go as he shaved the different parts of his face, telling him to be careful of that pimple. When he was finished the barber wiped his face with a towel, not too hot but just the way Ol Abe liked it, then carefully rubbed in skin cream and a special after shave lotion. Then Abe had his mustache trimmed and the hair in his nose cut. He stepped out of the chair and looked at himself in the mirror, combing his hair and adjusting the waves, and flashed a couple of bills into the barbers hands. He stayed for a while with the boys, listening to and singing along with the music, telling the boys about the fine chicks hes got after him and the cool brownskinned chick that was givin him the eye last night and how he dumped some big mothafucka on his ass a few weeks ago in MELS, and ah mean he was big Jim, and he had a blade that long, but ah laid one onim and pow, he went down jus lake that, and showed them his fist and smiled and they all laughed and he waved again as he sauntered out the door. Yeah, they all liked Ol Abe. He looked at his watch, but it was still too early to pick up the Cadillac. Itll takem a few more hours to do a good job. Too bad, cause this was the kindda day you lake to take a ride and just cruise around and dig the music on the radio and maybe pick somethin up. Too bad that chick wasnt around now. They could go for a little drive . . . yeah, man, a little drive, hehehe . . . well, maybe we do a little drivin tonight . . . He snapped his fingers, sheeit . . . He stopped outside the movie and studied the signs advertising the movies being shown. Two cowboy pictures were playing so Ol Abe decided hed kill the afternoon in the movie and sheeit, he always did dig cowboy pictures and when he got out the Cadillac would be ready.

*   *   *   *   *   *   *

269

THE PLAYGROUND

Most of the kids were out now, running around, knocking or being knocked down, depending upon their size. Some picked up a few bags of garbage that were lying around the halls and started a fire, running around it yelling, picking up pieces of burning garbage and throwing it at each other until a few doors opened and they were told ta get the fuck outta there ya little mothafuckas and they kicked the fire around the hall, yelled fuck you, and ran down the stairs, screaming, and out of the building. Others put strips of paper in the mail boxes with mail, then lit the paper and jumped up and down gleefully as the mail burned and the flames blackened the wall. When all the mail had been burned they rang as many bells as they could reach then ran screaming from the building. Heads popped out of windows and the kids were told theyd get their goddamn asses kicked if they didnt stop that shit and a bag of garbage and an empty bottle were thrown at them and the kids laughed and said up yur ass and ran to the playground where the smaller ones climbed up the sliding pond, knocking off the even younger kids, stamping on the hands of those who tried to climb the ladder, yanking another one off, kicking another in the face; then they made the rounds of the seesaws, flipping kids off, banging one in the face with the seesaw, the younger kids lying on the ground crying until a few parents, sitting in the sun, looked over and yelled, then the kids ran away to another part of the playground; and some of the bigger kids took a basketball away from the kids on the court and when the owner of the ball started crying for his ball they finally hurled it at him smashing his nose and making it bleed and one of his friends yelled at the fleeing kids calling them black bastards and they came back and told him he was black-eran shit and the other kids said they had black bedbugs and the other kid said his mother fucks for spicks and the kid pulled out a nailfile and slashed the other kid across the cheek and then ran, his friends running with him; and in the far corner of the playground a small group of kids huddled quietly, keeping to themselves, ignoring the fighting and screaming, their arms of comradeship around each others shoulders, laughing and smoking marijuana.

*   *   *   *   *   *   *

HURRYUP AND DRESS THE KID. I WANNA TAKE JOEY FOR A HAIRCUT. WHATAYA MEAN HAIR-CUT? SHAKING HER HAND IN HIS FACE. WHATS THE MATTA HE GOTTA TAKE A HAIRCUT? SOMETHING WRONG WITH HIS HAIR, EH? WHATZA MATTA YOU WANNA CUT IT OFF? ITS TOO LONG, THATS WHATZA MATTA. LOOK, HES GOT CURLS LIKEA GURL, PULLING JOEY BY HIS HAIR, ALMOST LIFTING HIM OFF HIS FEET, THE KID YELLING AND KICKING AT VINNIE. ITS TOO LONG, THATS WHATZA MATTA. MARY GRABBED A HANDFUL OF HAIR AND SAID WHATZA MATTA WITH THE CURLS? YOU DONT LIKE CURLS SO THE KID GOTTA TAKE A HAIR-CUT? NO, I DONT LIKE ALL THOSE CURLS, VIO-LENTLY SHAKING THE HAND HOLDING JOEYS HAIR. I DONT WANIM LOOKIN LIKE NO GURL. HES GONNA TAKE A HAIRCUT. YURAZ HES GONNA TAKE A HAIRCUT. I LIKE HIS HAIR LONG AND CURLY AND ITS GONNA STAY LIKE DAT, PULLING SO HARD ON JOEYS HAIR SHE LIFTED HIM FROM THE FLOOR AND HE SCREECHED AND SCRATCHED HER HAND SO

HARD SHE OPENED IT AND HE TURNED AND
KICKED HIS FATHER AND SCRATCHED HIS
HAND AND VINNIE LET GO OF HIS HAIR AND
SLAPPED HIM ON THE BACK OF HIS HEAD AND
MARY KICKED HIS ASS AND THEY YELLED AT
HIM, BUT JOEY DIDNT MIND, HE JUST KEPT
RUNNING AND THEY TURNED BACK TO EACH
OTHER. VINNIE YELLED AGAIN TA GET THE
KID DRESSED SO HE COULD TAKEIM FOR A
HAIRCUT AND MARY SAID HE DONT NEED ONE.
MEEEEEE. WHAT A FUCKIN JERK. THE KIDS
HAIRS DOWN TA HISZASS AND SHE SAYS HE
DONT NEED NO HAIRCUT. YEAH. I SAY. I SAY.
IT LOOKS NICE. I LIKE IT. HE AINT SUPPOSEDTA
LOOK LIKE A GURL. WHO SAYS, EH? WHO SEZ.
AND ANYWAY HE DONT LOOK LIKE NO GURL.
HE LOOKS CUTE. VINNIE SLAPPED HIS HEAD
AND GROANED. MEEEEEE, HE LOOKS CUTE.
WHAT KINDDA CUTE WITH ALL DOZE CURLS.
WHATSAMATTA WITH CURLS, EH? WHATSA-
MATTA? DIDNT YA BRODDA AUGIES KID HAVE
CURLS AND DIDNT ROSIE MAKE IT STAY LONG,
EH? EH? SO WHAT THE FUCK YAYELLIN
ABOUT? YEAH. YEAH. AND YA SEE HOW
CREEPY THE KID IS. LONG HAIR MAKES A KID
CREEPY. THAT'S WHAT IT DOES. GODFABID MY
KID GROWS UP LIKE THAT. ID GIVEM A SHOT
IN THE HEAD. joey peeked at them from his room.
WHO YA GONNA GIVE A SHOT IN THE HEAD,
EH? WHO? WHATTAYAMEAN WHO? ILL GIVE
YAONE TOO. YA THINK SO, EH? YEAH. GO-
AHEAD. GOAHEAD. ILL SPLIT YA FUCKIN
SKULL. WHOSE SKULL YA GONNA SPLIT. EH?
YOU MAKEIM TAKE A HAIRCUT. GOAHEAD,
MAKEIM. YOULL SEE. I SAY HES GOTTA TAKE

A HAIRCUT SO SHUT UP, YEAH? WAVING HIS HAND IN HER FACE AND MARY HIT HIM ON THE FOREHEAD AND YELLED SHE DIDNT WANT JOEY TA TAKE A HAIRCUT AND VINNIE SHOVED HER, GO WAAAAAAY, AND WENT TO JOEYS ROOM JOEY WAS SITTING IN THE CORNER WATCHING THE DOOR AND STARTED TO SCREAM WHEN VINNIE PICKED HIM UP AND CARRIED HIM TO THE CLOSET AND STARTED YANKING CLOTHES OFF THE HANGERS. HE SAT THE KID ON THE BED AND STARTED DRESSING HIM WHEN MARY CAME IN AND SHOVED HIM AWAY FROM JOEY AND TOLD HIM TA LAY OFF, HE DIDNT HAVE TA TAKE A HAIRCUT, AND VINNIE SHOVED HER AGAINST THE WALL AND TOLD HER TA LEAVEIM ALONE, YEAH? AND CONTINUED DRESSING JOEY AND MARY CAME BACK AND SCREECHED IN HIS FACE AND STARTED SHOVING AND HE SHOVED BACK WITH ONE HAND WHILE TRYING TO DRESS JOEY WITH THE OTHER AND JOEY SAT ON THE BED KICKING HIS FEET AND YELLING AND THE YOUNGER KID CRAWLED IN FROM THE LIVING ROOM AND SAT BY THE BED FOR A MOMENT THEN HE TOO STARTED YELLING AND VINNIE SHOVED MARY HARDER AND SHE FELL BACK, TRIPPING OVER THE BABY, FALLING ON THE FLOOR AND SHE JUMPED BACK UP AND STARTED KICKING VINNIE AND HE BACKHANDED HER HARD ACROSS THE FACE AND JOEY TWISTED AWAY FROM VINNIE AND LAY ON HIS STOMACH CRYING AND KICKING AND THE BABY WAS SILENT FOR A SECOND AS MARY FELL OVER HIM THEN STARTED WAILING EVEN LOUDER AND MARY SAID TA LEAVE THE

273

FUCKIN KID ALONE AND VINNIE GRABBED
HER BY THE SHOULDERS AND SHOOK HER
AND ASKED WHATZAMATTA YA CRAZY AND
SHOVED HER AGAINST THE WALL AGAIN AND
JOEY FELL FROM THE BED ONTO THE FLOOR
AND HE KICKED THE FLOOR SCREAMING, HIS
HANDS POUNDING THE FLOOR AND VINNIE
LEANED OVER THE BED AND PICKED HIM UP
AND STARTED DRESSING HIM AGAIN AND
MARY PUMMELED HIM OVER THE HEAD WITH
HER FISTS AND VINNIE KEPT SHOVING HER
AWAY AND DRAGGING CLOTHES OVER THE
KIDS ARMS AND LEGS AND WHEN HIS SHIRT
RIPPED AND VINNIE PULLED HIS ARM TOO FAR
HE LET GO OF THE KID FOR A MINUTE AND
PUNCHED MARY ON THE JAW AND SHE WENT
STAGGERING THROUGH THE DOORWAY,
BOUNCED OFF A WALL AND FELL TO THE
FLOOR AND THE BABY WATCHED, STILL WAIL-
ING AND JOEY STOPPED KICKING FOR A
MINUTE AND VINNIE DRAGGED SOMEMORE
CLOTHES ON THE KID, THEN JOEY STARTED
YELLING AGAIN, BUT HE WAS ALMOST
DRESSED NOW AND MARY WAS STILL UNCON-
SCIOUS AND VINNIE WAS STILL MUMBLING TO
HIMSELF ABOUT THE KID GOTTA TAKE A HAIR-
CUT, HE AINT GONNA LOOK LIKE NO CREEP
AND AUGIE WAS GODDAMN MAD ROSIE DIDNT
MAKE THE KID TAKE A HAIRCUT AND HE AINT
GONNA HAVE NO SHIT LIKE THAT AND HE
FINALLY GOT ENOUGH CLOTHES ON JOEY
AND MARY STARTED TO MOAN AND VINNIE
YELLED TA SHUTUUUUUP AND HE DRAGGED
JOEY FROM THE ROOM INTO THE OTHER BED-
ROOM AND VINNIE GOT A JACKET AND PUT IT

ON AND THE BABY HAD CRAWLED OVER TO
MARY AND WAS SLAPPING HER ON THE STOM-
ACH AND GIGGLING AND MARY OPENED HER
EYES AND VINNIE AND JOEY CAME OUT OF
THE ROOM AND SHE TRIED TO GRAB VINNIES
LEG AS HE STEPPED OVER HER, BUT HE JUST
SHOOK IT LOOSE AND SHE WATCHED THEM
LEAVE THE APARTMENT, SLOWLY GETTING
TO HER FEET AND SHE FINALLY MADE IT TO
THE LIVING ROOM WINDOW JUST AS VINNIE
AND JOEY WERE LEAVING THE BUILDING,
JOEY STILL YELLING, BUT NOT AS LOUD, AS
VINNIE DRAGGED HIM ALONG AND MARY
OPENED THE WINDOW AND YELLED COME
BACK YA FUCKIN SONOFABITCH AND VINNIE
SHOOK HIS HAND AT HER SHUTUUUUUP,
YEAH? AND HE CONTINUED DOWN THE PATH
TO THE STREET, MARY STILL SCREAMING
FROM THE WINDOW. . . .

* * * * * * *

Johnny almost drove Lucy crazy in the supermarket.
Robert sat quietly in the shopping cart, but Johnny
skipped ahead looking at the shelves, stopping to stare
at people and talk with other children. It seemed like
every few minutes she had to drag him away from some
child and he would skip off as soon as she freed his hand
and when she looked around again he would be with some
child, kneeling and looking under shelves or playing with
some kitten or the Lord knows what. And then, of course,
he wanted candy and Lucy finally had to twist his arm
and tell him to behave or she would beat him. O, how
she hated the weekends; having to shop in the crowded
stores (Louis was home for two whole days (sometimes),

and he was always in a hurry to go to bed, but he wouldnt sleep and wanted to fool around all night), and the laundromat was so crowded. She finally finished shopping and left the store. She rushed along the street carrying Robert, dragging her cart and Johnny, who was running to keep up and turning every few minutes to look in a store window or to watch kids play. She was doubly irritated by the people who strolled along leisurely enjoying the warm weather and the bright sun. Ada smiled at her when she passed her bench but Lucy ignored her (the filthy jew. Never changes her clothes) and rushed past her. She had to literally drag Johnny away from the children playing in front of the building and slapped his arm when he wanted to know why he couldnt stay down and play. She snarled in his ear and he ran in the building. Of course the elevator was still messed and she had to climb the stairs to the apartment. She couldnt understand why someone didnt clean the mess, after all everyone knew the porter wouldnt be back until Monday. The least someone could do would be to cover it.

Louis was sitting at the table drinking coffee and reading. She let the door slam and plopped in a chair. She took the childrens coats off and they ran yelling to their room and Lucy told them to play quietly. She poured herself a cup of coffee and plopped back in the chair. O, Im exhausted. Louis sipped his coffee (she usually doesnt pull that until we get to bed), continued reading and grunted. Im just worn out. Ive had to climb the stairs twice today with that heavy cart. Uh? Yes, twice. Lucy was slightly peeved at Louis/s lack of interest in her discomfort, but reminded herself that he had to study. She waited until he looked at her before continuing. Finally Louis reached the end of a paragraph and turned to her. Whats that? I had to climb the stairs twice, speaking in an exasperated tone. Yeah?

Yes. She told him about the mess in the elevator. Louis said he thought it would be easier to wait until you got home than do that. Then he smiled as he imagined how funny the person must have looked as he squatted in the elevator, shitting. Lucy said she didnt think it was so funny, not when you had to climb the stairs, but Louis continued to smile, wondering what would have happened if someone else had walked in the elevator just at that time. They sure wouldve been caught with their pants down. Louis laughed and Lucy frowned. Johnny came rushing out of the room shouting. Robert trailing behind, DA DA. Lucy grabbed Johnny and demanded to know what they were doing. Johnny stared at her and said playing. Well, why cant you play quietly? why must you always make so much noise—just playin cowboys. I dont care. Just play quietly. Do you have to run around like a ragamuffin? Now go in your room and play quietly. The children went back to their room and Lucy sighed. That boy sure can be nerve-racking. Hes under my feet all day long, always arunnin—running around the house yelling. O, it aint so bad as all that. Lucy almost corrected his using –all–, but hesitated knowing Louis would get mad. But I have him all day, everyday. You do not know how it is. Then why dont you just letim go out an play? Lucy cringed. Caus—Because I do not want him playing with any patched pants kids, thats why. Louis squirmed in his chair. He knew what was coming and he was determined to avoid an argument. If we lived somewhere else and had a bigger apartment it wouldnt be so bad. Louis said nothing, but breathed deeply and lit a cigarette—somewheres where I could let him out or where theres enough room so he wouldnt be underfoot all day. Four and a half rooms arent enough. And I dont even have any friends here (you dont have any anywhere). I have no body to talk to—O, what doya mean? Theres plenty a people to talk to around here. Why just look out the window, theres people all ovuh. *I* do not want to talk with those people (the word is ov*er*). Well, *ah* dont see anything wrong with living here and its goddamn cheap. And ah aint gonna move. But you dont know how it is all day. Already Louis was sorry he had allowed himself to argue, again, with Lucy, but he couldnt stop. Every weekend she starts a argument about something. Look, ah says we stay. This place suits me fine an if we moved we couldnt have no car an ah aint givin up the car. He got up and poured himself another cup of coffee and Lucy argued on. He sat back at the table and tried to ignore Lucy and wished there was a goddam baseball game on tv. Lucys voice droned on and he sat smoking and drinking trying not to hear her, not wanting to argue about the same old shit again and have her get pissed off and turn her back on him for a month when they went to bed. It was hard enough as it was to get her in the mood. She always had some kind of excuse and he was too tired to go out looking tonight. But he was damned if he was gonna give up the car—the children started yelling at each other and Lucy ran into their room—and anyway, school was only another few months. And once he got out hed have it made. And when he got himself a good job and a few bucks ahead, then maybe theyd move to a Middle Income Project, but he wasnt going to leave school now (and he wasnt getting rid of the car. If he didnt have that he might never get laid), especially after all the money hed paid them. And it was the best tv/radio repair school in the city—Lucy came back moaning about the kids always fighting over a toy—and hed get a job like *that,* and everybody knew how easy it was to knock down money repairing radio and tv sets. Lucy continued talking and

Louis refused to argue, thinking, and having thought all day, of tonight, and wishing to hell there was a ball game on.

*   *   *   *   *   *   *

WOMENS CHORUS II

The women were still on the bench, looking at a couple who had just sat down on a bench across from them. I wonder how they fuck? The woman was short with braces on both legs. a small hump on her back and she walked with crutches. Her husband had a wooden leg and walked with a twisted limp. Maybe he unscrews his leg and fuckser with the stump. Laughter. I wonder if she hitsim with her crutches when she comes . . . The *cripples* looked at them and smiled and the women nodded and smiled. Maybe he tapser on the hump when he wants ta get humped. Laughter. They smiled again at the cripples, then the smiles left all their faces and they groaned as they saw Mr. Green approach. His wife had had a stroke and was in the hospital and whenever he came out of the apartment he stopped the first one he saw and told them the entire story, and whenever he came in sight everybody ran, but the women were too lethargic to move. It was a funny thing how the stroke happened. We were just sitting in the parlor and all of a sudden she looks funny—you know, very pale like—and she moans and dribbles a little at the mouth and I helped her to the couch and she kind of passed out—I called her and shook her, but she didnt move—and I got one of the chairs from the kitchen and took it over to the couch—I couldnt move a big chair—and I sat there with her—I wouldnt leave her side for anything—I guess I sat there for over 4 hours, then I went next door and asked that nice young girl next door to come in and look at my wife—I dont know what I would have done without her—and she looked at her and said right away to call a doctor—such a nice young girl and smart as a whip too—so I did and they took her to the hospital. They gave her all kinds of examinations and they told me she had a stroke. I couldnt even see her until the next day. Shes been in the hospital 3 weeks now, but shes getting better. She ate very well yesterday, even had a second helping of the stew—she says it was very good—(the women continually looked at each other. giggling and moaning, hoping the old creep would go away and one of the women started looking through anothers hair, scraping off large hunks of dandruff, trying to get the dandruff out of the way so she could look for nits. The large hunks she just flipped away, but the smaller ones she cracked with her finger nail to see if they were just dandruff or a nit. If it snapped she showed it to the woman and told her she got one) she had two helpings of stew and she had a very good bowel movement this morning. It was soft and very dark. I guess the pills they give her make it dark like that. If she keeps improving they may let her come home soon. . . Mr. Green talked on and the women groaned and squirmed (the hunter completely absorbed in her work) and finally he finished and left, stopping someone else as he left the building and telling him the story. The women couldnt understand why he was so upset, the crazy ol bastard, he couldnt get it up for 20 years, or maybe more. Yeah. They cut the bone outta that a long time ago.

*   *   *   *   *   *   *

Mike got up from the table occasionally, taking his glass of beer with him, and looked out the window. He glanced at the other windows, but not with any real interest or expectation. It was too late to catch some broad walking around in an open bathrobe. He just looked out the window. He noticed the many people walking around and sitting on the benches and remembered that it was Saturday and that his friend Sal would be over. Probably with a bottle. Yeah. Sal would be over and they could get high. Great! He finished his beer then went back to the table and refilled his glass. There was no need to nurse his beer now. Sal should be there by the time he finished the beer and a few shots would set him straight. He turned the radio up and drummed on the table with his fingers. He felt better already. Yeah. Now there was something to do. He cleared the dirty dishes from the table and piled them in the sink. Helen asked again if she could go out and play and Mike almost said yes, but when he looked at her he realized he would have to dress her and he was in no mood to go diggin around looking for shirts, coats and all that shit. No. You can go out tomorrow. What the hell, it wasnt his fault he didnt know where all the clothes were. If Irene would put things out for him in the morning it would be different, but why should he have to go looking for the kids clothes? Irene could take her out tomorrow. Thank krist Irene was off the next two days. At least he wouldn't have to take care of the kids. And if it was a nice day maybe hed go out somewhere. Take in a show or somethin. Irene usually broke his balls when she was home, always asking him to help her with this or that, and she/d go running around the joint bitchin because she had to wash clothes or clean the house. What did she think he was, a goddamn house maid or somethin. Fuck her. Thats her job. Why should I do it? Its not my fault Im out of work. Maybe he and Sal would go and pick up some quiff tonight. Yeah. Maybe we/ll make the rounds of the bars. I could use a little nookie. Thats what I need, a good piece of ass. He rubbed his cock with the palm of his hand. Thats what he needed. Irene had the rag on for a week and he couldnt even get some of the old stuff. He drank his beer and smiled thinking of picking up a nice lookin head and takin her home and layiner —Helen asked if she could have something to eat. Im hungry. O for krists sake. Why do ya always have ta bother me, trying to still think of the nice head he would pick up, but the image faded quickly and he couldnt bring it back to mind as he looked at Helen and listened to her. He buttered her a piece of bread and slapped some jelly on it and handed it to her. She walked away licking the jelly and when Arthur saw her eating he started whining and Mike got mad as hell. Why dontya stay out here and eat. Why do ya have ta break my balls all the time. Helen stared at him for a minute then slowly started walking back to the kitchen, but Arthur continued to whine: OK, OK goddamn it. Mike took the bottle out of the crib and filled it with milk. Here, goddamn it. Now shut up. Krist, I/ll be glad when Irene gets home so I can get you kids off my back.

Irene didnt bother smiling at the customers when they asked her questions. She just told them how much it was; no they didnt have it in green; and that will be 2¢ tax; and she took money, gave change, dropped articles in bags and handed them over the counter. Saturday was always so busy. If it wasnt for all the crazy crowds on Saturday she wouldnt even think of the days off. There was always so much to do at home. That Mike wouldn't do anything. The bastard. By the time Tuesday came she was glad to go to work. The job wasnt bad. Especially now that she was used to it. It was just getting up in the morning. And she had a few girl friends at work. But Saturdays were terrible. But the day was more than half

282

gone. And at least her period was over. She didnt tell
Mike, but she was a week late this time. She was sure
she was pregnant. That night the rubber broke. She
was really frightened. She didnt want another kid. Not
now, anyway. But if she did, whatthehell. She supposed
Mike would get a job. If he really had to. But that was a
good night. The best they had in a long time. Maybe
theyd have another one like it tonight. She was always
so horny after her period. Mike might be drunk when
she got home. He usually was on Saturday. She hoped
he wouldnt drink too much. At least not so much he
couldnt get it up. She wondered if Mike would get a job
if she was pregnant. O well, theyd get by somehow. It
didnt make much difference. Theres always Home Relief. But she didnt want to quit her job. It was better
than staying home. The kids get on your nerves sometimes. If only she didnt have so much to do at home.
She/d talk to Mike about it again. When they were in
bed tonight. She hoped he wouldnt be too drunk.

Sal had been there for a while, having brought a bottle
and a bag of potato chips, just in case they got hungry,
hahaha. Mike took a couple of quick shots, chasing it with
the remainder of the beer, and he was feeling good.
Arthur was quietly playing in the crib and Helen didnt
bother him anymore about going out and was playing in
her room coming out occasionally for a potato chip and
Mike smiled at her and patted her head and told her she
was a good girl. Sal had a few bucks and they figured
theyd hit a few joints tonight and see what they could
pick up. After the first few shots they didnt drink too fast,
not wanting to get too high, it was too early yet, so they
sat at the table sipping their whisky, listening to the radio,

waiting for Irene to come home so she could take care of
the kids; and waiting for night to come when they would
go out and have a ball and get some ass. Yeah!

* * * * * * *

PROJECT NEWSLETTER
EVICTIONS
The following is a list of evictions from the
Project during the last two months:

Morals	7
Dirty Housekeeping	3
Non Payment of Rent	2
Criminal	9
Disturbing the Peace	4
Miscellaneous	8

Be sure you do not break any of the Rules. We
want this Project to be a safe and Happy place
in which to live. Only you can help.

* * * * * * *

THE LESSON

A couple of the kids were sparring with each other, the
others standing around forming a ring. They hit with open
hands and each time one scored all the kids yelled. One of
the kids fathers looked out the window and saw them and
rushed from the building yelling at the other kids to leave
his son alone and yelling at his son for fighting. The kids
stared at him for a moment, not moving, then the other
kids said they wasnt fighting, they was just foolin around.
He was teachin Harold how to fight. The father grabbed
his son by the arm and yanked him to his side and slapped
his head, telling him he had been warned about fighting

284

and hanging out with those crummy kids. Dont you know we could be evicted if you get in trouble? He pointed his finger at the other kid and told him to leave his son alone, that if he caught him hitting his son again hed take a strap to him. Harold stood pinned to his fathers side afraid to look at him and ashamed to look at his friends. His father continued yelling at the other kid and the kid told him again that they wasnt fightin, that he was just teachin him how to box. The father continued waving his finger in the boys face and told him he didnt have to teach his Harold how to fight. I/ll teach him how to fight. I/ll teach him how to kill, thats what 1/ll do. Im not going to have my son hit by lousy kids like you. If he wants to learn how to fight I/ll showim. He started shaking Harold by the arm and told him if ever those kids bothered him again to pick up a stick and bash in their heads. Or a rock. The kids just stared at him until he stopped and, dragging Harold by the arm, left. When the door closed behind him another kid took Harolds place and the exhibition continued.

*　　　*　　　*　　　*　　　*　　　*　　　*

Abraham sat through the movies and the cartoons, continually looking at his watch until he got involved in the movie. One of the movies had a real bad cat who was shootin up everybody and Abraham was greatly impressed by the way he had everybody in the town shittin green until that bad bastard from Texas got on his ass and burndim. Ol Abe knew that cat couldnt fuck around with that Texas stud. He chuckled when the guy got his lumps at the end. When he left the theater he walked quickly to the garage to pick up his Cadillac. He looked it all over inside and out and smiled when he saw the big black body shining and the whitewalls gleaming. He paid the bill and gave the stud a buck tip and jumped in and drove off. He drove around for a while, just cruising around the streets, listening to the purr of the motor, feeling the steering wheel in his hands, digging the sounds on the radio. Even while driving he could see the whitewalls and the bigass fins in the back and he felt good. Real great. He drove past MELS BAR and stopped, honked the horn and waved to the guys inside, then slowly drove home. He parked the car, but didnt leave at once. He sat behind the wheel diggin the few cats who were still washing their cars. He stepped forth from his Cadillac and went home to lie down and rest for the night.

* * * * * * *

WOMENS CHORUS III

The women finished their shopping, took the beer home and returned to their bench. Mrs. Olson, who had had a stroke 2 years ago when her husband died, came out and as she hobbled by the women watched her and laughed. She leaned forward slightly as she walked and dragged her right foot. She was unable to lower her right arm and it was bent at the elbow and stretched across her chest, her hand partially closed and jerking up and down. The women loved to watch her, wondering if she picked up chewing gum and dog shit with her right foot. She oughtta wear steel toe shoes. She probably got that way from jerking her husband off. Laughter. Maybe thats what killedim. One of the women looked up at the window on the fourth floor then called the others and pointed to a baby that had crawled out the window and was kneeling on the ledge. The women watched the baby as it crawled around on the ledge and window sill. Maybe he thinks hes a bird. Hey, ya gonna fly? Laughter. Others looked up and someone screamed and someone else yelled get back, O my God, O

my God. Ada covered her face with her hands. The
women continued to laugh and wonder when it would fall.
People ran frantically in circles under the window; someone ran up the stairs and banged on the door, but no one
answered. They banged again and listened at the door for
a sound, hearing something, a murmuring, yet still no
answer. They ran back down stairs and people asked if
anyone was home? are you sure no one was in? Heard
something . . . maybe kids . . . I dont know . . . what
can we do . . . O my God . . . Hes moving . . . I cant look
. . . call the cops . . . The people continued running in
circles, some running to the street looking for a police car;
someone else had called the Office and the women stopped
laughing now that there were so many people around, but
still looked anxiously, waiting for the small body to slowly
slip over the edge of the ledge and fall down, down . . .
then plop on the ground or in a hedge; and Ada looked
at the window with every screech from the crowd, covering her eyes quickly after each peek; and the baby rocked
back and forth on the ledge and seemed to be toppling
and two men ran under the window to try to catch it and
others raised their arms (the women still hoping for a
little more excitement) and yelled go back—O my God—
go back, and the baby leaned forward a little more and
seemed to be looking down at the crowd and hysterical
screechings came from them and the baby leaned back
and the crowd sighed and someone yelled for the cops,
theyre never here when you need them—O why dont they
hurry, and someone ran back upstairs and pounded on
the door and yelled, still no answer; and someone suggested lowering a rope from the window above and have
someone lowered; then 2 Housing Authority Policemen
came running up and yelled to the 2 men under the window to stay there and they ran up the stairs and opened
the door with a pass key, rushing past the 3 children

huddled by the door and into the room where the baby knelt on the ledge, and stopped a few feet from the window, then carefully and silently tiptoed the last few feet trying not to draw the babys attention fearing it might turn and fall, holding their breaths as one inched his arms out the window and grabbed the baby by the arms and quickly jerked him inside . . . held him for a moment . . . closed the window (the crowd still staring (the women annoyed that it was all over and that the kid didnt fall) then slowly lowering their eyes as the window was closed then slowly walking away). Then the policemen carried the baby to the living room and sat down, taking off their hats and wiping their foreheads. Christ, that was a close one, his body starting to tremble. The other nodded. The baby started to cry so they put him on the floor and he crawled over to his brothers and sister. The children stared, frightened, at the cops and the policemen smiled at them and asked them where their mommy was. They continued to stare at the cops and said nothing. Then one tottered over to them and asked if they really was policemen? and they said yes and the boy laughed. They asked him where his mommy was and he said out. Wheres your daddy. The youngster laughed and said mommy says hes drunk and he clapped his hands, laughing, and his sister added quickly that her daddy was gonna get a job on the boats and bring home lots of food and get a tv. The other 2 boys said nothing, continuing to stare at the policemen. I guess we/d better take them down to the office and call Welfare, eh Jim. I guessso. I/ll see if I can get some clothes on them. He asked the children where their clothes were and they showed him, saying nothing and remaining silent as they were being dressed. As they were about to leave the oldest boy, about 5 years old, asked them not to tell their mommy what happened. She said not to let nobody in and if she see somebody came in she/ll beatus. The cops reasurred the children, left a note stating where the children would be, and left.

*   *   *   *   *   *   *

MARY STARED AT JOEYS HEAD WHEN VINNIE TOOK THE BOYS HAT OFF. SEE, NOW HE LOOKS LIKE A BOY. NOT LIKE SOME GODDAMN SISSY. MARY LOOKED AT JOEYS HEAD. YOU SONOFA-BITCH. LOOK WHAT YADID. WHATTA YAMEAN WHAT I DID. I DIDNT DO NOTHIN. I TOOKIM FOR A HAIRCUT. WHATSZAMATTA. YOU DONT LIKE THE HAIRCUT? YA SONOFABITCH, YA CUT ALL HIS HAIR OFF. ALL THE NICE CURLS HE HAD. YA CUTEM ALL OFF. HE LOOKS LIKE HES GOTTA BALDY. AW SHUT YAMOUT. YEAH? HE AINT GONNA TAKE NO MORE HAIRCUTS. joey went to his room. YA STAY AWAY FROM ME YA SONOFABITCH. YA TINK SO, EH? I/LL BREAK YA FUCKIN LEGS. GO AHEAD. GO AHEAD. I/LL KILLYA. MEEE, SHES REALLY ASKIN FORIT. YEAH? YOULL SEE. YOULL SEE. JUST TRY. I/LL CUTCH YAFUCKIN COCK OFF. WHOSE COCK YOULL CUT OFF, EH? WHOSE? YA CRAZY FUCK I/LL BREAK YA FUCKIN LEGS. VINNIE SHOOK HIS HAND IN MARYS FACE THEN TURNED AWAY AND SLAPPED HIS FORE-HEAD, MARONE AME, WHATTA IDIOT, AND WENT OUT TO THE KITCHEN AND HEATED THE COFFEE. MARY WENT INTO THE KIDS ROOM AND PICKED JOEY UP, HOLDING HIM AT ARMS LENGTH FROM HER AND A LITTLE OVER HER HEAD, TURNING HIM TO LOOK AT ONE SIDE THEN THE OTHER. WHAT THEY DO TA MY

JOEY? THEY CUT ALL YA PRETTY CURLS OFF JOEY? YA FATHAS A STUPID. ALL THOSE NICE CURLS AND YA LOOKED SO CUTE. JOEY STARTED TO SQUIRM AND SQUINT SO MARY DROPPED HIM TO HIS FEET. I got a lollypop from the man. WHATTAYA MEAN LOLLYPOP? WHAT MAN? What cut my hair. I cried and he gave me a lollypop. SHE STORMED OUT TO THE KITCHEN. WHATTA YAMEAN GIVIN THE KID A LOLLY-POP, EH? WHATTA YAMEAN? WHATS AMATTA WITH A LOLLYPOP? MEEE, YA THINK IT WAS GONNA KILLIM OR SOMETHIN. I TOLDYA I DONT WANT THE KID TA HAVE NO LOLLYPOPS. WHATTA YA MEAN? WHATTA YAMEAN NO LOLLYPOPS? ALL THE KIDS GOT LOLLYPOPS. WHY HE CANT HAVE ONE? I SAID. A KID CAN CHOKE TA DEAT ON A LOLLYPOP YA STUPID BASTAD. DONT YAKNOW NOTHIN? EVERY-DAY SOME KID DIES FROM A LOLLYPOP. WHATTA YAWANT FROM ME? THE KID WAS CRYIN SO THE GUY GIVEIM A LOLLYPOP. HE DIDNT DIE DID HE? THE KID CRIED. THE KID CRIED. IF YADIDNT TAKEIM TA THE BARBAS HE WOULDNTA CRIED. HE DIDNT WANT NO HAIR-CUT. WHY DONT YALEAVE THE KID ALONE? WHY DONT YASHUT UP, YEAH? THE KID TOOK A HAIRCUT OK. NOW HE DONT LOOK LIKE NO CREEP. AND YA GIVEIM A LOLLYPOP LIKE A REAL JERK. SUPPOSE HE HADDA DIED, EH? SUP-POSE HE DIED? WHAT KINDDA DIED. MEEE. THIS FUCKIN BITCH IS CRAZY. HOWS HE GONNA DIE FROM A LOLLYPOP? HE COULD SUCK IT RIGHT DOWN HIS THROAT AND ITD GET CAUGHT, YA FUCKIN STUPID. MARONE AME, SHAKING HIS HAND IN FRONT OF HIM. YA

SOME FUCKIN NUT. YEAH? YA TINK SO, EH?
JUST DONT COME TO BED THATS ALL. YA STAY
OUT HERE TANIGHT. I/LL SLEEP IN THE
FUCKIN BED AND DONT YA TRY TA TELL ME
NOTHIN. joey and his brother played with plastic trains,
tooting and whistling as loud as they wanted. They were
having a fine time. YEAH? JUST TRY IT. I/LL
BREAK YA LEGS. I SWEAR TA JESUS. I/LL
BREAK YA FUCKIN LEGS.

*   *   *   *   *   *   *

BABYS BURNED BODY BARED

The burned remains of an infant, judged to
be about 10 days old, was found in the incinerator of one of the Citys Housing Projects
today. George Hamilton, 27, of 37-08 Lapidary
Avenue, a porter in the Project, was cleaning
out the ashes of the incinerator when he came
across the remains. He immediately notified the
authorities. The police investigating the incident think that the body must have been
dropped in the incinerator sometime during the
night. The Housing Authority expressed the
opinion that the baby did not belong to any of
the tenants in the Project. The Police are can-
vassing the neighborhood and the Project, but
as yet no additional information has been released by any of the Authorities involved. This
is the second body of a baby found in the Project this month.

*   *   *   *   *   *   *

WOMENS CHORUS IV

The women sat back on the bench after the baby had been taken safely from the ledge. It was fun while it lasted. Sure was a shame the cops had ta come so soon. Maybe he really woulda flyed. Laughter. Wait till the cops get on *her* ass, leavin the kids alone like that. I guess theyll reporter to Relief. Yeah, itll server right. I hope they kicker off. Boy, theyre really gettin tough on Relief now. We had anotha inspector around yesterday. She looked at the beer bottles and wanted ta know what they was doin here. Yeah, they got some nerve. I toler some friends boughtem. They usually come at the beginnin of the month and I get rid of all those things. Yeah, theyre always nosen around. How come they come back so soon? The inspector said someone had reported Charlie was workin. Thank krist he was off yesterday. Aint he workin steady? What for? 2 days a weeks enough. With Relief we make out good. The guy dont take no social security or nothin, so they cant check up. Yeah. Henry gets a couple a days a week like that too. I hope no investigator comes around when *hes* workin. Charlie work today? No. Hes upstairs sleepin. Gettin plenty a rest for tanight, eh? Laughter. Yeah I/ll give Henry a couple of beers and he/ll be good for a while. Try puttin some Geritol in his beer. I hear it puts the bone back in. The women continued talking until they decided to go home and fix supper. They parted at the entrance to the building hoping each other was lucky tonight then went to their apartments and put the beer in the refrigerator, piled the dishes from the day in the sink and started supper.

*   *   *   *   *   *   *

Ada remained on the bench as long as it was in the sunshine. There were a few people walking about and a few children still played, but all the other benches were vacant. She sat alone. A few people had said hello and smiled, though none had sat and talked with her. Yet it hadnt been too lonely a day. There were people around, and children, and the sun was bright and warm. Sometimes on days like this while the sun was still shining and the cool evening breeze was just starting to blow she and Hymie would stand in front of the store and watch the sun go down behind the building and watch the people rushing home from work . . . and the cars and trucks along the avenue . . . and it used to smell so nice and fresh, like sheets that had been on the line all day, and then she would go inside and fix supper and Hymie would eat his soup and smile . . . God bless poor Hymie.

The sun had gone down behind the building and the street lamps had been turned on. The breeze was cooler. Soon it would be dark. Ada got up and slowly left her bench and climbed the stairs to her apartment. She hung up her coat, closed all the windows then stood by her window. There were still a few children in the playground and she watched them, but soon the entire playground was in shadows and they too left. Cars and trucks passed along the avenue, but she ignored them and just watched the buses stop at the corner and people get off and rush home. She couldnt see the sun set, but she knew what it looked like and she imagined the purples, pinks, reds, laying on each other and mixing, just as she used to see it and as it looked in the picture puzzle she had of a ship on the ocean with the sun setting, the puzzle she put together and took apart, and put together again time after time after time all through the long cold heartless winters . . . and even some-

times in the spring when it rained for days and even looking from her window afforded no comfort. It was getting
dark fast now and it seemed very cold outside, the trees
barely visible from their shadows, the birds seeming to be
jumping for warmth. There was nothing much to see now,
just an occasional person rushing home, the cars and
trucks which she ignored, and the waving ovals of light
cast by the street lamps. She left her window and went to
the kitchen. She fixed her supper and sat down at the
table, still conscious of the empty chair opposite her. So
long hes dead now and still it seems like yesterday we
would sit and Hymie would put a big piece of sweet
butter on an onion roll. She smiled remembering how
much Hymie had loved onion rolls, and the way he would
spread the butter. God bless him, hes happy now. No
more suffering for him . . . only for me. She ate slowly
and lightly then sat for a few minutes remembering
how Hymie and Ira used to kid her because she took
so long to eat. I could eat two times before youre finished
Momma. That what Ira would say. I could eat two
times. And all the cookies they sent Ira while he was in
the Army. So many cookies. How many did he ever eat?
Maybe he was dead a long time and we sent cookies.
And he always wrote and said thanks Momma for the
cookies . . . Such a good boy, God bless my Ira . . . She
went into the bedroom, turned down the bed cover, laid
out her nightgown and Hymies pajamas and went into
the living room to listen to the radio for just a little while
before going to bed.

    *   *   *   *   *   *   *

Irene came home from work glad Saturday and her period
were over. She was hoping maybe Mike would go to the
store for supper, but she didnt expect it. But she didnt

mind because she was in a good mood and it was nice out. Especially after being in the store all day. Before she opened the door she could hear the radio and wasnt suprised when she did open the door to see Mike and Sal sitting at the table drinking. She said hello and went straight to the bedroom and threw her jacket on the bed, then picked up Helen who had run after her. Helen told her everything she did and Irene oooood and aaaaad and they both went in to see Arthur. She stayed with the children a few minutes then came out and, smiling, asked Mike how he was doing. Pretty good babe. Sal came over a little while ago and weve had a few drinks, hahahaha. She smiled again and wondered if she should ask him if Helen had been out. You want something to eat Sal? Of course he does. Ya think he dont eat? Irene shrugged her shoulders. I was just askin. How about gettin us a steak, handing her some money and smiling at Sal, making sure he understood that he was the boss in his house and just because Irene worked didnt mean he had to take any shit. Go getus a steak babe. Irene went to get her jacket, her good humor leaving her, feeling at that exact moment, humorless, and ready any second to lose her temper. He could have at least asked and not show off so damn much. She stopped in front of the table and asked him, attempting a slight nonchalance, how come Helen didnt have her overalls on? Didnt she go out today? No, she didnt go out today. Why not? It was a beautful day. Because I didn't feel like trying ta find where ya hid her clothes. So what? not able to return her stare and turning his head to look at Sal, increasing the scowl on his face. Irene clenched her teeth and left the apartment. The bastard. Wont go to the store; wont clean the house (probably get too drunk tonight); wont even let the kid out. She hustled from one store to the other, buying what she needed; rushed home; prepared and served the meal in silence; Mike ignoring her, feeling he had made his point with Sal; he and Sal leaving as soon as the meal was over.

*   *   *   *   *   *   *

THE DASHER

A young girl was waiting alone for a bus. She stood smoking and looking down the street for the bus. She had to meet her friends in a few minutes and she was late. She kept stepping off the curb to look down the street. A car stopped a few feet from the curb and the guy in the car yelled, can I takeya somewhere baby? The girl looked at the car, then down the street, but no bus was coming. Comeon, I/ll takeya where ya wanna go. She looked at the guy for a minute wondering if he would take her to 5th avenue or if hed start fuckin around. She thought she/d take a chance, hoping the guy wouldn't kick her out when she said no. He yelled again and she started to walk to the car when she saw the bus turn a corner 2 blocks away. She stepped back on the curb and turned her head. He yelled again and she said, go on, beat it. He mumbled something and she flipped her cigarette at the car and told him ta get the fuck outtahere. The guy started the car and drove away, but stopped a few hundred feet up the street and got out of the car. He whistled and yelled at the girl and when she turned and yelled at him ta go screw he opened his fly and took his cock out and waved it at her, still yelling and whistling. She told him ta shove it up his ass and he finally got back in his car and drove away. The young girl watched the car go up the street then turned as the bus approached. What a fuckin creep.

*   *   *   *   *   *   *

Nancy and the kids were still eating when Abraham got up. She asked him did he want some supper and he said hell no. He didnt want to eat none a her slop. He filled the tub and sat in the water smoking a cigarette, gently rubbing himself with the soap with his free hand, thinking of the brownskin gal and contemplating his stiffened dick. After he finished his cigarette he lathered himself up good, carefully and gently lathering his crotch so it would be sure to smell sweet (kissen sweet, hehehe), then rinsed and dried himself. Then he put deodorant under his arms and balls; massaged skin cream into his face; splashed after shave lotion on his face, neck and chest; rubbed pomade between the palms of his hands and rubbed it on his hair, then spent 20 minutes combing it carefully and adjusting his waves. Ghuddamn if he wasnt a sharp lookin stud. He checked the back of his head with the small mirror then satisfied that each wave was in its proper place he washed his hands and went back to the bedroom to dress. He put on his new white on white shirt with the Hollywood Roll collar and tied his silk lavender and purple tie in a large windsor knot. He selected his brown suit, the one he had made last year, and man its a sharpass suit. Put me back a 100 clams. He carefully adjusted the waist of his shirt before pulling the thin belt tight. He put on the jacket, buttoned it and rolled the lapels, fixed the handkerchief, and straightened out the things in his pockets. Then he took down the cool tan top coat, checked his shoes, put the coat on, then carefully placed his hat on his head. Man, he was ready. He left the house and didnt stop till he opened the door of his bigass Cadillac. He sat behind the wheel and pulled the door closed, smiling as he heard the heavy thud of the door. Sheeit. This is gonna be a night. I mean a *night* Jim . . .

❋   ❋   ❋   ❋   ❋   ❋   ❋

WHATTA YAMEAN THE SAUCES NO GOOD? THATS WHAT I SAID, THE SAUCES NO GOOD. WHATS THE MATTA, YA DONT UNDERSTAND ENGLISH? ITS NO GOOD. NO GOOD, NO GOOD. WHATTA YAKNOW ABOUT SAUCE? MEEEE, WHATTA I KNOW? I KNOW IT STINKS. NOT ENOUGH GARLIC. ITS GOT THE SAME GARLIC. JUST LIKE ALWAYS. THE SAME 8 CLOVES OF GARLIC AND YA SAY NOT ENOUGH GARLIC. YUR A FUCKIN DUMMY. ITS GOOD SAUCE. DONT TELL ME ITS NO GOOD. WHOSE A FUCKIN DUMMY? EH? WHO? I/LL GĪVEYA A RAP IN THE MOUT IM A DUMMY. YA CANT EVEN MAKE A SAUCE. WHY DONTCHA EAT AND SHUT UP, YEAH? I DONT LIKE THE SAUCE, banging his fork down on the table and shaking his hand in Marys face. ITS A FUCKIN IRISH SAUCE. NO GARLIC. NO GARLIC. little ralphy picked up a string of spaghetti and dropped it on the floor. joey picked it up and put it back on his plate. ralphy threw another string down and joey picked it up. DONT TELL ME. THERES NOT ENOUGH GARLIC. I LIKE GARLIC IN MY SAUCE. SO SHUT UP OR I/LL RAPYA OVA THE HEAD. AAAA, WHATTA-YAKNOW, EH? WHATTAYAKNOW? little ralphy picked up a handful of spaghetti and threw it hitting joey in the face. joey yelled to stop and slapped ralphys hand. ralphy yelled and threw another handful in his face. joey hit ralphy with a handful . . . GET ME ANOTHA MEATBALL. I CANT EAT THE MACARONI. YA CANT EAT, YA CANT EAT? WHATTAYA, A KING OR SOMETHIN? YA CANT EAT. GET ME AN-OTHA MEAT BALL AND SHUTUP. WHATTSA-MATTA YA CANT GET THE MEATBALL YA-SELF, EH? WHATTA YAMEAN GET IT MYSELF?

GET ME ANOTHA MEAT BALL OR I/LL BREAK
YALEG. AAAA, GETTING UP AND LADLING
ANOTHER MEATBALL OUT OF THE POT AND
PLOPPING IT ON VINNIES PLATE. MAYBE I CAN
EAT THIS. CANT EVEN MAKE A SAUCE.

*   *   *   *   *   *   *

Lucy said little during the meal, just reminding Johnny to
eat from time to time and asking Louis to pass something.
Halfway through the meal Robert decided he didnt want
to eat any more and Lucy forced food into his mouth in
between feeding herself and telling Johnny to eat. When
she had finished she started clearing the table, forcing the
last bit of food on Roberts plate into his mouth. Louis
just left the table and turned on the tv. Johnny started
playing with his food and Lucy yelled at him sharply
and Johnny whined and started eating and Lucy told him
to hushup and eat. Louis felt like telling her to stop yellin,
ghuddamn it, and rap her side the head. Seemed like she
was always yellin about somethin. Especially on the weekends. He just stared at the tv thinking about goin for a
drive tomorrow (maybe alone), and hoping the next few
hours would pass fast. Lucy finally shoved the last spoon-
ful of food in Johnnys mouth then did the dishes, leaving
the kitchen occasionally to tell the children to be quiet
(Louis squirming in his chair), then finishing the dishes
she put the children to bed and sat in the living room,
saying nothing, and watched tv. Louis turned to her
once in a while and made a comment about the show
hoping to get her in a good mood before they went to bed,
but Lucy only grunted, thinking how soon she would
have to go to bed with him and it would start like every
weekend (and many week nights too) and just the
thought made her muscles tighten and her flesh get

clammy. Lucy just grunted so Louis figured the hell with
it. Theyd be going to bed soon and maybe tonight will be
different.

* * * * * * *

THE QUEUE

The Welfare checks were cashed and there were long lines
outside the Liquor Store across the street from the Project.
The owner had his 2 sons and brother helping him as he
did every Saturday night. The store was in the middle of
the street and the two lines went out of sight around each
corner, and the cop on the beat stood near the entrance so
a fight wouldnt start as people pushed their way into the
store. Yet even with the cop there there was much pushing
and cursing. The clerks in the store worked as fast as they
could and wrapped the bottles quickly, but still the lines
were out of sight around both corners. Those at the end
of the line would step out occasionally and look to the
front wondering how much longer they would have to
wait and then finally they would turn the corner and
eventually they would come in sight of the lighted window
and then they could at least look at all the bottles on
display and then the time seemed to pass faster with their
goal in sight. Someone tried to get in ahead of time, but
someone else pulled him out of the doorway and an argument started and everyone yelled for them to clear the
front of the store so they could get in and the owner came
out and frantically yelled at them to stop (the people in
the store becoming nervous when the owner left the
counter fearing something would happen to prevent them
from getting their bottles after having waited on line for
so many hours) and finally the cop came over and yanked
them both out and told them to beat it. They pleaded to

300

be allowed to get their bottles or at least to get on the
end of the line (offering the cop money), but the cop refused (not wanting to louse up the beautiful deal he had
with the owner) and they finally walked off, sneaking
back and giving money to friends to get them a bottle.
Before the last customer was taken care of the clerks
were soaked with perspiration and completely knocked
out, but soon the last few customers were in the store.
Many parties had already started and as the last customers bought their bottles and walked happily toward
home the bells in a nearby church tolled midnight.

*   *   *   *   *   *   *

Abraham stepped into MELS and stood by the door for a
moment digging the scene, his hands in his coat pockets, a
coolass stud man, and every cat in the joint knew it. He
waved to his boys, hung up his hat and coat and went to
the bar, ordered a scotch and tossed a bill on the bar. He
leaned sideways against the bar and dug the scene. The
bar was not too crowded and the brownskinned gal wasnt
there yet. He went in the back and sat at a table and
ordered some of those fine ribs that were so great at
MELS and sucked each rib dry then sat back sucking his
teeth and smoking. Man he felt great. He paid the check
and went to the bar, saw the brownskinned gal and went
up to a cat he knew who was standing near her. He patted
the cat on the back, called the bartender, give my man
here a drink, ordered another scotch and tossed a 20 dollar bill on the bar. Man that chickll have big eyes now.
He knew how to play it cool. Yeah, ol Abe was a cool
ass stud. He let his change lay on the bar and when he
finished his drink he ordered another and told the bartender to give the young lady a drink. He smiled at her
and when they got their drinks he slid over next to her

and told her his name was Abe. Ol honest Abe, hahaha.
Mahns Lucy. He asked her to dance and he winked at
the cats at the bar as they walked to the dance floor.
Sheeit, nothin to it when you operate like ol Abe. They
danced and he told her she danced real great and she must
be new around here, he comes here all the time and he
never seen her before and she smiled and said yes she/d
only been here a few times before and they danced and
drank and ol Abe smooth talked her and he was in
and he told her he had a Cadillac, with whitewalls and
would she like something to eat and when you with ol
Abe you move and he knew this would be a great night
and hed fuck the ass off this bitch.

* * * * * * *

Nancy put the kids to bed and got out the bottle of wine
she stashed in the closet. She sat down and watched tv for
a while, taking slugs from the bottle, then went to bed and
lay there drinking, smoking and playing with her crotch.
She wisht the fuckin Abe would come home and lay her.
The sonofabitch aint fucked me but oncet in the last
month and nobody else ever come around this house. If
she could get somebody to sit with the kids she could go
out, but she couldnt get nobody. Sheeit. She was tired.
Almost felt like going to sleep. But it was too early yet.
Still almost half a bottle left too. She/d drink that first.
Somebody might come around looking for Abe. No sense
in waiting for him though. He/ll be gone all night. Sheeit.
Ah need me some cock. She finished the bottle and threw
it down the incinerator then went back to bed and lay
down, remembering how big and hard Abes cock was
and how it felt going in.

* * * * * * *

THE WORSHIPPERS

A woman screeched hysterically, AH LOVESSIM, AH
LOVESIM and she rolled on the floor, beating the floor
with her fists. The people in the adjoining apartments
listened, laughing. COME DOWN! COME DOWN! and
someone beat a drum, someone else pounded on a table,
OOOOOOO AH LOVESIM! AH *DIE* FORIM! and
other voices screeched and a roar came through the
walls, the people on the other side listening and laughing.
OOOOO JESUS! JESUS! OOOOO JESUS! and the other
voices roared a HAAAAL LAY LOOOOOO YAAAA!
WE *LOVES*YA! O *JES*US! WE *LOVES*YA! and the
beating of drums and table grew louder and a voice
moaned AH SINNED! AH SINNED! OOOOO LORD,
AH SINNED! FORGIVE ME LORD! another body fell
to the floor and groveled and beat its fists and the drum-
mer beat frantically and the clanging of a pot joined the
drum and table and other bodies fell to the floor and they
rolled and beat and kicked and the voices screeched and
boomed and roared AH LOVESIM! AH LOVESIM!
HAAAAL LAY LOOOOO YAAAA! OOOOO LORD!
LORD! HAAAL LAY LOOOOO YAAAA-DA-DUM-
DADUMDADUMDADUMDADUMDADUM - WEES
YO CHILLEN LORD! O BLESS US LORD-AH SIN-
NED! AH SINNED! FO GIVE ME LORD! OOOO
OOO LORD FOGIVE A MISERABLE SINNER! (ears
pressed against the wall, hands raised for silence, laugh-
ter)—AN JOSHYA TUMBLED THE WALLS! OOOO
*JER*ICHO! O *JER*ICHO!—BABUMBABUMBABUM
BABUMBABUMBABUMBABUM — EEEEEEEEEEE
AAAAAAAAA—OOOO MERCY! OOOOO MERCY!
FOGIVE YO CHILREN LORD! FOGIVE WE SIN-
NERS—COME DOWN! COME DOWN *JES*US!—

HAAAAL LAY LOOOOO YAAAA (a door was opened slightly to hear better)—AH *LOVES*IM! AH *LOVES*IM—HAAAAL LAY *LOOOOO* YAAAA—A MISERABLE SINNER—COME DOWN—OOOOOO OO—IN THE FIERY FURNACE—O LORD! LORD! —DRRRRRR—COME DOWN—BLESSUS! BLESS-US!—*JESUS! JESUS! JESUS! JESUS! JESUS JESUS!* —HAL LAY LOOOOOOO YAAA! LORD—THE PEARLY GATES—WE *LOVES*YA—COME DOWN— EEEEEEEAAAAAA — O *JESUS* — BLESSUS — AH LOVESIM—YO CHILREN—SINNERS—FOGIVE— AMEN!—AMEN LORD! AMEN! and the door was closed.

* * * * * * *

THE CONTEST

The street was quiet and a gang of young spades on one corner started walking toward a gang of spicks on the other, each gang ripping the aerials off the parked cars; some carrying rocks, bottles, pipes, clubs. They stood a few feet apart in the middle of the street calling each other black bastards and monkey mothafuckas. A car came along the street, horn blowing, trying to pass, but they didnt move and finally the car had to back out of the street. The few people on the street ran. The gangs remained in the middle of the street. Then someone threw a rock, then another was thrown and 30 or 40 kids were screaming, throwing bottles and rocks until there were none left, then they ran at each other swinging clubs and whipping the car aerials, cursing, screaming, someone crying in pain, a zip gun being fired and a window breaking and people yelled from windows and one of the kids went down and was kicked and stomped and knots of kids

304

formed, swinging, clubbing, kicking, yelling and a knife was stuck in a back and another one went down and a cheek was cut to the mouth with an aerial and the ragged flesh of the cut cheek flapped against the bloodied teeth and a skull was opened with a club and another window was broken with a rock and a few tried to drag another away as three pairs of feet kicked at his head and a nose was smashed with a pair of brass knuckles and then a siren was heard above the yelling and suddenly, for a fraction of a second, everyone stood still then turned and ran, leaving three lying on the street. The cops came and people came back to the street and the cops kept them back, asking questions and finally the ambulance came and two were helped in the ambulance the third being carried. Then the amublance left, the cops left, and it was quiet once again.

*   *   *   *   *   *   *

As soon as they got in the door the guy grabbed her ass. Goddamnit, cant yawait, pushing him away. She staggered and leaned against the wall, the guy leaning over her kissing her neck as she yanked open a closet door looking for a bottle, then slammed it shut when no bottle could be found. She looked around trying to figure out what was wrong. Somethin was wrong. Maybe her husband came home. She called. Called again and still no answer. She pushed the guy away and staggered into the bedroom to see if he was there, but he wasnt. Guess he aint here. Somethin sure as hells wrong. Then she remembered her kids. They should be here. She looked in their room and called, but they were gone. Shit, whered them little bastards go. I toldem ta stay put. She went back to the kitchen, the guy still behind her pulling her coat off and grabbing her ass. She looked around the kitchen and the living room, reaching behind her and bouncing the guys balls with her fingertips, the guy slobbering over her, groping and mumbling. Finally she saw the note left by the Police. Well, fuckem then. They can stay the night. She went back to the bedroom, the guy behind her. They undressed, fell onto the bed and fucked.

*   *   *   *   *   *   *

Mike and Sal made the rounds of a few joints, but couldnt score. They had danced with a couple of broads, but nothing else. Not even a phone number or a date for the next weekend. Sal wanted to try a spick joint on Columbia street, but Mike didnt feel like walking that far and anyway he didnt trust the spicks. So they stood at the bar drinking, hoping something might come in that they could latch on to, getting drunker. Mike laughed at Sal and toldim he could go home and get laid and Sal had to pull his prick. Sal laughed and said that was ok, hed rather pull his prick than take care of a couple a kids all day. Thats ok man, at least I get mine. They had another drink and Mike was getting tired of hanging around, and was too goddamn horny to wait any longer. He told Sal he was gonna leave and asked him if he was goin. No, I think I/ll hang around a while. Nothin ta do home. Mike told him not ta pull it too much, he was goin home ta get laid (and by krist he was, rag or no rag). The apartment was dark and Mike let the door bang then stumbled toward the bedroom, cursing the fuckin chairs for bein in his way. Irene woke when Mike came in and listened for a moment to hear if the kids woke up, then waited for Mike. She said hello and he flopped on the bed and started undressing, throwing his clothes onto a chair. You still awake? You woke me up when you came in. Whatid ya want me ta do, crawl

through the key hole, determined he wouldnt take any
shit off her tonight and if she said a word hed knocker
teeth in. I didnt say anything Mike. Comeon, come to bed.
He finished undressing and flopped over toward her and
she put her arms around him. He tried to kiss her, but he
missed her mouth and kissed her nose and mumbled
something about her staying still and she finally directed
him properly and she kissed him and Mike fumbled
around her crotch and they kissed and Irene ran her hand
along the inside of his thigh and Mike squirmed and
grabbed her crotch and they continued kissing and
squirming and Irene worked steadily and expertly with
her hands and tongue, but after 15 minutes Mike still
couldnt get a hardon so he cursed and rolled over on her
and tried to get it in anyway, but it kept bending and
flopping out and he tried to stuff it in with his finger but
it was useless and Mike cursed her for a useless bitch,
still trying, still stuffing, until he eventually passed out and
rolled off her. Irene pulled her arm from around him and
sat up looking at him, listening to him breathe, smelling
his breath . . . Then she lay down and stared at the
ceiling.

*　　*　　*　　*　　*　　*　　*

Naturally Lucy smiled demurely when Abe asked her if
she/d like to cut and asked where theyd go and ol Abe
said theyd make a party of their own and Lucy hesitated
and ol Abe turned the sweet talk on that chick and told
her, come on baby, we/ll have a time and he giver the
BIG smile and she started to waver and ol Abe knew, as
he had known all along, that he would make another
conquest. Sheeeit, theres no bitch livin that ol Abe couldnt
fuck. They left MELS and Abe let her look his Cadillac
over before he opened the door. He wanted to be sure

she saw those bigass fins and the whitewalls. Abe flipped on the radio and handed her a cigarette and they took off. They drove downtown and stopped at a hotel and when they got up to the room ol Abe tipped the boy big and asked for a bottle of whisky and some ice. He came back with it in a few minutes and by the time Abe poured the drinks Lucy was undressed and in bed. Ol Abe stared at those fine tits and set the drinks down and undressed. As he rolled over on her the first time he smiled thinking how hed have that bitch callin him DADDYO before that night was ovuh. After fucking her once Abe wanted to have a drink and a smoke, but Lucy wasnt the type of girl who believed in rest periods so ol Abe sunk it again and this time he really concentrated on his work, but he didnt have his drink and smoke until he had fucked her 3 times and by then ol Abe was even thinking of a little sleep. Not much, just a little. Lucy finally gulped her drink down and put out her cigarette and rolled over on Abe and though he was a little beat he did justice to the girl, but he was thinking hed have to stop for a while. After the fourth piece they did stop for a while, but Lucy wouldnt let him sleep, continually playing with his ear, kissing his neck, caressing his balls, playing with his cock until it was hard and then she pulled him over again an ol Abe fucked, but he wasnt concentrating too hard and was thinking that the ghuddamn bitched fuckim ta death.

    *   *   *   *   *   *   *

Most of the parties in the Project were over and the only lights lit were in those apartments where pay-parties were being thrown where the guests played cards and dice and the host cut the game and supplied beer at 35¢ a can, gin at 60¢ a shot, wine at 30¢ a glass, sandwiches 50¢ each and a real fine chicken dinner with rice and yams for a buck and a half. Occasionally someone got too drunk and accused someone else of cheating and started an argument or pulled a knife, but the host was always fast and cooled the scene with a quick rap on the head with a small club and so no real disturbances occurred. The rest of the Project was dark and quiet, the only noise caused by a passing drunk or someone being mugged, the victim, when regaining consciousness, usually yelling like hell for the cops, but this didnt happen more than once or twice on a weekend night and bothered no one. VINNIE AND MARY HAD STOPPED ARGUING, VINNIE FI-NALLY PULLING HER LEGS APART AND GET-TING A PIECE BEFORE GOING TO SLEEP, AND THEY ROLLED NOISILY IN THE BED, THE SPRINGS SQUEAKING AS THEY SLEPT UNDER THE PICTURE OF THE BLESSED MOTHER; Lucy and Louis had been asleep for hours, their backs to each other, her body still stiff and tense, Louis grumbling in his sleep; Mike rolled and grumbled drunkenly, but Irene eventually fell asleep; Ada slept, after kissing Hymies and Iras pictures, with one hand touching the pajamas on the other side of the bad; and Nancy dropped off with her clothes still on and her hand still on her crotch; and even ol Abe was eventually allowed to sleep for a while.

*　　*　　*　　*　　*　　*　　*

Abe was dragged from sleep with the hardening of his prick. He had trouble focusing his eyes and could feel something brushing lightly against his thighs and stomach. He raised his head slightly and could see the fine nipples of Lucys tits caressing him as she sucked his cock. When she saw his head move she got up and sat on his dick and rotated, smiling at Abe, his eyes opening wider with each gyration. She sat on it grinding away and leaned over and took two cigarettes from the table, stuck one in her mouth and one in Abes, then lit them. You want a drink daddyo. Abe shook his head, moving automatically in perfect time and rhythm with her grinding. He took a few drags of the cigarette then put it out and started to fuck with concentration . . .

*　　*　　*　　*　　*　　*　　*

The sun rose behind the Gowanus Parkway lighting the oil filmed water of the Gowanus Canal and the red bricks of the Project. Church bells announced the beginning of services. Ada looked out her window for a while before starting breakfast; Louis got up planning on getting out as early as possible, alone, and going for a ride; Irene woke up before Mike and laid in bed listening to him grumble and wondering how he would feel when he woke up; VINNIE GOT UP FIRST AND YELLED FOR THE KIDS TA KEEP QUIET, YEAH? AND DRAGGED MARY BY THE ARM ACROSS THE BED AND TOLDER TA GET UP: Nancy woke, scratched her crotch then smelled her finger and yelled for the kids to shutup. When ol Abe got home the kids were sitting at the table yelling and eating and he told them to be quiet, he wanted to sleep and went into the bedroom, staggering slightly, his eyes red and barely open. He carefully took off his clothes and hung them up, put on his hairnet and went to bed. Nancy came in and lay down beside him and started tickling his asshole. He shoved her away, laughing at her, and told her to get the fuck out and leave him alone. She told him she werent goin, that she was gonna have some cock and he backhanded her across the face and toler ta go get a banana and she called him a no-accountblackniggabastard and he punched her in the motherfuckin face, knocking her off the bed, and toler ta

310

get her ass outta there or I/ll bust ya apart woman, and rolled her out of the room. She crawled out to the kitchen and pulled herself up, holding onto the edge of the sink, still yelling he was a blackniggabastard, then let cold water run over her head. Her daughter came over to help her and Nancy continued yelling and then the frustration started her crying and her daughter told her not to cry, Jesus loves us Mommy. Nancy told her to get the fuck away from her.

Abraham slept.